The LOVES of CHARLES II

The Stuart Saga

Jean Plaidy

THREE RIVERS PRESS
NEW YORK

Published in the United States by Three Rivers Press, an imprint
of the Crown Publishing Group, a division of Random House, Inc., New York.
www.crownpublishing.com

THREE RIVERS PRESS and the Tugboat design are registered trademarks
of Random House, Inc.

Originally published as three separate works in hardcover in Great Britain
by Robert Hale, London, in 1956 and 1957.

Library of Congress Cataloging-in-Publication Data
Plaidy, Jean, 1906–1993
The loves of Charles II : the Stuart saga / Jean Plaidy.—1st American pbk. ed.
1. Charles II, King of England, 1630–1685—Fiction. 2. Great Britain—History—Charles II, 1660–1685—Fiction. 3. Catherine, of Braganza, Queen, consort of Charles II, King of England, 1638–1705—Fiction. 4. Cleveland, Barbara (Villiers) Palmer, Duchess of, 1641–1709—Fiction. 5. Great Britain—Kings and rulers—Fiction. I. Title: Loves of Charles the Second. II. Title: Wandering prince. III. Title: Health unto His Majesty. IV. Title: Here lies our sovereign lord. V. Title.
PR6015.I3A6 2005
823'.914—dc22 2005005922

ISBN-13: 978-1-4000-8248-3

ISBN-10: 1-4000-8248-X

Printed in the United States of America

Design by Meryl Sussman Levavi

10 9 8 7 6 5 4 3 2 1

First American Paperback Edition

Contents

Part One

THE WANDERING PRINCE

Henriette d'Orléans
and Lucy Water

". . . I think that no joys are above
the pleasures of love."

CHARLES STUART

ONE

It was late afternoon on a July day in the fourth year of the Great Rebellion. The sun was hot; the grass banks were brown; and the purple nettle-flowers and the petals of the woundwort were peppered with fine dust.

A small party—two men and two women—trudged slowly along the road, looking neither to right nor to left, their eyes fixed on the ground. One of the women was a hunchback, and it was this deformed one who carried a sleeping child.

Sweat ran down her face; she caught her breath as she saved herself from tripping over a stone and going headlong into one of the numerous potholes which were a feature of the road. She wiped the sweat from her face but did not lift her eyes from the ground.

After a while she spoke. "How far from the inn, Tom?"

"We'll be there within the hour."

"There's time before dark," said the other woman. "Let's stop for a rest. The boy's heavy."

Tom nodded. "A few minutes will do no harm," he said.

The hunchback spoke again. "Only let us rest if you are sure there's time, Tom. Don't let the dark overtake us. There'll be robbers on the road at twilight."

"There are four of us," answered Tom, "and we look too poor to rob. But Nell's right. There's time for a rest."

They sat on the bank. Nell took off her boots and grimaced at her swollen feet while the hunchback laid the child gently on the grass. The others would have helped, but she waved them aside; she seemed determined that none but herself should touch the child.

"Here's the best spot for you," said Tom to the hunchback. "The bush makes a good support." But the hunchback shook her head and looked at him with some reproach. He smiled and sat down at the spot he had chosen as the best. "We should be in Dover long before this time tomorrow," he added.

"Call me Nan," said the hunchback.

"Yes . . . Nan . . . I will."

"You must remember to call me Nan. It is short for Nanette. Ask my husband. Is that not so, Gaston?"

"Yes . . . that is so. Nan . . . it is short for Nanette."

"And that is my name."

"Yes, Nan," said Tom.

"There is someone coming," said Nell quickly.

They were silent, listening to the sound of footsteps on the road. A man and a woman came into sight, and the hunchback's eyes went to the sleeping child beside her; her right hand moved out and rested on its ragged clothes.

The man and woman who were approaching carried bundles, and their dress proclaimed them to be of slightly higher social standing than the group on the bank. The man who wore his hair cut short so that his pink and rather prominent ears could be seen, might have been a tradesman. The woman was plump and puffing with exertion; it was clear that she was finding the heat uncomfortable.

"Here's sensible people," she was grumbling, "taking a rest by the roadside. I declare I'll do the same, for my feet won't carry me a step farther until I give them a short rest."

"Now come along, Kitty," said the man. "If we're to be in Tonbridge in time for the wagon there's no time for dallying."

"There's time enough, and my feet won't go a step further." The fat woman was smiling as she plumped herself down on the bank, and her husband had no choice but to do the same, for it was too hot to stand and argue.

"God be with you," said the fat woman.

"God be with you," murmured Tom and his companions, but they did not look at the newcomers; they kept their eyes fixed on the opposite bank. Unlike the fat woman they did not wish for roadside chatter; but the fat woman was one who usually achieved that which she desired.

"A pretty child . . ." she began.

The hunchback smiled and bowed her head in acknowledgment of the compliment.

"I've a weakness for little girls . . ."

"This . . . is a little boy," said Nan, and her accent was unmistakably foreign.

"You sound like a foreigner," said the woman.

"I am French, Madame."

"French?" The man shot a suspicious glance at the party. "We don't like the French much here."

His wife continued to smile. "Lee says that when our King went and got married to a French wife the trouble started, and now look what she's brought him to. That's what you say, eh, Lee?"

"Where is she now?" demanded Lee. "In France . . . kicking up her heels and dancing the new dances, I'll warrant. A fine wife she's been to our King Charles and a fine brewing of trouble she's brought him!"

"I'm sorry that the Queen should be French," said Nan. "For myself I am a poor woman. My husband here and my child . . . with these two fellow servants, go to join our master. The poor in France are much like the poor in England."

"There's truth in that, I'll swear," said the woman.

"A master or a mistress says 'Go here . . . Go there . . .' and their servants must go . . . even if it is to service in another country. My husband is a valet to a gentleman. That is so, is it not, Gaston?"

Gaston agreed that it was so, in English slightly less fluent than that of the hunchback.

"And we all serve in the same household," put in Nell.

"Ah," said the man Lee, "there's going to be a turnabout in this country ere long. Things will be different for some of us when the Parliament is victorious. We're for the Parliament . . . as all the poor should be. Are you for the Parliament?"

"Please?" said the hunchback.

"For the Parliament," said Lee in a louder tone.

"I do not always understand. I am not English. You will forgive me."

Lee turned to Tom. "Are you French too?"

"No, I am English."

"Then you'll think as I do."

"How old is the child?" interrupted Lee's wife.

"He has two years," said the hunchback. She had unconsciously laid her hand on the child.

"What a fine-shaped hand you've got," said the woman. She studied her own gnarled one and its broken nails with a distasteful grimace.

"She's a lady's maid," explained Nell.

"What! Dressing and curling the hair and sewing on ruffles. You'll be used to high-life."

"High-life?" said the hunchback. "What is that?"

"High society, balls and masques," said Tom.

"Fine ladies and gentlemen making merry while the poor starves," said Lee.

"I am sorry that that should be so," said the hunchback gravely.

" 'Tis no fault of yours. The poor stands together . . . times like these. Where are you making for?"

"We are joining our master's household at Dover."

"And all on foot!" cried Lee, "with a child to carry!"

"That's how the rich look after their servants," added his wife.

"We have to be there tomorrow," said Tom, "to set the house in order. We've little time to lose."

"A nice way to treat you!" the woman went on grumbling. "Walking all the way! Where have you come from?"

"Well . . ." began Tom; but the hunchback said quickly: "From London."

"And carrying a child all that way!"

"The child is mine . . . mine and my husband's," said the hunchback. "We are glad to be able to have him with us."

"Why," said Lee, "you ought to get the stage wagon. That's where we're going now. To Tonbridge to catch the wagon."

"Lee's a much travelled man," said his wife admiringly.

"Yes. I don't mind telling you it's not the first time I've travelled on the stage wagon. Once I went from Holborn to Chester . . . travelling the whole of six days. Two miles the hour and a halfpenny the mile, a wagoner to hold the horses and lead them all the way while you sat on the floor of the wagon like a lord. 'Tis a wondrous thing to travel. Hist! I think I hear riders coming this way."

The hunchback shrank nearer to her friends as once again her hand hovered over the sleeping child. They were all silent for some seconds while the sound of horses' hoofs grew louder; and soon a party of riders came into sight. They were soberly dressed and their hair scarcely covered their ears, thus proclaiming them to be soldiers of the Parliamentary forces.

"God go with you!" called Lee.

"God be with you, friend," answered the rider at the head of the cavalcade.

The dust raised by the horses' hoofs made the hunchback cough; the child started to whimper. "All is well," murmured the hunchback. "All is well. Sleep on."

"I heard," said Lee's wife, "that the King won't hold out much longer. They say he's gone to Scotland. He hadn't a chance after Naseby. Best thing he could do would be to join the Frenchwoman in France."

"Mayhap he would not wish to leave his country," said Tom.

"Better for him to leave for France than the next world," put in Lee with a laugh.

The child sat up and gazed at the Lees with an expression of candid distaste.

"All is well," said the hunchback hastily. She put her arm round the child and pressed its little face against her.

"No, no, *no*!" cried the child, wriggling away.

"A fine temper," said Lee's wife.

"It's so hot," replied the hunchback.

"I see you spoil him," said Lee.

"Let's have a look at the little 'un," said his wife. She took hold of the child's ragged sleeve. The child tried to shake her off, but she only laughed, and that seemed to enrage the little creature. "You're a spoiled baby, you are," went on the woman. "You'll never grow into a fine soldier to fight for General Fairfax, you won't. What's your name?"

"Princess," said the child haughtily.

"Princess!" cried Lee. "That's a strange name for a little boy."

"It is Pierre, Monsieur," said the hunchback quickly.

"That in English is Peter," added Gaston.

"He does not speak the very good English," went on the hunchback. "His words are not very clear. We talk to him sometimes in our own tongue . . . sometimes in English . . . and our English, as you see, Madame, is sometimes not very good."

"Princess!" repeated the child. *"Me* . . . Princess!"

There was silence while all looked at the child. The Lees in puzzlement; the four companions of the child as though they had been struck temporarily lifeless. In the distance could be heard the sound of retreating horses' hoofs. Then the hunchback seemed to come to a decision; she rose and took the child firmly by the hand.

"We must go," she said. "We shall not reach our lodging by nightfall if we stay longer. Come, my friends. And good day to both of you. A pleasant journey and thank you for your company."

The other three had risen with her. They closed about the child.

"Good day to you," murmured the Lees.

The child turned to take a last look at them, and the big black eyes showed an angry defiance as the lips formed the words: "Princess. *Me* . . . Princess!"

❁ ❁ ❁

They did not speak until they had put some distance between themselves and the man and woman on the bank. The hunchback had picked up the child so that they might more quickly escape.

At length Nell said: "For the moment I was ready to run."

"That would have been unwise," said the hunchback. "That would have been the worst thing we could have done."

"If we could only make . . . the boy understand!"

"I have often been relieved because he is so young . . . too young to understand; and yet if only we could explain. . . . But how could one so young be expected to understand?"

The child, knowing itself to be the subject of discussion, was listening eagerly. The hunchback noticed this and said: "What will there be to eat at this inn of yours, Tom? Mayhap a little duck or snipe . . . peacock, kid, venison. Mayhap lampreys and sturgeon . . ."

"We must remember our stations," said the hunchback.

The child wished to bring the conversation back to itself. The little hands beat the hunchback. "Nan . . . Nan . . ." said the child. *"Dirty* Nan! Don't like dirty Nan."

"Hush, dearest, hush!" said the hunchback.

"Want to go home. Want clean Nan . . . not dirty Nan."

"Dearest, be good. Only a little while longer. Remember you are Pierre . . . my little boy."

"Little *girl*!" said the child.

"No, dearest, no! You are Pierre . . . Pierre for Peter."

"No Pierre! No Pierre!" chanted the child. "Dirty Nan! Black lady! Want to get down."

"Try to sleep, my darling."

"No sleep! No sleep!"

Two soldiers had rounded the bend and were coming towards the party, who immediately fell silent; but just as the two men drew level with them, the child called to them: "Me . . . Princess. Dirty frock . . . not mine . . . Me . . . Princess!"

They stopped. The hunchback smiled, but beneath the grime and dust her face grew a shade paler.

"What was it the little one said?" asked one of the soldiers.

It was the hunchback who answered. "Your pardon, Messieurs. I and my husband do not speak the English very well. Nor does our son. He is telling you his name is Pierre. That is Peter in English."

One of the soldiers said: "I thought the boy said he was a Princess."

The child smiled dazzlingly and chanted: "Princess! Princess! Don't like black lady. Want clean Nan."

The soldiers looked at each other and exchanged smiles. One of them brought his face near to that of the child. "So you're a Princess, eh, young fellow?" he said. "I'll tell you something." He nodded his head in the direction of his companion. "He's Oliver Cromwell and I'm Prince Charley."

"Forgive, Monsieur," said the hunchback quickly. "We mean no harm. We are walking to Dover to the house of our master."

"To Dover, eh!" said the soldier. "You're on the right road but you've many hours journey before you yet."

"Then we must hasten."

The second soldier was smiling at the child. "Listen to me, little 'un," he said. " 'Tis better in these days to be the son of a hunchback than the daughter of a King."

"Ah, Messieurs!" cried the hunchback. "You speak truly. I thank God these days that I am a poor hunchback, for I remember there are others in worse case."

"God's will be done," said the soldier.

"God be with you," said the hunchback.

"And with you, woman. And with you all. Farewell, Princess Peter."

The child began to wail as they continued along the road. "Me Princess. Want my gown. Don't like dirty Nan."

Again that silence; again that tension.

Nell said: "Can it go on? Shall we be so lucky every time?"

"We must be," replied the hunchback grimly.

❁ ❁ ❁

It was dusk when they came to the inn. They were glad of that, for the daylight was disturbing; moreover the child slept.

Tom went across the inn yard and found the landlord. He was a long time gone. The rest of the party waited uneasily beneath the hanging sign.

"Mayhap we should not have come here," said Nell. "Mayhap we should have made beds for ourselves under the hedges."

"We shall be safe enough," murmured the hunchback. "And we'll leave at daybreak."

At length Tom called to them to come forward. The landlord was with him.

"So this is the party," said the landlord. "Two women and two men and a young boy. I don't make a practice of taking foot passengers . . . nor those that come on the stage wagon. My inn is an inn for the quality."

"We can pay," said Tom quickly.

"There's comings and goings these days," said the landlord. "We had a troop of soldiers in here only this day."

Tom took out his purse and showed it to the innkeeper. "We'll pay in advance," he said. "We're tired and hungry. Let us make a bargain here and now."

"Very well, very well," said the landlord. "What'll you eat? It'll be at the common table, I reckon, and that'll cost you sixpence a-piece."

Tom looked at the hunchback, who said: "Could we have the meal served for us alone? Mayhap we could have a room to ourselves."

The innkeeper scratched his head and looked at them.

"We'll pay," said Tom.

"Well then . . . it could be arranged. Please to wait in the inn parlor, and you'll be called to table in good time."

He led the way into the parlor, and Tom went out with him to settle where they would sleep, what they would eat, and to pay the innkeeper what he asked.

There were several people in the inn parlor. The hunchback noticed this with dismay and she hesitated, but only for a second; then she went boldly forward holding the sleeping child in her arms, with Nell and Gaston on either side of her.

Several people, who sat at the tables and in the window seat, and who were talking together, called a good day to them. The eyes of a plump lady bedecked with ribbons went to the child.

"Looks worn out," she commented. "Poor little mite! She fast asleep?"

"It's a little boy."

"There now! So he is! Have you come far?"

"From London."

The rest of the people went on talking about the war; they were sighing for the good old days of peace and blaming "The French Woman" for all their troubles. There was one large man with short hair who had taken upon himself the task of mentor to the rest. He was explaining to the company why it had been necessary to wage war against the Royalists. His knowledge of affairs was imperfect, but those present who might have corrected him dared not do so.

"The Queen would make us all Catholic if she could," he was declaring. "You, Sir, and you, Madam, and you, my comely wench. Aye, and you who have just come in . . . the hunchback woman and the boy there . . . she'd make us all Catholic if she dared."

"We'd die rather," said another man.

"Why," went on the first, "on St. James' day this Queen of ours walked afoot to Tyburn to honor Catholics who had died there. And I tell you, friends, by the gleam in her eyes it was clear she'd like to see done to some of us good Christians what was done to idolators at Tyburn gallows. If I'd been at Exeter I'd not have let her give *me* the slip. I'd have found her. I'd have carried her to London . . . aye, that I would. I'd have made her walk to Tyburn gallows . . . and it wouldn't have been to honor idolators!"

"She's a very wicked woman," volunteered one of the women. "They say the French are all wicked."

"It won't be long," said the large talkative man, "before we've done with kings and queens in England. Kings and queens have no place in England today."

"If the King was to be killed in battle . . . or after," said a short fat man, "there'd still be his children to make trouble."

"I saw the Prince of Wales once," said the beribboned woman.

"An ugly fellow!"

"Well, that's as may be," said the woman with a smile.

"And what would you mean by that?"

"Oh . . . he was dark . . . dark to swarthiness . . . He had a big nose and a big mouth . . . He was a boy and yet . . ."

"Sounds as if you're a Royalist, madam," said the large man accusingly.

"Oh no, I wouldn't say that. He was naught but a boy . . . Prince Charles . . . and he was riding through our town with his brother, young James. It would have been just before Edgehill, I reckon."

"We nearly got those boys at Edgehill," grumbled the man. "If I'd have been there . . ."

The woman was wistful. "No, he wasn't really ugly . . . not when he smiled. And he smiled at me . . . straight at me and doffed his hat as though I were a lady of the Court. There was a woman with me who declared the smile and the hat-doffing was for her . . ."

"You're bedazzled by royalty!" sneered the man.

"Not me! It was only the Prince himself. There were others there. Gentlemen . . . dukes . . . lords . . . Handsome they might be called, but it was the Prince . . . that boy . . . that dark and ugly boy . . . Mayhap it was because he *was* just a boy . . ."

"Tush!" said the man. "His Royal Highness! He'll not be Highness much longer. It won't be long before he'll want to forget he was Prince of Wales and once heir to a kingdom that will have none of him. People will be ashamed to talk of kings and queens, I tell you. We'll choose our Lord Protector and if he doesn't please us we'll rid ourselves of him and choose another. Royalty! I'd have the heads off the lot of them!"

"Except the prince of Wales . . ." murmured the woman.

Tom looked in at the door and beckoned to his party; gladly they followed him out of the parlor.

He whispered as the door shut on them: "We're to have an attic to ourselves to sleep in. The landlord is having straw put up there now. Food is being prepared for us, and that we can have by ourselves in one of the small rooms. I have paid him well. I think he is a little suspicious of how we can pay for what we want; but his eyes glistened at the sight of the money."

"Then let us eat quickly and retire to our attic," said the hunchback.

As they walked across the hall they heard a man's voice, shouting to a groom. It was a loud and arrogant voice. They were all straining their ears to listen.

"Come, boy! Where's mine host? I'm famished. And I want a room . . . the best room you have . . ."

The innkeeper was bustling into the yard; they could hear the rise and fall of his voice as he obsequiously placated the newcomer.

"Come along," said the hunchback; and they went into a small room where a meal of duck and boar was laid out for them, with ale to drink. The child awakened and sleepily partook of the meal. They spoke little while they ate, and before the others had finished—as the child had fallen asleep again—the hunchback said she would go up to the attic room with him and there she would stay till morning; for the two of them must not be separated.

"I'll show you the way," said Tom. " 'Tis right at the top under the eaves."

As they came out into the hall the arrogant newcomer was leaning against the wall shouting instructions and looking with distaste at his surroundings. His eyes flickered over the hunchback and the child; he paused for a second and then gave them a look of distaste. The hunchback hastily followed Tom up the stairs and, as she did so, she heard the drawling voice: "God's Body! This is no inn! 'Tis an ale house. This is no place for the quality. Hunchback beggars and their brats stay here. Plague take you! Why did you not tell me, man?"

The hunchback did not look round as she followed Tom up the narrow staircase. Tom indicated a door and they went in. It was a long, low-ceilinged room; a dark room, and the thatch showed through a small unglazed window. On the floor were two piles of straw which would serve as beds. It was rough but it would do for a night.

"Go back to your food," said the hunchback. "I will stay here with the child. All of you join me when you have finished, but first eat your fill."

Tom bowed and when he had left her she laid the child on one of the heaps of straw and gently put her lips to the small forehead. Then she threw herself down beside the child. She was worn out with the day's exertion. She laid her hand over her fast-beating heart. It should beat more peacefully now; here they would be safe until morning, and there were only a few more miles to Dover. Here they could sleep and refresh themselves, and at daybreak they would be on their journey again.

Suddenly the door opened and a groom came in. He hesitated. "Ah . . . I did not know there was anyone here. I have brought more straw."

"I thank you."

"There are four of you and the little girl?"

"Little boy," she corrected him.

As she spoke she had laid her hand on the child; it was as though when anyone spoke of it she had to touch it, fearing that someone might try to snatch it from her. The man came over and looked down at the sleeping child. He stared, and she remembered how the woman on the bank had noticed her finely shaped hands.

"A little boy," said the groom, "with the looks of a girl."

"He is young yet, and I am told that he resembles his mother rather than his father."

"He has an air," said the groom. "He might be the child of someone of high degree."

He was watching the hunchback in a manner which brought the flush to her cheeks, and in that instant, as the rich blood showed beneath the dirt, she was young and comely.

He lowered his voice. "Lady," he said, "there are some hereabouts who would be loyal to His Majesty."

She did not answer; her grip tightened on the child.

"Your hands are too fine, madam," he said. "They betray you. You should keep them hidden."

"My hands? I am a lady's maid."

"That would account for it, mayhap."

"Mayhap! It does account for it!"

"Your hump has slipped a little, lady. If you'll forgive my saying so, it is a bit too high. And you should bend over more."

The hunchback tried to speak, but she could not; her mouth was dry and she was trembling.

"I was with the King's army at Edgehill," went on the groom. "I was with the little Prince Charles and his brother James. There was that about him—Charles, I mean—which made me want to serve him. Boy as he was, I'll never forget him. Tall for his age and dark for an Englishman, and so ready to give a smile to a man that he didn't seem like a king's son. Just one of ourselves . . . and yet with a difference . . . He came near to capture at Edgehill . . . God bless him! God bless the Prince of Wales!"

"You're a bold man to speak thus before a stranger."

"These are days for bold deeds, madam. But you may trust me. I wish you Godspeed and a safe trip across the water."

"Across the water?"

"You go to Dover, madam. You will cross the water with the child and join the Queen."

"I have said nothing that should make you think this."

"They say the Queen is the cause of the King's troubles, madam. That may be so, but the Queen is devoted to the King's cause. Poor lady! It must be two years since she fled from England. It was a few weeks after the birth of her youngest, the little Princess Henrietta."

"This makes uneasy talk," said the hunchback.

"You may trust me, madam. And if there is anything I can do to serve you . . ."

"Thank you, but I am only a poor woman who, with her husband and fellow-servants, goes to join her master's household."

He bowed and went from the room; and when he had gone she was still unable to move, for a numbness had seized her limbs. On the road, passing the soldiers of the King's enemies, she had been less frightened than now. The walls of the attic became to her like prison walls.

When the others joined her, they found her sitting on the straw holding the child in her arms.

She said: "I am afraid. One of the grooms came to bring straw, and I am sure he knows who we are. And I . . . I cannot be sure whether or not we can trust him."

❁ ❁ ❁

The night was full of terrors. She shifted from side to side on her straw. The hump of linen hurt her back, but she dared not unstrap it. What if the hunchback were surprised without her hump! Had she been foolish in attempting this great adventure? What if she failed now? That virago, Queen Henrietta Maria, would never forgive her for exposing her youngest child to such dangers of the road. And yet there were times when it was necessary to take a bold action. The Queen herself had acted boldly, and because of that was at this moment in her native country where she might work for the King, her husband, instead of being—as she most certainly would have been, had she been less bold—the prisoner of the King's enemies.

Anne Douglas, Lady Dalkeith, had had to find some way of disguising her tall and graceful figure, and the hump had seemed as good a way as any; and to assume French nationality had seemed imperative since the little Princess could prattle and her lisping "Princess" sounded more like Pierre than any other name. If it had only been possible to make the child understand the danger she was in, how much easier would this task have been! But she was too young to realize why she must be hurried from her comfortable palace, why she must be dressed as a beggar's child, and that she must be called Pierre. If she had been younger—or older—the journey might have been less dangerous.

Anne Douglas had scarcely slept since she had left the Palace of Oatlands; she was exhausted now, but even with the others at hand, she dared not sleep. The groom had made her very uneasy. He had said she could trust him, but whom could one trust in a country engaged in a great civil war?

It would have seemed incredible a few years ago that she, Anne Villiers, wife of Robert Douglas who was the heir of the Earl of Morton, should be lying in such a place as this. But times had changed; and it occurred to her to wonder where the King slept this night or where the Prince of Wales had his lodging.

She had made the decision suddenly.

It was two years since the little Princess had been born. The Queen had been very weak at the time, and before she had risen from her bed news had come that Lord Essex—who was on the side of the Parliament—was marching to Exeter with the intention of besieging the city. Henrietta Maria had written to him asking for permission to leave for Bath with her child; Essex's reply had been that if the Queen went anywhere with his consent it would be to London, where she would be called before the Parliament to answer a charge of making civil war in England.

There had been only one course open to her—flight to France. How she had wept, that emotional woman! She had cried to Anne: "I must leave this country. If the Parliament make me their prisoner, my husband will come to my aid; he will risk all for my sake. It is better that my miserable life should be risked than that he should be in peril through me. I have written to him telling him this; and by the time he receives my letter I hope to be in France. The Queen of France is my own sister-in-law, and she will not turn me away."

She was all emotion; her heart was ever ready to govern her head, and this, Anne knew, was in a large measure to be blamed for the King's disasters; for, oddly enough, although the marriage of Charles and Henrietta Maria had begun stormily, they had quickly understood each other, and with understanding had come passionate affection. The Queen was passionate by nature; frivolous she seemed at times, yet how singlemindedly she could cling to a cause; and the cause to which she now gave her passionate energy was that of her husband.

"Take care of my little one, Anne," she had said. "Guard her with your life. If ill befall her, Anne Douglas, you shall suffer a thousand times more than she does." Those black eyes had snapped with fury as she had railed against a fate which demanded she leave her child; they softened with love for the baby and gratitude to Anne Douglas, even while she threatened her. Then, having made these threats, she had taken Anne in her arms and kissed her. "I know you will take care of my child . . . Protestant though you are. And if you should ever see the light, foolish woman, and come to the true religion, you must instruct my daughter as I would have her instructed. Oh, but you are a Protestant, you say! And the King will have his children brought up in the religion of their own country! And I am a poor desolate mother who must give up her newborn babe to a

Protestant! A Protestant!" She had become incoherent, for she had never bothered to learn the English language properly. Anne knelt to her and swore that, apart from her religion, she would serve the Queen and obey her in all things.

Poor sad Henrietta Maria, who had come to England as a girl of sixteen, very lovely and determined to have her own way, was now an exile, parted from her husband and children. But with God's help, there should be one child restored to her.

To Exeter the King had come, for he had not received his wife's letter and believed her to be still there in childbed; he had fought his way through the Parliamentary forces to reach her. It had been Anne's unhappy task to tell him that he was too late. Her eyes filled with tears now as she remembered him—handsome, even with the stains of battle on him, noble of countenance as he always would be, for he was a man of ideals; and if there was a weakness in that face, it but endeared him to a woman such as Anne Douglas. He was too ready to listen to the wrong advice; he was weak when he should have been strong, and obstinate when to give way would have been wise. He believed too firmly in that Divine Right of Kings which had grown out of date since the reign of Henry VIII; he lacked the common touch of Henry's daughter, Elizabeth, who had been able to adjust her rule to meet a more modern way of life. Weak though he might have been, a ruler unfit to rule, he was a man of handsome presence and of great personal charm; and it was moving to see his devotion to his family.

With him to Exeter had come the young Prince of Wales, a boy of fourteen then, who had none of his father's good looks, but already more than his father's charm. He was rather shy and sweet-tempered. It had been moving to see him take the baby in his arms and marvel at the smallness of her.

Anne wept afresh; she wept for the handsome King who was losing his kingdom, for the Prince, who would be heir to his father's lost throne, for the baby—the youngest of a tragic family.

"Poor little daughter," the King had said, "you have been born into a sorry world. You must be baptized at once."

"What name shall she be given, Your Majesty?"

"Let us call her Henrietta after my wife. But she must be baptized according to the rites of the Church of England."

And so the ceremony had taken place in the Cathedral of Exeter on a warm July day two years ago; then the King had left for Cornwall where he pursued the war with some success.

Later, when the baby was three months old, he returned to Bedford House in the city of Exeter where she was caring for the child, but only for a brief visit, and Anne had not seen him since. The Prince came to see his little sister a year later. The child, fifteen months old, was not too young to notice the tall dark boy who made so much of her; she was old enough to crow with pleasure when she saw him, and weep bitterly when he went away. The Prince had had to leave in a hurry because once more the Roundheads were marching on Exeter. Remembering Henrietta Maria's words, Anne had done her utmost to escape with the child to Cornwall, but her attempt to do so had been foiled. She had been surrounded by spies, and there had been nothing she could do on that occasion but shut herself and her servants up in the security of Bedford House and remain at the side of the Princess day and night.

From her exile in France an angry Queen, knowing that her precious child was in Exeter and that the town was being besieged by her enemies, had raved with fury against fate, the Parliament and that slothful traitress, Anne Douglas.

That was a cruel charge and Anne had suffered deeply. In vain did those about her tell her that she was foolish to attach such importance to the Queen's reproaches. Did she not know the Queen!

It was said of Henrietta Maria that she regarded unfortunate friends blameworthy, even as traitors were. Anne tried to understand. Henrietta Maria was beside herself with grief, wondering what was happening to her child in a besieged city where there would be little to eat, where death stalked the streets and there would be constant dangers. Henrietta Maria was like a child; when she was hurt she stamped her foot and struck out at those nearest.

Anne had told herself she must remember the Queen's grief and bear with her.

Sir John Berkeley, who had held the city for the Royalists, deciding they could hold out no longer, had surrendered the city on the condition that the little Princess and certain of her houschold should be allowed to leave Exeter; so they went, by the Parliament's order, to the Palace of Oatlands, and there they had been living for the last months at Anne's expense as the Parliament refused to grant money for the Princess's upkeep.

Oatlands, that royal pleasure house built by Henry VIII, had proved a refuge as pleasant as could be hoped for in the circumstances. But, since the day civil war had broken out in England, there had been no lasting peace for any member of the royal family; and there came that day when, leaving the garden and coming through the courtyard to the quadrangle with the machicolated gateway, Anne had met a messenger who brought her a letter from the House of Commons telling her that the Princess must be made ready to leave for London; there she was to join her sister, the Princess Elizabeth, and her brothers, Prince James and Prince Henry, in St. James

Palace, where they would be placed in the care of the Earl and Countess of Northumberland.

Then Anne had made her decision. She would not again incur the anger of her mistress. She had long determined that she would never give up the child to any but the Queen or her family. The wild plan had come to her then. Henrietta Maria had fled to France; why should she not follow her? Surely she could disguise herself more successfully than the Queen had done. A woman with a child . . . a beggar woman? No! For beggars were sometimes set upon and treated badly. A humble servant and her child would be better; and for company she would take with her French Gaston, who would pretend to be her valet husband; and Elinor Dykes and Thomas Lambert, servants of the household, should come with her.

They would slip out of Oatlands Palace and none should know that they had gone. She would write a letter which should be sent back to the palace by another of her servants whom she would take with her for this purpose, informing certain members of her household whom she believed she could trust; she would give them permission to share the Princess's clothes and some of her possessions among themselves, and warn them that they must give her three clear days before informing the Parliament that she and the Princess were missing. If they obeyed her, none would know of her flight until the fourth day; and by that time she should be safely on the water on her way to France.

It had not seemed so difficult; but how could she have foreseen the weariness of a gently nurtured lady after tramping the roads for three days; how could she have guessed that the little Princess herself, not understanding the danger, would insist on telling those whom she met on the road that the clothes she wore were not the fine garments to which she was accustomed, that her name was not Pierre nor Peter; but that she was the Princess?

Another day, thought Anne feverishly, and we shall be at sea. Only another day . . . but here we are in this attic, and the attic walls are like prison walls, for suspicion has been born in the mind of a groom.

❁ ❁ ❁

They were awakened by a clatter of hoofs in the courtyard. It was dark in the attic; but Anne, starting up, saw a patch of starry sky through the window.

"Tom . . . Nell! Are you awake?"

"Yes, my lady."

"Hush, Tom!"

"Yes, Nan; we're awake," said Nell.

"What was that noise?"

"Only newcomers arriving, I doubt not."

"It's late . . . very late."

"Can you not sleep?"

"I am thinking of that groom."

"But he said he was loyal to His Majesty."

"How can we know whether he was speaking the truth?"

"Do you think he suspected who the child is?"

"I am not sure. But if she had awakened and called herself 'Princess' we should certainly have been betrayed."

They were silent for a while. Then Anne started up again. "Listen! Steps on the stairs!"

" 'Tis new arrivals at the inn," said Tom.

"But they are on the attic staircase. It leads only to us. I am sure they are there. It is the groom. He has betrayed us."

The next seconds seemed like minutes. Anne held the Princess close against her. Little Henrietta began to whimper in her sleep. Tom was on his feet; the footsteps had stopped and they knew that someone was standing on the other side of the door.

Then there was a sudden nerve-shattering hammering against the wood.

Tom threw his weight against it. "Who's there?" he demanded.

"It is your landlord."

"What do you want of us at this hour?"

"Soldiers are here. They demand quarters. I have no room for them all."

"Open the door to him," said Anne, and Tom obeyed.

"Listen here," said the landlord. "I've got to find room for the soldiers. I told them that the inn was full, but they wouldn't have it. They demand shelter. Some of them have been drinking. Now there's an outhouse you can have for the rest of the night. I often let it to passengers from the wagon. It would serve you well."

"Cannot the soldiers use the outhouse?" asked Tom.

"I don't want trouble at my inn. There's a war raging in this country. In wartime we're in the hands of the soldiery."

Anne said quickly: "Let us go to this outhouse. I doubt not that it will suit us well."

"Thank you. You are a wise woman. Come quickly. The soldiers are drinking in the parlor."

He held his candle aloft and, gathering the sleeping child in her arms

Anne, with Tom leading and Nell and Gaston taking up the rear, followed the man down the staircase. When they were on the lower landing, a door opened, and there stood the elegant man who had made such a commotion earlier that night.

"By God's body!" he cried. "Cannot a gentleman be allowed to sleep? Comings and goings the whole night through! What is happening now, man?"

"Your pardon, your honor. It's the soldiers. They've just come in. That's how it is these days, sir. There's nothing a poor innkeeper can do."

He quizzed the party. "These hardly look like soldiers."

"Nay, sir. Some poor travellers I took in, sir, and let them have the attic. Now the soldiers want it and . . ."

"So you're turning them out into the night, eh?"

"No . . . no, your honor. They've paid for shelter and they shall have it. I am giving them an outhouse. 'Tis warm and comfortable and will seem cozy to such as they are, I'll swear."

With an oath the man shut his door and the party continued their descent. The landlord took them through the kitchens where, setting down his candle, he took up a lantern, and conducted them to the outhouse.

"You'll pass the rest of the night in peace and comfort here," he said. "You could not be more snug. See, there's straw for you all and 'tis a warm night."

"Can the door be barred?" asked Tom.

"Aye. You can lock it from the inside if you wish to."

"This will suit us for the rest of the night," said Anne quickly.

The landlord left them; and as soon as he had gone Tom turned the heavy key in the lock.

"I feel a little safer here," said Anne; but she was still trembling.

❁ ❁ ❁

They left early next morning as soon as the first sign of dawn was in the sky. All through the morning they walked, and in the afternoon they came into the town of Dover. Anne felt great relief as, looking out to sea, she caught sight of the Dover Packet-boat lying at anchor; the weather was undoubtedly favorable. Very soon her ordeal must be ended.

Henrietta was lively; she had ridden all the morning on Anne's back, and if Anne was tired, she was not.

"Water!" she cried.

"It is the sea, my precious one," Anne told her.

"Nan . . . want my own gown . . ."

"Soon you shall have it, little Pierre."

"No Pierre! No Pierre!"

"Just a little while longer, dearest."

"No Pierre!" chanted Henrietta. "Me . . . Princess. No Pierre! No Peter!"

"Let's pretend for a little longer. Let it be our secret, eh?"

Tom said: "I wish the Princess would sleep."

"She cannot sleep all the time."

"No sleep! No sleep!" chanted the Princess.

" 'Twould please me better if she slept as we passed through the town," persisted Tom.

A man passed them. He gave no sign of having recognized them, but he was the elegant gentleman whom they had seen at the inn and who had opened his door as they had passed along the corridor.

None of them spoke, but each was aware of him. He turned slowly and followed them. At the water's edge he called to a boatman in his arrogant manner. "Is that the Dover Packet lying there, fellow?"

"Yes, milord."

"Then row me out to her, will you? These people will go with us."

"Milord . . . ?" began Tom.

The man shook his head impatiently.

When they were in the boat the baby Princess showed clearly her appreciation of the elegant gentleman, but he did not glance at her as he gave orders to the boatman in his cool arrogant manner.

"How's the wind?"

"Set fair for France, milord."

"Then the Packet will be leaving soon, I'll swear."

"Waiting but for the turn of the tide, milord."

Now they were alongside and the party stepped aboard, obediently following the man who led the way.

He signed to Anne and led her and the child into a cabin. When they were alone, he bowed to her, taking her hand and kissing it. "You have done a marvelous thing, Anne," he said. "The Queen will love you forever."

"It was a great comfort to know that you were with us . . . though not of the party."

"There were some uneasy moments. The worst was last night when I opened my door and saw you being marched down the stairs. Well, that is over. Stay in your cabin during the crossing, and remain disguised until you are safely on French soil. I must go now. Assure Her Majesty of my untiring devotion."

"I will, John."

"Tell her the Berkeleys will hold the West against any number of Roundhead oafs."

"I'll tell her, John."

"Goodbye and good luck."

Sir John Berkeley kissed her hand and that of the Princess. Then he quickly returned to the boat and was rowed ashore.

Not long after, the Packet slipped away from the white cliffs on its way to Calais.

TWO

The Princess was happy. No sooner had she and her faithful little party set foot on French soil at Calais than her dear Nan discarded her hump, kissed her rapturously and called her Beloved Princess. The indignity she had suffered was now over; there was no need to remind people now that she was a princess. There were fine clothes to be worn, there were many to kiss her hand and pay her the homage she had missed when dressed as the child of a servant. The crowds welcomed her. They called to her that she was the granddaughter of great Henri, and therefore France was her home and all French men and women were ready to love her.

How she crowed and waved her little hands! How she smiled as she smoothed down the folds of her dress! Occasionally she would turn to Nan and look with happy pleasure at the tall and beautiful governess whom it seemed she had sought in vain to revive from those dirty rags. Henrietta was happy; she did not know that she came to France as a suppliant; that she was a beggar far more than she had appeared to be on the road to Dover.

"You are going to see your mother, the Queen," Anne told her.

The child was wide-eyed with wonder. Her mother, the Queen, was just a name to her. Nan, during the Princess's two years of life, had been the only mother she had known.

"You must love her very dearly," Anne explained. "She will be so happy to see you, and you will be the only one of all your brothers and sisters who may be with her to make her happy."

"Why?" she asked.

"Because the others cannot be with her."

"Why not?"

"Because your brothers, James and Henry, must stay with your sister Elizabeth; and your big brother, Charles, cannot stay with his mother in France because he has other matters to which he must attend. Your big sister, Mary, is the Princess of Holland, so she cannot be with your mother either."

But Henrietta did not understand. She only knew that she was happy again, that she had bright clothes to wear and that people called her Princess.

So she was escorted from Calais to Saint-Germain.

The news had spread that her infant daughter was about to be restored to the poor sad Queen. There was a romantic story of a brave governess who had brought the child out of a war-torn country under the very eyes of the King's enemies. The story was one to delight the warmhearted French. They wanted to see the little Princess; they wanted to cheer the brave governess. So they gathered along the route from Calais that they might cry "Good Luck" to the little girl, and let her know that as granddaughter of their greatest King, they were ready to welcome her to their country.

The people cheered her. "Long live the little Princess from England! Long live the granddaughter of our great Henri! Long live the brave governess!"

And the Princess smiled and took this ovation as her right; she had already forgotten her uncomfortable journey. Anne was worn out with fatigue, and now that her anxiety had lifted, she felt light-headed; she could not believe that the people of France were cheering her; and while she smiled she felt as though she were not really there in France but sitting on a bank while the Princess betrayed their secret, or that she was in an attic, terrified while a groom told her that her hump was slipping.

When they came to the château on the edge of the forest, Henrietta Maria was waiting to greet them. She had been granted the use of the château at Saint-Germain-en-Laye and she had her own apartments in the Louvre; she had been given a pension by her royal relatives of France, and at the time of Henrietta's arrival she lived at Court with all the state of a visiting Queen.

She was waiting in her salon—surrounded by her attendants and some of the exiles from England who visited her from time to time—magnificently dressed in blue brocade decorated with frills of fine lace and pearls; her black eyes were filled with tears, and her usually sallow cheeks were aflame. This was the happiest moment of her life since she had left England, she declared.

When the Princess was brought to her she gave a great cry of joy; she dispensed with all ceremony and swooped on the child, pressing her against her pearl-decorated gown while tears gushed from her eyes. She began to talk in French, which the little girl could not understand.

"So at last, my little one, I have you here with me. Oh, how I have suffered! You, my little one, my baby, whom I had to leave when I fled from those wicked men! But now you are back with me. Now you are here and we shall never be parted as long as we live. Oh see, this is my daughter, my youngest and my most precious. She is returned to me and it is such a miracle that I must give great thanks to God and all the saints. And I do so here in this happy moment." She turned her tearful yet radiant face to Cyprien de Gamaches, her priest, who stood beside her. "Père Cyprien shall instruct this child of mine. She shall be brought up in the true faith of Rome. Rejoice, for she is not only snatched from her enemies—those round-headed villains who would destroy her father—she is saved from a subtler enemy; she is saved for Holy Church!"

Henrietta wriggled; the pearls on her mother's gown were hurting her; she turned and held out her hand to Anne who was standing close by.

The Queen's brilliant eyes were now on the governess.

"And here is my dearest Lady Anne . . . my dear faithful servant! We shall never forget what you have done. All Paris, all France talks of the wonderful deed. You have behaved with great courage and I shall never forget you."

The Queen put down the child and would have embraced Anne, but as she was about to do so, Anne, worn out by the terrible fatigue of her long tramp and by all the anxieties of the previous days, sank fainting to the floor.

It seemed that her determination to hand over the Princess to none but the child's mother had kept her going; now that her task was completed she must pay the price of the mental strain and physical hardship she had suffered.

❁ ❁ ❁

Henrietta Maria sat with her niece Mademoiselle de Montpensier in her apartments in Saint-Germain. Henrietta Maria was a schemer; when she decided she wanted something, she could be very single-minded. There were several things she wanted very badly; the first was to see an end to the war in England, with her husband victorious; the second was to bring her children up in the Roman Catholic faith; and the third was to arrange suitable marriages for her children.

All of these seemed to her not only natural but virtuous desires. It was a fact that in their marriage contract, the King, her husband, had promised that their children should be instructed in the Catholic faith. In this he had not kept his word; the whole of England would have been against his keeping his word; England still remembered the reign of Bloody Mary, and the people had decided to run no risk of a recurrence of those terrible days.

Henrietta Maria loved her husband and was devoted to her family; but, she told herself, as a staunch Catholic, she loved her religion more. Fate had played into her hands by delivering to her the Princess Henrietta; here was one child who should not be contaminated by wrong teaching; Père Cyprien was already taking matters in hand. He had had a clear run so far, because the Protestant governess, Anne Dalkeith, had been seriously ill since her arrival at Saint-Germain, and had been unable to take a hand in the Princess's upbringing or to remind the Queen of the King's wishes which were those of the majority of the people of England. And she *would* have reminded her, thought Henrietta Maria grimly; even though her ears would have been boxed for it, even though she would have to protest to the Queen and the mother of the child, Anne would do what she considered her duty. It would have been a pity to quarrel with Anne so soon after her glorious adventure. Perhaps, as Père Cyprien said, the hand of God was in this; first, in bringing her daughter to France at an early age before the contamination of a hostile Church could be begun, and secondly, by striking the Protestant governess with a fever and so preventing her interference. Père Cyprien would go even further; he would say that the Great Rebellion and Civil War in England had doubtless been an act of God calculated to save the soul of the young Princess.

Henrietta Maria could not follow him as far as that, but she was at least satisfied that her young daughter would be safe from heresy and now she could turn her thoughts to the marriages of her children. There was one whose marriage was of the utmost importance: Charles, Prince of Wales.

He was a boy of sixteen, very young to marry; yet Princes married young. Henrietta Maria's illogical mind darted hither and thither, taking up one idea, rejecting it for another, and then returning to the first. If young Charles were to remain an exile, he would need a very rich wife; if he were to be King, he would need a royal wife. But riches were always useful; she had not thought of that until she found herself an exile from her adopted country. What would have happened to her, she wondered, if, instead of being the daughter of the fourth Henri of beloved memory, she had been the daughter of the despised third Henri. Who could say?

Now she studied the young woman before her, for she had decided on Mademoiselle as the most fitting bride for her son Charles, and she had received reports that Charles was on his way to Paris.

Mademoiselle de Montpensier, known throughout France as the Mademoiselle of the French Court, was Henrietta Maria's own niece, being the daughter of her brother, Gaston, Duke of Orléans. Mademoiselle unfortunately had a great opinion of herself. She was the richest heiress in Europe; she was a cousin of the young King Louis XIV; she believed herself to be peerless in charm and beauty and, although she was willing to be wooed by the Prince of Wales through his mother, she would give no assurance that she would even consider his suit.

Now she smoothed the folds of her rich brocade gown about her beautiful figure, and Henrietta Maria knew that she was thinking what a charming picture she made with her pink and white complexion and her abundant fair hair; the Queen knew that she considered herself not only the wealthiest heiress but the most beautiful young woman in France. Henrietta Maria's fingers itched to box her ears; Henrietta Maria's small foot tapped impatiently; there was a great deal of hot temper bottled up in the diminutive body of the Queen of England.

"My son will soon be with us," said the Queen. "I live for the day."

"Ah, my dearest Aunt, it must be wonderful for you—an exile from your country in a foreign land—to have your family escape from those villains."

"A foreign land!" cried the Queen. "Mademoiselle, I was born in this country. I am my father's beloved daughter."

"A pity he died before he could know you," said the malicious Mademoiselle.

"Aye! His death was the greatest tragedy this country ever suffered. I burn with indignation every time I pass through the Rue de la Ferronnérie where that mad monk pierced him to the heart."

"My dearest Aunt, you upset yourself for something that happened years ago . . . when you have so many present troubles with which to concern yourself."

Henrietta Maria flashed a look of irritation at her niece. Mademoiselle was clever; she granted her that; she knew how to make those little thrusts in the spots where they hurt most. There she was, the arrogant young beauty, reminding her aunt that she, Mademoiselle, cousin to the King, daughter of Monsieur de France, was really being rather gracious by spending so much of her precious time with her poor exiled aunt.

Henrietta Maria could subdue her anger when great issues were at stake.

"My son is of great height, already a man. They say he bears a striking resemblance to my father."

"In looks only, I trust, Your Majesty. Your father, our great King, Henri Quatre, was France's greatest King, we all know, but he was also France's greatest lover."

"My son will love deeply also. There is that charm in him which tells me so."

"Let us hope, for the sake of the wife he will marry, that in one respect he will not resemble your great father whose mistresses were legion."

"Ah! He has his father's blood in him as well as that of my father. There never was a more noble man, nor a more faithful, than my Charles. I, his wife, tell you that, and I know it."

"Then, dear Aunt, you were indeed fortunate in your husband. When I choose mine, fidelity is one of the qualities I shall look for."

"Beauty such as yours would keep any man faithful."

"Such as your father, Madame, would never be faithful to Venus herself. And as your son is so like him . . ."

"Tush! He is but a boy!"

"So very young that he need not think of marriage yet."

"A Prince is never too young to think of marriage."

"Mayhap while his affairs are in a state of flux, it would be wise to wait. A great heiress would more readily accept a King whose crown is safe than one who may live through his life with only the hope of regaining it."

Mademoiselle was smiling absently to herself. Her thoughts were of marriage, but not of one between herself and the young Prince of England. Henrietta Maria fumed silently. She knew what was in the minx's mind. Marriage, yes! And with her royal cousin, the King of France. And Henrietta Maria had already decided that Louis XIV was for her own Henrietta.

❁ ❁ ❁

The Princess Henriette—she had been Henriette from the moment she passed into her mother's care—loved her brother immediately she set eyes on him. He came into the nursery where she was with her governess, poor pale Lady Dalkeith, who had just risen from her sickbed to find herself fêted as the heroine of the year. Lady Dalkeith, serious-minded and conscientious, found little pleasure in the eulogies which came her way; she had discovered the Queen's determination to bring up the child in the Catholic faith, which was against the wishes of the King of England and his people; and this disturbed her so much that she could feel only apprehension in contemplating the fact that she, having successfully conducted the child to her mother, was indirectly responsible.

But the little Henriette was unaware of the storms about her; all she knew was that she had a brother, and that as soon as she saw him, and he held her in his arms and told her that he had known her when she was a very tiny baby, she loved him.

"Charles!" she would cry in her high-pitched baby voice. "Dear Charles!"

And he would call her his baby sister. "But," he said, "Henriette is such a long name for such a small person, and now I hear they are to add Anne to it out of respect for King Louis' mother. It is far too long. My little puss . . . my little love, you shall be my Minette."

"Minette?" she said wonderingly.

"It shall be my name for you. It is something we share, you and I, dear little sister."

She was pleased. "Minette!" she said. "I am Minette, Charles' Minette."

He kissed her and let her pull his long dark curly hair.

"I wondered when I should see you again, Minette," he told her. "I thought mayhap I never should."

"You are so big to be a brother," she said.

"That's because I'm the eldest of the family. I was fourteen years old when you were born."

She did not fully understand, so she laughed and clasped his arm to her little body to show how much she loved him.

He held her tightly. It was wonderful to be with one of his own flesh and blood. He wondered whether all his family would ever be together again. He was only a boy but he had been with his father in battle, and he knew that events were moving against his family. He was quiet and shy; he enjoyed the company of women, but they must not be haughty ladies like his cousin Mademoiselle de Montpensier; he liked humbler girls, girls who liked him because he was young and, although not handsome, had a way with him. He was particularly shy here in France because he knew that they laughed at his French accent; and although he himself was ready to laugh at it—for he knew it to be atrocious, and he never tried to see himself other than the way he was—he was too young, too unsure of himself, to be able to endure the ironic laughter of others. He remembered continually that he was a Prince whose future was in jeopardy, and that made him cautious.

So it was wonderful to be with this affectionate little sister; she was so frail but pretty, and she had the Stuart eyes and the promise of Stuart gaiety. It was good, Charles decided, to have a family.

He had escaped from his companion, his cousin Prince Rupert, who spoke French perfectly and was considered to be a fine soldier in spite of his defeat at Marston Moor. He had escaped from his mother and her continual prodding, her many instructions as to how he must set about wooing his cousin, Mademoiselle of France.

"I love you, little sister," he whispered, "oh, so much more than haughty Mademoiselle."

"Charles," murmured the little girl, as she pulled his black hair and watched the curls spring back into place, "will you stay with me, Charles?"

"I shall have to go away soon, Minette."

"No! Minette says no!"

He touched her cheek. "And Minette's commands should be obeyed."

Lady Dalkeith left them together; she was very fond of the Prince and rejoiced to see the signs of affection between the brother and sister. She thought: Perhaps I could speak to him about her religious instruction. He knows the wish of his father. But how could I go against the Queen? How could I carry tales of his mother to the Prince? The child is too young to absorb very much at this stage. I will wait. Who knows what will happen?

"Were you little once?" Henriette asked her brother when they were alone.

"Yes, I was little, and so ugly that our mother was ashamed of me; I was very solemn, so they thought that I was wise. Dear sister, when in ignorance remain silent and look wise. You will then be judged profound."

Henriette could not understand what he meant, but she laughed with him; her laughter came of contentment.

He talked to her as he could not talk to others. He talked wistfully of his youth. He talked of England, where he had once been the most important of little boys; he told of playing in the gardens of palaces with his brother James and his sister Mary; they had played hide-and-seek on wet days through the great rooms of Hampton Court and Whitehall, and on fine days in the gardens, hiding among the trees, stalking each other through alleys of neatly trimmed yews. Best of all he loved to watch the ships on the river; so he told her how he used to lie in the grass for hours at Greenwich, watching the ships pass by.

"But, Minette, you do not know of these things, and I am a fool to talk to you, for in talking to you I am really talking to myself, and that is a foolhardy thing to do when such talk brings self-pity; for self-pity is a terrible thing, dear Minette; it is the sword which is thrust against oneself; one turns the blade in the wound; one revels in one's own pain, and that way lies folly." He stopped, smiling at her.

"More! More!" cried Henriette.

"Ah, my little Minette, what will become of us . . . what will our end be, I wonder?" But it was not in his nature to be sad for long. He did not believe that his father could be victorious, but he still could turn a nonchalant face to the future. He could live in the moment, and at this moment he was discovering what a delightful sister was his; he was discovering the pleasures of family life. "Dearest Minette, you do not tell me I must go and court the haughty Mademoiselle, do you! You laugh at my maudlin talk as though it were precious wit. Small wonder that I love you, sweet Minette."

"Minette loves Charles," she said, putting her arms about his neck.

Then he told her of Mr. Fawcett who had instructed him and his brother James in archery. His mind raced on; he thought of his French master and his writing master, and the tutor who had made him read from his horn-book; he remembered, too, his mother, who had smothered him with her affection, and had impressed on him the importance of his position. "Never forget, Charles, that one day you will be King of England. You must be as great and good a King as your father." He smiled wryly. Would the people of England now say that his father was a great and good King when they were doing their utmost—at least thousands of them were—to rid themselves of him? Would they ever welcome young Charles Stuart as their King?

"Poor Mam," he said softly, "I have a feeling that she will never be satisfied. She is one of the unlucky ones of this world. It is a comfort to talk to you, sweet sister, because you are too young to understand all I say." He put his lips against her hair. "You are lovely, and I love you. Do you know, I would rather be with you than with all the fine ladies of the Court—or with the King and Queen, and Mam . . . all of them."

Then to amuse her he told her of the piece of wood which he always took to bed with him when he was a boy of her age. "In vain did they try to take it from me, for I would not let them. I loved my wooden billet, and I confess I kept it until it had to be taken from me by very force—and I knew then that I had long outgrown it. One day, Minette, I will tell you more. I will tell you of the fun we had—my brother and sister and I—and I'll tell you how we thought we should go on forever and ever, laughing, playing our games; and then, suddenly, we grew up, all of us on the same day. It was worse for them, as they were younger than I; Mary only a year younger, James four years younger, and little Elizabeth five years younger. I was the big brother. Henry was the baby then, and there was no little Minette in our family, for she had not yet put in an appearance."

"No Minette!"

"You cannot imagine a world without her, can you? Come, Minette, let us play a game together. I weary you with my talk."

"No. Stay like this!" she said.

And thus it was that Mademoiselle, accompanied by his cousin Prince Rupert, found them.

"Your mother would not be pleased that you should spend your time playing with a baby in the nursery," said Mademoiselle coquettishly. She told herself that she had little time to spare for this boy whose fortunes were in the balance, but she was never averse to a light flirtation, and there was something about him—in spite of his youth and inexperience—which interested her more than his cousin Rupert did.

"You must forgive me, Mademoiselle," said Charles. "My French is not good enough to answer you in that language."

She tapped his arm with her fan. "Are you not ashamed, cousin? You cannot speak French!"

"It is remiss of me. I fear I occupied myself riding and shooting at the butts when I should have been studying French, just as you, Mademoiselle, doubtless indulged in some pastime when you should have been studying English."

Rupert translated, and Mademoiselle pouted.

"What would you say if I said you might wear my colors, Charles?"

"I should say you are very gracious," he answered through Rupert.

"I might allow you to hand me into my coach."

"Mademoiselle is most kind."

"And perhaps to hold the flambeau while I am at my toilette."

"Pray tell Mademoiselle that I am overwhelmed by her generosity."

Mademoiselle turned to Rupert. "Do not translate this I only do these things because I am sorry for the poor boy. I would never marry him, as his mother hopes I will. I have set my aim higher . . . much higher."

"I am sure," said Charles, "that Mademoiselle is talking sound sense."

Rupert smiled. He knew that the Prince of Wales understood every word, and that it was only his shyness which prevented his speaking French with Mademoiselle.

"Tell him," said Mademoiselle, "that he may come to my apartment and sit at my feet while I am with my women."

When Rupert translated this, Charles replied: "Mademoiselle is overwhelmingly generous, but I have a previous engagement with a lady."

"A lady!" cried Mademoiselle.

"My little sister, Mademoiselle. My friend Minette."

Henriette guessed that the beautiful Mademoiselle was being unkind to her brother. "Go away!" she said. "Minette does not like you."

Mademoiselle answered: "I know she is young, but she should be taught how to conduct herself. She should be beaten for that."

Henriette, recognizing the word "beaten," put her arms about her brother and buried her face against him.

"No one shall hurt you, Minette," he told her. "No one shall hurt you while your brother Charles is here."

Mademoiselle laughed, and rising, commanded Rupert to lead her away.

"We will leave the boy to play with his sister," she said; "for after all, he is but a boy and still concerned, I doubt not, with childish things."

And when they were alone, Minette and her brother were soon gay again, and she loved him dearly.

❁ ❁ ❁

Each day they were together; each day he talked to her, and although she did not always understand what he said, she knew that he loved her as she loved him.

It had not occurred to her that life could change, until one day he came to her and sadly kissed her. "Minette," he said, "we shall always love one another—you and I." And the next day he did not come.

Angrily she demanded to know where he was. He had gone away, they told her.

She fretted; she would not eat; she so much longed for him.

Her mother warmly embraced her. "My dearest child, you are very young, but there are things you have to learn. Your father is fighting wicked men, and your brother must go to help him. Then, when they have beaten those wicked men, we shall all go home, and you will not only have one brother, but three—as well as a dear sister."

"Don't want three brothers," sobbed Henriette. "Minette wants Charles."

And all through the days which followed she was a sad little figure in the palace of Saint-Germain.

If any asked her what ailed her she would say: "Want Charles." And each day she knelt on the window seat watching for him to come again; she waited, so it seemed to her, for years; but she never forgot him.

In the palace of the Louvre, the Princess Henriette lay in her bed. Her mother sat beside the bed, and about her shoulders were three cloaks, and her hands were protected by thick gloves. It was bitter January weather, and outside the Louvre, in the narrow streets of Paris, Frenchmen were fighting Frenchmen in that civil war which had been called the War of the Fronde.

Little Henriette, who was but four years old, shivered with the cold; her mother shivered also—but not only from cold. As her friend, Madame de Motteville, had said to her: "This year a terrible star reigns for kings and queens."

Henrietta Maria was not thinking so much of the bloodcurdling shrieks which again and again reached her from the streets; her thoughts were across the Channel in her husband's country, for he was now the prisoner of the Parliament, and awaiting trial. She had begged to be allowed to see him, but this had been denied her. If she came to England, she was told, it would be to stand on trial with him, for the Parliament considered her as guilty as her husband of High Treason.

What was happening in England? She knew little for no messengers could reach her, France having its own civil war with which to contend. She was alternately full of self-reproach and indignation towards others. She accused herself of ruining not only her own life but that of her husband and children; then she would rail against the wicked Cromwell and his Parliamentarians who had brought such suffering to her family.

And here she was—Queen of England—without food and warmth in this vast palace, alone with her child, the child's governess, Père Cyprien and a few servants who were all suffering now as she and her daughter suffered.

Three of her children were prisoners in the hands of the Parliament—James, Elizabeth and Henry. Mary, she thanked God, had been safely married and out of England before the trouble grew beyond control; and Mary at the Court of Holland provided a refuge for her brother Charles and any of those who managed to escape thither. The family relied on Mary in these hard times.

When she had first come to France much honor had been given to Henrietta Maria; but little by little she had shed her pomp, her plate and jewels; her foremost thought had been to send all she possessed to her husband in England. If she was frivolous, if she had been in a large measure responsible for his downfall, at least she was wholehearted in her passionate desire to help him. Only now that she was separated from him did she realize the extent of her love for that good and noble man, the best of husbands and fathers, even if he were not the wisest of kings. And now what assistance could she hope for from her royal relatives of France? They had been forced to leave Paris; the little King, in charge of his mother, the Queen-Regent, had slipped away from Paris to Saint-Germain where they stayed during the siege of Paris. Mademoiselle de Montpensier had decided to place herself on the side of the Frondeurs, which was typical of her; trust Mademoiselle to call attention to herself in some way!

It was an evil star indeed which shone on kings and queens during that year. Henrietta Maria had in vain warned her sister-in-law. Had she herself not suffered so much because she had once believed as Anne believed, behaved as Anne behaved? It was hard to learn that their countries were moving forward, that new ideas had brought a new outlook. The Stuarts would have been as autocratic as the Tudors, but they did not understand the people, and that understanding had been at the very root of the popularity achieved by those great Tudor sovereigns, Henry VIII and Elizabeth. The common people denied the Divine Right of Kings to govern; there were some who remembered the revolt of the barons in an earlier century. The people wished to go back to those conditions when a king's power was limited. How easy it was to see mistakes when one looked back, and to say: "Had I done this, that would not have happened. Had we not made mistakes, Charles I and Henrietta Maria would be reigning in England now, living happily together."

And so it was with Anne of Austria, the Queen-Mother of France. The situation was tragically similar. Mazarin and the Queen-Regent had imposed crushing taxes on the people, and the people would have them know that the age when kings and queens could believe they ruled by Divine

Right was over. France was divided. Anne, frivolous, as Henrietta Maria had been, and as unrealistic, had laughed in the face of Paul de Gondi, the Coadjuteur of Paris; she had encouraged her friends to laugh at him because he was something of a dandy, and that accorded ill with the *soutane* he wore as a man of the Church. Paul de Gondi was a strong man; he had declared he would be master of Paris and he had prepared himself to bring about that state of affairs.

It was last July, in the heat of summer, when, below that apartment in which the Queen of England and her daughter now shivered, Parisians had barricaded the streets. Great barrels, filled with earth and held in place by chains, were placed at the entrances of narrow streets. Citizens were detailed to guard these streets. This was reminiscent, and indeed inspired by the "Night of the Barricades" of the previous century.

The War of the Fronde had started. It was typical of Parisian humor that the war should be so named. A law had recently been passed prohibiting young boys from gathering in the streets of Paris and attacking each other with the *fronde* (a sling for stones) then so popular. These games of stone-slinging had on more than one occasion proved fatal and there had been public concern. So it was that, during the heated discussions in the Parliament concerning the taxes about to be imposed by the hated Cardinal Mazarin, the favorite of the Queen-Regent, the President of the Parliament had begged the assembly to consider the terms which Mazarin was proposing. The President's son—he was de Bachaumont and known throughout Paris as a *bel esprit*—had said that when his turn came to speak he would *"frondera bien l'opinions de son père."* This *bon mot* was taken up and repeated; and *Frondeur* was adopted as the name of those who would criticize and "sling" rebellion against the Court party.

So, during those months, Paris was in danger; and the French throne seemed about to topple as had that of England. Henrietta Maria's pension had not been paid since the war started; she had run short of food and wood, and now that the winter was upon her suffered acute discomfort; yet, soothing her little daughter, putting her arms about her and cuddling her in an attempt to keep her warm, she was not thinking of what was happening immediately outside her windows but of her husband who was about to face his trial in London.

"Mam," said the little Princess, "I'm cold."

"Yes, little one, it is cold, but perhaps we shall soon be warm."

"Cannot we have a fire?"

"My love, we lack the means to light one."

"I'm hungry, Mam."

"Yes, we are all hungry, dearest."

The Princess began to whimper. She could not understand.

"Holy Mother of God," murmured the Queen, "what is happening to Charles?"

Anne, who was now Lady Morton as her husband's father had recently died, came into the room. Her lips were blue, her beautiful hands mottled with the cold.

"What is it, Anne?" asked the Queen.

"Madame, Monsieur le Coadjuteur is here to see you."

"What does he want of me?"

"He asks to be brought into your presence."

The Coadjuteur was at the door; this was not a time when Queens should be allowed to stand on ceremony, and he was master of Paris.

Henrietta Maria did not rise; she looked at him haughtily.

But Paul de Gondi had not come as an enemy.

He bowed before the Queen, and she looked into the face of the man who was temporarily king of Paris. It was a dissolute face though a strong one. Paul de Gondi, who from childhood had wished to be a great power in the land, had been destined for the Church. His uncle had been Archbishop of Paris, and it was intended that Paul should succeed him. But Paul, having no vocation for the Church, had tried to prove himself unsuitable for the office by riotous living and frequent dueling. Finding himself unable to avoid acceptance of the archbishopric he decided to become a learned man and rule France as Richelieu had done. First he had set about winning the people of Paris, and having done this with some success he found himself in his present position of power.

But when he looked at the poor suffering Queen of England, stoically shivering by the bed of her daughter, and thought of what was happening to her husband and other children, he was filled with pity for her.

"Madame," he said, "you suffer much."

"Monsieur le Coadjuteur," she replied, "if you have news for me, pray give it—I mean news from England."

"That I cannot give, Madame, but I can give some comfort. I can have food sent to you—food and firewood."

She said: "Monsieur, if you know anything, I beg of you give me news."

"I have no news. But it shall not be said that I stood by and allowed the daughter of Henri Quatre to starve."

Henrietta Maria shrugged her shoulders. "It is six months since I received my pension, and no one would supply me with food and the means to keep my apartment warm because I could not pay."

"But this is terrible!"

"I keep my little daughter company. It was too cold for her to rise today."

"Madame, I shall myself see that your daughter does not have to stay in bed for want of a faggot."

"What can you do, Monsieur?"

"First I shall have comfort sent to you; then I shall put your case before the Parliament."

"The Parliament!" Henrietta Maria laughed aloud and bitterly. "Parliaments do not love kings and queens these days, Monsieur."

"Madame, the Parliament will not allow it to be said that it denied food and firewood to a daughter and granddaughter of Henri Quatre."

The Queen wept a little after he had gone.

"Why do you cry, Mam?" asked the little girl. "Was the man cruel to you?"

"No, my sweetheart. He was not cruel; he was kind."

"Then why do you cry?"

"There are times, dearest, when unexpected kindness makes us cry. Ah, you look at your poor Mam with those big black eyes and you wonder at my words. But there is much you do not yet know of life. Yet you are learning; you are learning fast for a little one."

Paul de Gondi was as good as his word. That very day firewood and food were brought to the Louvre, and a few days later, at the instigation of de Gondi, the Parliament ordered that 40,000 livres should be sent to the Queen in memory of Henri Quatre.

In memory of Henri Quatre! Henrietta Maria could not help comparing her father with her husband. She could not remember her father, yet she had heard much of him; she had seen pictures of that great man, depicting the full sensuous mouth, the large nose, the humorous eyes and the lines of debauchery. She remembered stories she had heard of the stormy relationship between her father and mother; she had heard of the continual quarrels and the ravings of her mother whose temper she knew to be violent. She could imagine that angry temper roused to madness by the cynically smiling King; she knew that many times her mother had struck him, and she had heard how such blows reduced him to helpless laughter in spite of the fact that she was, as he himself said, "terribly robust." He had been called the ugliest man in France, but people would always add "and its bravest gentleman." They had loved him as they had loved no other King; the lecher (who, at the time of his assassination in his fifty-seventh year had been courting Angelique Paulet, a girl of seventeen) had declared, old as he was, that conquest in love pleased him better than conquest in war—and he was the most popular King who had ever ruled France.

This ugly man, this cynic, without any deep religion, ready to turn from the Huguenot faith to the Catholic faith (for "was not Paris worth a mass?") was the hero of France; and even after his death those who had rebelled against the Court remembered him, and for his sake would not let his daughter starve.

When he had been stabbed by a fanatical monk, all France had mourned him; his assassin had died the horrible death which the nation demanded as the penalty of such a deed. And yet in England a good and noble man, religious, faithful and striving to act in a manner he considered to be right, might die and the people would cry: "God's will be done."

❁ ❁ ❁

It was February of that tragic year. There was a little more comfort in the bare rooms of the Louvre than there had been during previous months. But a worse tragedy overhung the palace; the servants knew of it; Anne knew of it; but there was no one who dared speak of it to the Queen. So they kept her in ignorance.

Henrietta Maria, during those weeks, was subdued yet determined to be hopeful.

"I often wonder why there is no news," she would say to those about her. "But good it is that there should be no news. I know the people love the King, my husband. Perhaps they have already released him from captivity. Oh, it is a sad and wicked thing that he should be a captive. So good . . . so noble . . . the best husband any woman ever had. No child ever had a more kindly father. How happy we could have been!"

Towards the middle of February she would wait no longer. Paul de Gondi had shown his goodness to her; he would not deny her in her great need. She would ask that a messenger be sent to Saint-Germain where there would certainly be tidings of her husband.

Then they knew that they could withhold the truth no longer.

Anne asked Lord Jermyn, the Queen's most faithful adviser, to break the news to her. "For," she said, "you will do it better than any of us could. You will know how to soothe her."

He went to Henrietta Maria in her apartments. With her was the little Princess, Anne Morton and Père Cyprien de Gamaches.

Jermyn knelt before the Queen.

She said at once: "You have news from England?"

He lifted his face to hers; his lips quivered, and she knew, even before he spoke. A blank expression crept over her face; her eyes were mutely pleading with him not to speak, not to say those fateful words.

"Madame, dear Madame, on the 30th of January, the King, your husband, laid his head upon the block . . ."

She did not speak.

"Madame," resumed Jermyn, his voice broken with a sob. "Madame . . . Long live King Charles II."

Still she did not speak. Anne placed her hand on the shoulder of the little Princess who was looking at her with wondering eyes, and gently pushed her towards her mother. The Queen, putting out her hand, reached for her daughter and held her fast to her side; she still looked blankly before her and said not a word.

❀ ❀ ❀

The little Princess was bewildered. She was five years old; she lived in the great Palace of the Louvre, but the vast rooms were deserted and there was war in the streets. She could not understand her mother's sudden passionate embraces, the great floods of tears and what seemed to her the incoherent ramblings. Her mother had changed. She wore somber widow's mourning; she was constantly in tears; she referred to herself as *La Reine Malheureuse*; and little Henriette would cry with her, not knowing why she cried.

"Ah, you do well to weep!" the Queen would say. "Do you know that but for you I should not be here now. I should be with the Carmelite nuns in the Convent of the Faubourg Saint-Jacques; that is where I yearn to be, to pray for strength to help me bear this burden of living. Ah, *ma petite,* I pray that you will never feel as I do. I pray that you will never be beset with doubts as your poor mother is this day. There are many who say I brought him to this—that good and noble man! They say that had he never attempted to arrest the Five Members seven years ago, civil war would have been averted. *I* urged him to do that. I did not believe that any would dare oppose the King to the extent of going to war. I believed that we could govern without a Parliament. Oh, my little Henriette, have I, who loved him, brought him to the scaffold?"

Henriette did not know what to answer; she could only take her little kerchief and wipe away her mother's tears.

And now her mother had gone away to stay with the nuns, and she could only feel relieved because of this. She was left to the care of dear Anne Morton and Père Cyprien. But these two were beginning to cause her some anxiety; and their teachings often seemed to be contradictory. She was conscious of some vague strife between them, of triumphs enjoyed by one to the discomfiture of the other; and in some way, which she herself did not understand, she was involved in their polite warfare.

"I wish my brother would come," she often said to herself. "All would be well if he were here."

She thought of him constantly; he had always been kind and loving; he was so big and clever, yet not too big and clever to make a little girl feel she was of some importance to him.

And then, one day, he came to the Louvre.

He had grown up since she had last seen him; he was a young man of nineteen now. He was taller, but he still had the same luxuriant black hair and humorous eyes.

When he came into the apartment Lady Morton and Père Cyprien both fell on their knees, but Henriette ran to him and flung herself into his arms.

"My child," said Anne reprovingly, "you forget the respect due to His Majesty."

"But it is *Charles*!" cried the little girl.

"Come now. You should kneel to him. He is your King first . . . your brother second."

"A poor King, my Minette," he said, as he swung her up that her face might be on a level with his; "a King without a kingdom, but a brother rich in love. Which will you have?"

She did not understand him, but she had never had need to understand his words; she only knew that he loved her; his eyes told her that, as did his loving arms about her.

His mother, who hearing of his arrival had left the convent and returned to the Louvre, embraced him warmly. She wept afresh for his father. She was *La Reine Malheureuse,* she declared. "Life has nothing left to give me. I have lost not only a crown but a husband and a friend. I shall never regret enough the loss of that good man—so wise, so just, so worthy of the love of his subjects."

The young King smiled his melancholy smile. " 'Tis no use to weep, Mam," he said. "We must look forward as he would have had us do. We'll defeat them yet."

"Amen, my boy, my Charles, my King."

When the Queen-Mother of France heard that the King of England was at the Louvre, she asked the royal party to join the French Court at Saint-Germain.

"I have warned Queen Anne," said Henrietta Maria, "that my husband lost his life because he was never allowed to know the truth, and I have implored her to listen to her advisers before it is too late . . . before the crown of France goes the way of that of England."

Charles smiled ruefully. "It is difficult enough to learn through one's own experience, Mam, let alone the experience of others."

His mother smiled at him sadly. Even when he was a baby—an ugly, solemn little fellow—she had felt he was cleverer than she was. Now she hoped that was true. He would need to be clever. He had to fight his way back to his throne.

She had heard that there were plans afoot, that soon he would be returning to Scotland where he could hope for support which would help him make an onslaught on England.

"May God go with you then, dear son," she said. "You will need His help."

"That's true, Mam," he answered. "But 'tis better to die in such at enterprise than wear away one's life in shameful indolence."

"I heard rumors concerning your visit to The Hague."

"There will always be rumors concerning our family, Mam."

"This was concerning a young woman named Lucy Water. You know of such a one?"

"Yes, Mam. I know of such a one."

"They say she is a foolish little thing . . . though beautiful."

"I doubt not that they who say it are often foolish—and never beautiful."

"Now, Charles, this is your mother speaking, your mother who had you beaten when you would not take your physic."

He made a wry face. "That physic, Mam; it was no good to any. Lucy is not in the least like a dose of physic."

"A woman of easy virtue . . . too ready with her smiles and caresses, I understand."

"What should I want of one who was niggardly with the same?"

"You are no longer a boy, Charles. You are a King."

"You speak truth, Mam. I am a King. Pray thee do not think to make of me a monk. Come! We prepare ourselves for the journey to Saint-Germain. The crowds in the streets are ugly. But never fear. I shall be there to protect you. I must tell Minette that we are going."

"Henriette is a child. She will not understand."

He lifted his sister in his arms. "Minette will wish to know that we are going on a journey. Minette, do you wish to go on a journey?"

"Are you going, Charles?"

"I am taking you and Mam."

Henriette smiled. "Yes, please; Minette will go."

"Dearest, the crowds may shout at us as we pass through the streets. You'll not be afraid, will you, if I am there?"

She shook her head.

"Nobody would dare hurt Minette while King Charles is there to protect her. You know that, don't you?"

She put her arms round his neck and kissed him.

"How much do you love me, Minette?"

"Forty thousand livres," she answered, remembering that amount which Paul de Gondi had urged the Parliament to grant to her mother.

"Forty thousand livres! That's a lot of money."

She nodded happily. "But it's all for you—and something else."

"What else, Minette?"

"The silver laces in my shoes."

He kissed her. "And what shall I give you in return for those you give me, eh?"

She thought awhile, then she said: "Never go away."

"Ah, Minette," he said, "if only that could be! And if all loved me as you do what a happy man I should be!"

Then he thought of Lucy, charming, gay and very loving; Lucy who had initiated him into delights which he had scarcely been aware existed, and had promised more revelation; Lucy, practiced harlot, some said, but nevertheless his love.

He had much love to give; he loved them both—Lucy and Minette; he loved them with all the capacity of a nature deeply concerned with the pleasures of loving.

He continued to think of Lucy, who was now with child.

"Your child, Charles," she had said. "Your royal bastard—that is unless you marry me and so make an honest woman of your Lucy . . . and your bastard, heir to the throne of England."

He smiled. Lucy was amusing; Lucy was light, but Lucy was gay; he would look forward to enjoying her amusing and erotic company as soon as he possibly could.

But in the meantime he had his little sister to love, and deeply he loved her.

She sat with him and their mother in the coach which carried them through the dangerous streets of Paris; about them swirled the mob of angry men and women, and among them were those to whom Madame d'Angleterre—as they called Henrietta Maria—owed much money.

Minette felt safe; she did not fear the people, for there was her big brother, one hand on the door of the coach, the other on the hilt of his sword, ready to repulse any who dared come too near.

And so they came to Saint-Germain; and as the little girl observed the homage paid to her brother, she was thrilled with pride and pleasure.

And he, turning suddenly, caught her earnest eyes upon him.

Ah, he thought, if only I could be as sure that Lucy loves me as does my sweet Minette!

THREE

The first time Lucy set eyes on Charles he was merely Prince of Wales—a boy of eighteen. Lucy was also eighteen; but she seemed older. She was full of wiles and she had been born with them. There had always been admirers for Lucy from the days when, as a little girl, she had played in the grounds of Roch Castle. She was brown-skinned, brown-eyed, and her rippling hair was brown also; she was plump and indolent. Her father, watching her even as a girl of twelve, decided to marry her off quickly. She was a girl who was obviously ripe for marriage.

There were local squires in the neighborhood of Haverfordwest and St. David's who would have been ready enough to link their fortunes with those of the Waters, for Lucy's mother was a niece of the Earl of Carbery, and her family was not without fortune. Moreover, Lucy was as luscious as a ripe peach and wherever she went men's eyes followed her. Her voice had a soft lilting Welsh accent and it rose on a note of laughter at the end of her sentences; it was not that Lucy's conversation was so very amusing and witty; it was merely that she appeared to be ready to enjoy life. She was aware of her ripe young body; she was aware of the ripe young bodies of others. Lucy was longing for amorous adventures; she would lie in the grass on the mound at the top of which stood Roch Castle, and dream of lovers.

The war altered life at Roch Castle as it did everywhere else. Her father went off to fight for the Royalist cause, and Lucy remained at home—a girl of fourteen, restive, forced to sit at her needlework during long sunny afternoons, stitching reluctantly, the despair of her governess.

There was continual talk of the war. Lucy rarely listened to it with any great attention. She was a fervent Royalist because the Cavaliers, in their dashing clothes, their curls falling about their shoulders and their jauntily feathered hats, pleased her; and the soberly clad soldiers of the Parliamentary forces, with their round cropped heads and their text-quoting, did not attract her at all.

Lucy was filled with vague longings. She was not sure that she wanted to settle down to a married life. She had watched her mother looking after the servants, working in her still-room, arranging meals, having children. Such a life did not seem very attractive to Lucy. She had noticed at an early age how men's eyes followed her, and that pleased her. She would sit before a mirror tying ribbons in her brown hair, arranging her curls, aware that she was very pretty and remembering how the men looked at her; but she was only vaguely aware of what she wanted. It was more than admiration, more than warm glances; yet she did not want to be the chatelaine of a castle like that of her parents, to have children, a still-room, servants to command.

Lucy was lazy, it was agreed by all. She would not attend to her lessons; she could not even concentrate on her needlework. Her eyes would wander from her work, and her thoughts would wander too.

Then Lucy suddenly discovered what she wanted from life.

It was when a party of Royalists rode up to the Castle and asked for a night's shelter. There was always food and shelter at Roch Castle for the Cavaliers. The Captain of the troop was young and handsome; he was the most elegant man Lucy had ever seen; his curled moustache was golden; so was his pointed beard; his fair hair fell to his shoulders; he was a dashing figure in his doublet with its wide sleeves and narrow sash; in his wide-brimmed hat was a curling feather. He was the most handsome man she had ever seen, and her eyes told him so.

From the time the Cavaliers entered the house the Captain was aware of Lucy. She must wait on him at table because, said her mother, it was a symbol of loyalty to the cause that the daughter of the house should do this in place of the servants; and as she waited on him he took opportunities of touching her hand. Lucy's large brown eyes glistened. She was ripe and very ready for seduction on that day; and the handsome Cavalier was well aware of this. He was young—not yet twenty—and life was adventurous in wartime. Any day might be his last; he was no canting Puritan to think longingly of the next world; he was a Cavalier determined to make the most of this one.

They would stay the night at Roch Castle, these soldiers of the King, for Roch Castle was at the disposal of His Majesty's friends; and during that evening the handsome Cavalier was not absent from Lucy's mind one moment—nor was Lucy from his. Even in the presence of others he managed to suggest desire, and Lucy, inexperienced as she was, managed to convey her response.

It was a July evening—warm and sultry—and there was an air of unreality in the Castle. Everyone felt that the war had moved closer. If Royalist soldiers were in the neighborhood, it was probable that Roundheads were not far off. These handsome Cavaliers admitted that they were in retreat, that they had given their pursuers the slip near Brecknock, and that although their scouts had not seen a sign of them for several hours, it did not mean that the enemy had given up the chase.

At any moment there might be the sound of clattering horses' hoofs in the courtyard; at any moment rough soldiers might be demanding to search the Castle in the name of Oliver Cromwell.

It was not yet dark, but it soon would be; yet no one made preparations for settling down for the night. In the great hall the soldiers kept a lookout; there were men posted in the turrets.

Lucy was aware that at any moment this man who so excited her might ride away and never again be seen by her. His burning eyes watched her as she moved about the great dining hall, for once eager to help as she was bid.

With a quick glance at the Cavalier she made her way to the door and slipped out into the grounds. Almost immediately she heard footsteps behind her; she ran down the slope towards the moat and into the copse where as a child she used to hide from her governesses.

There she waited, and she had not long to wait. She stood, tense and breathless. He called her name softly. Then she felt his arms seize her; she was lifted up, violently kissed and quickly laid down among the bracken. She was aware of the urgency of the moment. There was no time for delay; he sensed that, even as she did; and it was she, he reminded himself, who had led the way to the copse.

Her first erotic adventure was all she needed to tell her for what she had been longing. It was not marriage; it was love, physical love, this sort of love—desire which came suddenly and must be swiftly satisfied. Lucy was perfectly contented lying there among the bracken. She was not frightened, though she was but fourteen; she knew that she had been born for this. She had been scolded for carelessness, laziness and stupidity; but in love she could attain perfection. Ignorant in many ways she might be, but now she needed no instruction. Entirely sensual, she was the perfect lover.

The young Cavalier looked at her wonderingly as she lay back in the bracken, her eyes wide and starry, her lips parted. It was he who had to remind her that they might be missed. For Lucy there was only the moment; consequences could not touch her in this mood of ecstasy.

"Which is your room?" he asked.

She told him.

"Tonight, when all is quiet, I will come to you."

She nodded. But the night was a long way off. She put her arms about his neck and pulled him down to her again.

The dusk had turned to darkness but they were unaware of it. They would have remained unaware had not the shouts and screams from the Castle become so insistent.

He started up and sniffed the air. He coughed, for the smoke had drifted into the copse.

"God's Body!" cried Lucy's lover. "They're here! Cromwell's men are at the Castle!"

Lucy looked at him, but even so she was only vaguely conscious of what he had said; she was dazed, lost in a maze of emotions. She had ceased to be a child; only that morning she had been ignorant and innocent, and in that state, dissatisfied; now she was fulfilled; now she knew herself.

He gripped her arm and drew her with him deeper into the copse.

"Don't you understand?" he said. "Cromwell's men are here. They are burning the Castle!"

❁ ❁ ❁

That was the beginning of a new life for Lucy. Roch Castle was burned down that night, Lucy had lost her home and her family; and she had nothing but her personal attractions.

There was only one course open to her and her lover—they must try to escape from Pembrokeshire. All that night they walked, and before dawn Lucy had led her lover to the house of a neighbor and friend to her family who lent them horses. The next day they began their journey towards London where, said her lover, Lucy could set up house for him, and he would visit her when his duties permitted him to do so.

Sometimes they slept under hedges, sometimes in friendly cottages, occasionally in big houses, the owners of which were faithful to the Royalist cause.

Lucy was a constant surprise to her lover; when he had first seen her he had planned a quick seduction before he passed on; now he found that it was Lucy who was in control of their relationship, Lucy whose big brown eyes rested ardently on other men, Lucy who would have smiled and bidden him a friendly farewell if he had suggested a parting. In vain did he tell her that she was a natural harlot. Lucy did not care. Lucy knew what she wanted, and it was becoming increasingly clear to her that she would never be obliged to go short of lovers.

Lucy was the perfect mistress of a fleeting passion, for her own passions were fleeting. She did not ask for gold or jewels but the slaking of her desire. This quality, added to voluptuous beauty, made her doubly desirable.

They came to London, and London enchanted Lucy. Her lover set her up in lodgings not far from Tower Hill, and she prided herself on being faithful to him when he could come to her. There were times, of course, when he could not visit her, but Lucy was never lonely, never long without a gallant.

London was a merry town at that time, for Puritanism had not yet cast its ugly pall over the city. The people were noisy; brawls were frequent; and opportunity for indulging in pageantry was eagerly seized upon. No one was safe after dark; but by day the streets were crowded. Fiddlers seemed always at hand to play a merry jig for any who cared to dance; ballad-sellers sang samples of their wares in high trebles and deep basses; carriages jingled through the narrow cobbled streets; London was everything but dull. The brothels were flourishing, and girls, scantily clad, painted and patched, talked to each other from the gables of opposite houses which almost met over the narrow streets; nor were these disorderly houses confined to Bankside and Southwark; they were appearing all over London from Turnbull Street at Smithfield to Ratcliff Highway and Catherine Street near the Strand—and, of course, they abounded in Drury Lane.

The most important highway of the city was Paul's Walk—the center aisle of the old cathedral. This was not so much a part of a church as a promenade and market. All kinds of people gathered there—merchants to sell their wares, prostitutes to offer theirs. The pillars were used to denote the centers for certain trades. If a man wanted a letter-writer he was to be found by the first pillar; horses would be sold at the second pillar; the money-lenders were farther along; and next to them was the marriage-broker, and after that the obliging gentleman who could arrange for a man to spend a night—or an hour—with one of the women he controlled; mercers showed their materials; and those who had something to sell announced the fact by sticking notices on the pillars.

Nor was Paul's Walk the only place where it was possible to mingle with the London world. There was the Royal Exchange and the New Exchange; and in each of these were the galleries where shopkeepers set up their stalls, where pretty young women not only sold trifles but made appointments with the dandies who strolled through the galleries. There were young men in velvet coats carrying swords with jeweled hilts; they wore gold buttons on their coats, brilliant feathers in their wide-brimmed beaver hats; their breeches were trimmed with fine point lace and held in at the knees with ribbons, and their hair was beautifully dressed and hanging in ringlets over their shoulders—the delight of the girls and the envy of every apprentice. The theaters had closed at the beginning of the war, but the London to which Lucy came was a very merry place.

Each day she would wander out into the street, would stroll through the Royal Exchange, buy herself a fan or a ribbon, give her peculiarly inviting smile to the ogling men, and if her lover were away, she would agree that the one she fancied most should come to her lodging.

She found a little maid—Ann Hill—who thought her wonderful and declared she would die rather than leave her service—as she probably would of starvation, being ill favored. Lucy was glad to take her in and, in her lazy way, was kind to her.

Lucy would have been content to go on in her pleasant way, but the war brought changes. Each year there was a difference in the London scene. There were more soldiers in the town, and now they were not swaggering Cavaliers; they burned beautiful buildings and praised God as they did so. Beauty had no place in the good life, they believed; they used the churches as sleeping quarters; they took possession of St. Paul's; they stabled their horses in the Cathedral and cut down the beams for firewood; they played ninepins in the aisles and shouted to each other throughout the night. Very few Cavaliers flaunted through the streets now. The King's cause was a lost one, said the people. Noll Cromwell was in command.

Lucy's lover had appeared at her lodgings in a great hurry; he had stayed there for several days and nights, for he dared not face the streets. London was less merry; people were subdued and no longer openly expressed an opinion unless it was favorable to Cromwell.

Lucy went out to buy food during those days, and she was watched, she knew, by a man who always seemed to be lounging in the gallery of the Royal Exchange. For several days she had seen that that man's eyes were on her. She was not sure how, but she knew him to be a Cavalier. His hair was cropped and his clothes were somber; yet there was that in his face which told her he was no Roundhead.

She liked his appearance; she more than liked it. She thought about him a good deal; if she had not already been harboring one man at her lodgings she would have invited him there.

Then one day he followed her. Lucy was not frightened so to be followed; she was only exhilarated. She understood the meaning of his glances. He wanted only one thing from her; and she believed she would be very willing to grant that; so what had she to fear?

He caught up with her in a deserted alley whither she had led him. He plucked her sleeve and, as she turned, he released it and bowed as only a Cavalier would bow.

"You would have speech with me?"

"You are Mistress Lucy Water?"

"That's true enough."

"You are the most beautiful woman in London."

Lucy smiled complacently. He kept his eyes on her face.

"I wish to know you," he said, "very well."

"You know my name," she answered. "Should I know yours?"

"I will tell you . . . in time."

"And now what would you have of me?"

"You have a lodging near here?"

She nodded.

"And you share it with . . . a friend?"

Her eyes flashed. "A very good friend."

He caught her arm; his touch pleased her because it excited her. "I know him," he said. "He served with me. Take me to him. I must have speech with him. Please believe me. There must be no delay."

To Lucy this was a new method of approach and she enjoyed novelty. "Come this way," she said.

When she brought the stranger to her lodgings her lover was overawed. There was no doubt that the man had spoken the truth.

"Let us talk," said the newcomer. "There is little time."

"Sit down, sir," said Lucy's lover. "Lucy, bring a stool."

Lucy obeyed; she sat at the table watching them, her plump hands supporting her chin, her dreamy eyes on the newcomer. He would be an exciting lover, she was telling herself. He *will* be an exciting lover! She knew that whatever he was implying, that was what he wished to be ere long; and that was what had brought him to their lodging.

He flicked his fingers. "Your life won't be worth that, if you're caught here, my dear fellow."

"No, sir, 'tis true."

"I am leaving this day . . . for The Hague."

"To join the Prince, sir?"

"Aye! To join the Prince. You would do well to make good your escape while there is yet time."

"But to journey to The Hague . . . I have not the means."

"Can you obtain two good horses?"

"I could . . . if I had the money, sir."

"Then get them. Make for Harwich. The coast is quiet there . . . and I will tell you how you can find a boat to carry you across."

"But, my lord . . ."

"You have but to tell the Prince that I have sent you, and you will be well received; you will be given a place in the Army there. Here is money." He turned to look at Lucy. "We shall meet in The Hague. If you bring Mistress Lucy Water to me safely there, you will not regret it."

"I will do as you say, sir. You will take a little wine?"

"I have no time. I have certain things that must be done before I leave for The Hague. Wait till dusk, then go. Mistress Water will crop your hair. Don't venture out with your lovelocks flowing. Mistress Water . . ." He stood up and Lucy stood up with him; he gripped her arms and looked into her face. "You and I will meet ere long. I eagerly await our next encounter."

He was gone and the two looked at each other in amazement.

"Why, my pretty Lucy," said her lover, "you have got yourself one of the quality this time. Do you know who that was? It was Algernon Sydney, son of the great Earl of Leicester. Get ready, girl. Don't waste time. We'll be out of this place as soon as night falls. We're going to Court . . . the Prince's Court. We're going to leave the sinking ship, my pretty. Come! Cut my hair. He's right, you know. You've got to make me into one of those ugly Roundhead fellows, and I'm to deliver you to your new protector, Lucy; and when I do my reward will be great."

But his smile was rueful while he jingled the gold in his silken purse.

❁ ❁ ❁

Lucy lay in bed watching her lover dressing. He was preparing himself to go to the little Court which the Prince had set up in The Hague.

Lucy had seen little of the place as yet. She had arrived after a tedious journey which had taken far longer than her ex-lover had anticipated. The journey to Harwich had been beset by difficulties; one of the horses had gone lame, and they had to procure another; everywhere they went they were under suspicion, as many were in England at that time; and then, when they had been ready to sail, the wind and weather had been against them. Meanwhile, in The Hague, Algernon Sydney eagerly awaited the girl who was being brought to him.

Lucy had discovered that he had paid fifty gold crowns to her lover, and that amused Lucy. He had paid for that which he could have had for nothing, had he waited to court her as a gentleman should. Not that Lucy would have needed much courting. She could quickly decide whether or not a man could appeal to her, and how far that appeal would carry him; Algernon Sydney need not have feared that he would fail to win that which he coveted.

Yet she would always laugh at the way things had turned out. She heard now, from Colonel Robert Sydney, how impatient his brother Algernon had been—watching the tides, riding three miles a day to Scheveningen where the boat was expected to make port, finding no satisfaction in any other woman, so that he had been the laughing stock of the whole Court.

Colonel Robert laughed with her, for after all he had come very well out of the affair.

"God's Body, Lucy!" he told her. "He almost wept, so vexed was he! He said there wasn't another woman in the world who would do; and worse still he had paid some rogue fifty gold crowns for you."

"Then he has none but himself to blame," said Lucy. "No man should pay another money for me. I'm not that sort of harlot."

Now, watching him dressing for his appointment at Court, she did not regret the way in which matters had turned out. Robert was a satisfactory lover and she doubted his brother could be better. When she thought of arriving from the boat, and being brought to this place, to the comfort of hot food, a warm bed and a lover, she was not sorry. Robert was handsome and bold; he had wasted no time in taking to himself his brother's preserves. "It is, after all, a family matter!" he had joked.

She had not known that her arrival and the fifty gold pieces had provided the amusing story of the moment. It was the sort which would amuse a band of exiles. They craved other amusement than continual dicing, and all were eager to see the young woman for whom Algernon Sydney had paid his fifty pieces. That he should have been called to join his regiment for service elsewhere and so been deprived of his prize, was a matter for the greatest hilarity.

Robert knew how all at Court were laughing over the affair; he also knew that his brother—whom he had always believed to have been something of a connoisseur where women were concerned—had not been deceived about this one. Robert was anxious to keep her to himself and not eager that she should be seen by the young roués who circulated about the Prince.

Lucy was happy enough; never very energetic she was content to lie about the apartment, eating the sweetmeats which Robert provided, trying on the pretty ribbons which he had procured for her.

So Robert went off to Court and Lucy lay in bed. Soon Ann Hill would come in—for Lucy had insisted on bringing Ann with her to The Hague—and her toilet would be made by the time her lover returned. Later, Lucy would explore the town, but not yet; she needed a few more days to recover from her journey.

Ann came in and sat on the bed and talked in her bright cockney way, which was such a contrast to Lucy's musical Welsh accent.

Ann had been out; she had seen something of the flat country and she dismally shook her head over it. There could not be anything more different from London, she assured her mistress. The land was so flat; the wind blew across the sand, forming it into dunes; and these people had built dykes to keep out the seawater. There were small lakes all along the coast, where the sea had defied all attempts to keep it out. The town itself was more interesting although quite different from London. She had seen the palace where the Prince's sister Mary lived; and she had heard that the Prince was with her there; she had seen the arched gateway which led to the prison. But this town was a poor place compared with London, and the fresh wind howled all the time. Yet there were many gallant gentlemen in the streets, and to see them in their fine clothes, and with their fine manners, one might be in London; moreover, these gentlemen were even finer than those they had been wont to see in London recently; yes, there were some who were very fine indeed.

Lucy's eyes shone as she listened. She said: "I think I shall dress myself and take a walk."

But as she rose from her bed she and Ann heard a voice singing outside the window; it was a deep, masculine voice and very musical. Lucy put her head to one side, listening, for the singer had stopped beneath her window.

"I loved a lass, a fair one,
As fair as e'er was seen;
She was indeed a rare one,
Another Sheba's Queen!
But fool as then I was,
I thought she loved me too:
But now, alas: she's left me,
Falero, lero, loo."

Lucy could not refrain from going to the window; she opened the casement wide and leaned out. Below was a very tall young man of about her own age with large brown eyes, the warmest and merriest she had ever seen; he had long dark curly hair, and as she looked down he stopped singing, swept off his beaver hat, and bowed low.

"Good day to you, mistress," he said.

"Good day," said Lucy, drawing about her the wrap she had slipped on—and which was all she was wearing—but making sure that it did not cover too much of her magnificently rounded shoulders.

"I trust you liked my poor song, mistress."

"It was well rendered, sir."

"At least it had the desired effect of bringing you to the window."

"So that is why you are singing there!"

"Why else?"

"Then you know me?"

"Everyone in this town has heard of the beauty of Mistress Lucy Water."

"You flatter me, sir."

"Nay, to flatter is to praise unduly. However great the praise accorded to you, it could not be undue. Therefore it would be impossible to flatter you."

"You must be an Englishman."

He bowed. "I am glad you recognize me as such. These Dutchmen are dull fellows. They are not our equals in eating, dicing or loving the ladies."

"I have no knowledge of your talents at the table, sir, nor with the dice, nor . . ."

"Who knows, I may be able to prove my talents in all three one day, mistress."

"You are bold."

"There again we differ from these Dutchmen. Bold they may be on the seas, but it would need an Englishman to be as bold as this."

Lucy gave a little scream, for he had swung himself up on to the parapet, and his long slender fingers, immaculately white and adorned with several flashing rings, were clinging to the sill.

"You will fall, foolish man!" She reached for him, and, laughing, he managed, with her help, to scramble through the window, which was no easy matter, the window being small and he being six feet in height.

Lucy's wrap had slipped from her shoulders in the effort; this but added to their pleasure in the adventure—his to see so much which was beautiful, hers to show it.

"You might have killed yourself," she reproved.

"It would take more than a fall from a window to kill one so strong as I."

"And all for a silly prank!"

"It was worth the slight discomfort. I see rumor has not lied. Mistress Lucy Water *is* the most beautiful woman in The Hague."

"I must send you away. You should not come here thus. What Colonel Sydney would say if he found you here, I dare not think."

"I will risk Colonel Sydney's displeasure."

"You are too bold, young man."

"I count boldness a virtue. It is a quality which such as I could not do without."

"I must tell you that Colonel Sydney is a very important man."

"I know of him, and you are right."

"Then have you no fear . . . ?"

He put his hands on her shoulders and, drawing her swiftly to him, kissed her lips, then her throat, then her breasts.

"This is too much," she stammered.

"Indeed, it is not enough."

"It is too much to be suffered!"

"That which cannot be helped must be endured."

"Sir . . . how dare you come thus to my chamber?"

"How dare I? Because you are beautiful; because I am a man; because I saw you at the window; because you heard my song and helped me in; because I have seen that which makes me long to see more; because I have kissed your lips and tasted that which I would savor to the full."

"I have a lover."

"I offer you a better one."

"You are insolent!"

"I am ardent, I confess."

Lucy tried to be stern, but how could she be? Colonel Sydney was a lover to her taste, but this young man was different from any she had ever known before. He was tall and strong; he could have overpowered her, and perhaps she would not have been sorry if he had; but he did no such thing, although he was somewhat arrogant and very sure of himself. He was not going to take by force, she realized, that which he knew would not long be denied him. There was a tenderness mingling with the passion she saw in his eyes, and such tenderness she had never before encountered. There was something lazy in his manner which matched her own laziness; his sensuality, she felt, was equal to her own; he was of her age; and yet he was by no means handsome; but Lucy's experience told her that he had more than good looks; he was the most charming person it had ever been her good fortune to meet.

Lucy said: "You must know that Colonel Sydney will consider it a great offense to force your way in here thus."

"Are we not to tell him that you helped me in then?"

"I did not mean to help you in. It was but to save your life. I feared you would fall."

"I thank you for my life, Lucy. How can I repay you?"

"By going quietly before Colonel Sydney returns and finds you here."

"Is that all I am to get for my pains . . . after risking my life to be near you as I did?"

"Please go. I am afraid the Colonel will arrive."

"You are beginning to make me fear the Colonel. Are you fond of him, Lucy? Is he good to you?"

"He is good to me and I am fond of him."

"But not so fond that you cannot spare a smile or two for a passing fancy, eh? Lucy, do you think you could grow as fond and fearful of me as you are of the Colonel?"

"You forget I do not know you. I saw you for the first time only a few minutes ago."

"We must put that right. From now on we will see a good deal of each other. I will risk Colonel Sydney's displeasure. Will you?"

"I might," murmured Lucy.

He took her hand and kissed it. "You are the most beautiful woman I have ever seen," he said; "and I have always been a close observer of women. Why, I remember an occasion—in the town of Oxford it was—when I was in church with my father, and he smote me on the head with his staff because, instead of listening to the sermon, I was smiling at the ladies. I am older now, but I have never ceased to smile at the ladies, and no amount of smiting on the head will stop me. So you see I know what I am talking about."

"I am sure you would always give a good account of yourself to women. There is no need to tell me that. Now go, I beg of you. I will order my maid to take you down by the back staircase. You must go at once."

"But I will have a kiss before I go."

"Then . . . you will go?"

"I swear it. But do not imagine we shall not meet again."

"I would do anything to be rid of you before Colonel Sydney returns."

"Anything!" His warm brown eyes were alert and hopeful.

"I would kiss you," she said firmly.

So he took her into his arms and kissed her, not once but many times, and not only on the lips as she pretended to intend. Lucy, flushed and struggling, was nevertheless laughing. It was an amusing adventure with the most fascinating man she had ever met. She hoped he would keep his word and visit her again.

She called Ann Hill.

"Ann," she said, "show this man out of the house . . . quickly . . . by way of the back staircase."

"Yes, mistress," said Ann.

Lucy watched him go regretfully. At the door he turned and bowed. He bowed more elegantly than any man she had ever known. "We shall meet again . . . very soon," he promised. "But not too soon for me."

Then he turned and followed Ann.

At the door he looked at Ann. She had lifted her face to his, for Ann too felt the power of his fascination. The warm brown eyes softened. Poor Ann! She was not well-favored, but she had seen the kiss he had given her mistress. 'Od's Fish! he pondered. She's envious, poor girl!

And because, ever since the days when his father had smitten him for his too-open admiration of the girls in church—and perhaps before then—

he had been unable to slight any woman, pretty or plain, lowly or high-born, he stooped quickly and lightly kissed Ann's cheek.

❁ ❁ ❁

Robert announced that Lucy was to be presented to the Prince.

"He has heard much of you," said Robert. "The talk of Algy's paying his fifty crowns and then being recalled before you arrived seems amusing to Charles. He says he must see the heroine of the story. So put on the dress I gave you and prepare yourself. You'll have to go to Court some day. In a place like this . . . all huddled together . . . exiles must necessarily mingle."

While Ann helped Lucy to dress they were both thinking of the tall dark man.

"Do you think he'll come back, mistress?" asked Ann.

"How can I know? He was too quick, was he not? He had the manners of a practiced philanderer."

"But of a gentleman too," murmured Ann.

"They often go together, I believe. Come, girl, my kerchief and my fan."

Even when she reached the palace in which the Prince had his apartments Lucy was still thinking of the tall dark man. She entered the palace with its wheel windows and gothic towers at either end; she walked up the staircase into the hall where the Prince was waiting to receive her.

She thought she was dreaming as he smiled at her, and kneeling before him she could not help lifting her eyes to look into that dark face with the glowing brown eyes which were now shining with mischief. She felt bewildered and, in that moment when she had knelt, she had not believed that he could really be the Prince. She thought it was some hoax, the sort of game he and his friends would like to play.

All about him were men—some young, some old—but he towered above them all, not only because of his height, but because of that overwhelming charm, that easy grace. It seemed incredible, but it must be true: the young man who had climbed through her window was Charles, Prince of Wales, and no other.

He was laughing merrily. "So, pretty Lucy," he said. "I stand exposed in all my perfidy."

"Sir . . ." she began.

He turned to those about him and said easily: "Lucy and I have already met, we find. We also find that we have a fondness for each other."

"Your Grace, I do not understand," said Robert.

"Then we must acquaint you with the facts, and as a good soldier, Colonel, I am sure you will know when the moment has come to retreat."

All those about the Prince began to laugh. Only Robert looked dismayed.

He bowed with dignity. Then he said: "I understand Your Grace's meaning and realize that I am in a position from which the only possible action is retreat."

"Wise Robert!" cried Charles. "And speaking of retreat, that is an order I give to the rest of you gentlemen."

Much laughter followed, and one by one the gentlemen left the apartment, pausing only to throw appreciative glances at Lucy.

So Lucy was alone with Charles.

And thus she became the willing mistress of the exiled Prince of Wales.

❁ ❁ ❁

She loved him truly; he was more to her than any other lover had been, for he was more than mere lover. It was that tender quality in him which moved Lucy. He was easygoing, full of wit, and if he did not always keep his promises, it was due to sheer kindness of heart which would not allow him to refuse anything which was asked of him.

As Prince's mistress her life changed yet again. It was true that he was a Prince in exile, but he was England's heir for all that. Although his eyes would never fail to light up when they rested on a pretty woman, he became devoted to Lucy; she was his chief love, and was content that this should be so. These weeks, she decided, were the happiest of her life.

She made the acquaintance of men whose names she had heard mentioned with awe; she heard the plots and intrigues which were in motion to win this second civil war, begun this year, and which one of these men—George Villiers, Duke of Buckingham—had helped to bring about. Buckingham had recently joined the Prince and was his closest companion. Charles told her that he and Buckingham had been brought up together, and when the elder Villiers died, King Charles I took his children into the royal household and Lord Francis and Lord George—as this Buckingham was then—had played with the royal children.

Lord Francis had been killed recently, as many people were killed in England; and the young Duke had escaped to join the Prince.

Charles enjoyed unburdening his mind to Lucy. He felt it was unimportant what he said to her, for Lucy only half-listened. He would smile on seeing the vague look which would come into her eyes at times, when she would nod and express surprise even when she had little notion about what he was talking.

"Why, Lucy," he said, "you'd never betray my secrets to others, would you, for the simple reason that you have never heard me betray them to you."

That amused him. Some might have been angry at her obtuseness; Charles was rarely angry. If he was inclined to be, some spirit of mischief would seem to rise within him and make him see himself partly in the wrong.

"Lucy," he would say, "I am like a man with an affliction of the eyes. They don't focus together; consequently I have two pictures of every scene—two views, you see, and of the same affair. That's very disturbing. Then I begin to wonder whether there are not many versions of the same picture, and whether the man with whom I have been so fiercely arguing has not as true a picture as mine. Lucy, you are not listening. You are wise, my love, for I am sure I talk much nonsense."

She wanted to please him; she wanted to show her gratitude. She would not look at other men—or hardly ever. He noticed this; he had a quick appreciation of such things, and he thanked her gravely.

He introduced her to his brother James who was not quite fifteen years old.

James liked to talk to Lucy; he talked often of his recent escape. To Lucy he would talk of it again and again, for she did not mind, and would appear to be interested on every occasion. It was the most exciting thing that had ever happened to him and he was so very proud of himself.

"To tell the truth, Lucy," he told her on one occasion, "I escaped because I dared stay no longer. There were messages from our mother, and she was ashamed of me for not managing to get away. Elizabeth—that is my sister—was also ashamed. She used to say: 'If I were a boy I should have found some means to escape.' But it was not easy, Lucy. We were at St. James' Palace where old Noll Cromwell had set guards to watch everything we did. They said they were going to make apprentices of Elizabeth and me, so that we could earn our living with our hands."

"So you ran away," said Lucy.

"Yes, I ran away. How I wish the others could have come with me! It was not possible, though, for the three of us to escape. Elizabeth was not strong enough. She was never strong after she fell and broke her leg. And Harry was not really old enough. He's only nine now. We made plans, but only one of us could get away in safety. So we planned a game of hide-and-seek. I was to run and hide, and so was Henry. Elizabeth would look for us. I ran back to the guard and pretended to hide; then Harry came running out and asked a guard to lift him to the top of one of the porches where Elizabeth would not easily find him. While they were doing this I managed to slip away to where my valet was waiting for me with horses. I changed my clothes and dressed up as a woman, Lucy. I nearly betrayed myself by raising my leg and plucking at my stocking as no woman would. But we got to Gravesend and so I went to Middleburgh and Dort and finally here."

"It was a wonderful escape," murmured Lucy.

"I'm glad you think so, Lucy."

His eyes were admiring; he was almost as fond of the ladies as his brother was; and perhaps, thought Lucy, when he was older he would be quite as fond. But, she decided, although she liked him very much, he would never have his brother's charm.

Yes, she was happy during those warm days of summer, and before September she knew that she was going to have a child.

❁ ❁ ❁

Lucy grew large and there was speculation throughout the Court of exiles. Men and women made bets with one another. Whose child is this, they asked—Charles' or Robert's? Who could be sure of Lucy?

Lucy heard the gossip; so did Charles.

"It is your child," she told him. "It could not possibly be that of another man."

He nodded gravely; whether or not he believed it she was not entirely sure. He would never *say* that he doubted her word. He would consider that most ungallant. Moreover she might weep, and there was nothing which distressed Charles more than the tears of women. They could upset him more, it was said, than bad news from England. And what did it matter whose child Lucy carried? The Prince would acknowledge it as his, for, considering his relationship with the mother, he would feel it to be most unchivalrous not to do so.

There were some who remembered his grandfather, Henri Quatre; and they declared that the resemblance between these two—in character, not in appearance, of course—was great. Both were great lovers of women and treasured conquests in love more than those of war; both were blessed, or tormented, by the ability to see many sides to all questions and disputes; both were easygoing and good-natured almost to a fault. Henri Quatre had been a great soldier and an even greater King. Those who wished the Royal House of Stuart well, hoped that Charles had inherited more from his maternal grandfather than these qualities.

There were times during those summer months when a deep melancholy would show itself in the Prince's face. The news from England was disastrous. Charles shut himself up with the letters his father sent from England.

He thought of the kindly man who had not, to his cost, possessed that gift of tolerance towards the opinions of others, but who had nevertheless been a loving father. He read the words Charles I had written.

"An advantage of wisdom you have above most Princes, Charles, for you have begun and now spent some years of discretion in the experience of trouble and the exercise of patience. You have already tasted the cup whereof I have liberally drunk, which I look upon as God's physic, having that in healthfulness which it lacks in pleasure . . ."

Charles had to face the truth. He knew that his father was the captive of his enemies. He feared greatly that he would never see his face again.

He thought of his family: little Henry and Elizabeth, prisoners of the Parliament in St. James Palace; James here with him after a miraculous escape; little Henriette—his dear Minette—after an equally miraculous escape, in Paris with his mother; and lastly, Mary, his eldest sister, whose hospitality he now enjoyed.

War was raging in England; war was raging in France; and both these wars were civil wars, the rising of the common people against their royal rulers.

What did the future hold for him—the penniless, exiled Prince? He could not say; and, because he was never one to trick himself with false beliefs, he dared not think.

He would go to Lucy; they would sport and play together. He thanked God for love, which could always enchant him, always make him forget his troubles. Lucy was a delight; he must be thankful for the gifts he had, for though he was a Prince without a kingdom and heir to a throne which would be denied him, he had certain gifts which would always bring him favor with women. So he would plunge into pleasure and try to forget his melancholy state.

❁ ❁ ❁

News came from England, which set a gloom over the Prince's Court.

Charles Stuart, King of England, stood convicted, attainted and condemned of high treason; and the penalty for high treason was death.

They would not dare! it was said.

But all knew that Cromwell and his followers had little respect for kings. To them, Charles Stuart was no ruler anointed by the Lord; he was a man guilty of treason to his country.

The Prince had lost his gaiety. He shut himself away from his friends. Even Lucy could not comfort him. His thoughts were all for the noble, kindly man. He thought of Nottingham, where his father's followers had tried in vain to raise the royal standard, and how the wind blew it down and seemed determined, so fiercely did it rage, that the King's colors should not be unfurled. An evil omen? it had been whispered. He thought of the skirmish at Copredy Bridge which had decided nothing and had led to the disaster of Marston Moor. He remembered the last time he had seen his father; it was in Oxford almost four years before.

And what could he do now to save his father? He was powerless; he depended on others for his very board. He was a beggar in a foreign country; his entire family was reduced to beggary. But at least he was a Prince, heir to a throne, and Cromwell would never feel at peace while he lived.

Impulsively he wrote to the Parliament of England; he sent them a blank sheet of paper which he sealed and signed Charles P. He asked them to fill in on that blank sheet any terms they cared to enforce; he would fulfil them; they might bring about his own disinheritance; they might execute him; but in exchange for his promise to deliver himself into their hands that they might do what they would with him, they must spare his father's life.

He despatched three messengers each with a copy of this document to ensure the message's reaching its destination; and he bade them depart with all speed to England.

Then there was nothing he could do but wait. He had done all that a son could do to save his father.

❁ ❁ ❁

One February day as he left his bedchamber he was met by one of his men, and was struck by the way in which the man looked at him before he fell to his knees and said in a solemn manner: "May God preserve Your Majesty!"

Then he knew what had happened to that kindly man, his father. He could not speak, but turned abruptly and went back to his bedchamber. There he threw himself upon his bed and gave way to passionate weeping.

Not until several days later could he talk of his father. Then he wished to hear of the heroic way in which he had died. He pictured it so clearly; it was engraved on his mind so that he would never forget it. He visualized his father, handsome and stately, brought to the Palace through St. James' Park; he pictured him walking with the guards before him and behind him, the colors flying ahead of him, and drums beating as he passed along. It was all so clear to him. He saw his father take the bread and wine which were brought to him; he saw him break the manchet and drink the claret just as Sir Thomas Herbert, his father's groom of the chamber, described the scene. He saw the crowds assembled; and as the King passed them on his last journey, his son knew that many in the crowds had muttered prayers and called: "God bless Your Majesty!" Never would Charles I have looked more noble than he did on that last walk to the scaffold; he would be noble to the end, even when he laid his head upon the block.

And ever after that, although the young Prince might be gay—and there were few who could be gayer than he—it seemed to those who observed him closely that a touch of melancholy never completely left him.

❁ ❁ ❁

Now Lucy was no longer the mistress of a Prince; she was a King's mistress; for although the Parliament of England would have none of him, he had been proclaimed King Charles II in Jersey.

Moreover, there came tentative offers to receive him in Scotland and Ireland.

It was a different matter being the mistress of the King from being merely that of a Prince.

Charles kissed her warmly and told her he must leave her. Business called him now—affairs of state. "Our ranks have risen, Lucy," he said; "and with new honors come new responsibilities. I must leave you for a time. I go to Paris to see my mother."

Then he told her he had another love in Paris. "Oh, Lucy, now you look hurt. You must not be, and you will not be when you hear who this is. She is not quite five years old, and she is my little sister. I am torn between my melancholy in leaving you and my delight in the prospect of seeing her. Lucy, you will be true to your King?"

Lucy declared she would. He wondered. Then he believed that she might until the child was born.

"Take care of yourself, Lucy, and of our child," he said.

She kissed him with passion, telling him that she loved him truly; she wept after he had gone.

Lucy knew she might not be faithful; it was not in her nature to be faithful, any more than it was in his; but she also knew that, though her body might demand other lovers, there would never be one to equal Charles Stuart—Prince or King.

❁ ❁ ❁

In a house in the city of Rotterdam, not far from Broad Church Street where Erasmus was born, Lucy lay in childbed. She was vaguely aware of the women about her, for she was quite exhausted by the ordeal through which she had just passed.

It was Ann Hill who held up the child for her to see.

"A boy, mistress. A bonny boy!"

Lucy held out her arms for the child and Ann laid him in them. There was a dark down on his head and he bawled lustily.

"He's one who will want his own way," said one of the women.

"The son of a King!" said Ann with awe.

Some of those about the bed raised their eyebrows, and their eyes asked a question: "The son of a King or the son of a Colonel? Who shall say?"

But Lucy did not see them and Ann ignored them.

"I shall call him James," said Lucy. "That is a royal Stuart name."

She bent and kissed the soft downy head.

"Jemmy," she murmured. "Little Jemmy—son of a King—what will you do in the world, eh?"

FOUR

The little Princess Henriette was bewildered. She sensed tension between two beloved people—her mother and her brother. It had something to do with Father Cyprien's instruction, which occurred daily. Charles was not pleased that it should take place, and her mother was determined that it should. It was Henriette's great desire to please her brother in all things; if he had said to her: "Do not listen to the teachings of Père Cyprien; listen to the words of Lady Morton!" gladly would she have obeyed. But her brother was careless—he was never really angry—while her mother could be very angry indeed. It was the Queen who put her arms about her little daughter and whispered to her that she was her mother's *"enfant de bénédiction,"* the Queen who told her that God had rescued her from heretics that she might become a good Catholic. Charles merely played with her, told her gay stories and made her laugh. She loved best of all to be with Charles, but it did not seem so imperative to follow his wishes as those of her mother, for if she obeyed her mother, he would merely be wistful and understand that she was by no means to blame; whereas if she obeyed Charles' wishes, her mother would be passionately angry, would rail against her and perhaps punish her. She was only a little girl and she must do that which seemed easiest to her.

So, to please her mother, she tried to become a good Catholic; she believed Père Cyprien when he had said that God had caused a great civil war so that she, Henriette, should escape from her father's country and come to France to learn how to be a good Catholic. She tried sincerely to thank God on her knees—through the saints—for having thousands of men killed, including her father, that her own soul might be saved.

Henrietta Maria had bought a house in Chaillot and thither she had taken several nuns from the Convent of Les Filles de Marie that she might found an order of her own. In this house Henrietta Maria had her own rooms which were always preserved for her, and it was her pleasure to spend a great deal of her time "in retreat" as she called it. It delighted her to take her little daughter there. Henriette would stand at the windows looking down on the gleaming Seine with the buildings of Paris clustered on either bank; but she knew that she was there for a more important reason than to admire the view; she was there to learn to be a good Catholic.

Lady Morton invariably accompanied her, and would often be present when she received her instruction. Lady Morton was very anxious about this instruction and Henriette was sorry for this. Why could they not all be pleased? What did it matter whether she was brought up in the religion of France or England? To tell the truth, Henriette herself could see little difference in those faiths about which others grew so fierce.

Henrietta Maria declared to Charles that she had been promised on her marriage that all her children should be brought up as Catholics. Again and again Charles reminded her that it would be against the wishes of his father. Then the Queen swore that her husband had promised her that, even if others of the family must follow the teachings of the Church of England, Henriette should become a Catholic.

"I swear it, Charles! I swear it!" she cried, tapping her foot as she did in moments of agitation. "He could deny me nothing. It was the last time I saw him. I swear to you, Charles. You would not wish to go against your father's wishes, would you?"

"No, Mam," was Charles' answer. "That is why I wish you to allow Lady Morton to supervise my sister's religious education in the faith of the Church of England."

"But it was your father's wish . . ."

The young King smiled gently at his mother. He was always extremely courteous to her, but he was not fond of her and he was too honest to pretend that he was. He loved his little sister dearly; but he also loved peace. A young King with a kingdom yet to be won had too many difficulties to face without making others with a fanatical Catholic such as his mother was. So Charles consoled himself with the thought: Minette is only a child. She will absorb little as yet. Later, something must be done. Perhaps then he could commission someone else to take up the struggle with his mother, and so escape the unpleasantness.

Meanwhile there was much to occupy him. Lucy had come to Paris with their son, and he was delighted with them both. Young Jemmy was a lusty youngster; Charles swore he had the Stuart eyes; he was certain that

Robert Sydney could not claim him as his son. He often said: "If I were not the King, I'd marry Lucy to make the boy my heir."

He had been alarmed because young Jemmy had already started to cause some trouble at The Hague. It was realized that he was a very important little boy, and there had been a plot to kidnap him which had nearly succeeded. Charles had declared that Lucy must come to Paris and bring the boy with her. This she had been quick to do. Paris suited Lucy better than The Hague—even Paris suffering from the disasters of the Fronde. So Charles, with plans for expeditions to the loyal territories of Jersey, Scotland and Ireland to be considered, and his playmate, Lucy, and his little son to enchant him, found it easy to shelve the problem of his sister's religion.

Henrietta Maria looked on with quiet satisfaction.

Let the boy amuse himself. Soon he would have little time for amusement. It was natural that he should wish to dally with a mistress. Was he not the grandson of Henri Quatre?

So Henrietta Maria kept her daughter with her, and often she would take the child against her knee and, embracing her fiercely, tell her that only by learning all that Père Cyprien had to teach her could her soul be saved.

"And what will happen to those whose souls are not saved?" asked Henriette.

"They burn in the fires of hell eternally."

"How long is eternally?"

"For ever and ever."

"And Lady Morton will burn forever and ever?"

"If she does not become a Catholic."

Tears filled Henriette's eyes. "Oh no! Not dear Nan! Please Mam, pray to God and the saints not to burn poor Nan."

"If she becomes a Catholic she will be safe. You must try to convert her."

"Oh, Mam, I will . . . I will!"

So Henriette went to her governess and put her arms about her neck crying: "Do be converted, dear Nan. Dear Lady Morton, you must be a Catholic to be saved. Do be a Catholic, and I will love you more dearly than ever."

"My dearest, we cannot easily change our convictions," said Anne Morton.

"But you must be a Catholic . . . you *must*! All those who are not cannot be saved. They are tormented forever and ever."

"So they have told you that, have they?"

"I cannot bear that you should be burned, dear Nan."

"Come, dry your tears. I promise you this: I shall not be burned."

"Then you will . . ."

"Let us not talk of this, my dearest. Might it not be that there are many ways to salvation?"

"But there is only one. Père Cyprien says so."

"It may be that he knows only one. Now I will tell you how we came out of England, shall I?"

"Oh yes, please . . . and how I kept telling people that I was the Princess and that the clothes I wore were not my own."

So she was appeased for the moment, and later she said to her mother: "I will tell Charles he must be saved, for, Mam, he too may burn eternally."

"Do not speak of these matters to your brother, *chérie.*"

"But, Mam, he will not be saved if he is not a Catholic."

Henrietta Maria was more brusque than she usually was with her little daughter. "Now . . . now . . . you talk too much. It is not for you to save souls. That is for Père Cyprien. You must learn what is told you. You are not yet ready to teach."

"But if I may try to save dear Lady Morton, why should I not try to save Charles?"

Henrietta Maria pinched the soft cheek affectionately. "I have said you must learn first. There is so much you do not understand."

Henriette nodded. She was content not to understand, for understanding, it seemed, could make people disagree, and that had already caused trouble between those whom she loved.

❁ ❁ ❁

It seemed to Henriette that any day might bring news which made her mother weep and declare that she was the most unhappy Queen in the world and that no woman suffered as she did.

The troubles of the Fronde endangered the lives of royal people. It was a long time since Henriette had seen her cousins, Louis the King and his brother Philippe, so that she had forgotten she had ever known them. Her own beloved Charles had left again; he had gone to Jersey where the people were loyal. Henriette quickly learned that it was a sad thing to be an exile in a strange land. And although her mother told her stories of the days when she herself was a little girl and Paris had been her home, still they were looked upon as strangers. When the French were angry with the English government much was made of Henriette and her mother; when they were indifferent to the English government they had nothing but sullen looks for the exiles.

"It is the saddest thing in the world to have no country," said Henrietta Maria.

"Shall we never have a country?" asked her daughter.

Her mother's eyes, with the dark shadows beneath them, gleamed as she enlarged on one of her favorite topics. "If you marry, the country of your husband will be your country."

Henriette nodded slowly; she knew that her mother had a husband in mind for her. It was a boy who would one day be the most important man in France. He was already a King, even as Charles was. He was Louis XIV. She had forgotten what he looked like so she began to picture him looking exactly like her brother Charles, although she knew that he was not so old. But he was a King, and people would kneel and kiss his hands as they kissed Charles'. She was not displeased at the thought of marriage with Louis since when she thought of him she thought of a boy who looked like Charles, spoke like Charles and indeed *was* another Charles—but instead of being called by that name he was Louis, and King of France instead of King of England.

Now, of course, on account of the Fronde, the little King and his brother did not come to Paris. Henrietta Maria and her daughter stayed there because they were not important and Paul de Gondi allowed them to.

So sometimes they were in the apartments of the Louvre, and sometimes they were in the house on the hills of Chaillot. Henriette studied; she found it easy to study and there were few distractions. She wanted to learn; there was so much to know. She wanted to understand why the people of England had killed her father and would not allow Charles to have his throne; she wanted to know why the people of France were threatening their monarch with the same treatment.

Mademoiselle de Montpensier visited them now and then. "La Grande Mademoiselle" she was called in Paris, for she was on the side of the Frondeurs; and she hoped to be remembered in the years to come as another Jeanne d'Arc who had saved France. She was very handsome and very anxious that everyone should pay homage to her, the cousin of the King, the richest heiress in Europe, and now . . . the heroine of the Fronde.

Henriette knew that her mother wanted La Grande Mademoiselle to marry Charles, and Henriette thought she was almost worthy of him as she looked at the handsome girl so exquisitely dressed in the fashions inspired by the Fronde—her long hanging sleeves were *frondées,* slung, not looped; her fan, gloves and kerchief were all *à la mode de la Fronde;* on her elaborate hat she wore an ornament which was the shape of a sling. The people cheered as her carriage drove through the streets: *"Vive la grande Mademoiselle!"*

Mademoiselle should, so said Henrietta Maria, look to her actions. Did she think that her attitude endeared her to the Queen Mother? Was this siding with the Queen's enemies a wise thing? It was true that the great Condé was on the side of the Fronde, and that many aristocrats had followed his example, but for a young woman who hoped to marry the little King to side with his mother's enemies, was surely unwise!

But Mademoiselle was unwise and Mademoiselle was arrogant. She thought herself grand and clever enough to do exactly as she pleased.

She was coquettish; she liked to talk to Henrietta Maria about Charles, for Charles was one of her many suitors, and although Mademoiselle considered him beneath her, she was not averse to hearing of his passion for her.

The little Princess liked to be present at these conversations between her mother and Mademoiselle; she liked to hear their talk of Charles, for, of course, they talked of him differently from the way in which they talked of him to her. There was so much she wanted to know about that most fascinating person, her beloved brother Charles.

"When he regains his kingdom his wife will be the Queen of England," Henrietta Maria constantly reminded her niece.

"Ah, when, dear Madame! When will that be?"

"Can you doubt that it will be ere long? The people of England will not endure forever that upstart Cromwell and his miserable rule."

"They say he has a way of enforcing that which is not palatable."

"Can you doubt that a young man so strong, so full of courage, so determined, will not soon win back his kingdom?"

"There are some who say he loves the company of women better than that of soldiers and statesmen."

"So did my father, but that did not prevent his conquering his enemies and bringing an end to civil war in France."

"But that happy state of affairs did not come about until he was well advanced in years. I should not care to spend the days of my youth an exiled Queen. Moreover, the King of England, even while courting me, brought his mistress to Paris."

"Bah! A man must have a mistress. What of that?"

"And treats her bastard as though he were a prince."

"He is at least the bastard of a King."

"I have heard that there is some doubt of that. This Lucy Water! Who is she? A King's mistress should have some quality, should she not?"

"He but amuses himself. And what ladies of quality were there, do you think, at The Hague where he found her?"

"Madame, she was his mistress in Paris."

"He is the sweetest natured man in the world. He could not turn her off because he was in Paris. You will see what grand mistresses he will have when he is in his own country."

"Madame, I would rather my husband were faithful to me than that he should have the grandest mistresses in the world. Your son cannot remain faithful to any woman. Why, even when he courts one, his eyes follow others. I hear now that he is causing some scandal in Jersey. There is a woman's name which is mentioned in connection with him—Margaret Carteret."

"Margaret Carteret!" interrupted the Queen. "She is merely the daughter of the Seigneur of Trinity. She is a young girl. My son stays at Elizabeth Castle, which is her father's residence, and because my son is there and a young woman is there . . ." Henrietta Maria's hands flew up in a gesture of inevitability.

"Wherever Charles Stuart is, Madame, there will be scandals concerning women."

"That is because he is so gallant and charming."

"And such a lover of women!"

"Mademoiselle," said Henrietta Maria, "I shall tell my brother to marry you to a monk. I can see that you do not wish for a man."

And with that Henrietta Maria rose and left her niece, taking short rapid steps which, to her daughter, conveyed her anger.

Little Henriette sat on, quietly thinking of her brother.

❁ ❁ ❁

Lucy, who had been lonely, was lonely no longer.

She had left Paris for The Hague—with her was the King and his little Court—for Charles had returned from Jersey and there were new plans afoot with the Scots. The Marquis of Montrose was awaiting him at The Hague with new propositions to lay before him. England would have none of her King; but Jersey had accepted him, and Scotland was prepared to do so—on terms. All Charles need do was sign the Oath of the Covenant, and he could be crowned at Scone.

Lucy did not understand why the King should be so perplexed. If he could not be King of England he could at least be King of Scotland. To be King of any land was surely better than to be King of none; and even Lucy could see that Charles was King in name only.

"You don't understand, Lucy," her lover tried to explain. "The Covenanters of Scotland are Presbyterian, and the Church of Scotland is the enemy of the Church of England, of which my father was head. There was trouble when my father sought to force them to accept the English liturgy. To sign the Covenant is, in a measure, to betray England. But what is the use of explaining, Lucy? You do not care for these matters, and perhaps in that you are wise. Lucy, I often think that if all the world were as careless of so-called great matters, and so absorbed in the pleasure of love, this Earth would be a happier place."

Lucy smiled; she knew how to turn him from his worries; and he was only too ready to be turned. He hated trouble; when it presented itself he always seemed to be looking for the easiest way out of it.

His friend George Villiers, the Duke of Buckingham, was at his elbow now. "Why not sign the Covenant?" he asked. "Better to have a country to rule over—even if it is that bleak and puritanical one—than remain an exile here!"

And so eventually he decided to sign. He knew that his mother would throw up her hands in despair, for the Covenanters' aim was to destroy Popery; he knew that there would be many to say that had he been a nobler man he would have preferred exile to siding with the Covenanters. He explained to Buckingham: "I am not a man who is so devoted to religion that he cannot set it aside for the sake of peace. My grandfather changed his religion that the wars of France might cease. There are times when I feel that I am my grandfather reborn."

"It is true you are as careless of religion," agreed George. "You are devoted to women. There is certainly a resemblance. But, Sire, you will have to work harder with the latter if you are to compete with your noble grandsire."

"Give me time," murmured the King. "Give me time."

The two young men could not be serious for long, and even the prospect of a sojourn in a land of Puritans could not curb their levity.

So Charles left for Scotland, whither obviously he could not take his mistress and little Jemmy. The Scots, said the King, so assiduously loved God that it gave them little time for loving others—even their wives; but he had little doubt that they took time off from their devotions to make love to their wives now and then, though it would be under cover of darkness and, as he had heard, for the sole purpose that more Puritans might be procreated.

Before he left he embraced Lucy and spent as long as he could playing with Jemmy.

"Take care of my boy, Lucy," he admonished, "and remember me when I am gone."

"I will never forget you, Charles," she told him.

"Nor I you, Lucy."

He did not promise that he would be faithful; although he broke so many promises, he did not make them callously. He doubted that he would be faithful, though he had heard that the Scottish women were as cold as their climate. There were always exceptions, as he well knew, and if there was one warmhearted woman in Scotland, he doubted not that he would find her.

So Lucy stood on the shore watching the ship sail away from Holland; then she returned to her apartments where she had so often entertained her royal lover, and declared to Ann Hill that no gentleman should enter her bedroom until her royal lover returned.

"You could not tolerate another after him," said Ann.

"Indeed I could not!" declared Lucy.

She believed this for two whole days. Then she began to feel lonely. Her big brown eyes would rest wistfully on several handsome men who still remained at The Hague; but always little Ann Hill would be there to remind her of Jemmy's father.

Lucy would sigh, and she and Ann would talk of Charles; and Lucy tried to be contented with that.

❁ ❁ ❁

There was great excitement at The Hague because the Duke of York had arrived. The Duke lacked the gay charm of his brother; he was not unhandsome—and Charles was far from handsome—yet James seemed unattractive when compared with the King. He was solemn and rather obstinate; but in one respect he did resemble his brother—his love of the opposite sex. He did not enjoy his brother's success with women, but he was determined to do so as soon as possible.

Lucy met Sir Henry Bennett soon after the arrival of the Duke. Sir Henry had come to Holland with James, and like James was looking for amusement at the quiet Court. As soon as he set eyes on Lucy he decided she could provide this, and when he learned something of her history, he could not believe—in spite of her association with the King—that she would be unwilling to become his mistress.

He called at her apartments, pretending to bring a message from his master. Ann Hill brought him to her mistress whose big brown eyes were wistful as they rested on his handsome figure, for if he had noticed Lucy, Lucy had also noticed him, and although they had not spoken at their first meeting, their glances told each other a good deal.

"Mistress Water!" said Sir Henry, bowing over her hand.

"Welcome to Holland, Sir Henry."

"I was loath to leave France for Holland," he said, his warm eyes full of suggestions, "but had I known I should find you here, Mistress Lucy, my reluctance would have immediately changed to delight."

"Men's tongues become sugar-coated at the French Court, I've heard."

"Nay, Lucy. They learn to appreciate beauty and are not chary of expressing that appreciation."

Lucy signed to Ann to leave them. Ann was hovering, and Lucy knew that she was trying to remind her of her royal lover. Lucy did not want to remember Charles just now; she had remembered him for four months—an age for Lucy—and none but Charles could have kept her faithful so long.

As soon as they were alone Sir Henry was beside her, taking her hands and covering them with kisses.

"You . . . you move too quickly, sir."

"Madame, in this world of change, one must move quickly."

"I would have you know of my position here."

"Do you think I do not know it? Do you think I did not make it my first business to know it, as soon as I set eyes on you?"

"There is a child in the next room who is the King's child."

"Poor Lucy! You have been long alone, for indeed it is long since His Majesty left for Scotland."

"I have been faithful to Charles . . ."

"Dear Lucy! What hardship for you! Come, I will show you that a knight in your arms is a better man than a king across the water."

"That sounds like treason, sir."

"Who'd not commit treason for you, Lucy!"

Lucy ran from him and made for the door, hoping he would catch her before she reached it, which he did very neatly. He kissed her with passion.

"How dare you, sir!" cried Lucy.

"Because you are so fair and it is a sin that all these charms should be wasted."

"You shall pay for this, sir."

"I'll pay with pleasure, Lucy."

"You will go at once and not dare come here again." Lucy's voice faded away; she gasped; she sighed; and she pretended to struggle as she was carried into the bedchamber.

❁ ❁ ❁

So Lucy was no longer alone. Lucy had a lover.

The little Court, amused, looked on. What was Charles doing in Scotland? They wondered; they had heard rumors. Was he thinking wistfully of his exiled Court? From all accounts the Covenanters were keeping a stern eye upon him. He must listen to prayers and sermons each day; he must not walk abroad on Sundays; he must spend long hours on his knees. It was a big price, all decided, to ask of a man such as Charles, even for a kingdom. And what of the women of Scotland? How could he elude his jailors—for it seemed they were no less—to enjoy that company in which he so delighted? It was said that he was not permitted even to play cards, and that he had been seen by a pious lady sitting at an open window doing so, and that she had immediately complained to the Commissioners of the Kirk. The King was sternly reprimanded. Cards on the Sabbath! The Scots would not allow that. One of the Commissioners had come in person to rebuke him and had read a long sermon on the evils of card-playing at all times, assuring him that it was a double sin to play on the Sabbath. But this Commissioner had seemed to be aware of the strain the Scots were imposing on the gay young King, for it was said that he whispered before he left: "And if Your Majesty must play cards, I beg of you to shut the window before commencing." From which it might be deduced that Charles had found some in Scotland to understand him a little.

He had not been crowned, and the Duke of Hamilton and the Earl of Lauderdale had been warned that he was not to mingle with the people on the streets, for that easy charm would, it was understood, win them to his side; and because he was such a feckless young man no one could tell what effect this might have. The Scots wished to keep Charles Stuart under their control; he was to be the figurehead they would use when they marched against Cromwell's England.

But, said the exiled Court, if there was an opportunity Charles Stuart would have found a mistress, and there were always women in any country; so it was certain that the warmth of Charles Stuart's charm would have dispersed even the frigid mists of Scotland.

In any case Charles might be hurt when he came back to find Lucy unfaithful, but he would understand. He could always understand. Warm and passionate himself, he would be ready to make allowances for Lucy's warm and passionate nature. It was true, Lucy assured herself, that no one of her temperament—or Charles'—could remain faithful to an absent lover for so long. So, after the first reluctant submission which Lucy liked to imagine had taken place by force, she would make assignations with her lover; she would deck herself with finery; she gave herself up to the arts of loving which she practiced so well, and in a month after the day when Sir Henry Bennett called at her apartments she found that she was to have his child.

❁ ❁ ❁

A small and solemn party was riding slowly towards Carisbrooke Castle. There were guards before and behind; there were a few servants and a tutor, and in the center of the party rode two children, the elder a girl of fifteen, the younger a boy of eleven.

As they rode along the boy would take surreptitious glances at the girl down whose cheeks the tears were quietly falling. The pale face of his sister frightened him; her tears worried him, for he knew that she was now even more unhappy than she had been before.

He had always been afraid of his sister, afraid of her passionate courage as well as her frequent tears. She could not be reconciled to their way of living as he could have been. He could have forgotten that he was a prisoner if she would do so.

"But no!" she cried passionately. "You must not forget. You always remember who we are, and above all you must remember Papa."

At the mention of his father's name the little boy was always moved to tears. When he was in bed at night he would make a pact with himself: "I will not think of Papa!" And to his prayers he added "Please God guard me this night and do not let me dream of Papa."

He was Prince Henry, but no one but his sister Elizabeth ever referred to his rank. To the servants and his tutor he was Master Harry, and his sister, instead of being Princess Elizabeth, was Mistress Elizabeth. It was said that they were to be made to forget that they were Royal Stuarts. Elizabeth was to be taught button-making and Henry shoe-making, that they might eventually become useful members of the Protector's Commonwealth.

"I would rather die!" cried Elizabeth, and indeed it seemed that if grief and melancholy could kill, Elizabeth would soon be dead.

Mr. Lovel, the little boy's tutor, whispered to him when they were alone that he was not to be afraid. The Protector's bark was worse than his bite, and he uttered these threats in order to humiliate the little boy's mother and brothers.

So, with Mr. Lovel to teach him and to give him comfort in secret, Henry could have borne his lot; but his sister was always there to remind him of what they had lost.

She, who was older than he was, remembered so much more of the glorious days. He scarcely remembered his mother; his father he remembered too well. Charles, James and Mary he had scarcely known, and his youngest sister, Henriette, he had never seen at all. Moreover he was physically stronger than Elizabeth, who had broken her leg when she was eight years old and had remained in delicate health thereafter; she grew paler and thinner, but her spirit of resentment against her family's enemies burned more fiercely every day.

"Elizabeth," he whispered to her now, "Elizabeth, do not weep so. Perhaps we shall be happy at Carisbrooke."

"Happy in prison!"

"Perhaps we shall like it better than Penshurst."

"Shall we enjoy living in that very place where *he* lived just before . . . just before . . ."

Henry's lips trembled. It would be impossible to forget Papa in the castle where he too had been a prisoner.

Elizabeth said: "They took Papa there before they murdered him, and now they take us there."

Henry was remembering it all so clearly as they rode along. He was sure that he would have more vivid dreams in Carisbrooke Castle. Perhaps he would ask Mr. Lovel to sleep in his room. Elizabeth would be angry with him if he did so. "You are afraid to dream of Papa!" she had cried scornfully, when he had told her of his fears. "I wish I *could* dream of him all through the days and nights! That would be almost like having him with us again."

Now the little boy was crying. He remembered it all so vividly, for it had happened only a year ago when he had been ten years old. One day—a bitterly cold January day—men had come to Syon House, which was the prison of his sister and himself at that time, and they said that the children were to pay a visit to their father.

When Elizabeth had heard this she had burst into bitter weeping, and Henry had asked: "But why do you cry? Do you not want to see Papa?"

"You are too young to understand," Elizabeth had sobbed. "Oh, lucky Henry, to be too young!"

But he was no longer young; he had ceased to be young that very day.

He could remember the sharp frosty air, the ice on the water; he remembered riding beside the frozen river and wondering why Elizabeth was crying since they were going to see their father.

And when they had arrived at the Palace of Whitehall, Henry had felt his father to be a different man from the one he had known before, and in his dreams it was the father he saw on that day who always appeared. Henry remembered vividly every detail of that last meeting. He could see his father's face, lined, sad, yet trying to smile as he took Henry on his knee while the weeping Elizabeth clung to his arm. He could see the velvet doublet, the pointed lace collar, the long hair which hung about his father's shoulders.

"So you have come to see me, my children." He had kissed them in turn. "Do not weep, beloved daughter. Come, dry your eyes . . . to please me."

So Elizabeth had dried her eyes and tried to smile; their father had held her tightly to him and kissed the top of her head. Then he had said: "I must have a little talk with your brother, Elizabeth. See, he is wondering what all this is about. He says, 'Why do you weep, when we are together thus? Is it not a time for rejoicing when we are together?' That's what Henry thinks; is it not, my little son?" Henry nodded gravely. "We wish to be with you more than anything," he had said. "Papa, let us be together now . . . and always."

His father had not answered that, but Henry remembered how his arms had tightened about him.

"My little son," he had said, "grave events are afoot. In these times we cannot say where we shall be from one day to another. I am going to ask you to remember this meeting of ours in the years ahead. I want you to remember what I say to you. Will you try to do that?"

"Yes, Papa."

"Then listen carefully. These are two things I have to say to you, and although you are but ten years old, you are the son of a King, which means that you have to remember much more than other boys. These are the two things I wish you to remember, and if you are ever tempted to forget them, think of this moment when you sit on my knee and your sister stands there trying not to weep, because she is older than you are. The first: You have two brothers. Never allow any to put you on the throne of England while either of them lives. The second is this: Never renounce the Faith of the Church of England in which Mr. Lovel has instructed you. There! That is what your father asks of you. Will you do these things for me, and if any should try to turn you from the wish to obey me, remember this day?"

Henry put his arms about his father's neck. "Yes, Papa. I will remember."

And shortly after that time he had grown up. He had begun to understand. He knew that the day after he had sat on his father's knee and made his solemn promise, men had taken the King outside the banqueting hall at Whitehall and there, before the eyes of many people, had cut off his head.

That was the specter which haunted his dreams—his beloved father, a father no more, but a headless corpse, those kind eyes glassy, staring and smiling no more.

If he could only forget his father's death, if he and Elizabeth could only escape from his father's enemies and join their mother, how happy he might be! He did not mean that he would forget his promise to his father; *that* he would never do. But he would be happy in his love for his mother and his brothers and sisters, and he would then be able to forget that last interview, those brooding eyes, so kind and tender and so heartbreakingly sad.

Perhaps one day Elizabeth would help him to escape as she had helped James. She had reproached James for not escaping before. She had mocked him for his cowardice. "Were I a boy and strong, I'd not long remain the captive of that beast Cromwell!" she had declared. And at last James had escaped and gone across the sea to their mother and brother Charles, who was the King of England now.

After they had been taken back to Syon House following that last interview, Elizabeth had changed. Then young Henry had seen his sister devoid of all hope.

Then to Penshurst where they had lived with the Earl and Countess of Leicester, who had been kind to them but forced to obey the instructions of the Parliament and treat the two children, not as the son and daughter of a King, but as other children of the household. Henry had not cared; it was Elizabeth who had suffered so cruelly.

And then, when she had heard she was to go to Carisbrooke, she had been stricken with horror. Henry had tried to comfort her. "It is near the sea, Elizabeth. It is very beautiful, they tell me."

"Near the sea!" she had cried. "Very beautiful! *He* was there. There he lived and suffered before they took him away to murder him. Every room is a room in which he has lived . . . and waited for them to come for him. He will have watched from the ramparts . . . walked in the courtyards. Are you blind, Henry? Are you quite callous? Are you completely without sensibility? We are going to our father's prison. One of the last places he was in before he was murdered. I would rather *die* . . . than go to Carisbrooke."

And so she grew paler every day. She begged that she might not be sent to Carisbrooke, but all her entreaties were in vain. "Send them to Carisbrooke!" said the Protector, and the Protector ruled England.

"Perhaps we shall escape as James did . . . as Henriette did," Henry whispered to her as they rode along.

"You may, Henry. You *must*!"

She knew she herself never would. She looked to Carisbrooke Castle as the place whither she would go to die.

If she died, pondered Henry, what of one poor little boy, fatherless and alone, cut off from his family?

Mr. Lovel rode up to him and tried to banish his melancholy. Did he not think this island was beautiful? He doubted not that the little boy would enjoy more freedom than he had in Kent. "For, Master Harry, this is an island and the water separates us from England." Henry was ready to be beguiled; but Elizabeth just stared straight ahead, seeming unaware of the tears which ran down her face.

Then Mr. Lovel began to talk of Carisbrooke, which he said was a British camp at the time when the Romans came to Britain. The land surrounding the castle was then covered with thick yew trees, for the Celtic word "Caerbroc" meant "the town of yew trees."

Mr. Lovel discoursed pleasantly of the Castle of Carisbrooke, which had faced the winds and storms of the Channel for so many hundreds of years; he told of Fitz-Osborne, the Norman who held the castle on condition that he defended it and the surrounding lands against all enemies, so that it was called The Honor of Carisbrooke. He told of Montacute, Earl of Salisbury, who had left his mark upon it in the reign of the second Richard, and of Lord Woodville who, years later, had enlarged the place. But Mr. Lovel could not continue with the Castle's history for the simple reason that it had played a part in the tragedy of Henry's father. So he came to an abrupt stop and spoke of other things.

Thus it had often been, Henry remembered. There were frequently those sudden terminations of conversation. It was as though people said: "Ah, now we are coming near to dangerous ground; we are approaching that terrible thing of which this little boy knows nothing."

At last they reached the Castle, and Henry lifted his eyes to the Keep, high on its artificial mound; the ramparts, the barbican and the battlements seemed impregnable as they looked down in arrogance at the cosier Priory. The walls of the fortress were in the shape of a pentagon with five bastions of defense. The little party crossed the fosse and in a short time were in the Castle Yard, where Henry saw the well with a great wheel turned by a donkey in the same way that a dog labored in a turnspit.

The servants came out to see them; they did not bow or kiss their hands. They merely nudged each other and made such remarks as: "Oh, 'tis Mistress Elizabeth and Master Harry come to Carisbrooke."

Elizabeth looked past them as though they did not exist, but Henry gave them a forlorn smile, for he understood, since Mr. Lovel had told him, that these people did not wish to be disrespectful to the son and daughter of the King; they had to remember that there was now no King and therefore no Prince and Princess; they were all citizens of the Commonwealth, and the Isle of Wight was a part of Cromwell's England.

He dismounted and walked beside Elizabeth who looked small and frail in the big hall of the Castle; the mourning clothes, which she had refused to lay aside since the death of her father, hung loosely on her form. She would not eat the food which had been prepared for them. Henry tried not to eat, but he was so hungry, and Mr. Lovel pointed out that he could not help Elizabeth by joining in her fast. And very soon Elizabeth retired to her bed and, when she was there, she asked that she might speak to her brother before she slept.

Henry was frightened more than ever when he looked at the pale face of his sister.

"Henry," she said, "I feel I shall not live long. I should not want to . . . in this prison. The happiest thing that could happen to me—since our enemies will not let me join our sister Mary in Holland—would be to join our father in Heaven."

"You must not talk thus," said Henry.

"Death is preferable to the lives we lead now, Henry. They are a dishonor to a line of Kings."

"One day my brother will come to England and drive the Beast Cromwell away."

Elizabeth turned her face to the wall. "I fear our brother lacks the strength of our father, Henry."

"Charles . . . !" stammered the boy. "But Charles is now the King. All loyal subjects proclaim him such."

"Our brother is not as our father was, Henry. I fear he will never live as our father lived."

"Would it not be better so, dear Elizabeth, since our father's way of life led him to the scaffold?"

"Our father's way of life! How can you say such things! It was not our father's way of life which led him there; it was the wickedness of his enemies. Father was a saint and martyr."

"Then," said the little boy gravely, "since our brother is not a saint he will not die as a martyr."

"It is better to die or live in exile than to do that which is unkingly."

"But our brother would not do that which is unkingly."

"He is in Scotland now. He has joined the Covenanters. He has made himself a pawn for the Scots for the sake of a kingdom. But you are too young to understand. I would have lived in poverty and exile . . . yes, I would have been a button-maker, rather than have betrayed our father."

Henry could not help being glad that his brother was not like his father. He personally knew little of Charles, but he had heard much of him. He had seen the smiles which came on to people's faces when they spoke of him. He had his own picture of Charles—a brother as tall as his father had been, with always a song on his lips and a shrug of the shoulders for trouble. Henry had always thought it would be rather wonderful to be with such a brother. He did not believe he would take him on his knee and talk of solemn promises. Charles was jaunty, a sinner of some sort, yet people loved him; he might not be good, as his father and Elizabeth were good, but he would be a happy person to be with.

Elizabeth put a thin hand on his wrist. "Henry, your thoughts stray. You do not give your mind to what I am saying. Here we are in this terrible place; here, in this room, our father may have paced up and down thinking of us all . . . our mother and brothers and sisters—all scattered, all exiles from the land we were born to rule! Henry, I cannot live in this Castle, I cannot endure these great rooms, these stone walls and . . . the spirit of our father. I cannot endure it."

"Elizabeth, perhaps we could escape."

"I shall soon . . . escape, Henry. I know it. I shall not be here long. This prisoner of Cromwell will soon elude him."

"Perhaps we could slip away from here. Perhaps there might be a boat to take us to Holland. I should have to dress as a girl, as James did. . . ."

Elizabeth smiled. "You will do that, Henry. You will do it."

"I should not go without you. This time you will come too."

"I have a feeling you will go alone, Henry, for there will be no need for me to go with you."

Then she turned her face to the wall and he knew that she was crying.

He thought: What good can come of crying? What good can come of grieving? They say Charles is always merry, that he does not let his sorrows interfere with his pleasures.

Henry longed to be with his gay brother.

Then, realizing how callous he was, he took his sister's hand and kissed it. "I'll never leave you, Elizabeth," he said. "I'll stay with you all my life."

She smiled then. "May God bless you, Henry," she said. "You will always remember what our father said to you, won't you?"

"I will always remember."

"Even when I am not here to remind you?"

"You will always be with me, for I shall never leave you."

She shook her head as though she had some special knowledge of the future, and it seemed that she had, for a week after her arrival at Carisbrooke Castle, Elizabeth developed a fever which, mingling with her melancholy and her desire for death, robbed her of her life, and from then on there was only one young prisoner at Carisbrooke Castle. He found a way out of his loneliness in dreams, and those dreams were always of his family. He fancied that his mother came to sit by his bed each night; he could almost feel her good night kiss upon his brow.

One day, he told himself, I shall be with them all.

In reunion he would come to perfect happiness, and looking forward to that happy day he forgot he was a prisoner.

❁❁❁

In her mother's apartments at the Louvre, Henriette sat with her governess, Lady Morton, who was teaching her to make fine stitches on a piece of tapestry, when Queen Henrietta Maria came into the room. Anne Morton was glad it was a needlework lesson; Henrietta Maria was suspicious of all that was taught the Princess and was apt to fly into a passion if she heard the governess say anything which she might construe as "heresy."

Lady Morton often thought of her own children in England who surely needed her; it was four years since, disguised as a servant, she had fled from England with the Princess on her back, and in those four years she had thought constantly of her own family. She knew she was fighting a losing battle against Henrietta Maria and Père Cyprien; they were determined to have this child for their Church, and they were succeeding.

But now Henrietta Maria had not come to talk of religion to her daughter and the governess. She burst in dramatically, for Henrietta Maria was dramatic by nature. Her black eyes were almost closed up with weeping; she was carelessly dressed and her tiny gesticulating hands betrayed her despair even more than the signs of grief on her face.

This was indeed *La Reine Malheureuse.*

She came straight to the Princess and, as little Henriette would have knelt—for the Queen was stricter in her observances of etiquette here in exile than she had ever been in her own Court of Whitehall—she lifted her in her arms and, bursting into bitter weeping, held the child's face against her own.

Henriette remained passively unhappy, patiently waiting for her mother to release her. There was new trouble, she concluded. It seemed to her that there was always trouble. At such times she longed more passionately than ever for her brother Charles, for whatever the trouble he never mourned about it; he would more often laugh at it with a lift of the shoulders; and that was how Henriette wanted to meet trouble when it came to her.

At first she was terrified that this bad news might concern Charles. He was in Scotland, she knew; her mother railed about it at great length; she had sworn that Charles had gone to Scotland without her consent; she was angry because Charles was now a man who could make his own decisions, no longer a boy to be guided by her. "His father listened to my advice!" she had cried when he had gone to Scotland. "He never will. Your father was a man with experience of ruling a kingdom. This is a boy who has never been acknowledged King by the English; yet he flouts his mother's advice."

Henriette began to pray silently that the trouble did not concern Charles.

"My child," cried Henrietta Maria, "you have lost your sister Elizabeth. News has come to me that she has died of a fever in Carisbrooke Castle."

Henriette tried to look concerned, but as she had never seen Elizabeth she could scarcely grieve for her; moreover she was delighted that it was not Charles who was in trouble.

"My daughter . . . my little girl!" cried the Queen. "What will become of us all? There is my son . . . my little Henry, left now in that Castle where his father suffered imprisonment before his murder. When shall I see my son Henry? What evil is befalling him in that place with his enemies about him? Oh, I am the unhappiest of women! Where are my children now? Am I to lose them as I lost my husband? My son Charles pays no heed to his mother. He goes to Scotland and makes terms with the Covenanters. He fritters away his time, I hear, in dicing and women . . ."

"Mam," said Henriette quickly, "what does it mean to fritter away his time with dicing and women?"

The Queen, as though suddenly aware of her daughter, gripped her so firmly that the little girl thought she would be suffocated. "My little one . . . my precious little one! You at least shall be saved for God."

"But Charles and his dice . . . and women?"

"Ah! You hear too much. You must never repeat what you hear. Lady Morton, you stand there weeping. That is for my little Elizabeth . . . my little daughter. . . . What will become of us all, I wonder? What will become of us . . . ?"

"Madam, I doubt not that one day King Charles will recover his kingdom. There are many in England who long to see him on the throne."

"But he has made this pact with the Covenanters."

"Mayhap they will help him to regain his kingdom."

"At what cost, at what cost! And my little Elizabeth . . . so young to die. We made plans for her at the time of her birth . . . my dearest Charles and I. Oh, I am the most unhappy of women. What would I not give to hear his voice again . . . to have him here to share this burden with me!"

"He had too many burdens in life, madam. This would but have added to them."

Henrietta Maria stamped her foot. "It would not have happened had he been alive. They have not only killed their King but their King's daughter."

"Madam, you distress yourself."

"You speak the truth, Anne. Prepare the Princess for Chaillot. I must go there at once. Only there can I find the comfort I need, the fortitude to bear the blows which God would seem to delight in dealing me."

The Princess turned to her mother. "Mam, may I not stay with Nan?"

"My dearest, I want you with me. You too will wish to mourn for your sister."

"I can mourn here, Mam. Nan and I can mourn together."

Henrietta Maria forgot her grief for a moment. She looked sharply at Lady Morton. What did she teach the little Henriette when they were alone? Père Cyprien had said that the child asked too many questions. It was perhaps time Lady Morton went home; she had her own children. A mother should not be separated from her own in the service of her Princess.

"Nay, child, you shall come with me to Chaillot. You too, shall have the comfort of those quiet walls."

"Madam," said Lady Morton, "if you would care to leave the Princess in my charge . . ."

Henrietta Maria narrowed her eyes. "I have declared she shall come with me to Chaillot," she said firmly. "Lady Morton, you have been a good and faithful servant. I shall never forget how you brought the Princess to me here in France. The saints will bless you forever for what you did. But I fear we trespass too much on your generosity and your loyalty. I often remind my daughter that you have children of your own."

Henriette was looking into her governess's face. Lady Morton had flushed slightly. The Queen had touched on a problem which had long given her cause for anxiety. It was four years since she had seen her family and she longed to be with them; yet she had never asked that she should be allowed to go home. She had felt it her duty to stay in France and do battle with Père Cyprien over the religion of the Princess Henriette.

The Queen and Père Cyprien were determined to make a Catholic of her; yet Lady Morton knew that it had been her father's wish that she should be brought up in accordance with the tenets of the Church of England. She could not have understood how Henrietta Maria, who wept so bitterly for her husband, could work against his wishes in this way, had she not understood the nature of the widowed Queen. Henrietta Maria was a Catholic first; and anything else took second place to that. Lady Morton knew that she would have beaten the little girl whom she now fondled so tenderly, if the child had shown any signs of refusing to accept the Catholic faith. Moreover Henrietta Maria had always been able to believe what she wanted to believe, and now she was able to assure herself—in direct contradiction of the facts—that the child's religious teaching had been left in her hands. And as Anne Morton looked at this fervent little woman with the snapping black eyes, she wondered once more whether Charles I might not still be alive had he married, instead of the French woman, the bride from Spain who had at first been intended for him.

Now there was a subtler meaning behind the Queen's words concerning Lady Morton. Was she thinking of dismissing her? It would seem so. She wanted Père Cyprien to take over the education of her daughter completely; she wanted no heretic to have a hand in it. Henrietta Maria would wave aside the valiant part Anne Morton had played in bringing her daughter to France; she would forget that which she had vowed never to forget, for it would be in the name of the Holy Catholic Church. She would forget her gratitude to Anne as she had forgotten the wishes of her husband whom she continued to mourn. Henrietta Maria was a tornado of emotions; and Lady Morton had to make up her mind whether her duty lay with her own children or with the Princess.

Henrietta Maria was watching her slyly, guessing her thoughts. Even in that moment of grief for her daughter Elizabeth, she would not swerve in what she called the battle for the soul of Henriette.

"And now," the Queen was saying, "we shall prepare for Chaillot. There we shall mourn together, dearest. Lady Morton, prepare the Princess. You will not accompany us, of course."

The Princess was led away, thinking sadly of the rigorous life at Chaillot, of the solemn nuns in their black garments, of the hard wood on which she had to kneel for so long, of the cold rooms and the continual ringing of bells. And what if Charles should come while she was there and go away again without seeing her?

She mentioned this to Anne, who said: "But he is in Scotland. He cannot come so soon. You will doubtless be back in the Louvre before he is again in Paris. Moreover . . ." She paused and Henriette had to urge her to go on. "It is nothing," she added. "I know nothing."

Henriette stamped her foot—a habit learned of her mother. "I will not have you start to tell me something and then stop. You do it often. I wish to know. I wish to know."

Then Anne Morton knelt down so that her face was on a level with that of the Princess. Anne was near crying, Henriette saw; she put her arms about her neck and kissed the governess. "Anne, are you crying for Elizabeth?" she asked.

"Not only for her, my darling. For us all."

"Why for us all?"

"Because life has become so hard for us."

"Are you thinking of your children in England?"

"Of them . . . and of you . . . I pray we shall soon all be in England."

"Do you think we shall?"

"Well, suppose the Scots helped your brother to regain his throne, and suppose he was crowned in London, and suppose you all went home . . ."

Henriette clasped her hands. "I will think of that, Anne. All the time I am at Chaillot I will think of that. Then the time will pass quickly perhaps."

But the time at Chaillot did not pass quickly. There was more bad news.

The Prince of Orange, who was the husband of Henriette's sister Mary, died, and there was more shedding of bitter tears. In vain did little Henriette try to comfort her mother. "But this is not so bad, dear Mam, is it? Not as bad as Elizabeth's death. Elizabeth was my own sister and your daughter, but the Prince is only the husband of Mary . . ."

"My child, you are but six years old, yet you have already known more sorrow than many know in a lifetime. This is a sad thing . . . in a way it is sadder than the death of Elizabeth for, my love, Elizabeth was but a little girl . . . a prisoner. We loved her dearly and her death hurt us in one way; but the death of your other sister's husband touches us more closely. Now that he is dead, your sister has not the same power, and there are men in her country who wish to be friends with Cromwell."

"The beast Cromwell?"

"The beast Cromwell!" Henrietta Maria spat out the words, and the Cromwell in the Princess's mind was an ape-like figure with terrible teeth and a crown on his head—her father's crown. "They are friends of the beast, so they will not offer the hospitality to your brothers that they have received in the Prince's day."

"Won't there be another Prince, Mam?"

"Yes. We hope that when your sister's child is born he will be the Prince."

"Then they won't dare be friends with the beast?"

"He will be but a baby. He can do little while he is so young. Oh, was there ever such an unhappy woman as your mother, child? Was there?"

"There was our Lady of Sorrows," said Henriette.

Then Henrietta Maria swept up her daughter in one of her suffocating embraces. "You comfort me, my daughter," she said. "You must always comfort me. You can, you know. A little girl like you can make up for all I have suffered.

"I will, Mam. I will make you *La Reine Heureuse* instead of *La Reine Malheureuse.*"

There were more close embraces; and Henriette could not understand why that which she had offered as comfort should open the gates to more floods of tears.

❁ ❁ ❁

There was one happy event which pleased the Queen: her daughter Mary gave birth to a son. He was christened William and there was great rejoicing, not only throughout Holland but in the convent of Chaillot. Henriette was delighted. Now there would be no more tears; now they could be gay.

The Queen talked frequently of her grandchild. "My first grandchild . . . my very first!" She thought fleetingly of that bonny boy whom Charles called Jemmy. If that boy had been the child of Charles' wife instead of that low woman Lucy Water, what a happy woman she would have been! Henriette too was thinking of Jemmy. She reminded her mother of him. "He is your grandchild too, Mam. And, Mam, it is said that Charles already has more than one son."

"Then they should have their tongues cut out for saying it!"

"Why, Mam? Is it not a matter for rejoicing when a king has many sons?"

"When a king decides to have sons he should first take the precaution of marrying."

"Why, Mam?"

"Because when a man is a king he should have sons who could follow him as kings."

Henriette as usual sought excuses for her brother. "Mayhap as he has no crown, he thought he need not have a marriage."

"He is a gay rogue, your brother."

Henriette laughed; she did not mind Charles being called that, when it was done in such a manner that "rogue" was almost a compliment.

"He is the most wonderful person in the world, Mam," she said. "How I wish he could be here!"

She looked eagerly at her mother, hoping that her attitude had softened towards her eldest son; but there were so many emotions to be seen in the Queen's face that it was impossible to know which train of thought she was following.

"Would the Prince of Orange had lived to see his son!" said Henrietta Maria fervently.

"Still, Mam, it is a good thing that he has left a son, even though he is not here to see him."

Shortly afterwards they returned to their apartments in the Louvre, and there a shock awaited the Princess, for Anne Morton came to her and told her she was going home to England.

"I have my own children who need me," she explained.

"But I need you," said Henriette, her eyes filling with tears.

"My dearest, I must go. I have outlived my usefulness to you."

"I'll not let you go, Nan. You are my Nan. Did you not bring me here? Nan, do not talk of going. Instead let us talk of the days when we left England and I insisted on telling everyone that I was a Princess."

"That was long ago, sweetheart. Now you have your mother and Père Cyprien to look after you, and you no longer need your Nan."

So, thought Henriette, Anne was leaving because of the conflict between her and Père Cyprien. Henriette threw herself into her governess's arms and begged her not to go. But Anne's mind was made up, and so was the Queen's, and beside those overwhelming factors, the tears and entreaties of a little Princess carried no weight.

❁ ❁ ❁

There came a wonderful day in the life of Henriette. It was during the October following her seventh birthday, and her mother and those about her had been more than usually somber for a long time.

Henriette had tried to discover what it was that saddened them, but no one answered her questions. She was just set to do her lessons under the guidance of Père Cyprien, to read the holy books he brought for her, and so to study how to be a good Catholic.

Then one day her mother said to her: "My daughter, we are going to meet someone. I want you to ride with me out of Paris to greet this person. Wear your prettiest clothes. You will be glad you have done this when you see who this person is."

One name trembled on Henriette's lips, but she did not say it; she was afraid that if she said that name her mother might shake her head and say impatiently: "How can that be! You know he is in Scotland."

So she waited, wondering who it could be; and on the road between Paris and Fècamp, she was suddenly gloriously happy; for it was Charles himself whom they had ridden out to meet.

She stared at him for some seconds before she recognized him. He had changed so much. His beautiful curls had all been cut off, and his hair was like a thick black cap that did not reach below his ears. He was bearded and seemed even darker than before. He was taller than she remembered, and gaunt; he was no longer a young man. His face was tanned with sun and wind; there were fresh lines about his mouth; his expression was less gentle, more cynical, and the strain of melancholy was more pronounced. But it was Charles. There were the same large eyes ready to twinkle, the mouth so ready to curve into a smile.

And when he saw her his expression became doubly sweet. He cried: "Why, if it is not my Minette! And growing fast! Almost a young woman."

She forgot her manners and cried: "Charles! Dear Charles! This is the happiest day since you went away!"

Then she was aware of her mother's eyes upon her, and hastily she knelt and kissed the hand of her King.

❁ ❁ ❁

They were together often in the apartment of the Louvre. She contrived to be with him whenever possible and he, characteristically, aided her in this. She would curl up at his feet or sit close to him on a window seat; and she would take his hand and hold it firmly between her own small ones as though to imply that if he tried to leave her she would hold him against his will.

"You have been a long time away, Charles," she scolded. "I was afraid you would never return."

" 'Twas no wish of mine, Minette, and constantly I thought of you," he told her. "How gladly would I have fled from those dreary Presbyterians to be in Paris!"

"Were they very gloomy, Charles?"

"Deadly. They preached all the time; I was called upon to say my prayers it seemed a hundred times a day."

"Like Chaillot," murmured Henriette.

"I'll tell you this, Minette. Presbyterianism is no religion for a gentleman of my tastes."

"Your tastes are for dicing and women," she told him.

That made him laugh aloud and she held his hand more tightly than ever. What could be said to Charles of Charles could produce nothing but hilarious laughter, whereas said to others it would bring shocked reproaches. She loved that quality in him.

"So you begin to understand your brother, eh?"

She nodded. "Tell me about Scotland, Charles."

"Oh that! It was dull . . . dull! You would go to sleep if I told you. No! I will tell you what befell me in England, shall I? That makes a more stirring tale."

"Yes, please, dear Charles, tell me what befell you in England."

"It is only due to miraculous providence that you see me here, Minette. There was not only one miracle, but many were required to bring your brother back to you. And the wonder is that those miracles happened."

"What would have happened if you had not come back?"

"At this hour my head would be on a pike on London Bridge and people passing would point up to it and say: 'There is Charles Stuart—the second Charles Stuart—who came to seek his crown and left us his head!' "

"No, no *no*!" she cried.

"There, Minette, it was but a joke. There is no need for tears. My head is firm on my shoulders. Feel it. See how firm it is. Charles Stuart will never lose his head . . . except when dealing with your sex."

"You must never lose it . . . never!"

"But to lose it in that way is not to have it cut off, sweetheart. It is just to love . . . so that all else seems of no importance. But I am talking foolishly as, alas, I so often do. No more of heads. I'll tell you what befell me in England, and you must have no fear of what is past. What's done is done, and here I am beside you. So while you listen to me remember this: I passed under the noses of my enemies and I came back here unharmed. Minette, I have been defeated by my enemies; but perhaps in some sense I have triumphed over them. I sought to win my crown, and in that I failed; they sought to make me their captive, and in that *they* failed. A stalemate, you see, therefore a victory for neither, and one day I will try again. Minette, there is something within me which tells me that I shall one day win my throne, that one day I shall be crowned England's King. 'Tis a fate well worth waiting for, eh? God's Body! 'Tis so indeed."

She listened to him, watching his lips as he talked, looking now and then into those gentle humorous eyes which were momentarily sad, but never for long.

He told her of marching down from Scotland to England, of the fierce battle he and his supporters had fought against the Parliamentary forces. She did not understand all he said; but it seemed to her that he brought a thousand pictures of himself and held them up for her to see, and she believed she would remember them forever; she would preserve them, and when he was not with her that would, in some measure, serve instead of his exuberant presence.

She saw him, tall and dark, sitting on his horse with his men about him; they would be sad and dejected, for they had suffered terrible defeat at Worcester, and many of his friends were in the hands of the enemy. He had escaped by the first of the miracles, and as the few survivors from the battle clustered about him, they would be wondering how they could escape from a hostile country where at any moment, from behind any bush, their enemies might spring upon them.

She pictured him, rising with the Catholic gentleman, Charles Giffard and his servant Yates, whom Charles' devoted supporter, the Earl of Derby, had produced to guide him through the dangerous country to Whiteladies and Boscobel, where there were many places in which a King might hide. She saw him stopping at an inn for a hasty tankard of ale and then riding on through the night, bread and meat in one hand, eating as he rode, because he dared not stay but must journey south since the enemy and their scouts were waiting for him at every turn. She felt she was with him in the saddle as, in the early morning light, he saw in the distance the ruined Cistercian convent of Whiteladies.

He was silent for a while, his face hardened because he was thinking it was a bitter thing that England's King should depend on the bounty of humble Englishmen for a night's lodging.

"Did you stay in the ruined convent, brother?" asked Henriette.

"It is not a convent now. It had been turned into a farmhouse. It was the property of the gentleman, Giffard, who had brought us there. We were not sure whom we could trust, sister. That was why every movement we made was perilous. I remember standing beneath a casement window which was opened suddenly and a man's head appeared. I knew this to be one of the Penderels, a family who had been servants to the Giffards, and who were now tenants of Whiteladies. There were three Penderel brothers living at Whiteladies, and this I guessed to be one of them.

" 'Bring you news of Worcester?' cried a voice as the head appeared. It was that of a young man.

"Giffard answered: 'Oh, 'tis you, George Penderel. The worst news from Worcester I could bring. The King is defeated!'

" 'What happened to His Majesty?' asked George Penderel.

" 'He escaped and waits your pleasure below!' I answered.

"Then, my Minette, we were brought into Whiteladies and, to appease my hunger and thirst I was given wine and biscuits; and never, Minette, had food tasted so good as that did. So I sat on the floor with Derby, Shrewsbury, Cleveland, Buckingham and Wilmot about me, and we discussed with Giffard and these Penderels what might next be done."

She clasped her hands together. "What wine was it, Charles?"

"Sack . . . the best in the world."

"It shall always be my favorite."

"Sister, you say such quaint and charming things that touch my heart and make me love you."

Then he told her how the Penderel brothers sent a message to Boscobel, and more Penderels came to the aid of the King.

"I changed my clothes, Minette. I wore a green jerkin and breeches, a doublet of doeskin and a hat with a steeple crown—oh, such a dirty hat! I was loath to put it on my head. And when I put on these clothes and my own were buried in the garden, the man under that greasy hat still looked like Charles Stuart and none other—so what do you think? It was Wilmot, merry Wilmot—who could never be serious, even at such a time—who said: 'We must shear the sheep, for by his curls shall they know him.' And by God's Body, without a by-your-leave, the rogue set about hacking my hair with a knife—and a pretty bad job he made of it—and there were those Penderels and those Yateses and their servants catching my curls as they fell, declaring they would put them away and keep them forever."

"I wish you had kept one of your curls for me, Charles."

"One of my curls! They are all yours, Minette—entirely and forever yours. And what would you want of one small curl when you have the whole of the man at your command?"

"For when you go away again."

"You must remind me to give you one when next I depart."

"I pray you do not talk so soon of parting."

"Nay, Minette, I shall stay here for as long as I can . . . having nowhere else to go and no money even to buy me a shirt. Here's a pretty pass! Would you believe I was the King of England—a King without a shirt or the wherewithal to buy one?"

"One day you will have as many shirts as you desire."

"Alas, dear Minette, so many of my desires go beyond shirts. Now I will tell you how Mistress Yates brought me a dish of eggs, milk, sugar and apples, such as I had never tasted before and which seemed good to me; and when I had eaten again, I stood up in my leather doublet and my greasy hat and learned to walk in a loping manner as a rustic would, and Yates taught me how not to betray myself by my speech. I was a sorry failure. I could not rid myself of Charles Stuart. There he was . . . always ready to leap out and betray me . . . in my speech . . . in my walk . . . my very gestures. We heard that a party of Roundheads was not far off, so I went and hid in the woods while they called at the house to ask if Cavaliers had ridden that way; one of the party, they stressed, was a tall, dark, lean man. George Penderel said that such a party had passed that way but had headed away to the north some hour or more since . . . and off they rode; and as soon as dusk fell I went back to the house and nursed little Nan Penderel while her mother cooked eggs and bacon for my supper."

"What was she like, Nan Penderel? Did you love her?"

"I loved her, Minette, because she reminded me of my own little sister."

He told her of his arrival at Boscobel, a hunting lodge, and the home of other members of the Penderel family.

"I had walked so far that my feet were sore and bleeding, and Joan Penderel—who was the wife of William and lived with him at Boscobel—washed my feet and put pads of paper between my toes where the skin was rubbed. I rested there and I ate again; but the neighborhood was full of Roundhead soldiers, and it was certain that soon they would arrive at the house. Staying at Boscobel was a friend and good Royalist, Colonel Carlis, who had escaped from the Battle of Worcester, and was so delighted to see me that he wept—partly with joy to see me alive, partly with sorrow to see me in these straits—and he and I went out and climbed a great oak tree. The leaves were thick and they hid us, but we could peep through and see all that went on below. And while we were up there, we saw the soldiers searching the woods for us; and that was another miracle, Minette. Had we hidden anywhere but in an oak tree we should have been discovered; but who would look for a King in an oak tree? So Colonel Carlis and I waited hidden yet watching, while below us the Roundheads wandered about searching for me."

"I shall love oak trees forever," said Henriette.

Charles kissed her and they fell silent. Henriette was seeing pictures of

Charles on a horse, riding for his life, a piece of bread and meat in his hand; Charles in a greasy hat, and pads of paper between his toes; Charles hidden in an oak, the leaves of which hid him from his enemies.

He was thinking of these things too; but he did not see them as Henriette did. He saw himself an exile, a King without a crown; he had left more than his curls behind him in England; he had left his youth, his lighthearted optimism; he felt jaded, cynical, and at times even careless of his crown.

Now he spent his time dicing and with women, as they had said of him in his little sister's hearing.

He burst into sudden laughter.

It was perhaps a more satisfying way of passing one's time than fighting for lost causes.

❁ ❁ ❁

At her lodgings in The Hague, Lucy heard of the King's return. She stared at her reflection in her mirror as Ann Hill tired her hair. Ann knew what she was thinking, and shook her head sadly. How differently she would have behaved had she been the King's mistress!

Lucy said suddenly: "Do not look at me thus, girl!"

"I am sorry, madam," said Ann, lowering her eyes.

"He has been away so long," said Lucy sullenly. "It was too long. I was faithful to him for many weeks."

"A long time for you, madam."

If it had not required so much effort, Lucy would have boxed the creature's ears.

"You are judging me, Ann Hill," she contented herself with saying. "Take care I do not send you back to the gutter."

"You would not do that. You and I could not do without each other now."

"Do not deceive yourself. I could find a woman as clever with her fingers as you are, and less impudent with her tongue."

"But not one that would love you as I do, and it is because I love you that I say what is in my mind."

"Because you love him, you mean."

"Madam, he is the King!"

"Oh, do not think of his rank. I have heard that he does not hesitate to take a serving wench, should the fancy move him."

Ann blushed and turned away.

"There!" cried Lucy. "You see how you are! It is small wonder that you lack a lover. Men love those who are prepared to adventure anywhere with them. They look at such as myself and say: 'Lucy is ready for anything! Lucy is the one for me!' And they are right, for, Ann, I cannot live without a lover. I soon discovered that. I took my first lover when my home was being plundered by Roundhead soldiers, and I had only met him an hour or so before. When you can make love in such circumstances you will be one of whom the men will say: 'Ah! She is the one for me!' "

"His Majesty, knowing that while he risked his life at Worcester, you were sporting with another man, will not be likely to say: 'She is the one for me!' I promise you that."

"You promise me? What right have you to promise me anything? But, Ann, you are right. He would not have minded a little falling into temptation—who could understand that more readily than he?—but there is Mary."

"Ah! There is Mary."

"Some would have seen to it that the child was never born. I could not do that. I was too tenderhearted."

"You are too lazy," said Ann.

"Come nearer, girl, that I may box your ears."

"Dearest mistress, how will you explain little Mary when His Majesty comes?"

"How can one explain a child? A child explains itself. There is only one way of begetting children. But I could say the child was yours."

Angry color rose to Ann's cheeks. "There is not one person in this town who does not know she is yours and the Colonel's. Did you not start to call yourself Mistress Barlow when you grew large, so that people would think you had gone through the married state at some time?"

"It's true, Ann. You cannot take credit for our little bastard. I believe I can hear her crying now . . . Go and see."

Ann went away and soon came back with the baby. A boy of two years old, with lively black eyes, followed her into the room.

"Ah!" she said. "And here is young Jemmy too."

Jemmy ran to his mother and climbed onto her lap. She laughed at his boisterous ways. He was the spoiled darling of the household, and his flashing dark eyes held a look of confidence that everything he wanted would be his.

Lucy kissed him fondly.

"Mamma," he said, "Jemmy wants sweetmeats."

His greedy little hands were already pilfering sweets from the dish beside her. She watched him, as he crammed them into his mouth.

The son of a King! she mused. And the sight of him brought back memories of Charles, which made her a little sad. She was wishing, not that she had been faithful to this boy's father—Lucy was not one to wish for the impossible—but that he had not gone away. She wished that the little girl, whom Ann was soothing, had had the same father as the boy. A sparkle of animation came momentarily to Lucy's face. Would it be possible to pass the girl off as Charles' daughter? Suppose she had arrived a little earlier. . . . But it was impossible. Too many people had noted her arrival, had laughed up their sleeves because Charles' mistress had taken a new lover. No! There was no way of explaining Mary; Charles would have to know.

"More sweeties! More sweeties!" cried the greedy Jemmy.

Lucy caressed the thick curly hair. At least Charles must be grateful for a boy like this one.

Henry came in and sent the children away with Ann, for naturally Henry had not come to see the children. His glowing eyes were appreciative of his plump mistress.

Later she said to him: "His Majesty is in Paris, Henry."

"It's true. Soon he will be seeking his Lucy. What then?"

"What then?" echoed Lucy.

"Sydney had to stand aside. I should not care to do that. I rejoice that we have the child to show him."

"What will the King say to that, think you?"

"He'll understand. Who better? That's Charles' way. He'll not blame us. How can he? He'll see how matters stood. How could he expect you to be faithful for so long? He knows how easy it is to fall into temptation. He loves us both, so he'll forgive us. You look sad, Lucy. Do you feel regretful for His Royal Highness? I'll warrant he has nothing I lack . . . apart from his royalty."

"He is a very kind and tender man."

"And I am not! Nay! You mean he is the King, and that counts for much. Come, cheer up! Be lighthearted as he will be, I am sure. I'll tell you of a sight I saw outside the town yesterday. 'Tis a statue to a woman who is said to have borne as many children as there are days in the year—and all at one time. What an achievement, eh? What if, instead of one proof of our love, we had 365 to show His Majesty? What do you think he would say to that, eh?"

Lucy began to laugh. She said: "This is what he would do. He would laugh. He always laughs."

"There is no need to fear the wrath of a man who is so ready to laugh as is our gracious King. Come, Lucy. Stop fretting. Three hundred and sixty-five all at one birth, eh? What manner of man was he to father such; what manner of woman she to bear them! I'll warrant they were no more skilled than we are, Lucy. How would you like to see a statue raised to you in this town, eh?"

So they laughed, and very soon they were kissing and caressing.

They had nothing to fear from a King who, being so skilled in the arts of loving, understood so much.

❁ ❁ ❁

In Paris Mademoiselle de Montpensier was discovering a new quality in the young King. He now spoke French without embarrassment; he had left his shyness behind him with his luxuriant locks.

He was skilled in the graceful art of paying compliments; even the young French gallants could not do so more graciously than he could, and with the words he spoke went such eloquent looks from those large brown eyes that Mademoiselle was tempted to consider him seriously as a husband.

Charles was certainly seriously considering her as a wife. She was handsome—though not as handsome as she believed herself to be—and she was rich and royal. He could not make a more suitable marriage, he believed, than with the daughter of the King's uncle.

He thought of Lucy now and then. He had little fancy for Lucy now. He was not the inexperienced boy who had been her lover; he had grown up since he had last seen Lucy. Adventures such as he had experienced since he had left the Continent had done much to change him. He had sobered considerably, though this was not outwardly visible; he had lost those wild dreams of easily regaining his kingdom; the defeat at Worcester had marked him deeply; not only had it set shadows beneath his eyes, etched new lines of cynicism about his mouth; it had touched the inner man.

He was indolent; he knew it now, and he blamed himself for his defeat at Worcester. He firmly believed—for his gift of seeing himself without self-bias had been heightened by his misfortunes—that a better man would not have suffered defeat.

He had had a chance and lost it. He did not blame the superior forces of the Parliament, ill-luck, bad weather, or any of the ready-made excuses of defeated generals; it was characteristic of him that he blamed none but Charles Stuart. Somewhere he had failed. He had failed in Scotland; he had failed at Worcester; and he blamed himself because of his inclination to shrug his shoulders and think of dancing, gambling and going to bed with women, rather than starting a new campaign. He often thought: If the first Charles Stuart had had the power of the second Charles to see himself as he really was, and the second Charles had had the noble inclinations of the first Charles, they would, combined, have made one Charles worthy to wear the crown of England. It was a distressing foible to know oneself too well.

He had thought of this when riding with Jane Lane through the Forest of Arden. Dear Jane! So beautiful, so aloof, yet so entirely conscious that she rode pillion with the King. William, she had called him—William Jackson, her humble servant, who must accompany her on a journey. He would never forget that journey, the beautiful girl riding pillion behind him. He had been dressed as a farmer's son in a gray cloak and high black hat; and for a week, Jane—and only Jane—had held his life in her hands. Yet never once had he attempted to make careless love to her, though when he said adieu to Jane, he had ceased to long for Lucy.

Lucy had a child now; he had heard that she was Sir Henry Bennett's mistress. He was fond of Henry—an amusing fellow. He wished Henry luck with Lucy; he wanted to see young Jemmy; but he believed he had finished with Lucy. He wanted a different sort of woman. So he would not seek out Lucy; a meeting between them might provoke an awkward situation, and he had lost none of his desire to avoid such happenings.

No! He would enjoy these weeks in Paris. He would play with his little sister; he would court Mademoiselle who, he could swear, was more inclined to listen to him now than she had ever been.

"My cousin," she said to him, as they walked through the gardens of the Tuileries, "you have grown up since you returned from England. You have ceased to be afraid of me."

"I was never afraid of you, fair cousin," he answered, "only afraid of myself."

"Those are meaningless words," she countered. "Afraid of yourself! What do you mean?"

"Afraid of the lengths to which my passion for you might lead me."

"When you went away you could not speak French. You go to Scotland; you go to England; and you return speaking it fluently. Pray, did they teach you French in those two countries?"

"They taught me much, but not French. I came away not caring what was thought of my French or myself."

"How was it you acquired such indifference to the opinion of others?"

"I suppose, Mademoiselle, it was because my opinion of myself was so bad that that which others had of me could not be much worse."

"You sound like a cynical old man. Were the sins you committed in England great?"

"No greater than those committed by others, I dare swear."

"Am I to conclude that you now have a contempt for the whole world?"

"Never! The world is made up not only of saints and sinners—both of which I have no doubt I should abhor—but also of beautiful women."

"Could not beautiful women also be saints . . . or sinners?"

"Nay! They are but beautiful women. Beauty is apart. It exonerates them from all charges of sin or saintliness."

"You are ridiculous, Charles. But you amuse me."

"You would have been amused far more to see me with servants in the kitchen, posing as a nailer's son from Birmingham. There I sat . . . one of them . . . so sure of myself—William, the nailer's son from Birmingham. God's Body! What a strange world this is, when it is better to be the son of a nailer from Birmingham than the son of a Prince of Scotland and Princess of France!"

Mademoiselle clenched her fists at the thought. She could not bear to contemplate insults to royalty. Charles noticed this and smiled. He was a King, and therefore it was easier to bear such insults than it was for poor Mademoiselle to contemplate them. Mademoiselle would never be a Queen in her own right; though she could achieve a crown mayhap by marrying him. Was this the moment to remind her of this? He doubted it.

He went on, "Unfortunately for me the meat-jack ran down. 'Now, William,' cried the cook, 'why do you sit there . . . as though you're a lord? Wind up the meat-jack and be quick about it!' I was eager to serve the cook, but although much time and care has been spent on my education, the winding of meat-jacks was never taught me, and I, William, the nailer's son, was exposed in my ignorance and called by that fat cook 'the veriest clownish booby in the world!' "

"You should have drawn your sword and run the fellow through."

"Then, dear lady, I should have left my head behind me on London Bridge. 'Tis better to be called a clownish booby—if you merit the name—than a corpse, to my way of reckoning. Howsoever, I fared better than Wilmot who, hiding in a malthouse, came near to being baked alive, while our enemies looked everywhere but in that spot for him."

"And this Jane Lane . . . doubtless she became your mistress?"

"This is not so."

"Come, Charles! I know you well."

"Not well enough, it seems. I was the lady's servant and as such I behaved."

"Some servants, possessing the necessary qualifications, have been known to lay aside the garments of servitude at certain times."

"Not such servants as William Jackson when serving such a mistress as Jane Lane. Ah! It is small wonder that you find me changed. You should have seen me trying to squeeze myself into a priest's hole. You should have heard me. That hole was made not only for a smaller man than I, but for one less profane. You should have seen me mingling with the ostlers and the serving men. It is not easy for me to disguise myself. My dark and ugly face seemed known to all. How often was I told that I had a look of that tall, dark, lean man for whom the Parliament was offering a thousand pounds!"

"Yes, assuredly you have had adventures, cousin."

"And one day, I shall succeed. You know that, dearest lady. One day I shall go to England and not return."

"Do you mean that you will settle down to a life of servitude with a charming lady—a Mistress Lane?"

"I hope to settle down with a charming lady, but as a king, Mademoiselle. Would you be that charming lady? I should be the happiest man alive if that could be."

"Ask me later, Charles. Ask me when you have won your crown."

Charles kissed her fingertips. He was by no means upset. Mademoiselle was too proud a young woman to make a comfortable wife. Moreover, he had caught sight of one of Mademoiselle's ladies-in-waiting, the young Duchesse de Châtillon. She was a lovely creature—calm, serene and so gentle. In some measure she reminded him of Jane Lane; she was warm and tender yet unapproachable, being completely in love with her husband.

The hopelessness of loving her suited the King's present mood.

He was happy to transfer his attentions from the haughty Mademoiselle to charming "Bablon" as he called the Duchesse.

❁ ❁ ❁

Life suddenly began to change for Henriette. When she was eight years old she renewed her acquaintance with the two most important boys in France. One was Louis, the King, who was fourteen years old; the other, Philippe, his brother, was aged twelve.

The excitement began suddenly. Her mother came to her, and Henriette had begun to know that when those black eyes—embedded in pouches and wrinkles—sparkled and gleamed with speculation, when those plump white hands gesticulated wildly, there were plans in her mother's mind.

"Great events are afoot," cried Henrietta Maria, and she immediately dismissed all attendants.

The little girl gave her some anxiety; she was so thin and was growing too rapidly; and although she was vivacious and intelligent, she lacked that conventional perfection which was recognized in the Court as beauty.

"What may well be a very important day in your life is approaching, my child!" cried the Queen.

"In *my* life, Mam?"

"You are the daughter of a King—never forget that. My dearest wish is to see you wearing a crown. That alone can compensate me for all I have suffered."

Henriette was uneasy. Her mother had a habit of imposing unpleasant tasks which had to be done for her sake, because she was *La Reine Malheureuse* who had suffered so much.

"The war of the Fronde is over. The King and his mother and brother are to return victorious to Paris."

"And this . . . is important to me?"

"Now, child, you are not showing your usual intelligence. Is it not important to all France that those wicked rebels are subdued, that the King returns to his capital?"

"But, Mam, you said for *me* . . ."

"For you in particular. I want you to love the King."

"All France loves him. Is that not so?"

"You must love him as the King of this land, of course; but you must love him in another way. But more of that later. Louis is the most handsome King that ever lived."

Henriette set her lips stubbornly. There was only one King who could be that to her.

Henrietta Maria shook her daughter. "Yes, yes, yes. You love Charles. He is your dear brother. But you cannot marry your brother."

"I . . . I am to marry King Louis?"

"Hush, hush, hush! What do you think would happen if any overheard such words? How do we know? This is the King of France of whom you speak. Oh yes, he is a boy of fourteen, but nevertheless he is a King. Do not dare talk of marrying him!"

"But you said . . ."

"I said you were only to think of it, stupid one. Only to think of it . . . think of it day and night . . . and never let it be out of your thoughts."

"A secret?"

"A secret, yes! It is my dearest wish. Mademoiselle, your cousin, hopes to marry him. A girl of her age and a boy of fourteen! It is a comedy! And what does she think will be her reception when the King and his mother come back to their own, eh? What will they say to Mademoiselle, who ordered the guns of the Bastille to fire on the King's soldiers? I will tell you, my child. Monsieur Mazarin declared that the cannon of the Bastille killed Mademoiselle's husband. That is true. When those shots were fired, she lost her chance of marrying her cousin. Foolish girl! And double fool for thinking herself so wise! She thinks she is another Jeanne d'Arc. The foolish one!"

"Mam, you were talking about me, and how important this is."

"And so I shall talk of you. Let the foolish ways of Mademoiselle be a lesson to you. I'll swear that when the Court returns, Mademoiselle will be requested to leave the Tuileries; she will be retired to the country. There let her toss her pretty head; there let her write in her journal; there let her wonder whether it might not be a good thing to turn to the King of England before it is too late—lest she lose him as she has lost the King of France. The

King of France! A woman of her age! Nay, she shall never have Louis. Ah, my little Henriette, how I wish we could plump you up! How thin you are! Bad child! You do not eat enough. I shall have you whipped if you do not eat."

"Please, Mam, don't do that. I eat very well, but it does not make me fat. It only makes me tall."

"Louis is tall. Louis is so handsome that all who see him gasp at his beauty. A King ten years . . . and only fourteen now. It is said that he is not mortal, that no one could be as perfect as this boy, and be human."

"And is he so perfect, Mam?"

"Of course he is. More beautiful than all other boys; taller, more full of health, high spirits and good nature. They say he is the son, not of his father, but of a god."

Henriette's eyes glistened; she clasped her hands together and listened ecstatically.

The Queen of England caught the child to her and kissed her fiercely. "No! You must forget you are eight years old. You must conduct yourself as a lady. You must never . . . never forget that, though exiled, you are the daughter of the King of England . . . and that only a daughter of kings would be worthy to mate with such as Louis. Our dear Mademoiselle is not quite that, eh? For all her airs and so-called beauty . . . for all her wealth . . . she is not quite that. She is the King's cousin, as you are, my little one, but there is a difference. Ah! There is a difference. You are the daughter of the King of England, and your mother is as royal as Louis' own father, for *their* father was one and the same—the great and glorious Henri Quatre of great fame."

Henriette shifted from one foot to the other; she had heard all this before.

"Now tomorrow His Majesty will ride into his capital, and you will be there to greet him. Beside him will ride your own brother—two young kings side by side."

"Charles!" cried Henriette gleefully.

Henrietta Maria frowned at her daughter. "Yes, yes, brother make you forget your homage to the King of France. It is all very well to love your brother . . . but it will be necessary for you one day to love another more than you love Charles."

Henriette did not tell her mother—for it would have made her angry—that never as long as she lived could she love another as she loved her brother Charles.

"You are eight years old," repeated the Queen. "Old enough to put away childish things. Time enough for a princess to think of her future."

Eight years old! Often Henriette thought of that time as the end of her childhood.

❁ ❁ ❁

The next day the King of France rode into his capital. Along the route from Saint-Cloud to Paris the crowd waited to cheer him. It was a year since he had left Paris, and the people did not forget that, although they had rebelled against the Court, they had never felt any resentment towards this beautiful boy—so tall, so physically perfect, so charming to behold that he only had to show himself to win their applause.

Everywhere was pageantry and color; the city guards in red-and-blue velvet led the procession, and following them rode the King, glorious in purple velvet embroidered with golden fleurs-de-lis, his plumed hat well back from his handsome face, his brown eyes alight with triumph and loving kindness towards his people; his beautifully shaped features looked as if they had been carved by a Greek sculptor out of stone, because of their very perfection; yet his clear, bright complexion showed him to be of healthy flesh and blood. Beside him, such an excellent foil to such celestial beauty, was the tall lean figure of the King of England, his dark, saturnine face alight with humor; he seemed ugly in comparison with that pink and white boy, and yet many women in the crowd could not take their eyes from him to look at the beautiful boy-King of France.

From the churches bells pealed forth. The war of the Fronde was over; there was peace in France; and men and women wept and told each other that this handsome King was a gift from Heaven and that he would lead France to prosperity. At the windows groups shouted and cheered; silken streamers hung from those windows; people climbed to roofs to get a better view of their monarch. One woman—ragged and dirty—pushed her way through the crowds that she might kiss the royal foot. The guards tried to prevent her, but the King merely smiled that smile which made the women cry "God bless him!," and all began to cheer the beggar woman with their King.

Behind the King rode the great Dukes of France—the Duc de Vendôme and Duc de Guise; then followed the Marshal; and after them the Lords in glittering apparel, followed by more guards on horseback.

The Swiss Guards followed just ahead of the Queen's coach. In this Anne of Austria sat back plump and arrogant, displaying her beautiful hands, jewel-covered; the crowds had few cheers for her; they had never liked her and they blamed her—not handsome Louis—for the troubles from which the country had just emerged. With her rode her second son,

Philippe—known as Monsieur—who was twelve years old and a little sulky now because of all the fuss which was being made of his brother. It was difficult for a younger son not to resent the fate which had decreed that he should be born after his brother. Philippe lacked the striking beauty of Louis, but he knew himself to be of a sharper intellect, and it was sad to have to take second place on every occasion.

His mother, watching him, reminded him that it was necessary to smile and bow to the people. Did he want them to think he was a sullen fellow, so different from his brother? So Monsieur smiled and bowed and hid his feelings; and the people murmured together that it was a marvelous thing that after twenty-two years God had blessed the union of Louis XIII and Anne of Austria with two such boys.

Now the guns of the Bastille and the salvos from the Place de Grève roared forth; lamps shone in the windows and bonfires were lighted in the streets of Paris.

The war of the Fronde was over; Louis was back in his Louvre. Now there would be a return of pageantry and gaiety such as the French loved.

So Paris rejoiced.

❁ ❁ ❁

In the great hall of the Louvre the King welcomed his guests.

Henrietta Maria was present with her daughter. Anne of Austria smiled on her sister-in-law, and Henrietta Maria had reason to believe that she was not averse to a match between their children.

That made Henrietta Maria's eyes sparkle; that made her almost happy.

If only one other could be here to see this day! she thought, and the tears gushed to her eyes. None must see them; they were all impatient of her grief, as people always are of the grief of others too long preserved.

If Charles could have the fortune of Mademoiselle, he could begin campaigning for the return of his kingdom. If Anne of Austria would agree to a match between Louis and the little Henriette . . .

All these were dreams; but surely not impossible of fulfilment?

Young Louis had an arrogant air. Would he obey his mother? He was surrounded by sycophants who told him he had been sent by Heaven to govern France; he had been a king from the nursery; none had ever dared deny him what he asked; the most sweet-tempered person in the world could not emerge without a little arrogance from an upbringing such as that which had befallen the boy-King of France. No! He would make his own choice within reason; and was it not likely that he would choose her little Henriette?

Henriette herself felt bewildered by all the pageantry; she had lived so quietly during the war of the Fronde when the Court was not in Paris; she had never in all her life been in such glittering company.

She was excited by it; she loved to see the flashing jewels and the brilliant garments of the men and women. And Charles was here, in a place of honor beside the King of France. That gave her great pleasure. It was wonderful to see the honor paid to him and to remind herself that he was, after all, her dearest brother whose hair she pulled, who tossed her in his arms and was never too much the King to remember that he was Minette's brother.

Now she must go forward and kneel to the King of France. She thought how handsome he was; he was all that she had been led to expect he would be.

She knelt and kissed his hand as she had been told to do.

"My little cousin," he said, "it makes me happy to see you here."

But his gaze flickered over her lightly and, looking up, she caught the eyes of his brother Philippe on her. Philippe studied her languidly and without great interest.

She thought in that moment of her mother's words; she remembered that she had to make this King love her and that she had to love him for the sake of *La Reine Malheureuse* who had suffered so much and must therefore not be allowed to suffer more.

How can I make this magnificent young man love *me*! she thought in panic, and she felt so forlorn and frightened that she hesitated for a moment when she should have passed on.

She was aware of the shocked silence about her. Etiquette was of the utmost importance at the Court of France. She could not think what she must do now. She began to tremble.

Then she turned her eyes to that beloved face; she knew that she could rely on him.

The eyes crinkled up into that well-loved smile; the corners of the mouth turned up. She was appealing mutely to him for help, and, of course, she did not appeal in vain.

He was beside her, dispensing with etiquette, knowing that a breach on the part of the King of England was negligible compared with that of a little girl.

He laid his hand on her shoulder and drew her to one side, that the person who was waiting to kneel before the King of France might proceed.

"This is my own little sister," he said lightly. "I hope you will like her well, Louis, for I love her dearly."

Her hand curled round his finger. She felt safe and comforted. He kept her standing beside him, defiant of raised eyebrows.

I am growing up, thought Henriette, and growing up is frightening. I need not be afraid though . . . if Charles is near.

Charles' eyes sought those of his mother; his glinted with amusement. She was not displeased, and he was glad of that for Minette's sake.

She was thinking: Let all the Court be reminded that this little girl is the beloved sister of the King of England. Let the Queen-Mother also be reminded. Yes . . . it is a not unhappy little incident.

God's Body! thought the King of England. Mam is already trying to marry the child to the King of France. So Minette is leaving childhood behind her. My little sister is growing up.

FIVE

The carriage of the Queen-Mother of France was turning in at the Palais-Royal. Henrietta Maria was waiting impatiently to receive her, curbing the natural impatience which this flaccid-minded woman inspired in her, cautioning herself to remember that she was dependent on her sister-in-law's hospitality, on her sister-in-law's goodwill, if that for which she longed above all things was to come to pass.

Into the great reception room swept Anne of Austria, accompanied by her women. Poor creatures! thought Henrietta Maria. They looked worn out—worn out with having to listen to her inanities, having to adjust their minds to hers—quite a feat, for many of them were not only well-born but well-educated women. How relieved they must be at the end of the day after the Queen's *coucher* when they must chatter lightly to her until she had fallen asleep, for then they could escape from their bondage!

It was a great honor that she should condescend to call at the lodging of her exiled sister-in-law. Henrietta Maria's heart leaped with hope in contemplating the cause.

They embraced—the Queen-Mother of France and the exiled Queen of England. The ready tears came to Henrietta Maria's eyes.

"Such an honor . . . such an honor," she murmured. "Dearest Majesty, you make me forget I am an exile depending on your bounty."

Anne smiled. She was generous by nature and she loved to do little kindnesses if they did not involve taking too much trouble. She spent all the morning in bed and after that she prayed in her oratory for hours. She liked to be there alone, while her thoughts flitted lightly from one subject to another. What delicacies would her cooks have prepared for her that day? What new gossip was there in the Court? What new plays were being prepared for her? What was her darling doing at this moment? She must ask him to come to see her. *Ask* now—not command anymore. The beloved creature was no longer to be commanded. She could lie back in the sanctity of her oratory and think about his many perfections—her beautiful, beautiful son, of whom she never tired of thinking, whose handsome looks were a delight to her whenever her eyes fell upon him. Every queen in the world envied her her Louis. Any queen who had produced such a one had justified her existence, was entitled to give up her days to idling, gambling, watching plays, gossip . . .

She was doubly pleased with herself, for not only had she produced Louis, but Philippe. She laughed to herself sometimes when she thought of her late husband, now no longer here to plague her. Not that she thought of him often; he had been dead for nearly ten years. She was not one to brood on the past. She lightly skimmed over the years of marriage, his dislike for her, the urgent need for a child, which had forced Cardinal Richelieu to bring them together for a brief spell, and themselves to conform to his wishes; and the miracle, the birth of Louis—Louis Dieudonné—and later that of Philippe.

But why think of that other Louis—her husband—the cold, ugly misogynist who, after the first delights of fatherhood, had been irritated by the boisterous manners of his heir. Anne could smile at the memory of the little Prince's distaste when he had first seen his father in his nightcap. He had roared his dislike so that the King had turned furiously on his wife, accusing her of influencing the child against him, and he had even threatened to take the child from her.

Not that he had succeeded in doing that. He had been old; he was enfeebled; it had been clear that he was not long for this world.

It had seemed prophetic when, on the occasion of little Louis' christening at the age of two, his father had taken him on his knee when the ceremony was over and asked him: "Now what is your name, my child?" and the boy had answered boldly: "I am Louis XIV, Father." Then had the bitter mouth curled; then had the ugly eyes narrowed and a faint smile had touched the sallow face. "Not yet, Louis XIV," he had said. "Louis XIII is not dead yet. Aye, but mayhap you speak only a little too soon."

It was not long after that that the boy was indeed Louis XIV, and new power had come to Anne as Regent. Not that she had ever wished to alter her way of life. Politics bored her and she had her dear Mazarin to do for her what Richelieu had done in a previous reign. She was more concerned with the trivialities of life.

"Dismiss the attendants," she said now to Henrietta Maria. "Let us have a sisterly talk."

"This is an honor and a pleasure," said Henrietta Maria.

"Ah," said Anne, when they were alone, "it is good to be back in Paris. It is good to know that the troubles are over."

"And to see your son, His Majesty, gives me no less pleasure than it does yourself, I assure you, dear sister," said Henrietta Maria. "He grows in beauty. A short while ago it would not have seemed possible for any to be more handsome. But it was so. Louis of today is more beautiful than Louis of yesterday."

If there was one thing Anne liked better than lying abed, gossiping or having her hair combed, displaying her beautiful hands for admiration, partaking of the savory dishes and sweetmeats prepared for her approval, it was listening to praises of her son.

"You speak truth," she said now. "I confess his many perfections amaze me." She added condescendingly: "And your little daughter is not without her charm."

"My little Henriette! I have done my best. It has not been easy. These terrible years . . . I have devoted much time to her education. She is clever. She has also read much and she takes a delight in music. She can sing well; she plays, not only the harpsichord, but the guitar. Her brother, the King, adores her and declares he delights in her company far more than that of many ladies noted for their wit and beauty."

"He is a good brother to little Henriette. Poor child! Hers has been a hard life. When I think of her fate and compare it with that of my own two darlings . . ."

"Fortune has smiled on you, sister. There are some of us . . ." The ready tears sprang to Henrietta Maria's eyes.

But Anne, who did not care for exhibitions of grief, said quickly: "Well, the child is here with her family and, now that we have restored peace and order to the land, there will be changes at Court. It is of these matters that I have come to speak to you now. My sons take great pleasure in fêtes and balls . . . and particularly in the ballet. They excel in dancing. Now why should not their little cousin join them in these sports and pleasures? Mademoiselle . . ." Anne's flaccid mouth had hardened a little . . . "will be staying in the country for a while."

Henrietta Maria could not hide her satisfaction.

"She was clever at devising these entertainments," went on Anne, "but as she will not be here . . . mayhap your daughter could be of some use."

"This *is* a great pleasure to me. Henriette will be delighted."

"She may come to the Louvre to help my sons plan an entertainment they wish to give. I am sure she will be very helpful."

Henrietta Maria almost forgot to be discreet; she wanted to draw her chair closer to that of the Queen-Mother of France; she wanted to chat—as mother to mother—about the charms and achievements of their offspring; she wanted to make delightful plans for linking Henriette and Louis. But her ambition came to her aid and for once she suppressed her impetuosity.

She sat listening while Anne talked, and the talk was of Louis. Louis at seven being reprimanded for using oaths; Louis at eight, in pink satin trimmed with gold lace and pink ribbons, dancing perfectly, outshining all with his grace and his beauty; Louis with the fever on him, when for fourteen days his mother had done nothing but weep and pray; the sweetness and patience of the sick child; how he had appointed certain boys-in-waiting to share his games; how he had selected one of the serving girls, a country wench, to play with; how he loved her dearly and liked to make her act King while he became the serving maid; how in disputes between the brothers, she had always insisted that Philippe should obey Louis; how he must always be mindful of the great destiny which was his brother's. And so on, until she rose to go.

Then Henrietta Maria sent for her daughter; she embraced her warmly.

"Mam, Mam, what has happened to make you so happy? Is there news of Charles?"

"You think of your brother first on every occasion! There are other people who should concern you now and then. You are to visit the King and his brother; you are to go to the Louvre tomorrow to help them devise a ballet for our entertainment."

"I . . . Mam!" Henriette shrank from her mother.

"No, no!" scolded the Queen. "You must not be foolish." She pinched her daughter's cheek. "Remember what I have said. Though you must always remember that you are a King's daughter, you should not be insensible of this great honor which is done you. My little daughter, here is great news! Mademoiselle who would wish to marry Louis, is sent to the country in disgrace, and you, my little one, are to take her place in sharing the amusements of Louis and his brother. Now you must agree always with everything Louis says. You must take his side if there is a disagreement between the brothers. You must remember what I have told you."

"Yes, Mam," whispered Henriette.

She wished Charles were in Paris that she might tell him how uneasy she felt. He would understand; he would soothe her; but without Charles she was alone and there was no one to whom she could turn.

❁ ❁ ❁

The two boys were waiting for their cousin. Louis was impatient.

"A little girl!" he said. "Here's a pretty pass! So now we must play with little girls! Why should I be asked to play with little girls!"

"Because her brother is the King of England," Philippe answered wryly.

"King of England! The English have a different tale to tell."

"As the French might have had, brother . . . not so long ago."

Louis shook his head in exasperation, but he was used to Philippe's dry comments. Philippe was in a state of continual pique because he was two years younger than his brother and merely Monsieur, Duc d'Orléans, instead of King.

Louis' annoyance did not last long. He was naturally sweet-tempered though often arrogant, for it would have been a miracle if he had been anything else. From the day he was five he had been told he was the most important person in the world. Only a short while ago his tutor had told him that God had given him something that even his illustrious grandfather Henri Quatre had not possessed—a handsome presence, a beauty that was almost unearthly in its perfection, a fine figure, a charm which delighted while it won respect. All through his life it had been the same. His tutors never forced him to learn anything, but allowed him to follow his inclinations; it was a wonder that he had acquired any knowledge at all, considering he loved sports so much. But with all his physical perfections there had been born in him a desire to do what was right, and occasionally this was uppermost. Then he would try to study for a while before his desire to play soldiers—his favorite game—came over him and he could not resist calling his army of young boys together for a mock battle. Alas, only a year ago his Company of Honor had been disbanded, for their exploits had become so realistic that his mother had grown terrified for his safety; and Mazarin had decided to risk the King's displeasure and put an end to these warlike games. Then had Louis turned to dancing and, in particular, the ballet.

He excelled in these, but he never forgot that the praise which came his way might not be entirely genuine; Monsieur de Villeroi his governor, never reproved him; if Louis asked for something, de Villeroi always said: Yes, he might have it, before he even knew for what the boy asked. Yet Louis loved far better his valet, La Porte, who often crossed him and had even on occasion forbidden him to do what he wanted. The most Monsieur de Villeroi would say, if La Porte advised against doing something, was: "La Porte is right, Sire." But his governor never actually reproved or forbade, even when the King had turned somersaults on his bed and had ended by falling and getting a most unpleasant bump on the head.

Louis had realized long ago that, surrounded by such sycophants, a great ruler of fourteen must be especially watchful.

"Those who are lenient concerning your faults," La Porte told him once, "are not so on your account, but on their own, and their object is merely to make you like them, so that they may receive your favors and grow rich."

Louis never forgot that warning.

He became very fond of La Porte; he still liked to have the valet read to him when he was in bed at night. The History of France sounded quite exciting when read by La Porte; and Louis always listened gravely to the valet's comments and criticisms of other Kings of France.

But on this day he was by no means pleased that there had been sent to him a little girl, eight or nine years old, to help him and Philippe contrive a ballet.

She came and knelt before him. She was tall for her age and thin—very thin. Louis thought her rather ugly, for he was beginning to be very conscious of the looks of women.

He had grown accustomed to tender looks all his life, but there was one lady of his mother's bedchamber who made him feel very extraordinary when his eyes rested on her. It was an odd sensation, for she had only one eye and was far from comely. She was years older than he was; he assumed she must be at least twenty years old; she was married, and she was fat; yet—he did not understand why—he could not stop himself looking her way.

"So you have come to help us with the ballet, cousin?" said Louis.

"Yes, Sire. On the orders of our mothers."

"Then rise, and we will tell you what we plan. It is to be a grand ballet which we shall call The Nuptials of Thetis and Peleus."

Henriette listened as he continued. Philippe, somewhat bored, had wandered away and was looking at himself in the great Venetian mirror, thinking how handsome he was, setting his curls so that they fell more to one side of his head; he was wishing that, instead of this quiet girl, they had asked some of the amusing young men to join them. Philippe smiled at the thought. De Guiche was *so* good looking and so understanding.

He turned to his brother who was scowling at him for leaving him to explain to the little girl who, of course, would know nothing of ballets and such things, having just come from the nursery—or so it seemed from the look of her.

But Henriette's face had flushed a little and, listening to the King, she caught his enthusiasm. "Your Majesty should appear as Apollo in the masque," she ventured.

"Apollo!" cried the King with interest.

"Yes, Sire. The Sun God. It would be the most enchanting role in the ballet. You would be dressed in gold . . . and about your head could be a halo from which light radiated so that all would know that you were the Sun God as soon as they set eyes on you."

"The Sun God!" murmured Louis. "You are cleverer than I thought, cousin."

"I have lived so quietly, Sire, that so much of my time has been spent in study."

"That is why you are so thin," said Louis. "You should have spent more time out of doors. Then you would enjoy more glowing health. Though I'll grant you you would not be so useful in arranging ballets."

Philippe had come over to them. "What part is there for me?" he asked. "I should like the part of a lady. I like wearing ladies' costumes . . . jewels in my ears and patches on my face."

He minced about in a manner which was quite feminine and which made the King laugh. Henriette, taking her cue from him, laughed also. "You would make a lovely shepherdess, cousin," she said.

"A shepherdess! While my brother is the Sun God!"

"Ah, but a shepherdess in silver tissue with ribands the color of roses . . . scented ribands mayhap, and a hat of black-and-white velvet with sweeping plumes, blue, the color of the sky on hot summer days. You could carry a gilded crook."

"I like the costume, but I do not care to be a shepherdess, cousin."

"Then be a goddess. Be the goddess of love."

"She has ideas, this cousin of ours," said Philippe.

"Yes," admitted Louis, "that is true." He looked a little wistful. They were educating her—those old nuns of Chaillot—while he and his brother were allowed to do whatever they wished. This little girl, six years younger than he was, four years younger than Philippe, might be shy and ignorant of great ceremonies, but she had in a few years assimilated more booklearning than he and Philippe had.

"Can you dance, cousin?" asked Louis.

"A little, Sire."

"Then you shall show us. Dance, Philippe."

Philippe turned haughtily away. "I am in no mood to dance, Louis," he said. "Why do you not dance with our cousin, the better to test her prowess?"

Louis shook his head impatiently. He was not going to demean himself by dancing with such a thin little girl.

His eyes narrowed slightly as they met his brother's, and Philippe felt waves of resentment rising within him. He was born only two years later and the King was his brother, yet, because of those two years' seniority, he must obey Louis even in their games. His mother had said so. Mazarin had said so.

For a few seconds the two brothers stood glaring at each other. Philippe thought of quarrels they had had. They did not often quarrel, but when they did he had always been the one who must take the blame. He remembered an occasion when the Court was on a journey and Louis had insisted that they share a bedroom. It was such a small room, quite different from those which they usually occupied, and in the morning, on awakening and finding his brother's bed so close to his own, the King had spat on it. Philippe, ever ready to take offense, had immediately spat on Louis' bed; this had enraged the King who immediately spat in his brother's face. Philippe had then jumped on his brother's bed and wetted it. Incensed, the King had repeated this action on his brother's bed. When their attendants rushed in a battle was in progress; the brothers were flinging pillows about and trying to smother each other with the sheets, and it was all poor de Villeroi could do to stop them. Only La Porte had dared separate them and call upon them to realize what little savages they had become; at which Philippe flew into a rage, biting and kicking; but he, Philippe, had been ready to forget the incident in a few hours. Not so Louis. He could not forget. He blamed himself and suffered great remorse because he had conducted himself in a manner disgraceful to a King of France.

He had borne no resentment towards Philippe; he remembered that he had begun the quarrel by spitting on his brother's bed. Within a week, when he was to continue the journey while Philippe stayed behind, he was melancholy at the separation, and during his absence had written notes to Philippe, begging for news of him and reminding him that he was his affectionate and kind little Papa Louis.

But it had not ended there, that quarrel in the bedroom; it was not Louis who had wounded Philippe's *amour propre.* It was his mother and the Cardinal who had blamed the younger boy for the scene, who had impressed on him that he must never again expose his brother to indignity; if Louis spat on his bed he must remember that he did so with royal spittle, and it was not for Philippe to object.

Philippe was sullen; but he could not, of course, blame Louis; he could only be envious of Louis.

Now he remembered this and sullenly took the hand of the little girl, while Louis called to a musician to come and play music that his brother and cousin might dance.

Little Henriette danced with grace, and Louis watched with mild pleasure. The Sun God! he was thinking, and he smiled at the picture of himself. The ballet would be devised to show his perfections; he would have the central part and, when it was over, everyone would fawn on him and tell him that he was no human; he was too perfect; he was divine.

But he would remember La Porte and try not to be too pleased with himself.

Philippe and Henriette had finished their dancing.

"Well done!" said Louis. "You shall have a part in the ballet, cousin."

Philippe had languidly dropped his cousin's hand. He said: "Louis, let us call in the others. Let us call de la Châtre, and the Coslin boys and du Plessis-Praslin . . . and de Guiche."

"Yes," said Louis, "have them brought. We will devise our ballet of the Sun God; and, cousin, I have promised you a part."

"Thank you, Sire," said Henriette shyly.

The King's playmates came into the apartment. Louis said: "I have thought of a ballet. I am to be the Sun God."

Philippe took de Guiche into a corner where they arranged each other's hair and giggled together. Louis' admirers closed about him.

Henriette stood apart. No one was very interested in the thin little girl.

❁ ❁ ❁

Henrietta Maria came to see her daughter. Henriette was faintly alarmed. She knew her mother so well that she guessed some fresh task was about to be given her.

"I have good news for you, *chérie.* Your brother is coming to France."

"Charles . . ."

"No, no, no! Always it is of Charles you think. You have other brothers. I refer to your brother Henry."

"Henry . . . my youngest brother. I have never seen Henry."

"Then that shall be remedied. You shall see him ere long, for he is coming to Paris."

"Oh, Mam, I am so pleased."

"I shall have yet another of my children with me. That pleases me. He is thirteen. I remember well the hot day he came into the world. It was in the Palace of Oatlands and your father . . ."

"Mam, I pray you do not speak of those days. They but distress you, and you must be happy now because Henry is coming."

"Yes; and there is something we have to do for Henry—you and I."

"I, Mam?"

"Yes, indeed. You are a fortunate girl. Do you realize that? You came to

France when you were but two years old and heresy had scarcely touched you. Your brother has been less fortunate. I fear his immortal soul is in danger. We must save him, Henriette. And in this I shall allow you to help me. You must explain to him what Père Cyprien has taught you so well. Together we will save his soul."

Henry arrived—a shy boy of thirteen, very happy to be reunited with his family. His mother was loud in her exclamations of pleasure. Her beloved child restored to her; this was one of the happiest days of her life. Then she burst into passionate weeping because Elizabeth could not be with them.

Henry wept with her, and his little sister took his hand and begged him not to cry.

"For you are here, Henry," she said. "That is one matter for rejoicing. Let us think of that and nothing else."

Henry was pleased to do this; he was a boy who had had too much sorrow.

When they were alone together Henriette sought to do what her mother had commanded. She made him tell her of his life with James and Elizabeth and how James had escaped during a game of hide-and-seek. Then he told her of that time when they had lived at Syon House; but he did not speak of that January day when he and his sister had been taken to Whitehall to see their father. Instead he told her of Carisbrooke Castle and how Mr. Lovel had been good to him and had been his main companion since the death of Elizabeth; he told her how he had longed above all things to be with his mother again.

"Brother," said Henriette, "you are not of our faith—Mam's and mine."

"I am of the faith of my father."

"Henry, Mam wishes you to be of our faith. Will you come with me and hear what Père Cyprien has to say tomorrow?"

The boy's mouth grew stern. "I beg of you, Henriette, do not ask me to do that. I did not tell you, but when we were at Syon House, Elizabeth and I went to Whitehall one day. It was a cold day and the river was frozen. It was the saddest day of my life, Henriette; but I did not know it then. We went to see our father. It was the day before he died."

"Do not speak of it, Henry," said Henriette shrilly. "I pray you, do not speak of it."

"I must speak of it because I must explain. Our father took me onto his knee and told me that I must remain in the faith in which I was baptized."

"That is not Mam's faith and mine."

"No. But it is the faith of my father and my father's country."

"I see, Henry."

"Oh, Henriette, tell no one of this, but Mr. Lovel has said to me that if our mother had been of our father's faith, if she had not tried to turn him into a Catholic, and our country into a Catholic country, our dearest Papa might be alive today."

"Is it true then, Henry? Can that be true?"

"It is what has been said . . . not only by Mr. Lovel, but by many. I could never turn to a faith which by its very existence was responsible for my father's death."

"But it is Mam's faith, Henry."

"I am of my father's faith and I will never be of another. I promised him, Henriette. Oh, you never knew him. It is so long ago, but I cannot think of him without weeping, Henriette. I cannot . . . I cannot . . ."

Henriette dried her brother's eyes with her kerchief.

"Dearest brother, I shall never again ask you to change your faith. I am afraid myself . . . I am afraid of a faith which could bring about our father's death."

"Perhaps I am wrong, Henriette. Perhaps it is not a faith that could do this. Perhaps it is the way in which people think of their faith. It is not a religion which brings heartbreak and bloodshed; it is something in men which says: 'I think this way and I will kill and torture all those who think otherwise.' That cannot be true religion, Henriette. That is pride . . . self-pride and perhaps . . . doubt. I do not know. But do not ask me to change my faith."

"I will not," declared Henriette emphatically. "I promise I never will again."

❁ ❁ ❁

Henriette had passed her tenth birthday. She was leading a gayer life now than ever before. The royal brothers of France, discovering that, though only a little girl, she could dance gracefully and play the lute, graciously allowed her to take part in the revels. At the ballet in which the King appeared, not only as the Sun God, Apollo, but also as Mars, taking as well the minor roles of dryad, fury and courtier to show his versatility, the Court appeared to grow restive when he was not to the fore. Little Henriette had played the part of Erato, the muse of love and poetry; crowned with myrtle and roses she had repeated verses which she had learned by heart. Such an enchanting figure did she present that the Court was loud in its applause, and Henrietta Maria told those about her that this was one of the happiest moments of her life; she had one grief and it was a great one; her martyred husband could not be here to witness his daughter's triumph. Even Anne of Austria, lolling in her chair, had taken her eyes off her Sun God for a brief moment to study the little girl.

She nodded her head. "How the costume becomes her," she said. "This little girl of yours will be a beauty yet, sister. Louis tells me that he is pleased with her dancing and that she plays the lute with a skill beyond her years."

Ah yes, that had been a happy day for Henrietta Maria who already saw the crown of France on her daughter's head; but she was not so pleased as she surveyed her youngest son.

Stubbornly he had determined to shut his ears to the truth with which Père Cyprien was trying to save him from perdition.

"But he shall be saved!" Henrietta Maria told herself, tapping her foot. "He shall! Or I will make him wish he had never been born to defy his mother and God."

Little Henriette had been delighted with her success. She loved to dance; she had learned her verses more easily than anybody, and Louis himself had been delighted with her. She found that Louis' praise made her very happy. When those large brown eyes were turned on her in appreciation, she felt that she could be perfectly happy if she could go on pleasing him. How different was Philippe! Philippe's dark, long-lashed eyes were quite scornful of her; being a clever little girl and sharper-witted than the two boys, she was aware that neither of them wished to play with a girl as young as she was; the difference was that Philippe was anxious for her to know that they despised her youth, while Louis was anxious to hide this fact from her. Louis was not only handsome; he was kind. Henriette was beginning to think that he was one of the kindest people she had ever known. She was moved because he was a king—a much cherished king—and yet had the kindness to care for the feelings of a little girl. She tried to think of new ideas for ballets, and if Louis liked them she was happy; if his interest was perfunctory—which meant that he liked them not at all—she was desolate and cried a little when she was alone at night because she had failed to please him. Sometimes, oddly enough, if she had pleased him she would cry—but with different feelings; perhaps this was because she wistfully longed to be older and more beautiful, so that he would like her better.

But her excitement in her companionship with the King was spoiled by her pity for her brother. Why could he not be allowed to continue in the faith of the Church of England? It was Charles' faith; therefore it was right that it should be Henry's; and as Henry had promised his father that he would never leave it, why could not Mam be satisfied with one little Catholic in the family?

Charles came to see her and she forgot even her new friendship with Louis. He kissed her affectionately and told her he was going away again. It was to Cologne this time.

"I am a wanderer on the face of the earth, Minette," he said. "I am not only a king without a crown, I am a man without a country. I cannot stay long in one place for fear of wearing out my welcome. So I just flit from place to place, never staying long anywhere lest, when I next wish to visit it, my previous visit may be remembered as a very long one."

"Here we love to have you."

"You do, Minette, I know. But this is not your home either. However, be of good cheer. One day we shall be together. Then I shall be a king with a crown, and you shall be my companion forever. How will you like that?"

"Let it be soon, I pray. It is what I should love more than anything on earth," said Henriette vehemently.

"Oh come, you are happy enough here. They tell me you have done well in the ballet and that Louis himself is pleased with you. There, Minette! You may bask in the rays of the Sun God, so what do you want with a poor wandering prince like me when you move in the radiance of the Olympians?"

"I would rather be in a hovel with you."

"Nay, Minette, do not say such things. Make the most of your good fortune. Louis is a good fellow. It makes me happy that you have pleased him. And now I must see Mam before I depart, and make her swear not to plague poor Henry."

Henrietta Maria listened to her son in cold silence before she brought out the old arguments. The King, her husband, she stressed then, had promised that her children should be brought up in her religion.

"Mam! Mam! Why cannot you leave this matter of Henry's religion and concern yourself with the ballet as does our little Henriette?"

"You are frivolous, Charles. It is small wonder that God does not crown your efforts with success. This is a child's soul for which we are battling."

The King was stern for once. He said: "Henry has given his solemn word to our father that he will not change his religion. Mam, you astonish me. Would you force the boy to break his word? I speak to you now as your King, Madam. I forbid you to plague the boy. I command that you obey."

Henrietta Maria pursed her lips together to keep back the angry words.

"My own son is against me," she complained bitterly to her daughter when Charles had gone. "It is small wonder that he is an exile . . . small wonder indeed. It is small wonder that God is on the side of our enemies."

"But *they* are not Catholics either, Mam," said Henriette gently.

And for once the Queen pushed her daughter away from her; she was in no mood for further argument.

Her mind was made up. Charles was the King and he had commanded her; but Charles was an exile and would soon be far away.

❁ ❁ ❁

Young Henry was bewildered. For so many years he had longed to escape from his father's enemies, to be with his family; and now that he had achieved this end he found that he was tormented as he never had been when he was in the hands of the Roundheads.

His mother gave him no peace. He must read this; he must study that; he must listen to the teachings of older, wiser men than himself. Père Cyprien was at his elbow; so was the Abbé Montague.

To all their talk he remained mute and faithful to the promise he had given his father; his mother did not see his attitude as fidelity; she called it stubbornness.

The little boy was only fourteen. He did not know what he would have done without his brothers and sisters. Charles was not only his brother but his King; and Charles supported him. But Charles had gone to Cologne for a brief spell. His brother James was in Paris, and he supported him.

"Mam is a loving mother," James had said; "she is fond of us all, but she has one real passion—her faith; and where that is concerned she is a regular tornado. Stay firm, brother. Those are Charles' commands, and he is the King. You promised our father. You do well to remember your promise, and in this you are in the right."

He knew that his sister Mary, the Princess of Orange, had placed herself on his side. He was certain that Elizabeth would have supported him had she been alive; Elizabeth would have died rather than break her word to her father.

"And so will I!" declared Henry on his knees. "And so will I. I swear it, Papa. I remember. I will remember."

And when his mother railed against him, he shut his eyes tightly and thought of that man in the velvet jacket and lace collar with the hair falling about his shoulders. "Never forget what I ask, Henry. . . ." He heard those words in his dreams. "Papa . . . Papa . . ." he sobbed. "I will remember."

Sometimes his little sister Henriette came to his bed and sat beside it, holding his hand.

She wanted him to be happy. She did not know whether she ought to obey her mother and try to bring her brother into the Catholic faith; but when she heard that Charles had commanded his mother not to molest Henry, she knew what she must do.

She soothed Henry; she did not say much—it seemed so wrong to speak against her mother—but Henry knew that his brothers and sisters without exception were on his side; and he continued to hold out.

❁ ❁ ❁

Henrietta Maria was growing impatient. She would sit glowering at her youngest son, tapping the floor with her foot, her eyes hard.

Obstinate fellow! she thought. What an unhappy woman I am! My children will not obey me. They flout me. They are fools. Had Charles become a Catholic he might have stayed here. He might have been helped to regain his kingdom; who knew, Mademoiselle might have married him. But this obstinate clinging to heresy . . . it is ruining my life! What an unhappy woman I am!

It was true that Anne of Austria was protesting against the celebration of the rites of the Church of England in the Louvre; it was true that she was ready to help Henrietta Maria in her battle for little Henry's soul; but no one in France was ready to go to war with the Protector of England to help the King regain his throne. Still, Henrietta Maria liked to believe that this was so.

And now the boy had dared, without his mother's knowledge, to dispatch a letter to his brother, the King; that was because she had dismissed his tutor Lovel—an evil influence if ever there was one.

Henrietta Maria now had Charles' reply to Henry in her hands, and she fumed with rage as she read it.

"Do not let them persuade you," Charles had written, "either by force or fair promises; the first, they neither dare nor will use; and for the second, as soon as they have perverted you, they will have their end, and then they will care no more for you . . . If you do not consider what I say unto you, remember the last words of your dead father which were 'Be constant to your religion and never be shaken in it'; which, if you do not observe, this shall be the last time you shall hear from

Dear brother,

Your most affectionate

Charles II."

Her own family banding against her! It was more than a mother could endure. She would not be treated thus. She would settle this matter of her youngest son's religion once and for all time.

She waited until they had dined that day; then, as they rose to leave the dining chamber, she went to Henry and embraced him warmly.

"My son," she said, "how grieved I am that I should be forced to deal so severely with you, but it is my love that makes me do it. You must know that well."

"Oh, Mam," said the little boy, his eyes filling with tears, "please understand. I gave my word to Papa."

"Please . . . please, Henry, don't talk to me of Papa. There are some days when the memory of him hurts me more than others. I knew him more than you did, child. We had years together before you were born. Any grief you have felt for Papa is a small thing compared with mine."

"Mam . . . then . . . it is because of him, you understand . . ."

"You are weary, my son," she interrupted, "of being talked to on this matter. God knows I am weary of it too. Let us shorten the trial. Go to your apartments now and I will send the Abbé Montague to you."

"Please, Mam, there is nothing I can do. Do understand me when I say . . ."

"Go now, my son. Listen to the Abbé, and then give me your final answer."

"It can make no difference."

She pushed him gently from her, wiping her eyes as she did so.

He went to his apartment where the Abbé came to him; wearily he listened, and again and again he reiterated his determination not to swerve from the faith in which he had been baptized, not to break his word to his father.

"This is going to hurt your mother, the Queen, so deeply that I fear what the result will be," warned the Abbé.

"I cannot heed the result," answered the boy. "I have only one answer to give."

So the Abbé left him and went to Henrietta Maria who was with her youngest daughter; together they were stitching an altar cloth for Chaillot.

"Your Majesty," said Montague, "I fear I have only bad news for you. The boy remains obstinate. He clings fast to heresy."

Henrietta Maria rose to her feet, letting the altar cloth fall to the floor.

Her daughter watched the purple blood disfigure her face as, clenching her hands together, she cried: "Very well! This is the end then. He shall see what it means to flout God . . . and me. Go to him. Tell him that he shall see my face no more. Go at once. Tell him that. Tell him I can bear no more sorrows. I am weary. I am going to Chaillot to pray . . . for there only can I find peace."

"Oh, Mam!" cried Henriette. "Mam, what are you saying? You cannot mean this."

"I do mean it. I never want to see his face again. I want to forget I bore him."

"But, Mam, he swore to our father. He *swore.* You must understand."

"I understand only that he wishes to flout me. I shall make him repent this ere long. Go to him at once, Abbé. Give him my message. The ungrateful boy! He is no child of mine!"

Henrietta Maria flung herself out of the room; Henriette slowly picked up the altar cloth; then she sat down on the stool and covered her face with her hands.

Was there no end to these troubles which beset her family?

❁ ❁ ❁

After a while she rose. She must go to Henry. Poor Henry, who had dreamed so often of reunion with his family!

She went along to his apartment. Montague was talking to Henry, whose face was white; he looked stricken yet incredulous. It was clear that he could not grasp what the man was saying; he could not believe his mother had really cast him off.

"Just think what this will mean," Montague was saying. "If your mother renounces you, how will you live? How will you supply your table with food? How will you pay your servants?"

"I do not know," said Henry piteously. "I cannot understand!"

"Then go to the Queen; tell her that you will be her very good son, and she will have a proposal to make which will set your heart at rest."

"I fear, sir," said Henry in a quavering voice, though his lips were determined, "that my mother's proposals would not have that effect upon me, for my heart can have no rest but in the free exercise of my religion and in the keeping of my word to my father."

James came into his apartment while Henriette was wondering what she could do to soothe her brother. When James heard the news he was astounded.

"But our mother cannot do this!" he cried. "I will go to see her. There has been some mistake."

He strode out of the apartment, and Henriette put her arm about Henry. "Be of good cheer, Henry," she begged. "There has been a mistake. You heard what James said. It *must* be a mistake."

But shortly afterwards James was back. "Our mother is in a fury," he said. "She declares that henceforth she will show her pleasure to neither of her sons, except through the medium of Montague."

"Then she discards us both, James," said Henry. "Oh, James, I almost wish they had not let me come to France. I was happier at Carisbrooke than here."

"I would there were something I could do," said Henriette. "I do not believe Mam means this. She flies into tempers, but they pass. Go to her, Henry. Speak to her. She will soon be leaving for Chaillot, where she is going for Mass. Speak to her before she goes."

James thought that their mother might be in a softened mood as she was departing for her devotions.

So Henry waylaid his mother; he knelt before her, entreating her not to turn away from him; but she pushed him angrily aside and would not speak to him.

The boy was heartbroken and uncertain what to do. James put his arm about him, and together they went to the service which was held in Sir Richard Browne's chapel for the English Princes.

"She'll get over her anger," James told him. "Don't fret, brother."

But when Henry returned to his apartment after the service, he found that all his servants had been dismissed. There was no place for him at the table.

Bewildered, he flung himself down and gave way to bitter weeping. His mother, for whom he had longed during the years of exile, had turned away from him and had declared her intention of looking on his face no more.

❁ ❁ ❁

Gloomily he walked about the palace grounds. He did not know what to do.

The day passed; he returned to the palace. He decided he would go to bed and try to make plans for the morrow. As he entered the palace his little sister ran to him. "Henry, what are you going to do?" she asked.

"I do not know. I must go away, I suppose. But I do not know where to go."

"Then you will resist . . . our mother?"

"I must, Henriette."

"Oh Henry. . . . Oh, my brother! Oh, my mother! What can I do? I shall never be happy again."

"So you too are afraid of her. She is only kind to you because you are a Catholic. If you were not, she would be as cruel to you as she is to me."

Henriette continued to weep.

Her brother kissed her. "I am going to my apartment," he said. "I shall try to rest. Perhaps in the morning I shall know what to do."

She nodded and kissed him fondly.

He broke down then. "It is because I so longed to be with her . . . so much . . ."

"I know, Henry. I know, dear brother."

She turned and fled; and Henry went up to his apartments, only to find that the sheets had been taken from his bed, and that all the comforts had been removed from his room.

His Controller found him there, staring about in a bewildered fashion; he reported that the horses had been turned out of the stables and that he himself had been dismissed and warned that he should expect no wages from the Queen while he remained in the service of Prince Henry.

"But I do not know what to do!" cried the boy.

James sought him out and James had good news.

"Fret no more, brother," he cried. "All will be well. Did you think Charles would forget you! He knows how fierce our mother can be when she is engaged in conversions. Charles has sent to you the Marquess of Ormonde who waits below. He has horses and instructions to take you to Charles in Cologne."

"Charles!" cried Henry, tears filling his eyes. "I am to go to *Charles*!"

"Charles would never desert you!" cried James. "He expected this. He wrote to you somewhat sternly because he knew that you would never be at peace if you broke your word to our father. He wished you to hold out against our mother, and he is proud that you have done so. But never think that he would desert you. Be of good cheer, brother. You will find life more agreeable with the King, your brother, than among the monks of a Jesuit college which Mam had in mind for you."

And that night, after taking fond farewells of his brother James and his little sister Henriette, Henry, an exile from his mother's care, set out to join that other exile in Cologne.

SIX

Anne of Austria delighted to see her son dance—an accomplishment he performed with such grace—and it pleased her often to give an informal dance, inviting just a few members of the highest nobility to her own private apartments in the Louvre. Here she would sit in her dressing gown, her hair hidden under a *cornette* to indicate that the occasion was an intimate one and by no means to be considered a ball. She would have the violins in one corner of the vast room, and her friends about her in another; and in the middle of the floor the young people danced while she gossiped with her friends who must constantly supply her with the latest scandal and compliments on her son's perfections.

To these dances she often invited Henrietta Maria and her daughter.

"Such a pleasure for the little girl!" she said. "For she grows so charming. How old is she now?"

"Eleven," said Henrietta Maria. "Yes, she is growing up. It is difficult to believe that it is eleven years since that terrible day when . . ."

Anne interrupted quickly: "Louis enjoys dancing so much. Ah, what it is to be young! And as for Louis, he is never tired. There never was such a one." Anne tittered. "Why, do you know, I shall soon begin to believe that it was Apollo who stole in on me while I slept and planted his seed within me!"

"You will soon have to think of his marriage," suggested Henrietta Maria.

"One constantly thinks of his marriage. It will be the most important of marriages. But who, dear sister, *who* will be worthy to mate with Louis? That is the problem."

"Only the best," said Henrietta Maria fervently. "Only the best."

Anne looked slyly at her sister-in-law. Now if none of these tragic events had occurred in England, she pondered, if young Henriette's brother were safe on the throne, there could be no objection to my son's marriage with her daughter. Of course it would depend on Louis.

Anne spoke her thoughts aloud. "Louis will make his own choice, I doubt not. I remember once I took him to the Convent of the Carmelites, and when he was in the community room and the nuns spoke to him, he took no notice of them because he was so interested in the latch of the door. He played with the latch and would not have his attention diverted from it. I was forced to scold him. I said: 'Leave that latch, Louis.' But he frowned and answered: 'It is a good latch. I, the King, like this latch.' I said: 'It is a fine thing for a King to sulk before ladies and not utter a word.' Then suddenly his face grew scarlet and he stamped his foot as he shouted: 'I will say nothing because I wish to play with this latch. But one day, I shall speak so loudly that I shall make myself heard.' Oh, what a bold little fellow he was! Yes, Louis will have his own way, depend upon that."

Louis would indeed have his own way. So, at the private dances in Anne's apartments, Henrietta Maria could scarcely contain herself as she watched the crescent friendship between her daughter and the King of France.

✿ ✿ ✿

Louis' valet was dressing him for an informal dance in his mother's apartments.

Louis was silent, smiling to himself as he was being dressed, but he did not see the handsome figure reflected in the mirror. He looked like a young god in his costume of cloth of silver-and-black velvet embroidered with golden lilies. He felt like a god.

Yesterday he had had an adventure. It was an adventure which had seemed to befall him by chance. It had happened last night, and the partner of his adventure had been Madame de Beauvais who had always fascinated him in some strange way: Now he knew why. He had been dancing with her. The night was warm, and something in her expression as she looked at him made him say: "Madame, I should like to know you better than I do." She had laughed and moved closer to him and had said: "That is a command. Should I come to your apartments or you to mine, Sire?" Oddly enough he had stammered like a nervous boy—he the King! She had laughed, strange, throaty laughter, which made his heart beat faster. "I'll come to you," she said. "The King cannot move without attracting attention. I will be in the antechamber when the guards are sleeping tonight, when all have retired."

He only vaguely understood; he was very innocent. His mother and Mazarin had determined to keep him so; they did not want him to give rise to scandalous rumors about himself, as his grandfather had done in his early teens. He was astonished that this should have happened. She was old; she was twenty or more; she was plump; she had only one eye; but she had such merry laughter—merry and kind. And the thought of what she might have to say to him made his heart beat quickly.

So he had cautiously joined her in the antechamber. Did any of the guards see him go? Perhaps. But if they opened one eye they would realize from his manner that he did not wish to be seen, and the wishes of Louis Quatorze were always obeyed.

He was remembering now; he had wondered what he would say to her, but there had been no need of words. She wore nothing but a loose robe which fell from her as she approached him. He gasped; this reminded him of the first time he had dived into deep water when learning to swim; he had been tremendously exhilarated and fearful on that occasion, as he was on this.

"So to me comes the honor of leading Your Majesty to the *doux scavoir*!"

He stammered: "Madame . . . Madame . . ."

And she had said: "But you are beautiful. I am to mate with a god. I never thought that I should be the one."

He was bewildered, but she was not. She was the kindest, most tender person in the world.

And afterwards they lay side by side until the dawn came; and then he said he had better leave her, but they would meet again. So he had tiptoed back to his apartments and lain in his bed, mazed, bewildered and enchanted.

He was grown up; the boy-King had become a man.

All that day he had gone about in a dream—a dream of power and pleasure. He could not help knowing that any beautiful woman on whom he cast his eyes would, he dared swear, be ready to share with him such an adventure as he had enjoyed last night with Madame de Beauvais.

This was exciting knowledge.

These were his thoughts as he prepared himself for the dance in his mother's apartments.

As he walked into the room all rose and fell to their knees, except the two Queens who sat side by side. He made his way to them and kissed, first his mother's hand, and then that of his aunt.

"My beloved, how splendid you look!" said his mother. "These apartments seemed so dull a moment ago. Now you have entered and the sun shines on us all."

"Your mother but voices the thoughts of everyone present, Sire," added Henrietta Maria.

Her eyes were on her young daughter. Oh dear, she thought, if only the child would plump up! How thin, she thought, if only the child would plump up! How thin she is! I would we had more money that she might be ade-Court and that she is not here like a bird of paradise putting us all to shame.

She glanced at her sister-in-law, informal in her brocaded dressing-gown and *cornette.* It was but an informal occasion. She doubted much whether she and Henriette would have been invited had it been a grand ball or a masque, since their favor was not high at Court.

Louis was gazing round the company. Now that he had arrived, the violins began to play, but no one would dance until the King led the way. According to etiquette he must dance with the lady of the highest rank, and since neither of the Queens would dance, Louis would be bound in duty to ask his little cousin to dance first.

But Louis seemed disinclined to dance. The violins played on. He stood there, smiling to himself. He thought: If *she* were here, I would go to her now and ask her to dance with me. I should not care that she is not of the highest rank; I care nothing for rank. That is what I would have her know. I care only for what we were to each other last night, and that is something I shall never forget as long as I live. I will give her estates when it is in my power to do so. I will give her titles . . . and all she can desire. For no one could have been so kind as she was, pretending not to notice my inexperience, making of a simple boy a man of experience in one night.

Oh, the ecstasy of that encounter! Again tonight? Why had he come to a stupid dance? He had no desire to dance. He wished only to lie with her in the dark . . . in that antechamber. Had not that which he desired always been granted?

She was not there, his dear, dear Madame de Beauvais. Perhaps it was well that she was not, for he would not have been able to hide his grateful love. Now he knew—and fresh gratitude swept over him—that for this reason she had stayed away: She did not wish him to betray himself! She understood. She was wise as well as tender; she was modest as well as sweetly full of knowledge.

He looked round the assembly. No! He would not dance with that thin little cousin of his. He was in no mood to talk to a child tonight. His newly-found manhood made demands upon him. Tonight he was in love with women—all mature women who understood the delights of the *doux scavoir.* He offered his hand to the Duchesse de Mercoeur, who was the eldest niece of Cardinal Mazarin, a young and handsome matron.

Anne gasped. There was one thing which could always arouse her from her torpor—a breach of etiquette.

This was impossible! Louis had overlooked the Princess Henriette.

She rose and went to her son's side. "My dearest," she whispered, "you have forgotten . . . Your cousin Henriette is here . . ."

The King frowned; now he looked like the little boy who had played with the latch in the Carmelite convent. "Tonight," he said, "I do not wish to dance with little girls."

Henrietta Maria felt faint with anxiety. The King was slighting her daughter. He did not want to dance with a little girl! Well, Henriette was young yet, and she was so thin—bad, bad child; she would not eat enough! But later on he might grow fond of her. In the meantime this was disastrous. What could she do?

She rose uncertainly and went to Anne and Louis.

"I must tell Your Majesties," she said, "that my daughter cannot dance tonight. She has a pain in her foot. It would be too painful for her to attempt to dance. I am sure that His Majesty was aware of this and for that reason asked the Duchesse to dance."

Anne replied: "If the Princess is unfit to dance, the King should not dance tonight."

The King's natural good temper seemed to have deserted him. There was an ominous silence throughout the apartment. All eyes were on the royal party. Henrietta Maria thought quickly: A scene must be avoided at all costs. This might result in our being banished from Court.

She said firmly: "My daughter *shall* dance. Come, Henriette."

Henriette, blushing and miserably unhappy, obeyed her mother.

For an instant the King did not move to take her hand. Why should he—a man as well as a King—be told with whom to dance? Why should he not choose whom he pleased? He was no longer a boy. Madame de Beauvais understood that; all the Court . . . all the world must understand it too.

Then he looked at the little girl beside him. He saw her lips tremble and he noted the misery in her eyes. He realized her humiliation and he was ashamed suddenly. He was behaving more like a spoiled boy than the man he had become last night.

He took his cousin's hand and began to dance. He did not speak to her. He saw that she was fighting back her tears, so he pressed her hand tightly. He wanted to say: it is not that I do not wish to dance with you, Henriette. It is just that I am in no mood for the company of children.

But he said nothing and the dance continued.

That night the Princess Henriette cried herself to sleep.

❁ ❁ ❁

Henriette was with her mother in the great Cathedral of Notre Dame de Rheims. It was an honor to be here, she knew; her mother had impressed that upon her. They were participating in the Coronation of the King of France to which they had been invited, although it seemed that there was very little hope of the royal house of England's ever reinstating itself.

Charles was wandering around Europe, never staying long in one place, now and then daring to hope that there might be a chance of a little help from some important monarch who had reason to dislike the Protector of England. Plans . . . plans . . . plans . . . which never seemed to materialize. Then he would return to his dicing and women. Rumor reached France that the profligacy of the roaming English Court was becoming notorious.

Henriette longed for news of him, longed to see his face again. Each day, she hoped, would bring some news of him. At least, when he idled with his profligate friends, he was not endangering his life.

Once she had found consolation for the loss of her brother in the exciting company of her magnificent royal cousin, but that had changed recently. She and her mother spent most of their time in seclusion now at the Palais-Royal, Chaillot or Colombes, this last being a pretty house on the Seine, which Henrietta Maria had acquired, and where it was pleasant to spend the hot summer months. Life was growing quieter. Henriette was studying a good deal; her education was opening out into a course hardly ever pursued by ladies of her rank. There was little to do but study. She was thinner than ever and growing too quickly. Already she was aware of a slight deformity in her spine. She dared not tell her mother of this. One could not add to the sorrows of *La Refine Malheureuse*. Henriette knew that her mother longed for her to grow plump, with rounded cheeks and limbs. She, the daughter of an exiled family, would have nothing to recommend her as a wife but rank and beauty; and at this stage it seemed that the latter would never be hers.

Sometimes she worked in a frenzy that she might please her tutors and Père Cyprien; her knowledge increased and her wits sharpened; for recreation she played the lute and harpsichord and also practiced singing. She improved her dancing, practicing often, sometimes alone, sometimes with her women; she wished to excel at that because Louis set such store by it. Her slenderness gave her grace, and she learned to disguise her slight deformity by the dresses she wore, so that only her intimate attendants were aware of it.

She longed to be able to please her mother. She dreamed sometimes that she had become a *bel esprit* of the Court; she devised clever remarks; she imagined that Louis himself laughed heartily at her *bon mots.* It was pleasant dreaming.

Often she was at Chaillot with her mother, and there she was able to please the Queen by waiting at table on the Abbess and her Filles de Marie. They all declared that she was charming, graceful and modest.

And now there had come this invitation to attend the Coronation. Henrietta Maria was delighted.

"So we are not forgotten!" she cried. "On an occasion they realize, do they not, that it would be a great breach of etiquette to ignore such close relationships."

It was not as her mother believed, Henriette was sure. Louis had wanted them to be present, for Louis—King though he was, haughty though he could be—was more sorry for them than anyone else at the Court. Henriette remembered how he had danced with her and that the frown on his face had meant that he was sorry he had slighted her. He was ashamed of what he had done. Therefore he would take great pains to be kind. That was the sort of boy Louis was. While he had strong desires, while the sycophants about him assured him that his conduct was as perfect as his person, he yet wished to do what was right in his own eyes.

He was sorry for his thin little cousin; therefore he made a point of graciously inviting her and her mother to his Coronation. That was all. Henriette kept reminding herself of this.

Now they were bringing Louis into the Cathedral.

At six o'clock that morning, two Bishops, preceded by the Canons of the Chapter, had gone to the Archbishop's Palace—where Louis had had his lodging—and up to the King's bedchamber. The Precentor had knocked on the door with his silver wand.

"What do you want?" the Grand Chamberlain had asked from within.

"We desire the King," said the Bishops.

"The King sleeps."

"We desire Louis, the XIV of that name, son of the great Louis XIII, whom God has given us to be our King."

Then they entered the chamber where Louis had been lying in the state bed, pretending to be asleep. He wore a cambric shirt and red satin, gold-braid-trimmed tunic slit in certain places to allow him to be anointed with holy oil. Over this he wore a robe of cloth of silver, and on his head there was a black velvet cap decorated with feathers and diamonds.

The Bishops and their followers then helped him to rise and conducted him to the Cathedral.

As he entered, between the Bishops, Henriette studied this beautiful boy. All eyes were on him; he was sixteen and the eulogists had not greatly exaggerated when they declared that his youthful beauty was unequaled.

Between the Swiss Guards the procession made its way to the chancel where the King's chair and *prie-dieu,* upholstered in purple velvet decorated with the golden lilies of France, had been placed on Turkey rugs.

As she watched the ceremony, Henriette thought of another man whom she loved very dearly indeed. If he could have been in a similar position, how wonderful that would be! If it were Charles who was being anointed with oil, and this ceremony was taking place, not in France but in England, she told herself, she would have felt complete contentment, for then he would take her home with him, and she would live at his Court where there would be no slights, no humiliations; she need not then be disturbed by her feelings for her cousin Louis; she could give herself up to the pleasure of the King of England's company and forget those incomprehensible longings which were aroused within her by the King of France.

The Bishops were asking those present if they were willing to have this Prince as their King; and the purple velvet sandals were being put on Louis' feet while he was helped into the robe and dalmatica, and the great ceremonial cloak of purple velvet embroidered with golden lilies was placed about his shoulders. Now he looked indeed magnificent. He held out his hands that the consecrated gloves might be slipped over them and the ring placed on his finger; then he took the Sceptre in his right hand and the Hand of Justice in his left, after which the great Crown of Charlemagne was set upon his head, and he was led to the throne, there to receive the homage of the peers.

"Long live the King!" echoed through the Cathedral and the streets beyond.

Louis XIV, the *Roi-Soleil,* had been crowned. It was an inspiring ceremony. Tears dimmed Henriette's eyes. She was praying fervently for the

King of England, but the magnificent image of the King of France would come between her and her prayers.

❖ ❖ ❖

How tired one grew of exile! thought Charles. How weary of moving from place to place in search of hospitality! One had to suppress one's finer feelings when one was a beggar.

"Ah," he said one day, as he looked on the river from his lodgings in the town of Cologne, "it is a mercy that I am a man of low character, for how could one of noble ideals tolerate my position? From which we learn that there is good in all evil. A comforting thought, my friends!"

He smiled at his Chancellor, Edward Hyde, who had joined him in Paris some years ago and had since been his most trusted adviser. He liked Hyde—a grim old man, who did not stoop to flatter the King in case he should one day come into his own.

That amused Charles. "Others," he said, "wish to ensure their future—not that they have any high hopes that I shall be of much use to them—but flattery costs little. Reproaches cost far more. That is why I will have you with me, Edward, my friend. And if there should come that happy day when I am restored to my own, you shall be well paid for those reproaches you heaped upon me when I was in exile. There! Are you not pleased?"

"I should be better pleased if Your Majesty would not merit these reproaches. I would rather have the pleasure of praising you now, than the hope of rewards in the future."

"Would all men had your honesty, Chancellor," said the King lightly. "And would I had a state whose affairs were worthy of your counsel. Alas! How do we pass our days? In vain hopes and wild pleasure. What new songs are there to be sung today? Shall we throw the dice again? Any pretty women whose acquaintance we have not made?"

"Your Majesty, could you not be content with one mistress? It would be so much more respectable if you could."

"I am content with each one while I am with her. Content! I am deeply content. One leaves me and another appears, and then I find contentment again."

"If Your Majesty would but occupy yourself with matters of state you would have less time for women."

"Matters of state! They are things to dream about. Women! They are to be possessed. One woman in Cologne is worth a million imaginary state papers in Whitehall."

"Your Majesty is incorrigible."

"Nay, Edward, merely resigned. I will tell you this: You have enemies here at my mock Court and they would seek to drive a wedge between us were that possible. Yesterday one said to me: 'Your Majesty, do you know what your respected Chancellor said of you? Most disrespectfully he spoke of you. He declared you are a profligate who fritters his time away in vices of all descriptions.' And how do you think I answered your calumniator, Edward? I said: 'It does not surprise me that he should say that once in a way to you, for he says the same of me to myself a hundred times a week!' "

Charles laughed and laid his arm about his Chancellor's shoulders. "There!" he continued. "That is what I think of you and your honesty. I can appreciate other things . . . I can love other things . . . besides beautiful women!"

"Let us talk of state matters," said Edward Hyde. "It would be better if your sister of Orange did not make her proposed visit to Paris to see your mother."

Charles nodded. "I see that, Edward."

"Now that we are entering into negotiations with Spain, and Ormonde has gone on a mission to Madrid, we do not wish Spain to think that the bond between ourselves and France is being strengthened. The Spaniards will know that your mother and sister are being treated with scant courtesy in France; therefore they will be more likely to favor us. Any who is out of favor with France should readily find favor with Spain."

"I will speak to my sister."

"You should forbid her to make the journey."

Charles looked uneasy. "I . . . forbid Mary!"

"You are the King of England."

"A King without a kingdom, a man who would often have been without a home but for Mary. What would have happened to us but for her, I cannot think. Holland was our refuge until, with the death of her husband, she lost her influence. Even now we owe the money, on which we live, to her; but for my sister Mary I should not have even this threadbare shirt to cover my shoulders. And you would ask me to forbid her making a journey on which she has set her heart!"

"You are the King."

"I fear she will think me an ungrateful rogue."

"It matters not what she thinks of Your Majesty."

"It matters not! My dear sister to think me an ungrateful oaf? My dear Chancellor, you astonish me! A moment ago you were complaining because the world looks upon me as a libertine; now you say it is a matter of little importance that my sister should find me ungrateful."

"Your Majesty . . ."

"I know. I see your point. Ingratitude . . . intolerance . . . are minor sins in the eyes of the statesman. If the outcome of these things is beneficial, then it is good statecraft. But to invite a pretty woman to one's bed . . . in your eyes, Edward, and in the eyes of Puritans, that is black sin; yet to me—if she be willing—it seems but pleasure. We do not see life through the same eyes, and you would be judged right by the majority, so it is I who am out of step with the world. Perhaps that is why I wait here, frittering away my time with dice and women."

"I should advise Your Majesty to speak to your sister."

Charles bowed his head.

"And if I were Your Majesty I would not continue to associate with the woman, Lucy Water, who now calls herself Mistress Barlow."

"No? But I am fond of Lucy. She has a fine boy who is mine also."

"She is mistress of others besides Your Majesty."

"I know it."

"There are many gentlemen of the Court who share your pleasure in this woman."

"Lucy has much to give."

"You are too easygoing."

"I am content to go where my will carries me. There is no virtue in my easy temper."

"The woman could be sent to England."

"To England?"

"Indeed, yes. It would be better so. She could be promised a pension."

Charles laughed.

"Your Majesty is amused?"

"Only at the idea of such a magnanimous promise from a man in a threadbare shirt."

"There are some who would help to pay the pension for the sake of ridding Your Majesty of the woman."

"Poor Lucy!"

"She would enjoy returning to her native land doubtless. If the Spanish project comes to anything, we should leave Cologne. She would not wish to stay here when all her lovers had gone. Have I your permission to put this proposition to her, Your Majesty?"

"Put it by all means, but don't force her to go back to live among Puritans, Edward."

"Then sign this paper. It is a promise of a pension."

Charles signed. Poor Lucy! He had ceased to desire her greatly. Occasionally he visited her in indolence or out of kindness. He was not sure which, and he did not care enough to find out. One never knew, when visiting her, whether one would startle her with a lover who might be hiding in a cupboard until the royal visitor had departed. Such situations were not conducive to passion.

But as he signed he was really thinking of Mary, and what he would say to her.

Was it possible that Spain might help him to regain his throne?

There were times when some wild scheme would rouse him from his lethargy, and he would once more be conscious of hope.

❁ ❁ ❁

Mary, the Princess of Orange, had all the Stuart gaiety. She had lost her husband; she was young and alone in a country which did not greatly love her; she was full of anxieties for her baby son; yet when she was with her brother she could fling aside her cares and laugh, dance and make merry.

She was looking forward to going to France as she had not looked forward to anything for a long time.

"Paris!" she cried. "And all the gaiety I hear is indulged in there! I want to enjoy all that. And most of all, I want to see our mother whom I have not seen for thirteen years, and dear little Henriette whom I have not seen at all. Poor Mother! She was always so tender and loving."

"To those who do her commands!"

"Charles, you have grown cynical."

"Realistic, my dear. The longer I live, and the farther I wander, the greater grows my respect for the truth. Ask poor Henry to tell you of our mother's tender love!"

"Poor little Henry! His was a sad experience."

"And entirely our mother's doing."

"You must not dislike her because she is a Catholic."

"It is not her religion that I hate. It is her unkindness to our brother. The boy was heartbroken when Ormonde brought him to me."

"Well, Charles, you have made up to him for what he suffered at our mother's hands. He may have been disappointed in her, but he is not so in his brother. He adores his King; and is it not pathetic to see how he tries to model himself on you?"

"It is more than pathetic—it is tragic. And so bad for his morals."

"You might try to prevent that by leading a more respectable life yourself, brother."

"I cannot attempt the impossible—even for young Henry."

Mary laughed. "Now you are looking stern," she said. "Now you are preparing to pass on Master Hyde's orders to me. You are going to forbid me to go to Paris."

"Mary, who am I to forbid you!"

"You are the King and the head of our house."

"You are the Princess of Orange, mother of the Orange heir. I am your out-at-elbows brother."

"Oh Charles, dearest Charles, you are not a very good advocate for your cause. You are a profligate, they say, and I know that to be true; you are careless; you are idle; but I love you."

"If the reward of profligacy is love, then mayhap I am not such a fool after all."

"Are you forbidding me to go to Paris?"

"I forbid nothing."

"But you ask me not to go?"

" 'Twill offend the Spaniards."

"Listen to me, Charles. You and our mother have quarreled over Henry. It is a bad thing in any family to quarrel—in ours it might well be disastrous. I wish to right these matters. For years I have longed to see our mother again."

Charles smiled. "Dear Mary," he said. "You must please yourself. Go, if that is what you wish."

"I am sure I am right. I do not believe the Spaniards will help you regain your kingdom. They'll not fight for you. They are just temporarily friendly with you because, for the moment, the French are not."

"I think you have the truth there."

"We must not have these rifts between members of our family. Our mother must love you again. She must love Henry. Oh, Charles, there are so few of us left now. Smile on my journey. I could not enjoy it if you did not."

"Then if my smile is necessary to your pleasure, you must have it, dear sister. Take a kiss to my dear Minette."

Mary embraced him warmly.

"Yes, Charles," she said. "Do you know you're my favorite brother? I would almost go further and, but for a small person who now resides in Holland, I would say you are my favorite man."

"I really begin to think," said the king, "that I am not such a fool as I believed myself to be."

"You're the wisest fool on earth. I shall take your Chancellor's daughter with me as a maid of honor. She is a pleasant girl, Anne Hyde. And I wish her to make herself very agreeable to our mother whom I would like to see reconciled to the girl's father. She declares Hyde advises you to act against her wishes, you know."

"You make me wistful. I would that I could go with you on this journey to France."

"What! Have you a fancy for the Chancellor's daughter?"

"Anne Hyde! Assuredly not."

"Then I am glad, because I think her father would have a high pride in her virtue."

"I was not thinking of being with Anne Hyde," said Charles. "I was thinking of the pleasure of seeing Minette again."

❁ ❁ ❁

Lucy was in bed nibbling sweetmeats. She could hear Ann Hill moving about whilst she cleaned the apartment. Lucy had coarsened slightly, but she was still beautiful. On the pillow beside her had rested, until a few hours ago, the fair head of one of the Court gentlemen. She did not know his name, but he had been a satisfactory lover.

Her clothes lay on the floor where she had flung them; Ann had not yet been in to tidy the room. Ann was angry with her mistress. Ann thought her mistress should not receive any gentlemen in her bed except the King.

But Lucy must have a lover; she might sigh for the King, but the King was not always at hand, and there were so many waiting to take his place.

Now she wondered whether the fair gentleman would visit her again this night. If he did not, another would.

Ann had come into the room and was clicking her tongue at the state of the apartment as she picked up the garments which lay about the floor.

"Don't frown!" cried Lucy. "It makes you look uglier than usual."

"If this is what beauty brings you to, I'm glad I'm ugly," muttered Ann. "A new man last night! I've never seen him before."

"He was wonderful!" murmured Lucy.

"What if . . ."

"What if the King had visited me? Oh no!" Lucy sighed and was momentarily sad. "He is pleasantly occupied elsewhere for the last week—and the next, I doubt not."

"It's wrong," said Ann, shaking her head. "Quite wrong."

"Is it? I never have time to think about it."

"You think of little else!"

"It seems that I am thinking of last night's pleasure until it is time to anticipate tonight's."

Ann said: "It's depravity . . . and everybody here seems to . . . to wallow in it."

"It is a pastime in which one cannot indulge alone."

"For the children to see such things is not right."

"They are too young to know."

"Mary may be. Jemmy is not. He begins to wonder. He is nearly seven. It is time you gave up this way of living and, settled down to quiet, and thought of looking after the children."

Lucy stared before her. She loved her children—both of them—but she adored Jemmy. He had such vitality, such charm, and he was such a handsome little boy. Moreover everybody who visited the house—and in particular the King—made much of him.

Settle down and be quiet! Look after Jemmy! As well ask a bird not to sing in the spring, a bee not to gather honey!

Ann went on: "There are rumors. There'll be another move soon."

"I dare swear we shall go to Breda."

"If there is another attempt . . ."

"Attempt?"

"You think of nothing but who your next lover will be. Don't you see they're only waiting here. One day they'll be gone . . . and then where will you be? They'll all be leaving here to fight with the King, and you'll be left with a few Germans to make love to you."

"You're in a bad mood today, Ann."

"It's all these rumors," said Ann. "We shall be moving soon, I know. I wish we could go home."

"Home?"

"To London. Fancy being in Paul's Walk again!"

Lucy's eyes were dreamy. "Yes," she said. "Just fancy! Fancy going to Bartholomew and Southwark Fairs."

"I'd like to walk by the river again," said Ann wistfully. "No other place is the same, is it? They don't look the same . . . don't smell the same . . . All other places are dull. They weary a body . . . and make her long for home."

"To walk down the gallery at the Royal Exchange again . . ." murmured Lucy.

Jemmy came running into the room. He wore a toy sword at his belt; it was a present from his father. "I'm a soldier!" he cried. "I'm for the King. Are you for the Parliament? Then you're dead . . . dead . . . dead . . ."

He took out his sword and waved it at Ann, who skillfully eluded him.

"Wars, wars, wars!" said Lucy. "It is always wars. Even Jemmy dreams of wars."

"I'm the Captain," said Jemmy. "I'm no Roundhead." He climbed onto the bed looking for comfits and sweetmeats which were always kept close by Lucy so that all she had to do was reach for them. Her lovers kept her well supplied; they were the only presents Lucy appreciated.

Jemmy sat on the bed, arranging the sweetmeats as soldiers and eating them one by one. "Dead, dead, dead," he said, popping them into his mouth. "Is my Papa coming today?"

"We do not know," said Ann. "But if you eat more of those sweetmeats you will be too sick to see him, if he does."

Jemmy paused for a second or so; then he continued to murmur "Dead . . . dead . . . dead" as he popped sweet after sweet into his mouth. He was remarkably like his father at that moment.

A serving maid came in to say that a gentleman was waiting to see Mistress Barlow.

"Hurry!" cried Lucy. "My mirror! My comb! Ann . . . quick! Jemmy, you must go away. Who is it, I wonder?"

"If it is my father, I shall stay," said Jemmy. "If it is Sir Henry, I shall stay too. He promised to bring me a pony to ride." He leaped off the bed. "He may have brought it."

The maid said that it was neither the King nor Sir Henry Bennett. It was an elderly gentleman whom she did not know and who would not give his name.

Lucy and Ann exchanged glances. An elderly gentleman who had never been here before? Lucy liked young lovers. She grimaced at Ann.

"I should put a shawl over your shoulders," said Ann, placing one there.

Lucy grimaced again and pushed the shawl away so that the magnificent bust and shoulders were not entirely hidden.

Edward Hyde was shown into the room. He flinched at the sight of the voluptuous woman on the bed. The morals of the Court—which he would be the first to admit were set by his master—were constantly shocking him. He thought of his daughter, Anne, and was glad that the Princess of Orange was taking her away. He thought: What I must face in the service of my master! And his thoughts went back to that occasion when, seeking to join Charles in France, his ship had been taken by corsairs, and he, robbed of his possessions, had been made a slave before he finally escaped.

"It is my lord Chancellor!" said Lucy.

Edward Hyde bowed his head.

"This is the first time you have visited my apartment," she went on.

"I come on the King's pleasure."

"I did not think that you came on your own!" laughed Lucy.

The Chancellor looked impatient; he said quickly: "It is believed that we shall not be here in Cologne much longer."

"Ah!" said Lucy."

"And," went on Hyde, "I have a proposition to make. Many people remain here because they dare not live in England. That would not apply to you. If you wished you could return there, set up your house, and none would say you nay."

"Is that so?"

"Indeed it is. And it would be the wisest thing you could do."

"How should I live there?"

"How do you live here?"

"I have many friends."

"English friends. The English are as friendly at home as in exile. The King has promised to pay you a pension of four hundred pounds a year if you return to England."

"It is for Jemmy," she said. "He wants Jemmy to be brought up in England; that's it, I'll swear."

"It would be a very good reason for your going."

"London," she said. "I wonder if it has changed much."

"Why not go and find out?"

"The King . . . ?"

"He will not be long in Cologne."

"No," said Lucy sadly. "He will go, and he will take the most gallant gentlemen with him."

"Go to London," said the Chancellor. "You'll be happier there, and one day, let us hope, all the friends you have known here will join you there. What do you say? Four hundred pounds a year; and you have the King's promise of it as soon as it is possible. A passage could be arranged for you. What do you say, Mistress Barlow? What do you say?"

"I say I will consider the offer."

He took her hand and bowed over it.

"The serving girl will show you out," she told him.

When he had left she called Ann Hill to her.

"Ann," she said, "talk to me of London. Talk as you love to talk. Come, Ann; sit on the bed there. How would you like to go to London, Ann? How would you like to go home?"

Ann stood still as though transfixed. She was smelling the dampness in the air on those days when the mist rose up from the Thames; she was hearing the shouts and screams of a street brawl; she was watching the milkmaids bearing their yokes along the cobbled streets; she was seeing the gabled houses on an early summer's morning.

And, watching her, Lucy caught her excitement.

❁ ❁ ❁

At the Palais-Royal, Henrietta Maria and her daughter were awaiting the arrival of Mary of Orange. The Queen felt happier than she had for some time; the royal family of France, although they had so long neglected the exiled Queen and her daughter Henriette, were preparing to give Mary of Orange a royal welcome.

"This is an honor of which we must not be insensible," said Henrietta Maria to her youngest daughter. "The King, the Queen, and Monsieur are all riding out to meet Mary at Saint-Dennis."

"It is Holland they honor, Mam, not us," Henriette reminded her mother.

"It is Mary, and Mary is one of us. Oh, I do wonder what she will be like. Poor Mary! I remember well her espousal. She was ten years old at the time, and she was married in the Chapel at Whitehall to the Prince her husband, who was a little boy of eleven. It was at the time when your father was forced into signing Strafford's death warrant; and the day after the marriage the mob broke into Westminster Abbey and . . . and . . ."

"Mam, I beg of you do not talk of the past. Think of the future and Mary's coming. That will cheer you."

"Ah, yes, it will cheer me. It will be wonderful to see her again . . . my little girl. A widow now. Oh, what sorrows befall our family!"

"But there is joy coming now, Mam. Mary will soon be with us, and I know her visit will make us very happy."

"Hers was a Protestant marriage." Henrietta Maria's brow darkened.

"Please, Mam, do not speak of that. She will soon be here with us. Let us be content with that."

They heard the shouts and cheers as the party approached.

Mary was riding between Louis and Queen Anne. Philippe was on the other side of his brother. This was indeed a royal welcome for Mary.

So the first time Henriette set eyes on her sister was a very ceremonious occasion; but there was time in between the balls and masques, which the royal family of France had devised for Mary's entertainment, for them to get to know each other.

Henriette discovered Mary to be warmhearted and delighted to be with her family again. She was merry and quick to joke, and in that she reminded Henriette of Charles; she talked continually of her little boy who was now five years old—her little William of Orange, such a solemn boy, a regular Dutch William! She spoke sadly of her husband. She had been loath to marry him, she told Henriette as they sat alone. "So very frightened I was. I was younger than you, Henriette; think of that! But he was frightened too, and far shyer than I was, and we soon learned to love each other. And he died of that dreadful pox. It was a great tragedy for me, Henriette, in more ways than one. I could not then offer your brothers the hospitality which I had shown them hitherto; but more than that, I had lost a husband and protector . . . the father of my little Dutch William."

Henriette shed tears for her sister's sorrow, but more often she was joining in her sister's laughter.

Each day there was some entertainment for Mary's pleasure. Even young Philippe gave a ball two days after her arrival. It took place in the Salle de Gardes, and Philippe himself had spent much time and trouble ensuring that the illuminations should be of the brightest. In the tapestry-decorated *salle,* it was King Louis who opened the ball with Henriette. Mary, of course, did not dance, as French etiquette, dictated by Queen Anne, decreed that widows should not dance at great balls, and only on private occasions should they be allowed to do so.

Louis composed a ballet for her pleasure. It was founded on the story of Psyche, and never, declared the courtiers, had the King danced with greater perfection. Chancellor Seguier gave a fête in her honor, and the galleries which led to the ballroom were lighted with three hundred torches.

Mademoiselle, who was still banished from the Court, invited the Princess of Orange to her country residence of Chilly where she sought to outdo in splendor all the previous entertainments which the Princess had seen.

Mademoiselle, resplendent in jewels, was a dazzling hostess.

"Why, Henriette," she said to her cousin on that occasion, "how thin you are! Worn out, I dare swear, by all this unaccustomed gaiety. You must be rather sad at Colombes and Chaillot and the Palais-Royal. So very quiet it must be for you!"

"And you too, Mademoiselle, here in the country."

"Oh, I know how to entertain myself. I have my own little Court here, you see, and I have heard that I shall very soon be invited back to Court. I shall go at my pleasure."

"I am glad of that, Mademoiselle," said Henriette. "I know how unhappy it must have made you to feel the King's displeasure."

"It is not Louis. It is his mother. What jewels your sister has! They rival anything I see here. And Henriette, there is something I would say to you. You should not, you know, go in to supper before me. I should take precedence over you."

"My mother says that is not so; and you know how important it is that everyone should walk in the right order."

"In the old days the Kings of Scotland gave place to the Kings of France. Your brother . . . if he had a crown . . . would be a Scottish King, would he not?"

"But also a King of England . . ."

"My dear Henriette, you really should step aside for me to go into supper before you."

"My mother would never allow me to. Nor would Queen Anne."

Mademoiselle pouted. "Such fusses!" she said. "And over such small details. The Queen gives too much thought to such matters. Well, we shall see who will have precedence. Mark you, I think it would be a different matter if your brother were a ruling king."

"In the eyes of the French Court he is still a king."

"Lately, I have wondered. But enough of this. Enjoy yourself, Henriette. My poor child, it must be enchanting for you. You only go to the little private dances at the Louvre now, don't you?"

Mademoiselle left Henriette and returned to her guest of honor.

"And how do you like the Court of France, Madame?"

"I am in love with the Court of France," Mary told her.

"It is very different from that of Holland, is it not?"

"Indeed yes. Mayhap that is one reason why I have fallen so deeply in love with it."

"You do not love the Court of Holland?"

"I will tell you this, Mademoiselle: as soon as my brother is settled in his kingdom, I shall go and live with him."

"Ah! When will that be?"

"I pray to God each night," said Mary vehemently, "that his return will not be long delayed."

"You think you would live in amity with Charles?"

"Any woman could live in amity with Charles. He is the sweetest-tempered man alive."

Henrietta Maria heard them as they talked of her son, and her eyes sparkled with intrigue. Mademoiselle might be temporarily out of favor at the Court, but she was still the richest heiress in Europe; and badly Charles needed money.

"Ah!" she cried. "I hear you talk of this poor King of England. So you wish to hear news of him, Mademoiselle?"

"Her Highness offered it without my expressing the wish," said the insolent Mademoiselle.

"He is foolish," said Henrietta Maria, "in that he will never cease to love you."

"And wise," said Mademoiselle, "in that he does not allow this devotion, which you say he has for me, to interfere with his interest in others."

"He bade me tell you how sorry he was that he had to leave France without saying goodbye to you. Why, Mademoiselle, if you were married you would be your own mistress."

"But the King, your son, would not give up any of his if I were!"

"You would do exactly as you pleased. He is, as his sister tells you, such a sweet-tempered person. It is impossible to quarrel with him."

"And you, Madame, have achieved the impossible!"

"It is because he is unhappy that we have quarreled. If you married him he would be so happy that he and I would be reconciled."

"If the King cannot live happily with you, Madame, I doubt whether he could with me."

Mademoiselle's brilliant eyes were turned on Louis who had begun to dance.

Henrietta Maria followed her gaze. She could scarcely hold back her anger. It was ridiculous. Mademoiselle was eleven years older than the King of France and Henrietta Maria meant Louis to marry her own Henriette.

Henrietta Maria knew that she must shelve her immediate desires—Charles' marriage with Mademoiselle and Henriette's with Louis. Her daughter Mary was as amiable as her brother and as eager to please and live peaceably with her family. She attended the Anglican church every day; but perhaps it was possible that Henrietta Maria might save her for the true Church.

"Dearest daughter," she said, "I want you to come to Chaillot with me tomorrow. I am sure a rest in the tranquil atmosphere there will do you so much good."

Mary smiled at her mother. Charles was right about her, she thought. She was the most affectionate of mothers when her children obeyed her. But, thought Mary grimly, she shall never make a convert of me.

"Yes, Mama," she said, "I will with pleasure come to Chaillot, but I shall not go to Mass there. As you know, I always attend the Anglican church."

Henrietta Maria frowned. "One should never shut one's ears and one's heart, Mary. It is well to listen to both sides."

"That is true enough, Mama. So I hope you will attend the Anglican church with me, as I shall come with you to Chaillot."

"That is *quite* impossible!"

Henrietta Maria's whole body seemed to be bristling with indignation. Then her eyes filled with tears. "I always think," she said, "that everything would have been so different had your father lived."

Mary was filled with pity. Poor Mother! she thought. It is sad. She lost her husband and she loved him dearly; she must continually be haunted by the fear that she was instrumental in bringing him to his end. That is why she so fiercely maintains her grief. All her children will disappoint her, I fear. Charles has quarreled with her. She has sworn she will never see Henry again. James—her favorite—will bring sorrow to her, I doubt not, for he was mightily taken with Anne Hyde when they met. And what will Mother say to a marriage with Anne Hyde, Charles' Chancellor's daughter? But perhaps it will not come to that. Let us hope that she will not disown James as she has Henry, and doubtless would Charles if she dared. I disappoint her because I will not turn Catholic. No wonder she dotes on our little sister. Henriette seems to be the only one who is able to please her. Now I foresee many arguments; she will call Père Cyprien and the Abbé Montague to deal with me. Dear Mother! I am so sorry. But I cannot give up my faith even to please you.

But those arguments did not take place, for within a few days news came that Mary's little Dutch William was ill, and the smallpox was feared.

She was beside herself with grief, and left at once for Holland.

❁ ❁ ❁

Charles was riding to Breda. Another move—and who could say how long he would stay at Breda?

It was more than five years since he had set foot in England. Five wandering years! How many more would he spend—an exile from his kingdom? He was accustomed now to dreaming dreams, making plans which became nothing more than dreams. "I have had so little luck since Worcester," he told his friends, "that I now expect none."

He had said goodbye to Lucy and his son. They would be in London now. He did not care to think of London; but he hoped Lucy would fare well there. But Lucy, he assured himself, would fare well in any place. She would always have lovers to provide for her. How was he going to pay the four hundred pounds a year which he had promised her? He had no idea. His purse was empty. "I am a generous man," he often said. "I love to give, and if the only things I am able to give are promises with little hope of fulfilling them, then must I give them."

Lucy had said a sad farewell to him . . . and to others; she had wept to leave him . . . and to leave others.

He had swung young Jemmy up in his arms, and he knew then that he dearly loved the boy. If he had been the son of himself and Mademoiselle or Hortense Mancini or the now-widowed Duchesse de Châtillon—someone whom he could have married—he would have been well content. It was a pity such a fine boy as Jemmy must be a bastard.

"What will you do in London, Jemmy?" he had asked.

"Fight for the King's cause!" had answered the sturdy little boy.

"Ah, my dear boy, you will best do that by keeping those fine sentiments to yourself."

"I shall do it with my sword, Papa. Dead . . . dead . . . dead . . . I'll cut off Cromwell's head."

"Take care of yourself, my son. That is how you will best serve your King."

Jemmy was not listening. He was fingering his sword and thinking of what he would do in London.

"You'll have to curb our young Royalist, Lucy," Charles told the boy's mother. "We have talked too freely before him, I fear."

So they had gone, and here he was riding on to Breda.

His sister Mary joined him in the little town. She had left the French Court in haste on hearing news of her son's illness, but now cheering messages were reaching her. Her little William was merely suffering from an attack of measles, and not the dreaded smallpox as had been feared.

Mary, released from fear, was full of gaiety. She declared she could not come near Breda without meeting her favorite brother.

They embraced affectionately, and Charles made her tell him in detail all that had befallen her at the Court of France. He was particularly eager for news of Minette.

"I wonder who loves the other more—you or your little sister," said Mary.

"Tell me—is she well?"

"Yes—well and charming; but she grows too fast; and life at the Court is not very happy for her and our mother. Mademoiselle makes herself unpleasant, demanding precedence whenever they meet."

"A curse on Mademoiselle!"

"I thought you wanted to marry the woman."

"Mam wanted it, you mean, and as for myself, I would marry her, I dare swear, if she would have me. I'm not enamored of her, but her fortune is too great to be turned lightly aside."

"Poor Charles! Is your purse quite empty?"

"Very nearly."

"I have brought twenty thousand pistoles for your use."

"Mary, you are an angel! One day I shall pay you back. That's a promise." He smiled wryly. "I would give you a fortune if I had one; alas, all I have to lay at your feet is a promise."

"One day you will in truth be King of England. I am sure of it, Charles. One day you will be restored to the throne. The people of England are not pleased with Puritan rule. How could they be? You know how they love gaiety. Now the theaters are closed; there is no singing, no dancing, nothing to do but contemplate their sins and wail for forgiveness. It is not the English man's or woman's way meekly to accept such constraint. They love pageantry above all things. They will soon decide to have no more of puritanism. They decided they would have no more Catholic rulers at one time; they will be equally firm, when the time comes, to ban puritanism. The Englishman does not like his religion to interfere with his pleasure."

"I am beginning to think," said Charles, "that I make a very good Englishman."

"You do indeed. And soon the English will realize this. Then they will implore you to return. They'll go down on their knees and beg you to return . . ."

"They will have no need to. They have but to lift a finger, to throw a smile to poor Charles Stuart, and he will be entirely at their service. Now let us talk of the family. It is so rarely that we meet and can be alone together. Let us indulge ourselves, Mary."

"I wish it were a happier subject. I am a little disturbed about James and Anne Hyde. Perhaps I should never have taken the girl with me."

"James . . . and Anne Hyde?"

"He has a fancy for her. She is a good girl, Charles."

"And James . . . is not so good?"

Mary sighed. "I can only hope that no ill comes of it. I think of our mother and what she would have to say."

"Poor Mam! We do not want her declaring that she will not see *James'* face again."

"She is so ambitious for us all. She has been plaguing Mademoiselle . . . trying to persuade her to take you."

Charles groaned. "No! Not again!"

"And Mademoiselle spoke quite emphatically. I think, Charles, that you have fascinated her a little. If you were not an exile, willingly would she marry you."

"There are hundreds who would willingly marry the reigning King of England, Mary. It is only when they consider Charles Stuart the exile, that they find him such an unattractive fellow."

"Never that!" said Mary fondly. "Threadbare and empty of purse you may be, but you are the most fascinating man in Europe. Mademoiselle's problem is that she would like to marry you, but her pride won't let her."

"True! And I thank God that Mademoiselle's pride is there to protect me from Mademoiselle."

"And, of course, our mother has hopes of Louis for Henriette."

"That is what I would wish for, Mary. It is a cherished dream of mine. Dear sweet Minette . . . the Queen of France! How think you she would feel about it? I should not care to see her unhappy."

"Louis is magnificent, Charles. He is physically perfect . . . a little stupid perhaps, by Stuart standards." They laughed together. "But he is so beautiful and not unkind. I think Henriette is fond of him. In fact I do not see how she could help being fond of him. She compares him with you. I know it. I know of it by the manner in which she speaks of you both in the same breath."

"Then must Louis' perfections be more obvious than ever!"

"No, Charles. That is not so. In her eyes you are perfect. I said to her: 'How perfectly Louis dances!' She answered: 'He dances well, but he is not so graceful as Charles.' I said: 'Louis is surely the most handsome man in the world.' She smiled and said: "That may be so. I am no judge. But he has not the wit of Charles.' It is always Charles. It should not be so: a Princess so to love her brother!"

"Dear Minette! She should not. I shall write to her and scold her for loving me too well. But I do not think she loves me one whit more than I love her. If ever I become King I shall bring my family home. We shall all be together. That is what I long for more than anything."

"But," said Mary pensively, "I do not think she is untouched by Louis' charm. Indeed, I think she is very fond of him. He is a charming boy and of good character. He must be, for never was one more flattered, and yet his arrogance is not overpowering, and he always gives the impression of wishing to do what he considers right."

"I doubt that he would marry Henriette while I am still an exile. Oh, Mary, if I regained my kingdom, what a difference that would make, eh? I doubt not that then my little Minette would become the Queen of France. What an excellent thing that could be for our two countries! What an alliance! For I would love the French more than ever if Minette were their Queen."

"And you would take Mademoiselle for wife?"

"Ah! I doubt it. I doubt it very much. There is a great obstacle which I feel may prevent Mademoiselle and me from joining hands at the altar. While I am an exile she cannot contemplate marrying *me;* and if I had a crown fixed firmly on my head I could not bring myself to take *her.* Now let us drink to the future. Let us hope that our dreams will come true."

"Our first step will be to put you on the throne of England, where you belong."

"Our first step! But what a step! Yet, who knows . . . one day it may come to pass."

✿✿✿

When Lucy arrived in London she found that a great change had taken place in the city since she had left it.

Now the clothes of the people were drab, and the people themselves were, for the most part, suppressed and sullen. Those who were not, seemed to wear an air of perpetual complacency. All the ballad singers had disappeared, and there were no spontaneous outbursts of pageantry which had been a feature of the old days. The only places which still flourished were the brothels, and their inmates still chattered to each other from windows of rooms which projected and almost met over the cobbled streets.

Lucy found rooms over a barber's shop near Somerset House. She was warmly received by the barber and, as she called herself Mistress Barlow, no one knew of her connection with the King, nor that the bright-eyed little boy was Charles' son.

Ann Hill had taken charge, and told the barber that her mistress was a lady who had been living abroad and been trying for a long time to return to her native country.

They had a little money, and for a few days Lucy was content to lie in the room looking out on the street; but she soon began to long for a lover.

Each day Ann discovered more of the changes which had befallen London. All the taverns were closed; bull-baiting was suppressed; all the pleasure gardens were closed except the Mulberry Garden. There had been no Christmas festivals in the churches for a long time. There was no dancing in the streets on May Day.

"Why did we come back?" wailed Lucy. "There was more fun at The Hague and in Cologne."

A few days after her arrival she dressed herself with great care and went out. Everyone stared at her; she was different from other women. She looked like a foreigner. She soon found a lover—a high-ranking soldier of Cromwell's Ironsides; but she did not enjoy her relationship with him as she had with the merry Cavaliers in exile. He was conscious of sin the whole time he was with her, and he felt compelled to make love under cover of darkness, slipping into the rooms over the barber's shop at dusk, and leaving before it was light. Lucy was beautiful, and beauty, she believed, was not meant to be hidden by darkness. She was restive. She was wishing she had not come to London.

Finally, she told her lover that she had had enough of him and his preoccupation with sin, and that he had best take himself off to repentance.

After that it had become her habit to go out and wander disconsolately in the Mulberry Garden; it was not what it had been, of course; but it was still a place in which to sit and watch the world go by, to take a little refreshment under the trees and perhaps pick up a lover.

She did not meet a lover in the Mulberry Garden; but as she sat at one of the tables a woman approached and asked if she might join her.

"I saw you sitting there," she said, "and I thought I should like to join you. It is rarely one sees such ladies as yourself in the Mulberry Garden in these days."

"Ah, these days!" said Lucy incautiously. "In the old days, it was different, I can tell you."

"I could tell you too!" sighed her companion. "The old days! Will they ever come back, do you think?"

"You would like to see them back?"

"Who would not? I was fond of the play. I was fond of a bit of fun . . . a bit of gaiety in the streets. Now it is nothing but prayer meetings . . . all day and every day. Will you take a little refreshment with me?"

"Thank you," said Lucy, warming to the company. The woman was rather flashily dressed; she was no Puritan; that much was clear.

They ate tarts with a little meat, which they washed down with Rhenish wine.

"You are a very beautiful woman," said Lucy's new friend.

Lucy smiled her acknowledgment of the compliment.

"And very popular with the men, I'll warrant!"

"Are there any men left in this town?" asked Lucy ironically.

"Yes. A few. They visit my house near Covent Garden occasionally. You must pay us a visit."

"I'd like to."

"Why not come along now?"

"I have a family who will be waiting for my return."

"A family indeed!"

"A boy and a girl. I have left them with my maid."

"Where do you live then?"

"Near Somerset House. Over a barber's shop."

"It hardly seems a fitting lodging for a lady like you."

"Oh, I have had some fine lodgings, I can tell you."

"I don't need to be told. I can guess."

"You would be surprised if I told you where I have lodged."

"You have been in foreign parts, eh?"

"Yes. At The Hague and Paris. And . . . Cologne."

"There were Englishmen at those places, were there not?"

"Indeed there were!"

"Real gentlemen, I'll warrant."

"You would be surprised if you knew."

"Nothing would surprise me about a beautiful woman like yourself."

"You are very kind."

"I but speak the truth." The woman lifted her glass and said: "I will drink to the health of someone whose name should not be mentioned."

Lucy seized her glass and tears shone in her eyes. "God bless him!" she said.

"You speak with fervor, madam."

"I do indeed. There is none like him . . . none . . . none at all."

"You knew him . . . in The Hague and Paris . . . ?"

"Yes, I knew him well."

The woman nodded, then said: "Do not speak of it here. It would not be safe."

"Thank you. You are kind to remind me."

"It is good to have a friend. I hope we shall meet again. We *must* meet again. Will you visit my house tomorrow?"

"If it is possible, perhaps."

"Please come. Come in the evening. We make merry then. What is your name?"

"Barlow. Mistress Barlow."

"Mistress Barlow, I hope we shall be great friends. I see we are two who think similar thoughts in this drab place our city has become. My name is Jenny. Call me Jenny. It's more friendly."

"I am Lucy."

"Lucy! It's a pretty name, and you have a pretty way of speaking. That's not the London way."

"No. I come from Wales."

"Barlow! Is that a Welsh name?"

"Yes. It is, and so is Water . . . my maiden name."

"Water, did you say?"

"Yes. My name before I married . . . Mr. Barlow."

"Lucy Water . . . recently come from The Hague. You will come to see me tomorrow, please. I shall look forward to your visit."

Lucy went home not ill pleased with her visit to Mulberry Garden. Perhaps she would go to Jenny's house next day. It would be interesting to meet some merry company again.

❁ ❁ ❁

Lucy did go, and it was a merry evening. She awoke next morning in a strange bedroom, and when she opened her eyes she was slightly perturbed.

Ann would guess that she had stayed the night, not caring to face the streets at a late hour, and she would look after the children, so there was nothing to fear on that score; but Lucy's lover of last night had not entirely pleased her. She missed the pleasant manners of the Court gentlemen. Yes, that was it; last night's lover had been too crude for Lucy.

There was another discovery she had made. Jenny's home was nothing but a bawdy house. She had begun to realize that, not long after she had entered it; but already by then she had drunk a little too much and felt too lazy—and, of course, it would have been very impolite—to leave abruptly.

As she lay there she understood that she had not enjoyed last night's lover. Love, such as undertaken in Jenny's establishment, was quite different from that which she had hitherto enjoyed. She had always been fastidious in choosing her lovers; something in them had attracted her or made a strong appeal to her sensuality. This was quite different. This was lust, to be bartered for and haggled over. Lucy was not that kind of loose woman.

Now she knew why Jenny had been so friendly in the Garden, why she had been so eager for her to visit her home. She was glad her companion of last night was no longer with her. She would rise and dress, thank Jenny for her entertainment and slip away, never to see the woman again.

She was dressed when there was a knock at her door.

"Come in!" she cried; and Jenny entered.

"Good morrow to you, Lucy. Why, you look as pretty by morning light as by candlelight, I swear. Were you comfortable in this room?"

"Yes, thank you. I was quite comfortable."

Jenny laughed. "I notice you took the most amusing of the gentlemen, Lucy."

"Was he the most amusing?"

"I could see that from the moment you set eyes on him, no other would do."

"I fear I drank too freely. I am not accustomed to overmuch wine."

"Are you not? It is good for you, and it gives you such high spirits, you know."

"My spirits have always been high enough without. Now I must thank you for my lodging and be off."

"Lucy . . . you'll come again?"

Lucy was evasive. She was telling herself that if she had not drunk so much wine, if she had not been so long without a lover, what had happened last night would never have taken place.

"Mayhap I will," she said.

"Lucy, I'll make you very comfortable here. Those rooms over the shop . . . they must be most unsuitable for a lady used to the comforts you enjoyed at The Hague and Cologne."

"I manage very well. I have my faithful servant to look after me, and my children to consider."

"You could bring them all here. I could use a new servant, or you could keep her merely to wait on you. The children would be welcome here. We are a very happy family in this house."

The woman was breathing heavily. Lucy smelt the stale gin on her breath, and was aware of the avaricious gleam in her eyes. Lucy was not clever, but she now understood that she had behaved with the utmost folly. Doubtless there had been gossip bandied about as to the life Charles led on the Continent, and her name might well have been one of those which were mentioned in connection with him; and she, stupidly, had betrayed who she was, and perhaps last night had babbled even more.

No wonder this woman was eager to make her an inmate of her brothel! She could imagine what a draw the mistress of Charles Stuart would be.

Then Lucy wanted to get away. She wanted to wipe the shame of the place from her mind. She wanted to forget that she had spent the night in a brothel. All her love affairs had been so different. She had discovered that last night—half tipsy though she had been.

She drew herself away. "Well, I will say goodbye now."

"But you'll come again?"

"I . . . I'll see."

The woman's eyes narrowed. She was not going to let Lucy escape as easily as that.

❁ ❁ ❁

Ann was reproachful. She guessed that Lucy had spent the night with a man. She said nothing, but she was a little frightened. Glad as she was to be in London, she was quicker than Lucy to realize that, in more ways than one, this was not the same London which they had left more than eight years ago.

Jenny called. She was wheedling, and then faintly threatening. She hinted that one who had come rather mysteriously from across the water and had clearly been a close friend of people who were regarded as the enemies of the Commonwealth, might find it convenient to shelter in the house of a good friend who would protect her.

"I am very comfortable here," Lucy told her.

"You may not always be so," retorted Jenny. "You may be glad of friends one day, and that day soon!"

"I shall not join you at your brothel," declared Lucy firmly.

Jenny's eyes gleamed. "You may find there are worse places than my house, Lucy Water."

"I have never been in one," said Lucy carelessly.

"You'll change your mind."

"Never!" cried Lucy, and for once her mouth was set into lines of determination.

The woman left, and Lucy lay thoughtfully nibbling sweetmeats.

Jenny called again on two other occasions; she sought to placate Lucy, but Lucy's determination not to join her household brought more veiled threats.

A few days later two men called at the rooms over the barber's shop. They were soberly clad, grim-faced men, servants of the Commonwealth. They came to search the rooms and Mistress Barlow's belongings, they said.

"For what reason?" demanded Ann on the threshold.

"For this reason," answered one of the men. "We suspect that the woman who occupies these rooms has recently come from the Continent, and that she is a spy for Charles Stuart."

Lucy rose from her bed, her flimsy draperies falling about her; but these men were not Court gallants to be moved by beauty in distress. They began to search the room, and in a box they found the King's promise to pay Lucy four hundred pounds a year.

One of them said: "Mistress, prepare yourself to leave this place at once." He turned to Ann. "You also. We are taking you all to another lodging."

Trembling, Ann prepared herself and the children, who were making eager inquiries.

"Where are we going?" said little Mary. "Are we going for a walk?"

"You must wait to see where we are taken," Lucy told her.

"Mama," cried Jemmy, "do you want to go? If you don't, I'll run them through with my sword."

The men looked at Jemmy without a smile. Jemmy hated them. He was used to caresses and admiration. He drew his sword from his belt, but Ann was beside him; she caught his arm.

"Now, Master Jemmy, do as you're told. That is what is best for your mother . . . and for us all. It is what your father would wish."

Jemmy fell silent. There was something in Ann's face which made him pause to think; he saw that his mother was in earnest too. This was not a game.

In a very short time they had left the barber's shop and were being taken towards the water's edge, to where a barge was waiting for them.

Slowly they slipped down the river, and soon Jemmy was pointing out the great gray fortress on its banks. "There's the Tower!" he cried.

"That's so," said one of the men. "Take a good look at it from the outside, my boy. Mayhap you'll be seeing nothing but the inside for a long time."

"What do you mean?" cried Lucy.

"Just that we are taking you to your new lodging, Mistress, your lodging in the Tower . . . the rightful place for friends of Charles Stuart who come to London to spy for him."

Lucy was ailing. The rigorous life of a prisoner did not suit her. She had been accustomed to too much comfort. She had grown thinner since her incarceration; she would sit listlessly at her barred window, looking out on the church of St. Peter ad Vincula, and every time she heard the bell toll she would be seized with a fit of shivering.

Ann looked after her as well as she could, but Ann too was frightened. She remembered the day, over six years ago, when the Parliament had beheaded the King. She wondered if the same fate was in store for them.

Their jailer would tell them nothing. He would bring their not very palatable fare each day, and they would eat it in their cell. There were no sweetmeats for Lucy now; worse still, there were no lovers.

Jemmy often flew into a rage. He was a bold boy and a spoiled one. He demanded that they be set free.

He told the jailor: "One day you will suffer for this. My father will see that you do. I will kill you dead with my sword, and when my father is King again . . ."

The jailor listened in horror. He had not heard such words since the close of the war, and to think that he had under his care the son of Charles Stuart—bastard though he might be—overwhelmed him with astonishment at the importance and responsibility of his task in guarding these prisoners.

The jailor had a son who helped him in his work—a youth in his teens. Lucy's interest was slightly stirred at the sight of him, for he was a good-looking boy; but her attempts to fascinate him were half-hearted; she missed her ribands and laces, her sweetmeats and her comfortable lodgings. She was almost always tired and listless; there was about her an air of bewilderment. She, who had always been so healthy as to be unconscious of her health, was now made uncomfortably aware of many minor ailments.

All the same she made the young man conscious of her fascination, and when his father was not present he would smile shyly at his pretty prisoner and exchange a few words with her. He even brought in some sweetmeats for her, and a blue riband to tie about her hair.

Ann thought: One night I shall doubtless find him sneaking in to lie on the straw with her. Will she sink so low?

But that did not happen, for it was quickly realized that Lucy was no subtle spy. She was merely one of Charles Stuart's mistresses and, said those in authority, if we are going to keep all such women under lock and key, we shall soon have no room in the Tower for others. What harm can this woman do? She is nothing but a stupid, wanton creature. Why should we waste good victuals on Charles Stuart's mistress and his bastards? Send them back whence they came, and warn them not to come to England again.

So it was arranged, and a few months after Lucy's arrival in England she found herself, with Ann and the children, on the way back to Holland.

❁ ❁ ❁

Henrietta Maria and her daughter had once more retired to the country and only made very brief appearances at state functions.

It was clear that the fortunes of the Stuarts were at their lowest. Cromwell, determined to fight the "Lord's battles," had sent his Ironsides to join with Marshall Turenne against the Spaniards who, he declared, were "the underpropper of the Romish Babylon"; which meant that the Protector was fighting with France. How could the royal family of France honor the enemies of their ally, the Protector? All Henrietta Maria and her daughter could do was remain in obscurity, while it was impossible for any of the Stuart men to set foot in France. In desperation Charles, James and Henry joined forces with the Spaniards. Charles had been reported wounded when fighting in Spain, but this rumor had proved to be false. A few months later James and Henry were actually in Dunkirk, which was in the hands of the Spaniards, and was taken after a siege by the French.

During this period Henrietta Maria could do little but lie on her bed and weep bitterly. In vain did Henriette try to comfort her mother. The Queen saw the dissolution of all her high and mighty schemes.

When an invitation came for the Princess to attend the fête given by the Chancellor Seguier, Henriette was loath to go, but her mother insisted.

"My child," she said, "I grow sick and ill, but you must go. What will become of us, I wonder. And, my dearest, whatever has happened, you are still a princess. You have your position to uphold, and the King and Queen will never forget what is due to you; I am sure of that."

But afterwards Henrietta Maria wished with her daughter that Henriette had never gone to the Chancellor's fête, for Mademoiselle was present and she was determined on this occasion to assert her rights.

As the party left the ballroom for the banqueting hall, very deliberately she stepped in front of Henriette.

This was noticed by many, and the next day the whole Court was buzzing with the news. Etiquette was one of the most serious topics of the day—Queen Anne would have it so; and this seemed a matter of major importance.

Mazarin and the Queen called Mademoiselle to their presence and demanded an explanation.

Mademoiselle was haughty. She was sure, she said, that she had the right to enter a room before the Princess of England.

"She is the daughter of a king, Mademoiselle," said Anne sternly.

"Your Majesty, the Kings of Scotland always stood aside for the Kings of France, and Charles Stuart is not even a king of Scotland. He is King in nothing but in name."

"This is most distressing," said the Queen. "I am annoyed with you."

"Your Majesty, I did not wish to make too much of the matter. To tell the truth, I caught her hand as we passed in, and to many it would seem that we walked together."

Philippe, who had been listening while studying the rings on his fingers, cried out suddenly: "And if Mademoiselle did step before the Princess of England, she was perfectly right to do so. Things have come to a fine pass if we are to allow people who depend on us for bread and butter to pass before us. For my part, I think they had better take themselves elsewhere."

Louis, who had been giving only half his attention to the dispute, was startled by his mother's sharp cry of protest.

Louis was not really interested in the question as to which of his cousins stepped aside for the other. Greater matters concerned him. Since Madame de Beauvais had initiated him into the *doux scavoir* he found no pastime to equal it. He would be grateful to Madame de Beauvais for the rest of his days; he would always feel tender towards her, but his desires strayed elsewhere. There were three beautiful nieces of Cardinal Mazarin: Olympia, Marie and Hortense. Louis, who had been violently in love with Olympia—quickly married off to the Count of Soissons—had now transferred his affections to Marie. He was eager to marry her. She was after all the niece of the Cardinal and she bewitched him. Louis could not think very much about his thin little cousin, who was only a child, when his thoughts and feelings were so deeply involved with the fascinating Marie.

All the same, he was sorry for the little Henriette. She and her mother were out of favor now because of foreign affairs, and it was certainly not the fault of the Princess. Philippe was wrong to speak of her so slightingly, for what he had said would surely be carried hither and thither until it reached the ears of the desolate Queen and her little daughter.

So Louis joined his mother in reprimanding Philippe, who slunk off in some annoyance to go and find his favorite de Guiche and tell him what had happened, to complain that Louis and his mother conspired together to humiliate him, and to receive de Guiche's assurance that he was the most charming and clever of princes even though he had had the misfortune to be born two years later than his brother.

Louis went on dreaming of the beauty of Marie Mancini.

Love! What a pastime! What a pleasure! He would not of course wallow in it as did his cousin, Charles of England. Louis must have more dignity; he had so much to remember, so much to live up to. He was no wandering exile. That was why he would try to persuade his mother and the Cardinal to agree to his marriage with Marie. Then he could enjoy legitimate love, which would be so much more gratifying since it would not involve a lack of dignity.

Marie! Beautiful, charming, voluptuous Marie! But if the occasion arose, and he remembered, he would be kind to poor little Henriette.

❁ ❁ ❁

In his bedchamber at Versailles, Louis awoke to a new day. His first thoughts were of Marie. He intended to plead with his mother to allow him to marry her; he would do so this very day, without delay. Marie was urging him. Marie loved him, but she was also very eager to be Queen of France.

Louis' morning in Versailles involved a ritual. As soon as he awoke he said his prayers and rosary in bed, and when his voice was heard, his attendants would come to his bedside; among them would be the Abbé de Péréfixe whose duty it was to read to him from the Scriptures. Sometimes the Abbé substituted a part of the book he was writing—a history of Louis' grandfather.

When the Abbé had finished his reading, the valets, La Porte and Dubois, would come forward; they would put his dressing gown about him and lead him to his commode, on which he made a habit of sitting for half an hour. On rising, he went back to his bedroom where the officials of state would be waiting for him; he would chat with them in that charming and easy way which made them all so delighted to be with him. He continued to chat while he washed his face and hands and rinsed his mouth; then prayers began. After that his beautiful hair was brushed and combed amid expressions of admiration, and he was helped into the light breeches and cambric shirt which he wore for his morning physical exercises. At these he excelled, but on this morning he showed less than his usual skill, so that it was clear to those about him that something was on his mind. He did not land on the seat of the wooden horse with his habitual agility, although the usher, seeing his mood, had taken the precaution of not winding it quite so high as usual. It was the same during the bout of fencing; Louis was not displaying his customary good judgement. Even during the drill with pike and musket he was absentminded. But no one reproached him. Even when he made a fault there came a chorus of admiration. Then followed the ballet dancing to which he usually looked forward with such pleasure. Now he imagined himself to be dancing with Marie; and although he ignored the instructions of Beauchamp, the foremost master of the ballet in the country, he danced with inspiration that morning.

Sweating from the dance, he returned to his chamber, there to change his clothes before eating breakfast.

After that he went to the apartments of Cardinal Mazarin to discuss state matters.

Cardinal Mazarin! He was quite excited to be with him, for the Cardinal had a special importance at this time, being Marie's uncle.

He wondered whether to approach the Cardinal on the matter of his marriage; surely the great man would be on the King's side and would wish to see his niece Queen of France. All the same, Louis did not entirely trust Mazarin, and dared not speak to him until he had laid his plans before his mother.

He went to her as soon as he had left the Cardinal. It was now eleven o'clock and she was still in bed, for Anne never rose early.

Her face lighted at the sight of her son. Each morning it seemed to her that he had grown in beauty; he was like one of those romantic heroes of whom Mademoiselle de Scudéry wrote so entertainingly; and indeed this was not to be wondered at, for all writers of the day saw in Louis the romantic ideal, and no man could be a hero—even in fiction—unless he bore some resemblance to the King.

This was one of the hours of the day which Anne enjoyed most. To lie in bed and receive the filial duties of her beloved boy; to watch him as he gracefully handed her her chemise; to chat with him while she consumed the enormous breakfast which was brought to her bed; these were indeed great pleasures. She almost wished that he were a small boy again, that she might pop titbits into that pretty mouth.

She was glad he was so physically perfect. What did it matter if he were not a bookworm or if, after he left her, he indulged in sports and devoted but an hour or so a day to books?

"I have something to say to you, dear Mama," he said.

"You would wish us to be alone?"

He nodded. She waved her hand, and in a few moments her chamber was deserted.

"Now, my beloved?"

"Madame, it is this: "I am no longer a boy, and it is time I thought of marriage."

"Dearest, that is true. I have thought of your marriage ever since you were in your cradle."

"I have now found one whom I would wish to make Queen of France. I love her, *chère Maman.* I cannot live without Marie."

"Marie?"

"Marie Mancini."

"My son! But you joke!"

"It is not a joke. I love her, I tell you."

"Oh yes, you love her. That is understandable. It is not the first time you have loved. But marriage . . . the marriage of the greatest King in the world, my boy, is not a matter to be undertaken lightly."

"I am not a boy. I am twenty and a man."

"Yes, you are a man, and marry you shall. But you shall have a wife worthy of you."

"I love Marie."

"Then love Marie. She will be honored to become your mistress."

"This is a different love, Mama. Marie is too good, and I love her too deeply . . ."

"Fortunate Marie! Now, my son, there is nothing with which to distress yourself. Have your Marie. She is yours . . . in all ways but that of marriage. Why, you demean yourself, Louis! You . . . the King of France . . . and such a King as never before sat on any throne! Why, none but a royal bride would do for you."

"If I married Marie I should make her royal."

Anne was so distressed she could not do justice to the delicious cutlets which she so enjoyed.

"Dearest, you love Marie, but you have a duty to your country. Think about this, and, with your good sense, you will see that a marriage between you and Marie Mancini is out of the question. You must have a royal bride. I thought you were going to tell me that you wished to marry your cousin Henriette."

"Henriette!" Louis' eyes were wide with distaste.

"Do you not like Henriette?"

"She is but a little girl."

"She is fourteen now . . ."

"She is quiet and oh . . . I think of her as a little girl. I do not like little girls. I wish for a woman . . . a woman like Marie."

"Then we will find you a woman like Marie . . . a royal woman. But if you had wished to marry Henriette, if you had been in love with Henriette, in spite of her brother's exile, we should have been ready to consider the match. For you see, dearest, you are the son of a line of Kings and you must continue that line. Your children must be royal. You understand that, beloved. Henriette is royal. She is a princess, and her grandfather was your own grandfather, great Henri. The people would not be displeased to see you united to his granddaughter, pitiable though the state of her country's affairs may be. But . . . I would not say that was the best marriage you could make. There are other royal houses in Europe which are not in eclipse. If we could make peace with Spain you might marry the daughter of the Spanish King."

In the King's mind, love battled with his sense of duty. He never forgot for a moment the responsibilities of his position. He was fully aware that he must not make a *mésalliance.* He wished to be perfect in all things; he must not fail in this matter.

"But I love Marie," he persisted. "It is Marie whom I wish to marry."

"But, dearest, you will do your duty, I know. And in a little while you will forget Marie. There will be so many women to love you. Believe me, dearest, the one you marry need not necessarily come between you and your pleasures. Give France royal sons; and give as many sons as you wish to others. You will enjoy the begetting, and there is no woman in France who would not be proud to bear the King's sons, even though they be bastards."

"Such behavior seems wrong."

"What is wrong for ordinary men is right for kings. Never forget, my loved one, your brilliant destiny. You are not to be judged as ordinary men. Oh, my beloved, do not turn from your mother because she cannot give you what you want. How willingly would I give my consent if I could! My one wish is to give you all you ask. There! See how I love you! I have been unable to eat my breakfast."

He stooped and kissed his mother's cheek.

"Then you do not blame me, dearest?" she said anxiously.

"I understand, of course," answered Louis. "But, Mama, I cannot marry Henriette. Do not ask that of me."

"Why are you so much against her?"

"I think it is because I am sorry for her. I do not like to be sorry for girls. I like to admire, not to pity. And she is too learned. She spends too much time in study. No! It must not be Henriette."

"How vehement you are against this poor child, Louis. One would think you hated her."

Louis shook his head. He did not understand his feelings for his cousin. He protected her when he could from slights and insults; but he was determined on one thing; he would not marry her.

Sorrowfully he left his mother and went to the riding school, where he forgot his problems temporarily as he galloped round the school, picking up rings on his lance and holding them suspended during the gallop.

He was an expert at such feats, but as the cheering of his attendants filled his ears that day he began to think of what he would tell Marie; yet he found that it was the tall figure of Henriette which troubled his mind.

❁ ❁ ❁

Shortly after that interview with her son, Anne, in panic, invited to the Court of France the Dowager Duchess of Savoy, a daughter of Henri Quatre. The Dowager Duchess had a daughter. This was the Princess Marguerite, a small, dark-skinned girl, very plain, and, knowing the purpose of her visit to the French Court, very nervous.

Louis received her with all the courtesy he could muster, but it was impossible to hide his feelings of distaste. It seemed to him that, the more he saw of other women, the more he was in love with Marie.

"I shall not marry my cousin Marguerite," he told his mother. "I could not entertain the idea."

"You need see very little of her," said Anne. "And you would soon grow accustomed to her."

"Dear Mother, that is not my idea of marriage."

"You will have neither Marguerite nor Henriette then!"

"Neither," he said firmly.

The Cardinal would have liked to see a marriage between his niece and the King, but he realized that such an alliance was inadvisable. He knew that if the royal tradition of the house of France was so flouted, not only the nobility but the people would rise against him. They would blame him, as they were always ready to blame him for France's troubles. He remembered the wars of the Fronde, and the unpopularity he had suffered at that time; and he could see that such a marriage would do him more harm than good.

"Sire," he said, "if you should persist in making this marriage against my advice, I should have no alternative but to give up my office as your minister."

Louis was morose; he felt inadequate to deal with the situation. He thought continually of Henriette, because he knew that if he declared he would marry her, there would be no objection.

He wished that he had studied more assiduously; he wished he was more learned. It was all very well to be able to leap and vault to perfection, to outstrip all others in the hunt. But there was more to life than that. If he had had more book-learning, he might have been able to confute the Cardinal's arguments; he would certainly have been able to state his feelings with more clarity; he realized that well-chosen words were weapons which he had never before appreciated.

His cousin Marguerite returned to Savoy, and the Cardinal decided to send his niece away from Court.

Louis did not protest; he knew that what had been done was right for the King of France, no matter how disappointing it was to Louis the man.

He declared himself heartbroken, and then he found a lady of his mother's bedchamber who comforted him with great skill, and he was soon feeling as grateful to her as he had, during a previous period, been to Madame de Beauvais.

❁ ❁ ❁

Court gossip reached Henriette at Colombes. Her attendants chattered about the King's passion for the Cardinal's niece and the arrival of his cousin Marguerite.

"She was small and plain . . . and Louis would have none of her."

"It would have been such a suitable match," murmured Henriette.

"Ah yes, but he could not find it in his heart to love her. And he is so handsome . . . so romantic . . . so made for love."

Henriette pictured that poor plain Marguerite who had failed to charm the King. She was very sorry for her; she knew how the poor child must have suffered.

Henriette wept silently for Marguerite . . . and for herself.

❁ ❁ ❁

Lucy was tired, but she still walked through the streets of Paris. She was frequently ill now; she knew that she had changed, all in a few short months. She grew breathless at the least effort, and worse, she was suffering from an illness which she knew would not allow her many more months of life.

There were times when her mind wandered a little, when she thought she was back in the past, when men and women whom she had known would seem to walk beside her and talk to her.

Her father was often there. He said: "We shall have to marry that girl quickly." And her mother nodded and understood.

I was born that way, Lucy told herself. 'Twas no fault of mine. It was something which had to be. It was as natural to me as breathing. If I had been born ill favored like poor good Ann Hill, I should have been different. So who should blame such as I? Is it our fault that some of us are born with bodies which demand the satisfaction of physical love with such an intensity that we are not strong enough to deny it? Some have a love of mental exercise, and they become wise and are applauded; others have great skill in the art of war, and they win honors; but those who love—and love is all taking and giving pleasure, for the two go hand in hand—come to this sad end.

She would wander past the new houses in the Place Royale and the Place Dauphine; she did not notice the fruit trees and the flowers which grew in the gardens and nearby meadows. She was looking at the men who passed her by. They scarcely threw her a look nowadays—they who had once sought her so eagerly. She had sauntered through Paris; she had wandered along the north and south banks; she had strolled from the Place de Carrousel to the Porte St. Antoine, from the Porte du Temple to the Porte Marceau, and she found not one man who was ready to be her lover even for an hour.

To this had she sunk.

The roundness had left her face, and her cheeks hung in flabby folds; there were dark shadows under her still beautiful, large brown eyes. Her hair had lost its luster, and she had no money to buy colored ribands with which to adorn it.

Her good health had begun to desert her during her stay in the Tower; but her troubles had been slight then. When she had arrived in Holland she had still been a comely girl. There were lovers in Holland, but it seemed to her that one followed another in too rapid succession; they grew a little less courtly, less of the gentleman.

"I dislike this country," she had declared to the faithful Ann. "I hate the flatness and the wind."

By degrees they had made their way to Paris, going from town to town. Ann worked in some of the big houses, sometimes in gardens, often in the fields. Lucy plied the only trade for which she had any aptitude. And eventually they had come to Paris. But how changed was everything! She had hoped to find the King there, for she heard little news during her wanderings. She thought: He will not desert me. He will want to help me, if only for Jemmy's sake.

But there were rumors in Paris. The King of England never came there now. The French were friendly with his enemies. The Queen of England and the Princess Henriette were rarely seen in the capital; they attended few state functions; they lived in obscurity.

And so here was Lucy in Paris, trying to find lovers who would support her and her children, feeling too old and too ill to struggle any longer.

She sat on the bank and stared at the river.

It would have been better, she thought, if I had stayed in London.

Jenny, the brothel keeper, was right. I should have been better off had I followed her advice, for what is there for such as I when we grow old and ill and are no longer desirable!

She sat dreaming of her lovers. There were two whom she remembered best. The first because he *was* the first: she recalled the copse at twilight, the light in the sky, the shouts of Roundhead soldiers, and the sudden understanding of herself. She would never forget her first lover, and she would never forget Charles Stuart.

"Charles," she murmured, "where are you now? Yes, the most exalted of them all, would be the one above all others to help me now."

She thought of the children. What would become of them when she died?

Panic seized her, for she knew that she must soon die. She had known others who had contracted this disease which now threatened her life. She had seen how death came. It was the result of promiscuous pleasure. It was inevitable, mayhap, when one took lovers indiscriminately.

She must get back to her lodgings—the miserable room in a narrow cobbled street; she must get there quickly and talk to Ann. Ann was a good woman—a practical woman who loved the children. When Lucy died Ann must take them to their fathers and make sure that they were well cared for.

She struggled to her feet, and began to walk away from the river. As she neared that part of the town where she had her lodging, a fishwife, from whom now and then Ann bought scraps, called to her: "Have you heard the news then?"

"What news?"

"You'll be interested . . . since you are English. Cromwell is dead."

"Cromwell . . . dead!"

"Aye! Dead and buried. This will mean changes in your country."

"That may be so," said Lucy in her slow, laborious French, "but I'll not be there to see them."

She mounted the stairs to her garret and lay exhausted on the straw.

"This will mean changes for *him,*" she murmured.

When Ann came in with the children she was still lying there.

Ann's face fell into the lines of anxiety habitual to it now. She had been excited when she came in, and Jemmy was shouting: "Cromwell's dead . . . dead. Cromwell is dead!"

"Yes," said Lucy, "Cromwell is dead. Ann, there is something I want you to do without delay. I want you to leave at once . . . with the children. Find out where the King now holds his Court. Go to him. Tell him what has befallen me."

"We'll all go," said Ann.

"Where shall we go?" demanded Jemmy.

"We are going to the King's Court," Ann told him.

"To the King's Court?" cried Jemmy. He seized his sister's hand and began to dance round the garret. He was so strong and healthy that the life of poverty had scarcely had any effect upon him.

"Ann," said Lucy quietly, "mayhap the King will be going to England now. Who knows? You must find him quickly. You must not rest until you have found him and taken the children to him. He will do what has to be done."

"Yes," said Ann, "he will do what has to be done. Would to God we had never left him."

"Ann . . . leave soon. Leave . . . now."

"And you?"

"I think I can fend for myself."

"I'll not leave you. I'll never leave you."

Lucy heard Jemmy's shouts. "Cromwell is dead. We are going to see the King. You are Cromwell, Mary. I am the King. I kill you. You're dead."

"You have a fever," said Ann to Lucy.

"Leave tomorrow, please, Ann. It is what I wish . . . for the children."

"I'll never leave you," said Ann, and the tears started to run down her cheeks.

Lucy turned away. She said: "It has to end. All things have to end. It was a happy life, and all will be well for Jemmy and Mary. He will see to that. He is a good man, Ann, a good gay man . . . for a gay man can be as good as a somber one."

"There is none to equal him," said Ann.

"No," agreed Lucy. "None to equal him."

She lay still for a long time; and she fancied he was beside her, holding her hand, telling her not to be afraid. Life had been gay and merry; let there be no regrets that it had come to its end.

She whispered as she lay there: "In the morning, Charles, Ann will set out to bring the children to you . . . Jemmy who is yours, and Mary . . . who ought to have been yours. Look after Jemmy and see that Mary is well cared for. You will do it, Charles, because . . . because you are Charles . . . and there is none to equal you. In the morning, Charles . . ."

All night she lay there, her throat hot and parched, her mind wandering.

She fancied she heard the voices of people in the streets; they seemed to shout: "Cromwell is dead! Long live the King! God bless him!"

"God . . . bless . . . him!" murmured Lucy.

And in the morning Ann, with the two children, set out for the King's Court, for poor Lucy no longer had need of her.

SEVEN

It was almost two years since the death of Cromwell, yet the people of England showed no sign of recalling Charles Stuart to his throne, having installed Oliver's son Richard as Protector.

The excitement at the news of Oliver's death had still thrilled the King and his Court, who were then in Brussels, when Ann had arrived with the children.

Charles was silent for a few moments when he heard of Lucy's death. He embraced Jemmy warmly and, when the little girl, Mary, waited with such expectancy, there was nothing he could do but embrace her also.

He laid his hand on Ann Hill's shoulder. "You're a good girl, Ann. Lucy was fortunate in you . . . more fortunate than in some others. Have no fear. We will do our best to see you settled."

Ann fell on her knees before him and kissed his hand; she wept a little, and he turned away because the tears of all women distressed him.

Later he sent for Lord Crofts—a man whom he admired—and said to him: "My lord, you have this day acquired a son. I command you to take him into your household and bring him up as one of your own. I refer to my son James."

Lord Crofts bowed his head.

"I thank you with all my heart," said the King. "I know I cannot leave Jemmy in safer hands. Henceforth it would be better for him to be known as James Crofts."

"I shall obey Your Majesty's commands to the best of my ability," said Lord Crofts.

And so Jemmy was handed over to Lord Crofts to be brought up as a member of his family and to be taught all that a gentleman of high quality should know.

There still remained Mary.

"God's Body!" cried the King. "That child is no responsibility of mine."

He sent for Henry Bennet.

"Your daughter is at Court. What do you propose to do about her?" he demanded.

"Alas, Sire, I know of no such daughter."

"Come," said the King, "she is Lucy's girl. You knew Lucy well, did you not?"

"Even as did Your Majesty."

"I have placed my son in a household where he will be brought up in accordance with his rank. You should do the same for your daughter."

"Ah, the boy is lucky. It is a simple matter for a King to command others to care for his bastard. It is not so simple for a humble knight."

"It should not be a task beyond the strength of such as you, Henry."

"Poor little Mary! They have been brought up together, those two. It is a sad thing that one should have a future of bright promise and the other . . ."

"What do you mean, Henry? They're both bastards."

"But one is known to be the King's bastard. The other, bastard of a humble knight. A King's bastard is equal to any man's son born in wedlock. It is not such a bad fate to be a King's bastard. Poor Mary! And, for all we know, she might have been . . . she might have been . . ."

"She could not have been! I have a good alibi, Henry. I know I am far from impotent, but I am not omnipotent. My children are as the children of other parents. They grow as other children . . . before and after birth."

"Many have thought her to be your child, Sire. You can be sure Jemmy boasted that he had a King for a father."

"Are you suggesting that I should take upon myself the responsibility of fathering the child?"

"Sire, you have had children already, and there will be many more, I doubt not. Can one little girl make such a difference?"

"You're insolent, fellow! You would shift your responsibilities on to me, when it is a King's privilege to shift his responsibilities on to others. Did you not know that?"

" 'Tis so, Sire!" sighed Henry. "Alas, poor Mary! The poppet has set her heart on having a King for a father. Your Majesty has charmed her as you charm all others. She is, after all, a woman."

Charles said: "Oh . . . put the girl with a good family then. Give her a chance such as Jemmy will have."

"In Your Majesty's name, Sire? Mary will bless you all her days. She's Jemmy's sister, remember. You know how you love to please the ladies, and this little lady will be but one more."

"You may get you gone from my presence," said the King with a laugh. "First you steal my mistress when my back is turned; and not content with that you cajole me into fathering your daughter!"

He strode away laughing. He had been enchanted with little Mary; he wished she were in truth his child. But as Henry said: What did one more matter? The children would be well cared for, well nurtured; and Lucy—poor Lucy—could rest in peace.

He had thought at that time that his chances of regaining his throne had improved; alas, he had hoped too soon.

He went to Holland, where, on the strength of his hopes, the Dowager Princess of Holland smiled on his betrothal to Henriette of Orange. She was a charming girl, and Charles found it easy to fall lightly in love with her. But the romance was upset for two reasons: Most important, the Dowager Princess realized that Charles was not to be recalled and would doubtless remain an exile; and secondly, even while courting Henriette he had become involved in a scandal with Beatrix de Cantecroix, a very beautiful and experienced woman who was the mistress of the Duke of Lorraine.

Charles left Holland for Boulogne where he planned to journey to Wales and Cornwall, there to gather an army and fight for his throne.

But his plans were discovered by the enemy, and once again they came to nothing.

He decided then to see Mazarin and ask for France's help in regaining his crown.

Mazarin was already in negotiation for a peace with Spain, and Charles was treated with the utmost coldness.

And so it seemed that, nearly two years after Cromwell's death, his position was as hopeless as it had ever been.

❁ ❁ ❁

The French Court travelled south. In the eyes of Mazarin this journey was very necessary. There had been rioting in some southern towns, and a great deal of dissatisfaction had followed the arrest of certain men, some of whom had been hanged, others sent to the galleys.

Mazarin believed that a sight of the handsome King, together with his most gracious and benign manners, would rouse new feelings of loyalty in rebellious Frenchmen.

But that was not the only reason why the Cardinal so favored this tour.

He was considering a peace treaty with Spain, and his experience had always taught him that the best cement for securing peace was a marriage between the members of the two countries concerned.

Philip IV of Spain had a daughter—Marie Thérèse—and she would be a fitting bride for Louis.

Louis knew of this, and realized the importance of such a match. For two years there had been war between France and Spain; and unless real peace could be made between the two countries, doubtless ere long there would be war again. Marriage was one of a King's first duties, providing it was the right kind of marriage; and Louis was ever conscious of his duty.

When Marie Mancini had been sent away from the Court he had turned to her elder sister Olympia who had married the Count of Soissons.

He was soon deep in romantic love again, and gave balls in honor of the lady when he was not gambling in her house until three in the morning.

The Queen and Mazarin watched this friendship. "There is nothing to fear," said Anne to the Cardinal. "She is married, and he is safe with her. It is the romantic attachments to unmarried ladies which bother me. My Louis is so noble; he loves like a boy of sixteen still."

The Cardinal nodded; he was eager to reach the Pyrenean frontier.

Philippe was pleased because his favorite, the Comte de Guiche, travelled with the royal party.

The Comte was an extremely handsome young man with bold dark eyes and a dashing manner; Philippe had admired him from his earliest days and had commanded that the Comte should be his special companion. De Guiche was clever, witty and very sure of himself. Moreover, being a married man, he seemed knowledgeable in the eyes of Philippe. The young Comte had married—most reluctantly—when he was very young indeed, a child who was heiress to the great house of Sully; he had never had the slightest affection for his young wife, avoided her as much as possible, and was content to be the *bel ami* of the King's brother.

He was of the noblest family—that of the de Gramonts. His father was the Maréchal who enjoyed the affection as well as the respect of the royal family. The young Comte had grace of person; he excelled in social activities such as the ballet, which Louis had made so popular; he knew exactly how to please Philippe, and Philippe declared that he simply could not *exist* without his dear friend.

De Guiche had quickly discovered that one of Philippe's chief wishes was to be told that he was in reality as attractive as Louis. It was clear to the sly young Comte that Philippe had suffered much through his proximity to his royal brother. Louis was tall; Philippe was short. Louis was handsome in a masculine mold; Philippe was almost pretty in a girlish way; he had beautiful dark eyes, long lashed; he was graceful, almost dainty, and he accentuated his good points by means of jewels and cosmetics. Philippe must be constantly assured that he, in his way, was as attractive as Louis, and de Guiche's task was to assure him of this without saying anything which could be construed as disrespectful to the King. This was not easy, and there were occasions when de Guiche grew bold in his confidences with the young Prince.

As they journeyed through Marseilles—that turbulent town which had been more rebellious than most—and the people looked on their young King, those who had been ready to condemn the royal house experienced a quick change of mind. How could they do anything but express their love and loyalty to this handsome Apollo who rode among them, bowing and smiling, telling them that he was their "Papa Louis," that he was their King who loved them?

Philippe, watching his brother's triumph, scowled. The people did not cheer him as they did Louis; they did not admire him as they did the King. He fancied some of them tittered at his appearance. That was intolerable.

De Guiche knew that his royal friend was in special need of comfort and he wondered how best to give this.

It was a few evenings later, when they had rested at one of the châteaux on their road, that the two walked together in the grounds, and Philippe had his arm about de Guiche's shoulders.

"This journey is not so much in order to soothe these people by Louis' magnificent presence," said Philippe with a touch of anger as he referred to his brother, "as that there may be conferences between the ministers of Spain and our own."

"Monsieur is right as usual," said de Guiche. "It is Louis' marriage which is under consideration."

"I wonder if he will like Marie-Thérèse."

"I have heard rumors that she is very small and far from well favored," said de Guiche, to please his master.

Philippe laughed. "He'll not like that. He likes big plump women—matrons—with some experience to help him along."

De Guiche joined in Philippe's laughter, and Philippe went on: "Louis is the most innocent King that ever sat upon the throne of France."

"He has not Monsieur's quick mind," said de Guiche. "That has kept him innocent."

"You flatter, dearest Comte."

"It is no flattery. Is it not clear? See how he worships Madame de Soissons. She clearly loves the King because he is the King. And Monsieur de Soissons is so blind because his wife's lover is the King. But Louis thinks it is pure good chance that Soissons should not be in her apartment when he visits her. Louis is so romantic!"

Mayhap he will not feel so romantic when he is married to Marie-Thérèse. She is very thin; she is very plain. Why are all the girls whom princes may marry, thin and plain? Marguerite; Henriette; and now Marie-Thérèse.

"Henriette?" said de Guiche sharply.

"My cousin . . . the Princess of England."

"She is thin, yes," said de Guiche slowly; "but she has a charm."

"A charm! But she is so very thin . . . nothing but a bag of bones! And so quiet."

"There are some who are quiet because their discourse would be too profound to interest most of those who are at hand to hear it."

"But . . . Henriette . . . profound!"

"She has a quality," said de Guiche. "It is as yet hidden. She is not fifteen, your little cousin. Wait, Monsieur . . . ah, wait!"

"This is amusing. I think you but seek to make me laugh, dear Comte."

"No. I speak with great seriousness. She is a child yet, but she is clever. There is one thing: I have seen a certain sparkle in her eyes. She is sad because her life is sad. She has always lived in exile . . . like a plant in the shade. Ah, if the sun would shine on her! If she could let loose her natural gaiety! But she cannot. She is plagued all the time. She is an exile . . . a beggar at Court. Mademoiselle de Montpensier continually seeks to take precedence. Henriette's brothers wander the Continent; she never knows when they will meet their death. She is humiliated at every turn and, being so clever—so full of imagination—she is sensitive; so she remains in her corner, quiet and pale, and to those who have not the eyes to see, so plain. Do not underestimate Henriette, Monsieur. Your brother is not insensible to her charm."

"Louis!"

"Ah, Louis knows it not yet. Louis sees her as you do. Poor plain little cousin. 'Nothing but bones,' he said, and he thinks of his plump matrons. But Louis is romantic. He is a boy in heart and mind. You, Monsieur—forgive me; this sounds like treason, but between ourselves, eh?—you are so much cleverer than the King. You see more clearly. I'll wager this: One day Louis will not be insensible to the charms of little Henriette. Let her brother regain his throne; let her come out of her corner; let her dazzle us with *her* beautiful clothes, her jewels. Then we shall see her beauty shine. Do you remember that, in the ballets, it is she who often says: 'Wear this . . . it will so become you.' And how often is she right! Have you seen her, animated in the ballet, playing a part? Then she forgets she is the exiled Princess, the little beggar girl who may be snubbed at any moment. The true Henriette peeps out for a while to look at us; and, by the saints, there you have the most charming lady of the Court!"

"You speak with fervor, de Guiche. Are you in love with my cousin?"

"I? What good would that do me? I do not love women, as you well know. They married me too young, and so I lost any taste I might have had for them. I was merely telling you that the King is not insensible to the charms of his cousin."

"But he has refused to marry her; you know that."

"Yes. And she knows it. It has made her quieter than ever in his presence. But you have noticed the softness in the King's eyes when he speaks of her? Poor Henriette! he says to himself. He is sorry for her. He does not understand. He gambols with his plump matrons. He is like a child learning love . . . for he is far younger than his brother. He has spent his time in youthful sports; he is a boy yet. He has now acquired a certain taste for love, but at the moment he likes the sweet and simple flavors. Wait . . . wait until he demands something more subtle."

"Then you think . . ."

"He will one day greatly regret that he turned away from the Princess Henriette."

"I cannot believe that, Comte."

But Philippe was thoughtful; and his mind was filled with memories of Henriette.

❁ ❁ ❁

During the journey of the French Court to the Spanish border, Henrietta Maria and her daughter remained in Paris. Charles took advantage of the absence of the Court to visit his sister.

He came riding to Colombes where they were residing at that time. Unceremoniously he found his sister, and Henriette, giving a little cry of joy, ran into his arms.

She was laughing and crying, looking eagerly into his face, noting the changes, the fresh lines about the eyes and mouth which did not detract from his charm.

"Charles! Charles!" she cried. "What magic have you? That which makes others ugly merely adds to your charm."

"I was born ugly," said the King. "Those who love me, love me in spite of my face. Therefore they are apt to find something to love in my ill-favored countenance and they call it charm . . . to please me."

"Dearest brother, will you stay long?"

"Never long in one place, sister. I merely pay a flying visit while the coast is clear."

"It is wonderful to see you. Mam will be delighted."

Charles grimaced. "We are not the best of friends, remember. She cannot forgive me for taking Henry's side against her, and for not being a Papist. I cannot forgive her for the way she treated the boy."

"You must forgive her. There must not be these quarrels."

"It was to see you I came."

"But you will see her while you are here. To please me, Charles?"

"Dearest, can it please you to displease us both?"

"You would go away happier if you mended your quarrels with Mam.

Charles, she is most unhappy. She grieves continually. She thinks still of our father."

"She nurses her grief. She nourishes it. She tends it with care. I am not surprised that it flourishes."

"Try to understand her, Charles. Try . . . because I ask it."

"Thus you make it impossible for me to refuse."

So he did his best to mend the quarrel between himself and his mother. He could not love her; he could not tolerate cruelty, and when he remembered Henry's sorrow he was still shocked. But they did not discuss his brother, and he was able to spend many superficially pleasant hours in his mother's company.

It was not long after his arrival at Colombes that he betrayed to Henriette a secret excitement.

"I will tell you, sister," he said, "because if this should fail—as most projects have failed—I should not mind your knowing. Have you ever heard of General George Monk?"

"No, Charles."

"He was one of Cromwell's supporters, but I do not think my lord Protector ever entirely trusted him. I have heard that once when George Monk was in Scotland, Oliver wrote to him: ' 'Tis said there is a cunning fellow called George Monk who lies in wait to serve Charles Stuart. Pray use your diligence to take him and send him to me.' You see, Oliver was not without some humor."

"You speak as though you could even forgive Oliver."

"Forgive Oliver!" Charles laughed. "I thank God I shall never be asked to. He has passed beyond my forgiveness. I was never very skilled in judging and affixing blame. It is a matter of great relief to me that the judging of Oliver has passed into other hands. But more of Monk. He married his washerwoman—Mistress Anne Clarges; she must have a strong will as well as a strong arm for the tub, to induce the General to marry her. And do you know, Minette, Anne Clarges gives her support to me. She has a taste, not only for Generals, it seems, but for Kings; and I doubt not that she has urged her lord to favor me, with the same urgency as she once pressed him into marriage."

"Do you mean, Charles, that there is a General in England who would be ready to help you regain your kingdom?"

"I do, Minette. Aye, and do not speak of him as *a* General. He is the foremost General. He is a man who served the Protector well, but who, since the death of Oliver, has become disgusted with the Parliamentarians' rule. He has come to the conclusion that kings are slightly more attractive than protectors."

"What is happening? What is General Monk doing?"

"He has drunk in the presence of others to 'His Black Boy.' That is his name for me. He is reputed to have said that he is tired of the bickering in high places and that, if he had an opportunity of doing so, he would serve me with his life."

"Oh, Charles! If only it would come true!"

"If only, Minette! There have been so many 'if onlys' in my life. The sign of many failures, alas!"

"I shall hope and pray that Your Majesty soon comes to his kingdom. I shall pray that all health and happiness may attend Your Majesty."

"Come, come, do not treat me with so much ceremony. There should not be so many 'Your Majesty's between us two; there should be nothing but affection."

She clung to him, her eyes shining. Surely there must be some good fortune waiting for him at last! Surely the exile must soon be restored to his kingdom!

❁ ❁ ❁

Mademoiselle de Montpensier was faintly alarmed.

She had lost all hope of the exalted marriage for which she had longed. It was now common knowledge that Louis was to marry Marie-Thérèse, the daughter of the King of Spain. Negotiations were going ahead. Louis was reconciled to the fact that as a king he must do his duty. It would not be many months before the marriage would take place.

So I shall never be Queen of France! thought Mademoiselle.

There were other offers for her hand. She was still a granddaughter of France if not a daughter, she reminded herself, and she was the richest heiress in the world. A grand marriage was still possible for her. She was fascinated by Charles Stuart, but she certainly would not marry a roaming exile, and she had no wish to leave France. France was her home, and to have lived for years at the Court of France was to know that other Courts could never satisfy. No! Mademoiselle knew definitely what she wanted. She wanted to remain in France, and she wanted to make a brilliant marriage. There was only one other man worthy of her, in her opinion, now that she could not have Louis. A second best it was true, but it would still be a royal marriage—Philippe.

She and Philippe were good friends. They had been brought up together. She was thirteen years older than he was, but that was not an insurmountable difficulty. She had bullied him in childhood because it was Mademoiselle's habit to bully, but Philippe had accepted her domineering ways and even admired her for them. In the recent dispute over the right of precedence, Philippe had immediately placed himself on her side and demanded to know why people who depended on them for their bread should walk before them.

Mademoiselle was certain that she only had to make her wishes known to Philippe and he would be eager for their marriage.

It was strange how serving women seemed to know more of what was going on at Court than their masters and mistresses.

It was Clotilde, her maid, who first made her aware of the mistake she might be making concerning Philippe.

As she combed Mademoiselle's hair, she said: "Do you think Monsieur is serious in his attentions to the English Princess, Mademoiselle?"

"What is this? Monsieur . . . serious?"

"Oh yes, Mademoiselle. He is paying court to the Princess, it is said. He rides over to Colombes very often and . . . he is continually at the Palais-Royal."

"This is nonsense."

"It is, Mademoiselle?" Clotilde was silent. None dared contradict Mademoiselle.

"Well?" said Mademoiselle impatiently. "What else have you heard?"

Clotilde wished she had not spoken. She stammered: "Oh, 'twas a rumor, I dare swear, Your Highness. It is said that he is enamored of the Princess Henriette and is spending much time with her."

Mademoiselle's face was scarlet with mortification. She did not believe it. She would not believe it.

But she was uneasy.

Later, in the ballroom, when she was dancing with the King, she could not refrain from mentioning the matter to him. "Your Majesty is setting the fashion for marriage, I hear. Is it true?"

Louis raised his eyebrows. "Is what true?"

"Philippe, Your Majesty. I hear rumors. I wondered if they were true. I have heard that he has become enamored of that little bag of bones, Henriette."

Louis smiled. "Have you then? I doubt not that he will get her. Our aunt has tried in vain for the Grand Duke of Tuscany and the Duke of Savoy. They'll have none of our poor Henriette. I am sorry for that girl. A hard life she has had. If Philippe wants to marry her he is sure to do so . . . for no one else will have her, I fear."

"But . . . Your Majesty has heard these rumors?"

"Philippe has been thoughtful of late, and that is a sign of love. He rides often to Colombes, I hear; and Henriette is at Colombes."

"Your Majesty would give your consent to such a marriage?"

Louis hesitated. He would do nothing, Mademoiselle knew, without the agreement of his mother and Mazarin. Louis, for all his magnificence, was a boy in the hands of those two. He now said uncertainly: "I would her brother could regain his kingdom. If so . . . it would be an excellent match . . . an excellent match."

"There is little chance of that. And would Your Majesty allow your brother—Monsieur of France—to marry with the sister of an exile?"

"It would be hard to refuse," said Louis. "If they were really in love . . . I should find it hard to refuse."

Mademoiselle wished she could have slapped the sympathetic smile from the handsome face. It was all she could do to prevent herself doing so.

She was enraged. It would be intolerable if she lost not only Louis but Philippe.

❁ ❁ ❁

All Paris was *en fête.*

This was an occasion beloved by all, for on this hot August day the King was bringing his bride to the capital.

It might have been said that this year, 1660, was one when the stars of kings shone brightly.

Across the water there had been another great day—an even greater one for England than this was for France.

In London, a few weeks before, the streets had been decked with flowers and tapestries, fountains had run with wine, the citizens had shouted derisive farewells to the old *régime*; the life of pleasure and revelry was back, and there should be, all declared, more merriment than there had ever been before. The Black Boy was back; the Merry Monarch had returned; and his restoration was due to the will of his people—all except a few miserable Puritans.

Such rejoicing there had been that Charles, while he yet reveled in it, while he rejoiced to be home again and to be received with such wild enthusiasm, had stroked his lined face and remarked with a slightly cynical smile that it must have been his own fault he had not returned before, since every man and woman he met now assured him with tears and protestations of loyalty that they had always wished for the King's restoration.

So the exile was an exile no longer. He was back in Whitehall, full of gaiety and charm, delighting all who saw him—from the highest nobleman to the lowest fishwife.

The King had come home.

And what a difference the restoration made to his family abroad! No longer were Henrietta Maria and her daughter poor, exiled beggars depending on the hospitality of their relations. They were the mother and sister of the reigning King of England.

Now they sat beneath the canopy of crimson velvet on the balcony outside the Hotel de Beauvais, one on either side of Queen Anne. From other windows watched the ladies of the Court. Cardinal Mazarin also was at a window.

The procession passed along the streets—the gilded coaches; the mules with their silver bells; the magistrates in their red gowns; the musketeers in blue velvet with silver crosses; the company of light-horse in scarlet; the heralds carrying emblems the grand equerry who held aloft the royal sword with its scabbard of blue velvet and golden fleurs-de-lis. But all the brilliant color was eclipsed by the glory of Louis himself. Looking more handsome than even he had ever looked before, he rode his bay horse under a canopy of brocade. His face was benign as he moved forward, and the people roared in expression of their love and loyalty. Here was a King who was indeed a King. He was dressed in silver lace decorated with pearls and pink ribbons; his hat was kept on his head by means of an enormous diamond brooch, and the magnificent white plumes fell over his shoulders.

Behind him rode Philippe in a costume of silver embroidery; and behind Philippe came the Princes of the royal houses led by Condé.

Then came the bride—little Marie-Thérèse—in her coach, which was covered with gold lace. She was dressed in gold-colored cloth and was ablaze with jewels, so that eyes were dazzled as they looked at her. In those gorgeous garments, framed by the gold of her coach, she seemed like a fairy princess to the people of Paris; they cheered and exclaimed at her beauty.

Following her coach, Mademoiselle de Montpensier led the Princesses of France. Mademoiselle was trying to smile and to hide her bitter resentment. *She* should have been the Queen in that gilded coach. This should have been *her* day of triumph. She could smile—a little spitefully—to think of Marie-Thérèse, stripped of her finery. That was how Louis would have to know her, a silly little girl without that charm and wisdom which was an accomplishment acquired by those brought up in the Court of France.

A grand marriage with Spain! Let Louis enjoy it if he could.

Now the King had reached the royal balcony in which sat the two Queens and the Princess Henriette. Louis drew up his horse that he might salute the Queens and the Princess.

Henriette, her eyes dazzled with his beauty, suddenly understood her feelings for this man. She had grown up in that instant. She, a girl of sixteen, knew that she loved this man of twenty-two. Now she understood why she had wept so often after she had been in his company, why she had been hurt by his pity. It was not pity she had wanted from him.

Charles was now King of England; if he had been King of England last year . . . But Louis had never loved her; Louis would never have married her. But did he love little Marie-Thérèse?

Louis was looking into her eyes now. He saw the tears there and a faint flicker of surprise crossed his face. Why were there tears? he wondered. She had little to weep about now. Her brother was restored to the throne and it was very likely that Philippe would marry her; and what a suitable match this would be between the brother of the King of France and the sister of the King of England!

How pretty she was! He had never seen her dressed in such a grand fashion. He could realize now why Philippe was falling in love with her. Her beauty was not obvious as was that of Madame de Soissons . . . and others; but she had a certain charm, that little Henriette.

Louis was no longer sorry for her, and his pity had been replaced by another emotion which he did not fully understand, and as he rode on to receive the ceremonial congratulations of the Parliament on his marriage, it was not of Marie-Thérèse he was thinking, but of Henriette.

❁ ❁ ❁

Philippe was giving a ball at Saint-Cloud. He was pleased with himself. Saint-Cloud was a beautiful mansion, which Louis had recently brought from Harvard, his Controller of Finances, and presented to his brother. Moreover, Philippe's uncle Gaston had died that year, and on his death the duchies of Orléans, Valois and Chartres as well as Villers-Cotterets and Montargis, had fallen to Philippe.

He was young and handsome; he was rich; he was the brother of the King; it was his lot to be courted and flattered. Had he but been born a few years earlier, he would have been completely content.

But he was smiling to himself as, with his special friends about him, he was preparing himself for the ball. His valets loudly proclaimed that they had never served a more handsome master; some of his friends—far bolder—whispered to him that there was no one, simply no one, to equal him in beauty. They did not admire those pink-and-gold men who excelled at vaulting and the like; they preferred the subtler kind of masculine beauty—agility of mind, rather than body.

Philippe laughed. It was pleasant to be assured that not everyone found Louis more charming than his brother.

His head on one side, he criticized the set of his dalmatica. Was the sapphire brooch quite right? Would his dear Monsieur de Guiche decide whether ruby ornaments would be better? He thought after all that he would wear more emeralds.

Tonight was important. He would open the ball by leading the Princess Henriette out to dance. Henriette! He looked slyly at de Guiche. De Guiche was the cleverest man he knew. He saw further than did ordinary men. Henriette was charming. He realized that now. Occasionally he would be treated to those quick flashes of wit; he would see the sudden sparkle in her eyes. The restoration of her brother had acted as a tonic. She was no longer the plain little sit-in-a-corner. She had been too sensitive of her position; that was all that had been wrong with little Henriette.

And when he compared her with Marie-Thérèse he could laugh aloud. Marie-Thérèse might be the daughter of the King of Spain, but Henriette was the daughter of a King of England and now sister to the reigning King. There was no difference between the two girls in rank; but there were other differences. And what delight Philippe would enjoy when Louis became aware of the charms of Henriette!

"Come!" he said. "It is time I was greeting my guests. Do not forget that this is *my* ball. Tonight I am the host to His Majesty my brother, to his Queen and . . . the Princess Henriette."

❁ ❁ ❁

Henrietta Maria was in a flutter of excitement. She dismissed all their attendants and was alone with her daughter.

"My dearest," she said, "what joy is this! Sometimes I find it difficult to assure myself that I am not dreaming. Can this be true? Your brother has regained his crown! Oh, would I had been there to see him riding through the streets of London. What joy! If only his father had been there to see him proclaimed their King!"

"Then it would not have been Charles who was their King, Mam. Oh, I beg of you do not weep. This is too happy a time."

"Tears of joy, dearest daughter. Tears of joy. I must go to Chaillot and thank God and the saints for this happiness which has come to me. And, dearest, I wish to go to England. Charles wishes us to go. He wants us all to be together for a little while at least. It is his wish. It is his *command*—as we must say now."

"Oh, Mam! To go to London. That would be wonderful."

"To be received in London as a Queen, and to remember how I fled from England all those years ago!"

"Mam . . . I beg of you, look forward, not back."

"Yes, I must look forward. Dearest, you are the sister of a King who is indeed a King. You know that there has been talk of your marriage?"

"Yes," said Henriette, and her eyes as well as her voice were expressionless.

"It fills me with pleasure. It is a wonderful match. Few could be better."

"Philippe . . ." said Henriette slowly.

"Yes, dearest Philippe. The little playmate of your childhood. Oh, how happy you will be! Think, dearest. You will spend the rest of your life here . . . in great honor. You will be 'Madame' of the Court. You do not realize the extent of your good fortune. Your face tells me that. Do you know that there is no Court in the world to equal that of France . . . for elegance, for culture, for luxury? I can think of none other at which I would care to live except . . ."

"Except at home . . . at Charles' Court," said Henriette.

"Foolish child! How could you live at your brother's Court unless you remain unmarried? That you surely would not wish to do."

"Mam, I think I should like to live my life as Charles' sister."

"Holy Mother of God! What nonsense you talk! You should love your brother, it is true, but verily I believe you and he would carry to excess this affection you bear each other. Charles himself is delighted with the prospect of your marriage. I have heard from him on this matter."

"What . . . said he?"

Henrietta Maria came closer to her daughter. "He says he knows that if you marry Monsieur he will always have a friend at the French Court, one who will never forget the interests of England—and the interests of England are Charles' interests. He says it will be as though his other self is at the Court of France while he is in England. He says he will always love a country of which his dear sister is the Madame. He says he sees peace between France and England through a union which he would rather have for you than any."

"So he says all that?"

"He does indeed. And he is right. What an opportune moment this is! What glory! Why, had they kept him out of his kingdom another ten years, what would have become of us? What sort of a marriage would you have been able to make? Philippe is the most desirable *parti* in France. There is only one I would have rather seen you marry. And, mark you, if your brother had regained his kingdom a little earlier, who knows . . ."

"Mam . . . Mam . . . please do not speak of that."

"Why not, foolish one? We are alone. Moreover it is clear to any who give the matter a thought. Everyone knows that, while it is a good thing to be the wife of the King's brother, it would have been more desirable to have been the King's."

Henriette turned away.

Her mother must not see that she was too emotional to speak. How could she explain to Henrietta Maria that she longed to be Queen of

France, not for the glory of that title, not for the honors she would enjoy, but because as Queen of France she would also have been Louis' wife.

❁ ❁ ❁

Louis was conscious of his brother and Henriette. They were an attractive pair, he murmured to his wife.

She did not understand, of course. Her knowledge of the French language was limited.

He was smiling at everyone in his usual friendly manner; he accepted the congratulations on his marriage; he showed the utmost deference to his bride, and he would not admit, even to himself, that he was miserably disappointed in her. Louis was not given to frequent analyses of his feelings. Marie-Thérèse was his wife; she was the daughter of the King of Spain; his marriage was highly desirable. Mazarin considered that he had achieved a diplomatic feat of great importance to France by bringing it about; his mother had assured him that one of her dearest wishes was fulfilled. Louis must be pleased with his bride.

But how rigid was Spanish etiquette! And what a scrap of a thing was Marie-Thérèse, divested of her robes of state—small and brown and, it must be admitted, far from beautiful. Louis, who had enjoyed the luscious charms of more desirable and desiring ladies in his pursuit of the *doux scavoir,* could find little to attract him in his politically admirable match.

Marie-Thérèse never put ceremony aside, even in the bedchamber. During the day she seemed to wish to do nothing but eat, play cards and go to church. She was very greedy. In spite of her rigid adherence to etiquette, her table manners disgusted him. He would see those little black eyes watching the food; and when her own plate was filled she would still have her eyes on some favorite morsel in the dish, terrified lest someone else should be given it before she could announce her preference for it. There was another thing which was worrying Louis; shy and reluctant as she had been during the first night of their nuptials, she was fast overcoming her shyness and with it her reluctance. Often he would find her eyes fixed on him as though he were a dainty morsel in the dish.

She was going to fall in love with him and, as she did so, he was going to find her more and more repulsive.

But at present Louis would not admit this.

The Spanish marriage had been a good thing for France; therefore it was an admirable marriage. And the next marriage in the family should be between England and France. Two brilliant marriages—and so good for the state policy of Mazarin.

Philippe . . . and Henriette!

She had changed since her brother had regained his throne, and Louis was glad of it. She was less shy. Silly little Henriette, to have cared so deeply because of the humiliation she had suffered! He remembered the occasion when he had not wished to dance with her; he now reproached himself bitterly for that crude behavior.

Dancing in her blue gown, which was decorated with pearls, she was a charming sight. Philippe looked handsome too—and how ardent he was! Philippe ardent . . . and for a woman! It seemed incredible, but it was true.

He glanced at his bride. She looked well enough in her cloth of silver and multicolored jewels. He tried not to gaze in Henriette's direction; but his mother, sitting beside him, had noticed his interest in his cousin.

"Philippe and Henriette!" she said. "What a good match!"

"The best Philippe could make," replied the King.

"So he can be sure of Your Majesty's consent?"

Mazarin and his mother had already given it, Louis knew; but he kept up the pretence that he himself made all the decisions affecting the policy of France.

"I see no reason why such a marriage, so advantageous to France, should not take place."

"Philippe was afraid he might not have your consent," said Anne.

"He need not have been," snapped Louis, and his sudden rush of anger astonished him. "He'll get Henriette. Why, no one else would have her."

"That was before her brother's triumphant return. She is a more desirable *partie* now, my beloved."

"She . . . she has changed in more than her status."

"It has made a great difference to her and her mother, and I rejoice to see it. I never thought Henriette so charming before. She seems almost beautiful; and she is so frail, with such a look of innocence. Quite charming. Philippe is eager for the marriage, and it is small wonder."

Louis said in a mood of unaccustomed ill-temper: "Philippe should not worry. He shall marry the bones of the Holy Innocents."

Anne looked at him in amazement, but he was smiling fondly at Marie-Thérèse.

❁ ❁ ❁

Mademoiselle was furious.

The King was married; Philippe was to marry Henriette, and she had always thought that, if she lose Louis, Philippe would be hers for the taking.

What had come over her young cousin? This passion for Henriette had sprung up so suddenly. It was only a little while ago that he was taking sides against her.

Mademoiselle was no longer young. She was past the time for marriage. If she were not the granddaughter of France and its richest heiress she would be alarmed.

She must marry, and her marriage must be one which would not bring shame to her proud spirit.

There was one marriage which would please her more than any—except perhaps with Louis. Yet when she compared the two marriages she thought she would prefer the one still open to her. She would have wished to be Queen of France beyond anything, she supposed, because France was her native land and the Court well known to her; it would have been completely satisfying to spend the rest of her days in France. But to be the Queen of England—married to that fascinating rake, Charles Stuart—would be an exciting adventure.

Had she known he was to come into his kingdom, she would have married him ere this. But it was not yet too late, for he was still unmarried.

She went to his mother and, after kissing her hand, asked permission to sit beside her. Henrietta Maria graciously gave that permission.

No longer an exile! thought Mademoiselle. She is almost condescending to me now. I shall have to let these Stuarts know that I consider it my privilege to walk before their daughter, for the girl is not yet Madame of France.

Henrietta Maria's fond eyes were on Henriette now.

"A triumphant day for your daughter, Madame," said Mademoiselle. "I rejoice to see her so happy."

"Is she happy? She does not seem entirely so. Do you think she is as eager for this marriage as . . . others?"

"She will be. She is but a child. Philippe is eager . . . very eager." Henrietta Maria stole a malicious look at her niece. "He is as eager to marry her as others are to marry him."

"Let us hope she will be happy."

"Who could fail to be happy in such a match, Mademoiselle?"

"There will be matches in plenty in your family now, I doubt not."

"I doubt not," said Henrietta Maria. "My son, the King, will not hesitate now."

"She will be a happy woman whom he chooses."

"There was a time, Mademoiselle, when you did not consider his wife would ever be in such a happy position."

"Nor would she have been had he remained in exile."

"He will remember the days of his exile, I doubt not. He will remember his friends of those days . . . and those who were not so friendly."

"Here at the French Court there have always been many to offer him sympathy and friendship."

"He owes much to his sister Mary."

"A charming princess. She reminded me of Charles."

"So you found Charles charming then?"

"Who does not?"

"Many did not during the days of his exile. But I doubt not that the charm of a king—to some—is more obvious than that of a wandering beggar."

Mademoiselle was growing angrier. Was the Queen suggesting she was too late? Had she forgotten the vast fortune which Mademoiselle would bring to her husband! She had heard that the King of England still suffered from a lack of money.

Henrietta Maria was remembering it. She wondered what Charles would feel about marrying this woman. She must curb her impetuosity; it would not do to offend one who might become her daughter-in-law.

She turned her gaze on Henriette, and was soothed. *There* was one who was to make the best marriage possible—since Louis was married.

Mademoiselle followed her aunt's gaze, and her anger was turned to something like panic.

Too late for Louis; too late for Philippe. Could it be that she was too late for Charles?

❁ ❁ ❁

Henriette and her mother were ready to leave France on their journey to England. Henriette was longing to see her brother; but she was bewildered. Too much had happened to her in too short a time. The step from girlhood to womanhood had been too sudden. The thought of marriage alarmed her although as a princess she had been prepared for it, and she had been long aware that love played little part in the marriages of royal persons.

She liked Philippe; she continually told herself that. There had been one or two quarrels when they were children, but was not that inevitable? He had not always been kind to her; but he had been only a boy, and all that would be changed now that he was in love with her. She could not doubt his love; he made it so evident. His eyes scarcely left her and he was obviously proud of her. It was touching to see the way in which he looked at his brother as though he were comparing Henriette with Marie-Thérèse, to the disadvantage of the Queen. How ridiculous of Philippe! And yet she found it to be rather charming and very pleasant, after all the humiliations she had received, to be so loved by such an important person.

She would not wonder whether Louis was happy in his marriage; she would not think of Louis. Happily she was going to England and there it might be possible to talk with Charles, to tell him all that was in her mind and ask his advice.

She sought her mother, but when she reached the Queen's apartments she found Henrietta Maria lying on her bed, weeping bitterly.

"What is wrong?" cried Henriette in great alarm. Her thoughts had gone at once to Charles. Had he lost the kingdom he had so recently regained?

"Leave me with the Queen," said Henriette, and the women obeyed.

The Princess knelt by the bed and looked into her mother's face. The small dark eyes were almost hidden behind their swollen lids, but Henriette knew at once that her mother's grief was caused more by anger than sorrow.

"Can you guess what is happening in England?" she demanded.

"Tell me quickly, Mam. I cannot endure the suspense."

"There is danger of that woman's being received at Court."

"What woman?"

"That harlot . . . Anne Hyde!"

"You mean . . . Anne . . . Clarendon's daughter?"

"Yes, I do mean that rogue's daughter. That fool James has married her. Your brother has dared . . . without my consent . . . without the consent of his brother, the King, to marry her in secret!"

"He . . . he loves her."

"Loves her! She has tricked him, as she would well know how to do. He married her just in time to allow her bastard to be born in wedlock. And he . . . poor simpleton . . . poor fool . . . acknowledged the child to be his."

"Mam, it may well be that the child *is* his."

"My son . . . to marry with a low-born harlot!"

"Marriage with James will make her Duchess of York, Mam."

"If you try to soothe me I shall box your ears! I'll not be soothed. Thank God we can go to England to prevent further disaster. Can you believe what I have heard! Your brother Charles is inclined to be lenient over the affair and will receive the woman at Court as James' wife!"

"Yes," said Henriette, "I can believe it. It is what he would do."

"Charles is soft. There will always be rogues to get the better of him."

"No, Mam. He is kind. He says: 'They love each other; they are married; they have a child. So . . . let us all be merry together!' "

"For the love of the Virgin, daughter, let me not hear such nonsense from you. I thank the saints that we shall soon be in England and that I may be able to stop this folly."

"Mam, if Charles wishes to receive James' wife at his Court . . ."

"He must be made to see his folly. Does he want to lose that which he has just gained?"

Henriette shook her head sadly. How could she say to her mother: Nay. It was you with your bad temper, with your insistence on having your way, who lost your crown. Charles' kindness will make him popular with the people.

One did not say such things to Henrietta Maria. One let her rave and rant, and if one were like Charles, one avoided her as much as possible.

How regrettable this was! It seemed as though the visit to England would be spoiled. There would be trouble with James; and Henriette had been wondering what would happen when her mother and her brother Henry met again.

"Ah, it is high time I was at your brother's Court," continued Henrietta Maria. "I have had this news from your sister Mary. She and I see eye to eye in this. She is incensed that that Hyde girl . . . *her* maid of honor . . . should have dared marry your brother. She blames herself. She remembers that she brought the girl with her when she visited us. She remembers that it was in her retinue that your brother first set eyes upon her. She knew they were meeting; but she—considering the girl's lack of rank—thought her to be but the mistress of a few weeks. But to marry the girl . . . to legitimize her bastard!"

"Please, Mam, do not speak of them. Let us wait and see what Charles has to say. It is his Court after all. He will finally decide what has to be done."

Henrietta Maria's eyes narrowed. "He was never one to listen to his mother's advice."

"Mam," said Henriette, "I have been thinking of my brother Henry."

Henrietta Maria's face grew darker still. "You may consider you have a brother of that name. I have no son called Henry."

"But, Mam, you cannot at such a time continue to turn your face from him."

"I swore that I would not look at his face again while he persisted in his heresy. I have no reason to believe that he has discarded it."

"Please, Mam . . . he is but a boy. He swore to our father the day before he died, that he would not change his religion. You *must* receive him. You *must* love him. You must remember that he is young and eager for the love of his family . . . and in particular he would wish his mother to love him."

"Then he knows what to do."

"He was separated from you for so long. He looked forward so eagerly to be with you and then . . ."

"You make me angry, Henriette. I do not want to be disappointed in *all* my children. Would you have me break my vow?"

"Would you have him break his vow to his father? God would forgive you, Mam, if you broke your vow in order to make him happy."

"You horrify me, daughter. Have my nuns of Chaillot . . . have Père Cyprien and the Abbé Montague not taught you better than that?"

"Are we not told by God to love one another?"

"You think strange thoughts, child. Listen to me. I have sworn I will never look on Henry's face until he changes his religion. I shall keep my word."

Henriette turned away. Was the stay in England going to be so happy after all?

She need not have worried about the future of her brother Henry. They were on their journey to Calais when a message concerning him was brought to them.

Henry, Duke of Gloucester, had died the day before. He had been ill with the smallpox and had seemed to take the sickness lightly, so that all had hoped for a speedy recovery. He had been in the care of the King's doctors, who did all they could for him; he had been profusely bled and assiduously attended; but in spite of their efforts—or perhaps because of them—his illness had ended in death.

Henriette went to her mother, who was staring blankly, before her.

This is terrible for her, thought Henriette, for she will be unable to forget the last time she saw Henry.

She threw herself into her mother's arms and they mingled their bitter tears.

"Mam, you must not grieve," cried Henriette. "What you did you did for your Faith. You believed you were right, and perhaps we cannot be blamed for doing what we believe to be right."

Henrietta Maria did not seem to hear her. "So . . ." she said slowly, "I have lost my son. My daughter Elizabeth . . . my son Henry . . . They are both lost to me, and they both died heretics."

Then she burst into bitter weeping, moaning that she was indeed *La Reine Malheureuse.*

It may be, thought Henriette, that her regrets will make her lenient with James.

But this was not so. Henrietta Maria could not regret that she would never now have an opportunity of breaking her vow; she saw her action as the right one, the only one a good Catholic could take. All human emotions were subdued in her quest for converts. Now she wept, not because her son had died, but because he had died a heretic.

❁ ❁ ❁

James met them at Calais with a squadron of ships—the first outward sign of the glories which awaited them. Henriette anxiously watched her mother's greeting with her son, but it was formal and affectionate. The Queen had no quarrel with James; providing he would repudiate Anne Hyde she was ready enough to forgive him.

James was a good seaman, but in spite of his prowess they spent two days in crossing the Straits on account of the calm; and when they arrived at Dover, Charles, with a brilliant retinue, was waiting to receive them.

Henriette looked into his face and saw the difference which the restoration of his kingdom had made to him. He was jauntier than ever; but the cynicism with which the years of exile had endowed him would be with him forever; he was very affectionate with his dearest Minette, warning her that, even as a King returned to his throne, he would not tolerate too many "Your Majesty"s from her.

To his mother he was graciously polite and showed all that affection which was demanded of him. The people, who had gathered to watch the royal meeting, were a little cool in their reception of Henrietta Maria; the population of Dover was largely composed of Puritans and Quakers, and they looked with distrust on the King's Catholic mother; but the young Princess they thought charming, and they cheered her loudly, much to the delight of Charles.

"You see how my people wish to please me in all things," he whispered to her. "It seems they know that their appreciation of you pleases me far more than that which they have for any other."

He led his mother and sister into Dover Castle, where a great banquet was prepared for them. Charles placed his mother on one side of him, his sister on the other.

"This gives me great happiness," he whispered to Henriette. "Soon Mary will join us and then we shall all be together."

Later Henriette expressed the wish that Henry could have been with them.

"If he were here," said Charles, "we should have Mam turning her back on him."

"How did he die, Charles?" she asked. "Was he heartbroken? Did he long to speak to Mam before he died?"

"I was with him, Minette. I persuaded him not to grieve. You see, I am a profane man, and I said to him: 'If you side with Mam, you break your word to our father; if you do not break your word you are banished from our mother's favor. Side with yourself, brother. Do nothing that can offend yourself, and then, surely, in God's eyes, you have taken the right side.' "

"You are a good man, Charles—the best in the world."

"You joke, Minette. I am the world's biggest rake—or one of them. I doubt whether there is a man living who could compete with me. Now were my grandfather alive . . ."

"You are the world's kindest man, and it seems to me that kindness is one of the greatest virtues."

"If I am kind it is due to my laziness. That can scarcely be called a virtue. Nay, I beg of you, sister, do not see me as a better man than I am, for one day there may be disillusionment. Love me for my faults; for that is the only way in which a man such as I may be loved."

"What of James' trouble?"

"Trouble? James is in love, and his wife loves him. Can that be called trouble?"

"Mam will make trouble of it."

Charles groaned.

"She always hated Chancellor Hyde," went on Henriette. "She says if his daughter enters Whitehall by one door, she will leave by another."

"Poor Mam!" said Charles. "So she is bent on making trouble. Does she never learn? Have the years of exile taught her nothing then?"

It seemed not, for while they were at Dover—in that Puritan stronghold—she insisted that High Mass be celebrated in the great hall by Père Cyprien de Gamaches, whom she had brought with her.

Charles was in a dilemma. To forbid it would mean trouble; to allow it would be to offend the people.

Henrietta Maria, that diminutive virago, opposed to the Puritans of Dover! He smiled wryly. He feared his mother more, and hoped that in the excitement of the royal visit, in the pageantry so new to them after the years of Puritan rule, the people would overlook his mother's tactlessness. So he decided that it would be wiser to risk offending the people of Dover than to cross his mother, who must somehow be reconciled to James' marriage.

❁ ❁ ❁

In spite of the death of Henry, which cast a shadow over her pleasure, in spite of the apprehensive fears of the marriage which lay before her, this period seemed to Henriette the happiest of her life. In the grand entertainments which her brother had prepared for her she endeavored to forget the past and shut out thoughts of the future.

She discovered that she was like Charles; she could banish unpleasantness from her mind. She was very sorry for the Duchess of York, whose father was keeping her a prisoner in his house because the King's mother had been so furiously enraged every time her name was mentioned. But she was able to forget her in the joy she found in her brother's company.

Mary, the Princess of Orange, had arrived in England, and there were special balls and fêtes to honor her. She was almost as fierce in her denunciation of Anne Hyde as Henrietta Maria was; and Charles, although his sympathies lay with his brother, was too lazy to enter into long arguments with his strong-minded mother and sister. It was easier to shelve for a while the matter of the Duchess's banishment and give himself and his family the pleasure he had always promised this reunion should bring them.

Scandal spread about the Court concerning the Duchess. She was a harlot, it was said; the Duke was not the father of her child; it seemed there was nothing too bad that could be said of the Duchess. Henriette shuddered; but she did not know that there was scandalous gossip concerning herself and Charles. She had no idea that sly gossips were asking each other: "What is the nature of this affection between the King and his sister? Is it not a little too fond to be natural?"

There would always be scandals where there were Stuarts to provoke them.

If the King knew of these rumors he did nothing to refute them. He was too lazy for one thing, too wise for another. He often said that one could not alter people's thoughts, and to protest too strongly was often construed as evidence of guilt.

Henriette was fast passing out of childhood. One of those who hastened her steps in that direction was George Villiers, Duke of Buckingham. Almost as profligate as the King, he declared his infatuation for the young Princess and did all in his power to seduce her. He was sixteen years her senior, well versed in the art of seduction—having had plenty of practice—as cynical as his master, though lacking his lazy tolerance. Buckingham immediately recognized in the Princess that which had attracted de Guiche and so guided the attention of Philippe towards her.

She was not plump like most Court beauties, who looked so much alike, who were ready with the catchwords of the moment; she was ethereal, dainty and slender; her laughter was gay yet innocent; her wit was growing sharp. All the Stuart charm, which had been latent, was suddenly apparent. She danced with enthusiasm; she was as gay as any; she had grown vivacious and amusing. This was a new Henriette.

"By God's Body!" declared Buckingham. "She is incomparable, this little Princess. Having seen her, I find it difficult to see perfection in other women."

But all his practiced gallantry, all his polished charm, failed to move Henriette. She saw him as a rake and a libertine; Charles was as bad, she knew; but Charles was her beloved brother, and nothing she discovered about him could alter her love for him. But she was not ready to fall in love with a pale shadow of her brother. In love she demanded different qualities. There was one who possessed all that she would demand in a lover. He must be good to look upon, but he must be of high integrity; he need not be supremely witty, but he must be good-natured and kind at heart. She had met such a one, but she must not think of him, for he was not for her.

So she amused herself by listening to Buckingham's protestations of affection, flirting with him while making it perfectly clear that his desires concerning her would never be fulfilled.

" 'Od's Fish!" said her brother in high amusement. "You are leading poor old George Villiers a merry dance."

"Then it will do him much good to dance, as he has doubtless made others dance."

"I am sorry for poor George."

"I am sorry for his wife."

"I doubt not that Mary Fairfax can look after herself."

"To think it is only three years since she married him! How sad she must be to see him pursuing other women!"

"Three years!" cried Charles. "It is an eternity . . . in marriage."

"Would you not ask for three years' fidelity in a wife?"

"Dear Minette, I would not cry for the moon!"

"You are all very cynical here, and you, Charles, set the pace."

"That may well be. But don't fret for Fairfax's daughter. She was promised to Chesterfield, you know, and after the banns were published she eloped with Buckingham. We might say 'Poor Chesterfield!' There were those to say it once. Nay! Do not waste pity on others in this game of love, Minette. Only take care that there is none to say 'Poor Henriette!' "

"Charles, I am reminded that I must marry soon."

"It is a good match, Minette. There is none I would rather see you marry, now that you cannot have Louis."

"I am unsure."

"We are all unsure at such times, dearest."

"I cannot understand why Philippe so suddenly should want to marry me."

"You are very attractive, Minette, as well as being the sister of a King—one who has now a throne. You are a worthy match for Philippe, as he is for you."

"I wish I could love Philippe."

"Some would say 'That will come.' But we do not allow fictions to exist between us, do we, Minette? No. You should not think of love in conjunction with husbands. I do not, in connection with wives."

"You are being cynical again, Charles."

"There are some who turn from the truth when it is not pleasant and call it cynicism. Do not let us be of their number, Minette. Face the truth and you will find that if you study it well you may discover that there is some part of it which is not as unpleasant as you thought it."

"Must I marry Philippe, Charles?"

"It would be unwise not to."

"But could I not wait awhile? I am young yet."

"Mademoiselle de Montpensier told herself she was young yet, and now she is . . . not so young."

"She would give much to marry you now, Charles."

"And you see she comes too late. Do not follow Mademoiselle in that, Minette. Marry Philippe. We shall not be far apart then. We shall visit each other often. It is the best marriage you could make."

"Is it what you wish?"

"I dearly wish it."

"Then I will marry Philippe."

"And I will give you a handsome dowry—40,000 jacobuses and 20,000 pounds, that you may not be a beggar when you come to your husband. I wish all the world to know that, though I am the most inconstant man in the world, there is one to whom I am constant forever—my sweet Minette."

"Thank you, Charles. But, I pray you, let us talk no more of my marriage. Let us be gay and happy while we are together."

So she danced and was happy; she forgot Henry; she forgot the Duchess of York; she forgot that soon she must return to France where she must marry one royal brother while she loved the other.

❁ ❁ ❁

The King insisted that his mother and sister should not leave England until after the Christmas festivities. Christmas was celebrated with more gusto in England than in any other country, and this year's celebrations promised to be more exciting than ever, for under the rule of the Protector such revelries had been considered a sin. All Englishmen were going to make England merry once more; they were determined on it, and during that December there was high excitement in the streets of the capital.

The Princess Mary had thrown herself into the preparations with enthusiasm. There were to be ballets and masques.

"We must not fail Charles," she said to Henriette, "for he wishes his Court to rival that of Louis. We can help him achieve this, I am sure, although the English do not dance with the grace of the French."

Henriette agreed. She began feverishly planning the ballet. There would not be Louis to dance so gracefully, to enchant the spectators with his commanding presence; but she fancied they could give the English Court something it had never seen before.

As she and Mary sat together talking of the costumes they would wear, and the dances they would arrange, the verses which would have to be compiled, Mary said suddenly: "You look sad, sister."

And Henriette said in a rush of confidence: "It is this talk of the ballet. It reminds me of others. It reminds me that soon I must go back to France, and that . . ."

"Is it your marriage of which your are apprehensive?"

"Yes, Mary."

"We all are when our time comes. Our marriages are arranged for us, and we have nothing to do but obey. Oh, Henriette, you are more fortunate than many. At least you will not go to a stranger."

"Mary, sometimes I think that Philippe is almost a stranger."

"But you have known him from childhood."

"Yes. But it seems I knew a different Philippe."

"It is because he seemed then but a boy to you, and now he is the man who is to be your husband. I remember my own marriage. I was very young, but in time I came to love my husband."

Henriette turned to look at her sister. "It is such a comfort to have a family," she said. "I often think what a wonderful life ours might have been if everything had gone well for our father, and we had all been brought up together . . . Charles, James, you, Elizabeth, Henry and myself. I never knew Elizabeth. I saw very little of Henry . . . and now they are both dead."

"The rest of us must be good friends . . . always," declared Mary.

"And be happy together," said Henriette. "James is not very happy now, is he, Mary?"

Mary had put her hand to her head. She said: "I feel too tired to talk further, sister. I think I should like to rest awhile."

Henriette felt saddened, suspecting Mary was making excuses. Mary was as obstinate as their mother, over the affair of Anne Hyde.

Mary stood up. She swayed slightly and it occurred to Henriette that she really was feeling ill, so she helped her sister to bed and told her attendants that their mistress wished to rest.

"You have had too much excitement, Mary," she said. "You'll feel better in the morning."

But in the morning Mary was not better; and the news spread through Whitehall. The Princess of Orange was smitten with the smallpox, that dreaded disease which, so recently, had carried off her brother.

❁ ❁ ❁

Henrietta Maria was beside herself with anxiety. Henry dead. Mary ill. Smallpox in the Palace. Frantically she commanded her daughter to prepare to leave at once.

"Who will nurse Mary?" asked Henriette.

"Not you! You are to leave Whitehall at once. That is the King's command. I shall send you to St. James Palace, and there you must remain."

The King himself joined them. His face was grave. He took Henriette into his arms and kissed her solemnly.

"It is as if there is a blight on our family," he said. "First Henry . . . now Mary. Minette, I want you to leave Whitehall at once."

"I think Mary would wish to have some of her family about her."

"Mary is too ill to recognize her family, and you, my dearest, shall certainly not come within range of contagion."

"You are to leave at once," commanded Henrietta Maria. "I have arranged for you to leave in twenty minutes."

"And you, Mam," said the King, "must go with her."

"My place is at my daughter's bedside, Charles."

"Your daughter is sick. This is not the time for your conversions."

"A sickbed, Charles, is the place for conversions."

"Mary is very weak. She has been bled many times. Several of my doctors are with her. She is in no state to listen to your religious advice."

Henrietta Maria looked sternly at her son, but she knew him well enough to recognize the obstinate line of his mouth. Here was the little boy who had refused to take his physic. He was slack; he was easygoing; but suddenly he could make up his mind to stand firm, and then none could be firmer.

For a few seconds they glared at each other, and she gave way.

He was too good-hearted to make his victory obvious. He said: "Stay and look after Henriette, Mam. We should never forgive ourselves if aught happened to her."

"It may be you are right," agreed the Queen.

And she was thinking: Later, when Mary is a little better, I will talk to her; I will make her see the truth.

She left with Henriette and in the Palace of St. James eagerly they awaited the news.

It came. The Princess of Orange was improving. The doctors believed that the bleeding had proved efficacious.

Henrietta Maria made her youngest daughter kneel with her.

"Let us thank the Blessed Virgin and the saints for this recovery. It is a miracle that she is now on the road to good health. My prayers have been answered. I said: 'Holy Mother, I cannot lose two children . . . and so soon. I cannot lose them both in so short a time, and both to die heretics.' And, Henriette my child, my prayers have been answered. 'Give me my Mary's life,' I said, 'and I will give you her soul!' When she is well enough . . . a little later on, I will go to her and tell her that her life has been saved through prayer, and that she owes her soul to God."

Henriette, kneeling with her mother, was not listening to the Queen's words. The tears ran slowly down her cheeks.

"Thank God," she murmured. "Thank God we have not lost Mary too!"

❁ ❁ ❁

The King was at Mary's bedside. She had asked for a cordial that she might have the strength to receive the sacrament.

Charles could not keep back his tears. He knew that Mary was dying.

Only yesterday they had believed her condition to be improved, but they realized now that they had been too quick to hope.

"Charles," said Mary. "Are you there, Charles?"

"I am here, Mary."

"You should not be. It is dangerous."

"I am a tough fellow, Mary."

"Oh, Charles . . . my favorite brother . . ."

"Don't talk," he said. "Keep your strength to fight for your life."

"It is too late. The fight is over. You are weeping, Charles. Pray do not. We are an unlucky lot, we Stuarts. We don't live long, do we? Elizabeth, Henry, and now Mary. Only three left now. Three and poor Mam. Father went . . . long ago."

"Mary, I beg of you, save your breath."

"I'm not afraid of death, Charles. I regret dying only because of my boy. Charles, be a father to him."

"I will, to the best of my ability."

"My little Dutch William. He is a solemn boy."

"Have no fear. All shall go well with him."

She lay breathless on her pillows. Her glazed eyes looked up at him. "Charles . . . Charles . . . you should not be here. And you the King!"

"I have seen so little of you, Mary. I cannot leave you now."

"There will not be long for us to be together. I was cruel to James' wife, Charles."

"Do not think of that now."

"I cannot help it. I wish so much that I had been kind. She was my maid of honor. She was a good girl and I . . . in my pride, Charles . . ."

"I know. I know. You thought no one good enough for royal Stuarts."

"You are fond of her father, Charles."

"Aye! A good friend he has been. I am fond of his daughter too."

"You will have her recognized. Charles . . . you will make our mother understand how I feel now. Any day her time may come too. Don't let her feel as I do now. It is a terrible thing to have wronged someone and to come to your deathbed without setting that wrong right."

"I'll set it right, Mary. Think no more of it. I shall speak to Mam. I'll set that matter right. And Anne Hyde shall know that at the end you were her friend."

"Thank you, Charles. Thank you, my favorite brother."

He could not bear to look at her. He dashed the tears from his cheeks. They were giving her the sacrament, and she took it eagerly.

Afterwards she lay back on her pillows and quietly she died.

❁ ❁ ❁

That Christmas at Whitehall was a sad one, and arrangements were made for the return to France of Henrietta Maria and her daughter, for Philippe was urgently requesting that his marriage should be delayed no longer.

The King sought his mother in private audience soon after Mary's death; his face was stern, and Henrietta Maria was quick to notice the lines of obstinacy about his mouth.

"Mam," he said without preliminary ceremony. "I have come to ask you to accept James' wife as your daughter-in-law."

The Queen set her lips firmly together. "That is something I find it hard to do."

"Nevertheless you will do it," said the King.

She looked at him, remembering the stubborn boy who had taken his wooden billet to bed and refused to part with it, not with tears of rage, as most children might have done, but with that solemn determination which made him hold the piece of wood firmly in his small hands and look at those who would take it from him as though he was reminding them that he would be their King one day. He was looking at her like that when he said: "Nevertheless you will do it." She remembered that he had settled her yearly allowance and that she depended upon him for much. She knew that she would have to give way.

He was ready, as ever, not to humiliate her unduly. He did not want acknowledgment of his triumph. He merely wanted peace in his family. He said: "The rumors concerning poor Anne have been proved to be false. James loves her. They have a child whom I have proclaimed heir-presumptive to the crown. There remains one thing; *you* must receive her."

Henrietta Maria still did not speak.

"In view of all that has gone before," Charles continued, "it will be necessary for you to make public recognition of her. We are too unlucky a family not to be happy when we can be together. Fate deals us enough blows without our dealing them to each other. Mary realized that. On her deathbed she wept bitterly for the hurt she had done Anne Hyde. There will be a farewell audience at Whitehall before you leave, and during it James shall bring his wife to you. You will receive her, and do so graciously. I would have it seem that there has never been ill feeling between you."

Henrietta Maria bowed her head; she was defeated.

But she knew how to accept defeat graciously—in public at least, and when Anne Hyde was brought to her, she took her into her arms and kissed her warmly, so that it was as though there had never been aught amiss between them.

❁ ❁ ❁

The next day they left for France. As their ship tossed on the stormy seas, Henriette grew frightened—not of the death which the roaring winds and the angry waves seemed to promise, but of marriage with the Philippe who had become a stranger to her.

The visit to England had been a connecting bridge between childhood and womanhood. She had known it, and she was afraid of what was waiting for her.

Tossing in her cabin, she felt that her body was covered in sweat as she lay there, and suddenly it seemed to her that she was not in a boat at all. It seemed that she was flitting from one scene to another, and always beside her were the two brothers, Louis and Philippe. Philippe was embracing her, laughing slyly at her because she had believed he loved her; and Louis was turning away from her, looking with eager eyes at Madame de Soissons, Madame de Beauvais, Olympia and Marie Mancini—and dozens of others, all beautiful, all voluptuous. He was turning away from her, refusing to dance, and she was afraid because Philippe was waiting to seize her.

"Charles!" she cried. "Charles, save me, and let me stay with you."

Charles was somewhere near, but she could not see him, and her cries for help could not reach him.

Her mother was calling to her. "Henriette, my dearest. They have turned the ship. Thank God we have come safely in. You had a nightmare. We are back in England now. The Captain dared not continue the journey. My child, are you ill?"

Henriette closed her eyes and was only vaguely aware of being carried ashore. For fourteen days she lay at Portsmouth close to death.

❁ ❁ ❁

But she did not die. She refused to be bled as her brother and sister had been, and her malady proved not to be the fatal smallpox but only measles.

As she grew well she seemed to come to terms with life. She must marry. All royal persons must marry, and Philippe was a good match. The real Philippe was quite unlike the creature of her nightmare.

As soon as she was well enough to travel, they crossed the sea on a calm day, and on the way to Paris they were met by a royal party, at the head of which rode Philippe.

Henriette was received in Louis' welcoming embrace without betraying her feelings. She knew that her visit to England had not changed her love for him; growing up had but strengthened that.

She overheard him mention to his mother that poor Henriette was thinner than ever.

To her he said: "Now that you are in Paris, we shall soon have you strong, Henriette. We have some royal entertainments ready for you. I have a new ballet which I myself prepared for your return. Would you like to know the title?"

He was like a boy, she thought—youthful, eager to be appreciated, hoping that on which he had spent so much pains, would give her the enjoyment he had intended it should.

"Your Majesty is gracious to me," she told him with tears in her eyes.

"Well, you will be my sister in a few short weeks. It is fitting that I should welcome my sister on her return. The ballet is about lovers who have been separated too long and yearn for reunion. I have called it *L'Impatience des Amoureuxl.*"

"I am sure it will be very entertaining," said Henriette.

And the King was satisfied.

❁ ❁ ❁

The dispensation had arrived from the Pope; the wedding was arranged; but there was a postponement because of the death of Mazarin. Louis and his mother insisted on two weeks' Court mourning, during which time it was impossible for a Court wedding to take place. Buckingham, who had accompanied the Princess and her mother from England, was too obvious in his attentions to Henriette, and Philippe showed his jealousy. The Court was amused; so was Louis. It was amazing to see Philippe in love with a woman, and that woman his future wife.

Philippe insisted on Buckingham's being recalled to England, and Charles complied with his request. And all the time Henriette seemed to be in a dream, hoping that something would happen again to postpone the wedding.

But this time all went smoothly, and at the end of March the contracts were signed at the Louvre, and later that day at the Palais-Royal the betrothal took place before the King and Queens Anne and Henrietta Maria. All the nobility of France was present and, although owing to the recent deaths of the bride's brother and sister and the bereavement the royal family of France had suffered in the loss of Cardinal Mazarin, there were no balls and pageants such as were usually given to celebrate a royal wedding, the country showed itself delighted with the union, for all felt sure that it would bring peace between England and France, and moreover, the little Princess with her romantic story had always been a favorite in the land. La Fontaine wrote verses in which he told the story of her escape from England and the years of exile which had culminated in this brilliant marriage.

Charles was delighted; so was Louis. Philippe seemed completely happy; only the bride was filled with foreboding.

❁ ❁ ❁

So she was married. She was no longer the Princesse d'Angleterre, a shy young girl to be ignored and humiliated; she was Madame of the French Court and, after the little Queen Marie-Thérèse and Anne, the Queen Mother, she was the most important lady of France.

Terror had seized her when it was necessary for her to leave her mother and go with Philippe to the Tuileries.

He had been tender and by no means a demanding lover. She believed she had to be grateful to Philippe. He was kind during those weeks of the honeymoon; he had begged her not to be afraid of him. Did he not love her?

She reminded herself that all royal princes and princesses must face marriage. It was a duty they were called upon to perform. If there were love in their marriages they were indeed fortunate; it did not happen to many.

Philippe, she sometimes thought, was more in love with himself than with her. He liked her to admire his clothes and jewels. She believed it would not be difficult to live with Philippe. He was not very much older than she was, and she began to think she had been childish to feel so fearful.

Sometimes she would find his eyes upon her—alert, watchful, as though he were searching for something, as though he found her fascinating in a way he could not understand.

Once he said: "My lovely Henriette, you are charming. But yours is a beauty which is not apparent to all. They must look for it. They must seek it out. And then they find how very charming it is, because it is so different, so enchanting that the voluptuous beauties of the Court seem merely fat and vulgar when compared with you."

She said: "You are fond of me, Philippe, and thus you see perfection where others see what is imperfect."

He smiled secretly and after a while he said: "Now that all these perfections are mine, I should like others to see them and envy me my possessions."

She grew gay during those days of her honeymoon. She felt she had made an important discovery. There was nothing to fear from Philippe; he was kind and not excessive in his demands for a love she could not give him. It was as though, like herself, he accepted their intimacy for the sake of the children they must beget. She was no longer to suffer humiliation. He talked of the entertainments they would give as Monsieur and Madame of France; and she found herself waiting eagerly to begin the round of gaiety he was proposing.

"You were meant to be gay, Henriette," he told her. "You have suffered through living in the shade. Now that the sun will shine upon you, you will open like a flower. You will see; others will see." He went on, "We should not stay here in solitude too long. We must not forget that we are Monsieur and Madame, and there is one whom we must entertain before all others. I refer, of course, to my brother. Let us plan a grand ball and decide on whom we shall invite. The list will not include the Queen. Poor Marie-Thérèse! Her condition is just what the country would wish it to be, but I'll swear she looks plainer than ever. We'll have to provide another lady for Louis. That should not be difficult. Who shall it be? Madame de Soissons? Perhaps . . . But enough of Louis. This is your first appearance as Madame, and I wish it to be remembered by all who see it. Your gown . . . what shall it be? The color of parchment, I think. That will show your dark eyes. And there shall be slashes of scarlet on it . . . again for the sake of your *beaux yeux.* And in your hair there shall be jewels. Remember, Henriette, you are no longer an exile. You are Madame . . . Madame of the Court, the first lady of the ball; for my mother will not come, nor will yours; and poor little Marie-Thérèse must lie abed nursing the heir of France within her!"

"Philippe, I have rarely seen you so excited."

"I think of your triumph. How proud I shall be! Henriette, make me proud. Make all men envy me."

She laughed and threw herself gleefully into the preparations. There should be a dazzling ballet for the King's enjoyment. She and Philippe would dance together. Their first entertainment for the King should surpass all that had gone before.

She was gay. She wrote verses; she practiced the singing of them; she practiced the dance; her gown would be the most becoming she had ever possessed. For life had taken a new turn, and she was going to assume that gaiety which was her birthright and which had lain slumbering too long.

Philippe watched her, smiling, clapping his hands, kissing her lightly.

"All men will envy me this night!" he declared. "*All* men!"

❁ ❁ ❁

Animated, and vivacious as none had seen her before, she greeted Louis on his arrival, gracefully curtsying as he extended his hand for her to kiss.

He had said good night to his wife before he had left for the Tuileries; and he had thought how plain and sallow she was.

She was lying back in bed playing cards with her women, her greedy eyes turned from the dish of sweetmeats which were on the bed. She looked at him as though he were one of the sweetmeats, the biggest and the most succulent; and he had felt sick and angry because the daughter of the King of Spain did not look like Madame de Soissons.

Now Henriette stood before him. Such radiance! Such beauty! He had never before seen her thus. All his pity for his poor little cousin was swept aside and there remained feelings which he did not understand.

He said: "It shall be my privilege to open the ball with you, cousin . . . nay, you are my sister now."

He took Henriette's hand.

She thought how handsome he was, and she was momentarily wretched because it was his brother and not himself who was her husband. But now he was looking at her as he had never looked before, when the violins began to play and the dancers fell in behind them.

"You have changed," said Louis.

"Is that so, Your Majesty?"

"Marriage has changed you."

"Your Majesty knew me for a long time as the sister of an exiled King. Now Your Majesty sees me as the sister of a reigning King and . . . your brother's wife."

"Henriette," he whispered, "I'm glad you are my sister."

Her eyes filled with sudden tears, and he saw them.

Then suddenly understanding came to him. So many women had loved him; here was another.

He was silent as they continued the dance, but she was no longer silent. She was beautiful and vivacious tonight, and she knew that this was the beginning of a new life for her. She knew that all in the vast room watched her and marveled at the change in her. She could almost hear their voices, see the question on their lips: Is this little Henriette, the quiet little Princess who was so shy, so thin, so ready to hide herself in a corner? Has marriage done this? So all that charm and gaiety was hidden beneath those quiet looks!

Louis was enchanted. He did not notice Madame de Soissons. He could not bring himself to leave Henriette's side; and she felt recklessness sweep over her. She had been unhappy so long because he had failed to find her attractive.

Now she was happy; she could live in the moment. At last Louis had looked at her and found the sight a pleasing one.

He said to her: "Now that the Queen is indisposed, there is much you can do to help me. We shall need a lady to lead the Court. My mother has felt the Cardinal's death sorely, my wife is indisposed . . ."

"I shall do my best to prove a good substitute," she murmured.

"Substitute!" said Louis. "Oh . . . Henriette!"

"Your Majesty finds me changed. Have I changed so much? I am still thin."

"You are as slender as a willow wand."

"Still the bones of the Holy Innocents! Do you remember?"

"You shame me," cried Louis. "I am thinking what a fool I was. Henriette, what a blind, stupid fool!"

"Your Majesty . . ."

"I think of what might have been mine, and what is. I might have been in Philippe's place. I might . . ."

She broke in: "Your Majesty, what would I not have given to see you look at me thus a year ago!"

"So you . . ."

"Do you doubt that any who look upon you could fail to love you?"

"What can we do?" said the King. "What a tragedy is this! You and I . . . and to know this . . . too late!"

She said: "We are princes, and we have our duty. But that will not prevent our being friends. It is enough for me to be near you and see you often."

"Yes, often. It shall be so. Henriette . . . you are the most perfect being of my Court, and you are . . . Philippe's wife!"

So they were together and Madame was gay that night.

This is the happiest time of my life, she told herself.

Philippe watched his wife and his brother with immense satisfaction, for at last he had that which Louis coveted. Here was his revenge for all the boyhood slights.

Louis wanted Henriette, and Henriette was Philippe's wife.

EIGHT

Henriette began to be happy as she had never been happy before.

Louis loved her; he sought every opportunity of being with her. She was to reign over the Court with him; he reproached himself a hundred times a day because he might have married her, but had been a blind fool; he realized that he had never been indifferent to her, that those stirrings of pity which she had aroused in him had, in fact, been true love. He saw himself as a simpleton, a man who had never thought for himself because there had been others to think for him, a man who had never explored his own mind, because there were so many to tell him he was perfect, more god than man. He had never been given to self-analysis. Why should he? He had been told he was perfect. He had been taught to vault and ride, to show off his physical perfections rather than to study and use his brains.

He saw himself for the first time as a man who had been duped by his own simplicity. Beside him, loving him, had been the perfect companion, and he had failed to see in her more than a sad little cousin, worthy of his pity.

If Henriette had changed, so had Louis. He was no longer the puppet King. Mazarin was dead, and he intended to be the true King of France. He had grown up through the realization of his love for Henriette; he was a simple boy no longer; he was a man who would also be a King.

Now he began to show his mother that she could no longer lead him. He, Louis, would decide.

He seemed to increase his stature. He was at least three inches taller than most men at Court, but he seemed more than that in his high heels and his wig of stiff frizzed hair which rose straight up from his brow adorned with the broad-brimmed plumed hat. He was a magnificent figure, the leader of the Court, as he had never been before.

In those weeks it was enough for Louis—as it was for Henriette—to know themselves loved by the loved one. Their relationship seemed to them the more perfect because, as they saw it at this time, it could never reach its natural climax. It was romantic love which seemed to gain beauty from the fact that it could not reach that climax and therefore would go on forever at the same high level. Both Louis and Henriette were too well-versed in the etiquette of the Court to believe that Henriette could ever be his mistress—not only because of their marriage vows, but because of the close relationship which Henriette's marriage with Philippe had brought about.

Fontainebleau made a perfect setting for their romance. There in the gilded salons, Louis whispered to Henriette that he loved her; he told her the same thing as they wandered through the gardens. He enjoyed establishing an unceremonious rule at his beloved Fontainebleau, at this time his favorite palace. He would be there with Henriette, the Queen of his intimate Court; he would walk among his friends, joining their games of billiards and piquet when the fancy took him. Always Henriette was beside him, his hand resting lightly on her arm, his candid eyes alight with affection; they would discuss together the rebuilding of Versailles, planning the long gallery with its border of orange trees to be set in boxes of silver and to be lighted by candles in rock crystal lusters. Through the shrubberies and groves they wandered when they wished to be alone; under trees and past bushes which they planned to take from these woods of Fontainebleau to beautify the gardens of Versailles and make a charming setting for its statues and its waterworks.

And most vivid of all, it seemed, were the figures who moved about in this perfect setting. Jewels flashed; silks and satins rustled; blue, green and scarlet feathers drooped over shoulders and the air was filled with perfume. Fans were of brilliant colors and exquisite design; gloves were elaborately embroidered; swords were diamond hilted; spurs were of gold. In the center of all this magnificence were the royal lovers—Henriette, so different from others because she was frail and slender, yet vivacious and gay as she had never been before. She was able now to give expression to her natural elegance and good taste in clothes, and it was she who set the fashion. Louis, in cloth of gold, with black lace, in silks; velvets and satins, jewels adorning his handsome person, diamonds flashing in his hat, towered above them all—a fitting King of this paradise.

He could not honor Henriette enough. He must make up for all the years of neglect. He would have her take the Queen's place on Maundy Thursday in the hall of the Louvre at the ceremony of washing the feet of the poor. At the grand fêtes, he would open the ball with Henriette. "Where the King is," said the Court, "there is Madame."

She was just seventeen; she was romantically in love. Louis, in all his manly beauty and with his new authority, was all that she would ask in a lover. She did not seek sexual satisfaction; her experiences with Philippe had not made her desire to extend her knowledge in such matters. This was the perfect love; romantic, idealistic, untouched by the sordid needs of daily life.

She had a great influence over him. At her instigation he was turning to more intellectual pursuits. They wrote verses together and often read them aloud, when they were vociferously applauded by the courtiers.

Sometimes Henriette and her women would drive out to bathe in a stream in the forest; the King would ride through the trees to greet her returning from her bath that she might have an escort back to the palace. She was more beautiful than she had ever been; and she had always looked well on a horse, in her gold-laced habit with the brilliantly colored plumes in her hat shading her face. At the head of the retinue she and Louis would ride side by side.

Often there were picnics under the trees. She had inspired in him an appreciation of the arts, and sometimes musicians would play to them as they went along the river in a gondola decorated with purple velvet and cloth of gold. They would plan the entertainments for the next day as they sat side by side or rode through the forest. For Henriette that was an enchanted summer. Hunting was continued into the night, and Henriette and the King often went for long walks through the moonlight alone through the forest. If they did not meet each other every day they would write notes.

She had introduced to his notice many of the artistic personalities of the day. Lulli, the musician, must compose the music for his ballet; Molière must write the lyrics. Louis was reading the romances of Madeline de Scudèry and the dramatic pieces of her brother Georges. Because Henriette wished writers to be encouraged, Louis followed her lead, and, much to his delight, he found that a new world full of interest was opening to him.

The Court was changing; it was becoming more intellectual, and so more elegant than it had been for many years. "We are returning to the days of François Premier," it was said. "He loved writers more than any other men. He also loved his sister!"

It was impossible for this new relationship to pass unnoticed. There were sly glances and shaking of heads when the King was not present.

"So Madame is his newest mistress?" ran the murmurings. "What a situation! And, Monsieur! What does he think of his honeymoon's being interrupted?"

Philippe was more quickly aware of the sly looks, the whispered comments. All had worked out as he had been told it would. De Guiche had been right in his hints. Louis was in love with Henriette and had been for a long time, only he had been too simple to know it. The King of France envied his brother. That was quite satisfactory to Philippe. But it was not turning out quite as he had wished. Louis was not tormented by jealousy; Louis was indulging in a romantic love affair, and, it seemed, was content with life. Therefore Philippe was dissatisfied.

He walked in the gardens of Saint-Cloud with his dear friend de Guiche. He should have been contented. This palace was delightful, especially since those excellent architects, Lepante and Girard, had improved it that it might be ready for Philippe on his wedding. The beautiful parks and gardens had been designed by Le Notre himself, and the fountains, which equaled those of Fontainebleau, were the work of Mansart. From the terraces could be seen the river winding its way to Paris. Clipped yew hedges, arbors, palisades and parterres planted with orange trees and embellished with statues of Greek gods and nymphs, were an added glory. Saint-Cloud was indeed beautiful, and he was proud to possess it. Madame could spend as much time with the King as she liked—so he had thought—he would not object. He had his own friends to amuse and flatter him, and—constant gratification—Louis envied him his wife and compared her with the plain Spanish woman.

But it was not quite as he had planned.

"You were right," he said to his friend. "Louis was certainly in love with her. He needed her marriage to me to show him that."

"She has changed, has she not?" said de Guiche quietly. "Who would recognize her as the little Princess she was before her marriage? Now . . . she shows great charm. She has her brother's wit, I am glad to say, but not his looks—I am equally pleased to add. She is the natural friend of the most intellectual people at the Court. She has shown the Court that there is more to beauty than layers of fat. Henriette happy, is not only the most elegant, she is the most desirable woman at Court; and to be elegant and desirable—those are higher attributes than mere beauty."

"You speak as though you yourself are in love with my wife. If I did not know you so well, I should say you were. But it is not as I wished it to be—this love my brother has for my wife. They revel in it. She is changing him; she is ruling the Court. Now we do honor to those artists of hers. That fellow Molière would seem to be an intimate of the King . . . because Madame wishes it. Those de Scudèrys . . . this fellow he has taken from his band of violins . . . what is his name . . . Lulli? Old Corneille is made much of; and this young fellow, Racine . . . They surround the King; they swamp the King; he spends much time listening to their verses and their music. And it is at the command of my wife! It would seem to me that in marrying Henriette, I have made her Queen of France."

"A worthy Queen!" said de Guiche.

"I shall have to remind my brother that Henriette is Madame—not Queen—of France."

"You will dare do that?"

"I shall speak to my mother. She never cared for scandal which touched her own family—much as she loves it concerning others. She will make my brother see that there must be an end to these amorous talks tête-à-tête, these moonlight rambles, these dainty perfumed notes they send each other. I shall bring Madame back here to Saint-Cloud. She must be made to understand that she is not—although she and my brother may wish she were—the Queen of France."

"Alas! Madame makes an enchanting Queen!"

Philippe looked sharply at his friend.

If I did not know him so well, and that he does not love women, I should say he was in love with Henriette, thought Philippe.

But he did not entirely know his friend.

❁ ❁ ❁

Anne of Austria asked that she might see her son alone.

"Louis," she said, "my beloved, this is a delicate matter of which I must speak to you. Forgive me, I know that it is merely idle gossip which I repeat, but there must not be gossip concerning our great King."

"Gossip!" cried Louis. "What is this?"

"It concerns you and Madame."

"Who speaks this gossip? I will have him brought before me. I . . ."

"You cannot punish the whole Court, dearest. You will, I know, be your wonderful, reasonable self and, although there is no cause for this gossip, you will remove all excuse for it."

"What has been said of me . . . and Madame?"

"Merely that you are always together, that you treat her as your Queen, that you neglect the real Queen, that you write notes to each other if you are parted from her for a few hours at a time; in short, that you love your cousin who is the wife of your brother."

"This . . . this is monstrous!"

"Is it true that you spend much time in her company?"

"And shall continue to do so. Tell me who brought this news to you!"

"It was not one. I heard it from many. I beg of you be discreet. Do not give rise to such rumors. Have a mistress if you want one. Why should you not? And particularly while the Queen is indisposed. But let it not be your brother's wife. Philippe is jealous."

"Philippe! Let him return to his boys!"

"Henriette is his wife. It is the future we must think of, dearest. If she had a child . . . and it was believed to be yours . . ."

"This is foul!" cried Louis. "This is scandalous! That any should dare talk thus of Henriette!"

He strode from his mother's apartments and went to his own. He paced up and down, waving away all attendants. So they were talking about his devotion to Henriette! They were whispering sly things! They were besmirching his beautiful romance! It would never again be quite the same for him.

❁ ❁ ❁

Henrietta Maria tapped her foot and looked at her daughter.

"You must be more discreet. What an unfortunate thing this is! If Louis had but felt towards you a short time ago as he does today, what a wonderful thing that would have been! What glory! My son King of England; my daughter Queen of France! But this will not do. They are calling you the King's mistress."

"It is not true," said Henriette.

"Of course it is not true!" Henrietta Maria's arms were about her daughter, and Henriette received one of those suffocating embraces. "My daughter . . . so to forget herself . . . no! It is not true. But there must be no scandal. You and the King! Your husband's brother! You can see what scandal there could be! What if you were to have a child? We shall have them saying it is the King's! That would be intolerable."

Henriette said coldly: "These rumors are false. The King has never been anything but a good brother to me."

"Then I beg of you curb your affection for one another. You are too ostentatiously affectionate. You are too often in each other's company."

"I am tired," said Henriette. "I can listen to no more. I will do my best, I assure you, to see that you suffer no anxiety on my account."

She went to her apartment and asked her women to draw the curtains about her bed, shutting her in.

So . . . they were watching her and Louis! They were spying on their love.

It was true that she was going to have a child—Philippe's child. If only it had been Louis'!

Now she knew that she had passed the summit of her happiness. She knew the romantic idyll was less bright than it had been. She had been aware that it could not last forever. She buried her face in the silken cushions and wept.

❁ ❁ ❁

Louis sought her out. They did not always have to be asked to be left alone; discreet attendants withdrew. That was a sign, they both realized now, of the construction which was being put on their relationship.

He said: "Dearest, they are talking. There is scandal concerning us."

"I know it, Louis," she answered.

"My mother has warned me."

"Mine has warned me."

"What must we do?"

"We must never be alone together; we must give up our moonlight rambles. You must select a favorite and spend much time with her. You must treat me more as a sister."

"I could not do it, Henriette. Loving you as I do, I could not pretend not to do so."

"Yet it must be done."

"How I hate myself! We should have been free to make the most perfect marriage ever made by King and Queen . . . if I had been less of a fool!"

"Do not speak of yourself thus, Louis. If you were not exactly as you are, how could I love you? To me you are as perfect as your courtiers tell you you are—not because I think you are the wisest man in France, not because I think you write better verses than Moliere and Racine, but because I love you. I love you as you are, and would not have one little part of you changed."

He kissed her with passion. In future there must be no opportunities for such displays of feeling. They were both a little afraid of where such displays might lead them; they had both been brought up in the French Court by two mothers who had never failed to impress upon them the importance of their royalty. Etiquette was second nature to them and neither of them could act without being conscious of their royalty.

He released her and cried: "What are we going to do, Henriette? What shall we do, my love?"

It was to her that he had always turned for suggestions.

"There is only one thing we can do," she said. "We must make everyone believe that the affection we have for each other is pure . . . as pure as we know it to be. We must see each other rarely and never without others present."

"That I'll not agree to!"

"Then, Louis, you must come to see me, but it must appear that you are not interested in me, but in someone else."

"Would anyone believe that?"

"I have some pretty maids of honor."

He laughed at the suggestion and, taking her hands, kissed them fervently. "Henriette," he demanded, "why should we care? What should our positions matter to us? Has there ever been love such as ours? Why should we not ignore all those about us! Why should we not follow our inclinations! Life has cheated us."

"Nay, Louis," she answered sadly, "we have cheated ourselves."

"The fault is mine."

She stroked his face gently as though she longed to remember every detail of it. "I'll not have you blame yourself. The fault was mine. I was too proud. I was too conscious of my beggary. I hid myself away; I was shy and gauche."

"And I was blind."

"Nay, Louis, it is not true. I was there, but I was not awake then. I was only a child—a shy, proud child. I was not the person I am today. Nor are you. You, too, have changed.

"We have grown up, dearest. We have left childhood behind us. Why should we not be happy together?"

"I am trying to think of a means whereby we might continue our happiness. At the ball tonight we shall present the *Ballet des Saisons.* All the most beautiful women of the Court will either be among the spectators or taking part in the ballet. You must pretend to be mightily interested in one of them. There is a charming girl, Frances Stuart, one of the loveliest girls I ever saw."

"She will not seem lovely to me. I shall not see her."

"Dear Louis, you must see her . . . or one of them. There is young Marie-Anne, the youngest Mancini girl. She is charming."

"I shall dislike her. She will remind me how foolish I was with her sisters."

"There is a quiet little girl—only just sixteen. She is very shy, but she seems quite pretty at times. She would be enchanted if you but smiled at her. She will be carrying your Diana's train."

"I shall have eyes only for Diana."

"Please spare a glance for little Louise de la Vallière. She will be overcome with delight at the honor; and if you pay some attention to her, it will be said that Madame no longer draws to herself all the King's attention."

Then he held her against him and she clung to him. She had a feeling that there would be so few opportunities in the future.

"Dearest Louis," she said, "do not be jealous if you see me showing some civility to a friend of Philippe's, for I shall have to play my part. The Comte de Guiche will be to me as little Louise is to you; and you need not feel any jealousy, for he is one of Philippe's friends, and you know they have no interest in women."

"So . . . we must disguise our love. We must pretend to care more for others. . . ."

"It is the only way, Louis. You may trust me with de Guiche, and I shall trust you with the little Vallière."

❁ ❁ ❁

It was the most elaborate of all the fêtes, and the ballet, most appropriately, took place out of doors. The stage had been set on the lawn near the lake, and torches lighted in the avenues of trees.

The Queens Anne and Henrietta Maria were seated in state, surrounded by those members of the Court who were not taking part in the ballet.

First came beautiful nymphs, scattering roses on the grass as they sang and danced, and their songs were eulogies of the qualities of Diana the huntress. Then the curtain was drawn to show Henriette. A gasp of delight came from the spectators at the sight of her. She was clad in fine draperies and her hair hung loose about her shoulders; the silver crescent was on her brow and in her arms were the bow and quiver.

About her were green-clad beauties, and two of these were young girls whom Henriette had recommended to Louis: Frances Stuart who, it was clear, in spite of her youth, would be a great beauty, and the much less noticeable brown-haired girl, Louise de la Vallière.

The seasons of the year entered to pay tribute to Diana, and, dressed as Spring, in green and gold and ablaze with diamonds, came the King himself. He knelt before Henriette and lifted his eyes to her face. The chorus was singing verses in praise of Spring with such passion and verve that, if any had failed to recognize Louis in his verdant robes, it would have been known that Spring could only be the King.

Louis was not listening to the verses. He was looking at the young girl who stood with downcast eyes, not daring to glance his way.

Louise de la Vallière was very shy, and obviously in agony because she feared she would forget her words. Now came her cue to join Diana's handmaidens in a song, and Louise missed it.

She looked at the King and the King was looking at her; she blushed hotly and a wave of tenderness swept over Louis. Poor child! She was shy because she was taking part in a ballet with him, and he himself had seen that she was not so clever at the acting and singing as some of the girls.

He smiled, and he saw that it was all she could do to prevent herself falling on her knees before him. He raised his eyebrows. His lips formed the words: "I am not now the King; I am merely Spring." They seemed like part of the ballet. La Vallière smiled, tremulous and adoring; and Louis, accustomed as he was to admiration, was well-pleased.

❁ ❁ ❁

They walked about the gardens of Fontainebleau, the ladies and gentlemen of the Court. Henriette had changed Diana's draperies for a gown of cloth of silver and scarlet. Until today the King would have been beside her. With feelings of mingling relief and regret she saw that he was with a group which included La Vallière. It was as they had planned, but how she wished he had refused to carry out their plan! She imagined his coming to her and saying: "I care not for their gossip. I wish to be with you, and with you I shall be."

Armand, the Comte de Guiche, was beside her. "Madame," he said fervently, "may I congratulate you on a wonderful performance?"

"You are kind, Monsieur le Comte."

"It is you who are kind, Madame, to allow me to speak thus with you."

"Oh come, monsieur, we do not stand on ceremony on such occasions. Those are the King's orders. See how he himself mingles with his guests."

"It has been so difficult to speak with Madame," said de Guiche. "Usually the King is at her side. I am delighted to have this opportunity."

"The part you played in the ballet was considerable, Comte. You were a great success."

"I shall treasure such praise, coming whence it does."

"You have an air of melancholy. You have not quarreled with Monsieur, have you?"

"No, Madame."

"Then is anything amiss?"

"Amiss, Madame? I am the victim of a hopeless passion. I love a lady, the most delightful in the Court, and I have no hope that my passion will ever be returned."

"I am sorry to hear that. I did not know you cared for ladies."

"I never did until I saw this one."

"I am sorry she will have none of you. Have you courted her long?"

"I have seen her often, but there has been little opportunity for courtship. She is far above me. She is elegant; she is slender; and she is quite different from the plump beauties of the Court."

Henriette smiled. "Then I can only wish you the good fortune of falling out of love, since you cannot win this woman. Now, Monsieur le Comte, will you conduct me to the King? I wish to hear whether he himself is satisfied with our entertainment."

She was thinking: I cannot bear to be away from him. He has shown the arranged interest in La Vallière, and I mine in de Guiche; we have done our duty for this night, and we must not break away too suddenly.

She noticed how Louis' face lighted as she approached, and in that moment Fontainebleau was a very happy place for Henriette.

❁ ❁ ❁

Philippe faced his friend and demanded an explanation of his conduct. "You . . . flirting with Madame! What means this?"

"You have been misinformed."

"My eyes do not misinform me. I saw you. You were mincing along beside her, complimenting her like a young fop bent on seduction!"

"Does Monsieur think Madame would look my way?"

"It appears that she did."

"Only because . . ."

"Never mind why she smiled on you! Why did you smile on her?"

"She is enchanting."

"Armand!"

"Of what use to deny it?" said the Comte. "Of course I am in love with Madame. I was in love with her before anyone else saw how delightful she really was. I have always watched her; I have always understood her . . . known more of her than anyone. . . ."

"How dare you stand there and tell me you love my wife . . . you who are *my* friend!"

"Monsieur . . . Philippe . . . I am sorry. I love you. I have loved you since we were boys. This is different. It should not come between us. You, as her husband, should understand that."

"What has that to do with you and me?"

"You know her . . . how charming she is. I feel that I have helped to make her what she is today. I have helped to tear away that shyness, that *gaucherie* . . . but to me, even that was charming."

"Armand! I will not have you talk thus before me. Do not imagine that my favor is for you alone. There are others who would be only too ready to take your place in my affections. You may go away for all I care. And, in fact, if you are thinking of making love to Henriette, go you certainly shall! Do not imagine you can make me jealous by preferring my wife!"

De Guiche threw up his hands in a gesture of despair. "I see this is an impossible situation. I shall leave the Court, I shall go to the country. I cannot stay here any longer."

"Then go!" cried Philippe. "I have other friends to fill your place."

So Armand de Guiche retired to the country, and all the Court whispered that he did so because Monsieur had discovered his love for Madame.

❁ ❁ ❁

Louis had kept his part of the bargain. He had sought out the little Vallière. He enjoyed being kind to her because she was such a frightened little thing and overawed to have the attention of the King focused upon herself. She could not understand why, until other maids of honor told her that he was falling in love with her.

"It is impossible!" cried the little Vallière. "The King would never fall in love with me, when there are so many beauties of the Court all sighing for him."

But Louis continued to seek her out. He would be by her side when the Court rode together; he would join in the dance with her, for she was present at those informal occasions at Fontainbleau; he would say: "Come, Mademoiselle de la Vallière, come and watch the piquet."

Sometimes he himself would play, and when everything he did was applauded, La Vallière would clasp her hands together and her big brown eyes would be wide with adoration.

Louis thought: Poor child! She seeks too much to please. Oh, Henriette, if we could but be together! If only you were with me now!

The Queen was near her time. She spent much of the day lying in bed playing cards, in which she took great delight, still eating a great deal—far too much, it was said, for the good of the child.

Louis visited her as rarely as he could without calling attention to the fact that she bored him.

His mother was delighted because he was no longer constantly in the company of Henriette. She did not appear in public as frequently as before; she was content to leave state matters to Louis and his ministers. Like her daughter-in-law, her chief interest was in food and cards, although she had a love of the theater; she was content to keep certain ladies with her to gossip in her *ruelle* every night and bring her the latest scandals.

It was evening, and Louis was strolling through the grounds of Versailles with a little party of noblemen and ladies. Among the group was La Vallière.

The conversation was by no means profound; there were no literary allusions as there would doubtless have been had Henriette been present. The jokes were trivial and obvious, and everything the King said was greeted with hilarious laughter. He felt a longing to have Henriette beside him, to be free of these empty-headed sycophants.

Then he looked into the face of La Vallière who was close beside him. He knew that she was in love with him, and he was moved because of the sincerity of this young girl who could not hide her devotion; she was like a young fawn, fascinated yet apprehensive.

Louis realized that he had been faithful to Henriette ever since he had discovered that he loved her. He had had no mistress since then, and from those days when Madame de Beauvais had initiated him into the pleasure of the *doux scavoir* such delights had been a frequent need. He felt sexual desire upon him then like thirst in the desert or hunger after a long fast. It came to him as he stood there in the scented gardens with La Vallière beside him.

He looked at the girl, and felt pity for her. Pity! He had first felt that for Henriette, and in some ways this girl reminded him of Henriette—not as she was now, not Madame, but the shy Princess Henriette with whom he had once refused to dance.

He was unaware of the silence which had fallen about him, his large eyes had become a little glazed, and he was still looking at La Vallière.

He said, and although his voice sounded normal to him, it seemed to those about him—accustomed as they were to anticipating his moods—that it held a note of high-pitched excitement: "Mademoiselle de la Vallière, have you seen the new summer house I have had built near the ornamental grotto?"

La Vallière stammered, as she always did when directly addressed by the King: "N-no, Sire. Why . . . yes . . . I believe I have, Sire."

"Then let us go and make sure that you have."

By the time they reached the grotto the party which had accompanied them had lingered here and there, and there was none left but La Vallière and her King. They went through into the new summer house where were set out gilded chairs and a velvet-covered couch—scarlet, and decorated with golden fleurs-de-lis.

"So . . . you see it now," he said, and taking her hands he drew her to him and kissed her.

La Vallière trembled. The frightened fawn . . . the eager fawn . . . thought Louis. It is Henriette whom I love, but she is my brother's wife, and this timid little Vallière is so eager to be loved.

✿ ✿ ✿

Armand de Guiche soon returned to the Court. He found that his longing to see Henriette forced him to return. So he asked Philippe's pardon, which was graciously accorded him, and he became again the close friend of Henriette's husband in order that he might not be banished from Henriette's presence.

Henriette had an opportunity to speak a few words in private with the King while they danced together.

She said: "So we have produced the desired effect. There is talk of you and the little Vallière."

"Is that so?" said Louis.

"And I have heard my name is mentioned with that of de Guiche."

"I like that not," said Louis.

"Nor do I like to hear it said that you are in love with La Vallière."

"You could not believe that I would love anyone now . . . that I ever could, after I came to love you!"

"I hope not, Louis. I hope your love for me is like mine for you."

"Mine is infinite," declared the King; but he avoided meeting her eyes. He wished that he had not fallen into temptation with La Vallière. He wished that he did not keep remembering her little fluttering hands, her cries of protest and pleasure.

It should not happen again; he had promised himself that. He had not meant it to happen that second or third time, but it had been almost impossible to avoid it; she was so ready, so shy, so adoring. It would have been churlish not to. It was not love he had for the little one, he assured himself; it was pity . . . and the desire to honor her.

Henriette said: "Armand de Guiche came to my rooms this day, disguised as a fortune-teller. He is very bold. I had forbidden him to come near me. I thought there had been enough scandal, and I had no wish for more. Montalais, one of my maids of honor, came to me and said there was a teller of fortunes without, who had great things to tell me; and when I had him brought in I discovered it was de Guiche. I recognized him when he raised those mournful eyes to my face. I sent him off at once. I was thankful that none of the others present knew who my fortune-teller was."

"The insolent fellow!" exclaimed the King.

"Do not be hard on him, Louis. We chose to make use of him, remember."

Louis, heavy with the guilt of his affair with La Vallière, found that he was feigning anger against de Guiche which was greater than he felt. But Henriette was smiling tenderly; she felt it was wonderful to know that Louis could love her so much.

❁ ❁ ❁

In the streets they were singing songs about the amours of the Court. Madame was loved by Monsieur's *bel ami;* the King was neglecting his wife for one of Madame's maids of honor.

Mademoiselle Montalais, who loved to make mischief and knew more of her mistress's affairs than Henriette realized, whispered to her one day, "La Vallière is absentminded these days . . . They say it is her preoccupation with the King. She is afraid because she has surrendered her chastity to the King and, like all the pious, she seeks to justify her actions and tells herself that it would have been worse to have been a disloyal subject and refused him than to offend the laws of the church by lying with him in the summer-house."

"There is always gossip," said Henriette.

"There is some truth in this, I'll warrant," said Montalais. "I have heard La Vallière saying her prayers. She asks for courage to resist when the next time comes, and then in the same breath she seems to be asking that the next time may come soon . . . I could never endure pious harlots."

"I cannot believe this of . . . La Vallière!"

"Madame, it is true. The whole Court knows it. Though doubtless it is kept from you on account of your friendship with His Majesty."

Henriette dismissed the woman. Could it be true? Little La Vallière . . . the last person worthy of him, and yet her very timidity might make an appeal to Louis! She, Henriette, who loved him, knew him well.

Henriette hesitated to face the truth, yet she could not bear to remain in ignorance. She sent for La Vallière, and when the girl stood trembling before her, she said: "Mademoiselle de la Vallière, I have heard gossip concerning you. I do not want to believe that it is true. In fact I find it hard to believe, but I must ask you to tell me the truth. You are—as one of my maids of honor—in my care, and I should not wish to think that you had behaved wantonly while in my household."

Before the girl was able to speak she had revealed the truth to Henriette. First a wild anger possessed her—anger against Louis, against this girl, against herself for being such a fool as to recommend the girl to his notice, against Fate, which had been so cruel to her.

She stood trembling, her face pale, her hands clenched together; she could not look at the girl.

La Vallière had thrown herself at Henriette's feet and was sobbing out her confession.

"Madame, I did not mean it to happen. I could not believe that His Majesty would ever care for me. I know that I have done wrong . . . but His Majesty insisted and . . . I could not refuse."

"You could not refuse!" cried Henriette, pushing the girl from her. "You lie! You . . . you lured him with your seeming innocence. You feigned shyness . . . modesty . . . reluctance . . ."

"His Majesty is so . . . so handsome," stammered La Vallière. "Madame, I tried hard, but I could not resist him. No one could resist him once he had made up his mind. Even you . . . you yourself . . . could not have resisted him . . . had you been in my position."

Henriette cried in anguished fury: "Be silent, you wretched girl! You lying, hypocritical wanton, be silent!"

"Madame, I implore you. If you will speak to the king. If you could ask him to explain how it happened . . ."

Henriette laughed. "I . . . speak to the King . . . about you! You are of no importance to His Majesty. You are one of many . . . many!"

Henriette was trying to shut out of her mind pictures of Louis and this girl together; she could not. They would not be shut out. She saw Louis—passionate, eager, refusing to be denied.

Oh God, she thought, I cannot bear this. I could kill this silly girl who has had that for which I so longed. I hate her . . . I hate Louis for deceiving me. I hate myself for my folly. What a fool I have been! I gave him to her.

But she must be calm. All her life she had had to be calm. No one must know how she suffered. She must not be the laughingstock of the Court.

She said coldly: "Get up, Mademoiselle de la Vallière. Go to your apartment. Prepare to leave. I will not allow you to remain another night in my household. Not another night, I tell you. Do you think I shall let you stay here, corrupting others! You . . . with your sham humility! Prepare to leave at once."

La Vallière raised her tear-filled eyes to Henriette's face. "Madame, where shall I go? I have nowhere to go. Please Madame, let me stay here until I can see the King. Please see His Majesty yourself. He will tell you how he insisted . . ."

Henriette turned away; she was afraid that the girl would see the anguish in her face. "I have said Go!" she told her. "I never want to see your face again."

La Vallière rose, curtsied and hurried from the room.

When she had gone, Henriette threw herself onto a couch. She did not weep; she had no tears. There was no happiness left for her in the world. She had been brutal to La Vallière but her jealous fury had commanded her to be so. She hated herself and the world. She understood that Louis could not maintain their rarified devotion; he was not made for such idealism; he was young and lusty; he needed physical satisfaction. It was wrong to blame La Vallière, but how could she bear to see the girl daily!

"I wish I were dead!" she murmured. "I can see that life has nothing to offer me."

Her restless fingers plucked at the golden lilies embroidered on the velvet of the couch, but she did not see them; she saw nothing but Louis and La Vallière, locked in a lovers' embrace.

❁ ❁ ❁

Montalais brought her the news.

"The King is distracted, Madame. He has heard of the flight of La Vallière. He has himself gone in pursuit of her. Who would have thought that His Majesty would have cared so much for our silly little Vallière!"

"So," said Henriette, "he has gone in pursuit of her!"

"He is determined to find her," continued Montalais. "He is urging all his friends to join in the search. There will be rewards for those who uncover the hiding place of His Majesty's little inamorata."

"His Majesty has not mentioned the girl's flight to me."

"Has he not, Madame?" said Montalais, not without a trace of malice. "That is indeed strange. One would have thought you might have been able to tell him something of the girl's possible whereabouts, considering she was in your service."

Henriette said: "Doubtless the matter slipped his memory when he was with me."

"Doubtless, Madame," said Montalais.

They know! decided Henriette. They all know of my love for the King. They know he has turned from me to my maid of honor!

❁ ❁ ❁

A *calèche* drew up outside the Tuileries. From it alighted a man in a long concealing cloak and hood, and with him was a shrinking girl. The man demanded audience of Madame.

There were some who wanted to know how he dared storm the Tuileries at such an hour and peremptorily demand to see Madame d'Orléans.

But when the man threw back his hood and revealed his features, those who had asked the question fell on to their knees before him. They hastened to Madame's apartment to tell her that the King was on his way to see her.

Louis was already there, and Henriette saw that the shrinking creature who accompanied him was La Vallière.

Louis waved aside ceremony as Henriette would have knelt. He took her hand, looking earnestly into her eyes. "I have found little Mademoiselle de la Vallière," he said. "She was in a convent near Saint-Cloud whither she had taken refuge. Poor child! She was in a state of great distress. I know you will help me, Henriette."

"I . . . help Your Majesty!"

"I ask you to take her back into your service, to look after her, as your maid of honor. I want it to be as though she has never run away."

He turned to La Vallière, and Henriette felt as though her heart was breaking as she saw the tender looks he bestowed upon the frightened girl. Louis was so frank; he was incapable of deceit; he could not hide from her the fact that he was in love with this girl.

This is too much to be borne! thought Henriette. It is more than I can endure. Can it be that he has no understanding? Can he be as obtuse as he seems?

"Your Majesty," she said, steeling herself to speak calmly, "I cannot take this girl back. She admits that she has been guilty of an intrigue with a gentleman in a high place at Court."

"It was no fault of hers," said Louis.

"Your Majesty, I did not understand that she was the victim of rape."

Louis' eyes were full of anguish. He loved Henriette; she was the perfect woman, he told himself. If she could have been his wife he would have asked nothing more of life. But she was the wife of his brother; and between them there could never be the kind of love which was so necessary to him. His eyes pleaded with her: Understand me, Henriette. I love you. Ours is an ideal relationship. It is unique. You are my love. And the affair with this girl . . . it is nothing. It happens today and is forgotten tomorrow. But I am fond of her. She is so small and helpless. I have seduced her, and I cannot desert her now.

Poor Louis! He was so simple, so full of the wish to do right.

Help me, Henriette, said his pleading eyes. I beg of you show me the greatness of your love for me by helping me now. Surely love that exists between us is beyond the pettiness of an affair like this.

How I love him! thought Henriette. I love him for his simplicity. He has not yet grown up. Our great Sun God is but a child.

"Louis . . ." she murmured brokenly. "Louis . . ."

He laid his hands on her shoulders and gently kissed her cheek. Then he turned and, drawing La Vallière towards him, put an arm about her.

"Have no fear, my little one," he said. "You should not run away. Do you think you could hide from the King?"

Even as he looked at her, his desire was apparent.

What can she give him that I cannot? Henriette asked herself. The answer was clear: All that is so necessary to a man of his appetites.

"Madame is the kindest and greatest lady in the world," Louis was saying. "I give you into her care. She will love you and cherish you . . . for my sake."

Henriette said: "It is my one desire to serve Your Majesty." And she thought: I can do this for him . . . even this . . . so much do I love him.

❁ ❁ ❁

She did not sleep; she could eat very little. A great melancholy filled her.

Her mother visited her and was shocked by her appearance.

"What has happened?" she demanded. "You look so tired, and you are thinner than ever. And what is this I hear about your refusing to eat? This will not do, my child. I see that you need your mother to look after you."

Henriette Maria was seriously disturbed. She could not forget that in a comparatively short time she had lost three of her children. "You are coughing too much!" she cried. "How long have you coughed thus?"

Henriette wearily shook her head, but the sight of her angry mother, the quick rebukes, the tapping of the little foot, the bright darting eyes, had the effect of unnerving her. She, who had not shed a tear during all the weeks of jealous heartbreak, now burst into bitter weeping.

Once again she was held in her mother's suffocating embrace. Of all her children, Henrietta Maria loved best her youngest daughter. Henriette had been her darling since she had been brought to France from England and had become a Catholic.

"Oh, Mam . . . Mam . . . I wish we could go away together . . . you and I . . . just the two of us . . . to be together as we used to be. Do you remember, when we were at the Louvre and I had to stay in bed because it was too cold to be up? Oh, Mam, I wish I was your little girl again!"

"There, my love, my dearest," crooned the Queen. "You shall come with Mam. We will be together, and these hands shall nurse you, and this Queen, your mother, shall wait upon you. There has been too much gaiety . . . too many balls, and in your condition . . . ah, in your condition . . . But Mam will nurse you, my darling. You shall be with Mam and no one else. Not even Philippe, eh, my darling?"

"No, Mam. No one but you."

So Henrietta Maria sent for a litter and had her daughter conveyed from Saint-Cloud to the Tuileries, and there she nursed her.

During those weeks Henrietta had no wish to see anyone but her mother. She thought often of Charles. Her other love! She called him to herself. Charles . . . Louis! How different they were, those two men whom she loved beyond all in the world. Charles so adult, Louis such a boy; Charles the ugliest, Louis the most handsome King in Christendom; Charles clever and subtle, Louis so often naïve for all his grandeur, a man with a boy's mind, a man who had not yet grown up mentally.

There is only one thing which could make me happy now, she mused. To go to England . . . to be with Charles.

During her illness he wrote often. His letters were a source of great delight; he alone could make her laugh.

He wrote: "Do you suffer from a disease of sermons, as we do here? 'Od's Fish! What piety surrounds us! Dearest Minette, I hope you have the same convenience that the rest of the family has, of sleeping out most of the time, which is a great ease to those who are bound to hear them. But this sleeping has caused me some regret. South—he's an outspoken fellow, that one—had occasion to reprove Lauderdale when preaching last Sunday's sermon. Lauderdale's a man who can snore to wake the dead, and South stopped in the middle of his sermon to rouse him. 'My Lord,' he cried in a voice of thunder, 'you snore so loud you will wake the King!' "

Oh, to be with him! thought Henriette. Oh, to hear his voice again!

Her child—a daughter—was born prematurely. She had so longed for a son, and so had Philippe. Marie-Thérèse had borne a Dauphin; Philippe would be jealous now because Louis had a son while he had a daughter.

Perhaps, thought Henriette, my little daughter will one day marry Louis' son. In the years ahead mayhap I shall find peace, and these turbulent years will seem of no importance then.

It was thinking of Charles that made her aware of the compensations life had to offer. She longed to be with him, to hear his merry laughter, to listen to his witty comments on life, to enjoy that cynicism which veiled the kindest heart in the world.

❁ ❁ ❁

A few weeks after the birth of her child, Montalais came to Henriette to tell her that the Comte de Guiche was begging for an interview with her. His father, the Maréchal de Gramont, had arranged for him to be given command of the troops, and he was required to leave the Court at once.

Henriette, who had found the handsome young man a cultured companion, declared herself sorry that he was leaving, and received him.

He fell on his knees before her and kissed her hand.

He told her that he had been desolate when he had heard of her illness. He was saddened because he was ordered to leave the Court, and he knew this had been brought about by his enemies on account of his friendship with her. He would have her know that wherever he went he would carry with him the memory of her goodness and graciousness, and that he would never cease to love her beyond all others.

To Henriette such devotion came as balm in her humiliation. She was constantly hearing rumors of the growing passion of the King for La Vallière. It was even rumored that the shy maid of honor was with child by the King.

So Henriette could not help listening with sympathy and some pleasure to the declarations of the Comte.

He left her, protesting eternal devotion; but there were spies in Henriette's household, and it was not long before Philippe came to tell her that he had heard from his mother that she was very angry with her daughter-in-law. "It has come to her ears that you are receiving young men in your apartment."

"Young men!"

"De Guiche was seen leaving by a private staircase."

"This is ridiculous, Philippe. De Guiche is a friend of yours."

"But more of yours, it would seem."

"That is not so. He merely sees in me the wife of his beloved friend."

"So it is not true that you and de Guiche are lovers?"

"It most certainly is not true. Were I the wife of any but you, he would pay me no attention."

"Has he said so?"

"I believe it to be so," said Henriette.

Philippe smiled. "Poor de Guiche! To be banished from Court! He is desolate. Well, he will soon return, and it will be a lesson to him. Henriette, you are a very charming woman. I begin to think I am fortunate in my marriage. It is good to be a father. Though I would we had a son."

"You do not care that Louis should have what you lack, Philippe?"

"Louis!" he said. "The Queen is a plain creature. He loathes her. And La Vallière . . . she is no beauty either! It may be that he turns to her because he desires one other whom he dare not attempt to make his mistress. He has a son . . . but mayhap one day soon . . . I shall have a son. I have the most charming wife at Court. Why should I not have a son also? Eh, Henriette?"

He smiled at her and she shrank from him.

She thought: Oh, Charles, my brother, if I could but be with you at Whitehall!

NINE

Henriette lay on her bed. She was in need of rest, for she was pregnant again.

During last year she had plunged more deeply into the gay life at the Court; there had been a great need to hide the hurt she suffered. Louis was still devoted to La Vallière. In spite of his mother's protests he had refused to give her up, and even when she had been far advanced in pregnancy she had remained at Court.

But not the Queen, nor the King's mistress, had been the leader of the fêtes and ballets. It was Henriette who had been the center of the wildest amusements; she who had been more daring than any. She had taken the savants under her protection. Molière had dedicated his *L'Ecole des Femmes* to her. Certain holy gentlemen had declared that the playwright should be burned at the stake when *Tartuffe* had been produced, but Henriette had laughed at them and insisted on the King's attending a performance of the play at Villers-Cotteret. She gave audience to Molière, delighting in his conversation. She laughed heartily when he told her that he had named his hypocrite Tartuffe because one day he had seen two devout priests, palms pressed together, eyes raised heavenwards, when a basket of truffles was brought into the apartment wherein they were performing their religious duties. They went on praying, reminding God and the saints how they had subdued their earthly appetites while their eyes were on the truffles and the saliva ran down their chins. At length they could not stop themselves crying aloud: "Tartuffoli! Tartuffoli!"

Racine had dedicated *Andromaque* to her, declaring that but for her protection in his struggling days he could never have produced the work. La Fontaine had also received her patronage.

She was the benefactress of artists and, while she reigned with Louis ostensibly as his Queen, there was more culture in the Court of France than in any other in Europe, and again people recalled the days of François Premier and his sister Marguerite.

Charles wrote that he wished she could be with him to reign as Queen over his Court. He had married a wife from Portugal. She was no beauty, he admitted to his sister, but he had the good fortune to be able to compare her favorably with her maids of honor who accompanied her—six of them, all frights, and a duenna who was a monster. He was amusing himself, he told her, playing the good husband and, somewhat to his astonishment, not misliking the role. He had the plays of Wycherley and Dryden with which to amuse himself, and Sir Peter Lely to paint the beauties of his Court. He lived merrily but there would always be one thing he lacked to make his contentment complete—the presence of his beloved sister at his Court.

News came to Henriette of the troubles between his mistress-in-chief, the brazen Castlemaine, and his Queen Catherine. Charles and Louis were alike in one thing, it seemed.

She had tried to be content, lacking two things which would have assured contentment: Louis and Charles as her constant companions; for these two she loved beyond all else in the world.

She had not come unscathed through the scandals which had surrounded her. There were many stories circulating concerning her and de Guiche.

De Guiche had been wounded in Poland and had almost met his death. The story was that a case, containing Madame's portrait, which he carried over his heart, protected him from a bullet which would otherwise have cost him his life.

There had been many to notice the charms of Henriette, and since these scandals and her gay method of life suggested she was not inaccessible, many came forward to seek her favors. Among them were Monsieur d'Armagnac, of the house of Lorraine and Grand Ecuyer de France, and the Prince de Marsillac, son of the Duc de la Rochefoucauld. All were charming, all amusing, all certain that Madame could not prove continuously and tiresomely virtuous; but all were disappointed.

Then there was the Marquis de Vardes. Henriette found him more cultured, more amusing than any; and as a gentleman of the King's bedchamber, he had won Louis' regard, so she found herself often in his company.

He was a rake, but an extremely witty one, a companion of writers, artists and musicians; at this time he was the most popular man at Court. He had been involved in love affairs with Madame d'Armagnac and the Comtesse de Soissons, but he had now set his heart on the conquest of no less a person than Madame herself.

Henriette was at first unaware of this; indeed she believed him to be still involved with the beautiful Madame de Soissons who, since the King's favor had turned to La Vallière, had accepted him as her lover.

As she lay in her bed, Henriette was thinking of Louis. She had seen little of him for some weeks and then only in the company of others; those pleasant confidences which were the delight of her life were no longer offered. There were times when she fancied his glances were more than indifferent; they were cold.

He had turned against her.

She felt wretched and alone. Her mother had gone to England and was residing at Somerset House. She missed her sadly, although Henrietta Maria, disturbed by the gay life her daughter led and the fact that she had incurred the displeasure of Anne of Austria, had lectured Henriette so incessantly that she had longed to escape. If she could have explained to someone, how much better would she have felt! But how could one explain to Henrietta Maria? How could the fiery little Queen ever understand this passion of her daughter's? Henrietta Maria would never love as her daughter loved—secretly brooding, hiding her misery. Henrietta Maria had to parade hers that all might see it and commiserate with her.

Why had Louis suddenly turned against her? She had asked herself that question a hundred times. He had grown tired of their relationship and now he was not even taking the trouble to conceal that fact.

What satisfaction was there for her in the rounds of balls and fêtes? What did it matter if all complimented her on her elegant attire, her dancing in the ballet, her conversation? Louis had turned from her. He was not merely tired of her; he was beginning to dislike her.

And as she lay there, one of her women came to her and said that the

Comtesse de Soissons, who was ill and seemed to be near death, wished to speak to her. Would she be so good as to go to the Comtesse's bedchamber, as the Comtesse could not come to her?

Henriette rose from her bed then and followed the woman to the Comtesse's apartment.

It was difficult to recognize the beautiful Olympia Mancini, the woman who had enslaved Louis before her marriage and had been his mistress after it, in the thin wasted woman who now lay on the bed.

Henriette, full of sympathy for the sick since she herself did not enjoy the best of health, touched the Comtesse's hot forehead and begged her not to agitate herself.

"There is something I must tell you, Madame," said the Comtesse.

"Later will do."

"No, Madame. Later will not do. I feel so ill that I believe death to be near me, and I must warn you while it is in my power to do so."

"Of whom is it that you would warn me?"

"De Vardes."

"De Vardes! But he is my friend and your lover!"

"He was my lover, Madame. That was before he was determined to make you his mistress. When that determination came to him he vowed he would let nothing stand in the way of its fulfilment."

"It seems that *I* stood in the way, Madame de Soissons."

"Yes, Madame, you stood in the way. It is he who circulated the scandals about yourself and Monsieur de Guiche. He has carried these tales to the King."

"I . . . see," said Henriette.

"He believes that you love de Guiche, and has sworn to ruin you both."

"And how . . . does he propose to do this?"

"Madame, he has the ear of the King."

Henriette put her hand to her heart in a sudden fear that the violence of its beating might be betrayed to the sick woman.

"Does he think that the King would turn his favor from me if he believed I loved Monsieur de Guiche?"

"No, Madame." That answer hurt Henriette more than one in the affirmative would have done. "No, Madame; it is not the scandals he has uttered against Monsieur de Guiche. It is . . . the letters you receive from your brother."

"The letters of the King of England!"

"He says he has seen some of them."

"It's true. They are often witty. I remember being so amused with something my brother wrote that I showed the letter to de Vardes."

"Madame, de Vardes has accused you of betraying French secrets to your brother of England."

"But this is impossible!"

"Nay, Madame, it is true."

"And the King believes that . . . about me!"

"He knows how you love your brother. If Charles asked you to do little things for him it might be hard for you to refuse him."

"So Louis thinks I am my brother's spy! He thinks I would betray him to Charles!"

"He thinks you love your brother dearly."

Henriette turned her head away, but Madame de Soissons was stretching out her hand. "You will forgive me, Madame? You see, I loved the King . . . and then de Vardes. I should have told you how de Vardes determined to ruin both you and de Guiche. I should have told you before."

Henriette turned back to the sick woman. "You have told me now. That will suffice."

"Then, Madame, I have your forgiveness?"

Henriette nodded; she hurried from the sickroom.

She must see Louis as soon as possible. Those doubts and suspicions must not be allowed to remain between them.

❁ ❁ ❁

But before she saw him her child was born. This time it was a boy.

As she lay with the child in her arms, she felt that the boy would, in some measure, make up for all she had suffered.

Philippe was delighted; the King sent his congratulations and promised the boy a pension of 50,000 crowns. Anne of Austria declared her satisfaction at the birth of the boy, since the Dauphin was but a sickly child and his sister had recently died. Henrietta Maria was filled with more delight than she could express. As for Charles, he himself was suffering from a chill, having taken off his wig and pourpoint on a hot day, and was unable to write until almost a week later. Then he wrote of the extreme joy he felt because she had a son. Nothing, he said, could give him greater pleasure than that news.

She wanted to reply, telling him that she had fallen into disfavor with the King, and how unhappy this made her. She doubted whether he would understand. He would call her devotion to the King, folly. He loved easily and lightly—not one but many. Here again, Charles, perhaps, showed his wisdom.

It was not until she was up from her bed that she was able to secure the desired audience with Louis.

"I must," she insisted, "speak with Your Majesty alone."

Louis bowed his head in acknowledgment of her request, and she noticed with dismay how cold his eyes were.

As soon as they were alone, she cried out: "Louis, there has been a terrible misunderstanding, and I must make you see the truth."

He waited impassively.

She continued hurriedly: "It is quite untrue that I have conspired with my brother against you."

He did not answer, and she went on imploringly: "Louis, you cannot believe this to be so?"

"You are very fond of your brother."

"That is true."

"The affection between you has been marked by many."

"I know it."

"Brothers and sisters should have a certain regard for each other, but this affection between you and the King of England is unusual in its intensity, is it not?"

"I admit we are very fond of each other."

"I have talked freely to you of matters of state . . . state secrets . . . because I have admired your lively mind. I did not think you would so betray me as to discuss such matters with the King of another country, even though that King was your brother."

"You have been misinformed." She had broken down suddenly. The tears had started to stream down her cheeks. She stammered: "It is not so much that you should think these evil thoughts of me . . . it is that you should look at me so coldly."

Louis' pity was immediately aroused. She looked so frail after her recent ordeal; he went to her and laid his arm about her shoulders. "Henriette," he said, "if you have erred in this, mayhap it was due to thoughtlessness."

"I have never erred. I would never betray your secrets. Cannot you understand that my only wish is to serve *you*?"

"And to serve Charles."

"I love him, it is true. But he would never seek to embroil me in trouble. He would never ask me to do that which my regard for you would not allow me to."

"You say you love Charles," said Louis. "I know it. But what of Louis?"

"I love you both."

"Can one person love two others equally?"

"He is my brother."

"And I, Henriette?"

"You . . . you are the one beside whom I should have been content to live all the days of my life . . . had that been possible."

"Most women would love such a one more than a brother."

She did not answer, and he kissed her cheek gently.

"I have misjudged you, Henriette. Those who have slandered you shall not escape my displeasure. It may be that one day you will have an opportunity of showing me how much greater is the love you bear for the King of France than that you have for the King of England.

"I hope that day will not come."

He had taken her hands and was kissing them fervently. "It would be infinite joy for me to know that I held first place in your heart," he said. "Who knows . . . mayhap one day I shall ask you to prove that to me."

❁ ❁ ❁

For a long time after that Henriette was apprehensive.

The Comtesse de Soissons recovered, and seemed to regret her confidences. Louis had not redeemed his promise to punish de Vardes, and the man was still at large. Henriette knew that together he and the Countess planned to harm her in the eyes of the King; de Vardes because he knew that now she hated him and there was no hope of her becoming his mistress, the Countess because she was so infatuated with de Vardes that she was glad to help him in any way he wished.

Henriette realized how little Louis trusted her, and that he still believed she was in secret correspondence with her brother. It seemed to her that the most important thing was to win back Louis' faith and trust.

De Guiche had returned to Court. Louis had only allowed him to come back on condition that he did not attempt to see Henriette; but the foolish man could not resist writing to her, and de Vardes, feigning to be his friend, offered to deliver this to Henriette.

It was only a few weeks after the birth of Henriette's son, the little Duc de Valois, that she received a message from de Vardes. He assured her that he had been the victim of a terrible misunderstanding and implored her to grant him a short interview.

Disturbed and desirous of getting to the bottom of these intrigues, which were in progress to turn the King against her, Henriette agreed to see de Vardes and hear what he had to tell her.

De Vardes accordingly planned to visit her, but before going to Saint-Cloud he sought an audience with the King. He begged His Majesty's pardon for the intrusion, but if the King would walk with him the length of the gallery, he would show him something which would convince him that he, de Vardes, had been misjudged.

Louis frowned but said testily that he would grant the interview; and the two strolled off together.

De Vardes said: "Sire, I have been misjudged with regard to Madame."

"I have no wish to speak of Madame."

"Your Majesty, I beg of you, allow me to defend myself."

"On what grounds?"

"When I uncovered the perfidy of Madame in her relationship with her brother, my one thought was to serve Your Majesty. Your Majesty did not believe me, preferring to trust Madame." De Vardes bowed. "I can do no other than accept Your Majesty's decision. But Monsieur de Guiche has returned to Court, having promised on his honor not to see Madame again."

"You suggest that they are meeting?" demanded Louis.

"I have this letter—a profession of his undying devotion. He knows full well that he disobeys Your Majesty's command."

"He is a man in love," said Louis musingly.

"And Madame? Is Madame a woman in love?"

Louis was hurt and angry. It was true that La Vallière was his mistress whom he desired passionately, but for Henriette he had cherished an ideal love. If, while professing to love him, she was receiving a lover, it was more than he could bear. She had sworn to him that there were no lovers; she had in her way reproached him for lacking her own fidelity. And mayhap now she was laughing at him with de Guiche.

He said: "Take this letter to Madame. I will come with you, but you shall go to her and I shall remain hidden until you have handed her the letter. If she is my good friend—as she swears she is—she will not read the letter, which she knows comes to her in flagrant disobedience to my commands."

De Vardes bowed.

Louis took de Guiche's letter, read it and knew great jealousy.

He thought: I have been deceived. I have told myself that if I could have married Henriette, I should be the happiest man alive. I have idealized her; but if this man is her lover, she is unworthy of idealized love.

It was typical of Louis, openly unfaithful himself, to expect fidelity in others. Henriette had always known this side of his nature; but did she love him for his virtues? No more than she loved Charles for his.

And so the letter was brought to her, and the King was secreted in a closet to see and hear her reception of it.

When she saw what her visitor had brought, she turned away from him. "You bring me that which I have no wish to receive," she said. "I pray you take it back to him who gave it to you and tell him that he breaks the King's command by writing to me thus."

De Vardes fell on to his knees; he tried to take her hands; he exerted all his fascination, to the potency of which there were so many women at Court to bear witness, in an effort to make her betray some weakness to the watching King.

But Henriette had no love for either de Guiche or de Vardes, although she entertained a certain fondness for the former.

"Pray leave me," she said. "I wish to hear no more from either of you. I wish only to be left in peace; you have done me too much harm already."

De Vardes left and immediately Louis joined Henriette. She was shocked to realize she had been spied upon; but it was a great relief to know that Louis was her friend again.

"Now I have heard with my own ears and seen with my own eyes how you spurn these fellows. Can you forgive me for accepting their word against yours? I was jealous, Henriette. Oh, what an unhappy state is this in which we find ourselves!"

"If I may see you often," she said, "if I may enjoy your friendship, I could be happy."

"We shall be together as we were before. My favor is yours as it ever was. Henriette, we love and our love is a sacred passion . . . above more earthly loves."

Then she felt it was as it had been when they had first made that wonderful discovery regarding each other.

But still he did not carry out his threats to punish de Vardes; and he remained jealous of Charles.

❁ ❁ ❁

One of the noblemen of the Court was giving a masked ball, and as the King was not present on this occasion, the principal guests were Monsieur and Madame.

There was a great deal of excitement, as there always was at these affairs; flirtations were conducted under cover of wigs and masks. Henriette was glad of the anonymity.

She and Philippe went by coach to the nobleman's mansion—not in their own coach, which would have betrayed them, but in a hired one. Philippe scarcely spoke to his wife nowadays; he had ceased to show any great interest in her. He was pleased that she had given him a son who seemed to be more healthy than the Dauphin; he was pleased also that their daughter lived, although the King's had died. Henriette knew that such rivalry would always exist between them. Anne of Austria and Mazarin had perverted Philippe's mind during his childhood, when he had always been compelled to remember that his brother was his King.

When they arrived at the house Philippe gave his hand to the nearest lady, and a man immediately came forward to escort Henriette.

As she laid her hand on his satin sleeve she was aware of his excitement.

She said: "Have we met before, Monsieur?"

He answered: "Madame, we have."

"Then you know my identity?"

"Who could fail to recognize the most elegant and beautiful lady of the Court? Madame is like a slender lily compared with weeds."

Then since you know me, I pray you keep my identity secret. Remember this is a masked ball."

Then glancing down she caught sight of his hand, and she remembered hearing that, in the recent battle in which he had taken part, de Guiche had lost several of his fingers. The hand of this man was maimed.

Henriette caught her breath. How could she have been mistaken? He had a distinguished air, this de Guiche. He had a recklessness, something of the adventurer in him. He was taller than most men—though not as tall as Louis; now she saw that the large mask did not entirely conceal the well-shaped nose and sensitive mouth.

She thought: So he has dared to seek me out in this way! This is folly. If Louis were to hear of our meeting he would believe that I have been guilty of conspiring to bring it about.

"Monsieur," she said, "I wish you to leave me when we reach the top of the staircase."

"Madame . . . dear madame . . . I had hoped to be your companion for longer than that."

"You are a fool!" she cried. "I know who you are. So will others. And as you recognized me . . . so will they."

"Madame, I had to speak to you. I had to find some way. I could not endure those days without a sight of you."

"Monsieur de Guiche, you know you disobey the King's orders. If you have any regard for me, bring no more trouble on yourself . . . or me."

"It is not only to give myself the joy of seeing you and speaking to you which has brought me here. I know that to be dangerous. But I have to warn you; I do not believe you understand to the full the treachery of de Vardes and his mistress."

"I think I understand full well how those two have tried to harm me in the King's eyes."

"I beg of you, listen to me. De Vardes is determined to ruin us both. Madame de Soissons is jealous, not only of the King's regard for you, but because de Vardes desired you so passionately. De Vardes is not in high favor with the King, but Louis always has a soft spot for his mistresses, and

Madame de Soissons has his ear. She has this day told the King that, in secret correspondence, you have suggested to your brother that you take possession of Dunkirk in his name; also that this is my plan, and that I am ready to place my regiment of guards at your disposal."

Henriette caught her breath. "But this is madness."

"The madness of jealousy . . . envy . . . and those determined on revenge. The King already suspects you are more ready to serve your brother than to serve him. Madame, beware."

Philippe, who had reached the top of the staircase, had turned and was watching them.

Henriette whispered: "He knows you. He has recognized you. He has never forgiven you for turning from him to me. He too suffers from his jealousy. I beg of you, Monsieur de Guiche, as soon as we reach the top of the stairs, leave me. And leave this ballroom. It is unsafe for you to be here.

And when they reached the top of the stairs, she turned hastily from him and started to walk towards Philippe. In her haste her foot caught in her gown and she tripped and fell. It was de Guiche who leaped forward to catch her.

There were gasps of horror from those about her. Someone said in a loud voice: "Madame has fainted!"

Henriette realized that she was recognized, and in de Guiche's arms. She hastily disengaged herself; but as she did so she was aware of de Vardes' cynical voice beside her.

"There is no mistaking Madame. That beauty . . . that elegance cannot be hidden by a mask. But who is her savior? I think we may be forgiven a little curiosity on that score."

He stepped towards de Guiche and with a swift movement tore off his mask.

There was a murmur of: "De Guiche!"

"Our gallant soldier!" said de Vardes mockingly. "It is no great surprise that he should be at hand . . . when Madame needs him."

With great dignity de Guiche cried: "Monsieur de Vardes, my friends will be calling on you tomorrow."

De Vardes bowed: "Monsieur, they will be most welcome."

De Guiche then turned and walked haughtily through the press of courtiers and out of the ballroom.

Philippe, white-lipped with anger—for never had it seemed to him that de Guiche looked more handsome—gave his arm to his wife and led her away.

All through that evening, behind their masks, guests talked of this affair; and Henriette knew that, before the night was over, news of what had happened at the masked ball would reach the ears of Louis.

❁❁❁

She had implored the King to believe her guiltless. He was kind. He agreed on the villainy of de Vardes, but still he allowed him to go free. In her heart, Henriette knew that he did not entirely believe in her innocence.

Was there no one to whom she could appeal? There was only one person in the world whom she could entirely trust, and he was on the other side of the water.

At last she decided to ask for Charles' help, and she wrote to him:

> I have begged the Ambassador to send you this courier that he may inform you truly of the affair which has happened about de Vardes. This is a matter so serious that I fear it will affect the rest of my life. If I cannot obtain my object, I shall feel disgraced forever that a private individual has been allowed to insult me with impunity, and if nothing is done to punish this man, it will be a warning to the world in future how they dare attack me. All France is interested in the outcome of this affair. Out of your love for me, I beg you ask the King for justice. I am hoping that the consideration in which you are held here will settle this matter. It will not be the first debt I have owed you, nor the one for which I shall feel the least grateful, since it will enable me to obtain justice in the future.

She knew that her cry for help would not be in vain. Charles answered at once that she could rely on his assistance.

Two weeks later de Vardes was lodged in the Bastille.

❁❁❁

As for de Guiche, it was clear that he must not be seen at Court again. His father, the Maréchal de Gramont, advised him to beg one last audience with Louis, during which he must convince the King that he served no other master; after that he must depart and never see Henriette again.

This de Guiche promised to do, but he could not deprive himself of one last farewell. He dared not seek her in her apartments, so he dressed himself in the livery of one of the servants of La Vallière that he might see Henriette pass in her chair from the Palais-Royal to the Louvre.

This was the last he saw of her before he left for Holland and a brilliant military career.

The affair of de Guiche and de Vardes was closed, the King implied; but he continued to ponder on the relationship between Henriette and her brother.

TEN

A year had passed since the imprisonment of de Vardes and the banishment of de Guiche.

Louis was often in the company of Henriette. Always he was deeply affectionate, although at times she was aware of those suspicions which would return to his mind, and they always concerned her brother Charles.

Now that Louis was coming into his kingdom, now that he had made himself true ruler of France, he began to realize that he could use Henriette's influence with her brother in negotiations between the two countries. Moreover, Henriette's quick mind was as good as that of any statesman he possessed; and Louis was shrewd enough to know that a woman who was in love with him would make a better servant than anyone who worked for his own fame and glory.

There was only one doubt which arose now and then in his mind: Did the affection of Henriette for her brother exceed that which she had for himself?

He could not be entirely sure. It was a matter of great fascination and importance to him. This love between himself and Henriette was of greater interest to him than the more easily understood passions which he felt for La Vallière and her new rival, Madame de Montespan.

His mother, Queen Anne, was very ill, and he was aware that she could not live long. As he danced with Henriette, La Vallière or Montespan, his thoughts went often to his mother. He was fond of her, although lately she had interfered too much in his affairs, and she could not forget that he was her child, and continued to look upon him as such.

"Poor Mama!" he often murmured. "How she loves me! But she never understood me."

In the Palais-Royal, the great gallery of which was hung with mirrors and brilliant with torches, the new play by Molière, *Médecin Malgré Lui,* was performed for the first time, after the banquet.

Louis, with Henriette beside him, laughed loudly at the wit of his favorite playwright, and forgot his mother.

He was happy. He enjoyed such occasions. It was good to have a quiet little wife who adored him. She was not here tonight to admire him in his suit of purple velvet covered in diamonds and pearls, because she was in mourning for her father. He was glad she was absent, for the sight of his mistresses always distressed her, and La Vallière was pregnant again. It was good to have such a meek and tender mistress as La Vallière and such a bold and witty one as Madame de Montespan. And all the time he was enjoying a love affair on a higher plane with his elegant and clever Henriette. He enjoyed the pathos of their relationship; he did not see why it should not endure forever. Tonight she had arranged this entertainment for him; all the most brilliant fêtes, masks and ballets were arranged by Henriette for the pleasure of her King. If only he could have been entirely sure that her affection for him obsessed her completely, he would have been content.

But he was forever conscious of the dark witty man on the other side of the water, in whose capital city men were now falling like flies, stricken by the deadly plague.

❁❁❁

About the bedside of the dying Queen Mother of France were her children, Louis and Philippe, and with them stood their wives, Marie-Thérèse and Henriette.

All four were in tears. Anne had suffered deeply, and her death was by no means unexpected. The beautiful hands, now gaunt and yellow, plucked at the sheets, and her eyes, sunken with pain, turned again and again to the best loved of them all.

Louis was deeply moved; he was on his knees recalling that great affection which she had always given him.

Philippe was also moved. She had loved him too in her way, but, being a simple woman, she had not been able to disguise from him the fact that almost all the affection she had to give must go to her glorious firstborn.

Philippe took the hot hand and kissed it.

"Be good, my children," murmured Anne.

Henriette turned away because she could no longer bear to look on such suffering. She wished that she had not flouted Anne's advice; she wished that there were time to tell the dying Queen that she now understood how foolish she had been in pursuing gaiety, and so giving rise to scandals such as those concerning de Guiche and de Vardes. But it was too late.

"Louis . . . beloved . . ." whispered the Queen.

"My dearest Mother."

"Louis . . . be kind to the Queen. Do not . . . humiliate her with your mistresses. It is sad for a little Queen . . . so young . . ."

Marie-Thérèse, who was kneeling by the bed, covered her face with her hands, but Louis had placed his hand on her shoulder.

"I ask your forgiveness," he said, the tears streaming down his cheeks. "I ask both of you to forgive me . . ."

"Remember me when I am gone," said Anne. "Remember, my dearest, how I lived for you alone. Remember me . . ."

"Dearest Mama . . . dearest Mama . . ." murmured the King.

And all four about the bed were weeping as Anne of Austria ceased to breathe.

❁ ❁ ❁

Very soon after Anne's death, gaiety was resumed at Court. Louis was now free from all restraint. He planned a great carnival; it was to be more magnificent than anything that had gone before.

Henriette arranged the ballet.

The Queen came to her at the Palais-Royal, and when they were alone together she wept bitterly and told her sister-in-law how galling it was for her to see La Vallière and Montespan at Court.

"La Vallière is at least quiet," said Marie-Thérèse. "She always seems rather ashamed of her position. It is a different matter with Montespan. I believe she deliberately scorns me."

"Have no fear," soothed Henriette. "Remember the deathbed of the Queen Mother. Louis has promised to reform his ways. There will certainly be a part for you in the ballet."

"I am no good at dancing."

There will be little dancing for you. You will be seated on a throne, magnificently attired to receive homage."

"It sounds delightful."

"And La Vallière and Montespan will find that there are no parts for them."

"You are my good friend," said Marie-Thérèse. "I am glad of that, for you are a good friend of the King's, I know."

They embraced, and Henriette looked forward to her new friendship.

Through the window at which she sat with Marie-Thérèse she could see Philippe in the garden with his friend the Chevalier de Lorraine, who was a younger brother of Monsieur d'Armagnac. Lorraine was very handsome and Philippe was enchanted with him. They strolled through the grounds, their arms about each other, laughing and chatting as they went.

Henriette did not like Lorraine; she knew that he was determined to make mischief. He was insolent to her and it was clear that he wished to remind her that as Monsieur's *bel ami* he was more important to him than his wife. He was also the lover of one of her maids of honor, Mademoiselle de Fiennes, and scandalously he used this girl to make Philippe jealous. It was an unpleasant state of affairs.

Sometimes, thought Henriette, I feel I am married to the worst man on earth. What is the use of saying: If only I had married Louis, how different, how happy and dignified my life would have been!

Louis himself called at the Palais-Royal next day.

He was angry and did not bother to command a private audience. He came straight to her.

"I see, Madame," he said, "that there are no parts in the ballet for Mademoiselle de la Vallière and Madame de Montespan."

"That is so, Sire," answered Henriette.

"But you know our wish that these talented ladies should have parts."

"I understood from your promise to the Queen, your mother, that you had decided no longer to receive them at Court."

"Then you misunderstood my intentions, Madame."

Henriette looked at him sadly. "Then there is no alternative but to rearrange the ballet," she said quickly.

"Thank you, sister. That is what I would have you do."

"Mademoiselle de la Vallière is now scarcely in a condition to appear in the ballet, Sire."

"Let her take a part where she may sit down, and wear such a costume that shall disguise her condition."

"There is the Queen's part . . ."

"Yes, the Queen's part. Let that be given to Mademoiselle de la Vallière."

"But the Queen?"

Louis looked at her testily. "The Queen has no great love of the ballet."

Henriette's thoughts went to the sad little Queen who had wept so much because she must stand aside for the King's mistresses. She thought, too, of poor little La Vallière, who would soon be outshone by the more dazzling Montespan; it would be no use hiding in a convent then, for, if she did, Louis would not hasten to find her.

There he stood—magnificent even when peevish. Woe to those who love the Sun King! she told herself soberly.

Louis was saying: "There is another matter of which I would speak to you. It concerns my son."

"The Dauphin?"

"No. Mademoiselle de la Vallière's son. I would have him brought up at Court . . . perhaps here at the Palais-Royal or at the Tuileries. He should not live in obscurity since he is my son. He should enjoy royal honors. It is my wish that he should do so."

Henriette bowed her head. "I will do all that you command for him," she answered.

She saw now that the Queen's death was having its effect, even as had that of Mazarin.

Louis was in complete control now. La Vallière, large with child, should be in attendance on the Queen. La Montespan, brazen in her accession to the King's regard, would become Queen of the Court.

❁ ❁ ❁

Henriette was anxious. Charles was at war with Flanders, and relations between her brother and brother-in-law she knew to be very strained.

The Hollanders were holding out tempting promises to Louis; she, who was in his confidence in these matters, knew that a state of war between France and England was threatening.

Henrietta Maria, who had returned to France at the time of the great plague, was, with her daughter, horrified at the idea of hostilities between France and England.

The Queen and her daughter spent many hours together talking of state matters, and it seemed possible that Henriette's anxiety brought about her miscarriage.

The Queen nursed her daughter through her illness; she herself was ageing fast and suffered from a weak heart and sleeplessness. She was scarcely the most cheerful of companions, talking as she did continually of the old days and how her stay in England had revived her memories.

The news grew worse. Louis decided that Charles was no longer his friend, and French troops were sent into Holland against England's ally, Christian Bernard von Galen, Bishop of Münster.

Never in her life had Henriette been so wretched.

Her brother, whom she loved dearly, and the man whom she had longed to marry, were enemies, and each was expecting her to be his friend.

"Now," said Louis, "you have to decide between us. Which is it, Henriette?"

She looked into his handsome face. She said: "He is my brother, and nothing could make me do anything but love him. But I love you also, and you are my King."

Louis was well pleased with that answer. She would be useful when he made peace with England.

These warlike conditions between the two countries did not long persist, and by the May of that year both Kings were ready for peace. Henriette and her mother had done much to bring about this state of affairs.

"I hope and pray," said Henriette, "that I shall never see you two at war again."

Louis kissed her hand. "You will be loyal to me always, Henriette. That is so, is it not? You will remember our love, which is beyond earthly love, the noblest affection that was ever between two people."

"I will remember," she told him firmly.

She wished that she could have stayed at Colombes with her mother, and that there was no need to go back to Philippe.

❁ ❁ ❁

Sitting on a raised dais, Henriette, exquisitely dressed, her white and tan spaniel, Mimi, in her arms, was the central figure in the Ballets des Muses. She listened to the chanting of verses written by Molière; she watched the graceful dancing; and, as usual, her eyes rested on one figure, taller, more magnificent than all others—Louis, gorgeous and aglitter with jewels, his velvet dalmatica sewn with pearls, his high heels accentuating his height so that he stood above all, the Sun King, the Sun God, beautiful as Apollo himself.

She looked about and saw Mademoiselle de Montpensier, who was no longer Mademoiselle of the Court now that Philippe had a daughter to assume that title. Poor Mademoiselle! She was less proud now than she had been in her youth. None of those glorious marriages, whose worthiness she had doubted, had come her way. Now it was rumored that she was passionately in love with Lauzan, the dashing military commander, but a marriage between them would never be permitted.

Surely Mademoiselle was feeling sorry for herself, and yet perhaps even more sorry for Henriette. She had said that she would rather have no husband at all than one such as Philippe.

La Vallière was at Court again, recently delivered of a daughter, not entirely happy. She was very jealous of Montespan and greatly feared her rival. In protest she had retired from Court and gone into a convent; this time the King sent for her but did not go after her in person. Poor La Vallière! It seemed possible that her days as King's favorite were numbered.

And as Henriette sat there with the dancers circulating about her she did not see them. She was thinking of Charles and the terrible fire which, following the plague of last year, had ravaged his capital.

There was a great deal of misery in the world.

She stroked Mimi's silky ears. Even Mimi suffered; she had her jealousies and could not bear to see her mistress's attention turned to anyone or anything else. She would run away and hide out of very pique, if Henriette as much as picked up a book.

Roused from her reveries, Henriette noticed that one of the women was trying to catch her eye. Something was wrong.

She was glad when the ballet was over and she was free to listen to the woman.

"Madame, it is the little Duc de Valois. He has had a relapse."

❁ ❁ ❁

So she left the ball and drove with all speed to Saint-Cloud where her children were lodged.

The little boy's eyes lighted up when he saw his mother, but his appearance shocked her. She sank down by his bed and gathered him into her arms. In the service of the King, with the continual entertainments and ballets, she saw less of her children than she could have wished.

It was obvious that the little boy had a high fever and she turned appealingly to those about the bed.

"But his teeth came through quite well. I was told there was no longer need to worry. How did this happen? Why was I not informed?"

"Madame, the fever came on suddenly. The little Duc de Valois was playing yesterday with his sister. Then . . . suddenly he was in the grip of fever. The doctors have bled him continually. Everything has been done."

She was not listening. She was holding the precious child against her, rocking him to and fro.

I am weary of this life, she mused. I have had enough of balls and masques. I will nurse him myself. I will cease to be the slave of Louis. I will live differently . . . quietly. When I have nursed my boy back to health I will spend long hours with my children. I am tired. Each day I grow more quickly weary."

But while she thought thus the child's breathing grew more difficult and he did not recognize his mother.

Later she was aware of gentle hands that took the dead boy from her.

After that there arose the need to have another son. There was a return to the hateful life with a Philippe who was becoming more and more dominated by that vilest of men, the Chevalier de Lorraine.

❁ ❁ ❁

There was continual friction between Henriette and Philippe. Philippe seemed to be filled with hatred for his wife. To him it was a matter of great annoyance and envy that Louis should discuss with her those secret matters of state which concerned England.

Often he would cry: "You would have secrets from me? Is that the way in which to treat a husband? Tell me what passed between you and my brother."

"If he wished you to know he would tell you," Henriette would reply. "Why do you not ask him?"

"Is it meet that my wife should spend long hours closeted with my brother?"

"If the King wishes to command that it should be so, it *is* right."

"What is happening between our country and England? Should these matters be kept from me, yet imparted to my wife?"

"That is for the King to decide."

Philippe would fling away from her in a passion and seek out his dear friend Lorraine, who would console him and tell him that he was unfortunate indeed to be married to such a wife.

❁ ❁ ❁

At Saint-Cloud a new situation had arisen. One day Henriette asked for Mademoiselle de Fiennes, whom she had noticed was not amongst her attendants. She was told that the woman had gone away.

"Gone away? By whose permission?"

The answer was: "At Monsieur's orders. She did not wish to go, but Monsieur drove her from the house."

Henriette went to her husband's apartments. The Chevalier de Lorraine was sprawled insolently on his master's bed. Philippe sat in a window seat.

Neither rose when she entered. Lorraine was polishing a magnificent diamond on his finger—one of his latest presents from Philippe.

She was angry, but with admirable courage restrained herself from as much as glancing at her husband's favorite.

"Why have you sent Mademoiselle de Fiennes away?" she asked Philippe. "I found the girl useful."

"So did I, Madame," said Lorraine with a laugh.

"Monsieur de Lorraine, I know you are completely without the social graces of a gentleman in your position, but, I beg of you, do not address me until I speak to you."

"If I am to be treated in this way I shall leave," said Lorraine.

"I am glad you have given me an indication of how I may rid this place of your presence."

"But it is the house of Monsieur, Madame. Have you forgotten that?"

"Philippe!" cried Henriette. "Why do you sit there and allow this creature to behave thus to me?"

"It was you who were unpleasant to him in the first place," said Philippe sullenly.

"You may pamper the creature. I shall ignore him. I repeat: Why did you send Mademoiselle de Fiennes away?"

"I will tell you," cried Lorraine. "Yes, Philippe, I insist. *I* did not wish the girl to go. I liked her. I like women at times, and she was a pretty girl. It was Monsieur who sent her away. Monsieur could not endure her. It was because he thought I liked her too well." The Chevalier de Lorraine burst into loud laughter, and Philippe scowled.

"Do you expect me to endure this state of affairs?" demanded Henriette.

"You have no choice in the matter," answered Philippe. "And I will tell you this now, We leave for Villers-Cotteret tomorrow."

"*We* leave?"

"You, I and Monsieur de Lorraine."

"You mean you will carry me there by force?"

"You will find that you must obey your husband. I am weary of your spying servants. Our daughter's governess dared go to the King and complain about Lorraine and me, saying that we did not treat you in a becoming manner."

"At least she spoke the truth."

"And my brother has dared to ask me to mend my ways. And this, Madame, is brought about through your servants. Therefore we shall go where we shall not be spied on."

"I will hear no more."

"Hear this though. We leave tomorrow."

"I shall not come."

"Madame, you will come. The King does not wish an open break between us. And have you forgotten our need for a son?"

Henriette turned and left the apartment. She shut herself in her bedchamber and paced up and down.

What had she done, she asked herself, to deserve the worst husband in the world?

❁ ❁ ❁

Solitude was the happiest state she could hope for at Villers-Cotteret. Often she wept bitterly during the night.

If she had a son she would insist on breaking away from Philippe; she would no longer live with such a man. She wept afresh for the loss of her little boy.

It was fortunate that Philippe and Lorraine were soon tired of the solitude of Villers-Cotteret, and they returned to Court.

It was Christmastime and a round of festivities was being planned. Now she was able to find new pleasure, for there came into her presence one day a tall, handsome young man who brought a note from her brother. It ran:

"I believe you may easily guess that I am something concerned for this bearer, James, and therefore I put him in your hands to be directed by you in all things, and pray use that authority over him as you ought to do in kindness to me. . . ."

Henriette looked up into the dark eyes so like Charles', and embraced the young man.

James, Duke of Monmouth, had been sent by her brother to visit her. Charles was proud of his son; perhaps, could Lucy Water see her Jemmy now, she too would be proud.

Henriette knew that Charles had received him at the London Court, that he had given him a dukedom and that he loved him dearly; but this was the first time she had set eyes on him.

Now she became gay again; it was the best way of forgetting those humiliating days at Villers-Cotteret; and how easy it was to be gay with Charles' son!

In some ways he reminded her of Charles, but he lacked her brother's wisdom, that gay cynicism, and perhaps that underlying kindness. How could she have expected it to be otherwise? There was only one Charles in the world.

"James," she cried, "you must tell me about my brother. You must give me news of him. You must tell me every little detail: What time he rises . . . how he spends his days . . . Please, all these little humdrum things that take no account of state affairs. Talk to me . . . talk to me of my dearly beloved brother."

So James talked, and Henriette often drew him aside to hear the news of her brother's Court. She would have him show her the dances prevailing there, those quaint folk dances which seemed so strange to the French; but best of all she liked to hear news of Charles.

Lorraine seemed to grudge her even this pleasure.

"They talk in English," he pointed out to Philippe. "She is half in love with this handsome nephew of hers."

"Nonsense!" said Philippe. "He is but the son of the brother she loves so well."

"She loved the brother too well, some say. Now she loves the brother's son. These are the ways of the Stuarts . . . all know that."

So Philippe taunted his wife, and their life together became more intolerable than ever. Even the Duke of Monmouth's visit was spoiled for Henriette.

❁ ❁ ❁

In the June of that year Marie-Thérèse gave birth to a son. There was general rejoicing throughout the country. The Dauphin, though sickly, still lived.

Henriette was expecting a child in two months' time. She prayed for a son. If she had a boy she was determined to leave Philippe. She would speak of these matters to the King, once her child was born; and surely Louis would understand that no woman of her birth could endure to be treated as she was.

She was worried about her mother, who had aged considerably since her return from England. She had become ill through her anxiety when there had been trouble between England and France, and had spent many sleepless nights wondering about the future relationship between her son and nephew.

Henrietta Maria came to see her daughter at Saint-Cloud because at this time the birth of Henriette's child was imminent, and she herself could pay no visits. They did not speak of the state of friction between the two countries, nor of their private affairs; these subjects were too unhappy to be talked of. Henrietta Maria knew of her daughter's treatment at the hands of her husband—indeed the whole Court knew. So they talked of the child who would soon be born, of their hopes for a boy, and the Queen's malady.

"I do not know what it is that ails me," said Henrietta Maria. "But perhaps it is not a good thing to complain. I have always thought that to complain of illness did little good, and I do not care to be like some ladies who lament for a cut finger or pain in the head. But how I wish I could sleep! I lie awake and brood on the past. It parades before me. I fancy your father speaks to me . . . warns me . . . that I must curb the levity of Charles."

"Charles is popular, Mam. I should not worry about him. It may be that subjects like their Kings to be gay. It may be that they wish for these things. They grew tired of Cromwell's England."

"But the women at his Court! It is not that he has a mistress . . . or two. It is a seraglio."

"Mam, Charles will always be Charles, whatever is said of him."

"And no son to follow him! Only James Crofts . . . or Monmouth, as he now is."

"A charming boy," said Henriette.

"And likely to become as profligate as his father and mother."

"Lucy Water!" pondered Henriette. "I saw her once. A handsome girl . . . but with little character, I felt. Well, Charles loved her and he has kept his word to care for her son; and the little girl is well looked after, although many say that Charles is not her father."

"He is ready to accept all who come to him and accuse him of being their father."

"Dearest Charles! He was always too good-natured. Mam, I beg of you, cease to worry. I will send my physicians to you to prescribe something for your sleeplessness."

"My child, may the saints bless you. May they bring you through your troubles to happiness. May you have a happier life than your poor mother."

"I always remember that you had a good husband who was faithful to you, Mam. It would seem to me that that made up for so much."

"Ah, but to have such a one . . . and to lose him . . . to lose him as I did!"

Mother and daughter fell into silence, and after a while Henrietta Maria left for Colombes.

Four days later Henriette's daughter was born. Her mother did not come to see her; by that time she was feeling too ill to leave Colombes.

❁ ❁ ❁

Henrietta Maria lay in her bed while the physicians sent by her daughter ranged themselves around her.

"It is sleep Your Majesty requires," said Monsieur Valot. "If you could rest you would regain your strength. We shall give you something to ease your pain, Madame."

Henrietta Maria nodded her assent. She, who had complained bitterly of her unhappy life, bore pain stoically.

Monsieur Valot whispered to one of the doctors: "Add three grains to the liquid. That will send Her Majesty to sleep."

Henrietta Maria, hearing the talk of grains, raised herself on her elbow. She said: "Monsieur Valot, my physician in England, Dr Mayerne, has told me I should never take opium. I heard you mention grains. Are those grains you spoke of, grains of opium?"

"Your Majesty," explained Valot, "it is imperative that you sleep. These three grains will ensure that you do. My colleagues here all agree that you must take this sleeping draught, for you cannot hope to recover without sleep."

"But I have been strictly warned against opium on account of the condition of my heart."

"This dose is so small, and I beg of Your Majesty to accept the considered opinion of us all."

"You are the doctors," said Henrietta Maria.

"I shall then instruct the lady in attendance on Your Majesty to give you this dose at eleven o'clock."

Henrietta Maria felt a little better that day. She was able to eat a little, and soon after supper her women helped her to bed.

"I feel tired," she said. "I am sure that, with the aid of my sleeping draught, I shall sleep well."

"There are two hours yet before you should take it, Your Majesty," said her ladies.

"Then I shall lie and wait for it in the comfort that a good night's rest is assured me."

Her ladies left her, and two hours later one of them brought in the draught. The Queen was then sleeping peacefully.

"Madame," said the woman, "you must wake and drink this. The doctor's orders, Your Majesty will remember."

Half awake Henrietta Maria raised herself and drank. She was too sleepy to question the wisdom of waking a sleeping person to administer a sleeping draught.

When her attendants came to wake her in the morning, she was dead.

❁ ❁ ❁

Henriette held her child in her arms. Another daughter. Did this mean she must resume marital relations with Philippe? It was too much to ask. She would not do it. She hated Philippe.

Her woman came to tell her that Mademoiselle de Montpensier was on her way to visit her.

When Mademoiselle came in there were traces of tears on her face; she embraced Henriette and burst into tears.

"I come from Colombes," she said.

Henriette tried in vain to speak. Mam . . . ill! she thought. But she has been ill so long. Mam . . . dead! Mam . . . gone from me!

"She died in her sleep," said Mademoiselle. "It was a peaceful end. She had not been able to sleep; the doctors gave her medicine to cure her wakefulness, which it has done so effectively that she will never wake again."

Still Henriette did not speak.

❁ ❁ ❁

Louis came to Saint-Cloud. He was full of tenderness, as he could always be when those for whom he felt affection were in trouble.

"This is a great blow to you, my darling," he said. "I know how you suffer. My brother's conduct is monstrous. I have remonstrated with him . . . and yet he does nothing to mend his ways."

"Your Majesty is good to me."

"I feel I can never be good enough to you, Henriette. You see, I love you. When I am with you, I am conscious of great regret. I have a wife . . . and there are others . . . but you, Henriette, are apart from all others."

"It warms my heart to hear you say so."

"You and I are close, my dearest . . . closer than any two people in the world."

He embraced her tenderly. She was frailer than ever.

"I know you love me," went on the King. And then: "Your brother is asking that you may visit him."

She smiled, and jealousy pierced Louis' heart, sharp and cold as a sword thrust.

"He says that it is long since he saw you. He says that the grief you have both suffered makes you long to be together for a short while."

"If only I might go!"

"I have spoken to Philippe. He is against your going."

"And you, Sire?"

"Philippe is your husband. His consent would be necessary. It might be that we could force him to give it. Henriette, I wish to speak to you of secret matters. I know I can trust you to work for me . . . for me exclusively."

"I am your subject, Louis."

"You are also an Englishwoman."

"But France is my country. I have lived all my life here. You are my King."

"And more than your King?"

"Yes, Louis. You are my King and my love."

He sighed. "I wish to make a treaty with your brother. It is a very secret treaty. I think he may need . . . a certain amount of persuasion to make him agree to this treaty."

Henriette's heart was beating fast.

"There is none who could persuade him . . . as you could," Louis went on.

"What is this treaty, Louis?"

"I could only disclose it if I thought that you were entirely mine. There are few who know of its contents, and I trust you, Henriette. I trust you completely." He was looking into her eyes. She saw that his were brilliant—as brilliant as when they rested on one of his potential mistresses. But what was happening now was seduction of a different kind—mental seduction. He was as jealous as a lover, but he was jealous of her love for her brother; he was demanding her complete surrender, not to be his mistress but his slave—his spy.

She was overcome by her love for him; the love of years seemed to envelop and overwhelm her.

She knew that if she failed him now, she had lost him; she knew that, if she gave herself to him in this way, they would be bound together forever, that what he felt for his mistresses would indeed be light compared with what he felt for her, that what they could give would be as nothing, compared with her service. She had something which she alone could give: her influence with her brother. He was demanding now to know the extent of her affection for him, how great it was compared with that which she had for Charles.

She felt as though she were swooning. She heard herself say, "Louis . . . I am yours . . . all yours."

❁ ❁ ❁

There were quarrels at Saint-Cloud. Philippe was furious with his wife.

The King had had the Chevalier de Lorraine arrested and sent to the Bastille. He had insulted Madame, and that, in the King's eyes, was a sufficient reason.

Madame was the King's favorite now. It was as it had been in the old days. Where Louis was, there was Henriette. They walked through the groves and alleys of Fontainebleau and Versailles, Louis' arm through that of Madame. They spent hours together with one or two of the King's ministers. Madame was not only the King's dear friend, it seemed; she was his political adviser.

Philippe came upon them once, poring over a document, which was put aside as he entered. His rage was boundless.

"What does the King talk of with you?" he wanted to know. "Answer me! Answer me! Do you think I will allow myself—the King's brother—to be pushed aside!"

She replied coldly: "You must ask the King. He will tell you what he wishes you to know."

"Holy Mother! You are now such a minister of state that you shall ask for the release of Lorraine."

"I shall do no such thing."

"You will . . . you will! It is to please you that he has put my dear friend away. And the only way you shall live with me, Madame, is to live with him as well. We will be together—the three of us—and if you do not like that, you shall endure it!"

"I will endure no such thing. The King has not yet released him, remember."

"If you do not have him released, I will not allow you to go to England."

"The King wishes me to go to England."

"You shall not stay long, though."

She turned away, shrugging her shoulders.

"I shall divorce you!" he cried.

"That is the best news I have heard for a long time."

"Then I shall not divorce you. I shall make you live in hell . . . a hell upon Earth."

"You have already done that. Nothing you do to me in the future can be worse than you have done in the past."

"You are ill. Anyone can see that. You are nothing but a bag of bones."

"I know I cannot hope to compete in your eyes with your dear little friends, Monsieur de Marsan and the Chevalier de Beuvron."

"It is true you cannot."

"Then I hope they console you for the loss of your dear Lorraine!"

Philippe flung out of the room. His rage had brought him near to tears. It had always been the same, Louis always in the ascendant. The same story now, as it had been in their childhood! He wished he had not married Henriette.

❁ ❁ ❁

Henriette could not sleep.

Now she knew the terms of the treaty. She knew that for Louis' sake she must persuade her brother to do something which she knew it was wrong for him to do.

Sometimes she would whisper to herself: "I cannot do it." She recalled her father's terrible end. He had gone against the wishes of his people. Was Louis asking Charles to do the same?

She repeated the terms over to herself. Charles was to join Louis in the invasion of Holland. The French were not popular in England, and that would be a difficult thing for him to arrange; but it was not that clause which gave her the greatest anxiety.

Charles was to make a public confession of his conversion to the Roman Catholic faith. Louis would pay him a large sum of money on his signing the treaty, and would give him men and ammunition to fight his fellow countrymen, should they object to their King's decision.

Louis had said: "I hold that only with a Catholic England can we have a true alliance."

"But if the English will not accept a Catholic King?"

"We must see that they do."

"This could make tragedy in England."

"My dearest, we are concerned with France. Your brother was brought up to be more French than English. He is half French, and it is more natural for him to follow our faith. I have heard that he—as well as your brother James—has a fancy for it."

"But the people of England . . ."

"As I said, we must think of France first, England second, eh? Your brother will know how this may be arranged. We do not ask him to proclaim his conversion at once. He may do so at his own leisure. The time to announce it will be for him to decide. There will be great advantages for him."

But still she did not sleep.

"I love them both," she whispered. "I love France; I love England. I love Louis; I love Charles."

But she knew she was placing the safety of England in jeopardy for the sake of France, for she was going to beg Charles, whom she loved, to risk his crown for the sake of Louis, whom she loved even more.

❁ ❁ ❁

So with great pomp she arrived at Dover. There was one young girl in her suite whose freshness and beauty delighted Henriette. She kept the girl beside her, for it was pleasant to see her childish delight in all the sights and ceremonies. She was the daughter of a poor Breton gentleman, and her name was Louise de Kéroualle.

It was a wonderful moment for Henriette when her brother and Monmouth came on deck to welcome her to England.

She was held fast in Charles' arms, and she saw the tears in his eyes.

"Minette . . . it has been so long. And how frail you are, my dearest, my darling!"

After the ceremonial greetings, the banquet given in her honor, she found herself alone with him. He told her he was grieved to see her so frail. He had heard of her suffering, and that her married life was by no means a felicitous one. He had heard the rumors concerning Lorraine. He would like to lay his hands on that gentleman, he said.

How close they were in those hours!

He learned the terms of the secret treaty. She watched his lean, dark, clever face. Charles understood her anxiety; he understood everything; she might have known that she could keep nothing from him.

Moreover, he was aware that she understood what she was asking him to do in signing this treaty; he knew, therefore, that she was working not for him, but for Louis. It was characteristic of him that he should understand this. His mind was alert. He had said that if he were less lazy he would be a good statesman, and if he could feel as enthusiastic about state matters as he could about a woman's charms, he would be a better King but a far inferior lover.

So it was clear to him that Louis had sent Henriette on this mission because Henriette loved Louis.

Charles was momentarily angry. This was not because she had failed in her love for him—he was but her brother and there was certain to be another whom she must love more—but because of what she had suffered in France. He knew her proud spirit; he knew of the humiliations she had endured at the hands of Philippe. He knew that she must soon leave him and go back to France. There, her position would only be tolerable if she were the King's favorite. Charles loved her; he loved her far more than she loved him. A poor statesman, I! he thought. But a good lover.

He took her face in his hands and kissed it.

"I am entirely yours, Minette," he said.

His quick mind was working. If I sign, I shall receive Louis' pension. That is a good thing. I may declare my conversion at any time I wish. Also a good thing.

My grandfather said Paris was worth a mass. Is not the happiness of my dear sister—she whom I believe I love beyond all things—worth a signature to a treaty?

Then he held her against him.

"My dearest Minette," he said, "you must go back and enjoy your triumphs. Louis is your friend. You can never have a better friend in a country than that country's King—providing he knows how to keep his crown. And you, my sister, have two who love you. When you return to France with my signature on that treaty, the King of France will indeed love you. But I do not think it can be said that he will love you more than does the King of England. Fortunate Minette, to be so loved by two Kings!"

He would not release her. He did not wish to see her tears, nor her to see his.

Minette now had what she had come for. As for Charles, he would find his way out of this awkward situation, as he had on other occasions.

❁ ❁ ❁

The treaty was dispatched to France. Then the entertainments began. Charles was determined to show his sister that the Court of England was as full of wit and luxury as that of France. But the most wonderful thing in the world was, as he told her, for them to be together.

The days passed quickly and it was soon time for her to leave.

"I will give you a parting gift, Charles," she said. "I will give you something which will remind you forever of this meeting of ours."

She called to little Louise de Kéroualle to fetch her casket, that the King might select a jewel. But when the girl came, the King's eyes were not on the casket but on her.

"Pray choose, brother," said Henriette.

Charles laid his hand on the arm of the girl. "Give me this beautiful child," he said. "Let her stay at my Court. She is the only jewel I covet."

Louise's beautiful eyes were opened wide; she was not insensible of his charm.

"Nay," said Henriette. "I am responsible to her parents. I cannot leave her with you, Charles. Come . . . take this ruby."

But Charles and Louise continued to exchange glances, and before Henriette left for France he had managed to kiss the girl.

"I shall not forget you," he said. "One day you shall come to me."

On a hot June day Henriette took her last farewell of Charles; and those about them wept to see their sorrow at this parting, for, never, it was said, had royal brother and sister loved each other as these two did.

❁ ❁ ❁

Louis received her back in France with great warmth. She was his dear friend; now he would trust her forever; never again would he doubt to whom her love was given.

There should be balls, masques, fêtes, ballets; and the Queen of his Court should be his Henriette.

She was gay for a while—two short weeks. She enjoyed her triumphs; but at night she would think of the dark, clever face which she loved so well, and she knew that he—past master in the art of loving—had proved the better lover. He had signed for her sake, and for love of Louis she had made him sign. He understood, as he would always understand; as he would have said: "To love is not only a pleasure, it is a privilege."

He had written in the verses he had shown her:

". . . I think that no joys are above
The pleasures of love."

Yet she had betrayed him, and because of that she knew she would never be happy again.

Now those about her noticed the effect of the sleepless nights. She was too thin, too fragile for a young woman barely twenty-seven years of age.

Philippe worried her continually. Her influence with the King was great, he reminded her; she must bring about the return of Lorraine; he would make her very sorry if she did not.

She turned wearily away from him. He forced her to go alone with him to Saint-Cloud where he continued to make her life miserable, and only the command of the King could induce him to bring her back to Versailles; but as soon as possible he forced her to return once more to Saint-Cloud.

There she must endure his company, his continual complaints, and this she suffered, together with the reproaches of her own conscience.

She was coughing a good deal, and there were times when she felt almost too weary to care what became of her.

One evening, only a few weeks after her return, she was dining with Philippe and her ladies when she felt a strange lassitude come over her. When the meal was over she lay down on some cushions because, she said, she felt unusually tired. The day had been hot and she now slept, and while she slept she dreamed. She dreamed she was sailing towards Dover, and her brother was holding out his arms to her, but that she was turning away and crying because she was ashamed to go to him.

Coming out of her dream she heard voices. "How ill Madame looks! Do you see?"

Then she heard Philippe: "I have never seen her look so ill."

"It is the journey to England which has done this. She has not been well since she returned."

"Ah, that journey to England!" said Philippe. "I was a fool to allow it."

Henriette opened her eyes and said: "I want a drink."

Madame de Gourdon, one of her ladies, hurried away to bring her a glass of iced chicory water, which she drank; but no sooner had she done so than she was seized with violent pains in her side.

She cried out in agony: "I have such pains! What was in that glass? I believe myself to have been poisoned." As she spoke she fixed her eyes on Philippe, who had hurried to her side.

Her ladies unlaced her gown as she fell fainting onto her cushions.

She opened her eyes at length and murmured: "This . . . pain. I cannot endure it. Who has poisoned me?" Once more she turned to Philippe. He fell on his knees beside her.

"You must get well," he said. "You will get well, Henriette."

"You have ceased to love me, Philippe," she said. "You never loved me."

Philippe covered his face with his hands and burst into tears.

One of the ladies sent for her confessor; another saved the chicory water that it might be examined.

"Madame," murmured one of the women, "the doctors will soon be here."

"I have greater need of my confessor," she answered.

The ladies were looking at her with concern. Henriette, through the haze in her mind, which was the result of pain, was aware of their suspicions of her husband. They were sure that she had been poisoned, and they suspected Philippe of murder.

❁ ❁ ❁

A few hours passed. Philippe showed great distress, but Henriette was skeptical. She said to herself: "He has then tried to rid himself of me as he threatened he would. Did he plot this then . . . with Lorraine?"

"Madame . . . Madame . . . take this soup," begged one of her ladies. "It will make you stronger."

"Nothing will make me stronger now. I shall not be here by morning. I know it."

She closed her eyes and thought: Nor do I want to be. I do not want to live continually to reproach myself.

After a while she said: "There is one who will be heartbroken when he hears the news of my death. Do you know who that is? Do you know who loves me more dearly than any? It is my brother of England."

"Madame," she was told, "the King is on his way to see you."

❁ ❁ ❁

When Louis came she was lying back exhausted, and he could scarcely recognize her; she looked so small in her nightdress which had been loosened at the neck to allow her to breathe. Her face was deathly pale, her beautiful eyes sunken; already she appeared to be more dead than alive.

She found it difficult to see him. He seemed to swim before her eyes—tall, commanding, the most handsome man in the world.

"Louis . . ." Her lips managed to form the words.

"Henriette . . . my dearest."

"Louis . . . I am going . . . I am going fast."

"Nay!" he cried; and she heard his sobs. "Nay, you will recover. You must recover."

"The first thing you will hear in the morning is that I am dead."

"It shall not be. It must not be."

"Oh Louis, you are the King and accustomed to command, but you cannot command death to stay away when he has made up his mind to come for me."

Louis turned to the doctors. "Will you let her die without trying to save her?"

"Sire, there is nothing we can do."

"Louis!" she cried. "Louis, come back to me. For the last time, hold my hand."

His eyes were so blinded with tears that he could not see her. "Henriette," he murmured, "Henriette, you cannot leave me. You cannot leave me."

"I must leave you . . . both you and Charles . . . you two . . . whom I have loved so much. Louis, there will be many to comfort you . . . I grieve for Charles. I grieve for my brother. He is losing the person he loves best in the world. Louis, you will write to him. You will tell him of my end? Tell him how at the end I spoke of him. Tell him that . . . if in any way I wronged him . . . I loved him . . . I always loved him."

"I shall send word to him. I shall send him comfort. I shall send him that Breton girl who was with you . . . You told me how he wished her to stay. She will comfort him . . . She will remind him of you. I shall send her to his Court with my wishes for his comfort."

Henriette tried to shake her head. She understood the meaning behind those words. He would send the girl to do what she had done—spy for France.

"Louis . . ." she gasped. "No . . . no!"

"But you will get well," persisted the King stubbornly. "I command you to get well. You cannot leave me. I'll not allow it."

The Curé of Saint-Cloud arrived, bringing the Host with him. She received the Viaticum and asked for Queen Anne's crucifix to hold in her hand as she left this world.

All knew now that she could not live long.

Men and women, courtiers and servants, were crowding into the great hall, for the news that she was dying had spread through the Court.

And there at her bedside stood the King, the tears falling and great sobs racking his body.

"Kiss me, Sire, for the last time," whispered Henriette. "Do not weep for me, or you will make me weep too. You are losing a good servant, Louis. I have ever feared the loss of your good graces more than anything on earth . . . more than death itself . . . and if I have done wrong . . . so often it has been that I might serve you. Louis . . . remember me . . ."

He kissed her tenderly. He knelt by the bed and covered his face with his hands.

❁ ❁ ❁

Charles was stunned by the news. Henriette, who had been with him a few weeks before, dead!

Minette, his beloved sister, who had seemed to be ever present in her letters to him! Minette, whom he had loved beyond all others; for his passion for his mistresses was fleeting, whereas his love for his sister had endured all through his life. Minette . . . dead!

Rumors spread that she had been poisoned. Philippe and the Chevalier de Lorraine were suspected.

Charles, in indignant rage, demanded the satisfaction of an autopsy. Louis was only too glad to grant this.

"It is a sorrow we share," he wrote to Charles. "If a foul deed has been done, I am as eager to find and punish her murderer as you are."

The chicory water had been examined and even drunk by others, who suffered no ill effect; at the autopsy no poison was found in her body; it was remembered that it was long since she had enjoyed good health.

Were there not always rumors of poisoning when notable people died?

Charles was unable to control his grief. He could not bear to speak of her; he shut himself away from the pleasures of his Court.

Never has the King shown such grief, it was said.

Then there came to his Court one who, the King of France felt, would, while she reminded him of his sister, bring some comfort to Charles. She was the jewel he had coveted, said Louis, and it would have been Henriette's wish that her brother should possess this coveted jewel. It was hoped that the King of England would show his sister's maid of honor "a piece of tenderness" and cherish her at his Court.

In the lovely young Breton, Louise de Kéroualle, both Kings saw a substitute for Henriette.

Louis saw her as his spy at the court of England, who would serve him as Henriette had done. Charles delighted to see her again and, in his appreciation of her fresh young beauty, was able to subdue his grief. He would show her that "piece of tenderness," and she would remind him of Henriette, even as Lucy's boy—Monmouth—reminded him of Lucy.

There was pleasure in love, he had always said, and for him there always would be. There were many years ahead for him and for Louis, to indulge in the pleasures of love. There would be many women, the memory of whom would become as hazy as his hours with Lucy had now become; yet as long as he lived he would cherish the memory of his sweet Minette.

Part Two

A HEALTH UNTO HIS MAJESTY

Catherine of Braganza and
Barbara, Countess of Castlemaine

ONE

It was the month of May—the gayest and most glorious month, the people assured themselves, that England had ever known. This was the 29th, a day of great significance.

That morning, it seemed that the sun rose with more than its usual brilliance.

"A good omen!" people called to one another from the windows of houses, the overhanging gables of which almost met over the cobbled streets. "It's going to be a fine day."

In the country, as soon as the dawn showed in the sky, people were gathering on the village greens; there would be many to line the roads so that they should miss nothing when the time came.

"Listen!" one said to another. "Even the birds are mad with joy. Have you ever heard a blackbird or chaffinch sing like that before? They know the good times are back."

Others declared that the cherry trees had never borne such great masses of blossom in previous years. The flowers seemed more fragrant that spring. Children gathered buttercups and bluebells, celandines and lady's-smocks to strew along the road; they wore chains of daisies as necklaces and chaplets as they danced to the merry tunes of the fiddlers.

Now the bells were ringing from every tower and steeple between Rochester and London.

This was the happy month of May when the "Black Boy" had come home to his people.

❖ ❖ ❖

He rode in the midst of the cavalcade—tall, slim and elegant, his swarthy face prematurely lined, his dark eyes smiling, eager, alert, yet holding a hint of cynicism in their depth. He looked older than his years; he was thirty and this was not only the day of his entry into his capital, it was also his birthday. A meet and fitting day, all agreed, for his return.

With him came 20,000 horse and foot, swords held high, shouting to express their hilarious joy as they marched along. The cavalcade had become swollen with every mile, for there had been a welcome for His Majesty at every point: Morris dancers had wished to show him by the abandoned joy of their performance that they rejoiced in his return, which was a signal for the overthrow of solemnity; fiddlers had played the merriest jigs they knew till the sweat ran down their faces; even the dignified mayors in their robes of office were almost indecorously gay. Men and women of all conditions had come to add their loyal shouts to the general clamor.

At last they came into his capital, where the bells were making a merry peel and the streets were hung with tapestry, and the conduits flowing with wine instead of water. Citizens wept and embraced each other. "The drab days are over," they cried again and again. "The King is restored to his own."

There would be merrymaking again; there would be pageants and ceremonies. On May Days the milkmaids would dance again in the streets, their pails flower-decked, while a fiddler led them along the Strand; the pleasure gardens would be thrown open; the theaters would flourish. Bartholomew and Southwark Fairs would be enjoyed once more; cock-fighting and bull-baiting would take place openly again; laughter would be considered a virtue instead of a sin; and when Christmas came it would be celebrated with the old gusto. The great days were here again for His Majesty King Charles II had come home.

What a brilliant sight this was, with the Lord Mayor and aldermen and members of City Companies in their various liveries and golden chains; colored banners were held high; lines of brilliant tapestries were strung across the streets, while trumpet, fife and drum all sought to rival each other.

So great was the company that it took seven hours to pass any one spot. There had never been such pageantry in the City of London; and the citizens promised themselves that the revelry should continue for days to come. No one should be allowed to forget for a moment that the King had come home. It was eleven years since his father had been cruelly murdered; and for more years than that this dark young man had been a wandering exile on the continent of Europe. It was only fitting that he should know a right royal welcome was his.

He rode bareheaded, bowing this way and that, a faint smile about his mouth. He had remarked that it must surely have been his own fault that he had not returned before, as he had met no one, since he had stepped on English soil, who did not protest most fervently that he had always wished for the restoration of his King.

Now there were faint lines of weariness about his mouth. He had long dreamed of this day; he would never have believed that he could have come to it in this manner and that his restoration could have been brought about without the shedding of one drop of blood—and by that very army which had sent his father to the scaffold and rebelled against himself. This was to be compared with that miraculous escape after Worcester; it was the second miracle in his life.

But he was weary—weary, yet content.

" 'Od's Fish!" he murmured. "I have learned to live on easy terms with Exile and Poverty, but Popularity is such a stranger to me that I am uneasy in his presence. Yet I trust ere long that he and I shall become boon companions."

His eyes strayed again and again to the women, who waved flowers from the roadside as he passed or called a loyal welcome from their windows. Then the somber eyes would lighten at the sight of a pretty face, and the smile he gave would be very charming, the regal bowing of the head most elegant.

The people looked at him with tears in their eyes. A young King—a King who, during his thirty years, had suffered hardship and frustration, which must have made him sick at heart. Small wonder that rumors had reached England of his profligate habits; but if he was overfond of the ladies the ladies would readily forgive him that, and the men would not hold it against him. He was such a romantic figure: a King returned to his country after years of exile. Charles Stuart on his thirtieth birthday, on entering his capital city, seemed to all beholders a King worthy to be loved.

The people grew hoarse with their shouting. Again and again the procession was delayed that yet another expression of loyal homage might be laid before the King, and it was seven o'clock before he came to his Palace of Whitehall.

Now the lights were springing up all over the city. Bonfires were raised in every open space, and lighted candles showed in all the windows.

"Let us welcome the King," shouted a thousand voices. "Let us cry 'A Health Unto His Majesty.' "

The City was brilliant with thousands of candles which shone alike from the' windows of great houses and the humblest dwellings.

In every window there must be candles to welcome His Majesty, for gangs roamed the streets ready to smash any window which was dark.

Everyone must join in the welcome, for the Merry Monarch had returned to make England merry.

❁ ❁ ❁

In the Palace of Whitehall there was one who, with an impatience that she could not contain, waited to be presented to the King.

This was a tall young woman of nineteen, strikingly beautiful with rich, ripe coloring, bold flashing eyes that were almost startlingly blue; her rippling dark auburn hair was thick and vital; her features firm but beautifully molded. There was in her evidence of a fierce passion, which might have alarmed, but fascinated. Almost every man with whom she had come into contact had discovered her to be irresistible. Her rages came swiftly, and when they were upon her there was no knowing what turn they would take; she was beautiful and could be fierce as a tigress—an Amazon of incomparable beauty which was of a deep sensual kind. Barbara Villiers—now Barbara Palmer—was the most desirable young woman in London.

Now she fumed as she paced up and down the apartment in which she waited for audience with the King.

Her maids hovered some little distance from her. They were afraid to come too near, yet afraid to come too far from her. If they offended her, Barbara did not hesitate personally to apply corporal punishment. She would pick up the nearest article and fling it at the offender; and her aim was sure; all her life she had been throwing things at those who offended her.

She was not satisfied with the set of her dress at one moment; at the next her eyes glistened as she looked down at its smooth silken folds which fell seductively about her perfect figure. Her arms—very white and perfectly rounded—were bare from the elbow and the upper arm was visible here and there, for her wide sleeves were slit from the shoulder and loosely laced with blue ribbons. Her skirt was caught up to show a clinging satin petticoat. She was beautiful; and she wished to be more beautiful than she had ever been before. She patted those curls which had been arranged on her forehead and which were called, after the fashion of the day, "favorites." Those which rippled over her shoulders were "heartbreakers," and those nestling against her cheeks "confidants." They were all lustrous natural curls, and she was proud of them.

Her husband, Roger Palmer, came to her then. His eyes shone with mixed pride and apprehension; he had been proud and apprehensive of Barbara ever since he had married her.

She gave him one of her disdainful looks. Never had he seemed to her more ineffectual than he did at that moment, but even as she glanced his way a smile curved her lips. He was her husband and that was how she would have him. She had strength and determination enough for them both.

Roger said: "The press in the streets is growing worse."

Barbara did not answer. She never bothered to state the obvious.

"The King is worn out with the journey," went on Roger. "All that bowing and smiling. . . . It must be wearying."

Barbara still said nothing. All the bowing and smiling! she thought. Tired he might be, but he would be content. To think it had come at last. To think he was here in London!

But she was afraid. When she had last seen him he had been a King in exile, a very hopeful King it was true, but still an exile. Now that he had come into his own, her rivals would not be merely a few women at an exiled Court; they would be all the beauties of England. Moreover he himself would be a man courted and flattered by all. . . . It might well be that the man with whom she had to deal would be less malleable than that King who, briefly, had been her lover when she had gone with Roger to Holland.

That was but a few months ago, when Roger had been commissioned to carry money to the King who was then planning his restoration to the throne.

Charles had looked at Barbara and had been immediately attracted by those flamboyant charms.

Barbara too had been attracted—not only by his rank but by his personal charm. She had been sweetly subdued and loving during those two or three nights in Holland; she had kept that fierce passion for power in check; she had concealed it so successfully that it had appeared in the guise of a passion for the man. Yet he was no fool, that tall lean man; he was well versed in the ways of such as Barbara; and because he would never rave and rant at a woman, that did not mean that he did not understand her. Barbara was a little apprehensive of his tender cynical smile.

She had said: "Tomorrow I shall have to leave for England with my husband."

"Ere long," he had answered, "I shall be recalled to London. My people have been persuaded to clamor for my return, just as eleven years ago they were taught to demand my father's head. Ere long I too shall be in England."

"Then . . . sire, we shall both be there."

"Aye . . . we shall both be there. . . ."

And that was all; it was characteristic of him.

She was faintly alarmed concerning the changes she might find in him; but when she held up her mirror, patted the "favorites" which nestled on her brow, smiled at her animated and beautiful face, she was confident that she would succeed.

Roger, watching her, understood her thoughts. He said: "I know what happened between you and the King in Holland."

She laughed at him. "I pray you do not think to play the outraged husband with me, sir!"

"Play the part! I have no need to *play* it, Barbara," said the little man sadly. "If you think to fool me with others as you did with Chesterfield . . ."

"Now that the King is returned it might be called treason to refer to his Majesty as 'others.' You are a fool, Roger. Are you so rich, is your rank so high that you can afford to ignore the advantages I might bring you?"

"I do not like the manner in which you would bring me these advantages. Am I a complacent fool? Am I a husband to stand aside and smile with pleasure at his wife's wanton behavior? Am I? Am I?"

Barbara spun round on him and cried: "Yes. . . . Yes, you are!"

"You must despise me. Why did you marry me?"

Barbara laughed aloud. "Because mayhap I see virtues where others see faults. Mayhap I married you because you are . . . what you are. Now I pray you do not be a fool. Do not disappoint me. Do not tell me I have made a mistake in the man I married, and I promise you that you shall not come badly out of your union with me."

"Barbara, sometimes you frighten me."

"I am not surprised. You are a man who is easily frightened. . . . Yes, woman?" shouted Barbara, for one of her women had appeared at the door.

"Madam, the King wishes to see you."

Barbara gave a loud laugh of triumph. She had nothing to fear. He was the same man who had found her irresistible during that brief stay in Holland. The King was commanding that she be brought to his presence.

She took one last look at herself in her mirror, assured herself of her startling beauty and swept out of her apartment to the presence of the King.

❁ ❁ ❁

Barbara had learned what she wanted at a very early age, and with that knowledge had come the determination to get it.

She never knew her father, for that noble and loyal gentleman had died before she was two years old; but when she was a little older her mother had talked to her of him, telling her how he had met his death at the siege of Bristol for the sake of the King's cause, and that she, his only child, must never forget that she was a member of the noble family of Villiers and not do anything to stain the honor of that great name.

At that time Barbara was a vivacious little girl and, because she was a very pretty one, she was accustomed to hearing people comment on her lovely appearance. She was fascinated by the stories of her father's heroism and she determined that when she grew up she would be as heroic as he was. She promised herself that she would perform deeds of startling bravery; she would astonish all with her cleverness; she would become a Joan of Arc to lead the Royalists to victory. She was a fervent Royalist because her father had been. She thought of Cromwell and Fairfax as monsters, Charles, the King, as a saint. Even when she was but four years old her little face would grow scarlet with rage when anyone mentioned Cromwell's name.

"Curb that temper of yours, Barbara," her mother often said. "Control it. Never let it control you."

Sometimes her relatives would visit her mother—those two dashing boys of another branch of the family, George and Francis Villiers. They teased her a good deal, which never failed to infuriate her so that she would forget the injunctions to curb her temper and fly at them, biting and scratching, using all the strength she possessed to fight them; this naturally only amused them and made them intensify their teasing.

George, the elder of the boys, had been the Duke of Buckingham since his father had died. He was more infuriating than his brother Lord Francis, and it became his special delight to see how fierce she could become. He told her she would die a spinster, because no man would marry such a termagant as she would undoubtedly become; he doubted not that she would spend her life in a convent, where they would have a padded cell into which she could be locked until she recovered from her rages.

Those boys gave her plenty of practice in control. Often she would hide from them because she was determined not to show her anger, but she soon discovered that, she enjoyed her passions and, oddly enough, the company of her young relatives.

When Barbara was seven her mother married again and Barbara's stepfather was her father's cousin, Charles Villiers, Earl of Anglesey.

The marriage startled Barbara because, having always heard her father spoken of with reverence, it seemed strange that her mother could so far forget his perfections as to take another husband. Barbara's blue eyes were alert; she had always felt a great interest in the secret ways of adults. Now she remembered that her stepfather had for some time been a frequent visitor, and that he had seemed on each occasion always very affectionate towards her mother. She reasoned that her, father, whom she had thought to be perfect, must after all have been merely foolish. He had become involved in the war and had met his death. The King's Cause had gained little by his sacrifice; and his reward was a tomb and the title of hero, while his cousin's was marriage with the widow.

Barbara told herself sagely that she would not have been as foolish as her father. When her time came she would know how to get what she wanted and live to enjoy it.

The result of this marriage was a move to London, and Barbara was enchanted by London as soon as she set eyes on it. It was Puritan London, she heard, and not to be compared with merry laughter-laden London of the old days; but still it was London. She would ride through Hyde Park with her mother or her governess in their carriage, and she would look wistfully at the gallery at the Royal Exchange, which was full of stalls displaying silks and fans; she would notice the rendezvous of young men and women in the Mulberry Garden. "London's a dull place," she often heard it said, "compared with the old city. Why, then there was dancing and revelry in the streets. A woman was not safe out after dark—not that she is now—but the King's Cavaliers had a dash about them that the Puritans lack."

She was eager for knowledge of the world; she longed for fine clothes; she hated the dowdy garments she was forced to wear; she wished to grow up quickly that she might take her part in the exciting merry-go-round of life.

The servants were afraid of her, and she found it easy to get what she wanted from them. She could kick and scream, bite and scratch in a manner which terrified them.

Occasionally she saw George and Francis. George was haughty and had no time for little girls. Francis was gentler and told her stories of the royal household in which he and his brother had spent their childhood, because King Charles had loved their father dearly and when he had been killed in the Royalist Cause had taken the little Villiers boys into his household to be brought up with the little Princes and Princess. Francis told Barbara of Charles, the King's eldest son, the most easygoing boy he had ever known; and he talked of Mary who had been married to the Prince of Orange, after she was almost blind with weeping and hoarse with begging her parents not to send her away from Whitehall; he told her of young James, who had wanted to join in their games, and from whom they had all run away because he was too young. She liked to hear of the games which had been played in the avenues and alleys of Hampton Court. Her eyes would glisten and she would declare that she wished she had been born a man, that she might be a king.

There came a time when Francis ceased to visit her and she knew, from the way in which people spoke of him, that some mystery surrounded him. She insisted on getting the story from the servants. Then she learned that Francis was yet another victim of the King's Cause.

Lord Francis had lost his life, and his brother the Duke, who had lost his estates, was forced to escape to Holland.

Seven-year-old Barbara, keeping her ears open, heard that Helmsley Castle and York House in the Strand, which had both been the property of the Villiers family, had passed to General Fairfax, and that New Hall had gone to Cromwell.

She was infuriated with those Roundhead soldiers. She would thump her fist on a table or stool. Her mother often warned her that she would do herself some injury if she persisted in giving way to the rage which boiled within her.

"Do we stand aside and allow these nobodies to rob our family?" she demanded.

"We stand aside," said her mother.

"And," added her stepfather, "we keep quiet. We are thankful that the little we have is left to us."

"Thankful, with Francis dead and George running away to hide in Holland!"

"You are but a child. You do not understand these things. You should not listen to what is not intended for your ears."

It was a long time after that when she saw George again; but she heard of him from time to time. He fought at Worcester with Charles, the new King, for the old King had been murdered by his enemies. Barbara was ten years old at that time and she understood what was happening. She cursed the Roundhead soldiers whom she saw lounging in Paul's Walk, using the Cathedral and the city's churches as barracks or for stabling their horses, walking through the capital in their somber garments, yet swaggering a little, as though to remind the citizens that they were the masters now. She understood George well, for he was very like herself—far more like her than gentle Lord Francis had been. George Duke of Buckingham wished to command the King's army, but the King, on the advice of Edward Hyde who had followed him to the continent, had refused to allow him to do so. Buckingham was furious—like Barbara he could never brook frustration—and was full of wild plans for bringing the King back to his throne. He was too young for the command, said Hyde; and at that time Charles had agreed with all that Edward Hyde advised. And Barbara heard how Buckingham would not attend council meetings in the exiled Court, that he scarcely spoke to the King; how his anger turned sour and he brooded perpetually; how he refused to clean himself or allow any of his servants to do this, and would not change his linen.

"Foolish, foolish George!" cried Barbara. "If I were in his place . . ."

But George, it seemed, was not so foolish as she had thought him. He suddenly ceased to neglect himself, for the Princess of Orange, the King's sister Mary, had become a widow and George had offered himself as her second husband.

Barbara listened to the talk between her mother and her stepfather; moreover she demanded that the servants should tell her every scrap of gossip they heard.

Thus she discovered that Queen Henrietta Maria had declared herself incensed at Buckingham's daring to aspire to the hand of the Princess. She had been reported as saying that she would rather tear her daughter into tiny pieces than allow her to consider such a match.

Yes, George was a fool, decided Barbara. If he had wished to marry Mary of Orange he should have visited her in secret; he should have made her fall in love with him, perhaps married her in secret. She was sure he could have done that; he was possessed of the same determination as she was. And then he would have seen what that old fury, Queen Henrietta Maria (who, many said, was responsible for the terrible tragedy which had overtaken her husband King Charles I) would do!

Then for a time she ceased to think of George when she met Philip Stanhope, Earl of Chesterfield, who came on a visit to her stepfather's house. She had heard much talk of him before his arrival.

He was clever, it was said; he was one of the wise ones. He was not the sort to talk vaguely of what he would do when the King came home; he was not the sort to drink wistful toasts to the Black Boy across the water. No, Chesterfield would look at the new England and try to find a niche for himself there.

It seemed he was finding a very pleasant niche indeed, for he was betrothed to none other than Mary Fairfax, the daughter of the Parliamentarian General who, next to Cromwell himself, was the most important man in the Commonwealth.

Mary Fairfax was her father's darling and, good Parliamentarian though she might be, was bedazzled not only by the handsome looks and charming manners of the Earl, but by the prospect of becoming a Countess.

So this was one way in which a member of the aristocracy could live comfortably in the new England.

Barbara admired the man before she saw him, and he showed on the first day under her stepfather's roof that he was not indifferent to Barbara. She would look up to discover his eyes upon her, and to her surprise she found herself blushing. He seemed to sense her confusion. It amused him; and she, telling herself that she was furious with him for this, knew in her heart that she was far from displeased. His attention was reminding her that she was not a little girl any longer; she was a young woman; and she fancied that he was comparing her with Mary Fairfax.

She would ignore him. She shut herself into her own room; but she could not drive him from her thoughts. She saw the change in herself. She was like a bud which was opening to the warmth of the sun; but she was not a bud—she was a woman responding to the warmth of his glances.

He came upon her once on the staircase which led to her room. He said: "Barbara, why do you always avoid me?"

"Avoid you!" she said. "I was not aware of you."

"You lie," he answered.

Then she turned and tossed her long hair so that it brushed across his face, and would have darted up the stairs; but the contact seemed to arouse a determination within him, for he caught the hair and pulled her back by it; then he laid a hand on her breast and kissed her.

She twisted free and, as she did so, slapped his face so hard that he reeled backwards. She was free and she darted up the stairs to her room; when she reached it, she ran in and bolted the door.

She leaned against it; she could hear him on the other side of it as he beat on it with his fists.

"Open it," he said. "Open it, you vixen!"

"Never to you," she cried. "Take care you are not thrown out of this house, my lord earl."

He went away after a while, and she ran to her mirror and looked at herself; her hair was wild, her eyes shining, and there was a red mark on her cheek where he had kissed her. There was no anger in her face at all; there was only delight.

She was happier than she had ever been, but she was haughty to him when they next met, and scarcely spoke to him; her mother reprimanded her for her ill manners to their guest; but when had she taken any notice of her mother?

After that she began to study herself in the mirror; she loosened her curls; she unlaced her bodice that more of her rounded throat might be shown. She was tall, and her figure seemed to have matured since that first encounter. When she was near him she was aware of a tingling excitement such as she had never known before in the whole of her life. Feigning to avoid him she yet sought him. She was never happier than when she was near him, flashing scornful glances at him from under her heavy lids; it amused her in the presence of her mother and stepfather to ask artless questions concerning the beauty and talents of his betrothed.

She saw a responsive gleam in his eyes; she was wise enough to know that she was but a novice in the game she was playing; she knew that he stayed at her stepfather's house for only one reason, and that he would not leave it until he had captured her. This made her laugh. Not that she would avoid the capture; she had determined to be captured. She believed that she was on the point of making an important discovery. She was beautiful, and beauty meant power. She could take this man—the betrothed of Mary Fairfax—and drive everything from his mind but the desire for herself. That was power such as she longed to wield; and she had learned from those moments when he had touched her or kissed her, that surrender would be made without the slightest reluctance.

Barbara was beginning to know herself.

So one day she allowed him to discover her stretched out on the grass in the lonely part of the nuttery.

There was a struggle; she was strong, but so was he; she was overpowered and, when she was seduced, she knew that she would never find life dull while there were men to make love to her.

❁ ❁ ❁

From that moment Barbara was aware that her first and most impelling need would always be the satisfaction of her now fully aroused sexual desires; but there was one other thing she wanted almost equally: Power. She wanted no opposition to any desire of hers, however trivial. She wanted to ride in her carriage through London and be admired and known as the most important person in the city. She wanted fine clothes and jewels—a chance to set this beauty of hers against a background which would enhance rather than minimize it. In the clothes she was obliged to wear, her fine already maturing figure was not displayed to advantage; the color of her gown subdued the dazzling blue of her eyes and it did not suit the rich auburn of her hair. Clothes were meant to adorn beauty, yet she was so much more beautiful without hers; it would seem therefore that she wore the wrong clothes.

Clearly she must be free. She was sixteen and would be no longer treated as a child.

She thought of Chesterfield and wondered whether through him lay a means of escape. There had been more amorous encounters between them. Although there was little of tenderness in their relationship, both recognized in each other a passion which matched their own. Barbara at sixteen was wise enough to realize that her feelings for this man were based on appetite rather than emotion, and Barbara's appetite was beginning to be voracious.

Chesterfield was a rake and a reckless man. From an early age he had been obliged to fend for himself; he was not the man to sacrifice his life to an ideal. He was as ambitious as Barbara, and almost as sensual. His father had died before he was two years old and he had received most of his education in Holland. He was some eight years older than Barbara and already a widower, for Anne Percy, his wife, had died three years ago and the seduction of females was no unusual sport of his.

Barbara often wondered what sort of husband he had been to Anne Percy. A disturbing one, she fancied, and of course an unfaithful one. He did not speak of Anne, though he found a malicious enjoyment in discussing his betrothed Mary Fairfax with Barbara.

He dallied at the house, delaying his departure; and it was all on account of Barbara.

That was why she began to contemplate marriage with him as a means of escape. They were of a kind, and therefore suited. She would not ask him to be faithful to her, for she was sure she would not wish to be so to him. Already she found herself watching others with eager speculation; so she and Philip would not be ill matched.

He was betrothed to Mary Fairfax, but who was Mary Fairfax to marry with an Earl? Whereas Barbara, on the other hand, was a member of the noble family of Villiers.

She hinted that her family might not be averse to a match between them. He had visited her in her room—a daring procedure; but Barbara could be sure that none of the servants who might discover her escapade would dare mention it for fear of what might happen to them if their tattling reached their mistress's ears. Moreover she was growing careless.

So as they lay on her bed she talked of her family and his, and the possibility of a marriage between them.

Chesterfield rolled onto his back and burst out laughing.

"Barbara, my love," he said, "this is not the time to talk of marriage. It is not the custom, for marriages are not planned in bedchambers."

"I care not for custom," she retorted.

"That much is clear. It is a happy quality . . . in a mistress. In a wife, not so . . . ah, not so."

Barbara sprang up and soundly slapped his face. But he was no frightened servant. His desire temporarily satiated, he laughed at her fury.

He went on: "Had you intended to barter your virginity for marriage it should have been before our little adventure in the nuttery, not afterwards. Oh, Barbara, Barbara, you have much to learn."

"You too, my lord," she cried, "if you think to treat me as you would treat a tavern girl."

"You . . . a tavern girl! By God, you spit like one . . . you bite and scratch like one . . . and you are as ready to surrender. . . ."

"Listen to me," said Barbara. "I am a Villiers. My father was . . ."

"It is precisely because you are a Villiers, my dear Barbara, that you are a less attractive match than the one I am about to make."

"You insult my family!"

That made him laugh more heartily. "My dear girl, are you ignorant of the state of this country? There has been a turnabout; did you not know? Who are the great families today? The Villiers? The Stanhopes? The Percys? The Stuarts? Not The Cromwells! The Fairfaxes. . . . Yet these newly made nobles have a certain respect for old families, providing we do not work against them. I'll tell you a secret. Oliver himself once offered me the command of his Army; and what do you think went with it?—the hand of one of his daughters."

"And you would consider that, would you? You would take up arms against the King?"

"Who said I would consider it? I merely state the facts. No! I have declined the command of the Army, and with it the hand of either Mary or Frances Cromwell."

"I see," said Barbara, "that you are telling me you are greatly desired in marriage by families which could be of greater use to you than mine."

"How clearly you state the case, dear Barbara."

Barbara leaped off the bed and, putting on her wrap, said with great disdain: "That may be so at this time, but one day, my lord you will see that the man who marries me will come to consider he has not made so bad a match. Now I pray you get out of my room."

He dressed leisurely and left; it seemed that the talk of marriage had alarmed him; for the next day he left the house of Charles Villiers.

❁ ❁ ❁

Buckingham came to London at this time; he was depressed, and on his arrival had shut himself up in his lodgings and had his servants explain that he was too low in health to receive visitors.

Barbara's imperious insistence fought a way through the carrier he had set about him. When she saw him she was surprised at the change in him. It was a matter of astonishment to her that a Villiers, a member of her noble family, could give way so easily to despair.

Buckingham was amused with his vehement young relative, and found no small pleasure in listening to her conversation.

"You forget, my cousin," he said to her on one occasion when he had broken his seclusion by calling at her stepfather's house, "that we live in a changing world. At your age you can have known no other, yet you cling to old Royalist traditions more fiercely than any."

"Of course I cling. Are we not a noble family? What advantages can such as ourselves hope for in a country where upstarts rule us?"

"None, dear cousin. None. That is why I lie abed and turn my face to the wall."

"Then you're a lily-livered spineless fool!"

"Barbara! Your language is not only vehement, it is offensive."

"Then I am glad it rouses you to protest, for it is as well that you should be aroused to something. What of the King? He is your friend. He may be an exile, but he is still the King."

"Barbara, the King and I have quarreled. He no longer trusts me. He will have nothing to do with me, and in this he follows the advice of that Chancellor of his, Edward Hyde."

"Edward Hyde! And what right has he to speak against a noble Villiers?"

"There you go again! It is all noble family with you. Cannot you see that nobility serves a man ill in a Commonwealth such as ours?"

"There are some who would attempt to find the best of both worlds."

"And who are these?"

"My Lord Chesterfield, for one. He seeks to marry into the Fairfax family. He says that Oliver Cromwell offered him one of his daughters as well as a command in the Army. He refused the Protector's offer. He did not, I suspect, wish to set himself so blatantly on the side of the King's enemies. But a marriage with Fairfax's daughter is less conspicuous and brings him, he thinks, many advantages."

"A marriage with Fairfax's daughter," mused the Duke. "H'm! Chesterfield is a wily one."

"Why should not Buckingham be as wily?"

"Why not indeed!"

"George, you are the handsomest man in England, and could be the most attractive if you would but seek to make yourself so."

"There speaks your family pride."

"I'll wager Mary Fairfax would turn from Chesterfield if she thought there was a chance of marrying with one who is not only the handsomest man in England but a noble Villiers."

"Barbara, you seem interested in this match. What is Chesterfield to you?"

Her eyes narrowed and she flushed faintly. Buckingham nodded his head sagely.

"By God, Barbara," he said, "you're growing up . . . you're growing up fast. So Chesterfield preferred Fairfax's girl to Barbara Villiers!"

"He's welcome to her," said Barbara. "If he begged me on his knees to marry him I'd kick him in the face."

"Yes, cousin, I doubt not that you would."

They smiled at each other; both were thoughtful, and both were thinking of Mary Fairfax.

❁ ❁ ❁

Barbara was amused and exhilarated by the manner in which events followed that interview of hers with Buckingham.

Certainly George was handsome; certainly he was the most attractive man in England when he cared to be. Poor plain little Mary Fairfax found him so.

It had not been difficult to obtain access to her. Abraham Cowley and Robert Harlow, friends of the Fairfaxes, were also friends of Buckingham. It was true that the lady was betrothed to Chesterfield, but Buckingham was not one to let such a thing stand in his way. Nor was Mary, once she set eyes on the handsome Duke.

Chesterfield was haughty; he was of medium height—neither tall nor possessed of grace; he was, it was true, unusually handsome of face; accomplished in social graces but very condescending to those whom he considered his social inferiors. Desirous as he was to bring about the match with Mary Fairfax, he could not hide from her the fact that he felt he was vastly superior in birth and breeding, and Mary, though shy and awkward in his presence, was unusually intelligent and fully aware of his feelings.

How different was the charming Duke of Buckingham who was so humble and eager to please! How such qualities became a gentleman of birth and breeding! He showed that he understood full well that the reversal of a way of life had altered their positions; yet, with a charming nonchalance he could suggest that such difference would have been unimportant to him in any age.

Mary had been well educated; she was, she knew, excessively plain. Neither her father's nor her mother's good looks had come to her; her gift was a calm shrewd intelligence. Yet as soon as she set eyes on the handsome Duke she fell in love with him; and nothing would satisfy her but the marriage which the Duke was soon demanding.

Barbara, in the privacy of her own room, laughed merrily when she heard of the marriage. This was her first real triumph, her first dabbling in diplomacy—and as a result, her relative Buckingham had a bride, and her lover had lost one!

But when she next saw Chesterfield, although her sensuality got the better of her wish to remain aloof, and they were lovers again, she laughed at his desolate state and told him, although he made no such suggestion, that she would never marry him and one day he might regret the choice he had made.

❁ ❁ ❁

In the next two years Barbara blossomed into her full beauty. At eighteen she was recognized as the loveliest girl in London. Suitors called at her stepfather's house and, although it was said that Barbara's virtue was suspect, this could not deter these young men from wishing to marry her.

Oddly enough Chesterfield remained her lover. She was completely fascinated by the man, even while she declared she would never marry him. Others were more humble, more adoring; but it was Chesterfield who, having first roused Barbara's desires, continued to do so.

There was one young man whom she singled out from the rest because in his quiet way he was so eager to marry her. His name was Roger Palmer and he was a student at the Inner Temple. He was a modest man and unlike Barbara's other admirers, for she had attracted to herself people of a temperament similar to her own.

It was not long before he declared his feelings and begged her to marry him.

Marry Roger Palmer! It seemed to Barbara at that time that he was the last man she would marry. She had no intention of marrying yet. She was enjoying life too much to wish to change it. She had all the pleasures, she assured herself, and none of the boredom of marriage. Certainly she would not marry Roger Palmer.

Her mother and her stepfather tried to persuade her to marry Roger. They were growing alarmed by the wild daughter whose reputation was already a little tarnished; they were hoping that Roger or someone would take out of their hands the responsibility for such a vital and unaccountable girl. But the more they persuaded her, the more Barbara determined not to marry.

Her appearance was so startling now that wherever she went she was noticed. People turned to stare at the tall and strikingly beautiful young woman, with the proud carriage and the abundant auburn hair. She was voted the most handsome woman in London; many declared there could not be one to match her in the world. But her temper did not improve. She would, when her rages were on her, almost kill a servant who displeased her. Her lovers were terrified of her tantrums, yet so great was her physical allure that they were unable to keep away from her. She was like a female spider—as deadly yet as irresistible.

When she heard that Sir James Palmer, Roger's father, had said that he would never give his consent to his son's marriage with Barbara Villiers, she laughed poor Roger to scorn. "Go home to Papa!" she scolded. "Go home and tell him Barbara Villiers would die rather than have you!"

Only for Chesterfield did she feel some tenderness; she would be mad with rage at his treatment of her, yet still she continued to receive him. He was so like herself that she understood him; she was furious when she heard that Lady Elizabeth Howard shared the role of Chesterfield's mistress with her. His temper was as hot as hers. He had already been in trouble on two occasions for dueling. They quarreled; she took other lovers; but back, again and again, she went to Chesterfield, and the chief gossip in London concerned the scandal of Lord Chesterfield and his mistress Barbara Villiers.

"Do you realize," her parents pleaded with her, "that if you go on in this way, soon there will not be a man in England who will marry you?"

"There are many men in England who would marry me," she said.

"You think so. They say so. But what would their answers be if brought to the point of marriage, think you?"

Barbara rarely stopped to think; she allowed her emotions of the moment to govern all her actions.

"I could be married next week if I wished!" she declared.

But her parents shook their heads and begged her to reform her ways.

Barbara's answer to the challenge was to send for Roger Palmer. He came. His father had recently died and there was now no obstacle to their marriage; he was as eager to marry Barbara as he ever was.

Barbara studied him afresh. Roger Palmer, mild and meek, Roger Palmer, of no great importance, to be the husband of Barbara Villiers, the most handsome woman in London! It seemed incongruous, but Barbara would show them she was different from all other women. She would not look to her husband to provide her with honors; she would provide them for him and herself. How, she was not sure, but she would do it. Moreover, the more she studied him the more clear it became to her that Roger was just the husband for her. He would be dull and easy to handle. He would provide her with freedom—freedom to take her lovers where she wished. For Barbara needed lovers, a variety of lovers; she needed them even more than she needed power.

So she and Roger were married, to the astonishment of all, and then poor Roger realized how he had been used. The foolish man! He had believed that marriage would change her character, that a ceremony could change a passionate virago into a submissive wife!

He quickly learned his mistake and complained bitterly. But Chesterfield continued to be her lover until he was sent to the Tower during that year on suspicion of being involved in a Royalist plot; and after he was released at the beginning of the year 1660, he killed a man in a duel at Kensington and had to escape to France to avoid the consequences.

So at the beginning of the momentous year Barbara was missing her lover sorely when something happened which made their love affair seem of less importance.

Plans were afoot to bring the King back to England; Cromwell was dead, and the country was no more pleased with the Protectorate than it had been with Royalist rule. Cavaliers were disgruntled because of lost estates; the middle classes were groaning under heavy taxation and it was clear that the new Protector lacked the genius of his father; above all, the people were tired of the Puritans; they wanted the strict rules relaxed; they wanted to see pageantry in the streets; they wanted gaiety and laughter; they were weary of long sermons; they wanted singing, dancing and fun.

General Monk was in favor of the King's return; Buckingham had been working for it with his father-in-law, Lord Fairfax; and Roger Palmer was entrusted with a sum of money which he was to take to the King's exiled Court in Holland; not only money did Roger take, but his wife, and there were many even at that time who said that it was the lady who pleased the young King more than the gold.

As for Barbara, she had never been so delighted in the whole of her life. The tall dark man was a King and therefore worthy of her; he was as recklessly passionate as she was; in other ways his nature was completely opposed to hers, for he was tolerant, good tempered, the most easygoing person in the Court; yet while his eyes were upon her Barbara knew how to be sweetly yielding. She affected surprise that he could wish to seduce her; she reminded him that her husband would be most displeased; she hesitated and trembled, but made sure that there was plenty of time during her visit to Holland for the King not only to become her lover but to learn something of that immense satisfaction born out of her own great sensuality and complete abandonment to pleasure which she was fully aware she could give as few others could. Barbara was determined that the King should not only revel in a love affair which must necessarily be brief, that he should not forget her but look forward to repeating that experience as eagerly as he looked forward to wearing the crown.

Evidently she had succeeded, for on his first night in London the King had sent for her.

She went into his presence and knelt before him. She was fully aware that she had lost none of her beauty since they had last met. Rather had she gained in charm. She was magnificently dressed, and her wonderful auburn hair fell about her bare shoulders. The King's warm eyes glistened as he looked at her.

"It is a pleasure to see you here to greet us," he said.

"The pleasure is that of Your Majesty's most loyal subject to see you here."

"Rise, Mistress Palmer." He turned to those who stood about him. "The lady was responsible for great goodwill towards me during my exile . . . great goodwill," he repeated reminiscently.

"It is the utmost joy to me that Your Majesty should remember my humble service."

"So well do I remember that I would have you sup with me this night."

This night! thought Barbara. This very night when the whole of London was shouting its welcome; this first night when he had returned to his capital; this night when he had received the loyal addresses, the right royal welcome, the heartiest welcome that had ever been given to a King of England.

She could hear now the sounds of singing on the river, the shouts of joy.

Long live the King! A health unto His Majesty!

And here was His Majesty, his dark slumberous eyes urgent with passion, unable to think of anything but supping with Barbara Palmer.

"So," said the King, "you will sup with me this night?"

"It is a command, Your Majesty."

"I would have it also a pleasure."

"It will be the greatest pleasure that could befall a woman," she murmured.

She lifted her eyes and saw one in the King's entourage who, in spite of her triumph, made her heartbeats quicken.

There was Chesterfield. She hoped he had heard. She hoped he remembered now that he had once laughed at the idea of marrying Barbara Villiers. One day, thought Barbara then, and that day not far distant, Barbara Villiers would be the first lady in the land; for the King was half French by birth and all French in manners; and it was well known that the *maîtresse en titre* of a King of France was, more often than his Queen, the first Lady in the land.

Chesterfield was going to regret and wonder at his stupidity. He was going to realize he had been a fool to think Mary Fairfax a better match. She wondered too how he was faring in his recent marriages for he had had the temerity to marry again while he was in Holland—marry without consulting her! She wished him all that he deserved. She wondered how the simple little Lady Elizabeth Butler was going to satisfy a man like Chesterfield. If Lady Elizabeth, brought up in the affectionate home of her parents, the Duke and Duchess of Ormond, believed that all marriages were like those of her parents, she was about to be very surprised.

For, thought Barbara, even as she contemplated supping with the King, Chesterfield need not think that Barbara Villiers had finished with him.

The courtiers were looking at her boldly now. The King had brought French manners with him. They did not think it strange that he should openly claim her for his mistress before them all. In France the greatest honor that could befall a woman was to become the King's mistress.

Charles—and Barbara—would see that that French custom was forthwith adopted at the English Court.

❁ ❁ ❁

Far into the night the revelry continued. Throughout the Palace of Whitehall, which sprawled for nearly half a mile along the river's edge, could be heard the shouts of citizens making merry. Music still came from the barges on the river; and the lights of bonfires were reflected in the windows. Ballad singers continued their singing; it was not every day that a monarch came home to his capital.

The King heard the sounds of rejoicing and was gratified. But he gave them no more than a passing thought. He remembered that some of those who were shouting their blessings on him had doubtless called for his father's blood. Charles did not put any great trust in the acclamations of the mob.

But he was glad to be home, to be a King once more, no longer a wandering exile.

He was in his own Palace of Whitehall, in his own bed; and with him was the most perfect woman to whom it had ever been his lot to make love. Barbara Palmer, beautiful and amorous, unstintingly passionate, the perfect mistress for a perfect homecoming.

From the park of St. James', beyond the Cockpit, he heard the shouting of midnight revelers.

"A health unto His Majesty. . . ."

But his smile was melancholy until he turned once more to Barbara.

TWO

In his early morning walks through the grounds which surrounded his Palace of Whitehall, the King was often a melancholy man during those first few months after his restoration.

He would rise early, for he enjoyed walking in the fresh morning air and at such times he was not averse to being alone, although at all others he liked best to be surrounded by jesting men and beautiful women.

He walked fast; it was a habit unless there was a woman with him; then he never failed to fit his steps to hers.

This was a January morning. There was hoar-frost on the grass and it sparkled on the Palace walls and the buildings which rose from the banks on either side of the river.

January—and seven months a restored King!

He had wandered into the privy gardens where in summer he would set his watch by the sundial; but this day the sheltered bowling green was perhaps more inviting. He would, as was his custom, look in at the small Physic Garden where he cultivated the herbs with which he and Le Febre, his chemist, and Tom Chaffinch, his most trusted servant, experimented.

He was in an unusually pensive mood on this day.

Perhaps it was due to the coming of the new year—his first as King in his own country. Those last months which should have been the happiest of his life were touched with tragedy.

He looked back at the Palace with its buildings of all sizes—past the banqueting hall to the Cockpit. Whitehall was not only his royal Palace, it was the residence of his ministers and servants, the ladies and gentlemen of his Court, for they all had their apartments here. And that was how he would have it. The bigger his Court the better; the more splendid, the more he liked it for it reminded him sharply, whenever he contemplated it, of the change in his fortunes.

The stone gallery separated his royal apartments from those of his subjects; and his bedchamber—he had arranged this—had big windows, which gave him a clear view of the river; it was one of his pleasures to stand at those windows and watch the ships go by, just as, when a small boy at Greenwich, he had lain on the bank and delighted in the ships sailing by.

In the little chamber known as the King's Closet, to which only he and Tom Chaffinch had keys, he kept the treasures that he had learned to love. He was deeply attracted by beauty in any form—pictures, ornaments and, of course, women, and now that he was no longer a penniless exile he was gathering together pictures by the great artists of his earlier days. He had works by Holbein, Titian and Raphael in his closet; he had cabinets and jewel-encrusted boxes, maps, vases and, perhaps more cherished than any—except his models of ships—his collection of clocks and watches. These he wound himself and often took to pieces that he might have the joy of putting them together again. He loved art and artists, and he intended to make his Court a refuge for them.

He was already restoring his parks to a new magnificence. St. James' Park was no longer to be the shabby waste ground it had become during the Commonwealth; he would plant new trees; there should be waterworks such as those he had seen in Fontainebleau and Versailles. He wished his Court to be as elegant as that of his cousin Louis Quatorze. And St. James' Park should be a home for the animals he loved. He himself delighted to feed the ducks on his pond; he had begun to stock the park with deer; he would have goats and sheep there too, and strange animals such as antelopes and elks which would cause the people of London to pause and admire. And all these animals he loved dearly, as he loved the little dogs which followed him whenever they could and had even found their way into the Council Chamber. His melancholy face would soften when he fondled them, and when he spoke to them his voice was as tender and gentle as when he addressed a beautiful woman.

But on this January day, early in the morning, his melancholy thoughts pursued him, for those first months of his restoration had been overshadowed by tragedy.

The first trouble had been James' affair with Anne Hyde, the daughter of his Chancellor, the man whom he had trusted more than any other during the years of exile. James had married the girl and then sprung the news on his brother at a most inconvenient time, falling on his knees before him, confessing that he had made this *mésalliance* and disobeyed the rule that one so near the throne should not marry without the consent of the monarch.

He should have been furious; he should have clapped them both into the Tower. That was what his ancestors—those worthy Tudors, Henry and Elizabeth—would have done; and they were considered the greatest King and Queen the country had ever had.

Clap his own brother into jail! And for marrying a girl who was so far gone in pregnancy that to delay longer would have meant her producing a bastard, when the child might well be heir to the throne!

Some might have done it. Not Charles. How could he, when he could understand so well the inclination which had first led James to daily with the Chancellor's daughter (though to Charles' mind she was no beauty, yet possessed of a shrewdness and intelligence which he feared far exceeded that of his brother) and, having got her with child, the impossibility of resisting her tears and entreaties.

Charles saw James' point of view and Anne's point of view too clearly even to feign anger.

"Get up, James," he had said. "Don't sprawl at my feet like that. 'Od's Fish, man, you're clumsy enough in less demanding poses. What's done is done. You're a fool, but alas, dear brother, that's no news to me."

But others were not inclined to view the matter with the King's leniency. Charles sighed, contemplating the trouble which that marriage had caused. Why could they not take his view of life? Could they unmake the marriage by upbraiding James and making the girl's life miserable?

It was a sad thing that so few shared the tolerance of the King.

There was Chancellor Hyde, the girl's father, pretending to be distraught, declaring that he would have preferred to see his daughter the concubine rather than the wife of the Duke of York.

"A paternal sentiment, which is scarcely worthy of a man of your high ideals, Chancellor," Charles had said ironically.

He had begun to wonder about Hyde then. Was the man entirely sincere? Secretly he must be delighted that his daughter had managed to secure marriage into the royal house, that her heirs might possibly sit on the throne of England. There had been whispering about Hyde often enough; a man so high in the King's favor was bound to have his enemies. He had followed Charles in his exile and had always been at his side to give the young King his advice. Charles did not forget that when Hyde had left Jersey to come to him in Holland he had been taken prisoner by the corsairs of Ostend and robbed of his possessions, yet had not rested until he had effected his escape and joined his King. His one motive was, he had declared, to serve Charles and bring about his restoration; and Charles, believing him, had made the man his first adviser, had asked his counsel in all political matters, had made him Secretary of State in place of Nicholas, and later, when it seemed that one day Charles might have a country to rule, he had become Chancellor. The man had had many enemies who envied him his place in the King's counsels and affections; they had done all they could to poison the King's mind against him. But Charles had supported Hyde, believed him to be his most trusty servant because he never minced his words and was apt to reproach the King to his face concerning the profligate life he led. Charles would always listen gravely to what Hyde had to say, declaring that although he was ready to accept Hyde's advice on affairs of state he felt himself to be the better judge in matters of the heart.

Chief of Hyde's critics had been Henrietta Maria, the King's own mother, who traced all the disagreements—and they were many—which existed between herself and her son, to this man.

Still Charles supported Hyde; and only now, when the man declared himself to be so desolate because his daughter was the wife and not the mistress of the Duke of York, did Charles begin to doubt the sincerity of his Chancellor.

He made him Baron Hyde of Hindon, and had decided that at his coronation he would create him Viscount Cornbury and Earl of Clarendon, to compensate him for his years of loyal service; but he had decided he would not be quite so trusting as hitherto.

Poor James! Charles feared he was not the most courageous of men. He was afraid of his mother. Odd how one, so small and at such great distance, could inspire terror in the hearts of her grown-up children. Henrietta Maria had made a great noise in Paris concerning this marriage—weeping, assuring all those about her that here was another instance of the cruelty of fate which was determined to remind her that she was *La Reine Malheureuse*. Had she not suffered enough! Was not the whole world against her! Charles knew full well how the tirades had run, and who had borne the brunt of them—his beloved little sister Henrietta, his sweet Minette. So James had trembled in Whitehall although it was so far from the Palais-Royal or Colombes or Chaillot or the Louvre, wherever his mother had been when calling those about her to weep for her sorrows, and the saints to bring vengeance on those who persecuted her. Then there had been his sister, Mary of Orange, who was furious that James could so far forget himself, and who had blamed herself because it was while Anne Hyde was in the retinue that she had first met the Duke.

Poor James! Alas, no hero. Alas, possessing no true chivalry. Terrified at what he had done in bringing upon himself the wrath of his formidable mother and strong-minded sister, he had declared his mistake to the world; he had lent his ears to the calumnies, which those who hated the Hyde family were only too ready to pour into them. Anne was a lewd woman, he declared; she had trapped him; the child for whose sake he had rushed into marriage was after all not his.

And so poor Anne, deserted by her family and by her husband, would have been in a sorry state but for one person.

Charles shrugged his shoulders. He did not believe the calumnies directed against the poor girl, but he suspected that if he had, his reaction would not have been very different, for he could never bear to see a woman in distress.

So the one who had visited the Duchess at her lying-in, when all the world seemed against her, was the King himself; and it was the royal hand which had been laid upon her feverish brow with, as he said, the tenderness of a brother, and it was Charles who whispered to her to have no fear for all would come right for her, since it was the envious enemies of her family who, denigrating its special talents and good fortune, had sought to harm her.

Whither the King went so must the Court go too. How could the courtiers neglect one whom the King chose to honor? "Come, man!" he cried to Hyde. "This business is done with. 'Tis a fool who makes not the best of what cannot be mended!"

To James he said: "You shame me! You shame our family. The Duchess is your wife. You cared enough for her to make her that. Is your love for her then less than the fear you have for our mother? You know she is innocent of these calumnies. For the love of God, be a man."

Thus had that most unhappy matter been satisfactorily settled, and it was then that Charles had given Hyde his peerage to show where his sympathies lay.

The next disaster had been the death of his brother, Henry of Gloucester, the younger of his brothers, and the best loved. Death had come swiftly in the guise of the dreaded smallpox; and young Henry, strong and healthy one week, had been gone the next.

Such a tragedy coming so soon after his restoration—Henry had died in September, a few weeks after the trouble with James had blown up, and little more than three months after the King's return to England—dampened all pleasure, and even the sight of his beloved sisters could not entirely console him.

Minette he loved dearly—perhaps more dearly than any other person on Earth—and it was delightful and gratifying to receive her in his own country, which had now acknowledged him its King, to do honor to the lovely and sprightly girl who had suffered such humiliation as a poor relation of the French Court for so long. But with Minette came her mother; Charles smiled now at the thought of Henrietta Maria, the diminutive virago, eyes flashing, hands gesticulating, longing to give James a piece of her mind and assuring everyone that she would only enter Whitehall when Anne Hyde was ordered to leave it.

And to Charles had fallen the task of placating his mother; this he did with grace and courtesy, and some cunning. For she was dependent upon his bounty for her pension, and she had been made to know that the obstinacy of her eldest son still existed beneath the easy-going manners, and that when he had made up his mind that something should be done, he could be as firmly fixed in his purpose as that little boy who had refused to take his physic and who had clung to the wooden billet which it had been his custom as a small boy to take to bed with him each night.

So he had triumphed over his mother as gently as he could. "Poor Mam!" he told his little Minette. She has a genius for supporting lost causes and giving all her great energy to that which can only bring sorrow to herself." He had insisted on her receiving James' wife in public.

And then almost immediately the dread smallpox, which had carried off his brother Henry, had smitten his sister Mary, and in the space of a few short months, though he had regained his throne, he had lost a beloved brother and sister.

How the family was depleted! There was now his mother—but they had never really loved each other—his brother James—and James was a fool and a coward, as was obvious from his treatment of Anne Hyde—and Minette, his youngest sister, the best loved of them all; yet she was rarely met and the water divided them. He had said farewell to her but a few days ago, but how did he know when he would see her again? He would have liked to bring her back to England, to have kept her with him. Dear Minette! But she had her destiny in another country; she had a brilliant marriage to make; he could not ask her to forsake her affianced husband and come to England merely to be the King's sister. There was scandal enough concerning them already. Trust the malicious tongues to see to that!

So it was small wonder that he felt melancholy at times, for he was a man who liked to surround himself with those he loved. He could remember happy days when he had been the member of a family; and it had been a happy family, for there was affection between his parents, and his father was a noble man and loving father; but that was before he had found it necessary to oppose his overbearing mother; he remembered her from then as ever demonstrative, quick to punish but full of an affection which was outwardly displayed by suffocating embraces and fond kisses. Yes, Charles was a man who needed love and affection; he longed to have his family about him. He suffered their loss deeply as one by one they left this life.

He remembered now, as he bent to examine a herb in his Physic Garden, the terrible anxiety he had suffered when he had believed that Minette herself was about to die. Stunned by the loss of a brother and sister he had thought that life was about to deal him the most brutal blow of all. But Minette had not died; she had lived to return to France, where she would marry the brother of the French King and every week there would be, as in the old days, loving letters from her to remind him of the bond between them.

Yes, he still had Minette, so life was not all melancholy; far from it. He had his crown and he had his beloved sister, and there was much merriment to be had in the Court of Whitehall. A man could not have pleasure all the time, for if he became too familiar with it he would be less appreciative of it. The loss of his dear brother Henry and sister Mary had made him all the more tender to his sweet Minette.

There were other matters which gave him some uneasiness. Were the people a little disappointed? Had they hoped for too much? Did they think that with the King's restoration all the old evils would be wiped out? Did they look upon the King as a magician, who could live in perpetual royal state and give his people pageants, restore estates, abolish taxes—and all because he had found some magic elixir in his laboratories? Oh, the many petitioners who hung about in the stone gallery of Whitehall which led to the royal apartments! How many there were to remind him that they had been loyal supporters during the years of exile! "Sire, it was due to me . . . to me . . . to me . . . that Your Majesty has been restored." "Sire, I had a great house and lands, and these were taken from me by the Parliament. . . ." "Sire, I trust that Your Majesty's restoration may be our restoration. . . ." It was easy—too easy—to promise. He understood their different points of view. Of course he understood them. He wished to give all they asked. It was true that they had been loyal; it was true that they had worked for his restoration and lost their estates to the Parliament. But what could he do? How could he confiscate estates which were now the property of those who called themselves his loyal subjects; how could he restore property which had been razed to the ground?

It was his habit almost to run through the stone gallery to avoid these petitioners. They would drop on their knees as he passed, and he would say quickly: "God bless you! God bless you!" before he strode on, taking such great paces that none could overtake him unless they ran. He dared not pause; if he did, he knew he would be unable to stop himself making promises which he could not fulfil.

If they would but let him alone to enjoy his pleasures—ah, then he would forget his melancholy; then he would practice that delightful habit of sauntering through his parks followed by his spaniels and surrounded by gentlemen who must all be witty and ladies who need not be anything but beautiful. To listen to the sallies (and he had made it clear that they could disregard his royalty in the cause of wit) and to feast his eyes on the graceful figures of the ladies, whisper to them, catch their hands, suggest a meeting when there might not be quite so many about them to observe their little tendernesses—ah, that was all pleasure. He wished that he could indulge in sauntering more often.

In November the army had been disbanded at Hyde's wish. Charles was sorry to see that happen, but whence would come the money to keep it in existence? It seemed to the King that as a monarch he was almost as poor as he had been as an exile, for, although he had a larger income, his commitments had multiplied in proportion. Monk kept his regiments—the Coldstream and another of horse; and that was all, apart from another regiment which was formed from the troops which had been brought from Dunkirk. Charles christened this regiment the Guards and from it planned to build a standing army.

But there was one other matter his ministers were determined on, as fiercely as on that of reducing expenses, and it was one which gave him as little pleasure; this was revenge.

Charles alone, it seemed, had no wish for revenge. The past was done with; his exile was over; he was restored; let all the country rejoice in that. But No! said his ministers. And No! said his people. Murder had been done. The King's father was Charles the Martyr, and his murder should not go unpunished. So there had been a trial, and those men who were judged guilty were sentenced to the terrible death which was accorded to traitors.

Charles shuddered now as he had then. If he had had his will he would have acquitted the lot. They had believed they were in the right; in their eyes they had committed no murder; they had carried out the demands of justice. So they saw it; and Charles, still remembering with great affection the father whom they had murdered, still very close to the years of beggary and exile, was the one who alone had desired that these men should remain unpunished.

Ten men died the terrible death that October, and there were others waiting to meet it. But the King could bear no more. He cried: "I confess I am weary of hanging—let it sleep!"

So he prevailed upon the Convention to turn their attention away from humble men to those who had been his father's true enemies; those who were already dead. And so the bodies of Cromwell, Pride and Ireton were dug from their graves, beheaded, and their heads stuck on spikes outside Westminster Hall.

This was gruesome and horrible to a man of fastidious tastes, but at least their dead bodies could feel no pain. It was better to offend his fastidiousness than wound his tender nature.

Revenge, he had said, was enjoyed by the failures of this world. Those who achieved success spared little time for something which had become so trivial. He was now back in the heart of his country and the hearts of his people. He forgave those men who had worked against his family, as he trusted God would forgive him his many sins.

So with the King's indifference to revenge, the people satisfied themselves with gloating over the decaying remains of the great Protector and his followers, which were displayed exactly twelve years to the day after the death of Charles I.

There were difficulties still over religion. How his people discoursed one against the other on this subject! What hot words they exchanged, what angers were aroused; how they disputed this way and that! Why could they not, Charles asked them and himself, be easy in their minds? Why should not men who wished to worship in a certain way worship that way? What should another man's opinions matter to the next man, providing he was allowed to preserve his own?

Tolerance! It was a hateful word to these fierce combatants. They did not want tolerance. They wanted their mode of worship imposed on the country because, they declared, it was the right way.

The struggle continued between Presbyterians and Anglicans.

Charles exerted all his patience; he was charming to the Anglicans, he was suave to the Presbyterians; but at last he began to see that he could never make peace between them and because the Anglicans had supported him during his exile he shrugged his shoulders and went over to their side.

Had he been right? He did not know. He wanted peace . . . peace to enjoy his kingdom. He, who could see the fierce points of argument from both angles and many more, would have cried: "Worship as you please—but leave each other and me in peace."

But that was not the way of these earnest men of faith, and Charles' way was to take the easiest route out of a dispute which was growing tedious.

So now he had come to the end of those months, and the year was new, and who could say what fresh triumphs, what fresh pleasures and what fresh sorrows awaited him?

He must find a wife ere long. He was thirty-one, and a King should be married by that age if he were to provide his country with sons.

A wife? The thought pleased him. He was after all a man who loved his family. He pictured the wife he would have—gentle and loving and, of course, beautiful. He would discuss the matter with his ministers, and it might be well to discuss it now, while Barbara was less active than usual. She was expecting a child next month; his child, she said.

He lifted one side of his mouth in a half-smile.

It could be his, he supposed, though it might be Chesterfield's or even poor Roger Palmer's. None could be sure with Barbara.

It was time he grew tired of her. It astonished him that she had been almost his sole mistress since he had set foot in England. Yet he did not grow tired of her. Handsome she was—quite the most handsome woman he had ever known. Physically she was unique; the symmetry of her body was perfect and her person could not fail to delight such a connoisseur. Her face was the most beautiful he had ever beheld, and even her violent rages could only change it, not distort it. Her character was unaccountable; and thus there was nothing dull nor insipid about Barbara. He had tried others, but they had failed to interest him beyond the first few occasions. Always he must go back to Barbara, wild Barbara, cruel Barbara, the perfect animal, the most unaccountable and the most exciting creature in his kingdom.

He looked at his watch.

It was time the morning perambulation was ended.

He chided himself lightly for thinking of Barbara so early in the day.

❁ ❁ ❁

Barbara sat up in bed in her husband's house in King Street, Westminster. In the cradle lay her few-days-old child, a girl. Barbara was a little sulky; she would have preferred her firstborn to be a boy.

She smiled secretly. There should be three men who would come to visit her, and each would believe in his heart that the child was his. Let them have their secret thoughts; Barbara had long decided whom she would name as the little girl's father.

Roger, the first of the visitors, came early.

How insignificant he was! How could she have married such a man? people wondered. She smiled when she heard that. Her reasons were sound enough. Poor Roger, he should not suffer for his meekness. Unfortunately nowadays he was not inclined to be as meek as she could wish.

He stood at the foot of the bed and looked from her to the child in the cradle.

Barbara cried: "For the love of God, do not stand there looking like a Christian about to be sent to the lions! Let me tell you, Roger Palmer, that if danger came within a mile of you you'd be squealing to me to protect you!"

"Barbara," said Roger, "you astonish me. I should not have thought any woman could be so blatant."

"I have little time for subterfuge."

"You deliberately deceive me with others."

"I deceive you! When have I ever deceived you? I am not afraid to receive my lovers here . . . in your house."

"Shame, Barbara, shame! You, a woman just delivered of a child! Why, there are many who wonder who the father of that child may be."

"Then they need not wonder long. They shall know, when the titles due to this child are given to her."

"You are quite shameless."

"I am merely being truthful."

"I suppose, when you married me you had your lovers."

"You surely did not think, sir, that you could satisfy me?"

"Chesterfield . . . ?"

"Yes, Chesterfield!" she spat at him.

"Then why did you not marry Chesterfield? He was free to marry at that time."

"Because I had no wish to marry Chesterfield. Do you think I wished for a husband who was ready to draw his sword every me he thought his honor slighted?" She laughed the cruel laugh he had come to know so well. "Nay! I wanted a meek man. A man who would look away at the right moment, a man without any great title . . . or hope of one, except that which *I* should bring to him."

"You are a strange woman, Barbara."

"I'm no fool, if that's what you mean."

"Do not think that I should wish for any honors which you could bring me. Honours, did you say? They would be dishonor in disguise."

"Honors are honors, no matter how they come. Ah! I see the look in your eyes, Roger Palmer. You are wondering what His Majesty will do for you if you quietly father his child, are you not?"

"Barbara, you are vulgar and cruel, and I wonder . . . I wonder I can stay under the same roof."

"Then cease to wonder. Get out. Or shall I? Do you imagine that there are not other roofs under which I could shelter? Why do you not admit the truth to yourself, Roger Palmer? You are jealous . . . jealous of my lovers. And why? Because *you* wish to be my lover!" She laughed. "My lover *en titre*. . . . You wish to exclude all others!"

"I am your husband."

"My husband! What should I want of a husband except his complaisance."

He strode towards the bed; his face was livid with fury.

Barbara called to her women, who hurried into the room.

"I am very fatigued," she said. "I wish to rest. Arrange the pillows more comfortably. Roger, you must leave me now."

"You must not excite yourself at such a time, Madam," said one of her women.

She lay back upon her pillows and watched Roger as he went quietly to the cradle and bent over the sleeping infant. She knew he was telling himself that the little nose, small though it was, was yet a Palmer nose; and the set of the eyes, that was Palmer too.

Let him go on thinking thus, she mused, for what harm is there in thinking?

And when he had gone, she sent one of her women with a message to Lord Chesterfield at Whitehall.

❁ ❁ ❁

Barbara's messenger found the Earl of Chesterfield in his apartments at the Palace. The Countess was with him, and it was not the most propitious moment to deliver a message from Barbara; but all Barbara's servants knew that to disobey was quite out of the question, and she would be amused to know that Chesterfield's bride was present when he received his summons to call on his mistress.

Chesterfield still felt the power of her attraction, and he had not ceased to be her lover at intervals ever since their first encounter. There had been a time when Barbara had actually seemed to be in love with him; when she had so far subdued her personality as to write to him: "I am ready and willing to go all over the world with you, and will obey your commands whilst I live." That was after Barbara's own marriage but before the return of the King, before Chesterfield had fought that duel which had necessitated his leaving the country. Then she had compared him with the meek Roger and when she knew there could never be marriage between them, she had felt he was the only man who could please her.

That mood had not lasted. The King had come home, and the occasions when Barbara had been at home to Chesterfield became less frequent, although she had wished to receive him more often when she had heard of the beauty of his wife.

Barbara was a wanton, Chesterfield told himself; Barbara was cruel; but that did not prevent her from being different from all other women and very desirable. His common sense told him to have no more to do with her; his senses refused to release him.

Now he looked at the quiet girl who was his wife. She was about twenty years of age—the same age as Barbara—but compared with his mistress she seemed but a child. There was no guile about Elizabeth; she was pleasant to look upon but seemed dull when he compared hers with the flamboyant charms of Barbara. And of course he must compare her with Barbara, for Barbara was constantly in his thoughts.

"A message?" she said now. "From whom, Philip? I had hoped that you would spend an hour or so with me."

"It matters not from whom the message comes," he said coldly. "Suffice it that it is for me, and that I must leave at once."

Elizabeth came to him and put her arm through his. She was very much in love with him. He had seemed so handsome and romantic when he had come to Holland; she had heard the story of the duel; she did not know the cause, and she imagined that it was out of chivalry that he had fought and killed a man. He would not talk of it. That, she had told herself, is his natural modesty. He will not speak of it because he fears to appear boastful.

She had led a sheltered life with the Duchess her mother, who, horrified at the licentious exiled Court, had kept her daughter from it in an endeavor to preserve her innocence; she had succeeded in her task too well, for Elizabeth at the time of her marriage had no notion of the kind of man she had married, nor of the kind of world in which she would be expected to compete for his affections. The marriage had seemed a good one. The Earl was twenty-five years of age, the Lady Elizabeth nineteen. Chesterfield, a younger widower, needed a wife and it was time the Lady Elizabeth was married.

It was true that the Duchess, having heard rumors of the bridegroom's reputation, was a little hesitant; but those rumors were not so disturbing as they might have been, for at that time Barbara Palmer had not achieved the notoriety which she attained when she became the King's mistress; and, as the Duke pointed out to his Duchess, a young unmarried man must have a mistress; Chesterfield would settle down when he married.

So the marriage took place at The Hague a little while before the

Restoration; and Lady Elizabeth who, having seen the affection between her parents, had expected to enjoy the same happy state with her husband, met with bitter disappointment.

The Earl made it quite clear that the marriage was one of convenience and Lady Elizabeth found that her naive expressions of love were cruelly repulsed.

At first she was hurt; then she believed that he still thought of his first wife, Anne Percy. She asked questions about her of all who had known her; she tried to emulate what she heard of her rival, but her efforts seemed to win her husband's impatience rather than his kindness. He was brusque, cold, and avoided her as much as possible. He made it clear that any intercourse between them was undertaken by him because it was expected of him.

The naive and gentle girl, being in every way different from Barbara, irritated him beyond all measure because, in everything she did, by the very contrast, she reminded him of Barbara, and set him longing to renew that tempestuous relationship.

Even now when they had returned to London she was kept in ignorance of the life he led. Her mother, unknown to her, had spoken to the Earl asking that he treat her daughter with the deference due to her; at which he became more aloof than ever and Elizabeth, left much alone, continued to brood on the perfections of Anne Percy who she believed could charm from the grave.

But at this moment the Earl was beside himself with the desire to see Barbara—and not only Barbara. He was sure the child was his. He had visited Barbara at the time she became the King's mistress; he remembered the occasion when he had accused her of seeking royal favor; he remembered her mocking laughter, her immense provocation, her insatiable lust which demanded more than one lover at a time. Yes, the child could very possibly be his.

"Philip. . . ." Elizabeth was smiling at him in a manner which she fondly imagined was alluring.

He threw her off, and the tears came to her eyes. If there was one thing that maddened him more than an attempt at coquetry, it was her weeping; and there had been much of that since her marriage—quiet, snuffling crying which he heard in the darkness.

"Why do you plague me?" he demanded.

"I . . . plague you?"

"Why do you seek to detain me when you know full well I have no wish to be detained by you?"

"Philip, you talk as though you hate me."

"Hate you I shall if you will insist on clinging to me thus. Is it not enough that you are my wife? What more do you want of me?"

"I want a chance, Philip, a chance for us to be happy. I want us to be as husband and wife. . . ."

That made him laugh. The spell of Barbara was on him. He was sure she was a witch who could cast spells from a distance. It was almost as though she were there in the room, mocking him, scorning him for not telling this foolish little girl the truth.

"You wish us to be as husband and wife? To live, you mean, as do other wives and husbands of the Court? Then you should get yourself a lover. It is an appendage without which few wives of this Court find themselves."

"A . . . lover? You, Philip, my husband, can say that!"

He took her by the shoulders and shook her in exasperation. "You are like a child," he said. "Grow up! For God's sake, grow up!"

She threw her arms about his neck. His exasperation turned to anger. He found her repulsive—this fresh and innocent young girl—because she was not Barbara on whose account he had suffered bitter jealousy ever since the King came home.

"Know the truth," he cried. "Know it once and for all. I cannot love you. My thoughts are with my mistress."

"Your mistress, Philip!" Elizabeth was white to the lips. "You mean . . . your dead . . . wife?"

He looked at her in astonishment and then burst into cruel laughter. "Mrs. Barbara Palmer," he said. "She is my mistress. . . ."

"But she . . . she is the King's mistress, they say."

"So you have learned that? Then you are waking up, Elizabeth. You are becoming very knowledgeable. Now learn something else: the King's mistress she may be—but she is mine also. And the child she has just borne . . . it is mine, I tell you."

Then he turned and hurried away.

Elizabeth stood like one of the stone statues in the Palace grounds.

Then she turned away and went to her apartment; she drew the curtains about her bed and lay there, while a numbness crept over her limbs, and it seemed that all feelings were merged in the misery which was sweeping over her.

❖ ❖ ❖

Before Chesterfield arrived at the house in King Street, Barbara had another visitor.

This was her relative, George Villiers the Duke of Buckingham. He was now a gentleman of the King's bedchamber; his estates had been restored to him, and he was on the way to becoming one of the most important men in the country.

He did not look at the child in the cradle. Instead his eyes were warm with admiration for the mother.

"So Mrs. Barbara," he said, "you flourish. I hear that the King continues to dote. This is a happy state of affairs for the family of Villiers, I'll swear."

"Ah, George," she said with a smile, "we have come a long way from the days when you used to tease me for my hot temper."

"I'll warrant the temper has not cooled, and were it not that I dare not tease such a great lady as Mistress Barbara, I would be tempted to put it to the test. Do you bite and scratch and kick with as much gusto as you did at seven, Barbara?"

"With as much gusto and greater force," she assured him. "But I'll not kick and scratch and bite you, George. There are times when the Villiers should stand together. You were a fool to get sent back from France."

"It was that prancing ninny of a Monsieur. He feigned to be jealous of my attentions to the Princess Henrietta."

"Well, you tried to make her sister Mary your wife and failed, then you tried to make Henrietta your mistress and failed in that."

"I beg of you taunt me not with failing. Mayhap your success will not last."

"Ah! Had I not married Roger mayhap I should have been Charles' wife ere now."

George's thoughts were cynical. Charles might be a fool where women were concerned, but he was not such a fool as that. However, it was more than one dared say to Barbara. Roger had his uses. Not only was he a complaisant husband but he supplied a good and valid reason why Barbara was not Queen of England.

"It seems as though fortune does not favor us, cousin," said George. "And the lady in the cradle—is she preparing herself to be nice to Papa when he calls?"

"She will be nice to him."

"You should get him to own her."

"He shall own her," said Barbara.

"Roger spoke of the child as though there could be no doubt that she is his."

"Let him prate of that in public."

"The acknowledgment by her rightful father should not be too private, Barbara."

"Nay, you're right."

"And there is something more I would say to you. Beware of Edward Hyde."

"Edward Hyde? That old fool!"

"Old, it is true, my dear; but no fool. The King thinks very highly of him."

Barbara gave her explosive laugh.

"Ah yes, the King is your minion. You lead him by the nose. I know, I know. But that is when he is with you, and you insist he begs for your favors. But the King is a man of many moods. He changes the color of his skin like a chameleon on a rock, and none is more skilled at such changing than he. Remember Hyde was with him years ago in exile. He respects the man's judgment, and Hyde is telling him that his affair with you is achieving too much notoriety. He is warning him that England is not France, and that the King's mistress will not be accorded the honors in this country which go to His Majesty's cousin's women across the water."

"I'll have the fellow clapped into the Tower."

"Nay, Barbara, be subtle. He's too big a man to be clapped into the Tower on the whim of a woman. The King would never consent to it. He would promise you in order to placate you, and then prevaricate; and he would whisper to his Chancellor that he had offended you and he had best make his peace with you. But he will not easily turn against Edward Hyde."

"You mean I should suffer myself to be insulted by that old . . . old . . ."

"For the time, snap your fingers. But beware of him, Barbara. He would have the King respectably married and his mistresses cast aside. He will seek to turn the King against you. But do nothing rash. Work stealthily against him. I hate the man. You hate the man. We will destroy him gradually . . . but it must be slowly. The King is fickle to some, but I fancy he will not be so with one who has been so long his guide and counsellor. His Majesty is like a bumble bee—a roving drone—flitting from treasure to treasure, sipping here and there and forgetting. But there are some flowers from which he has drunk deep and to these he returns. Know you that he has given a pension to Jane Lane who brought him to safety after Worcester? All that time, and he remembers—our fickle gentleman. So will he remember Edward Hyde. Nay, let the poison drip slowly . . . in the smallest drops, so that it is unnoticed until it has begun to corrode and destroy. Together, Barbara, you and I will rid ourselves of one who cannot be anything but an enemy to us both."

She nodded her agreement; her blue eyes were brilliant. She longed to be up; she hated inactivity.

"I will remember," she said. "And how fare you in your married life?"

"Happily, happily," he said.

"And Mary Fairfax—does she fare happily?"

"She is the happiest of women, the most satisfied of wives."

"Some are easily satisfied. Does she not regret Chesterfield?"

"That rake! Indeed she does not."

"She finds in you a faithful husband?" said Barbara, cynically and slyly.

"She finds in me the perfect husband—which gives greater satisfaction."

"Then she must be blind."

"They say love is, Madam."

"Indeed it must be. And she loves you still?"

"As she ever did. And so do the entire family. It is a most successful marriage."

Barbara's woman came in and was about to announce that Chesterfield was on his way, when the Earl himself came into the room.

He and Buckingham exchanged greetings. Chesterfield went to the bed, and, taking the hand Barbara gave him, pressed it to his lips.

"You are well?" he asked. "You are recovered?"

"I shall be about tomorrow."

"I rejoice to hear it," said Chesterfield.

Buckingham said he would take his leave. Matters of state called him.

When he had gone, Chesterfield seized Barbara in his arms and kissed her with passion.

"Nay!" she cried, pushing him away. "It is too soon. Do you not wish to see the child, Philip?"

He turned to the cradle then. "A girl," he said. "Our child."

"You think that?"

"Yes," he said. "It is ours."

"You are proud to own her, Philip. Well, we must see that your interest in the little girl does not become known to your Lady Elizabeth."

His faced darkened at the memory of the scene he had so recently experienced with his wife.

"I care not," he said.

She tapped him sharply on the arm.

"*I* care," she said. "I'll not have you bruit it abroad that this child is yours."

"You are reserving her for a higher fate? Barbara, you witch!"

"Philip, soon I shall be well."

"And then . . ."

"Ah! We shall meet ere long, I doubt not. Why, you are a more eager lover than you once were!"

"You become a habit, Barbara. A habit . . . like the drink or gaming.

One sips . . . one throws the dice, and then it is an unbearable agony not to be able to sip or throw the dice."

"It pleases me that you came so quickly to my call."

He was holding her hands tightly, and she felt his strength. She looked into his face and remembered that occasion four years ago in the nuttery. "The first time," she said. "I remember. It was nothing less than rape."

"And you a willing victim."

"A most unwilling one. 'Twas forced upon me. You should have been done to death for what you did to me. Dost know the punishment for rape?"

The woman came in. She was agitated. "My lady, Madam . . . the King comes this way."

Barbara laughed and looked up at her lover.

"You had better leave," she said.

Chesterfield had drawn himself up to his full height.

"Why should I leave? Why should I not stay here and say, 'By God, Your Majesty, I am honored that you should come so far to see my daughter?' "

Barbara's face was white and tense with sudden anger. "If you do not leave this chamber this minute," she said, "I will never see you again as long as I live."

She meant it, and he knew she meant it.

There were moments when he hated Barbara, but, whether he hated or loved, the knowledge was always with him that he could not live without her.

He turned and followed the woman out of the chamber; he allowed himself to be led ignobly out through a back door that he might run no risk of coming face-to-face with the King.

❁ ❁ ❁

Charles stepped into the room while his accompanying courtiers stayed in the corridor.

Barbara held out her hand and laughed contentedly.

"This is an honor," she said. "An unexpected one."

Charles took the hand and kissed it.

"It pleases me to see you so soon recovered," he said. "You look not like one who has just passed through such an ordeal."

"It was a joyful ordeal," she said, "to bear a royal child."

Eagerly she watched his face. It was never easy to read his feelings.

He had turned from her to the child in the cradle.

"So the infant has royal blood?"

"Your Majesty can doubt it?"

"There are some who doubtless will," he said.

She was reproachful. "Charles, you can talk thus while I lie so weakly here!"

He laughed suddenly, that deep, low musical laugh. " 'Od's Fish, Barbara, 'tis the only time I would dare do so."

"Think you not that she is a beautiful child?"

" 'Tis hard to say as yet. It is not possible to see whether she hath the look of you or Palmer."

"She'll never have a look of Palmer," said Barbara fiercely. "I'd be ready to strangle at birth any child of mine who had!"

"Such violence! It becomes you not . . . at such a time."

Barbara covered her face with her hands. "I am exhausted," she murmured brokenly. "I had thought myself the happiest of women, and now I find myself deserted."

The King drew her hands from her face. "What tears are these, Barbara? Do they spring from sorrow or anger?"

"From both. I would I were a humble merchant's wife."

"Nay, Barbara, do not wish that. It would grieve me to see our merchants plagued. We need them to further the trade of our country, which suffers great poverty after years of Cromwell's rule."

"I see that Your Majesty is not in serious mood."

"I could be naught but merry to see that motherhood has changed you not a whit."

"You have scarce looked at the child."

"Could I look at another female when Barbara is at hand?"

Her eyes blazed suddenly. "So you do not accept this child as yours . . . ?" Her long, slender fingers gripped the sheet. Her eyes were narrowed now and she was like a witch, he thought, a wild and beautiful witch. "If I had a knife here," she said, "I would plunge it into that child's heart. For would it not be better for her, poor innocent mite, that she should never know life at all than know the ignominy of being disowned by her own father!"

The King was alarmed, for he believed her capable of any wild action. He said: "I beg of you do not say such things, even in a jest."

"You think I jest then, Charles? Here am I, a woman just emerging from the agony of childbed; in all my sufferings I have been sustained by this one thought the child I bear is a royal child. Her path shall be made easy in the world. She shall have the honors due to her and it shall be our delight—her father's and mine—to love her tenderly as long as we shall live! And now . . . and now . . ."

"Poor child!" said Charles. "To be disowned by one because she could be owned by many."

"I see you no longer love me. I see that you have cast me aside."

"Barbara, should I be here at this time if that were so?"

"Then you would take your pleasure and let the innocent suffer. Oh, God in Heaven, should such an unfortunate be condemned to live? As soon as I saw her I saw the King in her. I said, 'Through my daughter Charles lives again.' And to think that in my weakness that father should come here to taunt me. . . . It is more than I can bear." She turned her face from him. "You are the King, but I am a woman who has suffered much, and now I beg of you to leave me, for I can bear no more."

"Barbara," he said, "have done with this acting."

"Acting!" She raised herself; her cheeks were flushed, her hair tumbled, and she looked very beautiful.

"Barbara," he said, "I beg of you, control yourself. Get well. Then we will talk on this matter."

She called to her woman. The woman came nervously, curtsying to the King as her frightened eyes went from him to Barbara.

"Bring me the child!" cried Barbara.

The woman went to the cradle.

"Give the child to me," said the King. The woman obeyed. And because he loved all small and helpless creatures, and particularly children, the King was deeply touched by the small, pink, wrinkled baby who might possibly be his own flesh and blood.

He looked down at the serving woman and gave her one of those smiles which never failed to captivate all who were favored with them.

"A healthy child," he said. "Methinks she already has a look of me. What say you?"

"Why, yes . . . Your Majesty," said the woman.

"I remember my youngest sister when she was little more than this child's age. They might be the same . . . as my memory serves."

Barbara was smiling contentedly. She was satisfied. The King had come to heel. He had acknowledged her daughter as his, and once more Barbara had her way.

The King continued to hold the child. She was a helpless little thing; he could easily love her. He owned to many children; so what difference did one more make?

❁ ❁ ❁

Spring had come to England, and once more there was expectation in the streets of London. It was exactly a year since the King had returned to rule his country.

The mauve tufts of vetch with golden cowslips and white stitchwort flowers gave, a gentle color to the meadows and lanes which could be seen from almost every part of the city. The trees in St. James' Park were in bud and the birdsong there sounded loud and jubilant as though these creatures were giving thanks to the King who had helped to build them such a delightful sanctuary.

The last year had brought more changes to the city. The people were less rough than they had been; there were fewer brawls. French manners had been introduced by the King and courtiers, which subdued the natural pugnacity of the English. The streets had become more colorful. Maypoles had been set up; new hawkers had appeared, shouting their wares through the streets; wheels continually rattled over the cobbles. On May Day milkmaids danced in the Strand with flower-decorated pails. New pleasure-houses had sprung up, to compete for public patronage with the Mulberry Garden. Cream and syllabub was served at the World's End tavern in the village of Knightsbridge. There was Jamaica House at Bermondsey; there were the Hercules Pillars in Fleet Street and Chatelins at Covent Garden—a favorite eating house since it was French and the King had brought home with him a love of all things French. Chatelins was for the rich, but there were cheaper rendezvous for the less fortunate, such as the Sugar Loaf, the Green Lettuce and the Old House at Lambeth Marshes; and there were the beautiful woods of Vauxhall in which to roam and ramble and seek the sort of adventures which were being talked of more openly than ever before, to listen to the fiddlers' playing, and watch the fine people walking.

Yes, there were great changes, and these were brought about through the King.

There was a new freedom in the very air—a gay unconcern for virtue. It might be that the people of the new age were not more licentious than those of the old; but they no longer hid their little peccadilloes; they boasted of them. They would watch the King's mistress riding through the town, haughty and so handsome that none could take his eyes from her. All knew the position she held with the King; he made no secret of it; nor did she. They rode together; they supped together four or five nights a week, and the King never left her till early morning, when he would take his walks and exercise in the gardens of his Palace of Whitehall.

It was a new England in which men lived merrily and were more ashamed of their virtue than their lack of morals. To take a mistress—or two—was but to ape the King, and the King was a merry gentleman who had brought the laughter back to England.

Charles was enjoying his own. The weather was clement; he loved his country; his exile was too close behind him for him to have forgotten it; he reveled in his return to power.

He was a young man, by no means handsome, but he was possessed of greater charm than any man in his Court; moreover he was royal. Almost any woman he desired, be she married or single, was his for the asking. He could saunter and select; he could enter into all the pleasures which were most agreeable to him. He could sail down the river to visit his ships—himself at the tiller; he could revel in their beauty, which attracted him so strongly. He could take his own yacht whither he wished, delighting in its velvet hangings and its damask-covered furniture, all made to his taste and his designs.

He could spend thrilling hours at the races; he could stand beside his workmen in the parks, make suggestions and give commands; he could watch the stars through his telescope with his astronomers and learn all they had to tell him. He could play bowls on his green at Whitehall, he could closet himself with his chemist and concoct cordials and medicines in his laboratory. Life was full of interest for a lively and intelligent man who suddenly found himself possessed of so much, after he had lived so long with so little.

He longed to see plays such as he had seen in France.

He was building two new theaters; he wished to see more witty plays produced. There were to be tall candles and velvet curtains—and women to act!

These were great days of change, but there was one thing which existed in abundance in this colorful and exciting City: dirt. It was ever present and therefore, being so familiar to all, passed unnoticed. In the gutters decaying matter rotted for days; sewage trickled over the cobbles; servants emptied slops out of the upper windows, and if they fell onto passersby that merely added gaiety and laughter—and sometimes brawls—to the clamoring, noisy city.

Noise was as familiar as dirt. The people reveled in it. It was as though every citizen were determined to make up for the days of Puritan rule by living every moment to the full.

Manners had become more elegant, but conversation more bold. Dress had become more alluring, and calculated to catch the eye and titillate the senses. The black hoods and deep collars were ripped off, and dresses were cut away to reveal feminine charms rather than to hide them. Men's clothes were as elaborate as those of women. In their plumed hats and breeches adorned with frilly lace they frequented the streets like magnificent birds of prey, as though hoping to reduce their victims to a state of supine fascination by their brilliance.

And now the arches, which would be adorned with flowers and brocades, were being set up; the scaffolding was being erected. People stood about in groups to laugh and chatter of the change which had taken place in their city since the King came home. They would turn out in their thousands to cry "A Health Unto His Majesty" when the King rode by on his way to be crowned, and drink to him from the conduits flowing with wine.

❁ ❁ ❁

Charles, driving his chariot with two fine horses through Hyde Park, bowing to the people who called their loyal greetings to him, was, for all his merry smiles, thinking of a subject which never failed to rouse the melancholy in him: Money.

A Coronation was a costly thing, and these people who rejoiced to see the scaffolding erected, and talked of the changed face of London, did not alas realize that they were the ones who would be asked to pay for it.

Charles had a horror of inflicting taxes. It was the surest way to a people's disfavor. And, he thought, I like my country so well, and I have travelled so much in my youth, that I have no wish ever to set foot outside England. It would therefore grieve me greatly if I were asked to go travelling again.

Money! How to come by it?

His ministers had one solution on which they continually harped. Marry a rich wife!

He would soon have to marry; he knew that; but whom should he marry?

Spain was anxious that the woman he married should have some ties with their country. The Spanish ambassador had put forth some suggestions tentatively. If Charles would consider a Princess from Denmark or Holland, Spain would see that she was given a handsome dowry.

Charles grimaced. He remembered the "foggy" women of those capitals in which he had sojourned as an exile. His ministers wished him to take a rich wife; it was imperative for the state of the country's finances that he did so. And for the sake of my comfort, he had begged, let her be not only rich but comely.

His ministers thought this a frivolous attitude. He had his mistresses to be beautiful; suffice it that his wife should be rich.

Hyde was a strong man. He had deliberately flouted Barbara; and only a strong man would do that, thought Charles grimly. Hyde had forbidden his wife to call on Barbara, and Barbara remembered insults. She was going to be angry when she heard that the King was giving him the Earldom of Clarendon at the Coronation. Why do I give way to Barbara? he asked himself. Why? Because she could amuse him far more than any woman; because there was no physical satisfaction equal to that which Barbara could give.

And why was this so? Perhaps because in her great gusto of passion she herself could enjoy so wholeheartedly. One could dislike Barbara's cupidity, her cruelty, her blatant vulgarity, yet Barbara's lusty beauty, Barbara's overwhelming sensuality chained a man to her side; it was not only so with himself. There were others.

But he must not think of Barbara now. He must think of a means of raising money.

When he returned to the Palace Lord Winchelsea was waiting to see him. Winchelsea had recently returned from Portugal, and he had news for the King which he wished to impart to him before he did so to any other.

"Welcome, my lord," said the King. "What saw you in Portugal that brings such brightness to your eyes?"

"I think mayhap," said Winchelsea, "that I see the solution to Your Majesty's pecuniary difficulties."

"A Portuguese wife?" said Charles, wrinkling his brows.

"Yes, Sire. I had an interview with the Queen Regent of Portugal, and she offers you her daughter."

"What manner of woman is she?"

"The Queen is old and earnest, most earnest, Your Majesty."

"Not the Queen—I have not to marry her. What of the daughter?"

"I saw her not."

"They dared not show her to you! Is she possessed of a harelip, a limp, a squint? I'll not have her, Winchelsea."

"I know not how she looks, but I have heard that she is mightily fair, Your Majesty."

"All princesses are mightily fair when they are in the field for a husband. The fairness is offered as part of their dowry."

"Ah, Sire, the dowry. Never has there been such a dowry as this Princess would bring to England—should Your Majesty agree to take her. Half a million in gold!"

"Half a million?" cried the King, savoring the words. "I'll swear she has a squint, to bring me half a million."

"Nay, she is fair enough. There is also Tangier, a seaport of Morocco, the island of Bombay—and that is not all. Here is an offer which Your Majesty cannot afford to miss. The Queen of Portugal offers free trade to England with the East Indies and Brazil. Sire, you have but to consider awhile what this will mean to our merchants. The treasure of the world will be open to our seamen. . . ."

The King laid his hand on Winchelsea's shoulder. "Methinks," he said, "that you have done good work in Portugal."

"Then you will lay this proposition before your ministers, Sire?"

"That will I do. Half a million in gold, eh! And our sailors to bring the treasure of the world to England. Why, Winchelsea, in generations to come Englishmen will call me blessed. 'Twould be worthwhile even if . . ."

"But I have heard naught against the lady, Sire. I have but heard that she is both good and beautiful."

The King smiled his melancholy smile. "There have been two miracles in my life already, my friend. One was when I escaped after Worcester; the other was when I was restored to my throne without the shedding of one drop of blood. Dare I hope for a third, think you? Such a dowry, and a wife who is good . . . and beautiful!"

"Your Majesty is beloved of the gods. I see no reason why there should not only be three but many miracles in your life."

"You speak like a courtier. Still, pray for me, Winchelsea. Pray that I get me a wife who can bring much good to England and pleasure to me."

Within a few days the King's ministers were discussing the great desirability of the match with Portugal.

❁ ❁ ❁

On the scaffolding the people had congregated to watch a procession such as they had never seen before. They chattered and laughed and congratulated one another on their good sense in calling the King back to his country.

Tapestry and cloth of gold and silver hung from the windows; the triumphal arches shone like gold in the sunshine; the bells pealed forth.

The King left his Palace of Whitehall in the light of dawn and came by barge to the Tower of London.

On St. George's Day the great event took place. The procession was dazzling, all the noblemen of England and dignitaries of the Church taking part; and in their midst rode the King—the tallest of them all, dark and swarthy, bareheaded and serene with the sword and wand borne before him on his way to Westminster Abbey.

That was a day for rejoicing, and all through it the city was thronged with sightseers. They were on the river and its banks; they crowded into Cheapside and Paul's Walk; they waited to see the King, after his crowning, enter Westminster Hall, passing through that gate on which were the decomposing heads of the men who had slain his father.

"Long live the King!" they shouted; and Charles went into the building which was the scene of his father's tragedy. And when he sat at the great banqueting table, Dymoke rode into the hall and flung down the gauntlet as a challenge to any who would say that Charles Stuart, the second of that name, was not the rightful King of England.

Music was played while the King supped merrily, surrounded by his favorites of both sexes; and when it was over he took to his gilded barge and so to Whitehall.

But the merriment continued in the streets where the fountains flowed with wine; the bonfires which sprung up about the city cast a fantastic glow on the revelers.

Men and women drunk with wine and excitement lay together in the alleys and told each other that these were King Charles' golden days, while others knelt and drank a health unto His Majesty.

The glow of bonfires was like a halo over the rejoicing city, and from a thousand throats went up the cry: "Come, drink the health of His Majesty."

❁ ❁ ❁

A few weeks after his people had crowned him King, Charles called together his new Parliament at the House of Commons and welcomed them in a speech which charmed even those who were not outstandingly Royalist in their sympathies.

"I know most of your faces and names," said Charles, "and I can never hope to find better men in your places."

Charles had come to a decision. He had to find money somehow. The revenue granted him was not enough by some £400,000 to balance the country's accounts. Charles was grieved because the pay of his seamen—a community in which he was particularly interested, for indeed he considered them of the utmost importance to the Nation's security—was far in arrears. He had had to raise money in some way, and had borrowed from the bankers of the city since it was the only way of carrying on the country's business; and these bankers were demanding high rates of interest.

How wearisome was the subject of money when there was not enough of it!

So he had come to his decision.

"I have often been put in mind by my friends," he told his Parliament at that first sitting, "that it is high time to marry, and I have thought so myself ever since I came into England. If I should never marry until I could make such a choice against which there could be no foresight of inconvenience, you would live to see me an old bachelor, which I think you do not desire to do. I can now tell you that I am not only resolved to marry, but whom I resolve to marry if God please. . . . It is with the daughter of Portugal."

As the ministers had already been informed of what went with the daughter of Portugal the house rose to its feet and showed the King in boisterous manner that it applauded his choice.

❀❀❀

Barbara heard the news. She was perturbed. The King to marry! And how could she know what manner of wife this Portuguese woman would be? What if she were as fiercely demanding as Barbara herself; what if she resolved to drive the King's mistress from her place?

Barbara decided she was against the marriage.

There were many people to support Barbara. Her power was such that she had but to drop a hint as to her feelings and there would be many eager to set in motion any rumor that would please her.

"Portugal!" said Barbara's friends. "What is known of Portugal? It is a poor country. There is no glass in the windows even at the palaces. The King of Portugal is a poor simple fellow—more like an apprentice than a king. And what of the Spaniards who are the enemies of the Portuguese? Where will this marriage lead—to war with Spain?"

Barbara demanded of the King when they were alone together: "Have you considered these things?"

"I have considered all points concerning this match."

"This dowry! Her mother must be anxious to marry the girl. Mayhap she can only marry her to someone who has never seen her."

"I have reports that she is dark-haired and pretty."

"So you are already relishing your dark-haired pretty wife!"

" 'Tis well to be prepared," said the King.

Barbara turned on him fiercely. There was a flippancy about his manner which frightened her. Of all her lovers he was the most important by reason of his rank; the others might seek consolation elsewhere, and she would not care with whom; with the King it was another matter. There must be no woman who could in his estimation compare with Barbara.

"Ah," sighed Barbara. "I am an unfortunate woman. I give myself . . . my honor . . . and I must be prepared to be cast off when it pleases you to cast me aside. It is the fate of those who love too well."

"It depends on whom they love," said the King. "Themselves or others."

"Do you suggest that I think overmuch of myself?"

"Dearest Barbara, none could help loving you beyond all others—so how could you yourself help it?"

"It amuses you to tease me. Now tell me that you will not let this Portuguese woman come between us."

She put her arms about his neck; she lifted her eyes to his; they were wet with tears. Barbara was a clever actress and, even though he knew this, her tears could always move him. Barbara tender was almost a stranger.

He said: "There is only one, Barbara, who could prevent my loving you."

"And who is that?"

"Yourself."

"Ah! So I have let my feelings run away with me, have I? How easy it is for some to be calm and serene. . . . They do not love. They do not care. But when emotions such as mine are involved . . ." She threw back her head and laughed suddenly. "But what matters it! You have come to see me. We are here together. . . . This night we may be together, so let the devil take the rest of my life. . . . I still have this night!"

Thus she could change from tearful reproaches to urgent passion; always unaccountable, always Barbara.

Nothing should alter his relationship with her. He assured her of that. "Not a hundred Portuguese women who brought me ten million pounds, twenty foreign towns and all the riches of the Indies."

❁ ❁ ❁

That year passed pleasantly for Charles. There was business to be conducted, affairs of state to be attended to, there was sauntering in the Park, bowls and tennis; there was racing, sailing and all the pleasures that a King could enjoy who was full of health and vigor.

He had made inquiries of Portugal. He had written letters to Catherine of Braganza, charming letters, which reflected his own personality, the letters of a lover into which he was able to infuse the illusion that the marriage which was to take place was not as one arranged by their two countries but based on pure love.

By the end of the year Barbara was pregnant again. She was exultant.

"I am glad!" she cried. "I would have the whole world know that I bear your royal child. This time there shall be no doubts. Charles, if you doubt this one to be yours, I'll not have it, I swear. I'll find some means of destroying it ere it is born. . . . If that fails, I'll strangle it at birth."

The King soothed her. The child was his. He was as sure of that as she was.

"Then what will you do to prove it? How long shall I remain plain Barbara Palmer?"

It was more than a hint, and the King was not slow to act. It seemed only fair to him that Roger Palmer should be rewarded for his complaisancy.

It was during that autumn that Charles wrote to his Secretary of State: "Prepare a warrant for Mr. Roger Palmer to be Baron of Limerick and Earl of Castlemaine, these titles to go to the heirs of his body gotten on Barbara Palmer, who is now his wife."

Barbara was delighted when she heard she was to be the Countess of Castlemaine.

❁ ❁ ❁

Shc could not rest until she had sought out Roger.

She flung the news at him like a gauntlet.

"Now you see what marriage with me has brought you!"

"I know what marriage with you has brought me."

"Come, Roger, why do you not rejoice in your good fortune? How many women are there in the world who can bring an earldom to their husbands?"

"I had rather you remained plain Barbara Palmer."

"Are you mad? I, plain Barbara Palmer! You fool! I see I work in vain to bring honor to you."

"It is so easy . . . so natural for you to bring dishonor on all those connected with you."

"You sicken me."

"As your conduct does me."

"Roger Palmer, I despise you. You stand there, so sanctimonious . . . such a hypocrite. Do you think I see not the lust in your eyes? Why, I have only to beckon you and you'd be panting for me . . . dishonor or not. . . . You fool! Why should you not share in the honors and riches I can bring to us? Do not think that this is all I shall have. Nay! This is but the beginning."

"Barbara," he said, "be not too sure. There will be a Queen of England on the throne ere long. Then it may be that the King will be engaged elsewhere and may not come a-supping with you night after night."

Barbara flew at him, and the marks of her fingers lingered on his cheek long afterwards.

"Don't dare taunt me with that! Do you think I'll allow that miserable little foreigner to come between me and my plans?" Barbara spat over her shoulder; she liked to indulge in the crude manners of the street; it was as though it brought home to herself as well as others that she had no need to act in any way other than the mood of the moment urged upon her. "She's humpbacked, she squints! The only way her mother can find a husband for her is by giving away half her kingdom."

"Barbara . . . for the love of God, calm yourself."

"I'll be calm when I wish to be. And wild when I wish to be. And I'll tell you this, Master Roger Palmer—who cannot bend his stiff neck to say a gracious thank-you for the earldom his wife has conferred upon him—I'll tell you this: the coming of this Queen will make no difference to my relationship with the King." She put her hands on her stomach. "In here," she cried, "is his child. Yes . . . his . . . his . . . his! And by the saints, I swear this child shall be born in the royal apartments of Whitehall. Yes! even if my confinement should take place during the honeymoon of this Portuguese idiot."

Her eyes flamed. She turned away and paced the floor.

She was eager to tell the King of her plans for lying-in when her time came at his Palace of Whitehall.

❁ ❁ ❁

Christmas came. Charles had laughingly waved aside the question of Barbara's lying-in. It was six months away, and he never let events so far ahead cast a shadow over the pleasure of the moment.

Marriage plans were going forward. It seemed very likely that by the Spring the little Portuguese would be in England.

The thought of her excited him, as the thought of any new woman would. That again was an excitement for the future. In the meantime there was Barbara to be placated, and enjoyed.

Barbara was brooding, still determined to be confined in his Palace. He wondered if he had been right to confer a great title on her husband that she might enjoy it. To give a little was to be asked for much. His experience of a lifetime told him that.

Still, there were occasions when he could remind even Barbara that he was the King, and he foresaw that when he had a wife such occasions might occur with greater frequency.

That again was a matter for the future.

So it was a merry Christmas—the merriest since he had come into England, for last Christmas had been overshadowed by the deaths of his brother and sister. It was good fun to revive those merry customs which had been stamped out by the Puritans—the old revelries of Christmas and Twelfth Night.

There was sadness to come in the New Year. His aunt, Elizabeth of Bohemia, who was at his Court, died there, and it was to him that she turned in her last moments.

He was saddened; he was indeed a family man; he could not bear that any member of his family, which had been so tragically torn apart in his youth, should die.

He had been fond of his aunt.

"So few of us are left now," he pondered. "There is James and Mam and Minette . . . and Mam is ailing, and Minette has never been strong . . . as James and I are."

He wrote to his sister then: "For God's sake, my dearest sister, have a care of yourself and believe me that I am more concerned for your health than I am my own."

She understood him as, he often thought, no one else in the world had ever understood him.

She wrote to him that she was thinking of sending him a little girl to be a maid-of-honor to his Queen when she arrived in England. "She is the prettiest girl in the world," wrote Minette, "and her name is Frances Stuart."

The Earl of Sandwich was soon on his way to Portugal. Arrangements were being made to receive the King's bride in England; and there was always Barbara to placate.

He was spending as much time in her company as he ever had.

He was now supping at her house every night, and the whole city was talking of the King's infatuation for its most handsome woman, which did not diminish even though he was negotiating for a wife.

He but takes his fill of Castlemaine until the Queen arrives, said the people. Then we shall see the lady's handsome nose put out of joint.

Charles was treated to the whole range of Barbara's moods during that spring. She would plead with him not to let the Queen's coming make the slightest difference to her position; she would scorn him for a coward; she would cover him with caresses as though to remind him of the physical satisfaction which she alone could give.

She was determined to bind him more closely to her than ever.

She talked continually of the child—his child—which was to be denied its rightful bedchamber when it came into the world. She pitied herself; she flew into rages and threatened to murder the child before it left her womb.

She demanded again and again that she should have her lying-in at Whitehall Palace.

"That is impossible," said the King. "Even my cousin Louis would not so insult his wife."

"You did not think of your wife when you got me with child!"

"A King constantly thinks of his Queen!"

"So I am scorned.

"For the love of God, Barbara, I swear I cannot much longer endure such tantrums."

Then she wept bitterly; she wished that her child had not been conceived; she wished that she herself had not been born; and he was at his wit's end to stop her doing herself some damage.

But on one thing he was adamant. It seemed likely that her child would be born just at the time of his Queen's arrival in England and the child must be born in Barbara's husband's house.

"What will become of me?" wailed Barbara. "I see I am of no account to you."

"You shall have a good position at Court."

She was alert. "What position?"

"A high position."

"I would be a lady of the Queen's bedchamber."

"Barbara, that is almost as bad as the other."

"Everything I ask is bad. It is because you are tired of me. Very well. You no longer care for me. I shall take myself to Chesterfield. He is mad for me. He would leave that silly little wife of his tomorrow if I but lifted my finger."

"I will do much for you," said the King. "You know it well."

"Then promise me this. I will go quietly to my husband's house and there bear our child. I will not embarrass you while you receive your wife. And for that . . . I shall be made a lady of your wife's bedchamber."

"What you ask is difficult."

"Are you a King to be governed? Are you not a King to command?"

"It seems that you would command *me.*"

"Nay! It is that humpbacked, squint-eyed woman who would do that. Come, Charles. Show me that I have not thrown away all my love on one who cherishes it not. Give me this small thing. I shall be a woman of your wife's bedchamber and I swear . . . I swear that I will then be so discreet . . . so gracious . . . that she will never know that there has been aught between us two."

He was weary of her tirades. He longed to rouse the passion in her . . . He wanted to find the Barbara who returned his passion so gloriously when she was in that abandoned mood which made her forget to ask for what she considered to be her rights.

She was near that mood. He knew the signs.

He murmured: "Barbara. . . ."

She leaped into his arms. She was like a lovely animal—a graceful panther. He wanted her to purr; he was tired of snarls. "Promise," she whispered.

And weakly he answered, for now it seemed that the moment was all important to him, and the future a long way off: "I promise."

THREE

In the apartments at the Lisbon Palace sat Catherine of Braganza, her eyes lowered over a piece of embroidery, and it was clear to those who were with her that her attention was not entirely on her work.

She was small in stature, dark-haired, dark-eyed; her skin was olive and she had difficulty in covering her front teeth with her upper lip. She was twenty-three years of age and not uncomely in spite of the hideous garments she wore. The great farthingale of gaberdine was drab in color and clumsy, so that it robbed her figure of its natural grace; her beautiful long hair was frizzed unbecomingly to look like a periwig and, as it was so abundant, her barber was forced to spend much time and labor in bringing about this disfigurement. But, since this hairstyle and the farthingale were worn by all Portuguese ladies, none thought their Infanta was disfigured by them.

The two ladies who sat on either side of her—Donna Maria de Portugal, who was Countess de Penalva and sister of the Portuguese Ambassador to England, Don Francisco de Mello, and Donna Elvira de Vilpena, the Countess de Ponteval—were very conscious of the disquiet of their Infanta and, because of certain rumors of which Donna Maria had learned through her brother, she was gravely disturbed. Her outward demeanor gave no hint of this, for Portuguese dignity demanded that a lady should never betray her feelings.

"Sometimes it would seem," Catherine was saying, "that I shall never go to England. Shall I, do you think, Donna Maria? And you, Donna Elvira?"

"If it be the will of God," said Donna Elvira. And Donna Maria bowed her head in assent.

Catherine looked at them and smiled faintly. She would not dare tell them of the thoughts which came to her; she would not dare tell them how she dreamed of a handsome bridegroom, a chivalrous prince, a husband who would be to her as her great father had been to her mother.

Tears filled her eyes when she thought of her father. It had always been so. Yet she must learn to control those tears. An Infanta did not show her feelings, even for a beloved father.

It was five years since he had died. She had been seventeen at that time—and how dearly she had loved him! She was more like him than like her clever, ambitious mother. We were of a kind, dearest father, she often thought; had I been in your position I too should have wanted to shut myself away with my family, to live quietly and hope that the might of Spain would leave us unmolested. Yes, I should have been like that. But Mother would not have it. Mother is the most wonderful person in the world—you knew that, and I know it. Yet mayhap if we had lived quietly, if you had never been called to wrest our country from the yoke of Spain, if we had remained as we were at the time of my birth—a noble family in a captive country, a vassal of Spain—mayhap you would be here with me now and I might talk to you about the prince whose wife I may become. But, of course, had you remained a humble nobleman, I should never have been sought by him in marriage.

"I have a letter from him," went on Catherine, "in which he calls me his lady and his wife."

"It would seem now," said Donna Elvira, "that God has willed that the marriage should go forward."

"How strange it will be," said Catherine, her needle poised, "to leave Lisbon; perhaps never again to look from these windows and see the Tagus; to live in a land where, they say, the skies are more often gray than blue; where manners and customs are so different." Her face showed fear suddenly. "I have heard that the people are fond of merrymaking; they laugh often; they eat heartily; and they are very energetic."

"They need to be," said Donna Maria. "It keeps them warm since they rarely feel or see the sun."

"Shall I miss it?" mused Catherine. "I see it often from my window. I see it on the water and on the buildings; but I seem only to look on the sunshine, not to be in it."

"It would seem that you have a touch of it to talk thus," said Donna Elvira sharply. "What should the Infanta of Portugal be expected to do—wander out into the sun and air like a peasant?"

They had been with her—these two—since her childhood, and they still treated her as a child. They forgot that she was twenty-three, and a woman. So many were married long before they reached her age, but her mother had long preserved her for this marriage—marriage with England, for which she had always hoped, because in her wisdom Queen Luiza had foreseen that Charles Stuart would be recalled to his country, and as long ago as Catherine's sixth birthday she had decided that Charles Stuart was the husband for her daughter.

At that time the fortunes of the Stuarts were low indeed; yet, although Charles I had been in sore need of the money a rich Portuguese wife could bring him, he had decided against the match for his son. Catherine of Braganza was a Catholic and it may have been that he—at that time the harassed King—was beginning to understand that his own ill fortune might in some measure be traced to the fiercely Catholic loyalties of his own wife.

Disaster had come to the Stuarts and the first Charles had lost his head, yet, with that foresight and instinct for taking action which would be useful to her country, Luiza had still clung to her hopes for union with England.

"I do not think I shall miss the sun," Catherine said. "I think I shall love my new country because its King will be my husband."

"It is unseemly to speak so freely of a husband you have not seen," Donna Maria reminded her.

"Yet I feel I know him. I have heard so much of him." Catherine cast down her eyes. "I have heard that he is the most fascinating King in the world and that the French King, for all his splendors, is dull compared with him."

Donna Maria lifted her eyes momentarily to Donna Elvira's; both looked down again quickly at their work. But not before Donna Elvira had betrayed by the slightest twitch of her lips that she was aware of what was in Donna Maria's mind.

"I think," went on Catherine, "that there will be a bond between us. You know how deeply I loved my father; so must he have loved his. Do you know that when his father was condemned to death by the Parliament, Charles—I must learn to call him Charles, although in his letter to me he signs himself Carlos—Charles sent to them a blank paper asking them to write what conditions they would and he would fulfil them in exchange for his father's life. He offered his own life. You see, Donna Elvira, Donna Maria, that is the man I am to marry. And you think I shall miss the sun!"

"You talk with great indiscretion," said Donna Maria. "You, an unmarried Princess, to speak thus of a man you have never seen. You will have to be more discreet than that when you go to England."

"It is surprising to me," said Donna Elvira, "that you can so little love your mother . . . your brothers and your country as to rejoice in leaving them."

"Oh, but I am desolate at the thought of the parting. I am afraid . . . so very afraid. Please understand me. I sometimes awake with terror because I have dreamed I am in a strange land where the people are rough and dance in the streets and shout at me. Then I long to shut myself into a convent where I could be at peace. So I think of Charles, and I say to myself: No matter what this strange new land is like, he will be there. Charles, my husband, Charles, who stopped the people torturing those men who had killed his father; Charles, who said: 'Have done with hanging, let it sleep;'

Charles, who offered his life and fortune for that of his father. Then I am less afraid, for whatever awaits me, he will be there; and he loves me already."

"How know you this?" asked Donna Maria.

"His goodness, you mean? I have heard it from the English at our Court. And that he loves me? I have his letter here. He writes in Spanish, for he knows no Portuguese. I shall have to teach him, as he must teach me English; for the nonce we shall speak in Spanish together. I will read it, then you will stop frowning over that altar cloth and you will understand why the thought of him makes me happy."

" 'My, Lady and wife,' " she read. " 'Already at my request the good Count da Ponte has set off for Lisbon; for me the signing of the marriage has been great happiness; and there is about to be despatched at this time after him one of my servants charged with what would appear necessary; whereby may be declared on my part the inexpressible joy of this felicitous conclusion, which, when received, will hasten the coming of Your Majesty.

" 'I am going to make a short progress into some of my provinces; in the meantime, whilst I go from my most sovereign good, yet I do not complain as to whither I go; seeking in vain tranquility in my restlessness; hoping to see the beloved person of Your Majesty in these kingdoms, already your own; and that, with the same anxiety with which, after my long banishment, I desired to see myself within them. . . . The presence of your serenity is only wanting to unite us, under the protection of God, in the health and content I desire. . . .' "

Catherine looked from one woman to the other and said, "He signs this: 'The very faithful husband of Your Majesty whose hand he kisses. Carlos Rex.' "

"Now, Donna Elvira, Donna Maria, what say you?"

"That he hath a happy way with a pen," said Donna Elvira.

"And if," added Donna Maria, rising and curtseying before Catherine with the utmost solemnity, "I may have the Infanta's permission, I will retire, as there is something I wish to say to your royal mother."

Catherine gave the required permission.

She returned to her needlework.

Poor Donna Maria! And poor Donna Elvira! It was true that they would go to England with her, but not to them would come the joy of sharing a throne with the most fascinating prince in the world.

As a result of her interview with Donna Maria, the Queen Regent sent for her daughter and, when she arrived, dismissed all attendants that they might talk in the utmost privacy.

Catherine was delighted to dispense with the strict etiquette which prevailed at the Court of Portugal; it was great happiness to sit on a stool at her mother's feet and lean against her.

At such times a foretaste of great loneliness would come to Catherine, for she would suddenly imagine what life would be like in a strange country without her mother.

Queen Luiza was an unusual woman; strong and fiercely ambitious for her family as she was, she was the tenderest of mothers and loved her daughter more than her sons. Catherine reminded Luiza poignantly of her husband—tender, gentle, the best husband and father in the world, yet a man who must be prodded to fight for his rights, a man who could be persuaded more by his conscience than his ambition. But for Luiza, Portugal would have remained under the yoke of Spain, for the Duke of Braganza had, in the early days of his marriage, seemed content to retire with his wife and two sons to the palace of Villa Viçosa in the province of Alemtejo surrounded by some of the loveliest country in Portugal, and there live with his family the life of a nobleman. For a time Luiza herself had been content; she had savored with delight the charms of a life far removed from intrigue; there in that paradise her daughter had been conceived and, on the evening of the 25th November, St. Catherine's Day, in the year 1638, little Catherine had been born.

In spite of her practical outlook, Queen Luiza was something of a mystic. From the time the child was two she had believed that Catherine was destined to lead her country to security and be as important a factor in its history as she knew herself to have been. For it was on the child's second birthday that greatness was thrust upon the Duke of Braganza and, had it not been for his two-year-old daughter, it might have happened that the great opportunity to rescue Portugal from Spanish tyranny would have been lost.

Never would Luiza forget that November day when the peace of the Villa Vicosa had suddenly given place to ambition. Portugal had been a vassal state to Spain since the mighty Philip II had made it so, and during the course of sixty years of bondage there had crept into the minds of the new generation a lassitude, a dull acceptance of their fate. It needed such as Luiza to rouse them.

Into the Villa Viçosa had come Don Gaspar Cortigno; he talked long and eloquently of the need to break away from the Spanish tyrants; he brought assurances that if the Duke of Braganza, the last of the old royal line, would agree to lead the revolt, many of the Portuguese nobility would follow him.

The Duke had shaken his head; but Luiza had been filled with ambition for her husband, her sons and her daughter. They were happy, she agreed, but how could they be content, knowing themselves royal, to ignore their royalty? How could they ever be content again if they did not keep faith with their ancestors?

"We are happy here," said the Duke. "Why should we not go on being happy all the days of our lives?" His eyes pleaded with her, and she loved him; she loved her family; yet she knew that never would her husband be completely happy again; always there would be regrets, reproaches and doubts in his mind. She knew that it might well be their children who, on reaching maturity, would accuse their parents of robbing them of their birthright. Then beside her was her little daughter catching at her hand, begging to be noticed; and inspired with the certainty that this appeal must not be turned aside, Luiza caught the child to her and cried: "But, my lord, here is an omen. It is two years since this child was born. Our friends are with us to celebrate her birthday. This is a sign that it is the will of Heaven that your sons should regain the crown of which we have long been deprived. I regard it as a happy presage that Don Gaspar comes this day. Oh, my lord and husband, can you find it in your heart to refuse to confer on this child the rank of King's daughter?"

The Duke was struck by the glowing countenance of his wife, by the strange coincidence of the messenger's coming on the birthday of his daughter; and he thereupon agreed to relinquish his peaceful life for one of bloodshed and ambition.

Often he regretted that decision; yet he knew that he would have regretted still more had he had to reproach himself for refusing to take it. As for Luiza, she was certain that Catherine's destiny was entwined with that of Portugal.

It was for this reason that she had kept Catherine so long unmarried; it was for this reason that she had determined to wait for the conclusion of the match with England.

And, during the years which had followed the Duke's decision, success had come to his endeavors and he had regained the throne; but the struggle had so impaired his health that he had died worn out with his efforts; and since Don Alphonso, his elder son, was somewhat simpleminded, his mother Luiza was Queen Regent and ruler of Portugal, for so ably had she advised her husband that on his death, when the government of the country was left entirely in her hands, she continued to preserve Portugal from her enemies and became known as one of the ablest rulers in Europe.

But now, as she confronted her daughter and thought of the life which lay before her in what she knew to be fast gaining a reputation as the most profligate court in Europe, and a rival to the French, she was wondering whether she had been as wise in conducting her family affairs as she had been in managing those of her country. Catherine was twenty-three, a normal and intelligent young woman, yet so sheltered had her life been that she was completely ignorant of the ways of the world.

She had seen the felicitous relationship of her father and mother and did not realize that men such as the Duke of Braganza—faithful husband and loving father, gentle yet strong, full of courage, yet tender and kind—were rare indeed. Catherine in her innocence would think that all royal marriages resembled that of her father and mother.

"My dearest daughter," said the Queen, embracing Catherine, "I pray you sit here beside me. I would talk to you in private and most earnestly."

Catherine sat at her mother's feet and rested her head against her farthingale. It was in moments of intimacy such as this that she was allowed to give vent to her tender feelings.

Luiza let her hand rest on her daughter's shoulder.

"Little daughter," she said tenderly, "you are happy, are you not? You are happy because there is now every likelihood that this marriage will come to pass?"

Catherine shivered. "Happy, dearest mother? I think so. But I am not sure. Sometimes I am a little frightened. I know that Charles is the most charming King in the world, and the kindest, but all my life I have been near you, able to come to you when I was in any difficulty. I am happy, yes. I am excited. But sometimes I am so terrified that I almost hope the arrangements will not be completed after all."

"It is natural that you should feel so, Catalina, my dearest child. Everything you feel is natural. And however kind your husband is to you and however happy you are, you will sometimes long for your home in Lisbon."

Catherine buried her face in the serge farthingale. "Dearest mother, how can I ever be completely happy away from you?"

"You will learn in time to give all your devotion to your husband and the children you will have. We shall regularly exchange letters, you and I. Perhaps there may be visits between us. But they would be infrequent; that is the fate of royal mothers and daughters."

"I know. But Mother, do you think in the whole world there was ever such a happy family as ours has been?"

"It is given to few to know such happiness, it is true. Your father was deeply conscious of that. He would have lived peacefully in the Villa Viçosa and shut his eyes to his duty for the sake of the happiness he could have had with us. But he was a king, and kings, queens and princesses have their duties. They must not be forgotten for the sake of quiet family happiness."

"No, Mother."

"Your father agreed on that before he died. He lived nobly, and that is the way in which *we* must live. My dearest Catherine, it is not only that you will be marrying a very attractive King who will be a good husband to you, you will be making the best possible marriage for the sake of your country. England is one of the most important countries in Europe. You know our position. You know that our enemies, the Spaniards, are ever ready to snatch from us that which we have won. They will be less inclined to attack us if they know that our family is united in marriage with the royal family of England, that we are no longer alone, that we have a powerful ally at our side."

"Yes, Mother."

"So it is for the sake of Portugal that you will go to England; it is for your country's sake that you will do there all that is expected of a queen."

"I will do my best, dear Mother."

"That brings me to one little matter with which I must acquaint you. The King is a young man who will soon be thirty-two years of age. Most men marry before they reach that age. The King is strong, healthy and fond of gay company. It is unnatural for such a man to live alone until he reaches that age."

"To live alone, Mother?" said Catherine, puzzled.

"To live unmarried. He, like you, could only marry one who was royal, and therefore suitable to his state. It would have been unwise for him to marry while in exile. So . . . he consoled himself with one who cannot be his wife. He had a mistress."

"Yes, Mother," said Catherine. "I think I understand."

"It is the way of most men," said Luiza. "There is nothing unusual in this."

"You mean there is a woman whom he loves as a wife?"

"Exactly."

"And that when he has a wife in truth he will no longer need her? She will not be very pleased to see me in England, will she?"

"No. But her feelings are of no account. It is the King's which are all important. He might dismiss his mistress when he takes a wife, but it has come to my ears that there is one lady to whom he is deeply attached."

"Oh . . ." breathed Catherine.

"You will not see her, for naturally he will not let her enter your presence, and you must avoid all mention of her. And eventually the King will cease to require her, and she will quietly disappear. Her name is Lady Castlemaine, and all you have to do is avoid mentioning her name to anyone—anyone whatsoever—and foremost of all to the King. It would be a grave breach of etiquette. If you hear rumors of her, ignore them. It is a very simple matter really. Many queens have found themselves similarly placed."

"Lady Castlemaine," repeated Catherine; then she suddenly stood up and threw herself into her mother's arms. She was shivering violently, and Luiza could not soothe her for some time.

"There is nothing to fear, dearest," she murmured again and again. "Little daughter, it happens to so many. All will be well. In time he will love you . . . only you, for you will be his wife."

❁ ❁ ❁

Every day the arrival of the Earl of Sandwich was expected. He was to come to Lisbon with ships so that he might conduct Catherine and her entourage to England.

Still he did not come.

Catherine, bewildered by the sudden change the last months had brought, wondered whether he ever would. She had not left the Palace more than ten times in the whole of her life, so determined had her mother been to keep her away from the world. Exercise had been taken in the Palace gardens and never had she been allowed to leave her duenna; now that she was Queen of England—for she had been proclaimed as such since the marriage treaty had been ratified in Lisbon—she had left the Palace on several occasions. It had been strange to ride out into the steep streets, to hear the loyal shouts of the people and to bow and smile as she had been taught. "Long life to the Queen of England!" they shouted. She was now allowed to visit churches, where she prayed to the saints that her marriage might be fruitful, and that long prosperity might come to the sister countries of Portugal and England.

When she was alone she took out the miniature which had been brought to her by Sir Richard Fanshawe who was in Portugal to help further the match, and she would feel that she already knew the man pictured there. He was as dark and swarthy as her own brothers, so that she felt he was no foreign prince; his features were heavy, but his eyes were so kindly. She thought of him as the man who had offered his life for the sake of his father and, although she was frightened of leaving her home and her mother, although she was fearfully perplexed at the thought of a woman named Lady Castlemaine, she longed to meet her husband face to face.

But still the Earl of Sandwich did not come.

❁ ❁ ❁

Luiza, anxiously awaiting the arrival of the Earl, began to be afraid. This marriage with England meant so much to her. If it should fall through she could see that the honor and comparative security, which she and her husband had won for Portugal during the long years of endurance, might be lost.

The Spaniards were doing all in their power to prevent the marriage; that in itself showed how important it was. Already they were massing on the frontiers, ready for an attack, and she, being obliged to raise forces without delay, had been hard put to it to find the money to do this, so that it had been necessary to use some of that which she had set aside for her daughter's dowry—that very dowry which had made Catherine so attractive to the English King. The thought of what she would do when the time came for Catherine's embarkation and the handing over of the dowry gave her many a sleepless night; but she was a woman of strong character who had faced so many seemingly insurmountable difficulties in her life that she had learned to deal only with those which needed immediate attention, and trust in good fortune to help her overcome the others when it was absolutely necessary to do so.

There was another matter which gave her grave concern. She was sending her daughter into a strange country to a man she had never seen, without even the security of marriage by proxy.

"I send you my daughter the Infanta, unmarried," she had written, "that you may see what confidence I have in your honor."

But she doubted whether that would deceive the King of England and his ministers. They would know that the Papal See, which was still the vassal of Spain, had never acknowledged Catherine as the daughter of a king; the Pope, when he gave the dispensation for the Infanta to marry a prince of the Reformed Faith—and the marriage could not be performed in Portugal without such a dispensation—would give her title not as Infanta of the Royal House of Portugal, but merely as the daughter of the Duke of Braganza. And that, Luiza felt, was a greater shame than any which could befall her.

So she, a determined woman grappling with many problems, had decided to act boldly. But if the Earl of Sandwich did not come soon, the Spaniards would be marching on Lisbon.

So each day she waited, but in vain.

Had the English learned that she could not find the money for the dowry? How could she know what spies there were in her Court? The Spaniards were cunning; they had been conquerors for a long time; and she was a poor Queen fighting a lonely battle for the independence of her country and the glory of her royal house.

Soon news came to her. The Spaniards were on the march. They were forging ahead towards the unfortified towns on the Portuguese seaboard.

Luiza was in despair. This attack was to be stronger than any the Spaniards had ever launched against their neighbors. Their aim was to see that, by the time the King of England's ambassadors came to claim the daughter of the royal house of Portugal, there would be no royal house. They were throwing great forces into the struggle; forever since the defeat of their "invincible" Armada in the reign of the great Elizabeth, the Spaniards had held the English in dread, and it was their endeavor to prevent at all costs the alliance between little Portugal and that country whose seamen they feared beyond any mortal beings.

So all her schemes had been in vain, thought Luiza. Her people would fight; but they had never had to face such a mighty army as now came against them. She saw ahead years of weary warfare, of frustration and struggle, the English marriage repudiated, and Catherine growing too old for matrimony.

She could no longer bear to look ahead. She shut herself into her apartments. She wanted to be alone to consider her next move.

She would not give up. She would somehow send Catherine to England. The King had promised to marry her. He must marry her.

❁ ❁ ❁

She had said she was not to be disturbed, but Catherine came running into the apartment. Her face was flushed, and she ran as best she could, greatly impeded by her cumbrous farthingale.

"Catherine," said her mother sternly; for in that moment Catherine bore no resemblance to an Infanta of the royal house.

"Mother! Dearest Mother . . . quickly! Come and look."

"What has happened, my child? What has happened to make you so far forget . . ."

"Come, Mother. It is what we have been waiting for so long. The English are here. They have been sighted in the bay."

Luiza turned to her daughter and embraced her. There were tears on her cheek, for she too had forgotten the formal etiquette of the Court.

"They have come in time!" she said.

And she looked in wonder at this daughter who, she had always known, had been born to save her country.

❁ ❁ ❁

There was rejoicing throughout Lisbon as the English came ashore. The Infanta Catherine, the Queen of England, had been born to save them; and here was another sign from heaven to assure her people that this was so. The commanders of the Spanish army, having heard the news and remembering the terrible havoc wrought on their country's ships by the satanic *El Draque* in another century, would not stay to face the English. They turned back to the border and retreated as quickly as they could to safety. Some had seen the ships in the bay—the *Royal Charles,* the *Royal James* and the *Gloucester* with their accompanying fleet of vessels. To those Spanish soldiers, brought up on the story of that ill-fated Armada, which had broken the hopes of great Philip II when it came into conflict with a fleet of inferior vessels yet led by a man of supernatural powers, one glimpse was enough. The great ships seemed to have about them a quality which was not of this world, for it seemed that with them they had brought the spirit of Drake. So the army turned tail, and the Portuguese were saved from their enemies; and how would they dare attack again, knowing that the English were united with their little neighbor through marriage!

Luiza fell on to her knees and uttered prayers of thankfulness to God and His saints. The greatest danger was over; but there still remained the matter of the dowry. However, that could be shelved for the moment; since God had willed that her daughter should be born to save her country, Luiza doubted not that He would show her some way out of the difficulty.

In the meantime there must be a great welcome for the saviors of her country. The people did not need to be ordered to hang out their banners. They were wild with the happiness which comes from relief; they were ready to rejoice. The best bulls had already been brought to Lisbon in readiness for the welcome; it was only a matter of hours before the streets were hung with banners of cloth of gold and tapestry; crowds were on the banks of the river as Don Pedro de Almeida, Controller of Alphonso's household, rowed out in the royal barge to welcome the ambassadors of the King of England. The guns roared as the Earl of Sandwich and his friends were brought ashore. The people cheered as the King's coach carried him to the Palace of the Marquez Castello Rodrigo, where Alphonso was waiting to receive him.

Now the city of Lisbon showed the English what a royal welcome it could give to its friends. Banners, depicting the King of England and the Portuguese Infanta, hands joined, were carried through the streets; the bells of all the churches rang out; bullfight followed bullfight, and every Englishman was a guest of honor.

"Long live the King and Queen of England!" cried the people throughout the city of Lisbon, and that cry was echoed in those towns and villages which had so recently been spared the tyranny of Spain.

❁ ❁ ❁

Queen Luiza chose a moment when the Earl of Sandwich had returned from a lavish entertainment, given in his honor, to ask him to her council chamber. On the previous day he had suggested to her that his master was impatient for his bride, and that he wished not to incur His Majesty's displeasure by further delay. The Queen knew he had been late in arriving at Lisbon, because he had found it necessary to subdue the pirates of the Mediterranean, who must be taught to respect the English flag; moreover, taking possession of Tangier, the task with which he had been commissioned before coming to convey the Infanta to England, had not been accomplished as quickly as he had hoped. The Moors had offered some opposition, and it had been necessary to overcome that. He anticipated no further trouble there, but had been obliged to leave a garrison in the town. As he considered these matters he thought he should lose no time in making his preparations to return; and so was eager to begin immediately to get the dowry aboard.

Luiza had known then that there was nothing for her to do but to explain her difficulties. She therefore arranged this Council meeting to take place after the Earl had been assured once more of the love the Portuguese had for his master and his master's country.

The miracle for which she had hoped had not come to pass. There was no means of providing the money she had promised. There was therefore nothing to be done but admit the truth.

She faced him boldly. "My lord, in these last months we have faced troublous times. Our old enemy had determined to do all in his power to prevent the match which is so desired by both our countries. When the marriage was ratified the dowry was ready and waiting to be shipped to England, but our enemies stole upon us, and it was necessary to raise men and arms against them. For that reason we were forced to use part of the money, which was intended for our daughter's dowry, in the defense of our country."

The Earl was dumbfounded. He had been ordered to bring back with him that money which he knew to be the very reason why his impecunious master had found the Portuguese match so desirable.

Luiza, watching the expressions of dismay flit across his face, knew he was wondering whether he should abandon Catherine and return to England without her. Panic filled her. She visualized not only the retreat of the English, but ignominious defeat at the hands of the Spaniards. Then she remembered that Catherine was destined to save her country, and her confidence returned.

The Earl of Sandwich was meanwhile taking into consideration the fact that he had at some cost gained possession of Tangier, and had left an English garrison there. He was also calculating the cost of conveying that garrison back to England.

Meanwhile Luiza went on: "Half the portion shall be delivered on board the King of England's ships without delay, and I pledge myself to send the other half before another year has passed."

The Earl made a quick decision. Half the money was better than nothing; and the whole affair had gone too far for withdrawal; so, bowing before the Queen, he declared that, since it was his Queen in whom His Majesty of England was primarily interested, he would accept half the marriage portion now, and the other half within a year as the Queen had suggested; and, as soon as the moiety was on his ship he would be ready to convey the King's bride to England.

Luiza smiled. The rest would be simple. She would merely have bags of sugar and spices and such commodities shipped aboard the English fleet in place of the money, which it was quite impossible to supply.

❁ ❁ ❁

Luiza held her daughter in a last embrace. Both knew that they, who had been so close, might never see each other's faces again. Neither shed a tear; they knew they dared not, for if they once allowed any sign of weakness to be visible they would break down completely before all the grandees and *fidalgoes* of the Portuguese Court and the seamen of England.

"Always remember your duty to the King your husband, and to your country."

"I will, Mother."

Luiza still clung to her daughter. She was wondering: Should I warn her once more against that evil woman Castlemaine, for whom they say the King of England has an unholy passion? No! It is better not. Catherine in her very innocence may discover a way to deal with the woman. Better for her not to know too much.

"Remember all I have taught you."

"Goodbye, dearest Mother."

"Goodbye, my child. Remember always that you are the savior of your country. Remember always to obey your husband. Goodbye, my love, my little one."

I should not grieve, thought Luiza. All I wished for has happened. The Spaniards no longer molest us; we have the English as our allies, bound to us by the ties of affection and marriage.

That little matter of the dowry had been satisfactorily settled, although she had been afraid that the Earl of Sandwich was on the point of refusing to accept the sugar and spices in place of the gold. However, he had agreed to take it, after it had been arranged that Diego Silvas, a clever Jew, should accompany the sugar and spice to England and there make arrangements to dispose of it for gold which would be paid into the English Exchequer.

God and the saints be praised! thought Luiza. All difficulties have been surmounted, and I have nothing to fear now. There is just that grief which a mother must feel when parting with a beloved daughter.

How young Catherine looked! Younger than her years. Has she been too sheltered? Luiza anxiously demanded of herself. Does she know too little of the world? How will she fare in that gay Court? But God will look after her. God has decided on her destiny.

The last embrace, the last pressure of the hand had taken place, and Catherine was walking between her elder brother, the King, and her younger brother, the Infante. She turned before entering the waiting coach to curtsy to her mother.

Luiza watched them, and a hundred pictures from the past flashed through her mind as she did so. She remembered their birth, the happy days at Villa Viçosa and that important occasion of Catherine's second birthday.

"Goodbye," she murmured. "Goodbye, little Catherine."

Through the streets went the royal coach, under the triumphal arches past the cheering people to the Cathedral, where Mass was celebrated. Catherine, who had rarely left the seclusion of the Palace, felt as though she were living through a fantastic dream. The shouting, cheering people, the magnificence of the street, and their decorations of damask and cloth of gold, the images of herself and Charles were like pictures conjured from the imagination. After the ceremony the coach took her, her brothers and their magnificent retinue to the Terreira da Paço where she was to embark on the barge which would carry her to the *Royal Charles.*

Among those who were to go with her were Maria de Portugal and Elvira de Vilpena. "You will not feel lonely," her mother had said, "for you will have, as well as your suite of six ladies and duenna, those two old friends of your childhood who together will try to be what I have always been to you."

The ceremony of going aboard was a very solemn one. A salute was fired from the *Royal Charles,* which carried 600 men and 80 brass cannon, and all the noblest in the retinue, which had accompanied her to the Paço, knelt before her to kiss her hand. Catherine stepped into the royal barge, and to the sound of music and cheering was rowed out to the *Royal Charles.*

As she became conscious of the swell beneath her feet a feeling of terrible desolation swept over her. She had been living in dreams; she had thought continually of her husband—the perfect King, the gentle Prince who had offered his life in exchange for his father's, the lover who had written such tender notes. And now she became acutely aware of all that she was losing—her home, the love of her brothers and, most of all, her mother.

And Catherine was afraid.

Elvira was beside her. "Your Majesty should go at once to your cabin. And you should stay there until we set sail."

Catherine did not answer, but she allowed herself to be led to the cabin.

Maria said to her: "The King himself designed your cabin in this his best beloved ship. I have heard it is the most magnificent cabin that ever was in a ship."

Catherine was thinking: So it may be, but how can I think of my cabin now, even though he planned it for me? Oh, Mother. . . . I am twenty-three, I know, and a woman, but I am only a little girl really. I have never left my home before; I have rarely left the Palace . . . and now I have to go so far away, and I cannot bear it . . . I cannot . . . for I may never return.

Now they were inspecting the cabin. In it, they were saying, was all that a Queen could wish for. A royal cabin and a stateroom! Had she ever seen the like? Both apartments were decorated with gold, and lined with velvet. Would she take a look at the bed? It was red and white and richly embroidered. Could she believe that she was on board a ship! Look at the taffeta and damask at the windows, and the carpets on the floor!

Now she must rest, and stay in her cabin until the ship reached England, for it would not be meet for a Queen and lady of the royal house of Portugal to show herself to the sailors.

But Catherine had turned away. The closeness of the cabin with its rich decorations seemed to suffocate her. She could not remain there. She could not now consider Portuguese etiquette.

She turned and went onto the deck, determined to look at her native land as long as it was in view.

All that day and the night that followed, the *Royal Charles* with Catherine on board lay becalmed in the bay of Lisbon; but in the morning a wind sprang up and, accompanied by the *Royal James, Gloucester,* and fourteen men-of-war, the ship crossed the bar and sailed out to sea. It was a magnificent sight.

On the deck, waving aside all those who would come near her, was Catherine, Queen of England, Infanta of Portugal, straining to see, through the tears she could no longer restrain, the last of her native land.

❀ ❀ ❀

After seventeen days at sea, to the great relief of all aboard, the English coast came into view. Elvira had suffered from a fever during the voyage. Catherine herself felt exhausted and weak and as the days passed she was beset by many doubts. It was one thing to dream of the perfect marriage with the perfect man, but when to accomplish it meant leaving behind her home and beloved family, she could not experience complete joy.

She had even had doubts about her husband's virtues as the voyage progressed. It might have been that, in imminent peril of losing their lives, those about her had not succeeded in hiding their feelings as they had in calmer moments. Catherine knew that those who loved her were afraid for her; she knew that they were thinking of the woman Castlemaine, of whom she must never speak. She herself was afraid. As she lay in her cabin, tossed by the erratic movement of the ship, she had felt so ill that she had almost wished for death. But then it had seemed that her mother was near her, urging her to remember her duty, not only to her husband, but to Portugal.

She had wept a little; she had cried for her mother, cried for her home and the quiet of the Lisbon Palace.

It was well that her weakness could be kept secret from those about her.

But she had felt happier when they had come in sight of land and, as they approached the Isle of Wight, the Duke of York's squadron hove in sight. Immediately word was sent to her that the Duke, brother to the King, had sent a message craving her permission to come aboard the *Royal Charles* that he might kiss her hand.

Soon he had come, with the gentlemen of his suite; the Duke of Ormond, the Earl of Chesterfield, the Earl of Suffolk and other fine gentlemen.

They were all dazzlingly dressed, and as her brother-in-law approached to kiss her hand, Catherine was glad that she had disregarded Maria's and Elvira's injunctions to receive the visitors in her native dress. She realized that it would seem strange to these gentlemen and that they would expect her to be dressed as the ladies of their Court. So she wore a dress which had been provided for her by the indefatigable and so tactful Richard Fanshawe; it was made of white and silver lace, and Elvira and Maria held up their hands in horror at the sight of her. It was, they declared, indecent compared with her Portuguese costume.

But she refused to listen to them and, in the cabin, which had been hastily turned into a small presence chamber, she received these gentlemen.

The Duke set out to charm her, and this he succeeded in doing, for, although his manners with ladies were considered somewhat clumsy by the members of his brother's Court, Catherine sensed his great desire to please, and she was only too ready to be pleased.

They talked in Spanish and, as the Duke was eager to dispense with ceremony, Catherine was delighted to do so. She asked for news of the King, and James told her many things concerning her husband: how he loved ships, and what care he had spent in decking this one out that it might be worthy to receive his bride; how he loved on occasion to take a hand at the tiller himself; he told of the improvements he had made in his parks and houses; how he loved a gamble at the races; how he made experiments in his laboratories, and grew strange herbs in his physic garden; he told her a great deal about his brother and mentioned the names of many ladies and gentlemen of the Court, but never once did the name of Castlemaine pass his lips.

Catherine received him daily when he would be rowed out to the *Royal Charles* in his launch; and they talked together, becoming the best of friends, so that Catherine felt her fears diminishing. And when the *Royal Charles* sailed to Portsmouth, James followed and was at hand again, when she left the great ship, to accompany her to port in the royal barge.

Once on land she was taken to one of the King's houses in Portsmouth, where the Countess of Suffolk, who had been appointed a lady of her bedchamber, was waiting to receive her.

The Duke advised her to despatch a letter to the King, telling him of her arrival, when he would with all haste come to greet her.

Eagerly she awaited his coming.

She shut herself into her apartment and told all her attendants that she wished to be alone. Elvira was still suffering from her fever, and Maria was exhausted; as to her six ladies-in-waiting and their duenna, they too were feeling the effects of the journey and, like their mistress, were not averse to being left alone to recover.

Catherine lay in the solitude of her chamber and once more took out the miniature she had carried with her.

Soon he would be here. Soon she would see him in the flesh— this man of whom she had dreamed so persistently since she had known he was to be her husband. She knew what his face was like. He was tall, rather somberly dressed, for he was not a man who greatly cared for finery. This much she had heard. No! He would not care for finery; vanity in dress was for smaller men! He was witty. That alarmed her. He will think me so very stupid, she thought. I must try to think of clever things to say. No, I must be myself. I must apologize because I am simple and have seen so little of the world. He will have seen so much. He has wandered over Europe, an exile for years before he came into his kingdom. What will he think of his poor simple bride?

She prayed as she lay there: "Make me witty, make me beautiful in his eyes. Make him love me, so that he will not regret giving up that woman whose name I will not mention even to myself."

I shall walk in his parks with him and I shall love the plants and bushes and trees because he has planted them. I shall love his little dogs. I shall be their mistress as he is their master. I shall learn how to take clocks to pieces and put them back. All his interests shall be mine, and we shall love each other.

"He is the most easy-going man in the world," they said of him. "He hates unpleasantness. He avoids scenes and looks the other way when there is trouble. Smile always, be gay . . . if you will have him love you. He has had too much of melancholy in his life. He looks for gaiety."

I will love him. I will make him love me, she told herself. I am going to be the happiest Queen in the world.

There was commotion below. He had arrived. He had had news of her coming, and he had ridden with great speed from London.

She should have had time to prepare herself. She rose from her bed, called frantically to her women.

"Quickly! Quickly! Dress me in my English dress. Loosen my hair. I will wear it as the English wear it . . . just at first. Where are my jewels? Oh, come . . . come . . . we must not delay. He must see me at my best. . . . I should have been prepared."

The Countess of Suffolk hurried into the chamber as her women bustled about her.

"Your Majesty, a visitor has come to see you."

"Yes . . . yes . . . bring him in. I am ready."

She half closed her eyes. She would not be able to bear to look at him. This was the most important moment in her life. Her heart was fluttering like a frightened bird.

She heard the Countess say: "This is Sir Richard Fanshawe. He has letters for you . . . messages from the King."

Sir Richard Fanshawe!

She opened her eyes as Sir Richard came into the apartment.

He knelt. "Your Majesty, I bring letters from the King's Majesty. He sends loving greetings to you. He commands me to tell you that he will be with you as soon as he can conveniently travel. At this time imperative business detains him in London."

Imperative business! What business could it be, she wondered, to keep a man from the wife whom he had not yet seen, a King from his Queen who had undertaken a perilous journey to come to him? She wished that she could banish the name of Lady Castlemaine from her mind.

❁ ❁ ❁

The bells were ringing in London. The people stood about in groups, as they did when great events were afoot. The Queen had arrived at Portsmouth; and now it would not be long before the ceremony of marriage took place in England; there would be more pageantry; more revelry; and it would be amusing to see what would happen when the new Queen and Lady Castlemaine came face-to-face.

The King himself had received the news of the Queen's arrival. He had heard also of the bags of sugar and spices that she had brought with her.

He let the communication drop from his hands. So he had a wife at last; but the very reason for her coming—that half a million of money which he so badly needed—was to be denied him.

The Queen Mother of Portugal had promised the rest would follow. In what form, he wondered; fruit? More spices? He had been deceived by that wily woman, for she had known that the reason he had agreed to marry her daughter was that the dowry would help to save his country from bankruptcy.

He must see Clarendon, his Chancellor. But no. Clarendon had been against the match; Clarendon had wished him to marry a Protestant wife, and had only agreed to support the Portuguese marriage when he was overruled by the majority of the King's ministers. And why had they agreed to this marriage? Simply because of that half a million in gold.

So, said Charles to himself, I have a wife and much sugar and spice; I have a port on the coast of Morocco which is going to cost me dearly to maintain—did the sly woman wish me to have it because she could no longer afford to keep it?—and I have the island of Bombay, which I may discover to be equally unprofitable. Oh, my marriage is a very merry one, I begin to believe!

The Queen was here. She was waiting for him at Portsmouth, and he was expected to go and greet her . . . her and her sugar and spice.

Barbara was plaguing him; she had never given up the idea of having her lying in at Whitehall. Barbara might even by now have heard the story of the sugar and spices; if so, she would be laughing herself hoarse with merriment.

He strode up and down the apartment. Mayhap this Jew they had brought with them would soon set about converting the cargo into money. Mayhap the Queen of Portugal would fulfil her promises in due time!

'Tis no fault of that poor girl! he mused. 'Tis her mother who has tricked me. But a fine laughingstock I shall be when the story of the sugar and spice is bruited about.

He lifted his shoulders characteristically; and went to sup at Barbara's house.

Barbara was delighted to receive him.

She was now very large, for her confinement would take place within the next few weeks. She embraced the King warmly, having signed to all to leave them, for it was Barbara who on such occasions gave orders like a Queen.

She had had prepared his favorite dishes. "For," she told him, "I heard of the manner in which these foreigners had cheated you, and I was assured that you would come to me this night for comfort."

"It would seem," said the King with a frown, "that news of my affairs reaches you ere it comes to me."

"Ah, all know how solicitous I am for your welfare. Your troubles are mine, my dearest."

"And what else have you heard, apart from the description of the cargo?"

"Oh, that Her Majesty is small of stature and very brown."

"Your informants were determined to please you."

"Nay, I had it from those that hate me. They say that her teeth do wrong her mouth, and that her hair is dressed in a manner most comic to behold. She has a barber with her who spends many hours dressing it. I hear too that she wears a fantastic costume. It is a stiff skirt designed to preserve Portuguese ladies from the sleight of hand of English gentlemen."

Barbara burst into loud laughter, but there was an uneasiness in it which the King did not fail to detect.

"Doubtless," he said, "I shall soon see those wonders for myself."

"I marvel that you are not riding with all speed to Portsmouth."

"Had I not promised to sup with you?"

"You had. And had you not kept your word I should not have let you forget it."

"Methinks, Barbara, you forget to whom you speak."

"Nay, I forget not." Her jealousy of the Queen was too strong to be subdued. "No," she added on a louder note, "I forget not. I speak to the father of this child I carry, this poor mite who will be born in a humble dwelling unworthy of his rank. He will be born in this miserable dwelling instead of the Palace in which he belongs. But then—he is not the first!"

The King laughed. "You speak of the child as though he were holy. Od's Fish, Barbara, you bear no resemblance to the Blessed Virgin!"

"Now you are profane. But mayhap I shall not survive this confinement, for I have suffered so much during my pregnancy. Those who should cherish me care not for me."

"And the sufferings you have endured have been inflicted by yourself. But I do not come here to quarrel. Mayhap, as you say, I should be on my way to Portsmouth."

"Charles . . . pray sit down. I implore you. I beg of you. Do you not understand why I am nervous this night? I am afraid. Yes, it is my fear that makes me so. I am afraid of this woman with her cruel teeth, and her odd hair, and her farthingale. I am afraid that she will hate me."

"I doubt not that she would—should your paths cross."

Barbara had turned pale. She said quietly: "I beg you eat of this pheasant. I had it specially prepared for you."

She held out the dish to him; her blue eyes were downcast.

For the rest of the meal she did not mention the Queen; but she became gay and amusing, as she well knew how to be. She was soothing; she was the Barbara he had always hoped she would be, and her pregnancy had softened the rather hard beauty of her face; and lying on a couch, a brilliantly colored rug hid her awkwardness, and her lovely auburn hair fell loose about her bare shoulders.

After a while others came to join them, and Barbara was merry. And when they had gone, and left the King alone with her—as it was their custom to do—he stayed talking to her; and she was tenderly tearful, telling him that she was sorry for her vicious ways towards him, and that she hoped in the future—should she live—to improve her manners.

He begged her not to talk of dying, but Barbara declared she had a feeling that she might not be long for this world. The ordeal of childbirth was no light matter, and when one had suffered during the weeks of pregnancy as she had suffered, death was often the result.

"You suffered?" asked the King.

"From jealousy, I fear. Oh, I am to blame, but that did not lessen my suffering. I think of all the sins I have committed, as one does when one approaches death, and I longed for a chance to lead a better life. Yet, Charles, there is one thing I could never do. I could never give you up. Always I shall be there if you should want me. I would rather face damnation than lose you."

The King was disturbed. Not that he entirely believed her, but he thought she must be feeling very weak to be in such a chastened mood. He comforted her; she made him swear that he would not let this marriage interfere with their relationship; she must have a post which would result in her seeing him frequently; but she knew that, if she lived, she would have it, for had he not promised her the post in his wife's bedchamber? She would be content with that, but she could never give him up.

"No matter," she said, "if a hundred queens came to marry you bringing millions of bags of sugar and spices, still there would be one to love you till she died—your poor Barbara."

And to be with Barbara, meek and submissive, was an adventure too strange and exciting to be missed.

It was early morning before he left Barbara's house; and all London took notice that the King passed the night at his mistress's house while his Queen lay lonely at Portsmouth. Outside the big houses of the city, bonfires had been lighted in honor of the Queen's coming; but it was seen that there was none outside the door of that house in which the King spent the night with Lady Castlemaine.

❁ ❁ ❁

What was detaining him? Catherine wondered. Why did he not come? Imperative business? What was that? After the second day she ceased to care, for she was smitten with that fever from which Elvira had suffered during and just after the voyage. Her throat was so sore and she was so feverish that she spent the hours lying in her bed while her maids of honor brought her dishes of tea, that beverage of which she was particularly fond and which was rarely drunk in England.

She would lie in her bed thinking of him, wondering when he would come. She longed to see him, yet she did not want him to come and see her as she was now, with dark shadows under her eyes, and her hair lusterless. She was terrified that he might turn from her in disgust.

Lady Castlemaine, she supposed, would be very beautiful. The mistresses of kings were beautiful because they were chosen by the kings, whereas their wives were thrust upon them.

She knew that her maids whispered together and wondered, as she did, what detained him. Perhaps they knew. Perhaps among themselves they murmured that name which, her mother had impressed on her, must never pass her lips.

Could it be that he, in her imagination the hero of a hundred romances, could so far discard his chivalry as to neglect his wife? Was he so angry about the dowry? Each day there came for her those charming letters from his pen. He wrote like a lover; he wrote of his urgent business as though he hated it, so it surely could not be Lady Castlemaine. He longed to be with her, he declared; he was making plans for the solemnization of their nuptials; ere long he would be with her to assure her in person of his devotion. She treasured the letters. She would keep them forever. Through them lived again the romantic hero of her imagination: Yet the days passed—three . . . four . . . five—and still there was no news of the King's coming.

The fever left her, but, said the physicians, she was to remain in bed. And on the fifth day news came to her that the King had left his capital.

It was two days later, and she was still confined to her bed, but there had been a miraculous change in her. She wondered how long the journey from London to Portsmouth would take, and she pictured him, having done with his "imperative business," riding with all speed to her, and thinking of her as she thought of him.

It was afternoon and Catherine was sitting up in bed, her luxuriant hair falling about her shoulders, when Elvira and Maria came hurrying into her room to say that the King was below.

Catherine was flustered. "I must be dressed . . . at once. How can I receive him thus? I pray thee, Donna Maria . . . call my women. I must wear my English dress. . . . Or should it be my own? . . ."

"You are trembling," said Elvira.

"It is because I shall not be at my best when the King arrives."

Elvira said: "The doctors' orders are that you shall not leave your bed. Why, if you were to take a chill now . . . who knows what would happen? Nay! The King shall wait. We will let His Majesty wait to see you, as you have waited to see him."

But at that moment there was a knock on the door and the Earl of Sandwich was craving permission to enter.

Elvira stood back and he came into the room, bowing to the Queen.

He said: "The King has ridden from London that he may be with his Queen. Your Majesty, he is ready to wait upon you now. . . ."

Elvira said: "Her Majesty is indisposed. She has been ill these several days. . . . Mayhap tomorrow she will be well enough to receive His Majesty."

But at that moment there was the sound of footsteps outside. A low musical voice cried: "Wait until tomorrow? Indeed I'll not. I have ridden far to see the Queen, and I'll see her now."

And there he was, just as she had imagined him—tall, very dark, and smiling the most charming smile she had ever seen. He was as he had been in her dreams, only so much more kingly, she told herself afterwards, so much more charming.

Her first thought as he approached the bed was: Why was I afraid? I shall be happy. I know I shall be happy, because he is all and more than I hoped he would be.

Sweeping off the big plumed hat, he had taken her hand; his eyes had twinkled as he smiled at her.

Now the room was filling with his attendants. The ambassadors were there, the Marquis de Sande and his gentlemen who had accompanied him to England; there were the King's cousin, Prince Rupert, my lord Sandwich, my lord Chesterfield, and others. Elvira had grown pale with horror on seeing so many gentlemen in the bedchamber of a lady.

The King said: "I am most happy at last to greet you. Alas, I do not speak your tongue. Nor you mine, I understand. 'Tis a merry beginning. We must speak in Spanish, which means that I must needs pause to think before I utter a word. And that may not be a bad thing, do you agree?" He was still holding her hand, pressing it firmly, and his eyes said: You are afraid. Of what? Not of me! Look at me. Do you think you should ever be afraid of me? Of these men! They are of no account, for you and I are their King and Queen, to rule over them.

She smiled tremulously, and her dark eyes never left his.

"It grieves me much to see you indisposed," he continued. And then he did a strange thing which no Portuguese gentleman would have dreamed of doing: He sat on the bed as though it had been a couch; and he still kept his grip on her hand. He threw his hat from him. One of the gentlemen caught it.

He went on: "Catherine, my happiness on this occasion would have been greatly diminished had your doctors not assured me that there is no cause for anxiety concerning your indisposition."

"Your Majesty is graciously kind to be so concerned," she said.

He smiled and waved to the people who had come into the room to retire a little, that he and the Queen might converse together in more privacy.

The courtiers moved back and stood in little groups while the King turned to his Queen.

"We shall have time in the future," he said, "for more private conversation. Then we shall be quite alone. Just now it would seem that your duennas are eager that you and I should not be left quite alone together."

"That is so," she said.

"And are you as solemn as they are?"

"I do not know. I have never had any opportunity to be other than solemn."

"You poor little Queen! Then we must contrive many opportunities for making you the reverse of solemn. You shall see what I have planned for you. I thank God you have come to me in summertime, for our winters are long, and doubtless you will find them very cold. But we shall have sylvan entertainments; we shall have river pageants. I mean to show you that your new country can look tolerably well in summertime. I trust you will not be displeased with it."

"I know I shall be very pleased."

"It shall be our earnest endeavor to make you so. Ah! You smile. I am glad you smile so readily. I am an ugly fellow who likes those about him to look pleasant—and what is more pleasant than smiling faces?"

"But indeed you are not ugly," she said.

"No? Doubtless the light of your bedchamber is favorable to me."

"No. Never, never ugly. . . ."

"Ah, it would seem I have not made such an ill impression after all. . . . I rejoice in that. Now you must get well quickly, for your mother will expect our nuptials to take place as early as can be arranged. As soon as you are fit to leave your bed the ceremony must be performed."

"I shall soon be well," she promised him.

Her face was flushed, but not with fever, and her eyes were bright.

He rose from the bed. "Now I shall leave you, for this was a most unceremonious call. But you will soon learn that I am not overfond of ceremony. I wished to see my bride. I could contain myself no longer, so great was my eagerness. And now I have seen her, and I am content. I trust you too are not entirely disappointed?"

How kind he looked—eager, anxious, determined to tell her she must not be afraid!

It was as though that romanticized figure of her dreams had materialized; and in the flesh he was more charming than her dreams had fashioned him, for the simple reason that, before meeting him, she would not have believed so much that was charming and fascinating could be concentrated in one person.

"I am content," she said; and she spoke from the bottom of her heart.

Then he kissed her hand again.

She heard her women, whispering together after he had gone, and they were talking of him. They were shocked because he had come thus unceremoniously, but she did not care. She would not care what they said in future. She was only anxious that she should please him.

She whispered to herself: "I am content." He had said that; and she had answered: "I am content."

❁ ❁ ❁

The King was pensive as he left the apartment. He was pleasantly surprised. From some reports, and in view of the way the Queen Mother had cheated him over the dowry, he had half expected a bride who looked more like a bat than a woman. It was true that she was no beauty, and he was such an admirer of beauty; but he realized that he could hardly have expected a woman who was suitable as a wife to be also a suitable mistress.

He liked very much her manner; quiet, innocent, eager to please. That was such a change after the imperious conduct of Barbara. Had his Queen the temper of his mistress he would have visualized a very stormy life ahead.

No. He believed he had good reason to congratulate himself.

He could grow fond of his little Catherine; he could find it easy to forgive her for not bringing him the promised dowry—and indeed how could a man of his nature do aught else, since it was in truth no fault of hers?

He would be kind to her; he would help her overcome her fears; he would be a gentle lover and husband, for he knew that was what she would want. He would make her happy; and they would have a fine family—several sons as handsome as young James Croft, Lucy Water's boy—and he would no longer have any need to sigh with regret every time his eyes fell on that young man.

He smiled, thinking of her shyness. What a life she must have led in her solemn Portuguese Court; and if her mother was anything like those dragons who had come to guard her daughter, it was no wonder that the poor child was eager for affection.

Have no fear, little Catherine, he mused. You and I can bring much good to one another.

He was looking forward to the nuptials, for a new woman was always a new adventure. Her eyes are good, mused the connoisseur, and there is certainly nothing in her face which could in the least way disgust one. In fact there is as much agreeableness in her lips as I ever saw in any woman's face, and if I have any skill in physiognomy, which I think I have, she must be a good woman. Her voice is agreeable and I am sure our two humors will agree. If I do not do all in my power to make her happy—in spite of the spice and sugar—I think I shall be the worst man on Earth, and I do not believe I am that, although I am far from saintly.

It was not in his nature to grieve unnecessarily. He doubted not that this Jew, whom Queen Luiza had sent with the cargo, would be able to dispose of it satisfactorily; and it should be his pleasure to care for his new wife, to make her feel welcome in her new country, and perhaps in some measure compensate her for having led such a dull life before she came to England.

❁ ❁ ❁

The meeting with the King had had its effect on Catherine. The remains of her illness had disappeared by the morning; she felt radiantly happy.

During that day and night she thought continually of her husband. That was real affection she had seen in his eyes; he had spoken so sincerely when he had said he was glad to see her and they would be happy together. And how he had smiled! And the manner in which he had sat on her bed had been most amusing—and quite charming. He had thrown his hat from him for one of the gentlemen to catch, a somewhat boyish and unkingly act! she thought indulgently; yet in what a kingly manner he had done it! He was so perfect that every gesture, every word, had a ring of nobility and became exactly right just because they were his.

He came to her that morning early, to the room which he called her presence chamber. He chatted easily and familiarly, and his warm dark eyes watched her closely. She blushed a little under the scrutiny, for she did not quite understand the meaning behind those eyes and she was very eager for his approval.

If he did not love me, she thought, I should want to die. And she found that every minute in his company increased her wish to please him.

He told her that their marriage should take place that day. "For," he added, "your mother has shown great trust in me to send you to me thus." He did not add, though he felt a temptation to do so: "And in particular considering she has sent me spice and sugar instead of the money she promised." He could not say anything that might hurt her; he could see that she was vulnerable; and he had determined to make her happy, to keep from her anything that might prove hurtful, for he could well imagine how easily she could be wounded. She was a gentle creature and she should be treated gently.

"Catherine," he said, "the ceremony shall take place here in this house and be registered in the church of St. Thomas A'Becket here in Portsmouth. Unfortunately you and I are not of the same religion; and my people, I think, should not be reminded that my Queen is a Catholic. It would be an unfortunate beginning to your life here if the Catholic ceremonial should be performed. So, my plan is that we shall dispense with it, and that there shall only be our Church of England ceremony."

He was unprepared for the look of horror which came into her face.

"But . . ." she stammered ". . . to dispense with the ceremony of my church! It would be as though we are not married."

"None could say that, Catherine. In this country all would consider the church ceremony completely binding."

She looked about her in distress. She longed for her mother. Her mother would tell her what she ought to do. She feared to displease Charles, and yet she was sure her mother would never have agreed to her dispensing with the Catholic rites.

Charles regarded her with the mildest exasperation. Then he said: "Oh, I see you have set your heart on it. Well, we must find some means of pleasing you. It would not do for us to disappoint you on your first few days in our country, would it?"

She was immediately radiant. It amused him to see the fear fade from her face and joy take its place.

He took her hand and kissed it; then, with an expert gesture, he drew her towards him and kissed her on the lips. Catherine gasped with pleasure.

"There!" he said. "You cannot say I do not do my utmost to win your love! I will even submit to this ceremony—and I confess to you here and now that you will find me a wicked man who has no love for such ceremonies—and all to please you!"

"Oh, Charles . . ." she cried, and she felt as though she might weep or swoon with the delight which swept over her; but instead she laughed, for she guessed intuitively that that would please him more than any other expression of her pleasure. "I begin to feel that I am the most fortunate woman in the world."

He laughed with her. "But wait!" he warned in mock seriousness. "You do not know me yet!"

Then he embraced her—an action which both terrified and thrilled her.

He was gay and lighthearted; she felt so moved by her emotions that she told herself: "If I should die now I know that I have discovered more happiness than I ever hoped to possess."

❁ ❁ ❁

The Catholic rites were performed in her bedroom with the utmost secrecy. How he loves me! she thought. For this is not easy for him. It must be done in secret because his people do not love Catholics. He himself is not a Catholic, yet he submits to this because he knows it gives me solace. He is not only the most charming man in the world, he is the most kind.

He whispered to her when the ceremony was over: "Now see what you have done! You will have to marry me twice instead of once! Do you think you can bear that?"

She could only smile and nod her head. She was afraid to speak, lest before witnesses she should find the words escape her which she knew it would not be wise to utter. She wanted to cry: "I love you. Even the man of whom I dreamed, I realize now, was a poor thing compared with the reality. You are good, and never did one seek to cover his goodness as you do. Never did such a kindly courtly gentleman cover his virtues with a laugh and such disparaging remarks concerning himself. I love you, Charles. And I am happy . . . happier than I ever thought to be."

The Church of England ceremony took place in the afternoon of the same day.

Her six maids of honor helped her to dress in the pale pink gown cut in the English manner. This dress was covered in knots of blue ribbon, and secretly Catherine thought it most becoming, although all the Portuguese ladies were not so sure. They declared it almost gave her the appearance of the type of person modesty forbade them to mention. Perhaps, thought Catherine, it was the excitement of marrying the finest man in the world which made her look like that.

As soon as she was dressed, the King came to her and, taking her hand, led her into the great hall where there was a throne containing two seats set under an elaborately embroidered canopy. One end of the chamber was crowded with those of the King's ministers and courtiers who had come with him to Portsmouth.

Catherine was trembling as the King drew her down with him onto the throne; she scarcely heard Sir John Nicholas read the marriage contract. She was only aware of Charles' twinkling eyes, which belied the solemnity of his tones, as he plighted his troth before them all. She tried to speak when it was indicated that she should join in the responses, but she found she had forgotten the unfamiliar English words which she had learned.

She was afraid, but Charles was beside her to indicate with his smiles that it did not matter; she was doing well all that was expected of her.

She was thinking: All through my life he will be there to support me; I need never be afraid again. He is the kindest, most affectionate of men.

When the ceremony was over, all the people in the hall cried: "Long may they live!" And the King took her hand once more and whispered to her in Spanish that it was over; she was truly his wife, and she could not run home to Portugal now if she wished to.

If she wished to! She wondered whether her eyes betrayed to him the depth of her feeling. I would die rather than leave you, she thought; and was astonished afresh that she could love so deeply, so completely, a man whom she had only known a few hours. Ah, she reminded herself, but I knew him long ago. I have known for long that he offered his life for his father; I knew then that he was the only man in the world whom I could love.

"Now we must go to my apartments," he told her, "and they will all come to kiss your hand. I pray you do not grow too weary of kissing this day, for I would you should save a few to bestow on me this night."

Those words made her heart beat so fast that she thought she would faint. This night the nuptials would be consummated, and she was afraid. Afraid of him? Perhaps afraid that she would not please him, that she was ignorant and would be stupid and mayhap not beautiful enough.

In his apartment the ladies and gentlemen took her hand and kissed it as they knelt to her. She stood beside Charles and every second she was conscious of him.

He was making jocular remarks as though this were not a most solemn occasion. I am not witty enough, she thought; I must learn to laugh. I must learn to be witty and beautiful, for if I do not please him I shall wish to die.

The Countess of Suffolk took one of the bows of blue ribbons from Catherine's dress and said she would keep it as a wedding favor; and then everyone was demanding wedding favors, and Lady Suffolk pulled off knot after knot and threw the pieces of blue ribbon to those who could catch them.

And amid much laughter Catherine's dress was almost torn to pieces; and this the English—and the King in particular—seemed to find a great joke, but the Portuguese looked on in silent disapproval as though they wondered into what mad company their Infanta had brought them.

When the merriment was ended, the King was the first to notice how pale Catherine had become. He put his arm tenderly about her and asked if she were feeling well; and she, overcome by the excitement of the ceremony and her own emotions, would have slipped to the floor in a faint but for his arms which held her.

He said: "This has been too much for the Queen. We forget she is but recently up from a sickbed. Let us take her back to it that she may rest until she is fully recovered."

So the Queen was taken to her bedchamber, and her ladies disrobed her; and as she lay back on her pillows a feeling of despair came to her.

This was her wedding day and she had been unable to endure it. He would be disappointed in her. What of the banquet that was to be given in her honor? She would not be there. A wedding banquet without a bride! Why had she been so foolish? She should have explained: I am not ill. It was the suddenness of my emotions . . . this sudden knowledge of my love, which makes me uncertain whether to laugh or cry, to exult or to despair.

She could not bear that he should be disappointed in her, and she was on the point of calling to her women to help her dress that she might join the company in the banqueting hall, when the door was opened and trays of food were brought in.

"Your Majesty's supper," she was told.

"I could eat nothing," she answered.

"But you must," said a voice which brought back the color to her cheeks and the sparkle to her eyes. "I declare I'll not eat alone."

And there he was, the King himself, leaving his guests in the great banqueting hall, to sup with her alone in her bedroom.

"You must not!" she cried.

"I am the King," he told her. "I do as I will."

Once more he sat on the bed; once more he kissed her hands, and those dark eyes, which were full of something she did not understand, were smiling into hers.

So he took supper sitting on her bed, and he laughed and joked with those who served them as though they were his closest friends. He was intimate with all, it seemed, however lowly; he was perfect, but he was less like a great King than she would have believed anyone would be. Now all the ladies and gentlemen had left the banqueting hall and came to sup in her room.

And all the time he joked so gaily Catherine understood, from the very tender note which crept into his voice when he addressed her, that he was telling her he understood her fears and she was to dismiss them.

"You must not be afraid of me," he whispered to her. "That would be foolish. You see that these serving people are not afraid of me. So how could you be, you my Queen, whom I have sworn to love and cherish?"

"To love and to cherish," she whispered to herself. To share this merry life all the rest of her days!

What a simpleton she had been! She had not realized there could be joy such as this. Now the glorious knowledge was with her. There was no room for fear, there was no room for anything but joy—this complete contentment which came of giving and receiving love.

The royal honeymoon had begun, and with it the happiest period of Catherine's life.

Charles knew well how to adapt himself to her company; to Catherine he was the perfect lover, all that she desired; he was tender, gentle and loving, during those wonderful days when he devised a series of entertainments for her pleasure. There were river pageants and sunny hours spent sauntering in the fields about Hampton Court whither they had gone after leaving Portsmouth; each evening there was an amusing play to watch, and a ball at which to lead the dancers in company with the King. There was none who danced so gracefully as Charles; none who was so indefatigable in the pursuit of pleasure.

She believed that he gave himself to these pleasures so wholeheartedly because he wished to please her; she could not tell him that the happiest times were when they were alone together, when she taught him Portuguese words and he taught her English ones, when they burst into laughter at the other's quaint pronunciations; or when she was in bed and he, with a few of his intimates, such as his brother the Duke of York and the Duchess, sat with her and shared with her the delights of drinking tea, of which they declared they were growing as fond as she was.

But they were rarely alone. Once she shyly mentioned this to Charles because she wished to convey to him the tenderness of her feelings towards him, and how she never felt so happy, so secure, as at those times when there was no one else present.

"It is a burden we must carry with us, all our lives," said Charles. "We are born in public, and so we die. We dine in public; we dance in public; we are dressed and undressed in public." He smiled gaily. "That is part of the price we pay for the loyalty of our subjects."

"It is wrong to regret anything," she said quietly, "when one is as happy as I am."

He looked at her quizzically. He wondered if she were with child. There was hardly time yet. He could not expect her to be as fertile as Barbara was. He had had news that Barbara had been delivered of a fine son. It was a pity the boy was not Catherine's. But Catherine would have sons. Why should she not? Lucy Water had given him James Crofts, and there were others. There was no reason to suppose that his wife could not give him sons as strong and healthy as those of his mistresses.

Then he began to think longingly of Barbara. She would have heard of the life of domestic bliss he was leading here at Hampton Court; and that would madden her. He trusted she would do nothing to disturb the Queen. No, she would not dare. And if she did, he had only to banish her from Court. Banish Barbara! The thought made him smile. Odd as it was, he was longing for an encounter with her. Perhaps he was finding the gentle adoration of Catherine a little cloying.

That was folly. He was forgetting those frequent scenes with Barbara. How restful, in comparison, how charmingly idyllic was this honeymoon of his!

He would plan more picnics, more pageants on the river. There was no reason why the honeymoon should end yet.

As he was leaving Catherine's apartment a messenger came to him and the message was from Barbara. She was in Richmond which was, he would agree, not so far from Hampton that he could not ride over to see her. Or would he prefer her to ride to Hampton? She had his son with her, and she doubted not he would wish to see the boy—the bonniest little boy in England, whose very features proclaimed him a Stuart. She had much to tell him after this long separation.

The King looked at the messenger.

"There is no answer," he said.

"Sire," said the young man, fear leaping into his eyes, "my mistress told me . . ."

How did Barbara manage to inspire such fear in those who served her? There was one thing she had to learn; she could not inspire fear in the King.

"Ride back to her and tell her that there is no answer," he said.

He went to the Queen's apartment. The Duchess of York was with her. Anne Hyde had grown fat since her marriage and she was far from beautiful, but the King was fond of her company because of her shrewd intelligence.

The Queen said: "Your Majesty has come in time for a dish of tea?"

Charles smiled at her but, although he looked at her so thoughtfully and so affectionately, he was not seeing Catherine but another woman, stormy, unaccountable, her wild auburn hair falling about her magnificent bare shoulders.

At length he said: "It grieves me that I cannot stay. I have urgent business to which I must attend without delay."

Catherine's face reflected her disappointment, but Charles would not let that affect him. He kissed her hand tenderly, saluted his sister-in-law, and left them.

Soon he was galloping with all speed towards Richmond.

❁ ❁ ❁

Barbara, confined to her bed after the birth of her son, fumed with rage when she heard the stories of the King's felicitous honeymoon. There were plenty of malicious people to tell her how delighted the King was with his new wife. They remembered past slights and humiliations, which Barbara had inflicted on them, and they came in all haste to pass on any little scrap of gossip which came their way.

"Is it not a charming state of affairs?" the Duchess of Richmond asked her. "The King has at last settled down. And what could be happier for the Queen, for the country and the King's state of mind than that the person who should bring him so much contentment should be his own wife!"

"That crow-faced hag!" cried Barbara.

"Ah, but she is pretty enough when properly dressed. The King has prevailed upon her not to employ her Portuguese barber, and now she wears her hair as you and I do. And hers is so black and luxuriant! In an English dress one realizes that beneath that hideous farthingale she is as shapely as any man could wish. And such sweet temper. The King is enchanted."

"Sweet temper!" cried Barbara. "She would need to have when the King remembers how he has been swindled."

"He is, as you would know better than any, the most forgiving of monarchs."

Barbara's eyes glinted. If only I were up and about! she told herself. If I had not the ill luck to be confined to my bed at such a time, I would show this black bat of a Portuguese Infanta what hold she has on the King.

"I long to be on my feet again," said Barbara. "I long to see all this domestic bliss for myself."

"Poor Barbara!" said Lady Richmond. "You have loved him long, I know. But alas, there is a fate which often overtakes many of those who love Kings too well. Remember Jane Shore!"

"If you mention that name again to me," cried Barbara, suddenly unable to control her rage, "I shall have you banished from Court."

The Duchess rose and haughtily swept out of the room; but the supercilious smile on her face told Barbara that she for one was convinced that Lady Castlemaine would no longer have the power to decide on such banishment.

After she had gone, Barbara lay brooding.

There was the child in the cradle beside her—a bonny child, a child any man or woman would be proud of. And she had named him Charles.

The King should be at her side at such a time. What right had he to neglect his son for his bride, merely because they had chosen to arrive at the same time?

She thumped her pillows in exasperation. She knew that her servants were all skulking behind doors, afraid to come near her. What could she do? Only shout at them, only threaten them—and exhaust herself.

She closed her eyes and dozed.

When she awoke the child was no longer in his cradle. She shouted to her servants. Mrs. Sarah came forward. Mrs. Sarah, who had been with her since before her marriage, was less afraid of her than anyone in the household; she stood now, arms akimbo, looking at her mistress.

"You're doing yourself no good, you know, Madam," she said.

"Hold your tongue. Where's the child?"

"My lord has taken him."

"My lord! How dare he! Whither has he taken him? What right has he . . . ?"

"He has a right, he would say, to have his own son christened."

"Christened! You mean he's taken the boy to a priest to be christened? I'll kill him for this. Does he think to bring the King's son up in the Catholic religion, just because he himself is a half-witted oaf who follows it?"

"Now listen to Mrs. Sarah, Madam. Mrs. Sarah will bring you a nice soothing cordial."

"Mrs. Sarah will get her ears boxed if she comes near me, and her nice soothing cordial flung in her face."

"In your condition, Madam . . ."

"Who is aggravating my condition? Tell me that. You are—and that fool I married."

"Madam, Madam . . . there are scandals enough concerning you. Tales are carried to the people in the street about your rages. . . ."

"Then find out who carries them," she screamed, "and I'll have them tied to the whipping post. When I'm up, I'll do the whipping myself. When did he take my son?"

"It was while you slept."

"Of course it was while I slept! Do you think he would have dared when I was awake? So he came sneaking in . . . while I could not stop him. . . . At what o'clock?"

"It was two hours ago."

"So I slept as long as that!"

"Worn out by your tempers."

"Worn out by the ordeal through which I have gone, bearing the King's child while he sports with that black savage."

"Madam, have a care. You speak of the Queen."

"She shall live to regret she ever left her native savages."

"Madam . . . Madam. . . . I'll bring you something nice to drink."

Barbara lay back on her pillows. She was quiet suddenly. So Roger had dared to have the child baptized according to the Catholic rites! She was tired of Roger; he had served his purpose. Perhaps this was not a matter to be deplored after all, for she could see all sorts of possibilities arising from it.

Mrs. Sarah brought her a dish of tea, the merits of which beverage Barbara was beginning to appreciate.

"There! This will refresh you," said Mrs. Sarah, and Barbara took it almost meekly. She was thinking of what she would say to Roger when she next saw him.

Mrs. Sarah watched her as she drank. "They say the King is drinking tea each day," she commented, "and that the whole Court is getting a taste for it."

"The King was never partial to tea," said Barbara, absently.

Mrs. Sarah was not a very tactful woman. It seemed to her that Barbara had to become accustomed to the fact that, now the King had married, her position would no longer be of the same importance.

"They say the Queen drinks it so much that she is giving the King a taste for it."

Barbara had a sudden vision of teatime intimacy between the foolish simpering Queen and the gallant and attentive King. She lifted the dish and flung it against the wall.

As Mrs. Sarah was staring at her in dismay, Roger and some of his friends came into the room. A nurse was carrying the child.

Barbara turned her blazing eyes upon them.

"How dare you take my child from his cradle?"

Roger said: "It was necessary that he should be baptized."

"What right have you to make such decisions?"

"As his father, the right is solely mine."

"His father!" cried Barbara. "You are no more his father than any of these ninnies you have there with you now. His father! Do you think I'd let you father my child?"

"You have lost your senses," said Roger quietly.

"Nay! It is you who have lost yours."

Roger turned to the company. I beg of you, leave us. I fear my wife is indisposed."

When they were alone Barbara deliberately assumed the manner of an extremely angry woman but inwardly she was quite calm.

"So, Roger Palmer, my lord Castlemaine, you have dared to baptize the King's son according to the rites of the Catholic Church. Do you realize what you have done, fool?"

"You are legally married to me, and this child is mine."

"This child is the King's, and all know it."

"I demand the right to have my child baptized in my own faith."

"You are a coward. You would not have dared to do this had I been up and able to prevent you."

"Barbara," said Roger, "could you be calm for a few minutes?"

She waited, and he went on: "You must face the truth. When you get up from that bed, your position at Court will no longer be the same as it has been hitherto. The King is now married, and his Queen is young and comely. He is well pleased with her. You must understand, Barbara, that your role is no longer of any importance."

She was seething with rage but with a great effort she kept a strong control over herself. As soon as she was up she would show them whether a miserable little foreigner with prominent fangs, a little go-by-the-ground, who could not speak a word of English, should oust her from her position. But in the meantime she must keep calm.

Roger, thinking she was at last seeing reason and becoming reconciled to her fate, went on: "You must accept this new state of affairs. Perhaps we could retire to the country for a while. That might make things a little more comfortable for you."

She was silent; and Roger went on to talk of the new life they might build together. It would be foolish to pretend he could forget her behavior ever since their marriage, but might they not live in a manner which would stop malicious tongues clacking? They would not be the only married pair in the country who shelved their differences and hid them from public view.

"I have no doubt there is something in what you say," she said as calmly as she could. "Now leave me. I would rest."

So she lay making plans. And when she was up and about again she sought a favorable opportunity when Roger was absent for a few days, to gather together all her valuables and jewels; and, with the best of the household's servants, she left Roger's house for that of her brother in Richmond, declaring she could no longer live with a husband who had dared to baptize her son according to the rites of the church of Rome.

❁ ❁ ❁

The King was more attentive to his Queen than ever he had been. Our love is strengthened day by day, thought Catherine, and Hampton Court will always be to me the most beautiful place in the world because therein I first knew my greatest happiness.

Often she would wander through the gallery of horns and look up at those heads of stags and antelopes which adorned it; it seemed to her that the patient glass eyes looked sadly at her because they would never know—as few could—the happiness which was hers. She would finger the beautiful hangings designed by Raphael, but it was not their golden embroidery depicting the stories of Abraham and Tobit, nor the Cesarean Triumphs of Andrea Montegna, which delighted her; it was the fact that within these elaborately adorned walls she had become more than the Queen of a great country; she had found love, which she had not believed existed outside the legends of chivalry. She would look at her reflection in the mirror of beaten gold and wonder that the woman who looked back at her could really be herself grown beautiful with happiness. Her bedroom in the Palace was so rich that even the English ladies marveled at it, and the people who crowded in to see her, as was the custom, would gasp at the magnificence of the colorful hangings and the pictures on the walls as well as the cabinets of exquisite workmanship, which she had brought with her from Portugal. But most admired of all was her bed of silver embroidery and crimson velvet, which had cost £8,000 and had been a present to Charles from the States of Holland. To Catherine this bed was the most valuable of all her possessions because the King had given it to her.

Now, as the summer days passed, there seemed to be nothing he would not give her.

Tiresome state business often detained him, but on his return to her he would be more gallant, more charming than he had seemed before, if that were possible. Never, thought Catherine, did humble shepherd and shepherdess—who chose each other for love, without any political motive—lead a more idyllic existence.

She could have been perfectly happy but for her fears for her country. She had had news from her mother. The Spaniards had been frightened off by the sight of English ships in Portuguese waters, the danger to the country was less acute than it had been, now that Portugal and England were united by the marriage, but England was far away, and Spain was on the borders of Portugal.

When the King asked tenderly what was causing her apprehension, she told him.

Then greatly daring, for she knew that the request she was about to make was one which the monarch of a Protestant country would be loath to grant, she told him what was in her mind.

"It is because you are so good to me, because you are always so kind and understanding, that I dare ask."

"Come!" said the King. "What is this you would ask of me? What do you wish? I doubt if I shall find it in my heart to deny it."

He smiled at her tenderly. Poor little Catherine! So different from Barbara. Catherine had never yet asked for anything for herself; Barbara's demands were never ending. He was foolish to see her so often, foolish to ride so frequently to Richmond, foolish to have acknowledged the new child as his own. But what a charming creature that small Charles was! What flashing eyes, and there was such a witty look about the little mouth already! He was undoubtedly a Stuart, for how like a Stuart to get himself—the King's bastard—born at the time of his father's marriage! He was more foolish still to have acted as Sponsor to the boy, with the Earl of Oxford and the Countess of Suffolk, at the time of his christening in accordance with the rites of the Church of England. And now that Barbara had declared she would never again live with Roger Palmer, and Palmer himself had left the country in his fury, there was certain to be more trouble; but if he could prevent its touching poor little Catherine, he would do so.

His one concern was to keep from the Queen knowledge of the state of his relationship with Lady Castlemaine; and as all those about him knew this was his wish, and as he was a most optimistic man, he did not doubt his ability to do so.

In the meantime he wished to indulge Catherine in every possible way; it pleased him to see her happy, and it seemed the easiest thing in the world to make her so. Now he listened to her request almost with eagerness, so ready was he to grant it.

"It is my country," she said. "The news is not good. Charles, you do not hate the Catholics?"

"How could I, when that would mean hating you?"

"You are being charming as usual, and not saying all you mean. You do not hate them for other reasons?"

He said: "I owe much to Catholics. The French helped me during my exile, and they are Catholics. My little sister is a Catholic, and how could I hate her! Moreover, a Mr. Giffard, who did much to make possible my escape after Worcester, was also a Catholic. Indeed no, I do not hate Catholics. In truth, I hold it great folly to hate men because their opinions differ from my own. Women of course I should never hate in any circumstances."

"Charles, be serious to please me."

"I am all seriousness."

"If the Pope would promise his protection to my country, it would have less to fear from Spain."

"The Pope will support Spain, my dear. Spain is strong, and Portugal is weak, and it is so much more convenient to support that which is in little danger of falling down."

"I have thought of a way in which I might appeal to the Pope, and with your permission I would do it."

"What is this way?"

"I am a Catholic, here in a Protestant country. I am a Queen, and it may be that all the world knows now how good you are to me."

Charles looked away. "Nay," he said quickly. "Nay. . . . I am not so good as I ought to be. Mayhap the whole world but you knows that."

She took his hand and kissed it.

"You are the best of husbands, and I am therefore the happiest of wives. Charles, would you grant me this permission? If you did, it would make my happiness complete. You see, the Pope and others will know how you love me, and they will think I am not without influence with you . . . and thus this country. If I might write to the Pope and tell him that now that I am in England I will do everything within my power to serve the Catholic Faith, and that my reason for coming here was not for the sake of the Crown which would be mine but for the sole purpose of serving my faith, I think the Pope will be very pleased with me."

"He would indeed," said Charles.

"Oh, Charles, I would not attempt to persuade you to act against your conscience."

"Pray you, have less respect for my conscience. He is a weak, idle and somnolent fellow who, I fear, often fails in his duty."

"You joke. You joke continually. But that is how I would have it. It is that which makes the hours spent in your company the happiest I have ever known. Charles, if I could make the Pope believe that I would work for the Catholic Faith in England, I could at the same time ask for his protection of Portugal."

"Yes, that is so; and I doubt not that you would get it for such a consideration."

"And Charles, you . . . you . . . would agree?"

He took her face in his hands. "I am the King of a Protestant country," he said. "What think you my ministers would say if they knew I had allowed you to send such a letter?"

"I know not."

"The English are determined never to have a Catholic Monarch on their throne. They decided that, more than a hundred years ago on the death of Bloody Mary, whom they will never forget."

"Yes, Charles. I see you are right. It was wrong of me to ask this of you. Please forget it."

As he continued to hold her face in his hands, he asked: "How would you convey such a letter to Rome?"

"I had thought to send Richard Bellings, a gentleman of my household, whom I can trust."

"You suffer because of your country's plight," he said gently.

"So much! If I could feel that all was well there, I should be happy indeed."

He was thinking how sweet she was, how gentle, how loving. He wanted to give her something; he wanted to give all that she most desired. A letter to the Pope? What harm in that? It would be a secret matter. What difference could such a letter make to him? And how it would please her! It might be the means of securing Papal protection for the poor harassed Queen Regent of Portugal, who had trials enough with her half-imbecile son as King and the Spaniards continually threatening to depose the pair of them. What harm to him? What harm in promises? And he felt a guilty need to make Catherine happy.

"My dearest wife," he said gently, "I ought not to allow this. I know it well. But, when you ask me so sweetly, I find it mighty hard to refuse."

"Then Charles, let us forget I asked you. It was wrong of me. I never should have asked."

"Nay, Catherine. You do not ask for jewels or money, as so many would. You are content to give of your love, and that has given me great pleasure. Let me give something in return."

"You . . . give me something! You have given me such happiness as I never knew existed. It is not for you to give me more."

"Nevertheless I shall insist on granting this. To please me, you shall write this letter and despatch it. But do this yourself—let none know that I have any part in it, or the thing would be useless. Tell the Pope what you intend, ask his protection. Yes, Catherine, do it. I wish it. I wish to please you . . . greatly."

"Charles, you make me weep . . . weep with shame for asking more of you who have given so much . . . weep for the joy of all the happiness which has come to me, so that I wonder why Heaven should have chosen me to be so singularly blessed."

He put his arms about her and kissed her gently.

While she clung to him he remembered a paper he carried in his pocket, which he had meant to present to her at a convenient moment.

He patted her arm gently and disengaged himself.

"Now, my dearest, here is a little matter for you to attend to."

He took the scroll from his pocket.

"But what is this?" she asked, and as she was about to look over his shoulder, he handed it to her.

"Study it at your leisure. It is merely a list of ladies whom I recommend for appointments in your household."

"I will look at it later."

"When you can no longer feast your eyes upon your husband!" he said lightly. "You will find all these ladies worthy and most suitable for the posts indicated. I know my Court far better than you can in such a short time, so I am sure you will be happy to accept these suggestions of mine."

"Of a certainty I shall."

She put the scroll away in a drawer and they went out into the gardens to saunter with a few ladies and gentlemen of the Court.

It was some time later when Catherine took out the scroll and studied the list of names.

As she did so her heart seemed to stop and plunge on; she felt the blood rush to her head and drain away.

This could not be real. This was a bad dream.

At the head of the list which the King had given her was the name Barbara, Countess of Castlemaine.

It was some time before, trembling with fear and horror, she took a pen and boldly crossed out that name.

❁ ❁ ❁

The King came to the Queen and dismissed all attendants so that they were entirely alone.

He began almost suavely: "I see that you have crossed out the name of one of the ladies whom I suggested you should take into your household."

"It was Lady Castlemaine," said Catherine.

"Ah, yes. A lady to whom I have promised a post in your bedchamber."

Catherine said quietly: "I will not have her."

"But I have told you that I myself promised this post."

"I will not have her," repeated Catherine.

"Why so?" asked the King. His voice sounded cold, and Catherine had never known coldness from him before.

"Because," she said, "I know what relationship this woman once had to you, and it is not meet that she should be given this post."

"I consider it meet, and I have promised her this post."

"Should a lady have a post in the Queen's bedchamber against the wishes of the Queen?"

"Catherine, you will grant this appointment because I ask it of you."

"No."

He looked at her appraisingly. Her face was blotched with weeping. He thought of all he had done for her. He had played the loving husband for two months to a woman who aroused no great desire within him, and all because her naivety stirred his pity. Being considerate of her feelings he had never once reminded her of the fact that her mother had cheated him over the dowry. He had only yesterday given her permission to write a letter to the Pope, which he should not have done, and yet because he had wished to give her pleasure he had agreed that she should write it. And now when he asked this thing of her because he, in a weak moment, had promised the appointment to a woman of whose rages he was afraid, Catherine would not help him to ease the situation.

So she knew of his liaison with Barbara, yet she had never uttered a word about it. Then she was not so simple as he had thought. She was not the gentle, loving creature he had believed her to be. She was far more subtle.

If he allowed her to have her way now, Barbara's rage would be terrible and Barbara would take her revenge. Barbara would doubtless lay bare to this foolish Queen of his the intimacies which had taken place between them; she would show the Queen the letters which he had carelessly written; and Catherine would suffer far more through excluding Barbara from her bedchamber than by accepting her.

How could he explain to the foolish creature? How could he say, "If you were wise you would meekly accept this woman. You have your dignity and through it could subdue her. If you would behave now with calm, dignified decorum in this matter, if you would help me out of a difficult position in which I, with admittedly the utmost folly, have placed myself, then I would truly love you; you would have my devotion forever more. But if you insist on behaving like a silly jealous girl, if you will not make this concession when I ask you—and I know it to be no small thing, but I have given you in these last two months far more than you will ever know—then I shall love you truly, not with a fleeting passion but with the respect I should give to a woman who knows how to make a sacrifice when she truly loves."

"Why are you so stubborn?" he asked wearily.

"I know what she was to you . . . this woman."

He turned away impatiently. "I have promised the appointment."

"I will not have her."

"Catherine," he said, "you must."

"I will not. I will not."

"You have said you would do anything to please me. I ask this of you."

"But not this. I will not have her—your mistress—in my service . . . in my own bedchamber."

"I tell you I have promised her this appointment. I must insist on your giving it to her."

"I never will!" cried Catherine.

He could see that she was suffering, and his heart was immediately touched. She was, after all, young and inexperienced. She had had a shock. He should have prepared her for this. But how could he when she, in her deceit, had given him no indication that she had ever heard of Lady Castlemaine?

Still he realized the shock she had sustained; he understood her jealousy. He must insist on her obeying him, but he wished to make the surrender as easy as possible for her.

"Catherine," he said, "do this thing for me and I shall be forever grateful. Take Lady Castlemaine into your service, and I swear that if she should ever be insolent to you in the smallest degree I will never see her again."

He waited, expecting the floods of tears, the compliance. It would be so easy for her, he was sure. Queens had been asked to overcome these awkward situations before. He thought of Catherine de' Medici, wife of Henri Deux, who had long and graciously stood aside for Diane de Poitiers; he thought of the many mistresses of his respected ancestor Henri Quatre. He was not asking his wife anything to compare with what those monarchs had asked of theirs.

But he had been mistaken in Catherine. She was not the soft and tender girl. She was a determined and jealous woman.

"I will not receive her into my household," she said firmly.

Astonished and now really angry, the King turned abruptly and left her.

❁ ❁ ❁

Charles was in a quandary. It grieved him to hurt Catherine, yet less than it would have done a week before, for it seemed to him that her stubborn refusal to understand his great difficulty dearly showed that her vanity and self-love was greater than her love for him; he was able to tell himself that he had been deceived in her; and this helped him to act as he knew he would have to act. Charles wanted to be kind to all; to hurt anyone, even those whom he disliked, grieved him; revenge had always seemed to him a waste of time, as was shown by his behavior when those men who had been instrumental in bringing about his father's death and his own exile had been brought to trial; he wished to live a pleasant life; if some painful act had to be performed it was his main desire to get it over as quickly as possible or look the other way while someone else carried it out.

Now he knew that he was going to hurt Catherine, for he was sure that to allow Barbara to disclose to the Queen the intimate details of their relationship—which Barbara had hinted she might do, and he knew her well enough to realize that she was capable of carrying out her threat—would result in hurting Catherine more than would quietly receiving Barbara into her household.

Catherine had right on her side to a certain extent, but if she would only be reasonable, if she would only contemplate his difficulties instead of brooding on her own, she could save them all much trouble.

But she was obstinate, narrow-minded and surrounded by a group of hideous prudes; for it was a fact that those ladies-in-waiting and duennas of hers would not sleep in any beds unless all the linen and covers had been changed—lest a man might have slept there before them and so would, they believed, defile their virginity.

Catherine had to grow up. She had to learn the manners of a Court less backward than that ruled over by her stern old mother.

He would not plead with her anymore; that only resulted in floods of tears; but he was convinced that to allow her to flout him would be folly. It was bad enough to have Barbara flouting him. He had to be firm with one of them; and Barbara had the whip hand—not only because of the revelations she could make, but because of her own irresistible appeal.

So he made up his mind that if Barbara could be presented to Catherine—and Barbara had promised that she would behave with the utmost decorum, and so she would, provided she had her way—the Queen would not make a scene in front of a number of people; and then, having once received his mistress, she would find there was nothing very extraordinary in doing so.

Catherine was holding a reception in her presence room, and many of the ladies and gentlemen of the Court were with her there.

Charles was not present and Catherine, heartbroken as she was, could not prevent her gaze straying every now and then to the door. She longed for a sight of him; she longed to return to that lost tender relationship. She let herself dream that he came to her full of sorrow for the way in which he had treated her; that he implored her to forgive him and declared that neither of them should ever see or speak of Lady Castlemaine again.

Then she saw him. He was making his way to her, and he was smiling, and he looked so like the Charles he had been in the early days of their marriage. He laughed aloud and the sound of that deep attractive voice made her whole body thrill with pleasure. He had caught her eye now; he was coming towards her and his smiles were for her.

She noticed his companion then. He was holding her hand, as he always held the hands of those ladies whom he would present to her. But Catherine scarcely looked at the woman; she could see none but him, and absorb the wonderful fact that he was smiling at her.

He presented the lady, who curtsied as she took Catherine's hand and kissed it.

The King was looking at the Queen with delight, and it seemed in that moment of incomparable joy that their differences had been wiped out. He had stepped back, and the lady he had presented remained at his side; but he continued to look at Catherine, and she felt that only he and she existed in that large assembly.

Then quite suddenly she became aware of tension in the atmosphere; she realized that the ladies and gentlemen had stopped murmuring; it was almost as though they held their breath and were waiting for something dramatic to happen.

Elvira, who was standing behind her chair, leaned forward.

"Your Majesty," whispered Elvira, "do you know who that woman is?"

"I? No," said the Queen.

"You did not catch the name. The King deliberately mispronounced it. It is Lady Castlemaine."

Catherine felt waves of dizziness sweeping over her. She looked round at that watching assembly. She noted the smiles on their faces; they were regarding her as though she were a character in some obscene play.

So he had done this to her! He had brought Lady Castlemaine to her reception that she might unwittingly acknowledge his mistress before all these people.

It was too much to be borne. She turned her eyes to him, but he was not looking her way now; his head was bent; he seemed absorbed in what that woman was saying.

And there stood the creature—the most lovely woman Catherine had ever seen—yet her loveliness seemed to hold an evil kind of beauty, bold, brazen, yet magnificent; her auburn curls fell over bare shoulders, her green and gold gown was cut lower than all others, her emeralds and sparkling diamonds about her person. She was arrogant and insolent—the King's triumphant mistress.

No! She could not endure it. Her heart felt as though it were really breaking; she suffered a violent physical pain as it leaped and pranced like a mad and frightened horse.

The blood was rushing to her head. It had started to gush from her nose. She saw it, splashing on to her gown; she heard the quick intake of breath as the company, watching her, gasped audibly.

Then she fell swooning to the floor.

❁ ❁ ❁

The King was horrified to see Catherine in such a condition; he ordered that she be carried to her apartments, but when he realized that only the feelings of the moment—which he preferred to ascribe to anger—had reduced her to such a state, he allowed himself to be shocked by such lack of control.

He, so ready to seek an easy way out of a difficulty, so ready to accept what could not be avoided, felt his anger increasing against his wife. It seemed to him that it would have been so simple a matter to have received Barbara and feigned ignorance of her relationship with himself. That was what he himself would have done; that was what other Queens had done before her.

He knew that he must placate Barbara; he had promised to, and she would see that this was one of the promises he kept. He hated discord, so he decided that he would shift to Clarendon the responsibility of making Catherine see reason.

He sent for his Chancellor.

He was not so pleased with Edward Hyde, Earl of Clarendon, as he had once been. In the days when he had been a wandering exile he had felt unsafe unless Clarendon was beside him to give him the benefit of his wisdom and advice. It was a little different now that he was a King. He and Clarendon had disagreed on several matters since their return to England; and Charles knew that Clarendon had more enemies in England than he ever had in exile.

Clarendon wished to go back to the prerevolutionary doctrine. He believed that the King should have sole power over the militia; and he wished to inaugurate in place of Parliament a powerful privy council who would decide all matters of state.

The King agreed with him on this but on very little else. Clarendon continually deplored the King's wish to shape his own monarchy in the pattern of that of France. The King was too French in his outlook; he looked to his grandfather, Henri Quatre, as a model, not only in his numerous love affairs but in his schemes of government. Again and again Clarendon had pointed out that England was not France, and that the temperament of the two countries was totally different.

They also disagreed on religious matters. Clarendon thought Charles' policy of toleration a mistaken one. There were many in the Court who sensed the mild but growing estrangement between the King and his most trusted minister, and they were ready enough to foster that growth. Buckingham was one, and with him in this was his kinswoman, Lady Castlemaine.

Clarendon, as a wise old man, knew that his enemies were watching, quietly as yet but hopefully.

Still he persisted in his frankness with the King; and although he had been against the Portuguese marriage he now attempted to take the side of the Queen.

"Your Majesty is guilty of cruelty towards the Queen," he said; "you seek to force her to that with which flesh and blood cannot comply."

Charles studied the man. He no longer completely trusted him. A few years ago he would have listened respectfully and he might have accepted Clarendon's view; but he now believed that his Chancellor was not wholly sincere, and he looked for the reasons which had impelled him to take such views as he now expressed.

Charles knew that Clarendon hated Barbara. Was this the reason why he now urged the King not to give way to his mistress's cruel desires, but to support his wife? How could he be sure?

"I have heard you say," went on the Chancellor, "when you saw how King Louis forced his wife to receive his mistresses, that it was a piece of ill nature that you would not be guilty of, for if ever you had a mistress after you had a wife—which Your Majesty hoped you never would have—she should never come where your wife was."

"It is good for a man who has a wife not to have a mistress," said Charles testily, "but if he has, he has, and there's an end of it. We would all like to be virtuous, but our natures drive us another way. I hold that when such a matter as this arises the best road from it is for good sense to be shown all round. If the Queen had quietly received my Lady Castlemaine there would not then be this trouble."

"Your Majesty, I would beg you to please your wife in this, for she is the Queen and the other but your mistress. I can assure Your Majesty that Ormond and others agree with me in this. You should repudiate my Lady Castlemaine and never allow her to enter into your wife's household."

The King was rarely angry, but he was deeply so on this occasion. He remembered the hypocrisy of Clarendon when the Duke of York had married his daughter. Then he had said he would have rather seen Anne James' mistress than his wife. It seemed at that time he had a little more respect for mistresses, since he was eager to see his daughter one.

No! He could trust none. Clarendon, Ormond, and the rest urged him to repudiate Barbara, not because she was his mistress, but because she was their enemy. They would have been howling for the destruction of the

Queen if they did not think her an ineffectual puppet who could harm them not.

Then Charles fell into one of his rare moods of obstinacy.

He said: "I would beg of you all not to meddle in my affairs unless you are commanded to do so. If I find any of you guilty in this manner I will make you repent of it to the last moments of your lives. Pray hear what I have to say now. I am entered upon this matter, and I think it necessary to counsel you lest you should think by making stir enough you might divert me from my resolution. I am resolved to make my Lady Castlemaine of my wife's bedchamber; and whosoever I find using any endeavors to hinder this resolution, I will be his enemy to the last moment of his life."

Clarendon had never seen the King so stern, and he was shaken. He remembered all his enemies at Court, and how again and again when he was in danger from them it was the King who had come to his aid.

He hated Lady Castlemaine; he hated her not only because she was his enemy but because of the influence she had over the King. But he knew that in this instance, the King's will being so firm, he must remember he was naught else but the King's servant.

"Your Majesty has spoken," he said. "I regret that I have expressed my opinions too freely. I am Your Majesty's servant, to be used as you will. I beg you forgive the freedom of my manners, which freedom has grown out of my long affection for Your Majesty."

The King, regretting his harshness almost immediately, laid his hand on Clarendon's shoulder.

He gave a half-smile. "I am pledged to this. It's a mighty unpleasant business. Come, my friend, extricate me; stand between me and these wrangling women. Be my good lieutenant as you have been so many times before, and let there never more be harsh words between us."

There were tears in the older man's eyes.

The charm of the King was as potent as it had ever been.

Oddly enough, thought Clarendon, though one believes him to be in the wrong, one desires above all things to serve him.

❁ ❁ ❁

Clarendon made his way to the Queen's apartment and asked for audience.

She received him in bed. She looked pale and quite exhausted after her upset, but she greeted him with a faint smile.

Clarendon intimated that his business with her was secret, and her women retired.

"Oh, my lord," she cried, "you are one of the few friends I have in this country. You have come to help me, I know."

"I hope so, Madam," said Clarendon.

"I have been foolish. I have betrayed my feelings, and that is a bad thing to do; but my feelings were so hard to bear. My heart was broken."

"I have come to give you my advice," said the Chancellor, "and it is advice which may not please Your Majesty."

"You must tell me exactly what you mean," she said. "I can glean no help from you if you do not talk freely of my faults."

"Your Majesty makes much of little. Has your education and knowledge of the world given you so little insight into the conduct of mankind that you should be so upset to witness it? I believe that your own country could give you as many—nay more—instances of these follies, than we can show you here in our cold climate."

"I did not know that the King loves this woman."

"Did you imagine then that a man such as His Majesty, thirty-two years of age, virile and healthy, would keep his affections reserved for the lady he would marry?"

"I did not think he loved her still."

"He has the warmest feelings for you."

"Yet his for her are warmer."

"They would be most warm for you if you were to help him in this," said the Chancellor slyly. "I come to you with a message from him. He says that if you will but do what he asks on this one occasion he will make you the happiest queen in the world. He says that whatever he entertained for other ladies before your coming concerns you not, and that you must not enquire into them. He says that if you will help him now he will dedicate himself to you. If you will meet his affection with the same good humor, you will have a life of perfect felicity."

"I am ready to serve the King in all ways."

The Chancellor smiled. "Then all is well. There is no longer discord between you."

"Save," went on Catherine, "in this one thing. I will not have that woman in my household."

"But only by helping the King in this—for he has given a promise that it should be so—can you show that devotion."

"But if he loved me he could not . . . could not suggest it! By insisting on such a condition he exposes me to the contempt of the Court. If I submitted to it I should believe I was worthy to receive such an affront. No. No. I will not have that woman in my household. I would prefer to go back to Lisbon."

"That," said Clarendon quickly, "it is not in your power to do. Madam, I beg of you, for your own sake, listen to my counsel. Meet the King's wishes in this. It is rarely that he is so insistent. Pray try to understand that he has given his word that Lady Castlemaine should have a post in your bedchamber. Demean yourself in this—if you consider you should demean yourself by so obeying your husband—but for your future happiness do not remain stubborn."

Catherine covered her face with her hands.

"I will not," she moaned. "I will not."

Clarendon left her and her women came round her, soothing her in their native tongue. They cursed all those who had dared insult their Infanta; they implored her to remember her state; they swore to her that she would forfeit all respect, not only of the Court but of the King, if she gave way.

"I cannot have her here," Catherine murmured. "I cannot. Every time I saw her my heart would break afresh."

So she lay back and her women smoothed her hair away from her brow and spread cooling unguents on her heated face; they wiped away the tears which she could not restrain.

❁ ❁ ❁

That night the King came to her chamber.

Clarendon had failed, and Charles no longer felt impelled to pretend he cared for her. She had disappointed him. Her charm had been in her soft tenderness, her overwhelming desire to please. Now she was proving to be such another termagant as Barbara, and not nearly so handsome a one.

They are alike, thought the King; only the method of getting what they want is different.

"Charles," she cried tearfully, "I pray you let us have done with this matter. Let us be as we were before."

"Certainly let us have done with it," he said. "You can decide that quicker than any of us."

"I could not bear to see her every day in my chamber. . . . I could not, Charles."

"You who have talked of dying for me . . . could not do this when I ask it?" He spoke lightly, maliciously.

She said: "When you speak thus I feel as though a hundred daggers pierce my heart."

"That heart of yours is too easily reached. A protection of sound good sense might preserve it from much pain."

"You are so different now, Charles. I scarcely know you."

"You too are different. I feel I knew you not at all. I had thought you gentle and affectionate, and I find you stubborn, proud and wanting in your sense of duty."

"I find you wanting in affection and full of tyranny," she cried.

"You are inexperienced of the world. You have romantic ideals which are far from reality."

"You have cynical ideas which shock and alarm me."

"Catherine, let us have done with these wrangles. Let us compromise on this. Do this one thing for me and I promise you that Lady Castlemaine shall never, in the smallest way, show the slightest disrespect for you; she shall never, for one moment, forget that you are the Queen."

"I will never have her in my household!" cried Catherine hysterically. "Never . . . never. I would rather go back to Portugal."

"You would do well to discover first whether your mother would receive you."

Catherine could not bear to look at him. He was so aloof and angry, and anger sat so unfamiliarly on that dark face. That he could talk so coldly of her going home frightened her.

He went on: "Your Portuguese servants will soon be going back, so doubtless they could lay this matter of your return before your mother; then we should see whether she would be willing to receive you."

"So you would send my servants away from me—even that?"

Charles looked at her in exasperation. She was so innocent of the world, so ignorant of procedure. She thought that in sending her servants from her he would be guilty of another act of cruelty; she did not understand that in all royal marriages a bride's servants stayed with her only until she was settled into the ways of her new country, and that it was considered unwise for them to stay longer since they created jealousy and were inclined to make great matters of small differences—such as this one—which arose between a king and his queen.

He did not explain to her; he was exasperated beyond endurance. Moreover it seemed to him she was ready to misconstrue all his actions and doubtless would not believe anything he told her.

"I did not know," she said, "that you could find it in your heart to treat me so ill. My mother promised me that you would be a good husband to me."

"Your mother, alas, made many promises which were not fulfilled. She promised a handsome dowry which has not yet been delivered."

He immediately hated himself for those words, for he had told himself again and again that the defalcation of her mother was no fault of Catherine's.

He longed to be done with the matter. It was absurd. A quarrel between two women, and he was allowing it to give him as much anxiety as the threat of a major war. He was wrangling with her through the night in such loud tones that many in the Palace would hear him.

It was undignified; it was folly; and he would do it no more.

He hurried from the apartment, leaving Catherine to weep through the rest of the night.

❁❁❁

The days passed most wretchedly for Catherine. She seldom spoke to the King. She would see him from the windows of her apartment sauntering with his friends; she would hear their laughter; it seemed that wherever he was there was merriment.

She was lonely, for, although she was the Queen, there was no one in the Palace who did not know of the estrangement between herself and the King, and many who had been eager to please her in the hope of receiving her favor, no longer considered her capable of bestowing benefits.

She knew something of what was said of her. The King's devotion of the last two months had been given out of the kindness of his heart: there had been no real love, no passion. How could there be? There were many ladies of the Court more beautiful than the Queen, and the King was deeply affected by beauty.

For two months he had given his affections exclusively to her, and she, being simple and ignorant, had not realized what a great sacrifice that was for the King to make.

She was humiliated and heartbroken. She did not know how foolish she was; she did not realize that, since there could be no happiness for her while the King was displeased with her, she could quite easily win back his grateful devotion. Charles hated to be on bad terms with anyone, particularly a woman; his tenderness for her sex was apparent in all he did; even to those women who attracted him not at all he was invariably courteous. He was sorry for Catherine; he understood her difficulties; he knew she was an idealist while he was very much a realist; and if at the time she had given way in this matter, if she had understood his peculiar problem, if she had been able to see him as the man he was—charming, affable, easy-going, generous, good-natured but very weak, particularly in his relationship with women—Catherine could have won his affectionate regard for all time; and although she could never have roused his passion she could have been his very dear friend. But her rigid upbringing, her lack of worldly knowledge, her pride and the influence of her prudish Portuguese attendants robbed her of not only her temporary peace of mind but of her future happiness.

So she sat aloof, sometimes sullenly, sometimes weeping bitterly; and the King ignored her, his courtiers following his example. Thus Hampton Court, the scene of those first weeks of triumphant happiness, became the home of despair.

❁❁❁

Henrietta Maria, the King's mother, arrived in England; she wished to meet her son's wife and let the whole world know how she welcomed the marriage.

Then it was necessary for Charles to behave towards Catherine as though all was well between them.

They rode out from Hampton Court side by side while a brilliant cavalcade accompanied them. The people lined the roads to cheer them, and Catherine felt new pride stir within her when she realized how the English loved their King.

That was a happy day, for Charles was chatting with her as though there had been nothing to disturb their relationship; and when they arrived at Greenwich, Henrietta Maria, determined to dispense with ceremony, took her daughter-in-law in her arms and assured her in her volatile way that this was one of the happiest moments in the life of one whose many sorrows had made her call herself *la reine malheureuse.*

She accepted a fauteuil and sat on the right hand of Catherine. Charles sat next to his wife, and on his left hand sat Anne Hyde the Duchess of York, while the Duke stood behind his mother.

It was Henrietta Maria who talked continually, studying the face of her daughter-in-law, trying not to let her eyes betray the fact that she was wondering if she were yet pregnant. Those lively dark eyes missed little, and she could see no signs of a child.

"This is indeed a pleasure, my dearest daughter. And how like you your country, eh? I thank the saints that you have come to it in summer weather. Ah, I remember my first visit to this country. That was in the days of my youth . . . the happiest time of my life! But even then I had my little worries. I was so small—smaller than you, my dear daughter—and it grieved me lest my husband should wish me taller. How we suffer we princesses sent to strange lands! But I found my husband to be the best man in the world . . . the kindest and most faithful husband . . . the best of fathers. . . ."

Charles interrupted: "I beg of you, Mam, say no more. My wife will expect too high a standard of me."

"And why should she not expect you to be like your father! I trust that you may bring her as much happiness as he brought me . . . though . . . through my love of him I suffered much. But is not that the way with love? To love is to suffer. . . ."

Catherine said fervently: "It is true, Your Majesty. To love is to suffer."

"Well, let us not talk of suffering on such a happy occasion," said the King. "Tell me, Mam, how is my sister?"

Henrietta Maria frowned. "She has her trials. Her husband is not kind to her."

"I am sorry for her," said Catherine.

" Ah . . . indeed, yes. When I think of the regard the King of France has for her . . . when I think of what might have been. . . ."

"It is useless to dwell on what might have been," said the King. "It grieves me that my sister is not happy."

"You must not be jealous of his love for his sister," said Henrietta Maria to Catherine. "I declare that my daughter's husband is jealous of hers for him. They have been devoted all their lives."

The Duke of York joined in the conversation and Henrietta Maria chattered on in her garrulous way; her manner was faintly cool to the Duchess of York whom Charles had forced her to accept, but James had always been a favorite of hers. She made little attempt to veil her likes and dislikes. She asked how fared that man Hyde—she refused to give him his title of Earl of Clarendon—and she asked if her son was still as strongly under his influence as he always had been.

The King turned aside her awkward remarks with his easy manner, and Catherine felt more deeply in love with him than ever before.

She could not be unhappy while they were together thus, for although it might only have been for the sake of etiquette, the King would turn to her again and again, and it was delightful to enjoy the warmth of his smiles and his tender words once more.

She felt desolate when it was time to return to Hampton Court, but she found that the King's manner towards her did not change as they rode away from London. He remained friendly and charming; though of course she knew that he would not be her lover.

Even then she did not see how much happier her life might have been had she given way on this one matter; and although she had been able to set aside her misery during the visit to Greenwich, still she determined to nurse it, and the matter of Lady Castlemaine's admittance to the household was still between them.

Henrietta Maria visited the King and Queen at Hampton Court, and during the month of August Catherine made her first public entry into the capital of her new country.

She rode down the river in the royal barge; and by her side was Charles, delighted to be on water, and returning to his capital. Full of charm and gaiety he was tender and affectionate. The Duke and the Duchess of York were with them in the brilliantly decorated barge, as well as those Princes, cousins of the King, Rupert and Edward, with the Countess of Suffolk; other members of the royal household followed. All along the riverbanks cheering people watched them; and when they were within a short distance of London they left the barge for a large boat with glass windows. The awnings were covered in gold-embroidered crimson velvet.

Now they were ready for the triumphal entry.

"And this," Charles told his wife, "is all in honor of you."

The river was crowded with craft of all description, for the Lord Mayor and companies had turned out in force to play their Queen, to the tune of sweet music, into her capital. On the deck of their boat, beneath the canopy which had been made in the form of a cupola with Corinthian pillars decorated with flowers, sat Catherine and Charles.

To Catherine it was inspiring and thrilling. The music enchanted her as did the shouts of the people acclaiming their loyalty to the royal pair; but what delighted Catherine more than anything else was the fact that Charles was beside her, her hand was in his, and his affable smiling face turned again and again from his cheering people to herself.

It was possible to believe that their differences were forgotten, that all was well between them, and that they were lovers again.

And so to Whitehall, of which the King had often talked to her, where the public crowded into the banqueting hall to watch the royal party dine.

Catherine realized now how much a part of this merry boisterous existence Charles himself was, how his ready smiles to the humblest, how his quick retorts, his dispensing with royal dignity, appealed to the people. They were delighted—those who crowded about Whitehall and came into the private apartment to see their royal family—with the easy manner of their King and his friendliness to all; they were enchanted with the extravagance of his Palace and glittering splendor of the gentlemen of his Court and the beauty of the ladies.

They loved their King not only because of his good nature—and when he had returned to England he had brought with him a colorful way of life—but also for his weaknesses, for providing them with many a titbit of scandal; they loved him for his love affairs, which could always be relied upon to raise a laugh in any quarter, and were such a contrast to the dull, drab and respectable existence of men such as Cromwell and Fairfax.

Now he joked with the Queen and his mother at the royal table, and the crowd looked on and enjoyed his wit.

Catherine was shocked when, before them all, he discussed the possibility of her bringing an heir to England.

"I believe he will soon put in an appearance," said Charles.

"This is wonderful news!" cried Henrietta Maria.

Catherine looked from one to the other, trying to follow the conversation which was taking place in English.

The King turned to her and explained what had been said.

Catherine blushed hotly, and the people laughed.

She stammered in English: "You lie."

At which the whole assembly burst into loud laughter on hearing the King so addressed; and none laughed more heartily than the King.

He said: "And what will my people think of the way in which I am treated by my wife? These are the first words in English she has uttered in public." His face wore a look of mock seriousness. "And she says I lie!"

He then turned to her and said that she must talk more in English, for that was what his people would like to hear; and he made her say after him such phrases as set the people rocking with hilarious laughter in which all the noble company joined.

❁ ❁ ❁

But Catherine's joy was short-lived, for it was not long before Barbara appeared at Whitehall. No more was said as to her becoming a lady of the bedchamber; she was just there, always present, brilliantly beautiful; so that whenever Catherine compared herself with Charles' notorious mistress she felt plain—even ugly—quite dull and completely lacking in charm.

She grew sullen; she sat alone; she would not join any group if Barbara were there, and, as the King always seemed to be where Barbara was, all the brilliant and amusing courtiers were there also.

Almost everyone deserted the Queen; the Earl of Sandwich, who had been so charming when he had come to Portugal, no longer seemed to have any time to spare for her; young Mr. James Crofts, a very handsome boy of about fifteen, scarcely noticed her at all, and moreover she felt that the fact that he was received at Court was an affront to herself, for she knew who he was—the son of a woman as infamous as Lady Castlemaine. And the boy's features, together with a somewhat arrogant manner would have proclaimed him to be Charles' son—even if the King did not make it openly obvious that this was so.

James Crofts was often with the King; they could be seen sauntering in the Park, arm in arm.

Catherine heard what was said of the King and this boy. "Greatly His Majesty regrets that he was not married to the mother of such a boy, for it is clear that handsome Mr. James Crofts is beloved by his father."

James gave himself airs. He was at every state occasion magnificently dressed, and already ogling the ladies. He was a fervent admirer of Lady Castlemaine and sought every opportunity of being in her company; and there was nothing this lady liked better than to be seen with the King and his son, when they laughed and chatted together.

There were some who said that young James' feeling for his father's mistress was becoming too pronounced, and that the lady was not displeased by this, but that when the King realized that this boy of his was fast becoming a man he would be less fond of Master James. The King however was human and, like all parents, took far longer than others to become aware that his son was growing up.

Although the King was outwardly affectionate to his wife, all knew of his neglect of her. It was said that he was pondering whether he might not proclaim Mr. Crofts legitimate, give him a grand title, and make him his heir. If he did this it would mean that he had decided no longer to hope for an heir from the Queen; and all understood what that implied.

So Catherine grew more and more wretched during those summer months. It seemed to her that she had only two friends at Court. Most of her attendants were returning to Portugal and all her most intimate friends were to leave her, with the exception of Maria the Countess de Penalva for, it was said, the King thought Maria too old and infirm to influence Catherine and support her in her stubbornness.

That other friend was a younger brother of the Earl of Sandwich—Lord Edward Montague—who held the post of Master of Horse in her household.

Edward Montague had by his demeanor shown his sympathy with her and had told her that he considered she was shamefully treated.

She found some pleasure therefore in listening to his words of sympathy, for it was comforting to think that in the royal household there was at least one who understood her.

When she said goodbye to her servants she continued to believe that Charles had deprived her of their company in order to spite her. She would not accept the fact that custom and the wishes of English members of the household demanded their departure.

She withdrew herself more than ever; she began to see that in refusing to accept Lady Castlemaine she had brought nothing but sorrow to herself. She had lost the King's affection, which had been given to a meek and gentle woman; and at the same time Lady Castlemaine had become a member of her household in spite of her dissent. Now James Crofts was made Duke of Monmouth, and was taking precedence over every other Duke in the kingdom with one exception—that of the King's brother James.

She herself was of no account; she had brought no good to her husband; her dowry was unpaid; her country was begging for England's military help; valuable English ships were kept in the Mediterranean to assist Portugal should Spain attack.

She was the most wretched of Queens for, in spite of all she had suffered, she continued to love her husband.

❁ ❁ ❁

She paced up and down her apartment.

Her country was in danger, she knew. If Charles withdrew his fleet Portugal would be once more the vassal of Spain. All the political advantages which this marriage had been intended to secure would be lost.

And it was due to her obstinacy. Was it obstinacy? She did not know. Was it her pride? Was it her vanity? She had dreamed of his chivalry; she had set him up in her mind and heart as the perfect man; and when she had met him in the flesh she had discovered him to be—so she had thought—more lovable than her ideal. That ideal had been noble, a little stern; she had never thought of his making merry. The reality had seemed noble but never stern; he was fond of laughter; lie was affectionate—the kindest man in the world.

And suddenly one night as she lay alone, the knowledge came to her. She loved him; she would always love him; she loved him not only for his virtues but for his faults. She no longer wanted that ideal; she wanted Charles the living man. Suddenly she realized that she was married to the most fascinating Prince in the world and that, although she was not sufficiently beautiful or charming, so kindly was his nature that she could still expect much affection from him.

He had asked one thing of her, and she had failed to give it because it had seemed impossible to give. He had asked her to accept him as he was—frail, a lover of women other than herself—and she had failed him in the one important thing he had asked of her.

She remembered now the kindness with which he had first received her; she remembered how, when he had come into her bedchamber, he had made her feel that she was beautiful and desirable, not because he found her so, but because he knew that that was what she wished to be. He would deceive in order to please; she had failed to appreciate that. She had set him stern rules, conventional rules; she had tried to make a saint of the most charming sinner in the world, little realizing that saints are often uncomfortable people and that their saintliness is often attained at the cost of that kindly good nature which was an essential part of Charles' character.

She saw clearly his side of their disagreement, as she had never thought to see it, and she cursed herself for a fool because she had failed him when he asked her help.

She loved him; any humiliation was not too much to suffer for the sake of his affection.

She determined to regain that affection. She would not tell him of her decision; she would startle him by her friendly manner towards Lady Castlemaine. Mayhap it was not too late.

❁ ❁ ❁

In the early hours of the morning as he left his mistress's apartment in the Cockpit and strolled back to his own in the main Palace, Charles was thinking of Catherine. He wondered how many people in the Court knew of these nightly wanderings of his to and from Barbara's apartment. Did Catherine know? Poor Catherine! He had been wrong to show coldness to her. He had asked too much of her. Could he have expected an innocent and ignorant girl, brought up as she had been, to understand his *blasé* point of view?

No! Catherine had acted in accordance with what she had considered to be right. She had clung to her duty. He, who would have sought an easy way out of the difficulty, must admire her for her strength of purpose. She had endured his neglect without much complaint, and he had behaved very badly.

She was the Queen, and he must put an end to this state of affairs. Barbara was often unbearable. He would tell her she must leave the Court. That should be his first concession to Catherine. Gradually he would let her see that he wished them to return to a happier relationship.

Poor homely little Catherine! She was a good woman, though a stubborn one, but well within her rights he doubted not.

"I will see what may be done about remedying this difference between us," he mused.

And so, salving his conscience, he returned to his apartment.

❁ ❁ ❁

Catherine's change of manner towards Lady Castlemaine caused great astonishment.

It was so sudden, for not only did she speak with her as hitherto she had not done, but she seemed actually to enjoy that lady's company more than that of any other. She referred to Barbara as "my friend Lady Castlemaine."

Poor Catherine! So eager was she for the King's regard that, having once made up her mind to turn about, she could not do so quickly enough.

Those few who had sought to curry favor with the Queen for what it might be worth, were now alarmed and tried to remember what derogatory remarks they had made about Barbara. Those who had ignored Catherine were equally astonished.

Clarendon thought her inconsequent and unreliable. "This," he said to Ormond, "is the total abandonment of her greatness. She has lost all dignity; for, although I continued to warn her against her stubborn conduct, yet I was forced to admire it. In future none will feel safe with her. The Castlemaine herself is more reliable."

The King, too, was astonished. He had not asked for such affability. He would have preferred her to have been cool with Barbara. It seemed folly to have expressed such abhorrence and now to have assumed a completely opposite attitude.

I was a fool, he told himself. I worried unduly. She is not the woman I thought her. She gives way to sudden passions. Her persistent refusal to receive Barbara did not grow out of her sense of rightness; it was pure perversity.

He shrugged his shoulders and decided to let matters take their course.

❁ ❁ ❁

It was the end of the year—Catherine's first in England—and the King gave a grand ball in his Palace of Whitehall to mark the passing of the old year and the coming of the new.

Into the great ballroom the public crowded to watch the dancing. There was the King, the most graceful dancer of all, more merry than any, clad in black with flashing diamonds adorning his person, surrounded by his fine courtiers and beautiful ladies. A little apart sat the Queen with Edward Montague and a few of her friends; and although she smiled often, chatted in her quaint English and seemed to be enjoying the ball, it was noticed how her eyes wistfully went back and back again to the tall figure of her husband.

She watched him leading the Duchess of York out for the brantle. And how ungainly was the poor Duchess beside such an elegant partner! The Duke led the Duchess of Buckingham, poor Mary Fairfax, for whom Catherine had a feeling of deep sympathy, for Mary was plain, ungainly and so eager to please the brilliant handsome man she had married; Catherine noticed how all eyes were on that other pair which joined the brantle with the King's group. Tall, dark James Crofts, the Duke of Monmouth, looking amazingly like his father, had chosen for his partner the most strikingly handsome woman in the ballroom. There were gasps from the people who had come in from the streets to watch the royal party at their pleasure; there was a titter of grudging admiration for the auburn-haired beauty with the flashing blue eyes.

Her jewels were more brilliant than those of any woman in the room, and she held herself imperiously as though conscious of her power; and now she was amused because she knew that the King was aware of the warm looks of this very young boy who was her partner in the dance.

A murmur went through the crowd. " 'Tis my Lady Castlemaine! Was there ever such a woman, such beauty, such jewels?"

The courtiers followed her with their eyes. None could refrain from looking at Barbara. Some of the jewels she was now wearing had been Christmas presents to the King, but already Barbara had grasped them with greedy hands. And as she danced in the brantle the King watched her, Monmouth watched her, and Lord Chesterfield watched her, but none watched her quite so closely nor so sadly as the Queen of England.

The brantle over, the King led the dancers in a coranto; and when that was ended and more stately dances followed, the King, with more energy than that possessed by most of his courtiers, signed to the fiddlers to play the dances of old England, with which country dances, he declared, none could compare.

"Let the first be 'Cuckolds all awry!' The old dance of old England."

The Court grew very merry in the light of tall wax candles, and the crowds cheered and stamped with pleasure to see the old English dance; and they laughed and shouted to one another that Charles was indeed a King, with his merry life and his bland good humor, and the smiles he lavished freely on his subjects; they wanted no saint on the throne, who knew not how to laugh and found a virtue in forbidding pleasure to others.

They looked at the sad-faced Queen who did not seem to share in the fun; and from her they turned their gaze on dazzling Barbara.

The King was a man whom the English would never cease to love. And at the great Court ball in Whitehall Palace on the last night of the year 1662, all those present rejoiced once more that their King was a merry monarch and that he had come home to rule his kingdom.

FOUR

In the great ballroom at Windsor Castle the most brilliant ball of the year was taking place. This was to celebrate not only St. George's Day but the marriage of the young man whom the King delighted to honor, his son, the Duke of Monmouth.

Catherine watched the dancers, and beside her sat the little bride, Lady Anne Scott, the heiress of Buccleugh and one of the richest in the kingdom; but the bridegroom seemed more interested in Lady Castlemaine than in his bride, and the young girl gazed at the pair with apprehension.

How sad it was, thought the Queen, that so many seemed to love those who were not their lawful partners! No wonder the King with sly humor liked to summon them all to dance "Cuckolds all awry." Was he the only man who knew that he could rely on the good faith of his wife? Yet he seemed not to love her the more for her fidelity, and to love Barbara none the less for the lack of it in her. It was said that Sir Charles Berkeley and George Hamilton were Barbara's lovers now and it seemed as though, before many weeks were out, young Monmouth might be; for the youth of the latter would be no deterrent to Barbara. She would look upon that as piquant. Catherine heard that she took lovers on the spur of the moment merely because some novelty in them appealed to her. She did not care whether they were noble or not; a lusty groom, she had been heard to say, was a better bedfellow than an impotent noble lord. The King also would hear these rumors, yet they seemed to affect him little; he still visited her on several nights each week and was often seen coming back early in the morning and all alone through the privy gardens. How could one hope to please such a husband as Catherine's by one's chastity?

Chastity! Who at Court cared about that? Their King clearly did not, and the courtiers were only too ready to follow his lead.

The Court was growing extremely elegant; Charles was introducing more and more French customs; he wrote continually to his sister, the wife of the French King's brother, asking her to send him any novelties which had appeared in the Court of her brother-in-law. Making love was the main pursuit, it seemed, of all; rarely did any drink to excess at the Court; there again the custom of the King was followed. There was less gambling now, although this was a sport much loved by Lady Castlemaine. The King would anxiously watch her at play; he had good reason, for she was a reckless gambler, and who would pay her debts but himself? He did not forbid her or any of the ladies whom he so admired, to gamble; he could not bring himself to spoil their pleasure, he admitted; but he tried to lure them from the gaming tables with brilliant balls and masquerades. How indulgent he was to the women he loved!

Why could they not be content with the partners whom they had married? Catherine wondered. She looked at little Anne beside her and felt a wave of tenderness for her. Poor child! She was young yet, but Catherine felt that if she ever grew to love her handsome young husband she was going to suffer deeply.

Lady Chesterfield was standing beside the Queen's chair and Catherine turned to her and smiled. A very charming lady—Elizabeth Butler now Lady Chesterfield—and married to that man who had seemed as much a slave of Barbara's as the King himself.

Catherine had been sorry for Elizabeth Chesterfield; she had felt she understood her sadness for she had heard how innocent she had been when she had married the profligate Earl, and how she had tried to win his love only to be repulsed.

Catherine said in her faltering English: "I rejoice to see you look so well, Lady Chesterfield."

Lady Chesterfield bowed her head and thanked Her Majesty.

Yes, she had changed, thought Catherine; she had lost her meek looks. Her dress of green and cloth of silver fell from beautifully rounded shoulders, and her thick hair was in ringlets falling about them; her eyes sparkled and she watched the dancers almost speculatively.

So she had come to terms with life, thought Catherine. She had decided not to grieve because her husband preferred the evil beauty of Lady Castlemaine.

The Earl of Chesterfield had come to his wife's side, and would have taken her hand to lead her into the dance, but Elizabeth had withdrawn it and seemed not to see him standing there.

Catherine heard the whispered words.

"Come, Elizabeth. I would lead you to the dance."

Elizabeth's voice was lightly mocking. "Nay, my lord, your place is by the side of another. I would not deprive you of your pleasure in her company."

"Elizabeth, this is folly.

"Nay, 'tis sound good sense. And I advise you to watch what is afoot, for your dear friend seems mightily taken with the young Duke. You endanger your chances with her by dallying with me. Ah, here comes my cousin George Hamilton to claim me in the dance. George, I am ready."

And the graceful creature had laid her hand in that of George Hamilton, her cousin, who, it was said, had lately been the lover of my Lady

Castlemaine. Chesterfield stood watching them with a frown between his eyes. It was like a mad dance, thought Catherine, in which, after a clasping of hands and a merry jig, they changed partners. Was Chesterfield more interested in the wife who flouted him than in the one who had been ready to love him? Or was it merely his pride which was wounded?

She noticed, however, that as the evening progressed his eyes were more frequently on his wife than on Lady Castlemaine.

Nor was he the only one who had seemed to change the course of his affections.

Catherine, whose eyes never strayed far from the King, saw that he was giving much of his attention to one of her maids of honor.

Frances Theresa Stuart was a distant relative of the King's; she was the daughter of Walter Stuart, the third son of Lord Blantyre, and Henrietta Maria had brought her to England when she came over, and had left the girl with Catherine to act as maid of honor.

Henrietta Maria had told Catherine that Louis Quatorze had been interested in her, and had suggested that she remain in his Court. "But," said Henrietta Maria, "I thought it well not to leave her there; for her family lost much during the Civil War and I have a duty to them. I would not wish to see her become one of Louis' mistresses. She has been brought up to live virtuously, so I pray you take her into your household and let her serve you."

Catherine had not wondered then whether removing Mrs. Stuart from the lecherous orbit of Louis to that of Charles was not after all somewhat pointless, because at that time she had regarded the King's attachment to Lady Castlemaine as largely the result of an evil spell which that woman had put upon him. Now she was beginning to understand her husband and to realize that if there had been no Lady Castlemaine there would have been others.

Previously Frances had been looked upon as little more than a child, but it seemed that in her dazzling gown and the few jewels she possessed, this night she had become a young woman; and Catherine realized that if Barbara's beauty had a rival it was in this lovely girl.

Frances's hair was thick, fair and hung in curls over her shoulders; her pink and white complexion was dazzling; her eyes were blue; and she was tall and very slender; Barbara had a rare beauty with which any woman would find it difficult to compete, but Frances, in addition to beauty, was possessed of an elegance which she had acquired during her education at the French Court; her manners were gentle and quite modest—a complete contrast to the vulgarity of Lady Castlemaine. Barbara was, of course, full of wiles, full of cunning and, compared with her, Frances Stuart seemed simple as a child. It was perhaps these qualities, as much as her youth, which had made Catherine regard her as a little girl.

But on this night she seemed to have grown up, and the King was noticing the change in her.

Others were noticing it too. Barbara's enemies, ever on the watch for her decline, were triumphantly asking each other and themselves: Could this be the end of her long domination of the King? Never had they seen Charles so completely absorbed in another woman, while Barbara was present, as he was in Frances.

Catherine was sad at heart. She had believed that one day the King would come to notice what a vulgar woman Barbara was and, full of shame and repentance, he would turn to his wife and they would resume that idyllic relationship they had enjoyed at Hampton Court.

Now she must wonder whether he ever would turn to her again, whether she had lost him forever when she had failed to do that one thing which he had asked of her.

She continued to watch Lady Chesterfield who, flushed and triumphant, had many admirers now, including her husband perhaps. There was the Duke of York, watching her with dark, slumberous eyes. James was so clumsy in his devotions to women that he always aroused the amusement of the Court, and particularly of Charles. Catherine doubted not that ere long there would be whispers concerning the attraction Lady Chesterfield was exerting over the susceptible Duke.

It was a strange world, this Court of her husband. She was once more reminded that it was a Court in which beauty and the power to charm were of greater importance than virtue. Lady Chesterfield provided an example. Could Catherine herself follow it?

There was young Edward Montague who was often at her side. But were his feelings for her inspired by pity for her plight rather than admiration for her person?

Now she must dance, and here was the Duke of Monmouth, in whose honor the ball was held, ceremoniously asking for the hand of the first lady of the Court.

Catherine rose and put her hand in his. He was a very graceful dancer, and Catherine, who loved to dance, found herself enjoying this one.

How like Charles he was! A younger, more handsome Charles, but lacking that kingliness, that great elegance, that wit, that charm. In comparison Monmouth was merely a pretty boy.

And as he danced with her—holding his plumed hat in his hand, since he danced with the Queen—Charles came to them and, there before the whole assembly, in an access of tenderness for this boy whom it was his delight to honor, stopped the dance, took the boy in his arms, kissed him on both cheeks and bade him put on his hat and continue the dance.

Everyone was astonished at this action of the King's. It could mean only one thing, it was whispered. The King so doted on his handsome son that he had determined to make him legitimate. Then the Duke of Monmouth would be heir to the throne.

Rumor began to grow. Had the King truly married Lucy Water? Had the creature prevailed upon him to go through a ceremony of marriage? Charles had been an exile then, and all knew how easy-going he was with his women.

Catherine sadly continued to dance; she feared that the King's regard for her was so slight that he was telling her—and the Court—that whatever children she might bear him, they could not mean more to him than did young Monmouth.

❁ ❁ ❁

In the little octagonal building which was part of Whitehall Palace and was called the Cockpit, Barbara had her apartments and here she held court. Hither flocked those ambitious men who believed that through Barbara lay the way to glory.

The chief of these was George Villiers, the Duke of Buckingham and Barbara's second cousin once removed; he was recognized, not only as one of the most handsome men of the day, but one of its most brilliant statesmen.

He saw in close association with Barbara a means of getting that power for which he had always longed, and there was one man whom he felt stood between him and his goal; that man was Clarendon, and in their hatred of the Chancellor, he and Barbara were united.

There in her rooms at the Cockpit they would meet frequently, and about them would gather all those who hoped to follow them to power. In the light of candles they would make merry, for, in addition to being a wily statesman, Buckingham was a man of many social graces: he was one of the most entertaining men at Court, and his imitations of well-known figures could set guests laughing so much that they became almost hysterical, so clever was he at caricaturing those little vanities and dignities of his enemies to make them appear utterly ridiculous. He used this gift in order to bring ridicule to those he disliked, and his caricature of Clarendon was in constant demand.

Another great enemy of Clarendon's who came to Barbara's parties was the Earl of Bristol. He was bold and vivacious but somewhat unreliable. He had written a book about the Reformation and, during the course of writing this, had become a Catholic; he was looked upon as the leader of the Catholic party in England and because of this was watched eagerly by those who hoped to see the Catholics more firmly established in the land. There was not a man at Court who hated the Chancellor more than did the Earl of Bristol.

Henry Bennet, who had been with the King in exile, was another; he was a clever, ambitious but rather pompous man who bore a scar on his nose of which he was so proud that he called attention to it by wearing a patch over it which was far greater than the scar warranted; this was meant to be a constant reminder to the King that he had been wounded in the Royalist Cause. Henry Bennet had shared Lucy Water with Charles when they were in Holland, and it was a matter of opinion whether Lucy's daughter Mary was Bennet's child or the King's. Barbara had included Bennet in her own little circle of men she could use, and it was largely through her that he had replaced Nicholas as Secretary of State.

It was these three men—Buckingham, Bristol and Bennet—with whom Barbara sought to intrigue after that New Year's ball during which the King had clearly shown his interest in Frances Stuart.

They all wished to bring about the downfall of Clarendon, and at the same time it was Barbara's desire to damage Frances Stuart in the eyes of the King.

Barbara was seriously alarmed about Frances Stuart. The girl had in the first place seemed to be a simpleton. She was young and artless and seemed unaware of the fact that there was not a woman at Court whose beauty could compare with hers; and in a Court where the King was instantly moved by beauty in any form—and in particular the beauty of women—that meant a passport to power.

Barbara watched Frances closely. Each day she seemed to grow in beauty. The girl was perfect; her figure was enchanting, her face, with that expression of supreme innocence, delightful. Had she not been the most beautiful girl at Court, her very grace of movement would have made her stand out among them all, and allied with this was a charming air of innocence. She laughed easily; she prattled of nothing in a lighthearted way; she seemed almost simpleminded in her childishness. But Barbara had her own ideas. She did not believe in Mrs. Stuart's innocence. She remembered the case of Anne Boleyn, who had remained haughty, pure and aloof, and had murmured to an enamored King: "Your wife I cannot be; your mistress I will not be."

Barbara was furious with the girl, but the situation was too delicate to allow her to give full vent to that fury. Barbara was in her twenties; Frances in her teens; Barbara lived riotously, never denying her senses what they craved; Frances slept the sleep of the innocent each night and arose in the mornings fresh as a spring flower.

Barbara had realized that where this sly little prude was concerned she would have to play a wary game.

So she took Frances under her wing. She believed that, if she had not, the King might have been found supping where Frances was and Barbara was not. She made Frances her little friend; she even had her sleep in her bed.

She knew, of course, that the King had made the usual advances to the girl—the languishing looks, the pressing of hands, the stolen kisses, the gifts. All these she had received with wide-eyed pleasure as though the insinuation which accompanied them was quite beyond her understanding.

So Barbara played those games which Frances loved, childish games which made the simple little creature shriek with pleasure. They played "marriage"—with Barbara the husband and Frances the wife, and they were put to bed with a sack posset and the stocking was flung. Unfortunately the King had come in while that game was in progress and had declared that it was a shame poor Frances had been married to one of her own sex. He was sure she would have preferred a man for her husband; he therefore would relieve Barbara of conjugal responsibilities and take them on himself. What shrieks of laughter from sly Mrs. Stuart! What nudging and whispering of those participating in the game! Had the bride been anyone else, Barbara knew full well that the frolic of that night would not have ended as it did. But sly, virtuous Mrs. Stuart knew when to draw back; and Barbara, with murder in her heart, believed the sly creature was contemplating very high stakes indeed.

So the dearest wish of Barbara's heart was to see Mrs. Stuart exposed in the eyes of the King as a wanton. She knew that he was growing more and more tender towards the girl, that he believed in all that innocence, and that it was having a devastating effect which might prove disastrous to Barbara. Dearly as she wished to see the fall of Clarendon she wished even more to see the fall of Mrs. Stuart.

It was in the Cockpit that she conferred with her friends.

"It should not be difficult now," she said, "for you gentlemen to assure the King of how this man works against him."

"The King is too easy-going," growled Bennet.

"Yet," said Buckingham, "his opposition to the Declaration of Liberty for Tender Consciences has, I am certain, incensed the King."

"I have assured him," said Barbara, "that Clarendon opposed the Declaration, not because he believed it to be wrong, but because of his hatred towards those who promoted it."

"And what said he to that?"

Barbara shrugged her shoulders. "He said that Clarendon was a man of deep conscience. He had reason to know it, for he knew the man well."

"Still he was displeased with Clarendon."

"Indeed he was," said Bristol, "and it was solely because of his need for money that he agreed to those laws which deal harshly with all who differ from the Act of Uniformity."

"And now," said Buckingham, "he has been forced to proclaim that Papists and Jesuits will be banished from the kingdom, although I have good reason to believe that he will do everything in his power to oppose the banishing. You know his great wish for tolerance, and it is solely because he needs money so badly that he is forced to fall in with the Parliament's wishes."

"But he loves them all a little less for forcing him to agree," said Barbara. "And he knows that it is Clarendon who has led those against him."

"So," cried Bristol, "now is the time to impeach the fellow. If the King fails to support him as he failed to support the King, all those who feign friendship towards him will drop away like leaves in an autumn gale."

"Yes," said Barbara, "now is the time."

"There is another matter," said Bristol. "I am a Catholic and I know how friendly the King has been to Catholics. There are rumors—and always have been—that one who can be so lenient towards Papists must surely be of their Faith."

"It is nonsense," said Barbara. "He is often more lenient when he does not agree. It is due to some notion he has of suspecting all points of view."

"Clarendon deplores his tolerance," said Buckingham. "I have it! Someone has been spreading reports of the King's devotion to the Catholic cause. It might well be Clarendon."

"It shall be Clarendon!" said Barbara.

"Moreover," said Bristol, "I have heard that a correspondence has taken place between the Queen and the Pope. His Majesty is weary of the Queen; that much is certain. There is no sign of a child. Doubtless the woman is unfruitful; princesses often are. And the King has proved his ability—nay his great good fortune—in getting children elsewhere. It may be that he would wish to rid himself of the Queen."

Barbara's eyes were narrowed. Could it be that these friends of hers were concocting some plot of which she was not acquainted? Had Bristol betrayed it; and could it by any chance concern Frances Stuart?

"Nay," she said quickly, "I warn you. If you should try to turn the King against the Queen you would be greatly mistaken."

Better, thought Barbara, a plain little Portuguese Catherine as Queen than beautiful Frances Stuart.

"Barbara is right in that," said Buckingham. "Let us not take the plot too far as yet. Let us settle this one matter first, and we will deal with others afterwards. Let us rid ourselves of the Chancellor; let us set up a new Chancellor in his place. . . ." Buckingham looked at Bristol, and Bristol looked at the ceiling. Why not Buckingham? thought Buckingham. Why not Bristol? thought Bristol. Bennet was smugly content as Secretary of State.

They parted soon afterwards. Barbara was hoping the King would call upon her.

❁ ❁ ❁

A few days later she had an opportunity of speaking to Buckingham alone.

She immediately began to discuss Frances.

"Do you believe she is as virtuous as she feigns to be?"

"There is no proof that she is otherwise."

"Mayhap no one has tried hard enough."

"The King is a skillful player. Would you not say he is trying very hard indeed?"

"George, you may not be the King, but you are the handsomest man at Court."

Buckingham laughed.

"Dear cousin," he said, "I know full well how mightily it would please you should I take the Stuart for my mistress. It is galling for one of your high temper to see His Majesty growing more deeply enamored every day. It would be pleasant for me to bask in your approbation, Barbara, but think what goes with it: the fury of the King."

"Nay, he'd not be furious. It is her seeming virtue that plagues him. He only half believes in it. Prove it to be a myth and he'll love you better than he loves the silly Stuart."

"And you too, Barbara?"

But Buckingham went away thinking of this matter. He *was* a handsome man; he was irresistible to many. Might it not be that for all his royalty, Charles as a man had failed to appeal to Frances? Might it not be that she realized that Charles in pursuit might be more amusing—and profitable—than Charles satisfied?

He decided to cultivate the fair Stuart.

❁ ❁ ❁

Barbara whispered to Sir Henry Bennet: "She is beautiful, is she not—Frances Stuart?"

"She is indeed. Apart from yourself, I would say there is not a more handsome woman at the Court."

"I know that you admire her."

" 'Tis a pity she is determined not to take a lover."

"So far!" said Barbara.

"What mean you by that?"

"Mayhap the man she would wish for has not yet claimed her!"

"The King, it is said, has had ill fortune in his pursuit of her."

"The King may not always be victorious. I have heard it said that Lucy Water, who knew you both well, had a more tender heart for Henry than for Charles."

Bennet was a vain man. He postured and laughed aloud at the memory of Lucy Water.

And when he left Barbara, he was thoughtful.

❁ ❁ ❁

The plot to discredit Clarendon failed completely, largely through Charles' interference. Charles fully realized that the charge had been brought against him, not because those who brought it believed that Clarendon was working against him and the country, but because the plotters were working against Clarendon.

The Chancellor's judges decided that a charge of high treason could not be brought by one peer against another in the House of Lords; and that even if those charges against Clarendon were true, there was no treason in them. The House of Lords therefore dismissed the charges.

Bristol, who had been the prime mover against Clarendon in this case, seeking to justify himself with the King and believing that Charles wished to rid himself of Catherine, added a further charge against Clarendon, declaring that he had brought the King and Queen together without any settled agreement about marriage rites, and that either the succession would be uncertain, in case of Catherine's being with child, for want of the due rites of matrimony, or His Majesty would be exposed to suspicion of being married in his own country by a Romanish priest.

When the King heard of this he was indignant.

"How dare you suggest that there would be an inquiry into the secret nuptials between myself and the Queen?" he demanded.

"Your Majesty, I thought that in raising this point I should be acting as you wished."

"You carry your zeal too far."

"Then I crave Your Majesty's pardon."

"It would be easier to grant it if I did not have to see you for a little time. I would have you know—and all those who are with you—that I will not have slights cast on the Queen."

"There was no desire to slight the Queen, Your Majesty."

"Then let us hear no more of the matter. It is astonishing to me that you, a Catholic yourself, should have added this article to the impeachment of Clarendon. What caused your conversion to Catholicism?"

"May it pleasure Your Majesty, it happened whilst I was writing a book for the Reformation."

The King turning away, said with a half smile: "Pray, my lord, write a book for Popery."

It was necessary after that for the Earl of Bristol to absent himself from Court for a while.

The people in the streets and about the Court had said that Bristol and his friend had cast the Chancellor on his back past ever getting up, but Clarendon retained his post, although the rift between the King and his Chancellor had widened.

❁ ❁ ❁

The Queen had become very happy. She was certain now that she was to have a child.

This made the King very tender towards her; he longed for a legitimate heir. He had not proclaimed Monmouth legitimate and he had denied the rumors that he had married Lucy Water. He was seen often in company with the Queen; but he was deeply in love with Frances Stuart.

He still continued to visit Barbara, who retained her hold over him, and she kept her title as his first mistress.

She made no attempt to control her temper, and she was pregnant again.

"It would seem," she said, "that I have no sooner borne a child than the next is conceived. Charles, I hope our next will be a boy."

"*Our* next?" said Charles.

"Indeed it is our next!" shouted Barbara.

The King looked about him. Barbara was not the only one who had her apartments in the Cockpit, for the building was large and had been built by Henry the Eighth to lodge those whom he wished to keep near him. Clarendon had a suite of rooms there; so had Buckingham.

Charles knew that these people were quite aware of the stormy nature of his relationship with Barbara, but he did like to keep their quarrels private.

"I doubt it," said Charles. "I very much doubt this one to be mine."

"Whose else could it be?"

"There you set a problem which you might answer more readily than I, though I confess you yourself might be hard put to it to solve it."

Barbara looked about for something that she might throw at him; there was nothing to hand but a cushion; she would not throw that; it would seem almost coy.

"Oh, Barbara," said the King, "let another man father this one."

"So you would shift your responsibilities!"

"I tell you I do not accept this responsibility."

"You had better change your mind before the child is born . . . unless you would like me to strangle it at birth and set it up in the streets with a crown upon its head proclaiming it the King's son."

"You're fantastic," said the King, beginning to laugh.

She laughed with him and leaping towards him threw her arms about his neck. In the old days such a gesture would have been a prelude to passion, but today the King was pensive and did not respond.

❁ ❁ ❁

In Frances Stuart's apartment the light of wax candles shone on all the most favored of the gallant gentlemen and beautiful ladies of the Court.

The King sat beside Frances who looked more beautiful than even she had ever looked; she was dressed in black and white, which suited her fair skin, and there were diamonds in her hair and about her throat.

From her seat at another table Barbara watched the King and Frances.

Frances seemed unaware of everything except the house of cards she was building. She was like a baby! thought Barbara. Her greatest delight was in building card houses; and everyone who sought to please her must compete with her in the ridiculous game. There was only one who could build as she did; that was Buckingham.

They built their card houses side by side. The King was handing Frances her cards; Lady Chesterfield was handing Buckingham his; all the other builders of card houses had given up the game to watch these two rivals. Frances was breathless with excitement; Buckingham was coolly cynical; but his hand was so steady that it seemed that his calmness would score over Frances's excitement.

Imbecile! thought Barbara. Is she really so infantile that a card house can give her that much joy? Or is she acting the very young girl in the hope that the King is weary of such as I? We shall see who wins in the end, Mrs. Frances.

Lady Chesterfield caught Barbara's attention momentarily; she had changed much since those days when she had first married Chesterfield and had been another simpleton such as Frances would have them believe she was. Simplicity had not brought Lady Chesterfield all she desired. Now George Hamilton sought to be her lover—and he had been Barbara's lover too—and the Duke of York was paying her that attention with which he was wont to honor ladies; it consisted of standing near them and gazing longingly, at them in a manner which made all secretly laugh, or writing notes to them which he pushed into their pockets or muffs; and as the ladies concerned were not always willing to accede to his advances, there had been much amusement when the notes had been allowed to fall, as though unnoticed, from muff or pocket and left lying about for any to read.

Barbara thought of Chesterfield, her first lover, her first experience in those adventures which were more important to her comfort than anything else. Chesterfield had been a good lover.

She realized with some dismay that it was a long time since he had been to see her. She verily believed that he was more interested in another woman than he was in herself; and it was rather comic that that woman should be his wife.

Ah, but he had turned too late to Lady Chesterfield, who would not forget the humiliation she had suffered at his hands. It delighted her now to be cold to him, to accept the admiration of George Hamilton and to return the yearning gazes of the Duke of York, to set new fashions in the Court such as this one of green stockings which had begun with her appearing in them.

The King's attention was all for the fair Stuart; Chesterfield's for his wife; and Buckingham—for naturally Barbara and Buckingham had slipped into amorous relationship now and then—was also paying attention to the Stuart, although, Barbara reminded herself, it was at her suggestion he did this.

Three of her lovers looking at other women! It was disconcerting.

George Hamilton too, she remembered, was paying attention to Lady Chesterfield and hoping to persuade her to break her marriage vows.

Could it be that Barbara, Countess of Castlemaine, was finding herself deserted?

Not deserted, never deserted. There would always be lovers, even if she chose one of her grooms—although she would not do that unless he was a very appealing fellow. Yet it was disconcerting to find so many of those who had once sought her favors eagerly looking elsewhere. It was certainly time Frances Stuart was exposed to the King as a hypocrite and humbug. He would find it harder to forgive her infidelity than he ever had Barbara's, for Barbara's he took for granted. He knew Barbara; she was like himself. They could not curb their desires; he understood that of her as she did of him. They were not the sort to wrangle if the other took an odd lover or two.

The building of card houses was over; Buckingham had allowed Frances to win, and now was singing one of his songs set to his own music. He was a good performer and he sang in French and Italian as well as English. His poor, plain Duchess looked on with wistful tenderness as he performed. They were rarely together, but Frances liked husbands and wives to come to her gatherings; she was so very respectable, thought Barbara cynically.

Now there was dancing; and it was left to Monmouth to partner Barbara.

A spritely young fellow, thought Barbara, but she had not allowed him to become her lover; she was not sure how the King would feel about that. Monmouth, as his son, would be in a different category from other men; and she was not going to offend Charles more than she could help at this point.

When they were tired of dancing, Frances called on Buckingham to do some of his imitations, and that night the Duke excelled himself. He did his favorite—Clarendon, carrying a shovel in place of the mace, so full of self-importance, slow and ponderous; and this made the company roll and bend double with merriment; then he did the King, the King sauntering, the King being very gallant to a lady—who, of course, it was implied, was Frances herself. Charles led the laughter at this. And finally the versatile Duke approached Frances and began to make what he called a dishonorable proposal. It was Bennet to the life. The phrases were Bennet's, slow, flowery and wordy, spiced with those quotations with which Bennet liked to adorn his parliamentary addresses.

Frances shrieked with laughter and clutched the King in a very paroxysm of merriment—all of which delighted the King mightily; and made of that evening a very merry one.

The French ambassador who was present was, after the merriment subsided a little, so delighted with the company that he whispered to the King that he had heard Mrs. Stuart was possessed of the most exquisite legs in the world, and he wondered whether he dared ask the lady to show him these—up to the knee; he would dare ask for no more.

The King whispered the request to Frances, who opened her blue eyes very wide and said but of course she would be delighted to show the ambassador her legs. Whereupon, still in the manner of a very young girl, she stood on a stool and lifted her skirt as high as her knees that all might gaze on the legs which had been proclaimed the most beautiful in the world.

The King was quite clearly enchanted with Frances's manners, with her ingenuity and with the grace she displayed.

The French ambassador knelt and said that he knew of no way in which to pay homage to the most beautiful legs in the world except to kneel to them.

Then was the whole assembly made aware of how deep was the passion of the Duke of York for Lady Chesterfield, for he said in his somewhat ungracious way that he did not consider Mrs. Stuart's legs the most beautiful in the world.

"They are," he declared, "too slender. I would admire legs that are plump, and not so long as Mrs. Stuart's. Most important of all, the legs I most admire should be clothed in a green stocking."

The King burst into merry laughter, for, like everyone else, he knew that the Duke was referring to Lady Chesterfield who had introduced the green stocking to Court; Charles clapped his brother on the back and pushed him in the direction of the lady.

Barbara continued to watch this horseplay. She saw Lord Chesterfield's angry glance at the royal brothers.

To think, thought Barbara, in rising fury, that I should ever live to see Chesterfield in love with his own wife!

She looked about her for the man whom she would invite to her bed that night. It would not be the King, nor Buckingham, nor Chesterfield, nor Hamilton.

She wished to have a new lover, someone young and lusty, who would take the memory of this evening with its warning shadows from her mind.

❁ ❁ ❁

The Chesterfield scandal burst suddenly on the Court. It was astonishing to all, for Chesterfield was known as a rake and a libertine, and none would have suspected him of having any deep feelings for a woman, least of all for his own wife.

Music was the delight of the Court, and Tom Killigrew, one of the leading lights in the theatrical world, had brought with him from Italy a company of singers and musicians who had a great success at Court. One of these, Francisco Corbetta, was a magnificent performer on the guitar, and it was due to this that many ladies and gentlemen determined to learn the instrument. Lady Chesterfield had acquired one of the finest guitars in the country, and her brother, Lord Arran, learned to play the instrument better than any man at Court.

Francisco had composed a Sarabande, and this piece of music so delighted the King that he would hear it again and again. All at Court followed the King's example, and through courtyards and apartments would be heard the Sarabande, in deep bass and high sopranos, played on all kinds of musical instruments, but the favorite way of delivering the Sarabande was to strum on the guitar and to sing at the same time.

When the Duke of York expressed his desire to hear Arran play the

Sarabande on his sister's guitar, Arran immediately invited the Duke to his sister's apartments.

Chesterfield, hearing what was about to happen, stormed into his wife's chamber and accused her of indulging in a love affair with the Duke of York.

Elizabeth, laughing inwardly, and remembering that occasion when she had first discovered that the husband she loved was in love with the King's mistress, merely turned away and would neither deny nor admit that the Duke was her lover.

"Do you think," cried Chesterfield, "that I shall allow you to deceive me . . . blatantly like this?"

"My thoughts are never concerned with you at all," Elizabeth told him.

She sat down and took up the guitar, crossing those plump legs encased in green stockings for which the Duke had displayed public admiration.

Chesterfield cried: "Is he your lover? Is he? Is he?"

Elizabeth's answer was to play the first notes of the Sarabande.

She looked at him coolly, and she remembered how she had loved him in the first weeks of their marriage, how she had sought to please him in every way, how she had dreamed of a marriage as happy as that enjoyed by her parents.

And then, when she had known that Barbara Castlemaine was his mistress—that woman of all women, that blatant, vulgar woman of whom there were so many stories current, that woman who had lost count of her lovers—when she had allowed herself to imagine them together, when she had seen how foolish she had been to hope for that happy marriage, quite suddenly she had ceased to grieve, she had come to believe that she would never care about anything anymore. It had seemed to her that in loving there could only be folly. The Court was corrupt; chastity and fidelity were laughed at even by the kindly King. Her feeling for her husband died suddenly. She had stood humiliated as a simple fool; and she would be so no longer.

Then she had discovered that there was much to enjoy in the Court; she had found that she was deemed beautiful. Gradually this understanding had come to her, and it was amusing to dance, to flirt, to astonish all by some extraordinary costume which, on her beautiful form, was charming. Like any other beautiful woman at Court she could have her lover. The King's brother now sought her; mayhap soon the King himself would.

As for her husband, she could never look at him without remembering the acute humiliation he had inflicted on a tender young spirit which had been too childlike to bear such brutality.

One of her greatest joys henceforth would be to try to inflict on him a little of the torture he had carelessly made her suffer. She had never thought to accomplish it; but now the perverse man was, in his stupidity, ready to love a wife who would be cold to him forever more, although he had turned slightingly away from her youthful love.

That was life. Cynical, cruel. The Sarabande seemed to explain it far better than she could.

"I ask a question!" cried Chesterfield. "I demand an answer."

"If I do not wish to answer you, I shall not," she said.

"So he comes to hear the Sarabande! What an excuse! He comes to see you."

"Doubtless both," she said lightly.

"And that brother of yours has arranged this! He is in this plot against me! Do you think I'll stand aside and allow you to deceive me thus?"

"I told you I do not think of you at all. And I do not care whether you stand aside or remain here. Your actions are of the utmost indifference to me."

She was very beautiful, he thought, insolent and cold, sitting there with her pretty feet and a green stocking just visible below her gown. He often wondered how he could have been such a fool as not to have recognized her incomparable qualities; he had been mad to prefer the tantrums of Barbara to the innocence of the young girl whom he had married. He remembered with anguish her jealousy of his first wife. If he could only arouse that jealousy again he would be happy. Yet he knew that he would never arouse anything within her but cold contempt.

There was no time to say more, for at that moment the arrival of the Duke of York with Arran was announced. The Duke was flatteringly attentive to Lady Chesterfield and it was clear that he was far more interested in her than in her guitar.

Chesterfield refused to leave the little party to themselves, and stood glowering while Arran instructed the Duke in the playing of the famous Sarabande.

But, before the lesson had progressed very far, a messenger arrived to say that Chesterfield's services as Lord Chamberlain to the Queen were required in the royal apartments, as the Muscovite ambassadors were ready to be conducted to her.

Furious at being called away at such a time, Chesterfield had no choice but to comply with instructions and leave Arran as chaperone for Lady Chesterfield and the Duke. When he arrived in the Queen's presence chamber, to his complete horror, he found that Arran was there. The Duke and Lady Chesterfield must be alone together, in her apartments!

A mad fury possessed Chesterfield. He could scarcely wait for the audience to end. He was convinced that a trick had been played on him and that he had been cunningly removed that the Duke might be alone with his wife.

So great was his jealous rage that he went straight to his apartments. Neither the Duke nor Lady Chesterfield were there; and the first thing his eyes alighted on was the guitar; he threw it to the floor and jumped on it again and again till it was broken into many pieces. Then he set about searching for his wife, and the first person he found was George Hamilton, his wife's cousin and admirer; and to him Chesterfield poured out the story of his miserable jealousy.

Hamilton, believing with Chesterfield that the Duke must certainly have succeeded with Lady Chesterfield where he had failed, nursed his own secret jealousy. He could not bear the thought of anyone's enjoying those favors for which he had long sought; he would prefer to lose sight of the lady rather than allow her to enjoy another lover.

"You are her husband," he said. "Why not take her to the country? Keep her where you will know that she is safe and entirely yours."

This seemed good sense to Chesterfield. He made immediate arrangements and, by the time he saw his wife again, he was ready to leave with her for the country; and she had no alternative but to fall in with his wishes.

So they disappeared from the Court and, in accordance with the lighthearted custom of the time, witty verses were written about the incident, and what more natural than that they should be set to the tune of the Sarabande and sung throughout the Court?

The Duke of York began pushing notes into another lady's muff. But Barbara could not forget that yet another lover had deserted her.

❀ ❀ ❀

Catherine was happier during those months than she had been since the days of her honeymoon. At last she was to bear a child; she saw in this child a new and wonderful happiness, a being who would compensate her for all she had suffered through her love for the King. She pictured him; for, of course, he would be a boy; he would have the manners of his father; yes, and the looks of his father; the kindliness, the affability and the good nature; but he would be more serious—in that alone should he resemble his mother.

She saw him clearly—the enchanting little boy—the heir to the throne of England. She built him as firmly in her imagination as, in the days when she was awaiting her marriage, she had pictured Charles. She found great happiness in daydreams.

And indeed the King was charming to her. He seemed to have

forgotten all their differences. He declared she must take the utmost care of herself; he was solicitous that she should not catch a chill; he insisted on her resting from arduous state duties. It was pleasant to believe that he cared, for her sake as well as for that of the child.

They rode hand in hand in the Park, and the people stood in groups to watch and cheer them. She was quite pretty in her happiness, and she heard the people confirm this to one another—for they were not a people to mince their words—as she rode forth in her white-laced waistcoat and her crimson short petticoat which was so becoming, with her hair flowing about her shoulders. Behind her and the King, rode the ladies, and of course Lady Castlemaine was there, haughty and handsome as ever, but just a little out of humor because she had not been invited to ride by the side of the King; and surely a little subdued, for previously she would have pushed her horse forward and made sure that she was seen riding near the King and Queen.

Her face under her great hat with its yellow plume was sullen; and, when she was ready to alight, she was very angry because no gentleman hurried forward to her aid but left her own servants to look after her.

Barbara's day is done, thought Catherine. Had this something to do with her own condition? Or was it because of the meek little beauty who rode with them and was even more lovely than haughty Castlemaine, determined that the people should not see *her* riding side by side with the King when his wife was present, and looking so charming, in her little cocked hat with the red feather, that everyone gasped at such beauty.

Good news came from Portugal of the defeat of the Spaniards at Amexial. The battle had been fierce, for the Spaniards were led by Don John of Austria, but the English and the Portuguese Allies had won this decisive battle on which hung the fate of Portugal. The English had fought with such bravery and resource that the Portuguese had cried out that their allies were better to them than all the saints for whose aid they had prayed.

Catherine, hearing the news, wept with joy. She owed the security of her country to the English; it was true that she had been born to be of great significance to Portugal. She looked upon Charles as the savior of her country; and when she thought of that, and all he had been to her since their marriage, she wondered afresh how she could have been so blind in the first days as to have refused him the one thing he asked of her. He had given her the greatest happiness she had ever known; he had saved her country from an ignoble fate, and when he had asked her to help him out of a delicate situation, she had not considered his feelings; she had thought only of her own pride, her own wounded love. She could weep for her folly now; but it was too late for tears; all she could do was wait for opportunities to prove her love, to pray that one day she might be able to win back his affection which her stupidity had made her throw away.

Her simpleminded brother had given the English soldiers a pinch of snuff apiece as a token of his gratitude, and she blushed for her brother. Pinches of snuff for a kingdom! The English soldiers had been outraged and had thrown the snuff on the ground; but Charles had saved the situation by ordering that 40,000 crowns should be distributed among them as a reward for their services to his Queen.

She knew how hard pressed he was for money, how often he paid the country's expenses out of his own personal income; she knew the constant demands made on him by women like Barbara Castlemaine, and how his generosity made it impossible for him to refuse what they asked.

She prayed earnestly that her child might be big and strong, a boy of whom he would be proud.

She looked into the future and saw a period of happiness ahead, for she was mellowed; she was no longer a hysterical girl who could not adjust herself to the exigencies of a cynical world.

❁ ❁ ❁

Barbara was thinking seriously.

It might, she supposed, be necessary to have a husband again. If she was to lose the King's favor, she would need the protection of Roger.

As the Queen grew larger, so did she; and was the King going to admit paternity of her child? It was true he came to her nurseries now and then, but that was to see the children who would clamber over him and search his pockets for gifts.

"I see," he had said on one occasion, "that you have your mother's fingers."

He would always look after the children—she need have no fear of that—but he was certainly growing cooler to their mother.

She could, of course, threaten him; she could print his letters. But what of that? All knew of their relationship; there was little fresh to expose.

Moreover, there was a possibility that he might banish her from Court. She knew him well. Like most easygoing people, there came to him now and then a desire to be firm, and then nothing could shake him. Barbara knew that although his great good humor could be relied upon, when he decided to stand firm none could be firmer.

She began to plan ahead and called a priest to her that she might make good study, she said, of the Catholic Faith, for there was something within her which told her that she ought to do this in preparation for a reconciliation with Roger.

The whole Court laughed at the thought of Barbara closeted with her priest; she declared he was teaching her the tenets of the Catholic Faith, but they ribaldly asked each other what *she* was teaching *him.*

Buckingham approached the King concerning his cousin. "Your Majesty, could you not forbid the Lady Castlemaine from this new religion?"

Charles laughed lightly. "You forget, my lord," he said, "I have never interfered with the *souls* of ladies."

Barbara heard this and was more alarmed than ever. She was becoming more and more aware that she was losing some of her power over the King.

❁ ❁ ❁

Buckingham had been sent from the presence of Frances Stuart. He was no longer her very good friend. He had dared make improper suggestions to her. She, who had professed to be so innocent, had been by no means at a loss as to how to deal with the profligate Duke.

He returned to the Cockpit and consulted with Barbara. "It would seem the lady is determined to be virtuous," he said.

Bennet tried his luck but, when he stood before Frances and made that declaration in the pompous tones which Buckingham had imitated so well, Frances was unable to contain her mirth, for, as she said afterwards, it was well nigh impossible to know whether she was listening to Bennet in person or Buckingham impersonating Bennet.

The King also made his proposals to the beautiful young girl. She was sad and remote. She did not think His Majesty was in a position to say such things to her, she declared; and even though she might incur his displeasure, she could only beg him not to do so.

The King, in exasperation, went to sup at Barbara's house.

She was delighted to see him and received him with warmth; she was determined to remind him of all that they had enjoyed together.

She succeeded in doing this so certainly that he was back the next night and the next.

Barbara's hopes began to rise; she forgot her priest and the need to accept the Catholic religion. She ordered a great chine of beef to be roasted for the King; but the tide rose unusually high and her kitchens were flooded, so that Mrs. Sarah declared she could not roast the beef. Barbara cried aloud: "Zounds! Set the house afire but roast that beef."

And Mrs. Sarah, far bolder with Lady Castlemaine than any other servant dared be, told her mistress to talk good sense, and she would carry the beef to be roasted at her husband's house; and as her husband was cook to my Lord Sandwich she doubted not that she could get the beef roasted to a turn.

This was done; and the King and Lady Castlemaine supped merrily, but all London knew of the chine of beef which had to be roasted in the kitchens of Lord Sandwich. It was known too that the King stayed with my Lady Castlemaine until the early hours of the morning.

❁ ❁ ❁

Catherine, resting in the Palace of Whitehall and shut away from rumor, was waiting for her baby to be born. She had allowed herself to believe that when the child came she and Charles would be content with one another. It was true that he was enamored of the beautiful Mrs. Stuart, but Frances was a good girl, who conducted herself with decorum and had made it quite clear that the King must give up all hope of seducing her.

When the child came he would forget his schemes concerning Frances Stuart, Catherine persuaded herself; he would give himself up to the joys of family life. He was meant to be a father; he was tolerant, full of gaiety and a lover of children. There would be many children; and they would be as happy a family as that in which she had been brought up—nay, happier, for they would not have to suffer the terrible anxiety which had beset the Duke of Braganza's.

All this must come to pass as she knew it could, once he was free of that evil woman. The name Castlemaine would always make her shiver, she feared. When she saw it she would always remember that terrible occasion when she had seen it written at the top of the list; and that other when she had given her hand to the woman to kiss, without realizing her identity; and the shame of the scene that followed.

But in the years to come the name of Castlemaine would be nothing but a memory, a memory to provoke a shiver it was true, yet nothing more.

So now she thought exclusively of the child, hoping it would be a boy; but if that should not be, well then, they were young, she and Charles, and they had proved themselves capable of getting children.

I knew I should be happy, she told herself. It was only necessary for him to escape from that evil woman.

The women below her window were giggling together. She wondered what this was about. She gathered it concerned a certain chine of beef. The stupid things women giggled about!

She turned away from the window, wondering when she would see Charles again.

Perhaps she would tell him of her hopes for their future—such confidences were often on her lips, but she never uttered them. Although he was tender and solicitous for her health, he was always so merry; and she fancied that he was a little cynical regarding sentimental dreams.

No! She would not tell him. She would make her dreams become realities.

Donna Maria came to her, and Donna Maria had been weeping. Old and infirm, hating the English climate, not understanding the English manners, Donna Maria constantly longed for her own country, although nothing would have induced her to leave her Infanta.

Poor Donna Maria! thought Catherine. She always had a habit of looking on the dark side of life as though she preferred it to the brighter.

"So you have heard this story of the chine of beef?" she asked.

"Well, I heard some women laughing over it below my window."

"It was for the King's supper, and the kitchens were flooded, so it must needs be carried to my Lord Sandwich's kitchens to be cooked."

"Is that the story of the chine of beef?"

"A noisy story because Madam Castlemaine cried out to burn the place down—but roast the beef."

"Madam . . . Castlemaine!"

"Why, yes, have you not heard? The King is back with her. He is supping with her every night and is as devoted to her as he ever was."

Catherine stood up. Her emotions were beyond control as they had been on that occasion when the King had presented Lady Castlemaine to her without her knowledge and consent.

All her dreams were false. He had not left the woman. In that moment she believed that as long as she lived Lady Castlemaine would be her evil genius as she was the King's.

"Why . . . what ails you?" cried Donna Maria.

She saw the blood gushing from Catherine's nose as it had on that other occasion; she was just in time to catch the Queen as she fell forward.

❁ ❁ ❁

The King stood by his wife's bed. She looked small, frail and quite helpless.

She was delirious; and she did not know yet that she had lost her child.

Donna Maria had explained to him; she had repeated the last words she had exchanged with Catherine.

I have brought her to this, thought the King. I have caused her so much pain that the extreme stress of her emotional state has brought on this miscarriage and lost us our child.

He knelt down by the bed and covered his face with his hands.

"Charles," said Catherine. "Is that you, Charles?"

"I am here," he told her. "I am here beside you."

"You are weeping, Charles! Those are tears. I never thought to see you weep."

"I want you to be well, Catherine. I want you to be well."

He could see by the expression on her face that she had no knowledge of the nature of her illness; she must have forgotten there was to have been a child. He was glad of this. At least she was spared that agony.

"Charles," she said. "Hold my hand, Charles."

Eagerly he took her hand; he put his lips to it.

"I am happy that you are near me," she told him.

"I shall not leave you. I shall be here with you . . . while you want me."

"I dreamed I heard you say those words." A frown touched her brow lightly. "You say them because I am ill," she went on. "I am very ill. Charles, I am dying, am I not?"

"Nay," he cried passionately. "Nay, 'tis not so."

"I shall not grieve to leave the world," she said. "Willingly would I leave all . . . save one. There is no one I regret leaving, Charles, but you."

"You shall not leave me," he declared.

"I pray you do not grieve for me when I am dead. Rejoice rather that you may marry a Princess more worthy of you than I have been."

"I beg of you, do not say such things."

"But I am unworthy . . . a plain little Princess . . . and not a Princess of a great country either. . . . A Princess whose country made great demands on you . . . a Princess whose country you succored and to whom you brought the greatest happiness she ever knew."

"You shame me." And suddenly he could no longer control his tears. He thought of all the humiliations he had forced her to suffer, and he swore that he would never forgive himself.

"Charles . . . Charles," she murmured. "I know not whether to weep or rejoice. That you should care so much for me . . . what more could I ask than this? But to see you weep . . . to see you so stricken with sorrow . . . that grieves me . . . it grieves me sorely."

Charles was so overcome with remorse and emotion that he could not speak. He knelt by her bed, his face hidden, bent over the hand that he held. As she drifted into unconsciousness, she felt his tears on her hand.

Donna Maria came to stand beside the King.

"Your Majesty can do no good to the Queen . . . now," she said.

He turned wearily away.

❁ ❁ ❁

He was at her bedside night and day. Those about the Queen marveled at his devotion. Was this the man who had supped nightly with my Lady Castlemaine, the man who was deeply in love with the beautiful Mrs. Stuart? He wished that his should be the hand to smooth her pillows, his the face she would first see should she awake, his the voice she should hear.

She was far gone in fever, and so light-headed that she thought she was the mother of a son.

Perhaps she was thinking of the tales she had heard of Charles' babyhood, for she murmured: "He is fine and strong, but I fear he is an ugly boy."

"Nay," said the King, his voice shaken with emotion, "he is a very pretty boy."

"Charles," she said, "are you there, Charles?"

"Yes, I am here, my love."

"Your love," she repeated. "Is it true? But I like to hear you say it as you did at Hampton Court before . . . Charles, he shall be called Charles, shall he not?"

"Yes," said the King, "he shall be called Charles."

"It matters not if he is a little ugly," she said. "If he be like you he will be the finest boy in the world, and I shall be well pleased with him."

"Let us hope," said the King, "that he will be better than I."

"How could that be?" she asked.

And the King was too moved to continue the conversation. He bade her close her eyes and rest.

But she could not rest; she was haunted by the longing for maternity.

"How many children is it we have, Charles? Three, is it? Three children . . . our children. The little girl is so pretty, is she not?"

"She is very pretty," said Charles.

"I am glad of that, for I should not like you to have a daughter who was not lovely in face and figure. You care so much for beauty. If I had been blessed with great beauty . . ."

"Catherine," said the King, "do not torment yourself. Rest. I am here beside you. And remember this: I love you as you are. I would not want to change you. There is only one thing I wish; it is that you may get well."

❁ ❁ ❁

Newly slaughtered pigeons were laid at her feet; she was bled continuously; a nightcap, made of a precious relic, was put upon her head; but the King's presence at her bedside seemed to give her more comfort than any of these things.

In the streets the people talked of the Queen's serious illness which might end in death; and it was generally believed that, if she were to die, the King would marry the beautiful Frances Stuart whose virtue had refused to allow her to become the King's mistress.

This thought excited many. Buckingham, in spite of his being banished from Mrs. Stuart's company on account of his suggestion that she should become his mistress, had been restored to her favor. No one could build card houses as he could; no one could sing so enchantingly, nor do such amusing impersonations; so Frances had been ready to forgive him on the understanding that he realized there were to be no more attempts at love-making. Buckingham, who thrived on bold plans, was already arranging in his mind for the King, on the death of the Queen, to marry Frances; and Frances's greatest friend and adviser would be himself.

Barbara, knowing these plans were afoot, was watching her relative cautiously. Buckingham had been her friend, but he could easily become her enemy. So Barbara was one of those who offered up prayers for the recovery of the Queen.

As for the King, he was so assiduous in his care for Catherine, so full of remorse for the unhappiness which he had caused her, that his mind was occupied solely with his hopes for her recovery.

The Duke and Duchess of York also prayed for Catherine's recovery, for it was said that she would be unable to bear children; and if this were true and she lived, it would mean that the King would be unable to remarry, thus leaving the way clear for their children to inherit the throne.

Speculation ran high through the Court and the country, but this ended when Catherine recovered.

One morning she came out of her delirium, and her anguish on discovering she was not a mother was considerably lessened by the sight of her husband at her bedside, and the belief that she might be a beloved wife.

He continued full of care for her, and the days of her convalescence were happy indeed. The King's hair had turned so white during her illness that he laughingly declared he looked such an old man that he must follow the fashion of the day and adopt a periwig.

"Could those gray hairs have grown out of your anxiety as to what would become of me?" she asked.

"Assuredly they did."

"Then I think mayhap I shall enjoy seeing you without your periwig."

He smiled, but the next time she saw him he was wearing it. He looked a young man with the luxuriant curls falling over his shoulders, although his face was lined and on his dark features there were signs of the merry life he lived. But he was tall and slender still and so agile. Then she remembered with horror that she had had all her beautiful hair cut off when the fever was on her, and that she must be plainer than she had ever been before.

Yet he seemed determined to assure her of his devotion; and when she was told that she must impute her recovery to the precious relics which had been brought to her in her time of sickness, she answered: "No. I owe my recovery to the prayers of my husband, and the knowledge that he was beside me during my trial."

FIVE

Alas, as Catherine's health improved the King's devotion waned. It was not that he was less affectionate when they were together; it was merely that they were less frequently together. Irresistible attractions drew him away from Catherine's side.

Barbara had been delivered of a fine son whom she called Henry. The King had refused to own him as his child, yet Catherine knew that he often visited Barbara's nurseries to see those children whom he did accept, and it had been reported to her that he was mightily wistful when he regarded the new baby, and that Barbara was hopeful.

What a cruel fate this was! Barbara had child after child; in fact it seemed that no sooner was one born than another was on the way; and yet Catherine, who so longed for a child, who so *needed* a child, had lost hers and she was so weak after her long illness that it was doubtful whether she would be fit to have another for some time.

It was a source of grief and humiliation to her to know that Barbara championed her, so little did the woman regard her as a rival. She had heard that Barbara had prayed fervently for her recovery—not out of love for her, of course, but because as a Queen she was so ineffectual that there was not the slightest need to be jealous of her.

The woman whom all were watching now, some with envy, some with speculation, was Frances Stuart. The King was becoming more and more enamored every day, and Frances's determination not to become his mistress, while it might have seemed laudable to some, was ominous to others.

The affair of the calash seemed significant.

This beautiful glass coach, the first of its kind ever seen in England, was a French innovation which Louis's ambassador, hoping to ingratiate himself and his country with the King, had presented to Charles. The entire Court was enchanted by the dazzling vehicle and, as Charles gave most of his presents to one of his mistresses—usually Barbara—it was Lady Castlemaine who immediately declared her intention of being the first to be seen in it.

Barbara visualized the scene—herself ostentatiously cutting a fine figure in Hyde Park with the crowd looking on. They would have heard of the presentation of the calash, and they would realize when they saw her within it that her favor was as high as ever with the King.

There had been a reconciliation between Charles and her, for, although the King was in love with Frances Stuart, he could not remain faithful to a woman who denied him her favors, and he was still supping now and then at Barbara's house, although often it was necessary for her to have Frances as a guest in order to ensure the King's attendance.

Barbara was pregnant again, and although the King had not yet accepted Henry, she was certain that he would do so ere long, and she assured him that the child she now carried was undoubtedly his.

It was evening of the day when Gramont had presented the glass coach, and the King and Barbara were at last alone. Barbara, remembering how soulful Charles had looked while he watched the simpering little Stuart building her card houses after she had insisted on the company's joining her in a madcap and very childish game of blindman's buff, had determined to show the Court and the world that her hold on the King was still firm.

"Tomorrow," she announced, "the calash should be shown to the people."

"Ah, yes," said the King absently. He was wondering whether Frances had seemed a little more yielding this evening. When he had kissed her during the game of blindman's bluff she had not turned away; she had just laughed on a note of shrill reproof which might not have been reproof after all.

"You know how they hate things to be hidden from them, and they will have heard of the calash. They will expect to see it in Hyde Park as soon as the weather permits."

" 'Tis true," said the King.

"I would wish to be the first to ride in it."

"I hardly think that would be meet," said the King.

"Not meet! In what way?"

"The Queen has said that she would wish to ride in it with my brother's wife. She says that is what the people will expect."

"The people will expect no such thing."

"You are right," said the King ruefully. "And that points to our bad conduct in the past."

"Bad conduct!" snorted Barbara. "The people want to see the calash, not the Queen."

"Then since it is the calash they wish to see, and the purpose of the ride is to please them, it matters not who rides in it. Therefore the Queen and the Duchess of York should do so."

Barbara stood up, her eyes flashing. "Everything I ask is denied me. I wonder that you can treat me thus!"

"I have always thought the truth much more interesting than falsehood," said the King. "You know you have been denied very little, and it is tiring to hear you assert the contrary."

Barbara's common sense warned her. Her position with the King was not what it had been. Her great sensuality could stand her in good stead only for the immediate future. She knew that Frances Stuart had first place in the King's heart. But it maddened her now to think that it might have been Frances herself who had suggested that the Queen should be the first to ride in the calash. The sly creature was forever declaring her devotion to the Queen; it was part of her campaign, like as not.

But Barbara was determined to ride in the calash.

She cried: "So you are tired of me! You have taken my youth . . . all the best years of my life . . . and now that I have born so many children . . ."

"Of whose parentage we must ever remain in doubt."

"They are your children. Yours . . . yours! It is no use denying your share in the making of them. I have devoted my life to you. You are the King, and I have sought to serve you . . ."

"Barbara, I beg of you, make no scenes now. I have had enough of them."

"Do not think to silence me thus. I am to have our child . . . our child, sir. And if you do not let me ride first in the calash I shall miscarry this child. Aye, and all the world shall know it was through the ill treatment I received from its father."

"They would not be very impressed," said Charles lightly.

"Do not dare to laugh at me, or I shall kill myself . . . as well as the child."

"Nay, Barbara. You love yourself too well."

"Oh, will I not!" She looked about her and called wildly: "A knife! A knife! Bring me a knife. Mrs. Sarah! Do you hear me?"

The King went to her swiftly and placed his hand over her mouth. "You will make it impossible for me to visit you," he said.

"If you did not, I should make you repent it!"

"I shall repent nothing. It is only the righteous who repent."

"You will. I swear you will. All the world shall know of what has been between us."

"Calm yourself, Barbara. The world already knows half and the other half it will guess."

"Don't dare talk to me thus."

"I am weary of quarrels."

"Yes, you are weary of everything but that smug-faced idiot. Do you imagine that she would interest you beyond a week? Even her simple mind realizes that. It is why she is so simperingly virtuous. She knows full well that once she gave way you'd be sick to death of her simplemindedness. Simpleminded! She is half-witted. 'Play a game of blindman's buff, sire?' " squealed Barbara and curtsied, viciously demure. " 'I do like a nice game of blindman's buff, because I can squeal so prettily, and say Nay, nay, nay when Your Majesty chases me!' Bah!"

In spite of his annoyance, Charles could not help laughing, for her mimicry, though cruelly exaggerated, had a certain element of truth in it.

"Charles," she wheedled, "what is it to you? Pray you let me ride in the calash . . . just once; and after that let the Queen and the Duchess take the air in Hyde Park. You know the people would rather see me than the Queen or the Duchess. Look at me. . . ." She tossed back her hair and drew herself to her full magnificent height. "Would the calash not become me, think you? 'Twould be a pity to let it take its first airing in the Park without the most becoming cargo."

"Barbara, you would wheedle the crown off my head."

And I would, she thought, but for my cursed husband! And while I am fettered to him, Miss Stuart stays coy and hopeful; and doubtless, in spite of all her piety and friendship for the Queen, she prays for Catherine's death.

Still, the calash, not the crown, was the immediate problem, and she believed that Charles was about to give way. She knew the signs so well.

Abruptly she stopped speaking of it and gave herself up to passion with such abandonment that she could not fail to win his response.

But when he left her in the early morning his promises about the calash were vague, and she was faintly worried.

❁ ❁ ❁

Many heard the loud quarrels between Charles and Barbara. Now the Court was saying that Barbara had declared her intention of miscarrying the child—which she insisted was the King's—providing she was not the first to ride in the calash.

The Queen heard this and remembered with humiliation her request to the King that she and the Duchess should be the first to use it.

What mattered it, thought Catherine, who rode in the coach? It was not the actual riding which was significant.

The King put off the decision. He wanted to please the Queen, yet he was afraid of Barbara. He could not be sure what she would do. She made wild threats; she was always declaring that she would strangle this child, murder that servant, if her whims were not satisfied. So far as he knew, she had not carried out these threats to kill, but her temper was violent and he could not be sure to what madness it would lead her.

The Court sniggered about the wrangle concerning the calash. The country heard and murmured about it. It was a great joke—the sort of joke with which the King so often amused his people. But the calash was not seen in the Park, simply because the King did not wish to offend the Queen and dared not offend Barbara.

A few evenings later the King was supping in the apartments of Frances Stuart, and as she was sitting at the table—with him beside her—Frances's beautiful blue eyes were fixed on the flimsy structure of cards before her, while the King's passionate dark ones were on Frances. She turned to him suddenly and said: "Your Majesty has often declared that you would wish to give me something which I dearly desired."

"You have but to ask, as you know," said the King, "and it is yours."

Everyone was listening. All were deciding: This is the end of her resistance. Frances has decided to become the King's mistress.

"I desire to be the first to ride in the calash," said Frances.

The King hesitated. This was unexpected. He was beginning to wish he had never been presented with the thing.

He was aware of Barbara's burning blue eyes on him; he saw the danger signals there.

Frances continued to smile artlessly and continued: "Your Majesty, the coach should be seen. The people long to see it. It would greatly please me to be the first to ride in it."

Barbara stepped up to the table. With an impatient gesture she knocked down the house of cards. Frances gave a little cry of dismay, but the eyes which looked straight into Barbara's were pert and defiant.

Barbara said in a low voice: "I have told the King that if I am not the first to ride in the coach I shall miscarry his child."

Frances smiled. "It is a pity," she said. "And if *I* am not the first to ride in the coach I shall never be with child."

It was a challenge. There were three contestants now. The Court laughed more merrily than before.

They were sure it would be a battle between Barbara and Frances.

The King, faintly exasperated by this public display of rivalry, said: "This calash seems to have turned all heads. Where is my lord Buckingham? Ah, my lord Duke, sing to us . . . sing, I pray you. Sing of love and hate, but sing not of coaches!"

So Buckingham sang; and Barbara's blazing eyes were fixed on the slender, youthful figure of Frances Stuart while he did so.

❁❁❁

The battle was over.

The Queen sat sadly in her apartments. She almost wishes that she had not recovered from her illness. She mused: While I was ill he loved me. If I had died then I should have died happy. He wept for me; his hair turned gray for me; it was he who smoothed my pillows. I remember his remorse for all the jealousy I had been made to suffer on his account. He was truly sorry. Yet, now that I am well, I suffer as I ever did.

Barbara's jealousy took another form.

She strode up and down her apartment, kicking everything in her path out of the way. No servants would come near her except Mrs. Sarah, and even she took good care to keep well out of reach.

All thought Barbara might do herself some injury; many hoped she would.

In her rage she tore her bodice into shreds; she pulled her hair; she called on God to witness her humiliation.

Meanwhile Frances Stuart was riding serenely in Hyde Park, and the calash made a very pleasant setting for such a beautiful jewel.

The people watched her go by and declared that never—even in those days when Lady Castlemaine had been at the height of her beauty—had there been such a lovely lady at the Court.

❁❁❁

Catherine, watching the game Charles played with the women of his Court, often wondered whether he were capable of any deep feeling. Barbara took lovers shamelessly yet remained the King's mistress; in fact, he seemed quite indifferent to her amatory adventures which were the scandal of the Court. He seemed only to care that she received him whenever he was ready to visit her.

Frances, after the affair of the calash, had continued to hold back. She had promised nothing, she declared; and her conscience would not allow her to become the King's mistress.

Catherine was unsure of Frances. The girl might be a skilful coquette—as Barbara insisted that she was, for Barbara made no secret of her enmity now—or she might indeed be a virtuous woman.

Catherine believed her to be virtuous. It certainly seemed to her that Frances was sincere when she confided to the Queen that she wished to marry and settle down in peace away from the Court.

"Your Majesty must understand," she had said, "that the position in which I find myself is none of my making."

Catherine determined to believe her, and sought to help her on every occasion.

She pondered often on the King's devotion to women other than herself. She remembered too the case of Lady Chesterfield. The Chesterfields remained in the country, but news came that the Earl was as much in love with his wife as he had been at Court, and that she continued to scorn him.

Catherine talked of this with Frances Stuart, and Frances answered: "It was only when he saw how others admired her that he began to do so. That is the way of men."

And I, thought Catherine, admired Charles wholeheartedly. I showed my admiration. I was without guile. He knew that no other man had ever loved me.

Edward Montague was often in attendance. He would look at her sadly when such affairs as that of the calash took place; it was clear that he pitied her. He was invariably at her side at all gatherings; his position as master of her horse necessitated that, but she was sure his feelings for her were stronger than those of a servant.

She often studied Edward Montague; he was a handsome young man and there was surely something of which to be proud in the devotion of such as he; so she smiled on him with affection, and it began to be noticed that the friendship between them was growing.

Catherine knew this, but did nothing to prevent it; it was, after all, a situation she had striven to create.

Montague's enemies were quick to call the King's attention to this friendship with the Queen; but Charles laughed lightly. He was glad that the Queen had an admirer. It showed the man's sound good sense, he said, because the Queen was worthy to be admired.

He was certainly not going to put a stop to the friendship; he would consider it extremely unfair to do so since he enjoyed so many friendships with the opposite sex.

Catherine, seeing his indifference to her relationship with her handsome master of horse, made another of those mistakes which turned the King's admiration for her to indifference.

Catherine's great tragedy was that she never understood Charles.

It so happened that, when she alighted from her horse and he took her hand, Montague held it longer than was necessary and pressed it firmly. It was a gesture of assurance of his affection and sympathy for her, and Catherine knew this; but when, longing for Charles' attention and desperately seeking to claim it, she artlessly asked what a gentleman meant when he held a lady's hand and pressed it, she was feigning an innocence and ignorance of English customs which were not hers.

"Who has done this?" asked the King.

She answered: "It is my good master of horse, Montague."

The King looked at her with pity. Poor Catherine! Was she trying to be coy? How ill it became her!

He said lightly: "It is an expression of devotion, but such expressions given to kings and queens may not indicate devotion but a desire for advancement. Yet it is an act of insolence for Your Majesty's master of horse to behave thus to you, and I will take steps to see that it does not happen again."

She believed she had aroused his jealousy. She believed he was thinking: So other men find her attractive; and she waited to see what would happen next.

Alas, Charles' attention was still on his mistresses and Catherine merely lost her one admirer.

Edward Montague was dismissed his office; not on account of the King's jealousy, but because Charles feared that Catherine's innocence might betray her into indiscretion if the man remained.

❁❁❁

The King's love for Frances did not diminish.

He was subdued and often melancholy; a listlessness—so unusual with him—crept into his behavior. He had accepted her reluctance at first as the opening phase in the game of love; but still she was unconquered; and he began to believe that she would never surrender.

His feelings were more deeply stirred than they had ever been before. For the first time in his life the King was truly in love.

Sometimes he marveled at himself. It was true that Frances was very beautiful, but she completely lacked that quick wit which he himself possessed and which he admired in others. Frances was just a little stupid, some might say; but that seemed to make her seem more youthful than ever. Perhaps she provided such a contrast to Barbara. She never flew into tantrums; she was invariably calm and serene; she rarely spoke in an ill-natured fashion of anyone; she asked for little—the affair of the calash was an exception, and he believed she may have been persuaded to that, possibly by Buckingham whose head was, as usual, full of the most hare-brained schemes; all she wished was to be allowed to play those games which delighted her. Frances was like a very young and guileless girl and as such she deeply touched the heart of the King.

It was Frances who now adorned the coinage—a shapely Britannia with her helmet on her charming head and the trident in her slender hands.

He brooded on her constantly and wrote a song to explain his feelings.

"I pass all my hours in a shady old grove,
But I live not the day when I see not my love;
I survey every walk now my Phyllis is gone,
And sigh when I think we were there all alone;
O then, 'tis O then, that I think there's no hell
Like loving like loving too well.
While alone, to myself I repeat all her charms,
She I love may be locked in another man's arms,
She may laugh at my cares, and so false may she be
To say all the kind things she before said to me;
O then, 'tis O then that I think there's no hell
Like loving too well.
But when I consider the truth of her heart,
Such an innocent passion, so kind without art;
I fear I have wronged her, and hope she may be
So full of true love to be jealous of me;
And then 'tis, I think, that no joy be above
The Pleasures of love."

And while the King brooded on his unfulfilled passion for Frances, state matters were not progressing satisfactorily. He would be called to hasty council meetings and there were long consultations with Clarendon, whose dictatorial manner was often irritating. But, like Clarendon, Charles was alarmed by the growing hostilities on the high seas between the Dutch and the English.

The Duke of York, who had won fame as an Admiral of the Fleet, was growing more and more daring. He had the trading classes of the country behind him; and it was becoming clear that these people were hoping for a war with Holland. The Duke had captured Cape Corso and other Dutch colonies on the African coast, a matter which had caused some concern to the Chancellor which he had imparted to Charles. These conquests, insisted Clarendon, were unjust and were causing bad blood between the two countries. The Duke's retort to Clarendon's warnings was to capture New Amsterdam on the coast of North America and immediately rename it New York. He declared that English property in North America had been filched by the Dutch, and it was only seemly that it should be filched back again. Meanwhile there were frequent hostile incidents when the ships of both nations met.

Charles could see that if events continued to follow this course there would indeed be war, for it seemed that he and the Chancellor were the only men in the country who did not wish for it. He himself was very much bound by his Parliament, and Clarendon was fast becoming the most unpopular man in the country. The Buckingham faction had set in progress rumors damaging to Clarendon, so that every difficulty and disaster which arose was laid at his door. It was now being whispered that the selling of Dunkirk to the French had been Clarendon's work, and that he had been heavily bribed for his part in this, which was untrue. Dunkirk had been sold because it was a drain on the expenses of the Exchequer which was in urgent need of the purchase money. Clarendon had only helped set the negotiations in motion once it had been decided that the deal should go forward.

So these were melancholy days for Charles. State affairs moving towards a climax which might be dangerous; Charles for the first time in love and denied the satisfaction he asked.

❁ ❁ ❁

Mary Fairfax, the Duchess of Buckingham, was giving a ball.

While her maids were dressing her she looked at her reflection in the Venetian mirror with a fearful pride. Her jewels were of many colors, for she liked to adorn herself thus and she knew she wore too many and of too varied colors, but she could never decide which she ought to discard. She was too thin, completely lacking the slender grace of Frances Stuart; she was awkward, and never knew what to do with her large hands, now ablaze with rings. She feared though that the jewels she wore did not beautify; they merely called attention to the awkwardness of those hands. Her nose was too large as was her mouth; her eyes large and dark, but too closely set together. She had always known she was no beauty; and she could never rid herself of the idea that brightly colored gowns and many jewels would help her to hide her deficiencies; it was only when she was in the company of some of the beauties of the Court—ladies such as Lady Chesterfield, Miss Jennings, Lady Southesk, Barbara Castlemaine and, of course, the most beautiful Mrs. Stuart—that she realized that all of them, including Barbara, had achieved their effects by less flamboyant means than she had employed.

She was neglected by her husband, the great Duke, but she never resented this; she was constantly aware that she, Mary Fairfax, was the wife of the handsomest man she had ever seen; not only was he handsome, but he was witty, amusing, sought after by the ambitious; and she continually told herself that she was the most fortunate of women merely to be his wife.

She was remembering, as her maids dressed her, that happy time immediately following her marriage, before the King's return to England, when the Duke had played the faithful husband, and her father had told her so often that he rejoiced in her marriage.

Mary's husband was a strange man. He was brilliant, but it seemed that always there must be some plot forming itself within his mind. What joy when that plot had been to marry Mary Fairfax; and afterwards, when he had planned to make Mary a good husband! They had lived quietly in the country—she, her dearest George and her father. How often had she seen them, her father and her husband, walking arm in arm while George talked of the book he was planning to write on her father's career. Those had been the happiest days of her life and, she ventured to think, of his. But the quiet life was not for him; and with the Restoration it was only reasonable that he should become a courtier and statesman. At Court it was natural that he should become the King's companion and the friend of those profligate gentlemen who lived wildly and consorted with women whose reputations were as bad as their own.

"Marriage," he had said, "is the greatest solitude, for it makes two but one, and prohibits us from all others." A different cry that from the words he had so often spoken immediately before and after their marriage. Nor did he accept this "solitude"; nor did he "prohibit himself from all others."

Life had changed, and she must accept the change; she was grateful for those occasions when she did see him, when, as on this one, he needed her help. It was rarely that he did so and it was not often that they were together.

Her father worried a great deal about the change in their relationship; he complained bitterly of the way in which George treated her. She was fortunate to be so loved by a great man like her father, but now he blamed himself because he had brought about this marriage; and again and again she soothed him and assured him that he had not wished for the marriage more than she had. All knew that Buckingham neglected her, that he had married her when his fortunes were at a low ebb and it had seemed as though the Monarchy would never be restored, but that marriage with the daughter of an old Parliamentarian was the best a man could make. She was glad that she had turned from Lord Chesterfield to Buckingham; she would never regret it, never, even though those who wished her well were sorry for her. Only recently one of the Duke's servants had made an attempt on his life when they had spent the night at the Sun Inn at Aldgate after returning from the Newmarket races. George had quickly disarmed the man. But the affair became widely known; and it was disconcerting that the point of the story should not be that the Duke was almost done to death by a mad servant, but that he should have been about to spend the night with his own wife.

Such slights, such humiliations, she accepted. They were part of the price which a plain and homely woman paid for union with one of the greatest Dukes in the country.

Now she asked her maids: "How like you my gown?"

And they answered: "Madam, it is beautiful."

They were sincere. They really thought so.

"Ah," said Mary quickly, "if I could but get me a new face as easily as I get me a new gown, then I might be a beauty."

The maids were excited because they knew that this was to be a very grand ball, and the King himself was to be present.

They did not know the purpose of the ball.

George had explained it to his wife. It was one of his plots and in this his conspirators were Lord Sandwich and Henry Bennet—who was now Lord Arlington.

"We cannot," George had said, "allow the King to become morose. He neglects his state business and he is not so amusing as he once was. The King wants one thing to make him his merry self again; and we are going to give it to him: Frances Stuart."

"How will you do this?" she had asked. "Is it not for Frances Stuart to make the necessary decision?"

"We shall be very, very merry," said the Duke. "There will be dancing and games such as Frances delights in. There shall be drink . . . potent drink, and we must see that Frances partakes of it freely."

Mary had turned a little pale.

"You mean that she is to be made incapable of knowing what she does!"

"Now you are shocked," said the Duke lightly. "That is your puritan stock showing itself. My dear Mary, stop being a hopeless prude, I beg of you. Move with the times, my dear. Move with the times."

"But this girl is so young and . . ."

"And wily. She has played her games long enough."

"George, I . . ."

"You will do nothing but be hostess to the guests; and make sure that we have a rich apartment ready for the lovers when they need it."

She had wanted to protest; but she could not bear his displeasure. If she *must* play such a part for the sake of her Duke, she had no alternative but to do so.

She took one last look at herself and went downstairs to be ready to greet her guests.

And when she was in that glittering assembly she knew at once that her jewels were too numerous, the bright scarlet of her gown unbecoming to one of her coloring; she realized afresh that she was the ugly Duchess of the most handsome of Dukes.

❁ ❁ ❁

Mrs. Sarah wanted a word with her mistress, and she wanted it in private.

Barbara left her friends to hear what her servant had to say. She knew that Mrs. Sarah, while often denouncing her to her face, was loyal.

Mrs. Sarah began: "Now, if I tell you something your ladyship won't like to hear, will you promise to hear me out without throwing a stool at me?"

"What is it?" said Barbara.

"Your promise first! It's something you ought to know."

"Then unless you tell me this instant I'll have the clothes torn from your back and I'll lay about you with a stick myself."

"Now listen to me, Madam."

"I am listening. Come closer, you fool. What is it?"

"There is a ball this night at my lord Buckingham's."

"And what of that? The fool can give a ball if he wishes to, without asking me. Let him sing his silly songs; let him do his imitations. . . . I'll warrant he has a good one of me."

"The King is to be present."

Barbara was alert. "How know you this?"

"My husband, who is cook to my lord Sandwich . . ."

"I see . . . I see. The King is there; and is that sly slug there with him?"

"She is, Madam."

"Playing card houses, I'll swear. Let them. That's all the game he'll play with that lily-livered virgin."

"Mayhap not this night."

"What do you mean, woman?"

"There is a plot to bring them together this night. My lord Arlington . . ."

"The pompous pig!"

"And my lord Sandwich . . ."

"That prancing ape!"

"And my lord Buckingham . . ."

"That foul hog!"

"I beg of you remember, Madam, stay calm."

"Stay calm! While that merry trio work against me? For that is what they would do, Sarah. They strike at me. They use that simpering little ninny to do so, but they strike at me. By God and all the saints, I'll go there and I'll let them know I understand their games. I'll throw their silly cards in their faces and I'll . . ."

"Madam, remember, so much is at stake. I beg of you do nothing rash. *She* remains calm. That is why she keeps his regard."

"Are you telling me what to do, you . . . *you* . . ."

"Yes, I am," said Sarah. "I don't want you to hurt yourself."

"Hurt myself! It is not I who shall get hurt. Do you think I do not know how to look after myself?"

"Yes, Madam, I do think that. I think that, had you been calmer and more loving and not so ready to fly into tantrums, His Majesty would have continued to love you even though, such being the royal nature, he hankered after Frances Stuart. Let me finish what I began to say. This night they plan to bring this affair to a conclusion. They will so bemuse Mrs. Stuart this night that it will be easy to overcome her resistance. And when that is done, there will be the apartment waiting and the royal lover to conduct her to it."

"It shall not be. I'll go there and drag the little fool away, if I have to pull her by her golden hair."

"Madam, think first. Be calm. Do not demean yourself. There is one other who would not wish for the surrender of Mrs. Stuart. Why not let her do your work this night? It would be better so if you would hold His Majesty's regard, for I verily believe that she who takes from him the pleasure he anticipates this night will not long hold his love."

Barbara did not answer immediately; she continued to look at Mrs. Sarah.

❁ ❁ ❁

The two women faced each other.

This is the woman, thought Catherine, who has destroyed my happiness. She it was who, as a mere name long ago in Lisbon, filled me with misgivings.

Barbara thought: I would not barter my beauty for her plain mien even though the crown went with it. Poor Charles, he is indeed gallant to feign tenderness for such a one. She could never have appealed to him during all those weeks when he played the loving husband.

Barbara said: "Your Majesty, this is not a time when two women should weigh their words. A plot is afoot this night to make an innocent young girl a harlot. That is putting it plainly, but it is nonetheless the truth. The young girl is Frances Stuart, and I beg of Your Majesty to do something to prevent this."

Catherine felt her heart beat very fast; she said: "I do not understand your meaning, Lady Castlemaine."

"Buckingham is giving a ball. The King is there. And so is Mrs. Stuart. It is the Duke's plan to make her so bemused that she will be an easy victim."

"No," cried Catherine. "No!"

" 'Tis so, Your Majesty. You know the girl. She is not very intelligent but she is virtuous. Can you stand aside and allow this to happen?"

"But no," said Catherine.

"Then may I humbly beg of Your Majesty to prevent it?"

"How could I prevent that on which the King has set his heart?"

"You are the Queen. The girl is of your household. Your Majesty, if you attended this ball . . . if you brought her back with you to your apartments, because you had need of her services, none could say you nay. The King would not. You know that he would never humiliate you . . . on a matter of etiquette such as this would be."

Catherine felt her cheeks burning. She gazed at the insolent woman, and she knew her motive for wishing to rescue Frances had nothing to do with the preservation of Frances' virtue. Yet she could not allow Charles to do this. She could not allow Frances to become his unwilling mistress.

She was not sure what it was that prompted her to act as she did. It might have been jealousy. It might have been for the sake of Frances's virtue, for the sake of Charles' honor. She was sure that in all his numerous love affairs there could never yet have been an unwilling partner.

She turned to Barbara and said: "You are right. I will go to the ball."

❁ ❁ ❁

It was three o'clock when the Queen arrived.

By this time the fun was fast and the games very wild and merry. Frances, the center of attraction, had been induced to drink far more than usual; she was flushed and her eyes bright with the excitement which romping games could always arouse in her.

The King had scarcely left her side all the evening. Three pairs of eyes watched Frances—Buckingham's, Arlington's and those of Sandwich—and their owners were sure that very soon Frances would be ready to fall into the arms of the King.

And then the Queen arrived.

Buckingham and his Duchess must declare their delight in this unexpected honor. They hoped Her Majesty would stay and join the dance.

She danced for a while, and then she declared that she would return to Whitehall and take Frances Stuart with her.

If Frances left there was nothing to detain the King at the ball; so the evening ended very differently from the way in which it had been planned, and Frances and the King left for Whitehall in the company of the Queen.

❁ ❁ ❁

Affairs of state were occupying the King continuously, so that he had little time for following pleasure. The Parliament were declaring that the damage inflicted on English ships was doing a great deal of harm to English trade. The merchants were demanding that the Dutch be taught a lesson. Dutch fishermen met English fishermen in the North Sea and fought to the death. On the African coasts Dutch and English sailors were already at war. In Amsterdam scurrilous pamphlets were published concerning the life of the King of England; and pictures were distributed showing a harassed King pursued by women who tried to drive him in all directions.

Charles was anxious. He loathed the thought of war, which he believed could bring little profit even to the victors. He had seen much of the sufferings due to war; his thoughts went back to that period of his life which would ever live vividly in his memory. He remembered Edgehill where he and James had come near to capture; but more clearly than anything that had ever happened to him would be the memory of disaster at Worcester and those weeks when he had skulked, disguised as a yokel, afraid to show his face in the country of which he called himself King.

But he knew that his wishes would carry little weight, for the whole country was calling out for war with the Dutch.

Every day, instead of sauntering in the Park he was on the Thames, inspecting that Fleet of which he was more proud than anything else he possessed.

He had told of his pride in it to the Parliament when he had asked them for money to maintain that Fleet.

"I have been able to let our neighbors see that I can defend myself and my subjects against their insolence. By borrowing liberally from myself out of my own stores, and with the kind and cheerful assistance which the City of London hath given me, I have a Fleet now worthy of the English nation and not inferior to any that hath set out in any age."

After that speech he had been voted the great sum of two and a half million pounds for the equipment and maintenance of the Fleet; and although his pride in it was high, he was fervently hoping to avoid making open war on the Dutch.

That winter was the coldest that men remembered; but the great news was not of the phenomenal weather; it concerned the exploits of Dutchmen, for if Charles had a great Fleet, so had they, and they were as much at home on the high seas as were the English.

Barbara had given birth to another child—this time a daughter whom she named Charlotte. She declared she was the King's child, and this time the King was too immersed in matters of state to deny this.

By March it was necessary to declare war on Holland, and the whole country was wild with excitement. The City of London built a man-of-war which they called Loyal London; and the Duke of York took command of the Fleet.

The spring came, warm and welcome after the long, hard winter, and all at home waited news of the encounter between the Dutch and English navies. In London the gunfire out at sea could be heard, and the nation was tense yet very confident. They did not know that the money voted by Parliament for the conduct of the war—a sum which seemed vast to them—was inadequate. There was one man who knew this and suffered acute anxiety. This was the King; he knew the state of the country's finances; he knew that he could not go on indefinitely subscribing to the maintenance of the Fleet in war out of his inadequate allowance; he knew that the Dutch were wealthier than the English, and that they were as worthy seamen.

When the news came of the victory over the Dutch, when the bells of the city pealed out and the citizens ran into the streets to snatch up anything that would make a bonfire, the King was less inclined to gaiety than any; he had heard news that Berkeley—recently become the Earl of Falmouth—had perished in the battle. He had known Berkeley, well, and he guessed that he would be but one of many to suffer if the war continued.

Then in the streets of London there appeared a more cruel enemy than the Dutch.

In that warm April a man, coming from St. Paul's into Cheapside, was overcome by his sickness, and lay down on the cobbles since he could go no farther. Shivering and delirious, he lay there, and in the morning he was dead; and those who approached him saw on his breast the dreaded macula and, shuddering, ran from him. But by that time others were falling to the pestilence. From the Strand to Aldgate men and women on their ordinary business would stagger and hurry blindly to their homes. Some of those stricken in the streets could go no farther; they lay down and died.

The plague had come to London.

❁❁❁

Who could now rejoice wholeheartedly? It was true that the English had taken eighteen capital ships from the Dutch off Harwich, and had destroyed another fourteen. It was known that Admiral Obdam had been blown up with his crew and would no longer worry the English. And all this had been achieved for the loss of one ship. It was true that many good sailors had been lost—Falmouth among them—with Marlborough and Portland and the Admirals Hawson and Sampson.

But the plague was on the increase, and its effect was already being severely felt in London. The weather was hotter than usual after the bleak winter. Stench rose from the gutters; refuse was emptied from windows by people who could not leave their houses since they kept a plague victim there. Men and women were dying in the streets. It was dangerous to give succor to any who fell fainting by the roadside. All indisposition was suspect. Many were frightened into infection in that plague- and fear-ridden atmosphere. Death was in the fetid air and terror stalked the streets.

The river was congested with barges carrying away from the City those who were fortunate enough to be able to leave the plague spots.

The Court had retired, first to Hampton, and then, when the plague stretched its greedy maw beyond the metropolis, farther afield to Salisbury.

Albemarle took command of London and, with the resourcefulness of a great general, made plans for taking care of the infected and avoiding the spread of the plague. He arranged that outlying parishes should be ready to take in all those who could arrive uninfected from the city.

London continued to suffer in the heat.

Grass was now growing among the cobbles, for the business of every day had ceased. Those merchants who could do so, left their businesses; those who could not, stayed to nurse their families and to die with them. Trade had come to a standstill and the City was like a dead town. Those who ventured into its streets did so muffled in close garments covering their mouths that they might not breathe the polluted air.

Almost every door bore a red cross with the inscription "Lord Have Mercy Upon Us" to warn all to keep away because the plague was in the house; by night the pest carts roamed the streets to the tolling of a dismal bell and the dreadful cry of "Bring out your dead."

By the time that terrible year was over about 130,000 people had died of the plague in England. The citizens returned to London to take possession of their property, but the losses of life and trade were so great that the country, still engaged in war, was in a more pitiable plight than it had ever been in during the whole of its history.

It was at this time that Catherine discovered she was pregnant, and her hopes of giving birth to an heir were high.

❁ ❁ ❁

The year 1666 dawned on a sorrowing people.

The plague had crippled the country more cruelly than many suspected. Since trade had been brought to a standstill during the hot summer months there was no money with which to equip the ships of the Navy. The French chose this moment to take sides with the Dutch, and England, now almost bankrupt and emerging from the disaster of the plague, was called upon to face two enemies instead of one.

The English were truculent. They were ready for all the "Mounseers," they declared; but the King was sad; he was alarmed that that nation, to which his own mother belonged and to which he felt himself bound so closely, should take up arms against his; moreover two of the greatest Powers in the world were allied against one crippled by the scourge of death which had lately afflicted it and by lack of the means to carry on a successful war.

In March of that year bad news was brought from Portugal, but on the King's advice it was not immediately imparted to the Queen.

"It will distress her," said Charles, "and in view of her delicate health at this time I would have the utmost care taken."

But it was impossible to keep the news long from Catherine. She knew by the tears of Donna Maria that something had happened, and she guessed that it concerned their country, for only then would Donna Maria be so deeply affected.

And at length she discovered the secret.

Her mother dead! It seemed impossible to believe it. It was but four years since they had said their last goodbyes. Much had happened in those four years, and perhaps in her love for her husband Catherine had at times forgotten her mother; but now that she was dead, now that she knew she would never see her again, she was heartbroken.

She lay in her bed and wept silently, going over every well-remembered incident of her childhood.

"Oh, Mother," she murmured, "if you had been here to advise me, mayhap I should have acted differently; mayhap Charles would not now regard me with that vague tolerance which seems so typical of his feelings for me."

Then she remembered all her mother had bidden her do; she remembered how Queen Luiza had determined on this match; how she had again and again impressed on her daughter that she, Catherine, was destined to save their country.

"Mother, dearest Mother, I will do my best," she murmured. "Even though he has nothing more than a mild affection for me, even though I am but the wife who was chosen for him and there are about him beautiful women whom he has chosen for himself, still will I remember all that you have told me and never cease to work for my country."

Tempers ran high during those anxious months.

When Catherine decreed that, in mourning for her mother, the Court ladies should appear with their hair worn plain, and that they should not wear patches on their faces, Lady Castlemaine was openly annoyed. She was affecting the most elaborate styles for her hair and set great store by her patches. Several noticed that, with her hair plain and her face patchless, she was less strikingly beautiful than before.

This made her ill-humored indeed; and in view of the King's continued devotion to Frances Stuart, her temper was not improved.

As Catherine sat with her ladies one day in the spring, and Barbara happened to be among them, they talked of Charles.

Catherine said she feared his health had suffered through the terrible afflictions of last year. He had unwisely taken off his wig and pourpoint when he was on the river and the sun proved too hot; he had caught a chill and had not seemed to be well since then.

She turned to Barbara and said: "I fear it is not good for him to be out so late. He stays late at your house, and it would be better for his health if he did not do so."

Barbara let out a snort of laughter. "He does not stay late at my house, Madam," she said. "If he stays out late, then you must make inquiries in other directions. His Majesty spends his time with someone else."

The King had come into the apartment. He looked strained and ill; he was wondering where the money was coming from to equip his ships; he was wondering how he was going to pay his seamen, and whether it would be necessary to lay up the Fleet for lack of funds; and if that dire calamity should befall, how could he continue the war?

It seemed too much to be borne that Catherine and Barbara should be quarreling about how he spent his nights—those rare occasions when he sought a little relaxation in the only pastime which could bring him that forgetfulness which he eagerly sought.

He looked from Catherine to Barbara and his dark features were stern.

Catherine lowered her eyes but Barbara met his gaze defiantly. "Your Majesty will bear me out that I speak the truth," she said.

Charles said: "You are an impertinent woman."

Barbara flushed scarlet, but before she could give voice to the angry retorts which rose to her lips, Charles had continued quietly: "Leave the Court, and pray do not come again until you have word from me that I expect to see you."

Then, without waiting for the storm which his knowledge of Barbara made him certain must follow, he turned abruptly and left the apartment.

Barbara stamped her foot and glared at the company.

"Is anybody here smiling?" she demanded.

No one answered.

"If any see that which is amusing in this, let her speak up. I will see to it that she shall very soon find little to laugh at. As for the King, he may have a different tale to tell when I print the letters he has written to me!"

Then, curbing her rage, she curtsied to the Queen who sat stiff and awkward, not knowing how to deal with such an outrageous breach of good manners.

Barbara stamped out of the apartment.

But on calmer and saner reflection, considering the King's cares of state and his melancholy passion for Mrs. Stuart, she felt she would be wise, on this one occasion, to obey his command.

Barbara left the Court.

❁ ❁ ❁

Barbara was raging at Richmond. All those about her tried in vain to soothe her. She was warned of all the King had had to bear in the last few years; she was discreetly reminded of Frances Stuart.

"I'll get even with him!" she cried. "A nice thing if I should print his letters! Why, these Hollanders would have something to make pamphlets of then, would they not!"

Mrs. Sarah warned her. She must not forget that although Charles had been lenient with her, he was yet the King. It might be that he would forbid her not only the Court but the country; such things had happened.

"It is monstrous!" cried Barbara. "I have loved him long. It is six years since he came home, and I have loved him all that time."

"Others have been his rivals in your affections, and fellow guests in your bedchamber," Mrs. Sarah reminded her.

"And what of *his* affection and *his* bedchamber, eh?"

"He is the King. I wonder at his tenderness towards you."

"Be silent, you hag! I shall send for my furniture. Do not imagine I shall allow my treasures to remain at Whitehall."

"Send a messenger to the King," suggested Mrs. Sarah, "and first ask his permission to remove your possessions."

"Ask his permission! He is a fool. Any man is a fool who chases that simpering ninny, who stands and holds cards for her card houses, who allows himself so far to forget his rank as to play blind man's buff with an idiot."

"He might not grant that permission," suggested Mrs. Sarah.

"If he should refuse to let me have what is mine . . ."

"He might because he does not wish you to leave."

"You dolt! He has banished me."

"For your insolence before the Queen and her ladies. He may be regretting that now. You know how he comes back again and again to you. You know that no one will ever be quite the same as you are to him. Send that messenger, Madam."

Barbara gazed steadily at Mrs. Sarah. "Sarah, there are times when I think those who serve me are not all as doltish as I once thought them to be."

So she took Sarah's advice and asked the King's permission to withdraw her goods; the answer she had hoped for came to her: If she wished to take her goods away she must come and fetch them herself.

So, with her hair exquisitely curled, and adorned by a most becoming hat with a sweeping green feather, and looking her most handsome, she took barge to Whitehall. And when she was there she saw the King; and, taking one look at her, and feeling, as Mrs. Sarah had said he did, that no one was quite like Barbara, he admitted that her insolence at an awkward moment had made him a little hasty.

Barbara consented to remain at Whitehall. And that night the King supped in her apartments, and it was only just before the Palace was stirring to the activities of a new day that he left her and walked through the privy gardens to his own apartments.

❁ ❁ ❁

All that summer the fear of plague was in the hearts of the citizens of London; the heat of the previous summer was remembered, and the dreadful toll which had been taken of the population. Through the narrow streets of wooden houses, the gables of which almost met over the dark streets, the people walked wearily and there was the haunting fear on their faces. From the foul gutters rose the stink of putrefying rubbish; and it was remembered that two or three times in every hundred years over the centuries the grim visitor would appear like a legendary dragon, demanding its sacrifice and then, having taken its fill of victims, retreat before the cold weather only to strike again, none knew when.

Catherine found this time a particularly anxious one. She was worried about her brother Alphonso who she knew was unfit to wear the crown; she knew that Pedro, her younger brother, coveted it; and now that the restraining hand of her mother would not be there to guide them, she wondered continually about the fate of her native country.

The condition of her adopted country was none too happy at this time. She knew of Charles' anxieties. She knew too that he was beginning to despair of her ever giving him an heir. Again her hopes had been disappointed. Why was it that so many Queens found it hard to give their husbands sons, while those same Kings' mistresses bore them as a matter of course? Barbara had borne yet another child—this time a handsome boy, whom she called

George Fitzroy. Barbara had, as well as her voluptuous person, a nursery full of children who might be the King's.

In June of the year which followed that of the great plague the Dutch and English fleets met. De Ruyter and Van Tromp were in charge of the Dutchmen, and the English Fleet was under Albemarle. There were ninety Dutch ships opposed to fifty English, and when the battle had been in progress for more than a day, the Dutch were joined by sixteen sail. Fortunately Prince Rupert joined the Duke of York and a mighty battle was the result; both sides fought so doggedly and so valiantly that neither was victorious; but, although the English sank fifteen Dutch ships and the Dutch but ten English, the Dutch had invented chain shot with which they ruined the rigging of many more of the English ships; and all the latter had to retire into harbor for refitting.

Yet a few weeks later they were in action once more, and this resulted in victory for the English, with few English losses and the destruction of twenty Dutch men-of-war.

When the news reached England, the bells rang out in every town and hamlet and there was general rejoicing in London which, but a year ago, had been like a dead and desolate city.

These celebrations took place on the 14th of August. Hopes were high that ere long these proud and insolent Dutchmen would realize who would rule the sea.

It was less than two weeks later when, in the house of Mr. Farryner, the King's baker, who lived in Pudding Lane, fire broke out in the early morning; and as there was a strong east wind blowing and the baker's house was made of wood, as were those of his neighbors, in a few hours all Pudding Lane and Fish Street were ablaze and the streets were filled with shouting people who, certain that their efforts to quench the raging furnace were in vain while the high wind persisted, merely dragged out their goods from those houses which were in danger of being caught by the flames, wringing their hands, and declaring that the vengeance of God was turned upon the City.

Through the night, made light as day by the fires, people shouted to each other to come forth and flee. The streets were filled with those whose one object was to salvage as many of their household goods as was possible; and the wind grew fiercer as house after house fell victim to the flames. People with blackened faces called to each other that this was the end of the world. God had called vengeance on London, cried some, for the profligate ways of its people. Last year the plague and the Dutch wars, and now they were all to be destroyed by fire!

Showers of sparks shot into the air and fell like burning rain when a warehouse containing barrels of pitch and tar sent the blaze roaring to the sky. The river had suddenly become jammed with small craft, as frantic householders gathered as many as possible of their goods together and sought the green fields beyond the City for safety. Many poor people stood regarding their houses with the utmost despair, their arms grasping homely bundles, both to leave their homes until the very last minute. Pigeons, which habitually sheltered in the lofts of these houses, hovered piteously near their old refuge and many were lying dead and dying on the cobbles below, their wings burned, their bodies scorched.

And all through the night the wind raged, and the fire raged with it.

❁ ❁ ❁

Early next morning Mr. Samuel Pepys, Secretary of the Navy, reached Whitehall and asked for an audience with the King; he told him all that was happening in the City, and begged him to give instant orders that houses be demolished, for only thus could such a mighty conflagration be brought to a halt. The King agreed that the houses which stood in the way of the fire must be pulled down, as only by making such gaps could the conflagration be halted, and gave orders that this should be done.

Pepys hurried back to the City and found the Lord Mayor in Cannon Street from where he was watching the fire and shouting in vain to the crowds, imploring them to listen to him, and try to fight the fire.

"What can I do?" he cried. "People will not obey me. I have been up all night. I shall surely faint if I stay here. What can I do? What can any do in such a raging wind?"

The Secretary, thinking the man was more like a fainting woman than a Lord Mayor, repeated the King's order.

"I have tried pulling down houses," wailed the Lord Mayor. "But the fire overtakes us faster than we can work."

They stood together, watching the flames which, in some places, seemed to creep stealthily at first, as tongues of fire licked the buildings and then suddenly, with a mighty roar, would appear to capture yet another; the sound of falling roofs and walls was everywhere; the flames ran swiftly and lightly along the thatches; now many streets were avenues of flame. People screamed as the fire drops caught them; flames spread like an arch from one side of London Bridge to the other; the air was filled with the crackling sound of burning and the crash of collapsing houses. It was almost impossible to breathe the dense smoke-filled air.

❁ ❁ ❁

On Tuesday morning the fire was still raging, and the King decided that he dared no longer leave the defense of his capital to the Lord Mayor and the City Fathers.

Fleet Street, the Old Bailey, Ludgate Hill, Warwick Lane, Newgate, Paul's Chain and Watling Street were all ablaze. The heat was so fierce that none could approach near the fire, and when a roof fell in, great showers of sparks would fly out from the burning mass to alight on other dwellings and so start many minor fires.

The King with his brother, the Duke of York, were in the center of activity. It was they who directed the blowing up of houses in Tower Street. The citizens of London saw their King then, not as the careless philanderer, but the man of action. It was he, his face blackened by smoke, who directed the operations which were to save the City. There he stood passing the buckets with his own hands, shouting to all that their help was needed and they would be rewarded for the work they did this day. There he stood, with the dirty water over his ankles, encouraging and, being the man he was, not forgetting to joke. It was while he stood in their midst that the people ceased to believe those stories which the Puritans had murmured about God's vengeance. This fire was nothing but the result of an accident which had taken place in a baker's kitchen and, on account of the high wind, the dry wood and thatch of the houses all huddled so closely together, had turned the fire in Pudding Lane into the Fire of London.

By Thursday the fire showed signs of being conquered. The heat from smoldering buildings was still intense; fires raged in some parts of the City, but that great ravaging monster had been checked.

It was said that day that all that was left of London owed its existence to the King and his brother James.

❁ ❁ ❁

Now it was possible to look back and see the extent of the disaster.

The fire, following so soon on the plague, had robbed the country of the greater part of its wealth. London was the center of the kingdoms riches, for more than a tenth of the population had lived in the Capital. Now the greater part of the City lay in ruins, and for months afterwards ashes, charred beams and broken pieces of furniture were found in the fields of the villages of Knightsbridge and Kensington; and the people marveled that the effects of the great fire could still be seen at such great distance.

But there were more terrible effects to be felt. In the fields the homeless huddled together, having nowhere to go. The King rode out to them, bags of money at his belt; he distributed alms and ordered that food and shelter should be found for these sufferers.

His heart was heavy. He knew that never before in her history had England been in such a wretched plight. There was murmuring all over the country and in particular throughout the stricken City. England was no longer merry, and people were beginning to think of the period of Puritan rule as the "good old days." The wildest rumors were in the air. New terrors stalked the smoldering streets. The fire was the work of Papists, said some. Those who were suspected of following the Catholic religion were seized and ill-treated and some were done to death by the mob. Feeling ran high against the Queen. She was a Papist, and trouble had started during the last King's reign, declared the people, on account of his Papist wife. Others said the profligate life led by the King and his associates was responsible for the fire.

"This is but the beginning," cried some. "The destruction of England is at hand. First the plague; then the war; and now the great fire. This is Sodom and Gomorrah again. What next? What next?"

The King realized that there was nothing to be done but lay up the Fleet, for where in his suffering country could he get means to maintain it? And to lay up the Fleet meant suing for peace.

Sailors were rioting in the stricken City's streets because they had not been paid. There was revolution in the air. Charles himself rode out to do what he could to disperse the groups of angry seamen. In vain did his Chancellor and those about him seek to restrain him. His subjects were in an ugly mood; insults had been hurled at the King on account of his way of life. But Charles insisted on going among them. He was bankrupt in all save that one thing which had stood him in good stead all his life; his charm was inviolate as was his courage.

So he rode out into the midst of the brawling crowds of angry sailors who stood about in the heart of the City amid the blackened buildings and heaps of ashes and rubble. He knew their mood; yet he was smiling, with that charming rueful smile. His manner was dignified, yet all those men were aware of the easy affability which had always been shown to any who came near him whatever their rank, and which had done much to make all submit to his charm.

They fell back before him; they would have expected him to come with soldiers behind him; but he came alone, and he came unarmed. So they fell back before him and they were silent as he spoke to them.

It was true they had not been paid. The King would remedy that as soon as it were possible to do so. They had fought gallantly. Would they tell themselves that they had fought for their country, and would that suffice for a temporary reward? He promised them that they should be paid—in time. They would be wise men to wait for that payment rather than to persist in acts which would lead themselves and others into misfortune likely to end in the traitor's fate on the gallows.

They had all suffered terribly. The plague last year; the fire this. Never in the country's history had such calamities befallen it. Yet had they not given good account of insolent Dutchmen? Let them all stand together; and if they would do this, their King doubted not that ere long they would have little cause for complaint.

Then suddenly someone in the crowd cried: "Long live the King!" and then others joined in and helped to disperse the mob.

On that occasion trouble had been avoided, but revolt continued to hang in the air.

The people looked about them for a scapegoat and, as usual at such times, their thoughts turned to the Chancellor. Crowds gathered outside the fine house he had built for himself in Piccadilly; they murmured to one another that he had built the palace with the bribes he had been paid by the French King to advise the selling of Dunkirk. It was remembered that he, the commoner, was linked with the royal family through the marriage of his daughter Anne Hyde with the King's brother. It was said that he had procured Catherine of Braganza for the King because he knew she would never bear children and thus leave the succession clear for the offspring of his own daughter. Everything that was wrong in the country was blamed on Clarendon; and this attitude towards the poor Chancellor was aggravated by such men as Buckingham—urged on by Lady Castlemaine—Arlington, and almost all the King's ministers.

A gibbet was set up on a tree outside the Chancellor's house, and on it was an inscription:

"Three sights to be seen—Dunkirk, Tangier and a barren Queen."

For the sale of Dunkirk, the possession of an unprofitable seaport and the Queen's inability to bear children successfully were all laid at Clarendon's door.

The King sought to throw off his melancholy and was already instructing his architect, Christopher Wren, to make plans for the rebuilding of the City; he was urging the Parliament to find money somehow for the refitting of his ships that they might, with the coming of spring, be ready to face their Dutch enemies. He sought to find consolation among the many ladies who charmed him, but he found that his desire for the still unconquered Frances Stuart made contentment impossible.

❁ ❁ ❁

There were men about the King now who, perceiving his infatuation for Frances Stuart, reminded him of how his predecessor, Henry VIII, had acted in similar circumstances. Chief among these was the Duke of Buckingham who, much to Barbara's annoyance, had made himself chief adviser and supporter of Frances Stuart.

What if there were a divorce? The Queen's religion displeased the people. After the disaster of the fire it could easily be suggested that this had been started by Papists. No English man or woman would desire then to see the King remain married to a member of that wicked sect. Moreover, the Queen was barren and surely that was a good enough reason for divorcing her. It was necessary for the King to have an heir and Charles had proved again and again that he was not to blame for this unfruitful marriage.

"It should not be difficult to obtain a divorce," said Buckingham. "Then Your Majesty would be free to marry a lady of your own choice. I doubt that Mrs. Stuart would say no to a crown."

The King was tempted. Frances had become an obsession. Through her he was losing his merry good humor. He was angry far more often than he used to be. He was melancholy; he wanted to be alone, whereas previously he had enjoyed company; he was spending more and more time in his laboratory with his chemists, but what compensation could that offer? It was Frances whom he wanted; he was in love. If Frances would become his mistress he was sure that he could forget, for long spells at a time, the sorry condition of his realm and all the troubles that were facing him.

Then he remembered Catherine—the Catherine of the honeymoon—so naively eager to please him, so simple, so loving. He had wronged her when he had made her accept Barbara. No! In spite of his love for Frances he would not agree to ill-treat Catherine.

He continued melancholy; but his temper blazed out when Clarendon again took up his tutorial attitude towards him.

"It is more important to Your Majesty to give attention to state matters than to saunter and toy with Lady Castlemaine." How often had the man said those or similar words, and how often had they been received with a tolerant smile!

Now the Chancellor was told to look to his own house and not try to set that of his master in order.

Clarendon was unrepentant; he prided himself on his forthright manners. He knew he was unpopular but he did not care; he said that all that mattered to him was that he should do his duty.

The Chancellor began to look upon Frances Stuart as an unhealthy influence, and thought that the best thing she could do was to marry. Her cousin, the Duke of Richmond—another Charles Stuart—was one of the many young men who were in love with her and having recently become a widower was eager to marry her. He was rich, of high rank, being distantly related to the King as Frances was. The Chancellor therefore called the young Duke to him and urged him to continue with his wooing. And when he had seen him and discovered that was just what the young man was most eager to do, he sought an audience with the Queen.

They looked at each other—Queen and Chancellor.

Catherine's appearance had not been improved by all she had suffered. She knew of the people's animosity towards herself; she knew that they hated her because she was a Catholic, and concocted rhymes about her which they sang in the streets; and that these rhymes were witty and ribald after the manner of the day.

She guessed too that certain of the King's ministers had spoken against her, because Charles had been particularly kind to her of late, which meant, she realized now that she had come to know him, that he felt sorry for her and was doubtless urging himself not to listen to his ministers' advice.

There was a numb desolation in Catherine's heart. She knew that they were advising him to rid himself of her. What would become of her? she wondered. Whither should she go? Home to Portugal where her brothers wrangled for the crown, a disgraced Queen, turned away by her husband because she could not bear him children and had failed to win his love and that of his subjects? No! She could not go back to Portugal. What was there for her, but a nunnery! She thought of the years stretching out ahead of her—she was a young woman still—of matins and complines, of bells and prayers; and all the time within her there would be longings which she must stifle, for whatever happened she would never forget Charles; she would love him until the day she died.

Last night he had stayed with her; he had resisted all temptation to go to one of his mistresses. She had been sick and overtaken with trembling, so fearful was she of what the future held for her.

How she despised herself! When she had the opportunity of being with him she was unable to make use of it. How could she hope to arouse anything but pity within him? His kindness she enjoyed was due, not to her attractiveness nor her cleverness, but merely to his goodness of heart. When she had been sick it was he who had brought the basin, and held her head and spoken soothing words; it was he who had called her women, to make her clean and comfortable, while uncomplaining he left the royal bed and moved to another room.

She could enjoy his kindness, but never his love.

Those were her thoughts when Clarendon was shown into her presence.

The Chancellor spoke in his usual blunt but somewhat pompous and authoritative manner.

"Your Majesty will have heard rumors concerning Mrs. Stuart?"

"Yes, my lord, that is true," agreed Catherine.

"I am sure Your Majesty will agree with me that the Court would be a happier place if Mrs. Stuart were married, and mayhap left it for a while. Her cousin, the Duke of Richmond, would be an excellent match. It would be well for those of us who wish Mrs. Stuart good to do all in our power to bring such a match about."

"You are right, my lord."

"Perhaps a word to the Duke from Your Majesty would be of use; and, as Mrs. Stuart's mistress, Your Majesty might see that the young people have every opportunity to meet."

Catherine clenched her hands tightly together and said: "I will do all in my power to bring this matter to a happy conclusion."

Clarendon was pleased. He, the Queen and the Duke of Richmond were determined to bring about this marriage. There was one other who would be equally delighted to see it take place. That was Lady Castlemaine. And if Frances herself could be made to realize the advantages of the match, it must surely come about.

❁ ❁ ❁

Barbara, whose spies were numerous, discovered that the Duke of Richmond was often in the company of Frances Stuart and that the conversations which took place between them were of a tender nature. Infuriated by the rumors she had heard of the King's contemplating a divorce that he might marry Frances, Barbara had one object in mind—and that was to ruin Frances in the King's eyes.

She did not believe that Frances was seriously contemplating marriage with her cousin, the Duke of Richmond. What woman, thought Barbara scornfully, would become a Duchess when the prospect of becoming a Queen was dangling before her?

She suspected Frances of being very sly and, in spite of her apparent ingenuousness, very clever. Barbara could be angry with herself when she came to believe that she, no less than others, had been duped by Frances's apparent simplicity.

No! said Barbara. What the sly creature is doing is holding on to her virtue where the King is concerned, following the example of other ladies in history such as Elizabeth Woodville and Anne Boleyn. It may even be that she is not averse to entertaining a lover in private!

One day she discovered through her spies that the Duke of Richmond was in Frances' apartment, and she lost no time in seeking out the King.

She waved away his attendants in a manner which annoyed him, but he did not reprove her for this until they had left.

Then she shouted at him: "Would you have them remain to hear what I have to say? Would you have them know—though doubtless they do already—what a fool Frances Stuart makes of you?"

The King's calmness could always be shaken by the mention of Frances, and he demanded to know to what she referred.

"We are so virtuous, are we not?" mimicked Barbara. "We cannot be your mistress because we are so pure." Her blue eyes flashed, and her anger blazed forth. "Oh, no, no, no! We cannot be your mistress because we think you may be fool enough to make us your Queen."

"Be silent!" cried the King. "You shall leave the Court. I'll never look on your face again."

"No? Then go and look on hers now. . . . Go and catch her and her lover together, and then thank me for showing you what a fool that sly slut has made of you."

"What is this?" demanded the King.

"Nothing. . . . Nothing at all. Merely that your pure little *virgin* is at this moment languishing in the arms of another Charles Stuart. It would seem that she hath a fancy for the name. Only one is a King and to be dangled on a string, and the other . . . is merely a Duke, so there is no sense in being *quite* so pure with him."

"You lie," growled the King.

"You are afraid of what you'll discover. Go to her apartment now. Go . . . Go! And then thank me for opening your besotted eyes."

The King turned and hurried from the room. He went immediately to Frances's apartments; he pushed aside her attendants and went straight into that chamber where Frances was lying on a couch and the Duke of Richmond was sitting beside her holding her hand.

The King stood, legs apart, looking at them.

The Duke sprang to his feet. Frances did likewise.

"Sire . . ." began the Duke.

"Get out of here," said the King ominously; and the Duke backed to the door and hurried away.

"So," said the King, turning to Frances, "you entertain your lovers alone at times. Did you find his proposals to your liking?"

Frances said: "They were honorable proposals."

"Honorable! And he here alone in your apartment?"

"Your Majesty must see that . . ."

"I know nothing of your behavior to this man," said the King. "I can only draw conclusions, and I see this: that you, who have been so careful not to be alone with me, employ not the same care in his case."

Frances had never seen Charles angry with her before, and she was alarmed; but she did not tremble before him; she knew he would not harm her.

She said: "Your Majesty, the Duke came hither to talk to me in an honorable fashion. He has no wife."

"How far has this gone?"

"No farther than you saw. How could it? I would never submit to any man except my husband."

"And you plan that he shall be that?"

"I plan nothing . . . yet."

"Then he should not be here in your apartments."

"Are the customs of the Court changing then?"

"We have always heard that you were set apart, that you did not accept the standards of the rest of us frail folk."

He took her by the shoulders suddenly; his face was dark with passion.

"Frances," he pleaded. "Have done with folly. Why do you so long hold out against me?"

She was frightened; she wrenched herself free and, running to the wall, clutched at the hangings as though childishly wishing to hide herself among them.

"I beg of Your Majesty to leave me," she said.

She realized that his anger was still with him. He said: "One day mayhap you will be ugly and willing! I await that day with pleasure."

Then he left her, and she knew that her relationship with the King had taken a new turn.

❁ ❁ ❁

Frances, her fear still upon her, sought audience with the Queen.

She threw herself at Catherine's feet and burst into tears.

"Your Majesty," she cried, "I beg of you to help me. I am afraid. I have aroused the wrath of the King, and I have never seen him angry before. I fear that when his wrath is aroused it is more terrible than in those to whom anger comes more often."

"You had better tell me what has happened," said Catherine.

"He disturbed me with the Duke. He was furious with us both. The Duke has fled from Court. I know not what to do. He has never looked at me as he did then. He suspected . . . I know not what."

"I think," said Catherine sadly, "that he will not long be displeased with you."

"It is not that I fear his displeasure, Your Majesty. He believes the Duke to be my lover; and I fear he will not have the same respect for me as hitherto."

"That may be true," agreed Catherine.

She felt then that she hated the beautiful face which was turned up to hers, hated it as much as she hated that other bold and arrogant one. These women with their beauty! It was cruel that they should have the power to take so easily that for which she longed, and longed in vain.

At that moment she would have given her rank and all she possessed to be in Frances Stuart's place, loved and desired by the King.

He was angry with this girl, she was thinking; yet with me he never cared enough to be anything but kind.

She was aware of a rising passion within herself. She longed to rid the Court of all these women who claimed his attention. She believed he was tiring of Barbara, whose continual tantrums were at last wearing him down; but this young girl with her matchless beauty and her girlish ways was different. He loved this girl; he had even contemplated making her his wife. Catherine was sure of this.

She said suddenly: "If you married the Duke you would have a husband to protect you. You would show the King that he was mistaken in thinking you had taken a lover. Would you marry the Duke? He is the best match you could make."

"Yes," said Frances, "if it were possible. I would marry the Duke."

"Can you keep a secret?"

"But of course, Madam."

"Then say nothing of this, but be ready to leave the Palace should the summons come."

"Whither should I go?"

"To marriage with the Duke."

"He has gone away. I do not know where he is."

"Others will have means of knowing," said the Queen. "Now go to your room and rest. Be ready to leave the Palace if need be."

When Frances had gone, Catherine marveled at herself. I have come alive, she mused. I am fighting for what I desire more than anything on Earth. I have ceased to sit placidly waiting for what I want. Like others, I go out to get it.

Then she summoned one of her women and bade her bring the Chancellor to her.

Clarendon came, and they talked long and secretly together.

The King's fury and sorrow, when he learned that Frances had eloped, was boundless.

He could not bear to think of Frances and her Duke together. He knew the young husband to be a worthless person, a devotee of the bottle, and he did not believe that Frances was in love with him. That she should have chosen such a man increased his rage. He declared he would never see

Frances again. He blamed himself for having caused that scene in her apartments; he suspected several people of being concerned in helping the lovers to elope, and he vowed that he would never forgive them. The only person he did not suspect was the Queen.

He believed Clarendon to be the prime mover in the affair, and both Buckingham and Barbara confirmed this belief.

Barbara was delighted. Not only was she rid of her most dangerous rival, but Clarendon was in disgrace because of it.

The King's natural easy temper deserted him on this occasion. He accused Clarendon and his son, Lord Cornbury, of conspiring to bring about the elopement, and for once would not let them speak in their defense. He was unable to hide his grief. All the Court now understood the depth of his feeling for Frances and that it was very different from the light emotions he felt for his mistresses.

This was the most unhappy time of his life. He dreaded the coming of the spring when his ships, still laid up and in need of repairs, would be required to set out to face their enemies; he did not know how he was going to make good the country's losses which were a direct result of the plague and the fire.

His position was wretched, and there was only one person at that time who could have made him feel that life was worthwhile. Now he had to think of her—for he could not stop thinking of her—in the arms of another man.

His rage and grief stayed with him; and at length he turned to one whose very outspoken vulgarity seemed to soothe him.

Barbara was in the ascendant again, and it seemed that the King was spending as much time with her as he had in the first days of his infatuation.

Barbara was determined that Buckingham should not go unpunished for his support of Frances Stuart, which was blatantly inimical to her interests.

Buckingham had become involved with a woman, notorious for her love affairs. This was Lady Shrewsbury, a plump, languorous beauty whose lovers were said to be as numerous as those of Barbara herself. She was a woman who seemed to incite men to violence, and several duels had been fought on her account. When he fell under her spell, Buckingham appeared to become more reckless than even he had been before, and was continually engaged in quarreling with almost everyone with whom he came into contact. His passion for Lady Shrewsbury increased as the months passed. He followed her wherever she went; and she was by no means loath to add the brilliant and witty, as well as rich and handsome, Duke to her list of lovers. On their first meeting, the Earl of Shrewsbury had quarreled with Buckingham, but neither Lady Shrewsbury nor Buckingham took the slightest notice of their marriage vows; and both the Earl and Lady Buckingham should, from their long experience, not have expected them to take such notice. Buckingham could not tear himself away from his new love; he was drinking heavily; he quarreled with Lord Falconbridge, and the quarrel threatened to end in a duel. He tried to quarrel with Clarendon; he attacked the Duke of Ormond; at a committee meeting he pulled the nose of the Marquess of Worcester; he insulted Prince Rupert in the street, whereupon the Prince pulled him off his horse and challenged him on the spot. Only the King could pacify his infuriated cousin. There was a quarrel at the theater whither he had gone with Lady Shrewsbury. Harry Killigrew, who was in the next box and was one of Lady Shrewsbury's discarded lovers, began attacking them both and shouting to all in the theater that Lady Shrewsbury had been his mistress—and declaring indeed there was not a man in the theater who might not aspire to the lady's favors, for she was insatiable in her demand for lovers—and that if the Duke believed he was her sole lover they could wager the very shirts on their backs that he was wrong.

The audience watched with great interest while the Duke ordered Killigrew to be quiet, and Lady Shrewsbury leaned forward in her box, sleepy-eyed, half smiling; for, next to getting men to make love to her, she liked setting them to fight each other; nor did she in the least mind being stared at.

Killigrew drew his sword and struck the Duke with the flat side of it. Buckingham thereupon sprang out of his own box and into Killigrew's, but Killigrew had already leaped out of his and was scuttling across the theater. The Duke flew after him, to the delight of the audience who found this far more entertaining than the play which was being performed on the stage. The Duke caught Killigrew, snatched off his periwig and threw it high in the air; then he set upon the man until he begged for mercy.

Killigrew was given a short term of imprisonment for the offense, and banished; and Barbara persuaded the King that her relative should also be banished until he learned to be less quarrelsome.

So Buckingham departed for the country, taking with him his wife and Lady Shrewsbury. There, he declared, he was content to stay. He had his music and his mistress, his chemists and his uncomplaining wife.

He knew though that Barbara was responsible for his banishment, and he promised himself that he would not let her escape punishment altogether, although he agreed that in trying to promote a marriage between Frances and the King he had not acted in the interest of his fiery cousin.

In his pastoral retreat he would have stayed, had not one of those men, who had professed to be his friends, made an accusation of high treason against him; the charge was of forecasting the King's death by horoscope.

He was ordered to return to London and sent to the Tower.

Barbara was now furious that a member of her family should be so imprisoned. She had merely wished that he should receive a light rap over the knuckles for having supported Frances's interest against hers.

She had forgotten that the King was no longer in love with her, and that it was only his acute sorrow in the loss of Frances which had made him turn to her. She believed her power to be as great as it had ever been, and she strode into his apartments, as soon as she heard the news, and cried aloud: "What means this? You would imprison your best servant on the false testimony of rogues!"

The King cried in exasperation: "You are a meddling jade who dabbles in things of which she knows nothing."

Barbara was furious. "You are a fool!" she shouted, not caring who heard her.

"Be careful!" he warned.

"Fool! Fool! Fool!" was Barbara's retort. "If you were not one, you would not suffer your business to be carried on by fools that do not understand it, and cause your best subjects and those best able to serve you to be imprisoned."

"Have done, you evil woman," cried the King.

He strode away and left her; she fumed up and down the apartment, declaring that ere long she would have her cousin free. It should be learned that any who dared imprison a noble Villiers was the enemy of the entire family.

By that she meant Clarendon.

And it was not long before Barbara had her way. No case could be proved against Buckingham. The paper on which he was supposed to have drawn up the horoscope was given to the King, who confronted Buckingham with it; but the Duke declared he had never before seen it, and asked the King if he did not recognize his (Buckingham's) sister's writing upon it.

"Why, 'tis the result of some frolic of hers about another person whose birthday happens to be the same as Your Majesty's. Your Majesty's name does not appear on the paper."

The King studied the paper afresh; he considered the whole matter to be too trivial for his attention, and he said so.

"Have done with this business," he cried. "There is no need to press the matter further."

Buckingham was released, though he was wise enough to know that he must not yet appear at Court.

Clarendon had imprisoned him. He decided, and Barbara agreed, that Clarendon's day must soon be over.

❁ ❁ ❁

The Fleet was crippled; the navy in debt to the extent of over a million pounds. There were two alternatives: not to repair the ships but to keep them laid up, and sue for peace; or bankruptcy.

Charles, with his brother, their cousin Rupert, and Albemarle passionately declared that the ships should be refitted at whatever cost to the nation; but the will of the Council prevailed.

The Dutch, however, were not prepared to make an easy peace. Why should they? They had had peaceful months in which to refit their ships; they had spent three times as much on the war as the English had. They believed that action was better than words at a conference table; and they were not going to lay up their ships merely because their enemy had been forced to do so.

It seemed to all Englishmen in the years to come that in June of the year 1667 there fell upon their land the greatest calamity which had ever touched its pride and honor.

On that warm summer's day some nine months after the Fire of London, the Dutch fleet sailed up the Medway as far as Chatham. They burned the *Royal Oak,* the *Royal James* and the *Loyal London,* together with other men-of-war; they blew up the fortifications and, towing the *Royal Charles,* they returned the way they had come, while their trumpeters impudently played the old English song "Joan's Placket is Torn"; and on either side of the river Englishmen looked on, powerless to prevent them.

Crippled by the great plague and the great fire of London, England suffered the most shameful defeat of her history.

❁ ❁ ❁

The people were numb with shame and anger.

They could not understand how such an insult could be aimed at them. They had believed they were winning the war against Holland. They had shown themselves to be seamen equal to—nay, better than—the Dutchmen. They had not been defeated in action. It was plague and fire which had defeated them, together with the threat of bankruptcy.

Revolution was again in the air. Much money had been raised for the conduct of the war; why then had it come to such a shameful end?

Someone was wrong. Someone must be blamed. And it was the custom to look to the most unpopular man in the kingdom on whom to fix blame.

Mobs pulled up the trees in front of Clarendon's Piccadilly house. It was true, shouted the people, that he had betrayed them. Was he not the friend of the French, and were the French not siding with the Dutch enemies of England? Who had sold Dunkirk? Who had married the King to a barren Queen that his own grandchildren might inherit the throne of England?

The people needed a scapegoat and, as Charles studied their mood, he knew that they must have him before Parliament reassembled.

Clarendon had been universally disliked since the early days of the Restoration; never had a man possessed more enemies. But for Charles' protection over the last years, he would have long ago been set down from his high post.

Now Charles himself no longer desired his services. He had grown tired of the man's continual reproaches. No Chancellor should speak to a King as Clarendon talked to his. Charles had always been ready to listen to reproaches from men of virtue, because he knew that he himself was far from virtuous. He had always maintained that every man had a right to his opinion and to the expression of that opinion. It was a view with which Clarendon had not approved. But, thought Charles, while those virtuous people, who spoke their minds freely concerning the faults of others, might in many cases have right on their side, they became increasingly unattractive; moreover it was other people's faults which they surveyed with such contempt, while they were apt to turn a blind eye to their own. Such as Clarendon believed that if a man lived a pious life and was faithful to one woman—and she his wife—intolerance, cruelty and carelessness of the feelings of others were no sins. That is where I differ, thought Charles; for I hold malice to be the greatest of sins; and I cannot believe that God would wish to make a man miserable for the sake of taking a little pleasure out of his way.

But Clarendon must go. The country was demanding it; and if he stayed, the people might be incited to revolution. Moreover, Charles did not feel inclined to protect a man who, he was sure, had done everything in his power to rob him of Frances Stuart.

But he did not wish Clarendon to suffer more than need be. He remembered the good advice the old man had given him when he was a wandering prince.

So he called the Duke of York to him—for, after all, James was Clarendon's son-in-law—and they talked together concerning the Chancellor.

"He has to go," said Charles.

James did not think so. James was a fool, alas. Charles wondered what would happen to him if he lived to wear the crown, which might easily come to pass, as he, Charles, was possessed, it would seem, of a barren wife.

"He is blamed for the conduct of the war," said Charles. "Did you not know that on the day the Dutch sailed up the Medway the mob broke his windows and pulled down the trees before his house?"

"He is not to blame. He took little part in the conduct of the war and only agreed to the suggestions of the experts."

"People rage against him. They say he has excluded the right men from ministerial posts and given those posts to those whom he considered to be of the nobility. Since you made his daughter a possible queen, he has, you will admit, been inclined to be haughty to the more lowly."

James' mouth was stubborn. Charles knew that in supporting his father-in-law he was obeying his wife, for James was known to be under Anne Hyde's control. Only a short while ago, Charles remembered, he had likened his brother to the henpecked husband in *Epicene,* or *The Silent Woman,* a play which had afforded him much amusement. Charles remembered ruefully that when he had mentioned this, one of the wits who surrounded him—and whom he had ordered to forget "His Majesty" in the cause of wit—had wanted to know whether it was better to be henpecked by a mistress than a wife.

That made him think momentarily of Barbara. He was wishing that he could rid himself of her. Her rages were becoming more and more unbearable; they ceased to amuse as they had once done. If only Frances were at Court, and amenable!

The memory of Frances turned his thoughts back to Clarendon who, he was sure, had done his best to arrange Frances' marriage.

He said: "The people accuse him of advising me to rule without a Parliament."

"That," said James, "was what our father tried to do."

"I have no intention of doing it. James, face the truth. The peace we have concluded with the French and Dutch at Breda is a shameful one. The people must have a scapegoat. They demand a scapegoat, and none will do but Clarendon. Do you know that I have been threatened with the same fate which befell our father if I do not part with him? As for myself, his behavior and humors are insupportable to me and all the world else. I can no longer live with it. I must do those things which must be done with the Parliament, or the Government will be lost. James, do you want to set out on your wanderings once more? Have you forgotten the Hague and Paris? Have you forgotten what it means to be an exile? But mayhap we were lucky to be exiles. Our father was less fortunate. Be practical, brother. Be reasonable. He is your father-in-law. He was my old friend. I forget not his services to me. Do not let his enemies seize him and make a prisoner of him. God knows what would be his fate if he were taken to the Tower. Go to him now. Urge him to retire of his own free will. I doubt not that then he will be saved much trouble."

The Duke at length saw the wisdom of his brother's plan and agreed to do this.

❁ ❁ ❁

After his interview with the Duke of York, Clarendon came to see the King. He still spoke in the manner of a schoolmaster. "And have you forgotten the days of your exile so soon then?" he asked. "Can you be so ungrateful as to cast off an old and faithful servant?"

Charles was moved to pity. He said: "I warn you. I am sure that you will be impeached when the next Parliament sits. Too many are your enemies. If you value your own safety, resign now. Avoid the indignity of being forced to do so."

"Resign! I have been your chief minister ever since you were a King in fact—and indeed before that. Resign because my enemies blame me for the Dutch disaster! Your Majesty knows that my policy was not responsible for that defeat."

Charles said: "The plague, the fire, our lack of money—they are responsible for our disasters. I know that, my friend. I know it. But you have many enemies, many who have determined on your ruin. You are growing old. Why should you not spend your remaining days in comfortable retirement? That is what I should wish for you. I implore you, give up the Seal on your own account, before they take it from you and inflict God knows what. They are in an ugly mood."

"I shall never give up the Seal unless forced to do so," said Clarendon.

Charles lifted his shoulders and left the apartment.

❁ ❁ ❁

Barbara knew that Clarendon was with the King; she knew that the old man was receiving his dismissal. She was hilarious in her delight. For years she had worked for this—ever since the day he had refused to allow his wife to visit her.

Now she waited in her bedchamber and joked with those who had gathered round her to witness what they knew to be the humiliating dismissal of the Chancellor.

"Who was he to forbid his wife to see me!" demanded Barbara. "I was the King's mistress; his daughter was the Duke's before she duped him into making her his wife. And do you remember how he disowned her . . . how he declared he would rather see her James' mistress than his wife! Yet he thought his family too fine . . . too virtuous to consort with me. Old fool! Mayhap he wishes he had not been so fine and virtuous now."

"He has left the King," cried one of her friends. "He comes across the gardens now."

Barbara ran out into her aviary that she might not miss the sight of the old man's humiliation.

"There he goes!" she called. "There goes the man who was the Chancellor. Look you! He holds not his head so high as he once did."

Then she broke into peals of mocking laughter, in which her companions joined.

Clarendon walked quickly on as though he did not hear them.

❁ ❁ ❁

Clarendon's enemies, led by Buckingham, were not content with Clarendon's dismissal. They were determined to arraign him on a charge of high treason. Charges were drawn up, among which was one accusing him of betraying the King's confidences to foreign Powers, and as this was nothing less than high treason it was clear that his enemies were after the ex-Chancellor's blood.

Charles was perturbed. He agreed that Clarendon was too old for his task, that his manner caused nothing but trouble to all those—including the King himself—who came into contact with him; he knew that his enemies had determined to destroy him.

He wished to be rid of Clarendon; yet he would not stand by and see an old friend forced to the executioner's block if he could help it.

He sent word in secret to Clarendon, telling him that unless he left the country at once he would find himself facing a trial for high treason.

Clarendon at last saw reason.

On the night after he had received Charles' message he was on his way to Calais.

❁ ❁ ❁

Barbara was delighted with the dismissal of Clarendon. She felt that her ascendancy over Charles was regained. She was congratulating herself on the disgrace of Frances Stuart who, she was sure, had wounded the King's *amour propre* to such an extent that she would never be taken back into favor again.

Barbara laughed over the affairs of Mrs. Stuart and Clarendon with her newest lover—little Henry Jermyn, one of the worst rakes at Court, and one of the smallest men to be met there; it was amusing to have for lovers the little Jermyn and the six-foot-tall King. Barbara was momentarily contented.

As for Catherine, she was hopeful. She did not believe that Charles was really in love with Barbara, and she knew that he was deeply wounded by the elopement of Frances; she often rode out with the King, and the people who, blaming Clarendon for the Dutch disaster, had taken Charles back completely into their affection, would cheer them.

Everywhere the King went was sung the latest song from the play *Catch that Catch Can* or *The Musical Companion*; and it was sung wholeheartedly.

"Here's a health unto His Majesty,
With a fa, la, la;
Conversion to his enemies,
With a fa, la, la.
And he that will not pledge his health,
I wish him neither wit nor wealth,
Nor yet a rope to hang himself,
With a fa, la, la."

Catherine would discuss with Charles his plans for rebuilding the City and, as he seemed to ceased mourning over past failures and had his eyes firmly fixed on the future, she found that she could follow his lead.

If only she could have a child! Then she believed that, with his own legitimate son and a wife who was ready to love him so tenderly, she and Charles could build a very happy relationship. God knew that she was willing and she could not believe that he, who was the kindest man in the world, could feel otherwise.

Charles believed that the new cabinet council would succeed where Clarendon had failed. This was already beginning to be called the "Cabal" because of the first letters of the names of the five men who were its members: Clifford, Arlington, Buckingham, Ashley and Lauderdale. He was seeing Christopher Wren every day, and it seemed that before long a new City would spring up to replace the old one of wooden houses and narrow streets.

Catherine was delighted to hear good news from her own country, and to learn that her brother, Don Pedro, had now succeeding in deposing his brother Alphonso; for Alphonso had become duller-witted as time passed and now, being almost an imbecile, it had seemed that unless there could be a peaceful abdication and the security of Portugal assured by Pedro, the Spaniards might march and subdue the disunited land.

Everything is working towards some good end, decided Catherine.

But one day Donna Maria asked her if she had noticed that the King was visiting the theater more regularly than usual. Donna Maria had heard that there was a reason for this, other than the play itself.

❁ ❁ ❁

Barbara was fuming.

"I can scarcely believe it!" she cried. "So His Majesty will demean himself as far as that! He will go to a theater and, because some minx on the stage leers boldly enough, the King is delighted. The King is in love with a low playing wench."

"Madam," said Mrs. Sarah, "I beg of you make no scenes in public."

Barbara slapped the woman's face, but not too hard. She valued Mrs. Sarah too much.

"Madam," said Mrs. Sarah, standing back a little and placing her hands on her hips, "the King is enamored of a wench at the play. She dances a merry jig, and that pleases him."

"A pretty state of affairs! No wonder the young men of this City are such that modest maidens dare not go abroad. No wonder no woman is safe!"

Mrs. Sarah had turned aside to hide a titter.

"Don't dare laugh at me, woman, or you'll wish you'd never been born."

"Come, my lady, *you're* not afraid to go abroad!"

"By God, no!" cried Barbara. "Nor to go to the theater and to order the crowd to pelt the lewd creature with oranges and to hoot her off the stage."

"The King would not be pleased."

"The King will not be pleased! And should I be pleased to see him so demean himself?"

Mrs. Sarah turned away. Even she dared not say that there were some who would consider he demeaned himself far more by his subservience to Lady Castlemaine than by any light fancy he might have for a play-actress.

Barbara demanded that her hat with the yellow plume be brought for her, her carriage called.

"You're not going to the play, my lady?" cried Mrs. Sarah.

"Of a certainty I am going to the play," retorted Barbara.

With the patch under her right eye to set off the brilliance of those features, and the small spot by her mouth to call attention to the fullness of her lips, and ablaze with jewels to the value of some £40,000, she set out to see Dryden's new play *The Maiden Queen,* for the part of Florimel was played by an Eleanor Gwyn, and it was said that the King was somewhat taken with the actress, although he was more deeply involved with another playgirl named Moll Davies.

"Play-girls!" muttered Barbara. "This is too much to be borne." She would sit in her box—next to the King's—and she would look haughtily at the stage, and then perhaps he would compare her with the low creature who, it was said, had caught his fancy with her merry jig and playing of a part.

She was aware of the interest of the pit as she took her place in the box. She looked over their heads and appeared to be concentrating on the stage. She liked the common people to stare at her, and she was glad she was glittering with jewels, and that the yellow plume in her hat so became her. The orange-girls stared at her in candid admiration; all eyes in the house were on her. The King and his brother, however, were watching the stage, and that maddened her.

And there was the girl—a small, bright, slender thing with tumbled curls and a cockney wit which the part would not suppress. A low-born player! thought Barbara; yet the King and the Duke were intent. And the player knew it; that was evident from the way in which she darted quick glances at the royal box.

The King knew Barbara was there; but he was growing very indifferent to Barbara—even to the scenes she would create. He kept his eyes on the stage.

But now one of the players had caught Barbara's attention. He was one of the handsomest men she had ever set eyes on, and what a physique! Her eyes glittered and narrowed; mayhap there was an attraction about these players.

She turned to the woman who had accompanied her, and pointed to the man.

"Charles Hart, my lady. Eleanor Gwyn, they say, is his mistress."

Barbara felt an inclination to laugh. She said to her woman: "You will go to Mr. Charles Hart and tell him that he may call on me."

"Call on your ladyship!"

"Are you deaf, fool? That was what I said. And tell him there should be no delay. I will see him at eight of the clock this night."

The woman was alarmed, but, like all those in Barbara's service, realizing the need for immediate obedience, left Barbara's box.

Barbara sat back, vaguely aware of the King in his box, of the girl on the stage, and the play which was about to end.

"I am resolved to grow fat and look young till forty," said the impudent little player, "and then slip out of the world with the first wrinkle and the reputation of five and twenty."

The pit roared its approval and called: "Dance your jig, Nelly. Dance your jig!"

The girl had come forward and was talking to them, and the King was laughing and applauding with all those in the pit.

Charles Hart! thought Barbara. "What a handsome man!" Why had she not come to the theater to look for a lover before now? And how piquant to take the lover of that brazen creature who was daring to throw languorous glances at the King!

❁ ❁ ❁

The King was visiting Barbara less frequently; his relationship with the Queen had settled into a friendly one, but Catherine knew that she was as far as ever from reaching that relationship which she had enjoyed during the honeymoon. And it seemed to her that morals at the Court were growing more and more lax with the passing of the years.

The affair of Buckingham was characteristic of the conduct of the times. The Earl of Shrewsbury had challenged the Duke to a duel on account of his misconduct with Anna Shrewsbury, and on a cold January day they met. Their seconds engaged each other and one was killed, another badly wounded, so Buckingham and Shrewsbury were left to fight alone. Buckingham fatally wounded Shrewsbury, and a week or so later Shrewsbury was dead. There was an uproar in the Commons against the duelists even before Shrewsbury died, and the King promised that he would impose the extreme penalty in future on any who engaged in dueling; sober people were disgusted that one of their chief ministers should have engaged himself in a duel over his mistress; and when Shrewsbury died, Buckingham came very near to being expelled from the Cabal. Wild rumors were circulated. It was said that Lady Shrewsbury, disguised as a page, had held her lover's horse and witnessed her husband's murder, and that the two lovers, unable to suppress their lust, satisfied it there and then while Buckingham was still bespattered with the husband's blood.

Buckingham was reckless and quite indifferent to public abuse. When Lady Shrewsbury was a widow he took her to Wallingford House, where the Duchess of Buckingham was living, and when she protested that she and her husband's mistress could not live under the same roof, he answered her coolly: "I did think that also, Madam. Therefore I ordered your coach to carry you back to your father's house."

Some of those who followed the course of events were shocked; more were merely amused. The King had his own seraglio; it was understandable that those about him should follow his example. Lady Castlemaine had never contented herself with one lover; as she grew older she seemed to find the need for more and more.

After her association with Charles Hart she discovered a fancy for other players.

One day, masked and wrapped in a cloak, she went to St. Bartholomew's Fair and saw there a rope-dancer—who immediately fascinated her. His name was Jacob Hill, she was told, and after his performance she sent for him.

He proved so satisfactory that she gave him a salary which was far greater than anything he had dreamed of earning; and thus, she said, he could give up his irksome profession for a more interesting one.

Like the King, she was learning that there was a great deal of fun to be had outside Court circles.

Catherine tried to resign herself, to content herself because the news from Portugal was good. Her young brother Pedro had contrived to establish himself firmly on the throne; he had arranged that his sister-in-law, Alphonso's wife, should obtain a divorce and marry him; Alphonso was put quietly away and all seemed well in Portugal. Catherine had hopes that one day the dowry promised by her mother would be paid to Charles; and she marveled at the goodness of her husband who never but once—and that when he was deeply incensed with her for denying him the one thing he had asked of her—had mentioned the fact that the dowry (the very reason for his marrying her) had not been paid in full.

So, saddened yet resigned, she continued to love her husband dearly and to hope that one day, when he tired of gaiety and his mistresses, he would remember the wife who, for the brief period of a honeymoon at Hampton Court, had been the happiest woman in the world because she had believed her husband loved her.

Then Frances Stuart came back to Court.

❁ ❁ ❁

The King received the news calmly. All were watching him to see what his reaction would be. Barbara was alert. She had her troupe of lovers, but she was as eager as ever to keep the favor of the King; she still behaved as *maitresse en titre,* but she was aware that the King knew of her many lovers, and the fact that he raised no objection was disconcerting. What would happen, she asked herself, now that Frances had returned? Frances, the wife of the Duke of Richmond and Lennox, might, as a married woman, find herself more free to indulge in a love affair with the King than she had been as an unmarried one. If she did, Barbara believed she would have a formidable rival indeed.

Catherine was uneasy. She knew that a faction about the King had never ceased to agitate for a divorce, and that the powerful Buckingham was at the head of this contingent. Catherine had proved, they said, that she could not bear children; the King had proved that he was still potent. It was unsound policy, declared these men, to continue in a marriage which was fruitless. England needed an heir. These men were influenced by another consideration: If the King died childless, his brother, the Duke of York, would follow him, and the Duke of York had not only adopted the Catholic religion but he was the enemy of many of these men.

Catherine knew that they were her bitter enemies. She was unmoved by the arrival of Frances. Frances could not now become the wife of the King since she had a husband of her own; and if she became the King's mistress, she would now be one of many.

But when the King and Frances met, the King received her coolly. It was clear, said everyone, that when she had run away with the Duke of Richmond and Lennox she had spoiled her chances with the King.

❁❁❁

It was not long after Frances's return to Court that all had an opportunity of understanding the depth of Charles' affection for his distant cousin.

Frances was now even more beautiful than when she had left. Marriage with the Duke had sobered her; she was less giddy; if she still played card houses it was with an abstracted air. The Duke, her husband, was not only besotted, he was indifferent; he had wished to marry her only because the King had so ardently desired her; in fact, Frances had quickly realized that her marriage had been one of the biggest mistakes of her life. She had her apartments in Somerset House, the home of the King's mother, Henrietta Maria, for she was not invited to take up residence in her old apartments in Whitehall. It was very different being merely the wife of the Duke of Richmond and Lennox and a woman who had offended the King so deeply that she would never be taken back into his favor again. There were fewer people to visit her and applaud all she did. Buckingham and Arlington, those devoted admirers, seemed now to have forgotten her existence. Lady Castlemaine laughed at her insolently whenever they met. Barbara was determined to flaunt her continued friendship with the King, which had lasted nearly ten years; Frances's spell of favor had been so very brief.

"The King must amuse himself," Barbara said in her hearing. "He takes up with women one week and by the next he finds it difficult to recall their names."

So Frances, the petted darling of the Court, the King's most honored friend, found herself neglected because she no longer held the King's favor.

There was no point in seeking to please her; for what good could her friendship bring them? It was astonishing how many of those who had sworn she was the most beautiful creature on Earth now scarcely seemed to notice her.

She was beautiful—none more beautiful at the Court; she was far less foolish than she had been, but her circle of friends had dwindled astonishingly and she was often lonely in her rooms at Somerset House. Now and then she thought of returning to the country.

Sitting solitarily, building card houses, she thought often of the old days; she thought of the charm of the King and compared it with the ungracious manners of her husband; she thought of the Duke's indifference to her and of the King's continual care.

She covered her face with her hands and wept. If ever she had been in love with anyone it had been with Charles.

She left her card house to collapse onto the table, and went to a mirror; her face looked back at her, perfect in contour and coloring; lacking the simplicity it had possessed when Charles had so eagerly sought her, but surely losing nothing of beauty for that.

She must go to Court; she must seek him out. She would humbly beg his pardon, not for refusing to become his mistress—he would not expect that—but because she had run away and married against his wishes, because she had flouted him, because she had been such a fool as to prefer the drunken Duke to her passionate, but so kind and affectionate King.

She called to her women.

"Come," she cried. "Dress me in my most becoming gown. Dress my hair in ringlets. I am going to pay a call . . . a very important call."

They dressed her, and she thought of the reunion as they did so. She would throw herself onto her knees first and beg his forgiveness. She would say that she had tried to go against the tide; she had believed in virtue, but now she could see no virtue in marriage with a man such as she had married. She would ask Charles to forget the past; and perhaps they would start again.

"My lady, your hands are burning," said one of her women. "You are too flushed. You have a fever."

"It is the excitement because I am to pay a most important call . . . I will wear that blue sash with the gold embroidery."

Her women looked at each other in astonishment. "There is no blue sash, my lady. The sash is purple, and the embroidery on it is silver."

Frances put her hand to her head. "Dark webs seem to dance before my eyes," she muttered.

"You should rest, my lady, before you pay that call."

Even as they spoke she would have fallen if two of them had not managed to catch her.

"Take me to my bed," she murmured.

They carried her thither, and in alarm they called the physician to her bedside. One of the women had recognized the alarming symptoms of the dreaded smallpox.

❁ ❁ ❁

The Court buzzed with the news.

So Frances Stuart was suffering from the smallpox! Fate seemed determined to put an end to her sway, for only if she came unscathed from the dread disease, her beauty unimpaired, could she hope to return to the King's favor.

Barbara was exultant. It was hardly likely that Frances would come through unmarked; so few people did, and Barbara's spies informed her that Frances had taken the disease very badly. "Praise be to God!" cried Barbara. "Madam Frances will no longer be able to call herself the beauty of the Court. Dolt! She threw away what she might have had when she was young and fair and the King sought her; she married her drunken sot, and much good has that done her. I'll swear she was planning to come back and regain Charles' favor. She'll see that the pockmarked hag she'll become will best retire to the country and hide herself."

The King heard the sly laughter. He heard the whispers. "They say the most beautiful of Duchesses has become the most hideous." "Silly Frances, there'll be no one to hand her her cards now." "Poor Frances! Silly Frances! What had she but her beauty?"

Catherine watched the King wistfully. She saw that he was melancholy, and she asked him to tell her the reason.

He turned to her frankly and replied: "I think of poor Frances Stuart."

"It has been the lot of other women to lose their beauty through the pox," said Catherine. "Her case is but one of many."

"Nay," said the King. "Hers is unique, for the pox could never have robbed a woman of so much beauty as it could rob poor Frances!"

"Some women have to learn to do without what they cannot have."

He smiled at Catherine. "No one visits her," he said.

"And indeed they should not. The infection will still be upon her."

"I think of poor Frances robbed of beauty and friends, and I find myself no longer angry with her."

"If she recovers it will bring great comfort to her to know that she no longer must suffer your displeasure."

"She needs comfort now," declared the King. "If she does not have it, poor soul, she will die of melancholy."

He was thinking of her in her little cocked hat, in her black-and-white gown with the diamonds sparkling in her hair—Frances, the most beautiful woman of his Court, and now, if she recovered, one of its most hideous. For the pox was a cruel destroyer of beauty, and Frances was suffering a severe attack.

Catherine, watching him, felt such twinges of jealousy that she could have buried her face in her hands and wept in her misery. She thought: If he could speak of me as he speaks of her, if he could care so much for me if I suffered the like affliction, I believe I would be willing to suffer as Frances has suffered. He loves her still. None of the others can mean as much to him as that simple girl, of whom it was once said: "Never had a woman so much beauty, and so little wit."

He smiled at Catherine, but she knew he did not see her. His eyes were shining and his mouth tender; he was looking beyond her into the past when Frances Stuart had ridden beside him and he had been at his wit's end to think of means to overcome her resistance.

He turned and hurried away, and a little later she saw him walking briskly to the river's edge where his barge was waiting.

Catherine stood watching him, and slowly the tears began to run down her cheeks.

She knew where he was going. He was going to risk infection; he was going to do something which would set all the Court talking; for he was going to show them all that, although he had been cool towards the lovely Frances Stuart because she had flouted him in her marriage, all was forgiven the poor, stricken girl who was in danger of losing that very beauty which had so attracted him.

For love like that, thought Catherine, I would welcome the pox. For love like that I would die.

❁ ❁ ❁

Frances lay in her bed. She had asked for a mirror, and had stared a long time at the face she saw reflected there. How cruel was fate! Why, she asked herself, should it have made her the most beautiful of women, only to turn her into one of the most hideous! If only the contrast had been less marked! It was as though she had been shown the value of beauty in those days of the Restoration, only that she might mourn its loss. Gone was the dazzling pink-and-white complexion; in its place was yellow skin covered by small pits which, not content with ravaging the skin itself, had distorted the perfect contours of her face. The lid of one eye, heavily pitted, was dragged down over the pupil so that she could see nothing through it, and the effect was to make her look grotesque.

Nothing of beauty was left to her; even her lovely slender figure was wasted and so thin that she feared the bones would pierce her skin.

Alone she lay, for none came to visit her. How was that possible, who would dare risk taking the dread disease?

And when I am recovered, she thought, still none will visit me. And any who should be so misguided as to do so will be disgusted with what they see.

She wanted to weep; in the old days she had wept so easily. Now there were no tears. She was aware only of a dumb misery. There was none to love her, none to care what became of her.

Perhaps, she pondered, I will go into a convent. How can I live all the years ahead of me, shut away from the world? I am not studious; I am not clever. How can I live my life shut away from the Court life to which I have grown accustomed?

How would it be to have old friends, who once had been eager to admire, turning away from her in disgust? There would be no one to love her; she had nothing to hope for from her husband. He had married the fair Stuart whom the King so desired because he had believed that, the King finding her so fair, she must be desirable indeed. Now . . . there would be none.

She could see from her bed the boulle cabinet inlaid with tortoiseshell and ivory. It was a beautiful thing and a present from the King in those days when he had eagerly besought her to become his mistress. She remembered his pleasure when he had shown her the thirty secret drawers and the silver gilt fittings. The cabinet was decorated with tortoiseshell hearts, and she remembered that he had said: "These are reminders that you possess one which is not made of tortoiseshell and beats for you alone."

Beside her bed was the marquetry table, ebony inlaid, and decorated with pewter—another of Charles' elaborate presents.

She would have these to remind her always that once she had been so beautiful that a King had sought her favors. Few would believe that in the days to come, for they would look at a hideous woman and laugh secretly at the very suggestion that her beauty could ever have attracted a King who worshipped beauty as did Charles.

All was over. Her life had been built on her beauty; and her beauty was in ruins.

Someone had entered the room, someone tall and dark.

She did not believe it was he. She could not. She had been thinking of him so vividly that she must have conjured him up out of her imagination.

He approached the bed.

"Oh, God!" she cried. "It is the King . . . the King himself."

She brought up her hands to cover her face, but found she could not touch the loathsome thing she believed that face to be. She turned to the wall and sobbed: "Go away! Go away! Do not look at me. Do not come here to mock me!"

But he was there, kneeling by the bed; he had taken her hands.

"Frances," he said, in a voice husky with emotion, "you must not grieve. You must not."

"I beg of you go away and leave me in my misery," she said. "You think of what I was. You see what I have become. You . . . you of all people must be laughing at me . . . you must be triumphant. . . . If you have any kindness in you . . . go away."

"Nay," he said. "I would not go just yet. I would speak with you, Frances. We have been too long bad friends."

She did not answer. She believed the hot, scalding smart on the face she loathed meant tears.

She felt his lips on her hands. He must be mad. Did he not know that there might still be danger of contagion?

"I came because I could not endure that we should be bad friends, Frances," he said. "You were ill and alone, so I came to see you."

She shook her head. "Now go, I beg of you. I implore you. I know you cannot bear to look at anything so ugly as I have become. You cannot have anything but loathing for me now."

"One does not loathe friends—if the friendship be a true one—whatever befalls them."

"You desired me for my beauty." Her voice broke on a cracked note. "My beauty. . . . I am not only no longer beautiful, I am hideous. I know how you hate everything ugly. I can appeal only to your pity."

"I loved you, Frances," he said. " 'Od's Fish! I did not know how much until you ran away and left me. And now I find you sick and alone, deserted by your friends. I came hither to say this to you, Frances: Here is one friend who will not desert you."

"Nay . . . nay . . ." she said. "You will never bear to look upon me after this."

"I shall visit you every day until you are able to leave your bed. Then you must return to Court."

"To be jeered at!"

"None would dare jeer at my friend. Moreover, you despair too soon. There are remedies for the effects of the pox. Many have tried them. I will ask my sister to tell me what the latest French remedies are for improving the skin. Your eye will recover its sight. Frances, do not despair."

"If I had been less beautiful," she murmured, "it would have been easier."

He said: "Let us talk of other matters. I will tell you of the fashions of which I hear from my sister. The French are far in advance of us and I will ask her to send French dresses for you. How would you like to come to Court in a dress from Paris?"

"With a mask over my face, mayhap I might," said Frances bitterly.

"Frances, this is not like you. You used to laugh so gaily when the card houses of others collapsed. Do you remember?"

She nodded. Then she said sadly: "Now my house has collapsed, and I see that cards were such flimsy things . . . so worthless with which to build a house."

He pressed her hands; and she turned to look into his face, hoping for what she could not possibly expect to find; the tenderness of his voice deceived her.

How could he love her—hideous as she had become? She thought of the flaming beauty of Barbara Castlemaine; she thought of the dainty *gamin* charm of the player with whom she had heard he was spending much time. And how could he love Frances Stuart who had had nothing but her unsurpassed beauty, of which the hideous pox had now completely robbed her?

She had caught him off his guard.

She had allowed him to see her once beautiful face hideously distorted, and he knew and she knew that, whatever remedies there were, nothing could restore its beauty; and she also knew that what had prompted him to visit her was nothing but the kindness of heart he would have for any sick animal. Thus would he have behaved for any of his little dogs or the creatures he kept in his parks.

Of all those who had courted and flattered her in the days when she had enjoyed the power her beauty had brought, there was only one who came now to visit her—the King himself; and, because of this, when she was well and no longer a danger to them, others would come, not because they cared what became of her, but because it was the custom to follow the King.

He had come in her affliction; she would always remember that. He had risked grave sickness and possibly death by coming to her when she had felt prepared to take a quick way out of this world.

Now he sat there on the bed and was trying to act a part; he was trying to be gay, trying to pretend that soon she would be back at Court, and the old game—she evasive, he persuasive—would begin again.

But although he was a tolerably good actor, there had been one moment of revelation when she had seen clearly that he had no feeling for her but one, and that was pity.

SIX

It was springtime, and Catherine was filled with new hope. If all went well this time she might indeed present an heir to the nation.

It was seven years since she had come to England, and she was more deeply in love with Charles than she had been during that ecstatic honeymoon. She no longer hoped to have his love exclusively; it would be enough for her if she might share it with all those who made demands upon it. He had so many mistresses that none was quite sure how many; he had taken a fancy to several actresses whom he saw at the theater; and, although his passion for these women was usually fleeting, he had remained constant to Eleanor Gwyn, who was affectionately known throughout the Court and country as Nelly. Barbara kept her place at the head of them, but that was largely due to Barbara herself; the King was too lazy to eject her from the position she had taken as a right; and until there came a mistress who would insist on his doing so, it seemed that there Barbara would remain.

As to Catherine, she allowed the King's seraglio to affect her as little as possible. She had her own court of ladies—among them poor, plain Mary Fairfax, who had suffered through her husband as Catherine had through hers. Catherine had her private chapel in the Queen Mother's residence of Somerset House; she had her own priests and loyal servants; the King was ever kind to her and she was not unduly unhappy.

Mary Fairfax, gentle, intelligent, and very patient, would sometimes talk of her childhood and the early days of her marriage which had been so happy, and how at that time she had believed she would continue to live in harmony with her husband all the days of her life.

They had much comfort to bring each other.

They talked of pleasant things; they never mentioned Lady Castlemaine, whom Mary Fairfax regarded as her husband's evil genius almost as much as Catherine regarded her as Charles'.

They talked of the coming of the child and the joy which would be felt throughout the country when it was born.

Lying back in her white *pinner,* the loose folds of which were wrapped about her thickening body, Catherine looked almost pretty. She was imagining Charles' delight in the child; she saw him as a boy—a not very pretty boy because he would be so like his father; he would have bright, merry eyes, a gentle nature and a sharp wit.

They talked together and an hour passed merrily, but when Mary

Fairfax rose to call her ladies to help the Queen disrobe, Catherine suddenly felt ill.

Her women came hurrying in, and she saw the anxiety on their faces; she knew they were wondering: Is the Queen going to miscarry again?

Catherine said quickly: "Send for Mrs. Nun. She is at dinner in Chaffinch's apartments. I may need her."

There was consternation throughout Whitehall. Mrs. Nun had been brought away from a dinner party in great haste at the Queen's command, and this could mean only one thing; the Queen's time had again come too soon.

Within a few days the news was out.

Catherine came out of her sleep of exhaustion, and the tears fell slowly down her cheeks as she realized that, once more, she had failed.

❁ ❁ ❁

The Duke of Buckingham called on Barbara.

When they were alone, he said: "So Her Majesty has failed again!"

"The King should have married a woman who could bear him children," declared Barbara.

"Well, cousin," said the Duke, "you have proved that you could do that. The only thing that would need to be proved in your case would be that the King had begotten them."

"It is only necessary for Queens to *bear* them," said Barbara.

"And does your rope-dancer still give you satisfaction?" asked the Duke.

"I'll be thankful if you will address me civilly," snapped Barbara.

"A friendly question, nothing more," said Buckingham airily. "But let us not quarrel. I have come to talk business. The King is gravely disappointed. He had hoped for a son."

"Well, he'll get over the disappointment, as he has been obliged to do before."

"It is a sad thing when a King, knowing himself to be capable of begetting strong healthy children, cannot get an heir."

Barbara shrugged her magnificent shoulders, but the Duke went on: "You indicate it is a matter of indifference. Know you not that if the King gets no legitimate son, one day we shall have his brother on the throne?"

"That would seem so."

"And what of us when James is King?"

"Charles' death would be calamity to us in any case."

"Well, he is full of health and vigor. Now listen to me, Barbara; we must rid him of the Queen."

"What do you suggest? To tie her in a sack and throw her into the river one dark night?"

"Put aside your levity. This is a serious matter. I mean divorce."

"Divorce!" cried Barbara shrilly. "That he might marry again! Another barren woman!"

"How do we know she would be barren?"

"Royal persons often are."

"Don't look alarmed, Barbara. It cannot be Frances Stuart now."

"That pockmarked hag!" Barbara went into peals of laughter, which the very mention of Frances Stuart's name never failed to provoke. She was serious suddenly: "Nay! Let the Queen stay where she is. She is quiet and does no harm."

"She does no good while she does not give the country an heir."

"The country has an heir in James."

"I'll not stand by and see the King disappointed of a son."

"There is nothing else you can do about it, cousin."

"Indeed there is! Ashley and others are with me in this. We will arrange a divorce for the King, and he shall marry a princess who will bring him sons."

Barbara's eyes narrowed. She was ready to support the Queen, because the Queen was docile. How did she know what a new Queen would do? Was her position with the King so strong that she could afford to have it shaken? And, horror of horrors, what if he looked about his Court and selected one of the beauties to be his Queen? It might so easily have been Frances Stuart. What if he should choose some fiery creature who would insist on making trouble for Lady Castlemaine?

She would have nothing to do with this plot. She was all for letting things stay as they were.

"The poor Queen!" said Barbara. "This is shameful. So you plot against her . . . you and your mischief-making Cabal. Keep your noses out of the King's marriage; meddle with matters more fitting. I tell you I'll do nothing to help you in this vile plot. I shall disclose it to the King. I shall . . ."

The Duke took her by the wrist, but she twisted her arm free and dealt him a stinging blow across the face.

"There, Master George Villiers, that will teach you to lay hands on me!"

It was nothing. There had been quarrels between them before; there had been physical violence and physical tenderness; they were of a kind, and they recognized that in each other.

Now they surveyed each other angrily, for their interests were divided.

Buckingham laughed in her face. "I see, Madam, that your standing with the King is in such bad case that you fear a new queen who might decide to banish you forever."

"You see too much, sir!" cried Barbara. "I have given you great support during the last years, but doubtless you forget this, as it suits you to. Do not forget that I, who have done you much good, could do you much harm."

"Your wings are clipped, Barbara. The King but allows you to stay at Court out of laziness, rather than his desire to keep you there."

"You lie."

"Do I? Try leaving and see then how eager he will be to have you back."

Fear was in Barbara's heart. There was some truth in Buckingham's words.

"Go and do your worst!" she cried. "See if, without my help—which you consider so worthless—you can rid the country of the Queen."

"So you have a fellow feeling with the Queen now," sneered Buckingham. "Two poor deserted women! Mrs. Nelly, they say, is an enchanting creature. She is young; she is very pretty, and she makes the King laugh."

"I pray you, leave my apartment," said Barbara with dignity; but almost immediately that dignity deserted her. "Get out, you plotting hog! Get out, you murderer! I wonder poor Shrewsbury does not haunt you, that I do. Get out and plot with Shrewsbury's widow."

"So you refuse to help me?"

"Not only that; I'll do all in my power to work against you."

"Think awhile, Barbara. You'll be sorry if you do anything rashly."

"You dare to tell me I shall be sorry? You'll be sorrier than I could ever be."

"We Villierses should stand together, Barbara. You said that."

"Not when it means bringing dishonor to an innocent woman," said Barbara in a virtuous tone which sent Buckingham into hysterical laughter. Whereupon he gave, for Barbara's benefit, an imitation of Barbara—the real Barbara, and Barbara, virtuous defender of the Queen.

Barbara was furious; she would have flown at him and dug her nails into his face, but he was quick, and before she could reach him he was through the door, and away.

❁ ❁ ❁

Buckingham sought out the King and intimated that he came from the Council with a matter of grave importance to discuss.

"Your Majesty," he said, "your Council and your country view with alarm the Queen's sterility."

Charles nodded. "It is a source of great disappointment to me. There was no reason for it. No accident. Nothing wrong. It is the same as that which happened previously. Again and again she loses the child she might have."

"It is the way with some women, Sire. You have but to look back and consider Henry VIII and what difficulties he had in getting an heir. It brought much inconvenience to him."

"And greater inconvenience to his wives, I fear," added Charles.

"There was much unrest regarding the succession, because of the sterility of those women."

"In my case I have a successor in my brother James."

"Your brother, Sire, has turned to the Catholic Faith. Your Majesty knows what dissatisfaction that causes in the country."

"James is a fool," said Charles.

"All the more reason why Your Majesty should make sure that he is not your successor."

"I have tried to make sure of that, George. God knows"—he smiled wryly—"I have tried very hard indeed."

"All know Your Majesty's labors have been tireless, But . . . there is no child, and it would seem that the Queen will never have one."

"Alas, it is a sad fate."

"Your Majesty would seem to accept it with resignation."

"I learned in my early youth to accept with resignation that which could not be avoided."

"There are means of avoiding most things, Sire."

"Are you back to the divorce?" asked the King.

"It is the only way in which we may reach a satisfactory conclusion to this affair of the succession."

"On what grounds could one divorce as virtuous a lady as the Queen has proved herself to be?"

"On her inability to bear an heir to the crown."

"Nonsense! Moreover she is a Catholic and would not agree to be divorced."

"She might be urged to go into a nunnery."

The King was silent, and Buckingham was delighted. He did not press the point. He would wait awhile. He believed the King greatly wished to be rid of his wife; it was not that he hated her; he was, in his way, fond of her; but because of her mildness, because of her resignation, she bothered him. She made him continually conscious of the way in which he treated her. He could no more deny himself the pleasure of falling in and out of light love affairs than he could stop breathing; but such was his nature that, knowing this hurt the Queen, he was uneasy in her presence; and it was of the very essence of his nature that he should avoid that which was unpleasant.

A divorce from the Queen! Catherine to spend the rest of her days peacefully in a nunnery!

It was a good idea. And for him the pleasure of choosing a new wife. This time he would choose with the utmost care.

When Buckingham left the King, the Duke's hopes were high indeed.

At all costs he must prevent his enemy, the Duke of York, mounting the throne—even if it meant making the bastard Monmouth heir of England.

Wild schemes formed in Buckingham's mind. What if Charles had really been married to Lucy Water! Then Monmouth would in truth be heir to the throne. What if a box were found . . . a box containing papers which proved the marriage to have taken place? An excellent scheme but a wild one.

It would be far, far better for the King to divorce Catherine, remarry, and let a new Queen produce the heir.

Well, he decided, he was moving forward. He had discovered something. The King would not be averse to a divorce. He sought out Lauderdale and Ashley to tell them the good news.

❁ ❁ ❁

Barbara's spies quickly brought the information to her.

She sat biting her lips and contemplating the possible danger to herself from a new and beautiful Queen.

I am satisfied with the Queen, she mused. I like the Queen—a mild and sensible lady who understands the King and his ways.

What if the King married? She pictured another such as Frances Stuart ruling the Court. The first thing such a woman would do would be to clear out the seraglio; and who would be the first to go? Those whom she most feared and whom the King was not determined to keep.

Barbara would certainly not allow these plans to proceed, for the deeper they were laid the more difficult they would be to frustrate, and it might well be that her persistent relative would set about making things so very uncomfortable for the Queen that she would sigh for the quiet walls of a convent.

Barbara sought audience with the Queen and, when she was with her, told her that what she had to say was for her ears alone.

She fell on her knees before Catherine and kissed her hand; then she lifted those bright flashing eyes to Catherine's face and said: "I have come to warn Your Majesty."

"Of what?" inquired Catherine. She spoke harshly. She was tormented by hundreds of mental pictures when this woman stood before her. She saw her in the arms of the King; she thought of his passionate lovemaking; she thought of all she had heard of this infamous woman, of the numerous lovers she took, and how she kept some as servants in her household so that she might call them instantly when she needed them. She thought of those days during her honeymoon, when Lady Castlemaine had been merely a name to be shuddered over and never mentioned.

Barbara boldly answered: "Of your enemies, who seek to destroy you. They would part you from the King."

Catherine turned pale in spite of her determination to remain controlled before this woman.

"How . . . how could they do that, Lady Castlemaine?"

"Madam, you have failed to give the King children."

Catherine winced and thought again of the many times this woman had been brought to bed, as she said, of the King's child.

"And," went on Barbara, "there are certain of his ministers who seek to have him set you aside. They talk of divorce."

"I would not agree."

"Your Majesty should never . . . never agree to that!"

"Lady Castlemaine, you have no need to urge me to my duty."

"Madam, you misunderstand me. Nor do you understand how wicked, how determined are these men who scheme to displace you. They will try persuasion at first, and if that fails they will seek to compel you."

"They dare not compel me. If they harmed me, they would have to answer to my brother."

Barbara raised her well-arched brows, indicating that Pedro of Portugal already had too many commitments to leave his country and sail across the seas in what would be a feeble attempt to defend his sister.

"But Madam, I came to tell you of plans I have discovered, plans which are indeed being set on foot to force Your Majesty from the throne."

"It is fantastic."

"Nevertheless, Madam, it is true."

"The King would not consent."

"The King must have an heir, Madam."

"He would never treat me thus."

"He can be persuaded."

"No . . . no. He is too noble . . . too good to agree to such a thing."

"Madam, I warn you. I beg of you, take my advice. The King has a tender heart; we both know that. You must win him to your side against your enemies. You must implore him to protect you against those who would destroy you. The King is tenderhearted. If you can move him with your tears . . . if you can but bring him to pity you, your enemies will have no power to harm you."

The two women looked at each other as though measuring each other's strength and sincerity.

Barbara was aging and the signs of debauchery were beginning to show on her handsome face, but however old she was, she would still be handsome. Catherine was pale from her miscarriage and in despair because she could not produce the heir so necessary to the country. They had been rivals for so long; they had hated each other; and now it was clear to them both that at last they must become allies.

"I must thank you, Lady Castlemaine," said the Queen, "for coming to me thus."

Barbara knelt and kissed the Queen's hand. For the first time Catherine saw Barbara humble in her presence; and she realized that Barbara feared the future even as she did.

❁ ❁ ❁

It was rarely, Catherine reflected bitterly, that she had an opportunity of being alone with the King. She had become resigned to the relationship between them; she had schooled herself not to show how hurt she was every time she saw him becoming enamored of a new woman. She had learned to hesitate before entering her own apartments, lest he should be there, kissing one of her maids, and she surprise them.

She had learned to subdue her jealousy; and now she realized that she would endure any humiliations which life with Charles brought her rather than suffer the lonely despair of life without him.

She waited for one of the nights when they were alone together. At such times she felt that he was more her husband than her King. He would then modify that brilliant wit of his and attune his conversation to suit her; he was unfailingly courteous. If she were ill he would tend her carefully; he never failed to be considerate of her health. She fancied that that expression of melancholy regret, which she saw so often on his face when he was in her company, meant that he was sorry because he could not be a better husband to her.

She now said to him: "Charles, it seems that there are many in your counsels who believe I am incapable of bearing children."

That light and easy smile flashed across his face as he prevaricated. "Nay, you must not despair. We have been unfortunate. There have been a few disappointments . . ."

She looked about the chamber of this apartment in Hampton Court and thought of other queens who had, within these very walls, despaired of their ability to produce an heir to the throne. Was there a curse on queens? she wondered.

"Too many disappointments," she said. "It does not happen with . . . others."

"They are stronger than you. You must take better care of your health."

"Let us be frank one with the other, Charles. There are men who plan to destroy me."

"To destroy you! What words are these?"

"They wish to rid you of me, that you may marry again. Buckingham, Ashley, Lauderdale . . . all the Cabal . . . and others. They offer you a new and beautiful wife who can give you sons. Oh, Charles, do not think I cannot understand the temptation. I am not beautiful . . . and you so admire beauty."

He was beside her; his arms were about her. "Now, Catherine, what tales are these you have heard? You are my wife. For you I have the utmost affection. I know I am not a good husband, but you took me, Catherine, and, Od's Fish, you'll have to stick to me."

"They seek to destroy me," she repeated blankly. "They seek to send me away from you. Do not deny it. You cannot deny it, can you, Charles?"

He was silent for a while; then he said gently: "They have thought that there is much of which you disapprove in our sinful Court. They have seen you so devout, and have thought that mayhap you would be happier in a nunnery."

She looked at him quickly, and she was overcome with anguish. Was that an expression of hopeful anticipation she saw on his face? Was he asking her to leave him for a nunnery?

Sudden determination came to her. She would not leave him. She would fight for what she wanted. She would never give up hope that one day he would turn to her for the love which she was but waiting to bestow upon him. Surely, when they were both old, when he had ceased to desire so many women, surely then he would understand the value of true love, the quiet affection which was so much more lasting than physical desire. She would wait for that. She would never despair of getting it; and she was going to fight all her enemies in this country until that day when Charles turned to her for what he needed most.

He was the kindest man she had ever known; he was the most attractive, the most tolerant; he would have been a saint, she supposed had he not been entirely sensual. It was that sensuality which caused her such misery, because she herself was not endowed with the necessary weapons to appeal to it in competition with such women as Barbara, Frances Stuart, Moll Davies, Mrs. Knight and Nelly.

But she would never give him up.

She turned to him: "Charles," she cried, "I will never willingly leave you."

"Of a certainty you shall not."

She threw herself at his feet. She was suddenly terrified. He was so careless, so easy-going, so ready with light promises; and those about him were ruthless men who stopped at nothing. She thought of Buckingham, determined to destroy her, his hands red with the blood of his mistress' husband. She thought of Ashley, that terrifying little man, with his elegant clothes, his head—adorned with a fair periwig—which seemed too big for his frail body, his sharp wit and that soft and gentle voice which belied the ruthless determination behind it; she thought of other members of the Cabal who had determined to provide a new wife for the King.

"Charles," she implored, "save me from those men. Do not let them send me away from you." She could no longer hide emotion. The tears streamed down her cheeks, and she knew that he could not bear to see a woman's tears. They never failed to move him deeply; he was even ready at all costs to stop the tears of women such as Barbara, who turned them on and off according to whether they would be effective.

"Catherine," he said in dismay, "you distress yourself unnecessarily."

"It is not unnecessary, I know. Charles . . . they will do anything to separate us. I know full well it is not merely their hatred of me which makes them determined to ruin me. What do they care for me! Who am I? A poor woman of no importance . . . unloved . . . unwanted. . . ."

"I'll not have you say that. Have I not cared for you?"

She shook her head sadly. "You have been kind to me. Are you not kind to all? Your dogs enjoy your kindness. . . . The animals in your parks benefit from it. And . . . so do I. Nay! They do not hate me. I am unworthy of hate . . . unworthy of love. They hate your brother. They are his sworn enemies. They are determined he shall not rule. They are determined on a Protestant heir. Oh, this is nothing so simple as their hatred for one poor woman. . . . It is a policy . . . a policy of state. But, for the sake of that policy, I shall be condemned to a life of misery. Charles, they will trample on my life as Buckingham trampled on Shrewsbury's. Charles, save me . . . save me from my enemies."

He lifted her in his arms and, sitting down, held her on his knee, while he wiped the tears from her face.

"Come, Catherine," he murmured, as though she were a child. "Have done with weeping. You have no cause to weep. Od's Fish! You have no cause whatsoever."

"You are gentle with me. But you listen to them."

"Listen to their roguery? I will not!"

"Then Charles, you will not let them turn me away?"

"I'll not allow it."

"My lord Buckingham makes many plots, and this is no less likely to be carried out than others."

"Nay! You listen to gossip. You and I will not allow them to separate us. If they come to me with their tales, I shall dismiss them from the Court. And, moreover, we'll foil them! They say we cannot have children. We'll show them otherwise."

He kissed her and she clung to him passionately.

He soothed her; he was adept at soothing hysterical women.

❁ ❁ ❁

Buckingham, Ashley and Lauderdale laid their plans before the King.

"Your Majesty, the Queen cannot bear children, and we fear that the country is growing restive because of this."

"The Queen is a young woman yet," murmured Charles.

"There has been more than one miscarriage."

" 'Tis true."

"If Her Majesty would be happy in a nunnery . . ."

"She has told me that she would never be happy in a nunnery."

Buckingham murmured in a low and wheedling voice: "If Your Majesty gave me permission, I would steal the Queen away and send her to a plantation, where she would be well and carefully looked after but never heard of more. The people could be told that she had left Your Majesty of her own free will, and you could divorce her for desertion."

Charles looked into the cunning, handsome face before him, and said quietly and with that determination which he rarely used: "Have done and hold your tongue! If you imagine that I shall allow an innocent woman to suffer through no fault of her own, you are mistaken."

Lauderdale began: "But Your Majesty would wish to take a new wife. Your Majesty could choose any beautiful princess."

"I am well satisfied with the ladies of my Court."

"But the heir . . ."

"My wife is young yet; and hear me this: If she should fail to get children, that is no fault of hers. She is a good and virtuous Princess, and if you wish to keen my good graces you will no more mention this matter to me."

The three statesmen were aghast.

They were determined that Catholic James should never have the throne. If he ever came to it, their ambitions would be at an end; moreover they foresaw a return to the tyranny of Bloody Mary.

Lauderdale then ventured: "The Duke of Monmouth is a brave and handsome gentleman. Your Majesty is justly proud of such a son."

"You speak truth there," said Charles.

"Your Majesty must wish," said Ashley, "that he were your legitimate son. What joy for England—if you had married his mother!"

"If you had known his mother you might not have thought so. I doubt whether the people of England would have accepted her as their Queen."

"She is dead," said Buckingham. "God rest her soul. And she gave Your Majesty a handsome boy."

"I am grateful to Lucy for that."

"If he were but your legitimate son, what a happy thing for England!"

Charles laughed lightly. He turned to Buckingham; he knew him to be a dangerous adventurer but, because he was the most amusing man at his Court, he could not resist his company.

"Have done with making trouble with my brother," said Charles. "Try cultivating his friendship instead of arousing his enmity."

"Your Majesty, I live in terror of the Duke, your brother," said Buckingham. "He threatens my very life!"

"I beg of you, no playacting," said the King, and he began to laugh. "I confess that to see you riding in your coach protected by your seven musquetoons for fear my brother will take your life . . . is the funniest thing I have witnessed for a long time."

"I am grateful to have brought a little sunshine into Your Majesty's life."

"George! Have done with your plotting and scheming. Let matters lie as they are. The Queen and I may yet get an heir. If not . . ."

"The Duke of Monmouth is a worthy heir, Your Majesty."

"A bastard heir for England?"

"We could discover that Your Majesty married his mother. Leave it to me, Sire. I will find a box in which are the marriage lines. . . . She begged you, she implored you . . . for the sake of her virtue . . . and Your Majesty, being the man you always are with the ladies, could not find it in your heart to refuse her!"

The King laughed aloud but his eyes were shrewd. He knew they were speaking only half in jest.

He said abruptly: "Have done! Have done! The Queen stays married to me. I'll not have the poor lady, who is the most virtuous in the land, plagued by you. As for Monmouth, I love the boy. I am proud of the boy. But he is a bastard and I'd see him hanged at Tyburn before I'd make him heir to my throne."

The members of the Cabal retired, temporarily defeated. And the matter of the divorce was dropped, for another more serious one arose. This concerned the secret treaty of Dover in which the King, unknown to his people and the majority of his ministers, agreed to become a Catholic and lead the country to do the same; for such services to Catholic France he would become the pensioner of that country. The matter had given Charles much grave thought. He was in dire need of money; he was verging on bankruptcy. There were two ways of raising money; one was by taxing his subjects, as Cromwell had done to such extent that they could bear little more; and the other was by making promises to the King of France—which might never be kept—and allowing France to wipe out England's deficit.

These matters occupied his mind continually and, when the sister whom he loved so tenderly came to England as the emissary of the King of France, when he realized how deeply she desired his signature to the treaty and all that his signature would mean to her, and how such a signature could make her unhappy life in France supportable through the love of Louis, he agreed—and the very few of his counsellors who were in the secret were of his opinion—that the best way out of England's troubles was the signing of the treaty.

There were fêtes and balls in honor of the King's sister, and Catherine was moved to see how tender was the love between Charles and Henriette of Orléans.

How sad he was when he bade farewell to his sister; and how much sadder he would have been, could he have known that he would never see her face again, for only a few weeks after her return to France Henriette died suddenly. During the King's grief at the loss of this beloved sister it was Catherine who brought him most comfort. She would sit with him, while he talked of Henriette, and of those rare occasions in her childhood when he had been able to enjoy her company.

He wept, and Catherine wept with him; and she believed that in his unhappiness she meant more to him than any woman of his Court.

She thought then: This is a foretaste of the future.

When he is old, when he no longer feels the need to go hunting every pretty thing that flits across the scene—like a boy with a butterfly net—then he and I shall be together in close unity; and those will be the happiest days of my life, and perhaps of his.

❁ ❁ ❁

Buckingham had not forgotten his threat to punish Barbara for not supporting him in the matter of the Queen's divorce. His spies had informed him that Barbara had whispered to the Queen of his plots against her, even telling her that he had suggested kidnapping her and taking her to a plantation—an idea too fantastic to have been meant in true earnest. And, because she had been warned, the Queen had been able to pour out her tears and pleadings to the King who, softened by these, had determined to turn his thoughts from the idea of divorce.

It was infuriating. For Charles was certainly tired of his Queen; he had never been in love with her; she was a plain little woman and by no means a clever one. Buckingham, Ashley and Lauderdale had several fascinating and beautiful creatures with whom to tempt the King; but they had been defeated by the Queen's tears which were the result of Barbara's perfidy.

Barbara should be shown that she could not work against her kinsman in this way; it should be borne home to her that her position at Court was far from secure.

When Charles' sister had visited him for the last time she had brought in her train a charming little Breton girl, named Louise de Kéroualle, who had taken Charles' fancy immediately; and, after the death of Henriette, Louis had sent the girl to Charles' Court, ostensibly to comfort him, but more likely to act as spy for France.

She was a very beautiful young girl, and it was clear that the King was ready to fall more deeply in love with her than was his custom.

This meant that Barbara would have a new and very serious rival; and the fact that the King had showered great honors on Barbara was an indication that he was expecting her to retire from Court. She had been created Baroness of Nonesuch Park, Countess of Surrey and Duchess of Cleveland; he had given her £30,000 and a grant of plate from the jewel house and, as she was already receiving an annual income of £4,700 from the post office, she was being amply and very generously paid off; but Barbara, while accepting these gifts and honors, omitted to remove herself from the Court and continued to pretend that she occupied the place of *maîtresse en titre.*

The King was uneasy. He saw trouble ahead between the newcomer—who, some said, had not yet become his mistress—and Barbara, now known by the grand title of Duchess of Cleveland.

Barbara continued to flaunt her jewels and her person at Court functions; she was often seen at the playhouse wearing her jewels, worth more than £40,000, so that all other ladies, including the Queen and the Duchess of York, seemed far less splendid than she.

She gave up none of her lovers and had even taken a new one—one of the handsomest men about the Court. Barbara's lovers were always handsome.

The latest was John, son of a Sir Winston Churchill, gentleman, of Devonshire. John Churchill had been a page to the Duke of York and had later received a commission as ensign in the Foot Guards. The Duke of York had shown him great favor, which might have been due to the fact that the Duke had cast a covetous eye on John's sister, Arabella.

Barbara had seen the young man and had immediately desired him as her lover. Barbara handsomely paid those whose services she used in this way; she lavished rich presents upon her young men, and made the way to advancement easier for them. If they could please the Duchess of Cleveland, it was said, their fortunes might be made; and John Churchill was soon on the way to making his.

Buckingham watched the affair, and considered that, if he could arrange for the King to catch them *flagrante delicto,* he would by such a device supply the King with a food excuse for ridding himself of a woman who was growing irksome to His Majesty; he would, moreover, be doing the King a good turn while letting Barbara see that she was foolish to work against her cousin.

It was not difficult to discover when the two would be together. Barbara had never made any great secret of her love affairs; and one afternoon, when Buckingham knew that Barbara was entertaining the handsome soldier in her apartments, he begged the King to accompany him thither.

The King agreed to go, and together they made their way to Barbara's apartment. When Buckingham saw the consternation of her women, he guessed that he had come at the right moment. Mrs. Sarah made excuses to delay them, saying that she would go to warn her mistress of their arrival, but the Duke pushed her aside and, throwing open the door of Barbara's bedchamber, could not repress a triumphant laugh.

Barbara was in bed, pulling the clothes about her; John Churchill, hearing the commotion without, had managed to scramble into a few of his more essential garments.

Taking one look at the Duke, and seeing the King behind him, the young lover could think of only one thing: escape.

He forthwith ran to the window and leaped out of it. The Duke of Buckingham burst into uproarious laughter; Barbara picked up an ebony-handled brush which lay on a table beside the bed and threw it at her cousin, while the King, striding to the window, called out after the departing figure of Churchill: "Have no fear, Master Churchill. I hold nothing against you. I know you do it for your bread!"

Barbara, furious at the insulting suggestion that she now found it necessary to pay her lovers, and mad with rage against the Duke, found herself for once without words to express her anger and indignation.

Nor did the King give her time to recover her calm. He strode out of the room. Only Buckingham turned to give a brief imitation of John Churchill, surprised and leaping to safety.

Barbara's rage was boundless and for some hours her servants dared not approach her.

She turned and pummeled her pillows, while Mrs. Sarah wondered which of those men she would have preferred to attack: the Duke for his perfidy in exposing her thus; John Churchill for running away; or the King for his cool and careless indifference to what lovers she might take.

It was clear that the King had ceased to regard her as his mistress; and very shortly afterwards her name failed to appear on the list of Ladies of the Queen's Bedchamber. Furthermore, when her daughter Barbara was born, and the girl was seen to bear a strong resemblance to John Churchill, the King flatly refused to acknowledge her as his.

Barbara's day was over.

SEVEN

It was sixteen years since Catherine had come to England, and in those years, during which she had lived through many fears, a little happiness and much heartbreak, she had never ceased to love her husband and to hope that one day he would turn, from those brilliant women who so enchanted him, to the plain little wife who adored him.

She had little hope now of bearing a child; and she knew that there were many of her husband's most important ministers who sought to ruin her. If they could have brought some charge against her, how readily would they have done so! But it seemed that, in the profligate Court, there was one virtuous woman, and she was the Queen. There was one matter which they held against her, and this was her religion. There was a growing feeling in the country against Papists and, whenever there was any trouble in this connection, there was always someone to remind the company that the Queen was a Papist.

Since the Duke of York had announced his conversion to the Catholic Faith there had been a strong and growing faction working against him, and these men never ceased to urge the King to rid himself of the Queen.

The chief of these was Ashley, who had now become Lord Shaftesbury. His principal enemy was the Duke of York, and his enmity towards him had increased since the Duke's marriage, on the death of Anne Hyde, to the Catholic Princess of Modena. The one aim of Shaftesbury's party was to prevent the Duke's becoming King and, since the Queen was barren, they could only hope to do this either through divorce or, as the only other alternative, by the acknowledgment of Monmouth as the heir to the throne.

They were certain that, but for the King's softheartedness, they could achieve this, and they had never ceased, over the last ten years, to work for it.

Catherine must therefore live in continual dread that one day they would succeed in their plans.

She was no longer plagued by Barbara, for Barbara was out of favor. It was true that the King had never dismissed her from the Court. It was beyond his nature to do that. Some said that he feared Barbara's threat to print his letters, but what harm would such an act do to him? All knew of his infatuation for her; all knew that she had behaved abominably to him and had not even pretended to be faithful. No, Catherine often thought, it is his sheer kindness of heart and his desire to live easily and comfortably without troublesome quarrels which have made him give no direct rebuff to Barbara, just as they compel him to keep me as his wife. To rid himself of either of us would make trouble. Therefore he says: Let Barbara stay at Court; let Catherine remain my wife. What matters it? I have many charming companions with whom to beguile my hours.

So that woman, Louise de Kéroualle, who had taken Barbara's place, was the Queen of England in all but name. It was she—now Duchess of Portsmouth—who lived as the Queen in Whitehall while Catherine retired to the Dower Palace of Somerset House.

She made excuses for him. He was half French; his mistress wholly so; and in France the King's mistress had invariably ruled in place of the King's wife.

It was true that his neglect of her, and the fact that—now that he no longer hoped that she would give him a child—he rarely visited her, meant that the hopes of her enemies were high; and they continued most energetically to plot for a divorce.

Barbara had gone to France, where she had indulged in a love affair with Ralph Montague, the King's ambassador. But now it seemed he had offended her and she was writing frequently to the King complaining of her ex-lover's conduct of English affairs.

Barbara had, after the installation of Louise de Kéroualle as the King's favorite, continued to amuse London with her many love affairs. She had turned again to the theater and had found one of the handsomest men in London, William Wycherley, the playwright, who dedicated his *Love in a Wood* to her.

But in spite of her numerous lovers she had found it insupportable to see another take her place with the King. The play-actress she accepted, but she could not tolerate the French woman. In vain did she call the woman a spy, and the King a fool. No one stopped her; they merely ignored her. That was why she had gone to France.

So, as Catherine looked out on the river from her apartments in Somerset House and her wistful gaze wandered in the direction of Whitehall, she told herself that she must be resigned to her position as wife of the King, the wife to whom he was so kind because he could not love her.

❁ ❁ ❁

It was a hot August day, and the King was shortly to ride to Windsor. He was leased at the prospect. Windsor was a favorite resort of his, and he was looking forward to a little holiday from state affairs. He had decided to take Louise and Nelly—those two whom he never greatly cared to be without—and set off as early as this could be arranged. He was eager to assure himself that his instructions were being carried out regarding the alterations he was having made there, and to see how Verrio's work on the fresco paintings was progressing.

He was about to take his quick morning walk through St. James' Park, with which he always liked to begin the day. With him were a few of his friends, and his dogs followed at his heels, barking their delight at the prospect of the walk.

But before he had taken more than a dozen steps a young man, whom he recognized as one who worked in his laboratories, came running towards him.

"Your Majesty," he cried, falling to his knees, "I beg of you, allow me to speak a few words to you."

"Do so," said the King in some astonishment.

"It would be well if, when walking in the Park, Your Majesty did not stray from your companions."

"Why so?" said Charles. He was faintly amused by the man's earnest looks. It was rarely that the King walked abroad and was not asked for something. That he should be asked to keep with his companions was a strange request.

"Your Majesty's life is in danger," whispered the young man.

Charles was not easily alarmed. He stood surveying the young man, who he now remembered was Christopher Kirby, a merchant who had failed in business and had begged the Lord Treasurer, the Earl of Danby, to employ him as a tax collector; as he had some skill as a chemist, he had been given work to do in Charles' laboratory; and it was in that capacity that the King on one or two occasions had come into contact with him.

"What is this talk?" asked Charles.

"Your Majesty may at any moment be shot at."

"You had better tell me all you know," said the King.

"Your Majesty, I can give you a full account. . . . I can give you many details, but to do so I must ask for a private interview."

"Go back to the Palace," said Charles, "and wait there in my private closet for my return. If any ask why you do so, tell them it is at my command."

The man came closer to the King. "Your Majesty, on no account leave your companions. Remember . . . men may at this moment be lurking among the trees."

With that, Kirby bowed and retired.

The King turned to his companions.

"Will Your Majesty continue the walk?" asked one.

The King laughed. "Ever since the gunpowder plot, in my grandfather's reign, there have always been plots which are purported to threaten the life of the King. Come! Let us enjoy the morning air and forget our chemist. I'll warrant this is nothing more than a dream he has had. He had an air of madness, to my mind."

The King called to his dogs who came running round him joyfully. He threw a stone and watched them race for it, each striving for the honor of bringing it back to him.

Then he continued his walk, and it was an hour later before he again saw Kirby.

❁ ❁ ❁

When the King returned to his closet, the chemist was waiting for him there.

The King listened to his story as patiently as he could, without believing a word of it.

Two men, according to Kirby, were lurking in the Park waiting for an opportunity of shooting the King.

"Why should they do this?" asked Charles.

"It is for the Jesuits, Your Majesty," replied Kirby. "Their plan is to murder you and set your brother on the throne."

Poor James! thought Charles. He has many enemies. Now these people would seek to add me to their number.

"How did you learn of these matters?" he asked, scarcely able to suppress a yawn.

"It was through a Dr. Tonge, Your Majesty. He is the rector of St. Michael's in Wood Street, and he has discovered much in the interests of Your Majesty. If Your Majesty would but grant him an interview he could tell you more than I can."

"Then I daresay we should see your Dr. Tonge."

"Have I Your Majesty's permission to bring him to the Palace?"

"You may bring him here between nine and ten this evening," said the King.

When Kirby had left, the King summoned the Earl of Danby and told him of all that had passed.

They laughed together. "The fellow is clearly deranged," said the King. "Let us hope this fellow Tonge is not equally so. Yet he was so earnest I had not the heart to deny him the interview. In the meantime keep the matter secret. I would not have the idea of murdering me put into the heads of people who previously have not given the matter a thought."

❁ ❁ ❁

At the appointed time Kirby arrived with Dr. Tonge, a clergyman and schoolmaster of Yorkshire; he was, he told the King, rector of the parishes of St. Mary Stayning and St. Michael's Wood, and because he had long known the wickedness to which the Jesuits would stoop—even to the murder of their King—he had made it his business to study their ways.

He then began to enumerate the many crimes he had uncovered, until the King, growing weary, bade him proceed with the business which had brought him there.

There were, said Dr. Tonge, Jesuits living close to the King, who had plotted his murder.

"Who are these men?" demanded the King.

Dr. Tonge thereupon produced a wad of papers and told the King that if he would read these he would find therein that which would shock and enrage him.

"How came you by these papers?" asked the King.

"Sire, they were pushed under my door."

"By whom?"

"By one who doubtless wished Your Majesty well and trusted that I would be the man to save Your Majesty's life and see justice done."

The King handed the papers to Danby.

"So you do not know the man who thrust these papers beneath your door?"

"I have a suspicion, Your Majesty, that he is one who has spoken to me of such matters."

"We may need to see him. Can he be found?"

"I have seen him lately, Your Majesty, walking in the streets."

The King turned to Danby. He was wishing to be done with the tiresome business, and had no intention of postponing the trip to Windsor because of another Papist scare.

"You will look into these matters, my lord," he said.

And with that he left.

❁ ❁ ❁

The Earl of Danby was a most unhappy man. He had many enemies, and he knew that a fate similar to that which had befallen Clarendon was being prepared for him. He was in danger of being impeached for high treason when Parliament met, and he was terrified that if there were an investigation of his conduct of affairs he might even lose his life.

He was fully aware that powerful men such as Buckingham and Shaftesbury would welcome a Popish plot. Since the Duke of York had openly avowed his conversion to the Catholic Faith there had been an almost fanatical resentment towards Catholics throughout the country. The Duke of York was heir to the throne, and there was a great body of Englishmen who had vowed never to allow a Catholic monarch to sit again on the throne of England.

Already the slogan "No Popery" had come into being; and it seemed to Danby that, by creating a great scare at this time, he could turn attention from himself to the instigators of the plot. The people were ready to be roused to fury at the thought of Catholic schemes to overthrow the King; some of the most important of the King's ministers would be ready to devote their great energy exclusively to discrediting the Duke of York and arranging a divorce for the King; and mayhap arranging for the legitimization of the Duke of Monmouth, thus providing a Protestant King to follow Charles.

The papers which he studied seemed to contain highly improbable accusations; but Danby was a desperate man.

He sent for Tonge.

"It is very necessary," he told him, "for you to produce the man who thrust these papers under your door. Can you do that?"

"I believe I can, my lord."

"Then do so; and bring him here that he may state his case before the King."

"I will do my utmost, sir."

"What is his name?"

"My lord, it is Titus Oates."

❁ ❁ ❁

Titus Oates was a man of purpose. When he heard that he was to appear before the King he was delighted. He saw immense possibilities before him, and he began to bless the day when Fate threw him in the way of Dr. Tonge.

Titus was the son of Samuel Oates, rector of Markham in Norfolk.

Titus had been an extremely unprepossessing child, and it had seemed to him from his earliest days that he had been born to misfortune. As a child he had been subject to convulsive fits, and his father had hated the shuffling, delicate child with a face so ugly that it was almost grotesque. His neck was so short that his head seemed to rest on his shoulders; he was ungainly in body, one leg being shorter than the other; but his face, which was purple in color, was quite repulsive, for his chin was so large that his mouth was in the center of his face; he suffered from a continuous cold so that he snuffled perpetually; he had an unsightly wart over one eyebrow; and his eyes were small and cunning from the days when he had found it necessary to dodge his father's blows. His mother, though, had lavished great affection on him. He had none for her. Rather he admired his father whose career he soon discovered to have been quite extraordinary. Samuel, feigning to be a very pious man, had, before he settled in Norfolk, wandered the country preaching his own particular brand of the gospels which entailed baptism by immersion of the naked body in lakes and rivers of the districts he visited. Samuel went from village to village; he liked best to dip young women, the more comely the better; and for this purpose he advised them to leave their homes at midnight, without the knowledge of their parents, that they might be baptized and saved. The ceremony of baptism was so complicated that many of the girls found that they gave birth to children as a result of it. But, in view of these results, dipping had eventually become too dangerous a procedure, and Samuel, after some vicissitudes, had settled down as rector of Hastings.

Meanwhile Titus pursued his own not unexciting career.

He went to the Merchant Taylor's School, where he was found to be such a liar and cheat that he was expelled during his first year there; afterwards he was sent as a poor scholar to a school near Hastings where he managed to hide his greater villainies; and eventually, having taken Holy Orders, he became a curate to his father.

The curate of All Saints, Hastings, quickly became the most unpopular man in the district. The rector was heartily disliked, and the people of Hastings would not have believed it was possible to find a man more detestable until they met his son. Titus seemed to delight in circulating scandal concerning those who lived about him. If he could discover some little peccadillo which might be magnified, he was greatly delighted; if he could discover nothing, he used his amazing imagination and an invention which amounted almost to genius.

Samuel hated his son more than ever and wished he had never allowed him to become his curate; therefore, there arose the problem of how to remove Titus. Titus had his living to earn; and it seemed that, if he remained in Hastings, not only the curate but the rector would be asked to leave. A schoolmaster's post would be ideal, decided Samuel; there was one in a local school, but unfortunately it was filled by a certain William Parker, so popular and of such good reputation that it seemed unlikely he could be dismissed to make way for Titus.

Father and son were not the sort to allow any man's virtues to stand in their way.

Titus therefore presented himself to the Mayor and told him that he had seen William Parker in the church porch committing an unnatural offense with a very young boy.

The Mayor was horrified. He declared he could not believe this of William Parker, who had always seemed to him such an honest and honorable man; but Titus, who was a lover of details and had worked on the plan with great thoroughness, managed to convince him that there was truth in the story.

William Parker was sent to jail and Titus, swearing on oath that he was speaking the truth, gave in detail all he alleged he had seen in the church porch.

Titus was eloquent and would have been completely convincing; but he was not yet an adept at the art of perjury, and he had forgotten that truth has an uncomfortable way of tripping up the liar.

Parker was able to prove that he was nowhere near the porch when the offense was alleged to have taken place; the tables were turned; Titus was in danger of imprisonment, and so he ran away to sea.

It was not difficult to get to sea, for His Majesty's Navy was in constant need of men and did not ask many questions. Titus became ship's chaplain, in which role he had opportunities of practicing that very offense of which he had accused Parker, and became loathed by all who came into contact with him; and after a while the Navy refused to employ him.

Samuel had been forced to leave Hastings after the Parker affair and was in London, where Titus joined him; but it was soon discovered that Titus was wanted by the law; he was captured and sent to prison, from which he escaped, only to find himself penniless once more. He joined a club in Holborn, where he made the acquaintance of several Catholics, and it was through their influence that he obtained a post of Protestant chaplain in the household of that staunch Catholic, the Duke of Norfolk.

It was at this time that the Catholic scare was beginning to be felt in England, and it had occurred to Titus that there might be some profit in exposing, in the right quarters, the secrets of Catholics. He thereupon set himself out to be as pleasant as he could to Catholics, in the hope of learning their secrets, and obtaining an authentic background for his imagination.

Dismissed from the service of the Duke of Norfolk, he was again in London where he made the acquaintance of Dr. Israel Tonge.

Dr. Tonge was a fanatic who was prepared to dedicate his life to the persecution of Jesuits. He had written tracts and pamphlets about their wickedness but, as so many had done the like since the conversion of the Duke of York, there was no sale for those of Dr. Tonge. This made him bitter; not against those who refused to buy them, but against the Papists. He was more determined than ever to destroy them; and when he renewed his acquaintance with Oates, he saw in him a man who could be made to work for him in the cause so near his heart.

Titus was at the point of starvation and ready enough to do all that was required of him.

The two men met often and began to plot.

Oates was to mingle with the Catholics who congregated in the Pheasant Coffee House in Holborn; Tonge had heard that certain Catholic servants of the Queen frequented the place. There Titus would meet Whitbread and Pickering, and other priests who came from Somerset House, where Catherine worshipped, in accordance with her Faith, in her private chapel.

There was one person whom those two plotters mentioned often; the condemnation of that person could bring them greater satisfaction than that of any other, for to prove the Queen of England a Papist murderer would enrage the country beyond all their hopes. If they could prove that the Queen was plotting to murder the King, then surely there was not a Jesuit in England who would not be brought to torture and death.

"The King is a lecher," said Oates, licking his lips. "He will wish to be rid of the Queen."

Dr. Tonge listened to the affected voice of his accomplice and laid a hand on his shoulder. He knew the story of William Parker and Titus' tendency to be carried away by his imagination.

He warned him: "This is no plot against a village schoolmaster. This is a charge of High Treason against the Queen. 'Tis true the King is a lecher, but he is soft with women, including his wife. We shall have to build up our case carefully. This is not a matter over which we can hurry. It may take us years to collect the information we need, and we shall accuse and prove guilty many before we reach the climax of our discovery which shall be the villainy of the Queen."

Tonge's eyes burned with fanaticism. He believed that the Queen must wish to murder the King; he believed in the villainy of all Catholics, and the Queen was devoutly Catholic.

Titus' sunken eyes were almost closed. He was not concerned with the truth of any accusations they would bring. All he cared for was that he should have bread to eat, a roof to shelter him and a chance to indulge that imagination of his which was never content unless it was building up a case against others.

Dr. Tonge's plan was long and involved. Titus should mix with Catholics; he should *become* a Catholic, for only thus could he discover all they would need to build the plot which should bring fame and fortune to them both, and win the eternal gratitude of the King and those ministers of his who desired above all things to see the Queen and the Duke of York dismissed from the Court.

Titus "became" a Catholic and went to study at a college in Valladolid. When he returned, expelled from the college, he brought with him little knowledge, but a fair understanding of the life lived by Jesuit priests; and he and Dr. Tonge, impatient to get on with their work, set about fabricating the great Popish plot.

They would begin by warning the King that two Jesuits, Grove and Pickering—men whom Titus had met at the coffee house in Fleet Street—were to be paid £1,500 to shoot the King while he walked in the park. The death of the King was to be followed by that of certain of his ministers; the French would then invade Ireland and a new King would be set up. This was to be the Duke of York, who would then establish a Jesuit Parliament.

That was the first plot. Others would follow; and when the people were fully aroused, and the King fully alarmed, they would bring forth evidence of the Queen's complicity.

Titus was excited. He saw here a chance to win honors such as had never before come his way.

So when Dr. Tonge returned to his lodgings and told Titus that the man who had uncovered the hellish Popish plot and had thrust the papers concerning it under the door of Dr. Tonge was ordered to appear before the King, Titus was eager to tell his story.

❁ ❁ ❁

Charles looked at Titus Oates and disliked him on sight.

Oates knew this but was unperturbed; he was accustomed to looks of disgust. He cared for nothing; he had a tale to tell, and he felt himself to be master of his facts.

He was glad now of the affair of William Parker as it had taught him such a lesson.

Beside the King was the Duke of York, for Charles had said he must be present since this matter of plots and counterplots concerned him as much as Charles himself.

"A preposterous tale," said Charles when he had read the papers. "False from beginning to end."

His eyes were cold. He hated trouble, and these men were determined to make it.

"So you have studied in Valladolid?" he asked Titus.

"It is true, Your Majesty."

"And you became a Jesuit, that you might mingle with them and discover their secrets?"

"That is so, Your Majesty."

"What zeal!" commented the King.

" 'Twas all in the service of Your Most Gracious Majesty."

"And when you were in Madrid you conferred with Don John of Austria, you say in these papers."

" 'Tis true, Your Majesty."

"Pray, describe him to me."

"He is a tall, spare and swarthy man, if it please Your Majesty."

"It does not please me," said Charles with a sardonic smile. "But doubtless it would please him, for he is a little, fat, fair man, and I believe would desire to appear taller than he is."

"Your Majesty, it may be that I have made a mistake in the description of this man. I have met so many."

"So many of the importance of Don John? Ah, Mr. Oates, I see you are a man much given to good company."

Titus stood his ground. Be could see that if the King did not believe him, others were ready to do so. The difference was that they wanted to, whereas the King did not.

"You say," went on the King, "that the Jesuits will kill not only me but my brother, if he should be unwilling to join them against me, and that they received from Père la Chaise, who is Confessor to Louis Quatorze, a donation of £10,000."

"That is so, Your Majesty."

Those about the King seemed impressed. It was true that Père La Chaise was Confessor to the French King.

"And that there was a promise of a similar sum from another gentleman?"

"From De Corduba of Castile, Your Majesty."

Again Titus was aware of his success. He made sure of facts. The visit to Spain had been well worthwhile. What if he had made a mistake in his description of a man; those about the King did not consider that to be of any great importance.

"So La Chaise paid down £10,000 did he? Where did he do this, and were you there?"

"Yes, Your Majesty. It was in the house of the Jesuits, close to the Louvre."

"Man!" cried the King. "The Jesuits have no house within a mile of the Louvre!"

"I doubt not," said Titus slyly, "that Your Majesty during your stay in Paris was too good a Protestant to know all the secret places of the Jesuits."

"The meeting is over," said Charles. "I will hear no more."

And, putting his arm through that of his brother, the King led James away, murmuring: "The man is a lying rogue. I am certain of it."

❁ ❁ ❁

But the news of the great Popish plot was spreading through the streets of London. The citizens stood about in groups discussing it. They talked of the Gunpowder Plot; they recalled the days of Bloody Mary, when the fires of Smithfield had blackened the sky and a page of English history.

"No Popery!" they shouted. Nor were they willing to wait for trials. They formed themselves into mobs and set about routing out the Catholics.

Coleman, who had been secretary to the Catholic Duchess of York, and one of the suspects at whom Titus had pointed, was found to be in possession of documents sent him by that very Père la Chaise, for Coleman was in truth a spy for France.

All the King's skepticism could do nothing to quiet rumor. The people's blood was up. They believed in the authenticity of the plot. The Jesuits were rogues who must be tracked down to their deaths; Titus Oates was a hero who had saved the King's life and the country from the Papists.

Oates was given lodgings in Whitehall. He was heard in royal palaces talking of Popery in his high nasal and affected voice interspersed with the coarsest of oaths; he was at the summit of delight; he had longed for fame such as this; he was no longer a poor despised outcast; he was admired by all. He was Titus Oates, exposer of Jesuits, the man of the moment.

The King, still declaring the man to be a fake, went off to Newmarket, leaving his ministers to do what they would.

And Titus, determined to hold what he had at last achieved, concocted fresh plots and looked for new victims.

❁ ❁ ❁

Catherine was afraid.

In her apartments at Somerset House she sensed approaching doom. She felt she had few friends and owed much to the Count of Castelmelhor, a Portuguese nobleman, who had been loyal to Alphonso and had found it necessary to leave the country when Pedro was in control. He had come to

Catherine for shelter and had brought great comfort to her during those terrible weeks.

Her servants brought her news of what was happening, and from her stronghold she would often hear the sound of shouting in the streets. She would hear screams and protests as some poor man or woman was set upon; she would hear wild rumors of how this person, whom she had known, and that person, for whom she had a great respect, was being taken up for questioning. "No Popery! No slavery!" was the continual cry. And Titus Oates and Dr. Tonge with their supporters were banded together to corroborate each other's stories and fabricate wilder and still wilder plots in order to implicate those they wished to destroy.

The King, disgusted with the whole affair and certain that Titus was a liar, was quick to sense the state of the country. He had to be careful. His brother was a confessed Catholic. It might be that that clause in the secret treaty of Dover was known to too many, and that he himself might be suspect; he was afraid to show too much leniency to Catholics. He was shrewd, and the tragic events of his life had made him cautious. He remembered—although he had been but a boy at the time—the feeling of the country in those days before the Civil War, which had ended in the defeat of his father, had broken out. He sensed a similar atmosphere. He knew that Shaftesbury and Buckingham with other powerful men were seeking to remove the Duke of York; he knew too that they plotted against Catherine and were determined either to see him divorced and married to a Queen who could provide a Protestant heir, or to see Monmouth legitimized.

He must walk very carefully. He must temporize by giving the people their head; he must not make the mistakes his father had made. He must allow those accused by the odious Titus Oates to be arrested, questioned and, if found guilty, to suffer the horrible death accorded to traitors.

He was grieved, and the whole affair made him very melancholy. He would have liked to have put Titus Oates and his friends in an open boat and sent them out to sea, that they might go anywhere so long as they did not stay in England.

But he dared not go against the people's wishes. They wanted Catholic scapegoats, and they were calling Oates the Savior of England for providing them. They must be humored, for their King was determined to go no more a-wandering in exile. So he went to Windsor and spent a great deal of time fishing, while he indulged in melancholy thought; and Titus Oates lived in style at Whitehall Palace, ate from the King's plate and was protected by guards when he walked abroad. All tried not to meet his eye, and if they were forced to do so, responded with obsequious and admiring smiles, for Titus had but to point the finger and pretend to remember an occasion when a man or woman had plotted against the King's life, and that man or woman would be thrown into jail.

Titus was content; for all those powerful men who had for ten years been seeking to bring about a divorce between the King and Queen saw Titus as a means of perfecting their plans, and to Titus they gave their support.

Catherine knew this.

She longed for the King to come and see her, but she heard that he was at Windsor. There was no one to whom she could turn for advice except those immediately about her, and they were mostly Catholics who feared for their own lives.

She began to realize that the trap into which many of her servants were in danger of falling was in reality being prepared for herself.

There came news that a certain magistrate of the City, Sir Edmund Berry Godfrey, had been murdered. He it was who had taken Titus' affidavit concerning the Popish Plot. He was known as a Protestant although he had Catholic friends, and the manner of his meeting his death was very mysterious. Titus accused the Papists of murdering him, and the magistrate's funeral was conducted with great ceremony while Titus and his friends did everything they could to incite the citizens to fury against his murderers, declared by Titus to be Catholics.

Charles had offered £500 reward for anyone bringing the murderer of Godfrey to justice, although he half suspected that the man had been murdered by Titus' agents for the purpose of rousing the mob to fresh fury, for it seemed that whenever this showed signs of lagging, some such incident would take place, some new plot would be discovered.

It was then that William Bedloe made himself known and came before the Council with a terrible tale to tell.

Bedloe was a convict, and he had met Titus when they were both in Spain. At that time Bedloe had been living on his wits and posing as an English nobleman, with his brother James acting as his manservant. He was handsome and plausible, and had managed during his free life to live at the expense of others, but he had served many sentences in Newgate and had just been released from that prison.

He was attracted by the King's promised reward of £500 and by the fact that his old friend Titus, whom he had last known as a very poor scholar of dubious reputation in Valladolid, was now fêted and honored with three servants at his beck and call and several gentlemen to help him dress and hold his basin whilst he washed.

Bedloe did not see why he should not share in his friend's good fortune, so he came forward to offer his services.

❁ ❁ ❁

It seemed to Catherine that she was always waiting for something to happen; she was afraid when she heard a movement outside her door. She believed that these men were preparing to strike at her, and she was not sure when and how the blow would fall.

It was dusk, and she had come from her chapel to that small chamber in which her solitary meal would be served. And as she was about to sit at her table, the door was thrown open and two of her priests came in to throw themselves at her feet.

"Madam, Madam!" they cried. "Protect us. For the love of God and all the Saints, protect us."

They were kneeling, clutching at her skirts, when she lifted her eyes and saw that guards had entered the chamber.

"What do you want of these men?" she asked.

"We come to take them for questioning, Madam," was the answer.

"Questioning? On what matter?"

"On the matter of murder, Madam."

"I do not understand."

"They are accused of being concerned in the murder of Sir Edmund Berry Godfrey."

"But this is not true. It is quite ridiculous."

"Madam, information has been laid with the Council that may prove them guilty."

"You shall not take them," cried Catherine. "They are my servants."

"Madam," said the guard who was spokesman, "we come in the name of the King."

Her hands fell helplessly to her side.

❁ ❁ ❁

When they had taken the two priests away, she went into her chapel and prayed for them.

Oh, these terrible times! she mused. What will happen next? What will happen to those two servants of mine? What have they done—those two good men—what have they done to deserve punishment, except to think differently, to belong to a Faith other than that of Titus Oates?

She was on her knees for a long time, and when she went back to her apartment she was conscious of the tension throughout her household.

She was aware of strained and anxious faces.

Walsh and le Fevre today. Who next? That was what all were asking themselves. And every man and woman in her service knew that if they were taken it would be because, through them, it might be possible to strike at the Queen.

They trembled. They were fond of their mistress; it would be the greatest tragedy in their lives if they should betray her in some way. But who could say what might be divulged if the questioners should become too cruelly determined to prise falsehood from unwilling lips!

"There is nothing to fear," said Catherine, trying to smile. "We are all innocent here. I know it. These cruel men, who seek to torture and destroy those of our Faith, cannot do so for long. The King will not allow it. The King will see justice done. They cannot deceive him."

No! It was true that they could not deceive him; but he was a man who loved peace; he was a man who had wandered across Europe for many years, an exiled Prince; he was a man whose own father had been murdered by his own countrymen.

The King might be shrewd; he might be kind; but he longed for peace, and how could they be sure whether he would bestir himself to see justice done?

And at the back of Catherine's mind was a terrible fear.

She was no longer young; she had never been beautiful. What if the temptation to put her from him was too great; what if the wife they offered him was as beautiful as Frances Stuart had been in the days before her disfigurement?

Who could tell what would happen?

The Queen of England was a frightened woman during those days of conspiracy.

❁ ❁ ❁

The Duchess of Buckingham brought her the news. She and Mary Fairfax had always been great friends, for there was much sympathy between them. They were both plain women and, if one had been married to the most charming man in England, the other had been married to one of the most handsome.

Mary Fairfax knew that her husband was one of the queen's greatest enemies; she loved her husband but she was too intelligent not to understand his motives, and she could not resist coming to warn the Queen.

"Your Majesty," she cried, "this man Bedloe has sworn that Sir Edmund Berry Godfrey was murdered by your servants."

"It cannot be true. How could they do such a thing? They were nowhere near the place where his body was found."

"They have trumped up a story," said Mary. "They declare that Godfrey was invited to Somerset House at five o'clock in the afternoon, and that he was brought into one of the rooms here and held by a man of my Lord Bellasis' whilst Walsh and le Fevre stifled him with the aid of two pillows."

"No one can believe such a tale."

"The people believe what they want to believe at a time like this," said Mary sadly. "They say that the body lay on your back staircase for two days. Many have been arrested. The prisons are full. The crowds are congregating outside and shouting for them to be brought out, hung, drawn and quartered."

The Queen shuddered. "And my poor innocent priests . . . ?"

"They will prove their innocence."

"These lies are monstrous. Will no one listen to the truth?"

"Your Majesty, the people are treating this man Oates as though he is a god. They are arresting all sorts of people. Do you remember Mr. Pepys of the Navy Office, who did such good service at the time of the great fire? He was taken up, and God alone knows what would have become of him had not one of his accusers—his own butler—come suddenly to his deathbed and, fearing to die with the lies on his lips, confessed that he had borne false witness. He is a good Protestant. Then why was he taken? Your Majesty might ask. Merely because he had been in the service of the Duke of York who thought highly of him."

"No one is safe," murmured the Queen. "No one is safe."

She looked at Mary and was ashamed of herself for suspecting her. But the thought had crossed her mind then; how could she be sure who was her friend?

Who was this man Bedloe who had sworn he had seen the body of a murdered man on her back stairs? Had he been here, disguised as one of her servants?

How could she know who were her enemies; how could she know whom she could trust?

❂ ❂ ❂

In the streets they were saying that the Queen's servants were the murderers of the City magistrate; and since these men were the Queen's servants, that meant that it was at the instigation of the Queen that the man had been murdered.

She was alone . . . alone in a hostile country. She did not believe now that they merely wished to be rid of her; they wished for her death.

They were going to accuse her of murder, and there was no one to stand between her and her accusers.

The country was feverish with excitement; plot after plot was discovered every day; armed bands walked the streets wearing the sign "No Popery" in their hats; and they all talked of the Papist Queen who had murdered the Protestant Magistrate.

Titus Oates went about the town in his episcopal gown of silk, in his cassock and great hat with its satin band; he wore a long scarf about his shoulders and shouted to the people that he was the savior of the nation.

He was ugly in spite of his finery, but none in those fear-ridden streets dared so much as hint that this was so. All who saw him bowed in homage, all called to him that England had been saved by him.

Catherine knew that the misshapen little man was thinking particularly of one victim whom he longed to trap; she knew he was waiting for the right moment, because she was such an important victim that he dared not pounce too soon.

Then suddenly she knew that she was not alone. She knew that she had not been mistaken, for the King came riding into the Capital from Windsor.

He had heard of the accusation against the Queen's servants, and he would realize to what this was leading.

He sent for Bedloe. He would have an exact description of what had taken place at Somerset House. Would the man describe the room in which the murder had taken place? Would he give the exact day on which this had happened?

Bedloe was only too willing to oblige. He gave details of the Queen's residence, for he had made sure of being correct on this.

But when he had finished, the King faced him squarely. "It is a strange thing to me," he said, "that I should have visited Her Majesty on the day you mention, and that I should have been at Somerset House at the very hour the murder took place."

"Your Majesty," began the man, "this may have been so, but Sir Edmund was lured inside while Your Majesty was with the Queen."

The King raised his eyebrows. He said lightly: "Since you and your friends startled my people with your stories of plots, my guards have been most careful of my person. I must tell you that, at the hour when the magistrate was said to have been lured into Somerset House, every possible entry was well guarded because I was there also. Could he have been lured past the guards, think you? And I will add that your tale lacks further conviction, for the passage, in which you say the body of the man lay, is that which leads to the Queen's dining chamber, so that her servants, when bringing her meals, must either have walked over the corpse or not noticed it, which I scarcely think is likely."

Bedloe was about to speak.

"Take this man away!" roared the King.

And Bedloe was hurried out, lest a command to send him to the Tower might be given. Charles was too shrewd to give such an order. He was aware that, as at the time of the war with the Dutch, revolution was in the air.

He could not stem the stream of accusations against the Queen, but he was there to give her his protection while he could do so.

❁ ❁ ❁

The people continued to believe that the Queen was guilty. Buckingham and Shaftesbury were bent on two things: the exile of the Duke of York and his Duchess; and the ruin of the Queen. The King had declined to rid himself of her by divorce; therefore there was only one other way of ridding the country of her.

Why should she not be accused of plotting against the King's life? Titus Oates had the people ready to believe any lie that fell from his lips. He must now uncover for them a plot more startling than any which he had given them before. It could be proved that the Queen had written to the Pope; she had done this during the first weeks of her arrival in England; she had offered to try to turn the King to Catholicism, in exchange for the Pope's recognition of her brother as King of Portugal. But more should be proved against the Queen.

She had refused to enter a nunnery; perhaps she would prefer the block.

Titus Oates, drunk with power, delighting in his eminence, knew what was expected of him.

He set out to concoct the plot to outshine all plots.

The country waited; those men who had determined on the ruin of the Queen waited. And Catherine also waited.

❁ ❁ ❁

Oates stood before the members of the Privy Council. He had grave matters of which to speak to them. He was a careful man, he reminded them; he was a man who had pretended to become a Jesuit for the sake of unearthing their wicked schemes; he was a brave man, they would realize from that, so he did not hesitate to make an accusation against a person however high that person stood in the land.

"My lords," he said in his high affected voice, "there are certain matters which I feel it my duty to disclose to you concerning the Queen."

"The Queen!"

The members of the Council feigned to be astonished, but Titus was aware of their alert and eager faces.

"Her Majesty has been sending sums of money to the Jesuits. They are always at her elbow . . . in secret conclave."

They were watching his face. Dare I? he wondered. It needed daring. He was uncertain, and this matter concerned no other than the King's own wife.

But Titus was blown up with his own conceit. He was not afraid. Was he not great Titus, the savior of his country?

He made his plots, and he made them with such care and with such delight that he came to believe in them even as he elaborated and made his sharp little twists and turns to extricate himself from the maze into which his lies often led him.

"I have seen a letter in which the Queen gives her consent to the murder of the King."

There was a sharp intake of breath as every eye was fixed on that repulsive, almost inhuman face.

"Why did you not report this before?" asked Shaftesbury sharply.

Titus folded his hands. "A matter concerning so great a lady? I felt I must make sure that that which I feel it my duty to bring to your notice was truth."

"And you have now made certain of this?"

Titus took a step nearer to the table about which sat the ministers.

"I was at Somerset House. I waited in an antechamber. I heard the Queen say these words: 'I will no longer suffer such indignities to my bed. I am content to join in procuring the death of the Black Bastard, and the propagation of the Catholic Faith.' "

"This were high treason," said Buckingham.

"Punishable by death!" declared Shaftesbury.

But they were uneasy.

"Why did you not tell this earlier?" asked one of the ministers.

"I have been turning over in my mind whether I should not first impart it to His Majesty."

"How can you be sure that it was the Queen who spoke these words?"

"There was no other woman present."

"So you know the Queen?"

"I have seen her, and I knew her."

"This is a matter," said Shaftesbury, "to which we must all give our closest attention. It may be that the King's life is in imminent danger—in a quarter where he would least expect it."

❁ ❁ ❁

Titus was elaborating his plot. Poison was to be administered to the King; and when he was dead the Duke of York would reign, and there would be a place of honor in the land for his Catholic sister-in-law.

In Somerset House the Queen was fearful. Rumor reached her. She knew that evil forces were working against her. What if, next time she was accused, the King could not save her?

What would he do then? she asked herself. Would he stand by and leave her to her fate?

❁ ❁ ❁

The climax came on a dark November day. Titus could contain himself no longer. His friend Bedloe had been pardoned for all his offenses, as payment for the evidence he had given against the Papists.

Titus, so happy in his episcopal robes, smoothing his long scarf, thinking of the happy days on which he had fallen after all the lean years, hearing the shouts of acclamation when he had been so accustomed to shouts of derision, was called to the bar of the House of Commons to give further evidence of plots he had unearthed.

He stood at the bar, and his voice rang out.

He said those fatal words which were meant to condemn an innocent woman to the block and to bring about the long hoped for conclusion of unscrupulous statesmen: "Aye, Titus Oates, accause Catherine Queen of England of Haigh Treason."

The words were greeted with a shocked silence.

Buckingham was heard to curse under his breath: "The fool! It is too soon as yet!"

And then the news was out.

All over London, and soon all over the country, the people of England were calling for the blood of the woman who had sought to poison their King.

❁ ❁ ❁

So this was the end. Catherine sat like a statue, and beside her was the Count Castelmelhor, whose expression of blank misery made it clear that he believed there was nothing more that he could do for her.

There would be a trial, thought Catherine; and her judges would find her guilty because they had determined to do so.

And Charles?

She understood his case.

His position was an uneasy one. The people were crying out for the blood of Papists, and she was a Papist. Revolution trembled in the air; she was fully aware that there was one day which Charles would never forget—that was a bleak January day when his father had been led to execution.

If he showed any leniency towards the Catholics now, the country would be screaming for his blood too. He knew it, and he had sworn that, at whatever cost, he would never go travelling again.

The people of England were repudiating her. She was a barren Queen; she was a Queen whose dowry had never been paid in full; and she was a Papist. The tall dark man with the melancholy face was no longer ruler of England; that role had fallen to a shuffling man with the most evil of countenances who went by the name of Titus Oates.

There seemed nothing to do but wait for her doom.

❁ ❁ ❁

Castelmelhor had news for her.

"The King has questioned those who accuse Your Majesty. He has questioned them with the utmost severity, and it is clear to all those who hear him that he is greatly displeased with those who would destroy you."

A gentle smile illumined Catherine's face. "Yes, he would be unhappy. That is like him. But he will do nothing. How can he? It would be against the people's wishes. And he must consider them now."

"He has insisted on a minute description of the room of this Palace in which Oates swears he overheard you plan to poison him; he says a woman would have to shout, for Oates to have heard her say what he declares he heard you say; he has said that you are a low-voiced woman. He is doing everything to prove your accusers liars."

Catherine smiled, and the tears started to flow gently down her cheeks.

"I shall remember that," she said. "When they lead me to the block I shall remember it. He did not pass by on the other side of the road. He stopped to succor me."

"Your Majesty must not despair. If the King is with you, others will follow. He is still the King. He is very angry that you should be so accused. They are saying now that Sir George Wakeman was to have brought the poison to you, and that you were to administer it to the King when he next visited you. The King has laughed the idea to scorn, and he says he will never suffer an innocent lady to be oppressed."

"I shall never forget those words," said Catherine. "I shall carry them with me to the grave. I know they have determined on my death, but he would have saved me, if he could."

"You underestimate the power of the King, Madam."

"My dear Castelmelhor, come to the window."

She took his hand and drew him there, for he was reluctant to go with her. Already the crowds were gathering. She saw their hats with the bands about them on which were written "No Popery! No Slavery!" They carried sticks and knives; they were a vicious mob.

They had come to mock and curse her on her journey to the Tower.

❁ ❁ ❁

A barge was on the river. The crowds hurried to its edge.

They have come to take me away, thought Catherine. I shall lie in my prison in the Tower as others have before me. I am guilty of the crime of Queens; I could not bear a son.

This was the end then—the end of that love story which was to have been so perfect, and of which she had dreamed long ago in the Lisbon Palace. She would sail down the river to the grim gray fortress into which she would enter by way of the Traitors' Gate.

It might be that she would never again set eyes on Charles' face. He would not wish to see her. It would distress him too much, for however much he wished to be rid of her, he would never believe her guilty of conspiring to poison him.

She heard the shouts of the people. She could not see the barge, for the crowds on the bank hid it; but now someone had stepped ashore. It was a tall figure, slender, black-clad, the dark curls of his wig falling over his shoulders, his broad-brimmed plumed hat on his head, while those about him were hatless.

Charles!

So he had come to see her. She felt dizzy with her emotion. He had come; and she had never thought he would come. He could have only one purpose in coming to her now.

With him were members of the Court, and his personal guards; he came from the landing stairs to the house with those so well-remembered quick strides of his.

"The King is here!" The words echoed through the house. It was as though the very walls and hangings were trembling with excitement—and hope.

He strode into the room; she tried to approach him, but her limbs trembled so that she could not move. She wanted to sink to her knees and kiss his hand. She merely stood mutely before him, looking up into that lined and well-loved face.

Then he put his hands upon her shoulders and, drawing her towards him, kissed her there before them all.

That kiss was the answer to all who saw it; it was the defiance of two people who were going to stand against all those who were the enemies of the Queen. They had not understood him. They had thought him too facile. They thought that he, being an unfaithful husband, was faithless throughout. They thought that he, finding it so easy to smile and make promises, could never stand firm.

"I have come to take you with me to Whitehall," he said. "It is not meet that you and I should live apart in these times."

Still she could find no words. She felt his hands gripping hers; she saw the tender smile which she remembered from the days of their honeymoon.

Come," he said, "let us go now. I am eager to show them that, whatever comes, the King and Queen stand together."

Then she could not suppress her emotion.

She threw herself against him and cried, half laughing, half in tears: "Charles, you do not believe these stories against me? Charles, I love you with all my heart."

He said: "I know it."

"They will seek to prove these terrible things against me. They will lie and . . . and the people listen to their lies."

"You are returning with me to Whitehall," he said, "whence we shall go to Windsor. We will ride through the countryside together, you and I; for I wish the people to know that in this turmoil there are two who stand side by side in trust and love and confidence: the King and his Queen in whom he puts his trust."

The crowds were gathering about the house. She could hear their shouts.

"Come," he said. "Let us go. Let us leave at once. Are you afraid?"

"No," she said, putting her hand in his, no longer afraid.

They left the house; the people stood back in a hushed silence; they stepped into the barge; the King was smiling at the Queen, and he kept her hand in his.

They sailed along the river to Whitehall and it was seen that never had the King paid more attention to any woman than he did at that time to his Queen.

Catherine felt then that those dreams which had come to her in the Lisbon Palace had materialized. She knew that it was such moments as this which made all that she had suffered worthwhile.

All through the years to come she would treasure this moment; she would remember that when she was lonely and afraid, when she was in imminent peril, that man who had come to her and brought her to safety was the one whom she loved.

EPILOGUE

Some twenty-four years after the reign of Charles had ended, Barbara, Duchess of Cleveland, lay in a house in the village of Chiswick; she was dying.

Sixty-eight years of age, an intriguante to the end, she had not ceased to look for lovers. So many of those who had witnessed the days of her glory were long since dead. Even Catherine the Queen, who had lived to an old age, had died four years before, just at the time when Barbara was contracting that most disastrous marriage with a man who had in his day been one of the most handsome rakes in London.

She lay on her bed, swollen to a great size by the dropsy which had attacked her. She felt too old and tired even to abuse her attendants; a sure sign, they felt, that the end was near.

She dozed a little and allowed her mind to slip back to events of the past. It was the only pleasure left to her. The greatest evil which could befall her had come upon her; she was old, no longer beautiful nor desirable; she remembered faintly that some member of the Court, with whom she had quarreled, had once declared that he hoped to see her come to such a state.

Well, it was upon her now.

She had lost the King's favor to her old enemy the Duchess of Portsmouth; she had had many lovers since then but she had never ceased to regret the loss of Charles. She had schemed to marry her children into the richest and most noble families of England; and only Barbara, her youngest and Churchill's child, had become a nun.

She thought of coming back to England just before Charles' death, with high hopes of returning to his favor. But he remembered too well the tantrums and furies of the past; he was happy with Louise de Kéroualle, his Duchess of Portsmouth, and Nelly the play-girl.

In place of the King she had found an actor lover, a gay adventurer, named Cardonell Goodman. Ah, he had been handsome, and what joy to see him strut across the stage as Alexas in Dryden's *All for Love,* or Julius Caesar or Alexander the Great. She had paid him well; and he had been grateful, for an actor's pay of six and threepence a day had been inadequate for the needs of such a man. No wonder he had loved her. No wonder he had refused to allow the play to start until his Duchess was in her box, even though the Queen herself had come to see it! He had tried to poison her children. Oh, he was a rogue, but an exciting one, and she had his child to remember him by.

But she was growing old and her body had become over-heavy; and the worst calamity which had befallen her was the death of Roger, for then she had been foolish enough to go through a form of marriage with Robert Feilding, who was known as "Beau."

The thought of that villain could rouse her from her torpor even now and bring the tumultuous blood rushing to her head. Be calm! she admonished herself. You do yourself harm by thinking of the rogue!

In Feilding she had found another such as she herself had been; but, being ten years her junior, he had the whip hand, and he used it. He had dared to dictate to her and, if she did not carry out his wishes, to lay about him with his heavy hands. He had dared to inflict bruises on the Duchess of Cleveland!

But Fate was kinder to her than perhaps she deserved; for she discovered that she was not after all his wife, since he had contracted a marriage with another woman some short while before he had gone through the ceremony with her.

And with Feilding had ended her matrimonial adventures. She had felt only one desire then—to live in seclusion.

So in the village of Chiswick she had come to end her days.

The room was growing dark; she could hear voices but she could no longer see the figures which moved about her.

She closed her eyes, and as her attendants bent over her bed, one murmured: "Was this then . . . this bloated creature . . . was she once the most beautiful of women?"

❁ ❁ ❁

It was four years before the death of Barbara when, in the quiet Palace of Lisbon, in that chamber to which no man must be admitted, Catherine of Braganza lay dying.

She was an old woman now, having reached her sixty-seventh year, and it was twenty years since Charles had died.

Now, as she lay in her bed with only Donna Inez Antonia de Tavora to wait on her, she felt life slipping away from her and was not always conscious of the room in which she lay.

It seemed to her that sometimes she was back in the Palace of Whitehall, enduring agonies of jealousy as she saw her husband become deeply enamored of other women. It had not been the end of jealousy when he had come to Somerset House and saved her from her enemies. He had not changed towards her. He was the same Charles as he had ever been. She had still remained his plain wife who did not attract him, who must be perpetually jealous of the beautiful women with whom he surrounded himself; but she had learned one thing: he would always be there when any dire peril threatened her.

He had saved her; it had been said, during the weeks which followed that journey from Somerset House to Whitehall: "The King has a new mistress—his wife."

Yet he had been unable to save her servants; he had been against the bloody executions which had followed, but he had done all he dared in saving his wife.

She recalled those unhappy days when England was ruled by a cruel rogue and wicked perjurer. She remembered the exile of the unhappy Duke of York, and later his defeat by his daughter's husband; she remembered the coming of William of Orange—and her own unhappy treatment at the hands of that sovereign and his wife Mary. She remembered returning to her native land and building this Palace of Bemposta; and she looked back on these last five years of her life as the peaceful years.

But there was one thing she remembered more vividly than anything, and that was the last time she had seen the man she had loved throughout her life. The pain he suffered could not disturb that wry smile; the agony of death could not quench the wit which came so readily to his lips.

She had wept and had begged that he would forgive her for failing him—for failing to bring him the dowry which he had so desired, for failing to bring him the beauty which he had so much admired, for failing to give him a son.

She would treasure his answer to the very end. "You beg my pardon? Do not, I pray you, for it is I who should beg yours, and this I do with all my heart."

Now she murmured those words to herself.

"He begged my pardon with all his heart. What need had he to beg my pardon with all his heart, when I loved him with all mine?"

The end was near. The room was now crowded; she was vaguely conscious of the last ceremonies, for it seemed to her that at the last there was one who stood beside her—tall and very dark, with a jest on his lips—who took her hand to lead her; and she was smiling, for thus she was not afraid.

Part Three

HERE LIES OUR SOVEREIGN LORD

Nell Gwyn and
Louise de Kéroualle

For Vivian Stuart

ONE

All through the spring of that year there had been growing tension in the streets of London. It had communicated itself to aged and young alike. The old woman with her tray of herrings on the corner of Cole-yard where it turned off Drury Lane, watched passersby with eagerness as she called: "Good herrings! Come buy my good herrings." If any paused, she would demand: "Is there news? What news?" The children, ragged, barefoot and filthy, playing in the gutters or trying to earn a coin or two by selling turnips and apples or helping the old woman dispose of her herrings, were alert for news. If any stranger rode by they would run after him, fighting each other for the privilege of holding his horse, demanding with their own brand of Cockney impudence: "What news, sir? Now Old Noll's departed, what news?"

Every day there were rumors. The observant noticed changes in the London they had known for the last ten years and more—small changes, but nevertheless changes. The brothels had flourished all through the Commonwealth, but discreetly; now, passing through Dog-and-Bitch Lane, it was possible to see the women at the windows, negligent in their dress, beckoning to passersby and calling to them in their harsh London voices to come inside and see what pleasures they might enjoy. Blood-sports were gradually coming back to London once again.

"We are getting back to the good old days," people said to one another.

On the cobbles outside one of the hovels in Cole-yard, three children sprawled. They were unusually good-looking, and none of them was marked by the pox or any deformity. The two elder children—a girl and a boy—were about twelve years old, the younger, a girl, aged ten; and it was this ten-year-old who was the most attractive of the three. Her bones were small and she was delicately formed; her hair fell in a tangle of matted curls about her shoulders; it was of a bright chestnut color; her hazel eyes were full of mischief; her nose, being small and *retroussé,* added a look of impudence to her face. For all that she was the youngest and so much smaller than the others, she dominated the group.

Beside the boy lay a torch. As soon as it was dark he would be at work, lighting ladies and gentlemen across the roads. The elder of the two girls was casting anxious glances over her shoulder at the hovel behind her, and the young girl was laughing at the elder because of the latter's fear.

"She'll not be out for a while, Rose," she cried. "She's got her gin, so what'll she want with her daughters?"

Rose rubbed her hand along her back reminiscently.

Her young sister jeered. "You should be smarter on your feet, girl. Shame on you! You an active wench, to be caught and pasted by an old woman full of gin!"

The child had leaped up; she found it hard to remain still for any length of time. "Why," she cried, "when old Ma turned to me with her stick I ran straight in to her . . . thus . . . caught her by the petticoat and swung her round till she was so giddy with the turning and the gin that she clutched me for support and begged me stop her from falling, calling me her good girl. And what said I? 'Now, Ma! Now Ma . . . You take less of the gin and be more ready with a kiss and a good word for your girls than with the stick. That's the way to have good and loving daughters.' She sat flat on the floor to get her breath, and it was not till she was fully recovered that she thought of the stick again. Then 'twas too late to use it, for her anger against me had sped away. That's the way to treat a drunken sot, Rosy girl, be she who she may."

As the girl had talked she had changed from the role of drink-sodden old woman to sprightly mischievous child, and each she had performed with an adroitness that set the others laughing.

"Give over, Nelly," said Rose. "You'll have us die of laughter."

"Well, we all have to die one day, whether it be of laughter or gin."

"But not yet, not yet," said the boy.

"Mayhap twelve years is a little too young, cousin Will. So I'll have mercy on you, and you shall not die of laughing yet."

"Come, sit down and be quiet awhile," said Rose. "I heard tales in Longacre Street this day. They say the King is coming home."

"If he comes," said Will, "I shall be a soldier in his Army."

"Bah!" said Nell. "A soldier to fight the battles of others? Even a link-boy fights his own."

"I'd have a grand uniform," said Will. "A beaver hat with a feather to curl over my shoulder. I'd have a silver chain about my neck, riding boots to the knee, and a red velvet cloak. I'd be a handsome gallant roaming the streets of London."

Nell cried: "Why not be the King himself, Will?" Will looked crest-fallen and she went on kindly: "Well, Will, who knows, mayhap you shall have your beaver hat and feather. Mayhap when the King comes home 'twill be the custom for every link-boy, from Aldgate Pump to Temple Bar, to have his beaver hat and feather."

"Nelly jokes," said Rose. "My girl, one day your jokes will land you into trouble."

"Better be landed in trouble by jokes than felony."

"You are too smart for your years, Nell."

There was a clatter of horse's hoofs as a man came riding by. All three children got to their feet and ran after the man on horseback who was pulling up at a house in Drury Lane.

"Hold your horse, sir?" said Will.

The man leaped down and threw the reins to Will.

Then he looked at the two girls.

"What news, sir?" asked Nell.

"News! What news should such as I have to give to a drab like you?"

Nell dropped a curtsy. "Drabs who would be ladies, and serving men aping their lords all have a right to news, sir."

"Impudent beggar's whore!" said the man.

Nell stood poised for flight.

"I am too young for the title, sir. Mayhap if you pass this way a few years later I shall have earned it."

The man laughed; then feeling in his pocket flung a coin at her. Expertly Nell caught it before it fell to the ground. The man passed on. Will was left holding his horse, while Nell and Rose studied the coin. It was as much as Will would earn for his labor, and Rose remarked on this.

"The tongue is as useful as a pair of hands," cried Nell.

"What will you do with the money?" asked Rose.

Nell considered. "A pie, a slice of beef mayhap. Mayhap. As yet I have decided on one thing only: It shall not buy gin for Ma."

As they strolled back to Cole-yard, their mother appeared suddenly at the door of the hovel.

"Rosy! Nelly!" she screeched. "You lazy sluts, where are you? I'll wallop you till you're black and blue, you lazy good-for-nothings, both of you. Come here at once . . . if you want to live another hour. Rosy! Nelly! Was ever a good woman cursed with such sluts?" Suddenly she saw them. "Come here, you two. You, Rosy! You, Nelly! You come here and listen to your own mother."

"Something has happened to excite her," said Rose.

"And for once it is not the gin," added Nell.

They followed Madam Eleanor Gwyn into the dark hovel which was their home.

❁ ❁ ❁

Their mother sat down panting on a three-legged stool. She was very fat, and the effort of coming to the door and calling them had tired her.

Rose pulled another stool up to her mother's; Nell spread herself on the floor, her legs and tiny feet swaying above her recumbent body, her vital heart-shaped face supported by her hands.

"There are you two, roaming the streets," scolded Mrs. Gwyn, "never giving a thought to the good days ahead."

"We were waiting for you to come out of your gin sleep, Ma," said Nell.

Mrs. Gwyn half rose as though to cuff the girl, but thought better of it.

"Give over with your teasing, Nell," she said, "and listen to me. There's good days coming, and shouldn't we all share in them?"

"The King's coming home," said Rose.

"You two don't remember the old days," said Madam Gwyn, lapsing into one of the sentimental moods which often came to her after consuming a certain quantity of gin. Nell found them less tolerable than her other phases, preferring a fighter any day to a maudlin drunkard. But now her keen eyes saw that this mood was a passing one. Her mother was excited. "No, you don't remember the good old days," she went on. "You don't remember the shops in the Royal Exchange, and all the merry girls selling their wares there. You don't remember seeing the young cavaliers about the streets. There was a sight for you—in their silks and velvets and feathers and swords! There was a life for a girl. When I was your age there was good sport to be had in this old city. Many's the time I've stood at a pillar in St. Paul's and met a kind and generous gentleman." She spat. "Kind and generous gentlemen—they went out with the King. They all followed him abroad. But things is different now—or going to be."

"The King's coming home!" cried Nell. She was on her feet, waving her arms and bowing. "Welcome, Your Majesty. And what difference are you going to make to two skinny girls and their gin-sodden bawd of a mother?"

"Be silent, Nell, be silent," warned Rose. "This is not the time."

"Anytime's the time for the truth," said Nell. She eyed her mother cautiously. Madam Gwyn returned her stare. Nell was too saucy by half, Madam Gwyn was thinking; but the girl was too spry to be caught and beaten, and in any case she wanted Nell as an ally now; she herself was the one who had to be careful.

And to think she's but ten years old, pondered Nell's mother. Her tongue's twice that age for all her small body and her child's face.

Madam Gwyn was filled with self-pity that she, a loving mother, always thinking of her girls, should be so treated by them; with cupidity, in assessing the value of these two girls in her proposed venture; and with admiration for herself because of the livelihood with which she was going to provide them.

"Nelly's right," she said placatingly. "It's always best to have the truth."

"When the King comes home," said Rose, "London will change. It'll be like the old London Ma knew as a girl. And if things change for London, they change for us. But it's a long time since Noll Cromwell died, and the King is still not home. I can remember, when he died, everybody said, 'Now the Black Boy will be home.' But he didn't come."

"The Black Boy!" cried Nell. "How black is he? And is he such a boy?"

"It's his swarthy skin and his way with women. He's as dark as a blackamoor and always a boy where the girls are concerned," said Madam Gwyn. She began to laugh. "And Kings set fashions," she added significantly.

"Let's wait till he's here before we line the streets to welcome him," said Rose.

"No," said Nell. "Let's welcome him now. Then if he does not come we've had the fun of welcome all the same."

"Put a stop to those clacking tongues," said Madam Gwyn, "and listen to me. I'm going to make this place into a nice house for gentlemen . . . There's the cellar below, where we'll put a few chairs and tables, and the gentlemen will come in to take their fill."

"Their fill . . . of what?" said Nell sharply.

"Of pleasure," said Madam Gwyn, "for which they'll pay right well. I'll let some of the girls hereabouts come in and help me build up a nice little house, and it'll all be for the sake of my girls."

"And a little extra gin," murmured Nell.

Rose was silent and Nell, who knew her sister well, sensed the alarm in her. Even Nell fell silent. And after a while Madam Gwyn dozed, and Nell and Rose went to the old herring-woman on the corner to help sell some of her wares.

❁ ❁ ❁

They lay side by side on their pallet. Close to them, on hers, lay their mother. She was fast asleep, but Rose could not sleep; she was afraid; and Nell sensed Rose's fear.

Nell's tongue was sharper than Rose's and Nell was bright enough to know that there were some things about which Rose must be—on account of her two years' seniority—better informed than herself.

Rose was alarmed at the prospect of the "house" which her mother was planning; and Nell knew that Rose was thinking of the part she would be called upon to play in it. This meant entertaining men. Nell knew something of this. She was so small that she appeared to be younger than she was, but that had not protected her from the attentions of certain men. Her pert face, framed by abundant curls, had not passed unnoticed. On more than one occasion she had been beckoned into quiet places and had gone, hoping to earn a groat or two, for Nell was often hungry and the smell of roasting flesh and hot pies which filled certain streets was at such times very tantalizing; but she had quickly retreated after inflicting kicks and a bite or two, and there had been a great terror within her which she had hidden by her indignant protestations.

"Rose," she whispered consolingly, "mayhap it won't come."

Rose did not answer. She knew Nell's way of not believing anything she thought might be unpleasant. Nell would play at the pageants and the excitement of the King's return over and over again, but of these plans of her mother's which might prove unpleasant she would declare—and believe—they would come to nothing.

Nell went on, for Nell found it difficult to hold her tongue: "Nay, Ma's house will come to naught. 'Tis many years since there has been this talk of the King's return. And is he here? Nay! Do you remember, Rose, the night of the storm? That was years and years ago. We lay here clinging one to the other in the very fear that the end of the world had come. Do you remember, Rosy? It had been a stifling hot day. Ugh! And the smell of the gutters! Then the darkness came and the thunder and the wind seemed as though it would tear down the houses. And all said: 'This is a sign! God's angry with England. God's angry with the Puritans.' Do you remember, Rosy?"

"Aye," said Rose. "I remember."

"And then just after that old Noll died and everybody said: 'God is angry. He sent the storm and now He's taken old Noll. The Black Boy will be home.' But that was long, long ago, Rose, and he's not here yet."

"It was two years ago."

"That's a long time."

"When you're ten it's a long time. When you're as old as I am . . . it's not so long."

"You're only two years older than I am, Rose."

"It's a great deal. A lot can happen to a girl in two years."

Nell was silent for a while; then she said: "You remember when the General came riding to London?"

"That was General Monk," said Rose.

"General Monk," repeated Nell. "I remember it well. It was the day after my birthday. It was a cold day. There was ice on the cobbles. 'A cold February,' everyone was saying. 'But a hard winter can mean a good summer, and this summer will surely bring the Black Boy home.' "

"And it looks as though it will," said Rose.

"What excitement, Rosy, when the General rode through London! Do you remember how they roasted rumps of beef in the street? Oh, Rosy, don't you love the smell of roasting rumps of beef? And there's one thing I like better. The *taste* of it." Nell began to laugh.

"Oh, what a time that was, Rosy," she went on. "I remember the bonfires—a line of them from St. Paul's to the Stocks Market. I thought London town was burning down, I did indeed. There were thirty-one at Strand Bridge. I counted them. But best of all were the butchers and the roasting rumps. That was a day, that was. I always thought, Rose, that it was for my birthday . . . coming so soon after it, you see. All those fires and good beef! I went with the crowd that marched to the house of Praise-God Barebone. I threw some of those stones that broke his windows, I did. And someone in the crowd said to a companion: 'What's it all about, do you know?' and I answered up and said: ' 'Tis Nelly's birthday, that's what it is, though a bit late; but Nelly's birthday all the same.' And they laughed in my face and someone said: 'Well, at least this child knows what it's all about.' And they laughed more and they jeered and were for picking me up and carrying me nearer to the bonfire. But I was scared, thinking they might take it into their heads to roast me in place of a rump . . . so I took to my heels and ran to the next bonfire."

"Your tongue again, Nell. Guard it well. That was the end of the Rump Parliament, and the General was for the King."

"It was not so long ago, Rose, and this time he'll be home. Then there'll be fun in the streets; there'll be games in Covent Garden, Rose, and there'll be fairs and dancing in the streets to the tunes of a fiddler. Oh, Rose, I want to dance so much I could get up now and do so."

"Lie still."

Nell was silent for a while. Then she said: "Rose, you're afraid, are you not? You're afraid of Ma's new 'house.' " Nell threw herself into her sister's arms. "Why, Rose?" she demanded passionately. "Why?"

This was one of those rare moments when Nell realized she was the younger sister and begged to be comforted. Once they had been more frequent.

Rose said: "We have to make a living, Nell. There are not many ways for girls like us."

Nell nodded fiercely; and a silence fell between them.

Then she said: "What shall I have to do in Ma's house, Rose?"

"You? Oh, you're young yet. And you're small for your age. Why, you don't look above eight. Keep your tongue quiet and none would think you were the age you are. But your tongue betrays you, Nell. Keep a fast hold on it."

Nell put out her tongue and held it firmly in her fingers, a habit of her very young days.

"You'll be well enough, Nell. Just at first you'll be called upon to do nothing but serve strong waters to the gentlemen."

The two sisters clung together in silence, rejoicing that whatever the future held for them, the other would be there to share it.

❁ ❁ ❁

Nell was there in the streets when the King came home. Never in all her life had she witnessed such pageantry. She had climbed onto a roof—urging Rose and her cousin Will to climb with her—the better to see all that was to be seen.

Nell's eyes shone with excitement as others, following her example, climbed the roof to stand beside the three children; Nell jostled to keep her place and let out such streams of invective that those about her were first incensed, then amused. She snapped her fingers in their faces; she was used to such treatment; she knew the power of her tongue which always made people smile in the end.

From where she stood she could see St. Paul's rising high on Ludgate Hill and dominating the dirty city, the hovels of which clustered about the fine buildings like beggars about the skirts of fine ladies. Even the wide roads were so much in need of repair that they were full of potholes; the small streets and alleys were covered in mud and filth. The smells from the breweries, soap-makers and tanneries filled the air, but Nell did not notice this; these were the familiar smells. On the river were boats of all descriptions—barges, wherries, skiffs, anything which could float. Music came from them, and shouting and laughter filled the air. Everyone seemed to want to talk of his pleasure in this day so loudly as to shout his neighbor down.

The bells were ringing from every church in the city; the roughness of the roads was hidden by flowers which had been strewn along the way the King would come; tapestry was hung across the streets and from the windows. The fountains were running with wine. All the people seemed to be congratulating each other that they had lived to see this day.

Over London Bridge and through the streets the procession came on its way to the Palace of Whitehall. There were all the fine ladies and gentlemen, all the noblemen and women who surrounded the King.

Nell leaped with excitement and was warned by Rose and Will that if she did not take greater care she would fall from the roof.

She paid no heed, for at that moment the cheering and shouting of the people had become so loud that she could no longer hear the pealing of the bells. Then she saw the King ride by, tall, and very dark—a veritable Black Boy—bareheaded with his black curls falling over his shoulders, his feathered hat in his hand as he bowed and smiled to the crowds who were shouting themselves hoarse in their welcome.

The dark eyes seemed to miss no one. All about her Nell heard the whisper: "He smiled at me. I swear it. He looked straight at *me* . . . and smiled. Oh, what a day is this! The King has come home, and England will be merry again."

Behind the King came all those who had followed him from Rochester, determined to accompany him into his capital, determined to drink his health in the wine flowing from London fountains, determined to show that not only in London did people welcome the King to his own.

Nell was quiet as she watched the rest of the procession. She was wishing she was one of the fine ladies she saw riding there. Those little feet of hers would look well in silver slippers. She longed for a velvet gown to replace her coarse petticoat; she would have liked to comb the tangles out of her hair and wear it in sleek curls as those ladies did.

Rose was wistful too. Rose had changed lately—grown secretive. Rose was now working in her mother's house, and Rose was reconciled. She was pretty and many men who came to the house asked for Mrs. Rose. Nell, hurrying from one table to another serving strong waters, eluded those hands stretched out to catch her; she could not curb her tongue and she knew how to use it to advantage—not to charm those men with the ugly lustful faces who gathered in her mother's cellar, but to anger them, so that they felt more inclined to cuff that slut Nelly than to caress her.

It was seven of the clock by the time the procession had passed and they could fight their way back to Cole-yard, where Madam Gwyn was waiting for them. There was free wine in the fountains that day, but all the same she anticipated good business in her cellar.

❁ ❁ ❁

It was early morning and there were still sounds of revelry in the streets.

Rose was not in the house in Cole-yard. She had gone off with a lover. "A fine and gallant gentleman," mused Madam Gwyn. "Ah, what I do for my girls!"

It was not easy to sleep. Nell lay on her pallet and looked at that mountain of flesh which was her mother. She had never loved her. How was it possible to love one who had cuffed and abused for as long as one could remember? What did Ma want now but a life of ease for herself—ease and gin, of course. She was meant to keep a bawdy-house. Sugary words came easily to her tongue when she talked to the gentlemen, just as abuse came when she scolded her daughters. All her hopes were in Rose—pretty Rose who already had found a lover from the casual callers at the house.

And, mused Nell, what else was there for a girl to do? Sell herrings, apples, turnips?

Rose had a fine gown given her by her lover, and she looked very pretty when she sauntered out into Drury Lane. The other girls were envious of Rose. Yet Nell did not want that life. Nell was going to remain a child—too young for anything but to serve strong drinks—for as long as she could.

"Ma," she said softly, "are you asleep?"

"There's too much noise outside for sleep."

"It's good noise, Ma. It means the King's home and things will change."

"Things will change," wheezed Madam Gwyn. Then she said: "Nell . . . there's nothing left in this bottle. Get me another."

Nell leaped up and obeyed.

"You'll kill yourself, Ma," she said.

Madam Gwyn spat, and snatched the bottle roughly. Nell watched her, wondering whether when she was young she had ever looked as pretty as Rose.

"I deserve my fancies," said Madam Gwyn. " 'Twas a goodly night. If all nights were as good as this one I'd be rich."

"Mayhap they will be, Ma, now the King's come home."

"Mayhap. Mayhap I'll have a true brothel. There's more to be made in a brothel than a bawdy-house. Mayhap ere long I'll have a place in Moorfields or Whetstone Park. Why should such as Madam Cresswell, Mother Temple, and Lady Bennet do so well, while I have my cold cellar and just a few sluts from the Cole-yard?"

"Well, Ma, you've done well. You've got the whole of this place now, and the rooms above this bring much profit to you."

"You're growing up, Nell."

"I'm not very old yet, Ma."

"I once thought you'd be every bit as good as your sister. I'm not so sure now. Don't none of the gentlemen ever have a word with you?"

"They don't like me, Ma." Madam Gwyn sighed, and Nell went on quickly: "You've got to have someone to serve the brandy, Ma. You couldn't get round quick enough with it yourself. And would you trust any but me with that fine Nantes brandy?"

Madam Gwyn was silent, and after a while she began to cry. This was the maudlin mood, and for once Nell was glad of it. "I'd have liked something better for my girls," mused Madam Gwyn. "Why, when you were born . . ."

"Tell me about our father," said Nell soothingly.

And her mother told of the captain who had lost all his money fighting the King's battles. Nell smiled wryly. All poor men in these days had lost their money fighting the King's battles; and she did not believe this story of the handsome captain, for what handsome captain would have married her mother?

"And he would give me this and that," mourned Madam Gwyn. "He spent all he had as soon as he got it. That was why he died—blessing me and his two girls—in a debtors' prison in Oxford town."

Madam Gwyn was crying noisily; outside in the streets the merry-making continued, and Nell lay wide-eyed yet dreaming—dreaming that some miraculous fate took her from her mother's bawdy-house in Cole-yard and she became a lady in a gown of scarlet velvet and silver lace.

❁ ❁ ❁

Nell stood watching the builders on that plot of land between Drury Lane and Bridge Street.

Will was with her. Will knew most things that went on in the city.

"You know what they're building here, Nelly?" he said. "A theater."

"A theater!" Nell's eyes sparkled. She had been to the play once in Gibbon's Tennis Court in Vere Street. It had been an experience she had never forgotten, and swore she never would. When she had left the place the enchantment had lingered and, having memorized most of the attractive roles, she had continued to play them out ever since, partly for the benefit of any who would listen and watch, chiefly for her own satisfaction.

What more exciting than to prance on a stage, to have all the people in the theater watching you, to hear them laugh at your wit, always knowing that their amusement might as easily turn to scorn. Yes, those laughs, those tender languishing glances from young gallants, might easily be replaced by bad eggs or offal, filth picked up in the streets. Nell's eyes sparkled still more as she thought of what she'd have to say to any who dared insult *her.*

And now they were building a new theater. Because, said Will, the King cared greatly for the theater and actors; he liked men who could make him laugh, and actors who could divert him with their play.

Gibbon's Tennis Court was no longer considered good enough for a King's Theater, and this was to be built. So Will had heard two gentlemen say, when he had lighted them across the road. It was going to cost the vast and almost unbelievable sum of one thousand five hundred pounds. "Mr. Killigrew is making all arrangements," added Will.

"Mr. Killigrew!" said Nell, and she laughed loudly. Rose had a new lover. He was a gentleman of high degree and his name was Killigrew—Henry Killigrew. He was employed by the Duke of York, the King's brother; but, more important still, he was the son of the great Thomas Killigrew, friend of the King, Groom of the King's Bedchamber and Master of the King's Theater. It was this great Thomas Killigrew who was responsible for the building of the new theater, and the fact that Rose's lover was his son gave Rose added luster in Nell's eyes.

She could scarcely wait to reach home and tell Rose what she had discovered, so bade a hasty farewell to Will, who looked hurt. Poor Will, he should be accustomed to her by now. Will was fond of her; he was afraid that one day her mother would succeed in making her work in the house as Rose worked, even though Nell was determined not to. Nell had her eyes on another life. It was not like her to be secretive, but this she kept to herself. She had started to dream ever since she had watched the King ride into his capital and had seen the fine ladies in their silks and velvets. She had wanted to be as they were and, perhaps because she knew that the nearest she could get to being a lady of quality was to act the part—and this she believed she could do so that none would know her home was a bawdy-house in Cole-yard—she had made up her mind to be an actress.

When she arrived at the house she realized with dismay that soon the gentlemen would be crowding into the cellar, and she would be running from table to table serving brandy, wine or ale, avoiding the hands that now and then sought to catch her, making use of her nimble feet either to kick or to run, and scowling—squinting too—to distort her pretty face.

She went to the room where the girls sat when they were not in the cellar. Rose was there alone.

Nell cried: "Rose, they're building a theater by Drury Lane and Bridge Street."

"I know," said Rose, smiling secretly. He told her, thought Nell.

"It's Henry's father, who is the King's Theater Master," said Nell. "He is having this done."

" 'Tis so," said Rose.

"Does he talk to you of the theater, Rose?"

Rose shook her head. "We don't have time for talking much," she said demurely.

Nell began to jig round the room. Rose looked at her intently. "Nelly," she said, "you're growing up." Nell stood still, some of the color drained from her face. "And . . . in your way . . ." said Rose, "you're a pretty wench."

The horror had frozen on Nell's face. "Mayhap," went on Rose, "you would miss my luck. 'Tis not every girl from Cole-yard who could find herself a gentleman."

"That's so," agreed Nell.

"You love the theater, do you not? You would like to go often. Why, I'll never forget the way you were when you came home after seeing the players—nearly driving us all crazy and making us die of laughing. Nell, how would you like to be in the theater while the players act?"

"Rose . . . what do you mean? Rosy, Rosy, tell me. . . . Tell me quickly or I'll *die* of despair."

"That's one thing you'd never die of. Listen to me: I know this, for Henry told me. The King's company have granted to Mrs. Mary Meggs the right to sell oranges, lemons, fruit, sweetmeats, and all manner of fruiterers' and confectioners' wares. That will be when the new theater opens. Oh, it's going to be such a place, Nelly!"

"Tell me . . . tell me about Mary Meggs."

"Well, she will need girls to help her sell her wares, that is all, Nelly."

"And you mean . . . that I . . ."

Rose nodded. "I told Harry about you. He laughed fit to die when I told him how you squinted for fear the gentlemen should be after you. He said he had a mind to try you himself. But he did not mean that," added Rose complacently. "I told him how you wanted to be in the playhouse all the time, and he said, 'Why, she'd make one of Orange Moll's girls.' Then he told me about Mary Meggs and how she wanted three or four girls to stand there in the pit and chivy the gentlemen into buying China oranges."

Nell clasped her hands together and smiled ecstatically at her sister. "And I am to do this?"

"I know not. You go too fast. Did you not always? If Mary Meggs makes up her mind that you will suit her, and if she has not already found her girls . . . well then, doubtless you will serve."

"Take me to her. Take me to her now. I must see Mary Meggs. I must! I must!"

"There is one thing you must not do—and that is squint. Mary Meggs wants pretty girls in the pit. No gentleman would pay sixpence for a China orange to a girl who squints."

"I shall smile . . . and smile . . . and smile. . . ."

"Nell, Nell, don't smile so downstairs, or you'll look too pretty."

"Nay," said Nell. "I shall look like this as I serve the waters." She made a hideous grimace, squinting diabolically, puffing down her lids with her fingers, and drawing her mouth into a snarl.

Rose doubled up with laughter. Rose laughed easily nowadays. That was because she was thinking of her lover, Harry Killigrew. Life was wonderful, Nell decided; one never knew what was coming. Poor Rose had been frightened of the cellar and the gentlemen, and now that work had brought her Harry Killigrew; and his connection with the King's players was to give Nell an introduction to Orange Moll Meggs and bring her near to her heart's desire.

Rose was sober suddenly. "There is no need for you to hurry to Mary Meggs. Harry will say: 'Mrs. Nelly is to sell oranges in the King's Theater because Mrs. Nelly is the sister of my Rose.' "

Nell flung herself into her sister's arms, and they laughed together as they had often laughed in the past, laughed for happiness and relief, which, Nell had said, were so much more worth laughing for than a witty word.

❁ ❁ ❁

Henry Killigrew did not come to the cellar that night. Rose was always anxious when he did not come. Nell was anxious now. What if he never came again? What if he forgot all about Rose and her sister Nell? What if he did not realize how vitally important it was that Nell Gwyn should become one of Mary Meggs' orange-girls?

Nell moved among the gentlemen with an abstracted look, but she was ever ready to elude their straying hands. She was sorry for poor Rose; for if her lover did not come, Rose would be forced to take another, provided he would pay the price her mother demanded.

Rose was no longer indifferent, because Rose was in love. It was as important now for Rose to elude those straying hands as it was for Nell to do so.

Nell felt sudden anger against a world which had nothing better than this to offer a girl, when others—such as those ladies in velvet and cloth of gold and silver—whom she had seen about the King on his triumphal entry into his Capital, had so much. But almost immediately she was resigned. Rose had her lover, and those ladies riding with the King had not seemed more radiant than Rose when she had been going to meet Henry Killigrew; and when she, Nell, was one of Mary Meggs' orange-girls she would know greater happiness than any of those women could possibly know.

Now her eyes went to Rose. A fat man with grease on his clothes—doubtless a flesh-merchant from East Cheap—was beckoning to her, and Rose must perforce go and sit at his table.

Nell watched. She saw the big hands touching Rose, saw Rose recoiling with horror, her eyes piteously fixed on the door, waiting for the entry of her lover.

Nell heard her say: "No . . . No. It is not possible. I have a gentleman waiting for me."

The flesh-merchant from East Cheap stood up and kicked the stool on which he had been sitting across the cellar. Others watched, eyes alert with interest. This was what they liked—a brawl in a bawdy-house when they could throw bottles at one another, wreck the place, and enjoy good sport.

Madam Gwyn had come from her corner like an angry spider. She raised her slurring gin-cracked voice. "What ails you, my fine gentleman? What do you find in my house not to your liking?"

"This slut!" shouted the flesh-merchant.

"Why, that's Mrs. Rose . . . the prettiest of my girls . . . Now, Mrs.

Rose, what has gone wrong here? You drop a curtsy to the fine gentleman and tell him you await his pleasure."

The flesh-merchant watched Rose and his little eyes were cruel.

"He's planning to hurt her," shouted Nell in panic.

Rose cried: "I cannot. I am ill. Let me go. There is a gentleman waiting for me."

Rose's mother took her by the arm and pushed her towards the flesh-merchant, who gripped her and held her to him for a few seconds; then he was roaring with rage, shouting at the top of his voice. "I see it now. She has my purse, the slut!"

He was holding a purse above his head. Rose had stepped back, staring at the purse with fascinated eyes.

"Where did you . . . find that?" she asked.

"Inside your bodice, girl. Where you put it."

" 'Tis a lie," said Rose. "I never saw it before."

He had caught at the drapery at Rose's neck, cut low to show her pretty bosom. He tore the charming dress which was a present from her lover.

"Lying slut!" cried the merchant. "Thieving whore!" He appealed to others sitting at the tables. "Must we endure this treatment? 'Tis time we taught these bawds a lesson."

He kicked the table; it was cheap and fragile, and it was smashed against the wall.

"I pray you, good sir," soothed Madam Gwyn, "I pray you curb your anger against Mrs. Rose. Mrs. Rose is ready to make amends. . . ."

"I never saw the purse," cried Rose. "I did not take the purse."

The merchant paused and ceremoniously opened the purse. "There's ten shillings missing from it," he said. "Come, give me what you've taken, slut."

"I have not had your money," protested Rose.

The man took her by the shoulders. "Give it me, you slut, or I'll bring a charge against you." His little pig's eyes were glistening. His face, thought Nell, was like a boar's head which had been pickled for several days. She hated him; if she had not grown accustomed to keeping herself under control in the cellar, she would have rushed at once to Rose's defence. But she was afraid; for that which she saw in the man's eyes was lust as well as the desire for revenge; and she was afraid of lust.

He had turned now to the company. He shouted: "Look to your own pockets. They lure you here; they drug their waters; how many of you have left this place poorer men than when you entered it? How many of you have paid too dear for what you've had? Come! Shall we allow these bawds to rob us?"

One of the men shouted: "What will you do, friend?"

"What will I do!" he screamed. He had caught Rose by the shoulder. "I'll take this whore and make an example of her, that I will."

Madam Gwyn was beside him, rubbing her fat hands together. "Mrs. Rose is my prettiest girl, sir. Mrs. Rose is longing for a chance to be kind to you."

"I doubt it not!" roared the man. "But she comes to her senses too late. I came here for a good honest whore, not a jailbird."

"I'm no jailbird!" cried Rose.

"Is that so, Miss?" snarled the man. "Then you soon will be. Come, my friends."

And with that he dragged Rose to the door. The men who were sitting about the tables rose and formed a bodyguard about him. "Take the thief to jail!" they chanted. "That's the way to treat a thief."

Rose was pale with horror.

Everyone was leaving the cellar. They could visit a bawdy-house at any time; but it was not so often that they could see one of the patrons drag a girl to jail.

"I've been robbed here more than once, I swear it," declared a little man.

"And I!" "And I!" the cry went up.

Nell moved then; she ran after the group who were pushing their way into the street. Already down in Cole-yard the flesh-merchant was calling out where he intended taking Rose, and crowds were gathering.

"A pickpocket whore!" Nell heard the words. "Caught stealing money."

" 'Tis a lie. 'Tis a lie!" cried Nell.

Nobody looked at her. She fought her way to Rose. Poor Rose, bedraggled and weeping so bitterly, her pretty gown ruined, her pretty lips begging, pleading, swearing that she was innocent.

Nell caught at the flesh-merchant's arm. "Let her go. Let my sister go!"

He saw her, and as she clung to his arm he raised it and swung her off her feet.

"It's the imp who serves strong waters. I'll warrant she's as quick with her fingers as the other. We'll take her along with us, eh, my friends?"

"Aye, take her along. Take the whole lot along. Have them searched, and have them hanged by the neck, as all thieves should be."

Nell caught one glimpse of Rose's anguished face. Nell's own was distorted with rage. She dug her teeth into the flesh-merchant's hand, gave him a kick on the shin, and so startled him that, letting out a cry of pain, he relaxed his hold on her.

She screamed: "Run, Rose. Run!" as she herself darted through the crowd. But Rose could not so easily make her escape; the crowd saw to that;

and in a few seconds the flesh-merchant had regained his hold upon her, and the shouting crowd carried Rose Gwyn to Newgate.

❁ ❁ ❁

Nell had never known such fear as now was hers. Rose was in jail. She was a thief, the flesh-merchant had declared; he had discovered his purse on her, and ten shillings were missing from it. There were even men to come forward and say they had seen Rose take the purse.

Rose had a fine dress, it was remarked. By what means had she, a poor girl in a low bawdy-house, come by such a garment? She had stolen the money to pay for it, of course.

Those who were found guilty of theft suffered the extreme penalty.

Nell walked the streets in her misery, not knowing which way to turn for comfort. Her mother drank more and more gin, and sat weeping through the day and night, for few people came to the cellar during those days. The rumor had spread that if you went into Mother Gwyn's house you might lose your purse. There had been many lost purses, and now Mother Gwyn as a result was going to lose her daughter.

Rose . . . in prison. It was terrible to think of her there—Rose who such a short while ago had been so happy with her lover, the man who thought so highly of her that he had promised to make her sister one of Orange Moll Meggs' girls.

There was only one person who could offer Nell comfort, and that was her cousin Will. They sat on the cobbles in the yard and talked of Rose.

"There's nothing can be done," said Will. "They've declared her a thief, and they'll hang her by the neck."

"Not Rose!" cried Nell, with the tears running down her face. "Not my sister Rose!"

"They don't care whose sister she is, Nelly. They only care that they hang her."

"Rose never stole anything."

Will nodded. "It matters not whether she stole or not, Nelly. They say she stole, and they'll hang her for that."

"They shall not," cried Nell. "They *shall* not."

"But how will you stop them?"

"I know not." Nell covered her face with her hands and burst into loud sobs. "If I were older and wiser I would know. There is a way, Will. There must be a way."

"If Mr. Killigrew had been there it would not have happened," said Will.

"If he had been there, he could have stopped it. Will, mayhap he could stop it now."

"How so?" said Will.

"We must find him. We must tell him what happened. Will, where can we find him?"

"He is Groom of the Bedchamber to the Duke."

"I will go to the Duke."

"Nay, Nelly. You could not do that. The Duke would never see *you*!"

"I would *make* him see me . . . *make* him listen."

"You would never reach him." Will scratched his head. Nell watched him eagerly. "I saw him last night," added Will.

"You saw him? The Duke?"

"Nay, Henry Killigrew."

"Did you tell him about Rose?"

"*I* tell *him*? Nay, I did not. I was holding a torch for a gentleman close by Lady Bennet's, and he came out. He was as close to me as you are now."

"Oh, Will, you should have told him. You should have asked his help."

"He has not been to Cole-yard since, has he, Nelly? He's forgotten Rose."

"I'll not believe it," declared Nell passionately.

"Rose used to say you only believed what you wanted to."

"I like believing what I want to. Then I can make it happen mayhap. Does he go often to Lady Bennet's?"

"I heard it said that he is mighty interested in one of the girls there."

"That cannot be. He is interested in Rose."

"Such as he can be interested in many at a time."

"Then I will go to Lady Bennet's, and I will see him and tell him he must save Rose."

Will shook his head.

Nell was the wildest thing he had ever seen. He never knew what she would do next. There was one thing he did know: it was folly to dissuade her once she had set her mind on something.

❀ ❀ ❀

So the small raggedly clad girl waited in the shadows of Lady Bennet's house. None of the gentlemen passing in and out gave her a second glance. She looked much younger than her thirteen years.

She knew that she would find Henry Killigrew there. She must find him there, and she must find him quickly, for Rose was in acute danger. If she could not find him at Lady Bennet's, then she would at Damaris Page's. She could be sure that it would be possible to find such a profligate as Rose's Henry undoubtedly was, at one of the notorious brothels in London.

Nell felt that she had grown up in these last days of her grief. She was no longer a child but a woman of understanding. Nothing she discovered of Henry Killigrew would surprise her as much as the fact that he had ever come to Cole-yard.

And it was outside Lady Bennet's that she came face-to-face with him. She ran to him, fell on her knees before him, and took his hand in hers. There was another gentleman with him who raised his eyebrows and looked askance at his companion.

"What means this, Henry?" he asked. "Who is the infant?"

"God's Body! I swear I've seen the child somewhere ere this?"

"You keep strange company, Henry."

"I'm Nell," cried Nell. "Mrs. Rose's sister."

"Why, now I know. And how fares Mrs. Rose?"

"Badly!" cried Nell in sudden rage. "And that seems small concern of yours."

"And should it concern me?" he asked flippantly.

His companion was smiling cynically.

"If you are not knave it should," retorted Nell.

Henry Killigrew turned to his companion. "This is the child who serves strong waters at Mother Gwyn's bawdy-house."

"And strong words with it, I'll warrant," said the other.

"A sharp-tongued vixen," said Henry.

Nell cried suddenly: "My sister is in prison. They will hang her."

"What?" said Henry's companion languidly. "Do they then hang whores? It will not do."

"Indeed it will not do," cried Henry. "Shall they hang all the women of London and leave us desolate?"

"God preserve the whores of London!" cried the other.

"They will hang her for what she has not done," said Nell. "You must save her. You must take her out of prison. It is on your account that she is there."

"On my account?"

"Indeed yes, sir. She was hoping you would come; you did not, but another did. She refused him and so he accused her of this crime. He was a flesh-merchant of East Cheap. Rose could not endure him . . . after your lordship."

"The vixen sets a drop of honey in the vinegar, Henry," murmured his friend, flicking at the lace of his sleeve.

"Do not mock," said Henry, serious suddenly. "Poor Rose! So this flesh-merchant had her sent to prison, eh . . . ?" He turned to his friend. "Why, Browne, we'll not endure this. Rose is a lovely girl. I meant to call on her this very night."

"Then call on her in jail, sir," begged Nell. "Call on her—and you, being such a noble gentleman, can of a certainty procure her release."

"The little vixen bath a good opinion of you," said Browne.

"And it shall not be misplaced."

"Where go you, Henry?"

"I'm going to see Mrs. Rose. I'm fond of Rose. I anticipate many happy hours with her."

"God will reward you, sir," said Nell.

"And Rose also, I pray," murmured Browne.

They walked away from Lady Bennet's while Nell ran beside them.

❁ ❁ ❁

Life was truly wonderful.

There was no longer need to hide her prettiness. Now she washed and combed her hair; it hung down her back in a cloud of ringlets. There was no longer need to squint and frown; she could laugh as often as she liked—an occupation which suited her mood more readily than any other.

On the day she walked into the King's Theater, she was the proudest girl in London. Lady Castlemaine, for all that she was the King's pampered mistress, could not have been happier than little Nell Gwyn in her smock, stays, and petticoat, her coarse gown and her kerchief about her neck; and she was actually wearing shoes on her feet. The chestnut curls hung over her bare shoulders; she looked her age now. She was thirteen, and even if it was a very small thirteen it was a very dainty one.

The men could look as much as they liked now, for, as Nell would be the first to admit, looks were free and any man who was prepared to pay his sixpence for one of her oranges could take his fill of looking.

If any tried to take liberties they would meet a torrent of abuse which seemed startling coming from one so small and so enchanting to the eye. It was said in the pit and the middle and upper galleries that the prettiest of all Moll Meggs' orange-girls was little Nelly Gwyn.

Nell was filled with happiness, for Rose was home now. She had been saved by the two gallants whom Nell had called in to help her. What a wonderful thing it was to have friends at Court!

A word from Henry Killigrew, Groom of the Bedchamber, to the Duke, a word from Mr. Browne who, it appeared, was Cup-bearer to the same Duke, and Rose was granted a pardon, and had merely walked out of her jail.

Moreover Mr. Browne and Henry Killigrew had been somewhat impressed by the wit and resource of Rose's young sister whom they addressed with mock ceremony as Mrs. Nelly; and Henry had been only too ready to see that Mrs. Nelly became one of Orange Moll's girls, for, as he said, it was such girls as Mrs. Nelly for whom Orange Moll was looking—and not only Orange Moll. He intimated that when he strolled into His Majesty's Theater he also would not be averse to taking a glance at Mrs. Nelly.

Nell shook her curls. She felt that she would know how to deal with Henry Killigrew, should the need arise.

In the meantime her dearest wish had been granted. Six days of the week she was in the theater—the King's Theater—and it seemed to her that, in that wooden building, the pageant of life at its most exciting passed before her eyes. She did not know which delighted her more, the play or the audience.

It was true that the King's Theater was a drafty place; its glazed cupola let in a certain amount of daylight, which in bad weather could make it somewhat uncomfortable for the occupants of the pit; sometimes it was cold, for there was no artificial heating; sometimes it was stiflingly hot from the press of bodies, and this heat was augmented by the candles on the walls and over the stage.

These were trifling matters. Gazing at the stage it was possible to forget that her home was still the bawdy-house in Cole-yard; here she could live in a different world by aping the actors and actresses; she could see the nobility, for often the King himself came to the playhouse. Was he not its chief patron, and did not all the actors and actresses of the King's house call themselves His Majesty's Servants? So, it was natural that he should often be there, sometimes with the Queen, sometimes with the notorious Lady Castlemaine, sometimes with others. She would see the Court wits—my lord Buckingham, my lord Rochester, Sir Charles Sedley, Lord Buckhurst. They all came to the play, and with them came the ladies who interested them at the time.

She had heard wild stories concerning them all, and to these she listened with relish. She had seen the Queen sail up London river with the King after his marriage; she had been with the crowd which had witnessed their arrival at Whitehall Bridge, while the Queen Mother, who was on a visit to her son, waited to receive the royal pair on the pier which had been erected for the occasion; and all were so gorgeously clad that the spectators had gaped with wonder.

She knew, too, that the King had forced the Queen to accept Lady Castlemaine as one of the women of her bedchamber. All London talked of it—the resentment of the Queen, the flaming arrogance of Lady Castlemaine, and the stubbornness of the King. She was sorry for the dark-eyed Queen, who looked a little sad at times and seemed to be trying so hard to understand what the play was about, laughing a little too late at the jokes, at which, poor lady, she might have blushed instead of laughed had she understood them.

Then there was the arrogant Lady Castlemaine, sitting with the King or in the next box and speaking to him in her loud imperious voice so that the audience in the pit craned their heads upwards to see and hear what she was at, and the galleries looked down for the same reason; for when Lady Castlemaine was in the playhouse few paid attention to the players.

There was often to be seen in their boxes those two rakes, Lord Buckhurst and Sir Charles Sedley. Lord Buckhurst was a good-natured man, a poet and a lover of wit, whose high spirits very often drew him into prominence. Sir Charles Sedley was a poet and a playwright as well. He was so slight in stature that he was nicknamed Little Sid. These two were watched with alert interest by the house. With Sir Thomas Ogle they had recently behaved with reckless devilry at the Cock Tavern, where, having eaten well and drunk still better, they had gone to the balcony of the tavern, taken off all their clothes, and lectured the passersby in an obscene and offensive manner. There had been a riot and as a result Little Sid was taken to court, heavily fined, and bound over to keep the peace for a year. So the audience watched and waited, no doubt hoping that these three rakes would repeat here in the theater the performance they had given at the Cock Tavern.

Here was Nell's first glimpse at the high life of the Court. And, in addition to watching at close quarters the highest in the land, she could practice her repartee on the gay young men in the pit. All those with a strain of puritanism, left over from the fifties, stayed away from the theater which, they declared, was nothing more than a meeting place for courtesans and those who sought them; and indeed the noblemen in the pit and the boxes, and women from the Court together with the prostitutes, made up the greater part of the audience. The women wore vizard masks (which were supposed to hide their blushes when the dialogue on the stage was too outspoken) and the lowest aped the highest; they chatted with each other, noisily sucked China oranges, threw the peel at each other and the players, showered abuse on the actors and actresses if they did not like the way the play was going, fought one another, and added to the general clamor. Courtiers, and apprentices aping courtiers, made assignations with the vizard masks. The side boxes, which cost four shillings, were filled with ladies and gentlemen of the Court and were only slightly raised above the pit, where the price of a seat was two shillings and sixpence. In the middle gallery where a seat cost a modest eighteen pence sat the quieter folk who wished to hear the play; and in the shilling gallery were the poorest section of the audience, and here coachmen and footmen, whose masters and mistresses were in the theater, were allowed to enter without charge towards the end of the play.

Each day Nell found full of incident. Never could one guess what would happen next at the playhouse, what great scandal would be talked of, or what great personage would quarrel with another during the course of the performance.

She could listen to the loud and often lewd conversation between courtiers in their boxes and vizard masks in the pit, conversation in which the rest of the audience would often join as they combed their hair or drank noisily from the bottles they brought in with them; some stood on the benches and jeered at the players, quarreled with the sentiments of the play, or even climbed onto the stage and attempted to fight an actor for his dastardly conduct in the play or mayhap on account of some real grievance.

It was all clamor, and color, and Nell loved it. Nor was this the sum of her excitement; for her, by no means least of the theater's attractions was the play itself.

And when the handsomest actor of them all, who was considered by many to be the company's leading man, played his parts he could often quiet the noisiest of the audience. He would strut the stage, not as himself, handsome Charles Hart, but as the character he played; and if that character were a king it would seem that Charles Hart was as much a king as that other Charles who sat in his box, alert and appreciative of one who aped his royalty with such success.

Nell thought Charles Hart godlike as he came from the back stage and stepped onto the apron stage, and by his magnetic presence demanded attention. She would stand very still watching him, forgetting her load of oranges, not caring if Orange Moll should see her staring at the stage instead of doing all in her power to persuade someone in the audience to buy a fine China orange. Nell had spoken to the great man once or twice. He had bought an orange from her. He had noted her dainty looks with appreciation, for Charles Hart was appreciative of beauty. He had never yet been made aware of the agility of Nell's tongue, for she had been reduced to unaccustomed silence in the presence of the great man. Yet he must have known that she had a ready gift of repartee since no orange-girl could have survived long without it.

This day he was playing the part of Michael Perez in *Rule a Wife and Have a Wife,* and many from the Court had come to see him. Nell was in a daze of admiration as she went into the tiring room to see if she could sell an orange or two to the actresses.

Several gallants were already there, for they were admitted to the tiring room on payment of an extra half-crown, and there it was possible for them to have intimate conversation with the actresses, perhaps make love to them there or make assignations for such lovemaking in more private places.

Nell was greatly attracted by the tiring room; she had heard that actresses were paid as much as twenty to fifty shillings a week—a fabulous sum to a poor orange-girl; they looked quite splendid off the stage as well as on it, for they had beautiful clothes which were given by courtiers—and even the King himself—for use in their plays. The gentlemen fawned on them, pressed gifts on them, implored them to accept their invitations; and the actresses gave answers as pert as any they used to their stage lovers.

"A China orange, Mrs. Corey?" cooed Nell. "So soothing, so cooling to the throat."

"Not for me, wench. Go along to Mrs. Marshall. Mayhap she'll get one of her gentlemen friends to buy her a China orange."

"I doubt she'll get much more from him!" cried Mary Knepp.

And Mrs. Uphill and Mrs. Hughes went into peals of laughter at Mrs. Marshall's expense.

"Here, wench," called Mrs. Eastland, "run out and buy me a green riband. There'll be a groat or two for your pains when you return."

This was typical of life in the green tiring room. Nell ran errands, augmenting her small income, and very soon took to wondering what Peg Hughes and Mary Knepp had that she lacked.

It was when she had returned with the riband and was making her way backstage, where Mary Meggs kept her wares under the stairs, that she came face-to-face with the great Charles Hart himself.

She curtsied and said: "A merry good day to Mr. Perez."

He paused and, leaning towards her, said: "Why, 'tis little Nell the orange-girl. And you liked Michael Perez, eh?"

"So much, sir," said Nell, "that I had forgot till this moment that he was an even greater gentleman—Mr. Charles Hart."

Charles Hart was not indifferent to flattery. He knew that he—with perhaps Michael Mohun as his only rival—was the best player among the King's Servants. All the same, praise from any quarter was acceptable, even from a little orange-girl, and he had noticed before that this orange-girl was uncommonly pretty.

He took her face in his hands and kissed her lightly. "Why," he said, "you're pretty enough to grace a stage yourself."

"One day I shall," said Nell; and in that moment she knew she would. Why should she not give as good an account of herself as any of the screaming wenches in the green room?

"Oh," he said, "so the girl hath ambition!"

"I want to play on the stage," she said.

He looked at her again. Her eyes were brilliant with excitement. There was a vitality which was rare. God's Body! he thought. This child has quality. He said: "Come with me, girl."

Nell hesitated. She had had similar invitations before this. Charles Hart saw her hesitation and laughed. "Nay," he said, "have no fear. I do not force little girls." He drew himself up to his full height and spoke the words as though he were delivering them to an audience. "There has never been any need for me to force any. They come . . . they come with the utmost willingness."

His fluency fascinated her. He spoke to her—Nell—as though she were one of those gorgeous creatures on the stage. He made her feel important, dramatic, already an actress, playing her part with him.

She said: "Willingly will I listen to what you have to say to me, sir."

"Then follow me."

He turned and led the way through a narrow passage to a very small compartment in which were hanging the clothes which he wore for his parts.

He turned to her then, ponderously. "Your name, wench?" he asked.

"Nell . . . Nell Gwyn."

"I have observed you," he said. "You have a sharp tongue and a very ready wit. Methinks your talents are wasted with Orange Moll."

"Could I act a part on the stage?"

"How would you learn a part?"

"I would learn. I *would* learn. I would only have to hear it once and I would know it." She put down her basket of oranges and began to repeat one of the parts she had seen played that afternoon. She put into it the utmost comedy, and the fine lips of Mr. Charles Hart began to twitch as he watched her.

He lifted a hand to stop her exuberance. "How would you learn your parts?" he said. Nell was bewildered. "Can you read?" She shook her head. "Then how would you learn them?"

"I would," she cried. "I would."

"The will is not enough, my child. You would be obliged to learn to read."

"Then I would learn to read."

He came to her and laid his hands on her shoulders. "And what would you say if I told you that I might have room for a small-part player in the company?"

Nell dropped on her knees, took his hand, and kissed it.

He looked at her curly head with pleasure. " 'Od's Fish!" he said, using the King's oath, for he played the part of kings now and then and had come to believe that in the world of the theater he was one, "You're a pretty child, Mrs. Nelly."

And when she rose he lifted her in his arms and held her so that her animated face was on a level with his.

"And as light as a feather," he said. "Are you as wayward?"

Then he kissed her lips; and Nell understood what he would require in payment for all that he was about to do for her.

Nell knew that she would not consider anything he demanded as payment. She had already learned to adore him from the pit; she was ready to continue in that adoration from a more intimate position. She laughed, signifying her pleasure, and he was satisfied.

"Come," he said, "I will go with you to Mary Meggs, for it may be she will by now be too ready to scold you, and it is my wish that you should not be scolded."

When Mary Meggs caught sight of Nell she screamed at her: "So there you are, you jade! What have you been at? I've been waiting here for you this last quarter-hour. Let me tell you that if you behave thus you will not long remain one of Orange Moll's young women."

Charles drew himself up to his full height. Nell found herself laughing, as she was to laugh so often in times to come at this actor's dignity. In everything he did it was as though he played a part.

"Save your breath, woman," he cried in that voice of thunder with which he had so often silenced a recalcitrant audience. "Save your breath. Mrs. Nelly here shall certainly not remain one of your orange-girls. She ceased to do so some little time ago. Nelly the orange-girl is now Nelly the King's Servant."

Then he strode off and left them. Nell set down her basket and danced a jig before the astonished woman's eyes. Orange Moll—none too pleased at the prospect of losing one of her best girls—shook her head and her finger at the dancing figure.

"Dance, Nelly, dance!" she said. "Mr. Charles Hart don't make actresses of all his women—and he don't keep them long either. Mayhap you'll be wanting your basket back when the great Charles Hart grows Nelly-sick."

But Nell continued to dance.

❀ ❀ ❀

Now Nell was indeed an actress. She quickly left her mother's house in Cole-yard and most joyfully set up in lodgings of her own; she took a small house next to the Cock and Pye Tavern in Drury Lane opposite Wych Street. Here she was only a step or two away from the theater, which was convenient indeed, for the life of an actress was a more strenuous one than that of an orange-girl. Charles Hart was teaching her to read; William Lacy was teaching her to dance; and both, with Michael Mohun, were teaching her to act. Mornings were spent in rehearsing, and the afternoons in acting plays which started at three o'clock and went on until five or later. Most of Nell's evenings were spent with the great Charles Hart who, delighted with his protégée, initiated her into the art of making love, when he was not teaching her to read.

Rose was delighted with her sister's success and she became a frequent visitor at the lodgings in Drury Lane. Nell would have liked to ask her to come and live with her; but Nell's small wages just kept herself—and as an actress it was necessary for her to spend a great deal of her income on fine clothes. Moreover Rose had her own life to lead and often a devoted lover would take her away from her mother's house for a while.

Harry Killigrew was one of these, as was Mr. Browne; and in the company of these gentlemen Rose met others of their rank. She was as eager to avoid flesh-merchants from East Cheap as she ever was, and continuously grateful to Nell who, she declared, had saved her from a felon's death.

Nell played her parts in the theater—small ones as yet, for she had her apprenticeship to live through. Charles Hart proved to be a devoted lover, for Nell was an undemanding mistress, never a complaining one; her spirits were invariably high; and she quickly learned to share Charles Hart's passion for the stage.

There were times when he forgot to act before her and would talk of his aspirations and his jealousies, and beg her to tell him without reserve whether she believed Michael Mohun or Edward Kynaston to be greater actors than he was. He often talked of Thomas Betterton, one of that rival group of players who called themselves The Duke's Men, and who performed in the Duke's Theater. It was said that Betterton, more than any man living, could hold an audience. "Better than Hart?" demanded Charles Hart. "I want the truth from you, Nell."

Then Nell would soothe him and say that Betterton was a strolling player compared with the great Charles Hart; and Charles would say that it was meet and fitting that *he,* Hart, should be the greatest actor London had ever known, because his grandmother was a sister of the dramatist, Will Shakespeare—a man who loved the theater and whose plays were often acted by the companies, and which, some declared, had never yet been bettered, surpassing even those of Ben Jonson or Beaumont and Fletcher.

Sometimes he would tell her how he had been brought up at Blackfriars and, with Clun, one of the other members of the company, had, as a boy, acted women's parts. He would strut about the apartment playing the

Duchess in Shirley's tragedy *The Cardinal,* and Nell would clap her hands and assure him that he was the veriest Duchess she had ever seen.

He liked to pour his reminiscences of the past into Nell's sympathetic ears. And Nell, who loved him, listened and applauded, for she thought him the most wonderful person she had ever known, godlike in his ability to raise the orange-girl to the green room, a tender yet passionate lover to introduce her into a milieu where, she was aware, she would wish to play a leading part.

She allowed him to tell his stories again and again; she would demand to hear them. "Tell me of the time you were carried off and imprisoned by Roundhead soldiers—taken while you were actually playing, and in your costume, too!"

So he would throw back his head and adjust his magnificent voice to the drama or comedy of the occasion. "I was playing Otto in *The Bloody Brother.* . . . A fine play. I'll swear Beaumont and Fletcher never wrote a better. . . ."

Then he would forget the story of the capture and play Otto for her; he would even take the part of Rollo, the Bloody Brother himself, and it was all vastly entertaining, as was life.

And in the boxes at the theater there appeared at this time the loveliest woman Nell had ever seen: Mrs. Frances Stuart, maid of honor to the Queen. The King gazed at her during the whole of the play so that his attention strayed from Charles Hart, Michael Mohun, and Edward Kynaston; and, what was more remarkable, neither tall and handsome Ann Marshall, nor any of the actresses could hold his gaze. The King saw no one but Mrs. Stuart, sitting there so childishly pretty with her fair hair, great blue eyes, and Roman nose, so that my lady Castlemaine was in such a high temper that she shouted insults to the actors and actresses—and even spoke churlishly to the King himself, to his great displeasure.

It all seemed remote to Nell; she had her own life to lead; and if it was less grand than those of these Court folk in their dazzling jewels and sumptuous garments, it was lively, colorful, and completely satisfying to Nell; for one of her great gifts was to be able to enjoy contentment with her lot.

And there came a day when she thought her joy was complete.

Charles Hart came to her lodging and, when she had let him in and he had kissed her, declaring that she was a mighty pretty creature in her smock sleeves and bodice, he held her at arms' length and said in his loud booming voice: "News, Nelly! At last you are to be an actress."

"You are insolent, sir!" she cried in mock anger, her eyes flashing. "Would you insult me? What am I indeed, if I am not an actress!"

"You are my mistress, for one thing."

She caught his hand and kissed it. "And that is the best part I have yet been called upon to play."

"Sweet Nelly," he murmured as though in an aside. "How this wench delights me!"

"As yet!" she answered promptly. "I beg of you to tell me quickly. What part is this?"

But Charles Hart never spoiled his effects. "You must first know," he said, "that we are to play Dryden's *Indian Emperor,* and I am to take the part of Cortes."

She knelt and kissed his hand in half-mocking reverence. "Welcome to the conquering hero," she said. Then she leaped to her feet. "And what part for Nelly?"

He folded his arms and stood smiling at her. "The chief female role," he said slowly, "is Almeria. Montezuma will sigh for her favors; Mohun will play Montezuma. She however longs for Cortes."

"She cannot help that, poor girl," said Nell. "And right heartily will she love her Cortes. I will show the King and the Duke, and all present, that never was man loved as my Cortes."

"Ann Marshall is to play Almeria. Nay, 'tis not the part for you. You are young yet to take it. Oh, you are learning . . . learning . . . but an orange-girl does not become an actress in a matter of weeks. Nay, there is another part—a beautiful part for a beautiful girl—that of Cydaria. I have said Nelly shall play Cydaria, and I have made Tom Killigrew, Mohun, Lacy, and the rest agree that you shall do this."

"And this Cydaria—she is of small account beside that other, played by Mrs. Ann Marshall?"

"Hers is the sympathetic part, Nelly. There is a pink dress come from the Court—a present from one of the ladies. You will well become it and, as you are the Emperor's daughter, you shall wear plumes in your hair. There is something else, Nelly. Cydaria wins Cortes in the end."

"Then," declaimed Nell, dropping a curtsy, "I must be content with Cortes-Hart and revel in this minor part."

❁ ❁ ❁

She was dressed in the flowery gown, her chestnut curls arranged over her shoulders. In the tiring room the others looked at her with envy.

"An orange-girl not long ago," whispered Peg Hughes. "Now, fa la, she is given the best parts. She'll be putting Mrs. Marshall's nose out of joint ere long, I'll warrant."

"You know the way to success on the stage surely," said Mary Knepp. "No matter whether you be actress or orange-girl—the way's the same. You go to bed with one who can give you what you want, and in the dead of night you ask for it."

Nell overheard that. "I thank you for telling me, Mrs. Knepp," she cried. "For the life of me I could not understand how you ever came to get a part."

"Am I a player's whore?" demanded Mrs. Knepp.

"Ask me not," said Nell. "Though I have seen you acting in such a manner with Master Pepys from the Navy Office as to lead me to believe you may be his."

Ann Marshall said: "Stop shouting, Nelly. You're not an orange-girl now. Keep your voice for your part. You'll need it."

Nell for once was glad to subside. She was sure that she would acquit herself well in her part, but she was experiencing a strange fluttering within her stomach which she had rarely known before.

She turned from Mrs. Knepp and whispered her lines to herself:

"Thick breath, quick pulse and beating of my heart,
All sign of some unwonted change appear;
I find myself unwilling to depart,
And yet I know not why I should be here.
Stranger, you raise such torments in my breast . . ."

These were her words on her first meeting with Cortes when she falls in love with him at first sight. She thought then of the first time she had seen Charles Hart. Had she felt thus then? Indeed she had not. She did not believe she would ever feel as Cydaria felt; Cydaria is beside herself with passion; wretched and unhappy in her love for the handsome stranger, fearing her love will not be returned, jealous of those whom he has loved before. There was no jealousy in Nell; love for her was a joyous thing.

She could wish for a merry part, one in which she could strut about the stage in breeches, make saucy quips to the audience, dance and sing.

But she must go onto the stage and play Cydaria.

❁ ❁ ❁

The audience was dazzling that day. The King was present, and with him the most brilliant of his courtiers.

Nell came on the stage in her Court dress, and there was a gasp of admiration as she did so. She glimpsed her companions with whom she had once sold oranges, and saw the envy in their faces.

She knew that Mary Knepp and the rest of them would be waiting, eagerly hoping that she would be laughed off the stage. They would, backstage, be aware of the silence which had fallen on the audience as she entered. There was one thing they had forgotten; orange-girl she may have been a short while ago, but now she was the prettiest creature who ever graced a stage, and in her Court dress she could vie with any of the ladies who sat in the boxes.

She went through her lines, giving them her own inimitable flavor which robbed them of their tragedy and made a more comic part of the Princess than was intended; but it was no less acceptable for all that.

She enjoyed the scenes with Charles Hart. He looked handsome indeed as the Spanish adventurer, and she spoke her lines with fervor. When he sought to seduce her and she resisted him, she did so with a charming regret which was not in the part. It called forth one or two ribald comments in the pit from those of the audience who followed the course of actors' and actresses' lives with zest.

"Nay, Nelly," called one bright fellow. "Don't refuse him now. You did not last night, so why this afternoon?"

Nell's impulse was to go the front of the stage and retort that it was no wish of hers to refuse such a handsome fellow and she would never have thought of doing it. The fellow in the pit must blame Master Dryden for that.

But Cortes' stern eyes were on her. My dearest Cortes-Charles, thought Nell; he lives in the play; it is this story of Princes that is real to him, not the playhouse.

" 'Our greatest honor is in loving well,' " he was saying. And she smiled at him and came back with:

"Strange ways you practice there to win a heart
Here love is nature, but with you, 'tis art."

No one had taken any notice of the interruption. There was nothing unusual in such comments on the actors and their private lives, and the play went on until that last scene when Almeria (Ann Marshall) brought out her dagger and, for love of Cortes, prepares to stab Cydaria.

There were cries of horror from the pit, cries of warning: "Nelly, take care! That whore is going to stab thee."

Nell reeled, placed the sponge filled with blood which she had concealed in her hand on her bosom, and squeezed it; she was about to fall to the floor when Cortes rescued her. There was a sigh of relief throughout the house, which told Nell all she wished to know; she had succeeded in her first big part.

When Almeria stabbed herself, and Charles Hart and Nell Gwyn left the stage arm-in-arm, the applause broke out.

Now the actors and actresses must come back and make their bows.

"Nelly!" cried the pit. "Come, Nelly! Take a bow, Nelly!"

And so she came to the apron stage, flushed in her triumph; and if her acting was not equal to that of Mrs. Ann Marshall, her dainty beauty found an immediate response.

Nell lifted her eyes and met those which belonged to a man who leaned forward in his box. His dark luxuriant curls had fallen forward slightly. It was impossible to read the look in the sardonic eyes.

But for those few moments this man and Nell looked at each other appraisingly. Then she smiled her impudent orange-girl smile. There was the faintest pause before the sensuous lips curled. Others in the theater noticed. They said: "The King liked Nelly in her new part."

❁ ❁ ❁

Now Nell was well known throughout London. When people came to the King's Theater they expected to see Mrs. Nelly, and, if she did not appear, were apt to ask the reason why. They liked to see her dance and show her pretty legs; they liked to listen to her repartee when someone in the pit attacked her acting or her private life. They declared that to hear Mrs. Nelly giving a member of the audience a rating was as good as any play; for Nell's wit was sparkling and never malicious except in self-defense.

There were many who believed she was well on the way to becoming the leading actress at the King's Theater.

Often she thought of the King and the smile he had given her. She listened avidly to all news of him. It was a great thing, she told herself, to perform before the King.

Elizabeth Weaver, one of the actresses, had a tale to tell of the King. Elizabeth held herself aloof, living in a state of expectancy, for once the King had sent for her. Nell had heard her tell the tale many times, for it was a tale Elizabeth Weaver loved to tell. Nell had scarcely listened before; now she wished to hear it in detail.

"I shall never forget the day as long as I live," Elizabeth told her. "My part was a good one, and a beautiful dress I wore. You reminded me of myself when you played Cydaria. Such a dress I had. . . ."

"Yes, yes," said Nell. "Have done with the dress. It's what happened to the wearer that interests me."

"The dress was important. Mayhap if I had another dress like that he would send for me again. I'd played my part; I'd taken my applause; and then one of the footmen came backstage and said to me: 'The King sends for you.' "

" 'The King sends for you.' Just like that."

"Just like that. 'For what?' I said. 'For what should the King send for poor Elizabeth Weaver?' 'He would have you entertain him at the Palace of Whitehall,' I was told. So I put on a cloak—a velvet one, one of the company's cloaks; but Mr. Hart said to use it since it was to Whitehall I was to go."

"Have done with the cloak," said Nell. "I'll warrant you weren't sent for to show a cloak!"

"Indeed not. I was taken to a grand apartment where there were many great ladies and gentlemen. My lord Buckingham himself was there, and I'll swear 'twas my lady Shrewsbury with him and . . ."

"And His Majesty the King?" said Nell.

"He was kind to me . . . kinder than the others. He is kind, Nell. His great dark eyes were telling me all the time not to be afraid of them and the things they might say to me. He said nothing that was not kind. He bade me dance and sing, and he bade the others applaud me. And after a while the others went away and I was alone with His Majesty. Then I was no longer afraid."

Elizabeth Weaver's eyes grew misty. She was looking back, not to the glories of Whitehall, not to the honor of being selected by the King, but to that night when she was alone with him and he was just a man like any other.

"Just a man like any other," she murmured. "And yet unlike any that I have ever known. He gave me a jewel," she went on. "I could sell it for much, I doubt not. But I never shall. I shall always keep it."

Nell was unusually quiet.

She is waiting, she thought, waiting and hoping that the King will send for her again. He never will. Poor Bessie Weaver, she is no longer as pretty as she must have once been. And what has she ever had but her youthful prettiness? There are many youthful pretty women to surround His Majesty. So poor Elizabeth Weaver will go on waiting all her life to be sent for by the King.

"A sorry fate," said Nell to herself. "Give me a merry one."

But she often found her thoughts going back and back again to the King who had smiled at her; and in spite of herself she caught her breath when she asked herself: "Will there ever come a day when the King will send for Nelly?"

❁ ❁ ❁

In the days following her success as Cydaria, Nell reveled in her fame. She would wander through the streets smiling and calling a witty greeting to those who spoke to her; she liked to stand at the door of her lodgings, watching the passersby; she would stroll in St. James' Park and watch the King and his courtiers at the game of *pelmel,* in which none threw as the King did; she would watch him sauntering with his courtiers, feeding the ducks in the ponds, his spaniels at his heels. He did not see her. If he had would he have remembered the actress he had seen at his playhouse? There were many to watch the King as he walked in his park or rode through his Capital. Why, Nell asked herself, should he notice one young actress?

But each day she hoped that he would come to see her perform.

Fate was against Nell then. She was ready to rise to the top of her profession, and suddenly the happy life was no more.

During the weeks which followed the production of *The Indian Emperor* there were rumors in the streets. The Dutch were challenging England's power on the high seas. That seemed far away, but it proved capable of altering the course of a rising young actress's life. When Nell saw a Dutchman whipped through the streets for declaring that the Dutch had destroyed the English factories on the coast of Guinea, she was sorry for him. Poor fellow, it seemed harsh punishment for repeating a tale which proved to be false. But a few days later England declared war on the Dutch, and then she began to realize how these matters could affect her life. The theaters were half empty. So many of the gallants who had sat in the pit and the boxes had gone to fight the Dutch on the high seas; the King came rarely to the theater, having matters of state with which to deal; and since the King did not come, neither did all the fine ladies and gentlemen. Thomas Killigrew, Michael Mohun, and Charles Hart, who had shares in the theatrical venture, began to look worried. Charles Hart recalled the days of the Commonwealth when it had been an offense to act, and actors had been deprived of their livelihood. Those were grim days, and even Nell's naturally high spirits were quelled by acting to half-empty houses and by a lover turned melancholy. Yet, ever ebullient, she prophesied a quick defeat of the Dutch and a return to prosperity. But that April there occurred an even more disastrous event than the Dutch war. Like the Dutch war it had broken gradually upon the people of London, for even towards the end of the year 1664 there had been rumors of deaths in the Capital which were suspected of being caused by the dreaded plague. With the coming of the warm spring and summer this fearful scourge broke out afresh. The gutters choked with filth, the stench of decay which filled the air and hung like a cloud over the city, were the best possible breeding conditions for the terror; it increased rapidly, and soon all the business of the town was brought to a standstill. A short while ago Nell and her companions had played to half-filled houses; now they had no audiences at all. None would dare enter a public place for fear that someone present might be infected. The theaters were the first places to close and Nell was deprived of her livelihood. Charles Hart was plunged into melancholy, more at the prospect of being unable to act than because of the danger of disease. He declared that they must leave London and go farther afield. In the sweeter country air it might be possible to escape infection.

"There are my mother and sister," said Nell. "We must take them with us."

Charles Hart had seen her mother; he shuddered at the prospect of even five minutes spent in her company.

" 'Tis quite impossible," he said.

"Then what will become of her?"

"Doubtless she will drown her sorrow at losing you, in the gin bottle."

"What if she takes the plague?"

"Then, my little Nell, she will take the plague."

"Who would care for her?"

"Your sister doubtless."

"What if she also took the plague?"

"You waste precious time. I wish to leave at once. Every unnecessary minute spent in this polluted place is courting danger."

Nell planted her small feet on the floor and, placing her hands on her hips, struck what he called her fish-wife attitude, since it was doubtless picked up when she sold fresh herrings at ten a groat.

"When I go," she said, "my family goes with me."

"So you choose your family instead of me?" said Hart. "Very well, Madam. You have made your choice."

Then he left her, and when he had gone she was sad, because she loved him well enough, and she knew that being unable to act he was a melancholy man. And she was a fool. What, she asked herself, did she owe to the gin-sodden old woman who had beaten and bullied her when she was able, and whined to her when she was not?

She went to Cole-yard; and as she passed into that alley Nell's heart was merry no longer, for on many of the doors were painted large red crosses beneath which were written the words "Lord have mercy upon us."

❁ ❁ ❁

Nell stayed in the cellar, with Rose and her mother, for several days and nights. Occasionally either Nell or her sister went out into the streets to see if they could find food. There was scarcely anyone about now, and grass was growing between the cobbles. Sometimes in their wanderings they would see sufferers by the roadside, struck down as they walked through the streets, displaying the fatal signs of shivering, nausea, delirium. Once Nell approached an old woman, because she felt she could not pass her by without offering help, but the woman had opened her eyes and stared at Nell, shouting: "You're Mrs. Nelly. Stay away from me." Then she tore open her bodice and showed the terrible macula on her breast.

Nell hurried away, feeling sick and afraid, aware that she could do nothing to help the old woman.

They lived this cellar existence for some weeks, occasionally venturing out and returning, feeling desolate and melancholy to see a great city so stricken. During the night they heard the gloomy notes of the bell which told them that the pest-cart was passing that way. They heard the sepulchral cry echoing through the deserted streets: "Bring out your dead." Nell had seen the naked bodies passed out of windows and tumbled into the cart just as they were, body upon body since there was no time to provide coffins; there were no mourners to follow the dead to their graves; the cart went its dismal way to the burial ground on the outskirts of the city where the bodies were thrown into a pit.

Then one day Nell cried: "We can no longer stay here. If we do we shall die of melancholy if not of the plague."

"Let us to Oxford," said her mother. "Your father has relations there. Mayhap they would take us in till this scourge be gone."

And so they made their way out of the stricken city. That night they slept in the shelter of a hedge; and Nell felt her spirits lifted in the sweet country air.

TWO

It was nearly two years later when Nell came back to London. Life was not easy in Oxford. She had gone back to selling fruit and fish when she could lay her hands on it. Rose worked with her, and the two girls from London, so sprightly and so pretty, were able to keep themselves and their mother alive during those two years.

News came from London—terrible news which set them all wondering whether they would ever return there. Travellers brought it to Oxford during the month of September, a year after Nell and her family had arrived there. Nell, eager for news of what was happening in Drury Lane and whether the players were back, heard instead of the disastrous fire which had broken out at a baker's shop in Pudding Lane and quickly spread until half the city was ablaze. The wild rumors reaching Oxford were numerous.

Many declared that this was the end of London, and that not a house was left standing; that the King and all his Court had been burned to death.

Nell for once was speechless. She stood still, thinking of Drury Lane and that squalid alley where she had spent most of her life, the old Coleyard; she thought of Covent Garden, the Hop Garden and St. Martin's Lane. She thought of the playhouse—that which she thought of as her own—and that rival house, both furiously burning.

" 'Tis the judgment of God on a wicked city," some people declared.

Rose cast down her eyes, but Nell was shrilly indignant. London had not been wicked, she cried; it was merry and full of pleasure, and she for one refused to believe that it was a sin to laugh and enjoy life.

But she was too wretched to retort with her wonted spirit.

Each day there came fresh rumors. They heard that the people had thrown the furniture from their houses and packed it into barges; that the flames had spanned the river; how the wooden houses on London Bridge had blazed; how the King and his brother the Duke had worked together to prevent the fire from spreading; that it had been necessary to use gunpowder and blow gaps in the rows of highly inflammable wooden houses.

And at length came good news.

It came from a gentleman riding through Oxford from London, a prelate who mourned the restoration of the King and looked yearningly back at the puritanism of the Protectorate.

Riding to Banbury, he stopped at Oxford and, seeing that he was a traveller who had doubtless come from London, Nell approached him, not to ask him to buy her herrings, but for news.

He looked at her with disapproval. No woman of virtue, he was sure, could look like this one. That luxuriant hair allowed to flow in riotous disorder, those hazel eyes adorned with the darkest of lashes and brows—such a contrast to the reddish tints in her hair—those plump cheeks and pretty teeth, those dimples and, above all, that pert nose, could not belong to a virtuous woman.

Nell dipped in a charming curtsy which would have become a lady of high rank and which Charles Hart had taught her.

"I see, fair sir, that you hie from London," she addressed him. "I would fain have news of that town."

"Ask me not for news of Babylon!" cried the good man.

"Nay, sir, I will not," answered Nell. " 'Tis of London I ask."

"They are one and the same."

Nell dropped her eyes demurely. "I hie from London, fair sir. Is it in your opinion a fit place for a poor woman to go home to?"

"I tell ye, 'tis Babylon itself. 'Tis full of whores and cutthroats."

"More so than Oxford, sir . . . or Banbury?"

He looked at her suspiciously. "You mock me, woman," he said. "You should go to London. Clearly 'tis where you belong. In that cesspool everywhere one looks one sees rubble in the streets—the evidence of God's vengeance . . . and these people of London, what do they do? They make merry with their taverns and their playhouses. . . ."

"You said playhouses!" cried Nell.

"God forgive them, I did."

"And may He preserve you, sir, for such good news."

A few days later she, with Rose and her mother, caught the stage wagon and, after a slow and tedious journey travelling two miles to the hour and sitting uncomfortably on the floor of the wagon as the wagoner led the horses over the rough roads, they were jolted to London.

Nell could scarcely help weeping when she saw the old city again. She had heard that old St. Paul's, the Guildhall, and the Exchange, among many other well-known landmarks, had gone; she had heard that more than thirteen thousand dwelling houses and four hundred streets had been destroyed, and that two-thirds of the city lay in ruins—from the Tower, all along the river to the Temple Church, and from the northeast gate along the city wall to Holborn Bridge. Nevertheless she was not prepared for the sight which met her eyes.

But she was by nature an optimist and when she remembered her last sight of the city, with the grass growing between the cobbles, with its red crosses on the doors and its pest-carts in the streets, she cried: "Well, 'tis a better sight than we left."

Moreover the King's Servants were back at the playhouse.

Nell lost no time in presenting herself at the playhouse, miraculously preserved; and indeed Thomas Killigrew had, during the time it had not been used, enlarged his stage.

❁ ❁ ❁

London was glad to see Nell back. She had changed in her two years' absence. She was no longer a child. At seventeen she was a poised young woman; her charms had by no means diminished; she was as slender and as dainty as ever; her tongue was as quick; but all who saw her declared that her beauty was more striking than ever.

She scored an immediate success as Lady Wealthy in James Howard's *The English Monsieur,* and later she played Celia in Fletcher's *Humorous Lieutenant.*

There was still great anxiety throughout the country; the plague and the fire had crippled trade, and the Dutch were threatening. In her lodgings in Drury Lane which she had taken again Nell thought little of these things. She gave supper parties and entertained her friends with her singing and dancing. These friends talked of the scandals of the Court, of the theater, and the roles they had played; it never occurred to them to give a thought to state affairs or to imagine that such matters could concern them.

To these parties came men and women of the Court; even the great Duke of Buckingham came. He was something of a mimic, and he declared he wished to pit his skill against Mrs. Nelly's. With him came Lady Castlemaine, who was graciously pleased to commend the little comedienne on her playing. She asked questions about Charles Hart, her great blue eyes rapaciously aglitter. Charles Hart was a very handsome man, and Nell had heard of the lady's insatiable hunger for handsome men.

One of the lampoons which was being quoted throughout the city concerned the King's chief mistress. It was:

"Full forty men a day provided for the whore
Yet like a bitch she wags her tail for more."

This was said to have been composed by the Earl of Rochester—who was Lady Castlemaine's own cousin and one of the wildest rakes at Court. He had recently been imprisoned for abducting an heiress; he was so daring that he cared not what he said even to the King; yet he remained in favor.

Henry Killigrew was there; he had been her friend since the days when she had begged him to help her obtain a pardon for Rose. Now she knew that he had been Lady Castlemaine's lover as well as Rose's and was the greatest liar in England. There was Sir George Etherege, lazy and good humored, known to them all as "Gentle George." Another who came to her rooms was John Dryden, a fresh-complexioned little poet who had written several plays and promised to write another especially for Nell.

This he did and, very soon after her return to London, Nell was playing in *Secret Love, or the Maiden Queen,* and the part of Florimel, which had been specially written for her, was the greatest success of her career.

All the town was going to see Mrs. Nelly as Florimel, for in Florimel Dryden had created a madcap creature, witty, pretty, full of mischief, expert in mimicry; in other words Florimel was Nell, and Florimel enchanted all London.

She could now forget the terrible time of plague; she could forget poverty in Oxford, just as in the beginning she had forgotten the bawdy-house in Cole-yard and her life as orange-girl in the pit. Nell knew how to live gloriously in the joyous moment, and to remember from the past only that which made pleasant remembering.

She had lost Charles Hart. He had never forgiven her for choosing her family instead of him. Nell shrugged elegant shoulders. She had loved him when she had known little of love; her love had been trusting, experimental. She was grateful to Mr. Charles Hart, and she did not grudge him the pleasure he was said to be taking with my lady Castlemaine.

What she enjoyed now was swaggering across the stage, wearing an enormous periwig which made her seem smaller than ever—a grotesque yet enchanting figure, full of vitality, full of love of life, full of gamin charm which set the pit bouncing in its seats, and every little vizard mask trying to ape Nell Gwyn.

And at the end of the play she danced her jig.

"You must dance a jig," Lacy had said. "Moll Davies is drawing them at the Duke's with her dancing. By God, Nelly, she's a pretty creature, Moll Davies; but you're prettier."

Nell turned away from his flattering glances; she did not want to seem ungrateful to one who had done so much for her, but she wanted no more lovers at this time.

She wanted no man unless she loved him, and there was so much else in life to love apart from men. She might have reminded him that Thomas Killigrew paid a woman twenty shillings a week to remain at the theater and keep his actors happy in their amorous moments. But being grateful to Lacy, she turned away as she had learned to turn away from so many who sought her.

And there were many seeking her. She was the most discussed actress of the day. There might have been better actresses on the stage but none was possessed of Nell's charm; though some admitted that that mighty pretty creature, Moll Davies, at the Duke's Theater, was the better dancer.

In the town they were quoting Flecknoe's verses to a very pretty person:

"She is pretty and she knows it;
She is witty and she shows it;
And besides that she's so witty,
And so little and so pretty,
Sh' has a hundred other parts
For to take and conquer hearts . . ."

The gallants quoted it to her; in the pit they chanted it. And they roared the last two lines:

"But for that, suffice to tell ye,
'Tis the little pretty Nelly."

And, although the times were bad and it was hard to fill a theater, those who could tear themselves from state matters came to see Nell Gwyn play Florimel and dance her jig.

❁ ❁ ❁

The King was melancholy. Frances Stuart, whom he had been pursuing for so long, had run away with the Duke of Richmond; and matters of greater moment gave him cause for anxiety. His kingdom, well-nigh ruined by the disastrous events of the last two years, was facing a serious threat from the Dutch. He had no money to refit his ships, so he negotiated for a secret peace; the French were joining the Dutch against him; but the Dutch, who had suffered no such hardships, had no wish for peace.

The King rarely came to the play; he did not even come for John Howard's new piece *All Mistaken or The Mad Couple,* in which Nelly had a comic part.

As Mirida she had two suitors—one fat, one thin—and she promised to marry the one if he could grow fatter, the other if he could lose his bulk. This gave her many opportunities for the sort of buffoonery in which she reveled. Lacy, stuffed with cushions, was the fat lover, and Nell and he had the audience hysterical with laughter. An additional attraction was Nell's parody of Moll Davies in her role in *The Rivals* at The Duke's; and with her fat lover she rolled about on the stage, displaying so much of her person that the gentlemen in the pit stood on their seats to see the better, so displeasing those behind them that this gave rise to much dissension.

There was one in his box who watched the scene with an avid interest. This was Charles Sackville, Lord Buckhurst, a wit and poet, and he was filled with a great desire to make Nell his mistress.

Consequently after the play the first person to reach the tiring room to beg Mrs. Nelly to dine with him was Charles Sackville.

❁ ❁ ❁

They dined at the Rose Tavern in Russell Street, and the innkeeper, recognizing his patrons, was filled with the desire to please them.

Nell had refused to ask the gentleman to her lodgings, as she had refused to go to his. She knew him for a rake and, although he was an extremely handsome one as well as a wit, she had no intention of giving way to his desires. Some of these Court gentlemen stopped at little. My lord Rochester and some of his boon companions, it was said, were beginning to consider seduction tame and were developing a taste for rape. She was not going to make matters easy for this noble lord.

He leaned his elbows on the table and bade her drink more wine.

"There's not an actress in the town to touch you, Nelly," he said.

"Nor shall any touch me—actress or noble lord—unless I wish it."

"You are prickly, Nell! Wherefore?"

"I'm like a hedgehog, my lord. I know when to be on my guard."

"Let us not talk of guards."

"Then what should we talk of, the Dutch war?"

"I can think of happier subjects."

"Such as what, my lord?"

"You . . . myself . . . alone somewhere together."

"Would that be so happy? You would be demanding, I should be refusing. If you need my refusal to make you happier, sir, you can have it here and now."

"Nelly, you're a mad thing, but a little beauty like you should have better lodgings than those in Old Drury!"

"Is it a gentleman's custom to sneer at the lodgings of his friends?"

"If he is prepared to provide a better."

"My lodging is on cold boards,
And wonderful hard is my fare.
But that which troubles me most
Is the impertinence of my host . . ."

sang Nell, parodying the song in *The Rivals*.

"I pray thee, Nell, be serious. I offer you a beautiful apartment, a hundred pounds a year . . . all the jewels and good company you could wish for."

"I do not wish for jewels," she said, "and I doubt you could provide me with better company than that which I now enjoy."

"An actress's life! How long does that go on?"

"A little longer than that of a kept woman of a noble lord, I imagine."

"I would love you forever."

"Forever, forsooth! For ever is until you decide to pay court to Moll Davies or Beck Marshall."

"Do you imagine that I shall lightly abandon this. . . ."

"Nay, I do not. It is after seduction that such as you, my lord, concern themselves with the abandonment of a poor female."

"Nell, your tongue's too sharp for such a little person."

"My lord, we all have our weapons. Some have jewels and a hundred a year with which to tempt the needy; others have a love of straight speaking with which to parry such thrusts."

"One of these days," said Charles Sackville, "you will come to me, Nell."

She shrugged her shoulders. "Who knows, my lord? Who knows? Now, if you would prove to me that you are a good host, let me enjoy my food, I beg of you. And let me hear a piece of that wit for which I hear you are famous. For the man from whom I would accept jewels and an apartment and a hundred a year must needs be a witty man, a man who knows how to play the perfect host, and that—so my brief spell in high society tells me—is to talk, not of the host's own inclinations, but of those of his guest."

"I am reproved," said Sackville.

He was exasperated, as he and his friends always were by the refusal of those they wished to fall immediate victims to their desires, but after that meal he was even more determined to make Nell his mistress.

❁ ❁ ❁

The King was furious with his players. It was unlike the King to lose his temper; he was, it was said by many, the sweetest tempered man at Court. But there was a great deal to make him melancholy at this time.

A terrible disaster had overtaken the country. The Dutch fleet had sailed up the Medway as far as Chatham. They had taken temporary possession of Sheerness; they had burned the *Great James,* the *Royal Oak,* and the *Loyal London* (that ship which London had so recently had built to ennoble the Navy). They had sent up in smoke a magazine of stores worth £40,000 and, afraid lest they should reach London Bridge and inflict further damage, the English had sunk four ships at Blackwall and thirteen at Woolwich.

The sight of the triumphant and arrogant Dutchmen sailing up the Medway, towing the *Royal Charles,* was, many sober Englishmen declared, the greatest humiliation the English had ever suffered.

So the King, who loved his ships and had done more than any to promote the power of his Navy, was melancholy indeed; this melancholy was aggravated by those who went about the country declaring that this was God's vengeance on England because of the vices of the Court. There came to him news that a Quaker, naked except for a loincloth, had run through Westminster Hall carrying burning coals in a dish on his head and calling on the people of the Court to repent of their lascivious ways which had clearly found disfavor in the eyes of the Lord.

Charles, the cynic and astute statesman, said to those about him that the disfavor of the Lord might have been averted by cash to repair his ships and make them ready to face the Dutchmen. But he was grieved. He could not see that the fire and the plague which had preceded it—and which in the crippling effects they had had on the country's trade were the reasons for this humiliating defeat—had any connection with the merry lives he and his followers led. In his opinion God would not wish to deny a gentleman his pleasure.

The plague came on average twice a year to London, and had done so for many years; he knew this was due to the crowded hovels and the filthy conditions of the streets, rather than to his licentiousness; the fire had been so disastrous because those same houses were built of wood and huddled so close together that there was no means—except by making gaps in the buildings—of stopping the fire once it had started on such a gusty night.

But he knew it was useless to tell a superstitious people these things, for they counted it Divine vengeance when aught went wrong and Divine approval when things went right.

But even a man of the sweetest nature could feel exasperated at times and, when he heard that in the *Change of Crowns* which was being done at his own playhouse John Lacy was pouring further ridicule on the Court, Charles was really angry. At any other time he would have laughed and shrugged his shoulders; he had never been a man to turn from the truth; but now, with London prostrate from the effects of plague and fire, with the Dutch inflicting the most humiliating defeat in the country's history and rebelion hanging in the air as patently as that miasma of haze and stench which came from the breweries, soap-boilers and tanneries ranged about the city, this ridicule of Lacy's was more than indiscreet; it was criminal.

The King decided that Lacy should suffer a stern reprimand and the playhouse be closed down for a while. It was incongruous, to say the least, that the mummers should be acting at such a time; and the very existence of the playhouse gave those who were condemning the idle life of the Court more sticks with which to beat it.

So, during those hot months, Lacy went to prison and the King's Theater was closed.

Once more Nell was an actress without a theater to act in.

❁ ❁ ❁

Afterwards she wondered how she could have behaved as she did.

Was it the desperation which was in the London air at that time? Was it the long faces of all she met which made her turn to the merry rake who was importuning her?

She who loved to laugh felt in those weeks of inactivity that she must escape from a London grown so gloomy that she was reminded of the weeks of plague, when she had lived that wretched life in a deserted city.

Charles Sackville was at her elbow. "Come, Nelly. Come and make merry," he said. "I have a pleasant house in Epsom Spa. Come with me and enjoy life. What can you do here? Cry 'Fresh herrings, ten a groat'? Come with me and I'll give you not only a handsome lover but a hundred pounds a year."

In her mood of recklessness, Nell threw aside her principles. "I will come," she said.

❁ ❁ ❁

So they made merry, she and Charles Sackville, in the house at Epsom.

There they were in pleasant country, but not too quiet and not so far from London that their friends could not visit them.

Charles Sedley joined them. He was witty and amusing, this Little Sid; and highly amused to see that Nell had succumbed at last. He insisted on staying with them at Epsom. He hoped, he said, to have a share in pretty, witty Nell. He would disclaim at length on the greater virtues of Little Sid as compared with those of Charles Sackville, Lord Buckhurst, and he was so amusing that neither Nell nor Buckhurst wished him to go.

They were wildly merry; and all the good people at Epsom talked of these newcomers in their midst. Little groups hung about outside the house hoping to catch a glimpse of the Court wits and the famous actress; and it seemed that a spirit of devilment came to all three of them, so that they acted with more wildness than came naturally even to them; and the people of Epsom were enchanted and shocked by turns.

Other members of the Court came down to see Lord Buckhurst and his newest mistress. Buckhurst was proud of his triumph. So many had laid siege to Nell without success. There was Sir Carr Scrope, squint-eyed and conceited, who made them all laugh by assuring Nell that he was irresistible to all women and, if she wished to be considered a woman of taste, she must immediately desert Buckhurst for him.

Rochester came; he read his latest satires. He told Nell that he set his footmen to wait each night at the doors of those whom he suspected of conducting intrigues, that he might be the first to compile a poem on their activities and circulate it throughout the taverns and coffeehouses. She believed him; there was no exploit which would be too fantastic for my lord Rochester.

Buckingham came; he was at this time full of plans. He swore that ere long they would see Clarendon out of office. He was working with all his mind and heart and he could tell them that his cousin, Barbara Castlemaine, was with him in this. Clarendon must go.

And so passed the weeks at Epsom—six of them—mad, feckless weeks, which Nell was often to remember with shame.

It was Sir George Etherege—Gentle George—who came riding to Epsom with news from London.

Lacy was released; the King had pardoned him; he could not remain long in anger against his players; moreover he knew the hardship this brought to those who worked in his theater. The ban was lifted. The King's Servants were playing once more.

Nell looked at her player's livery then—a cloak of bastard scarlet cloth with a black velvet collar. In the magnificence of the apartment which Buckhurst had given her, she put it on; and she felt that the girl she had now become was unworthy to wear that cloak.

She had done that which she had told herself she would never do. She had loved Charles Hart in her way, and if her feeling for him had not proved a lasting affection, at least she had thought it was at the time.

She accepted the morals of the age; but she had determined that her relationship with men must be based on love.

And then, because of a mood of recklessness, because she had been weak and careless and afraid of poverty, she had become involved in a sordid relationship with a man whom she did not love.

Buckhurst came to her and saw her in the cloak.

"God's Body!" he cried. "What have we here?"

"My player's livery," she said.

He laughed at it and, taking it from her, threw it about his own shoulders. He began to mince about the apartment, waiting for her applause and laughter.

"You find me a bore?" he asked petulantly.

"Yes, Charles," she said.

"Then the devil take you!"

"He did that when I came to you."

"What means this?" he cried indignantly. "Are you not satisfied with what I give you?"

"I am not satisfied with what there is between us."

"What! Nelly grown virtuous, sighing to be a maid once more?"

"Nay. Sighing to be myself."

"Now the wench grows cryptic. Who is this woman who has been my mistress these last weeks, if not Nelly?"

" 'Twas Nelly, sure enough, and for that I pity Nelly."

"You feel I have neglected you of late?"

"Nay, I feel you have not neglected me enough."

"Come, you want a present, eh?"

"Nay. I am going back to the playhouse."

"What, for a miserable pittance?"

"Not so miserable. With it I get back my self-respect."

He threw back his head and laughed. "Ah, now we have become high and mighty. Nelly the whore would become Nelly the nun. 'Tis a sad complaint but no unusual one. There are many who would be virtuous after they have lost their virtue, forgetting that those who have it are forever sighing to lose it."

"I am leaving at once for London."

"Leave me, and you'll never come back!"

"I see that you and I are of an opinion. Good day to you, sir."

"You're a fool, Nelly," he said.

"I am myself, and if that be a fool . . . then Nelly is a fool and must needs act like one."

He caught her wrist and cried: "Who is it? Rochester?"

Her answer was to kick his shins.

He cried out with pain and released her. She picked up her player's cloak, wrapped it about her, and walked out of the house.

Charles Hart was cool when she returned to the theater. He was not sure, he told her, whether she could have back any of her old parts.

Nell replied that she must then perforce play others.

The actresses were disdainful. They had been jealous of her quick rise to fame; and even more jealous of her liaison with Lord Buckhurst and the income which they had heard he had fixed upon her. They were delighted to see her back—humbled, as they thought.

This was humiliation for Nell, but she refused to be subdued. She went on the stage and played the smaller parts which were allotted to her, and very soon the pit was calling for more of Mrs. Nelly.

"It seems," said Beck Marshall, after a particularly noisy demonstration, "that the people come here not to see the play but my lord Buckhurst's whore."

Nell rose in her fury and, facing Beck Marshall, cried in ringing tones as though she were playing a dramatic part: "I was but one man's whore, though I was brought up in a bawdy-house to fill strong waters to the guests; and you are a whore to three or four, though a Presbyter's praying daughter."

This set the green room in fits of laughter, for it was true that Beck Marshall and her sister Ann did give themselves airs and were fond of reminding the rest that they did not come from the slums of London but from a respectable family.

Beck had no word to say to that; she had forgotten that it was folly to pit her wits against those of Nell.

The dainty little creature was more full of fire than any, and had the weapon of her wit with which to defend herself.

They all began to realize then that they were glad to have Nell back. Even Charles Hart—who, though in the toils of my lady Castlemaine, had regretted seeing Nell go to Buckhurst—found himself relenting. Moreover he had the business of the playhouse to consider, and audiences were poor, as they always were in times of disaster. Anything that could be done to bring people into the theater must be done; and Nell was a draw.

So, very soon after her brief retirement with Lord Buckhurst, she was back in all her old parts; and there were many who declared that, if there was one thing which could make them forget the unhappy state of the country's affairs, it was pretty, witty Nell at the King's playhouse.

All through that autumn Nell played her parts.

Meanwhile the country sought a scapegoat for the disasters, and Clarendon was forced to take this part. Buckingham and Lady Castlemaine were working together for his defeat, and although the King was reluctant to forsake an old friend he decided that, for Clarendon's own safety, it would be wiser for him to leave the country.

So that November Clarendon escaped to France, and Buckingham and his cousin Castlemaine rejoiced to see him go, and congratulated themselves on bringing about his eclipse.

But it was not long before Buckingham and his cousin fell out. Lady Castlemaine with her mad rages, Buckingham with his mad schemes, could not remain in harmony for long. The Duke then began to make further wild plans, and this time they were directed against his fair cousin.

He conferred with his two friends, Edward Howard and his brother, Robert Howard, who wrote plays for the theater.

Buckingham said: "The Castlemaine's power over the King is too great and should be broken. What we need to replace her is another woman, younger, more enticing."

"And how could this be?" said Robert. "You know His most gracious Majesty never discards; he merely adds to his hand."

"That is so; but let him add such a glorious creature, so beautiful, so enchanting, so amusing, that he has little time to spare for Castlemaine."

"He would fain be rid of her and her tantrums now, but still he keeps her."

"He was ever one to love a harem. Our gracious Sovereign says 'Yes yes yes' with such charm that he has never learned to say 'No.' "

"He is too good-natured."

"And his good-nature is our undoing. If Castlemaine remains mistress *en titre* she will ruin the country and the King."

"Not to mention her good cousin, my lord Buckingham!"

"Aye, and all of us. Come, we are good friends—let us do something about it. Let us find the King a new mistress. I suggest one of the enchanting ladies of the theater. What of the incomparable Nelly?"

"Ah, Nelly," said Robert. "She's an enchantress, but every time she opens her mouth Cole-yard comes out. The King needs a lady."

"There is Moll Davies at the Duke's," said Edward. Buckingham laughed, for he knew Moll to be a member of the Howard family—on the wrong side of the blanket. It was reasonable that the Howards should want to promote Moll, for she was a good choice, a docile girl. She would be sweet and gentle with the King and ready to take all the advice given her.

But Buckingham was the most perverse man in England. It would be such an easy matter to get Moll Davies into the King's bed. But he liked more complicated schemes; he wanted to do more than discountenance Castlemaine. Moreover how would Moll stand up to her ladyship? The poor girl would be defeated at every turn.

No, he wanted to provide the King with a mistress who had some spirit; someone who could deal with Lady Castlemaine in a manner to make the King laugh, if he should witness conflict between them, and there was one person he had in mind for the task.

Let the Howards do all in their power to promote the leading actress from the Duke's Theater; he would go to the King's own playhouse for his protégée.

Mrs. Nelly! She was the girl for him. She had at times the language of the streets. What of it? That was piquant. It made a more amusing situation: a King and a girl from the gutter.

He turned to the Howards. "My friends," he said, "if there is one thing His Majesty would appreciate more than one pretty actress, it is two pretty actresses. You try him with Moll; I'll try him with Nelly. 'Twill be a merry game to watch what happens, eh? Let the pretty creatures fight it out for themselves. Her ladyship will be most disturbed, I vow."

He could scarcely wait to bid them farewell. Nor did they wish to delay. They were off to the Duke's to tell Moll to hold herself in readiness for what they proposed.

Buckingham was wondering whether he should first call Charles' attention to Nell or warn Nell of the good fortune which awaited her. Nell was unaccountable. She had left Buckhurst and gone back to the comparative poverty of the stage. Mayhap it would be better to speak to Charles first.

He began to frame his sentences. "Has Your Majesty been to the playhouse of late? By God, what an incomparable creature is Mrs. Nelly!"

Buckingham was in high spirits by the time he reached Whitehall.

THREE

The King took several brisk turns round his privy gardens. It was early morning; it was his custom to rise early, however late he had retired, for his energy outstripped that of most of his courtiers, and when he was alone in the morning he walked at quite a different pace from that which he employed in his favorite pastime of sauntering, when he would fit his steps to those of the ladies who walked with him, pausing now and then to compliment them or throw some witty remark over his shoulder in answer to one of the wits who invariably accompanied him at sauntering time.

But in the early morning he liked to be up with the sun, to stride unattended through his domain—quickly round the privy garden, a brisk inspection of his physic garden, perhaps a turn round the bowling green. He might even walk as far as the canal in the park to feed the ducks.

During these walks he was a different man from the indolent, benevolent Charles whom his mistresses and courtiers knew. Those lines of melancholy would be more pronounced on his face as he took his morning perambulation. Sometimes he recalled the carousal of the previous day and regretted the promises he had made and which he knew he would not be able to keep; on other occasions he meditated on the virtuous and noble actions which he had left undone and all the subterfuges into which his easygoing nature and love of peace had led him.

It was more than seven years since he had ridden triumphantly into Whitehall, and this city had been gay with its flower-strewn streets, the banners and tapestries, the fountains flowing with wine, and most of all its cheering hopeful citizens.

And during that time how far had his people's hopes been realized? They had suffered plague in such degree as had rarely been known in all previous visitations; their capital city had been in great part destroyed; they had suffered ignoble defeat by the Dutch and had experienced the humiliation of seeing Dutchmen in their own waters. They had deplored the Puritan spoilsports but what had they in place of them? A pleasure-loving King who more frequently dallied with his mistresses and the debauched Court wits who surrounded him, than attended to affairs of state! The fact that he was in full possession of a lively mind, that he could, if he had been less indolent and more in love with politics than with women, have grown into one of the most astute statesmen of the times, made his conduct even the more to be deplored.

But even while he walked and considered himself and his position in his country, a sardonic smile curved his lips as he remembered that when he went into the streets the people still cheered him. He was their King and, because he was tall and commanding in appearance, because the women at the balconies who waved to him as he passed recognized that overwhelming charm in him, because the men, in their way, recognized it no less and were compensated for all the hardships they suffered when the King addressed them in the easy familiar way he had towards his subjects, rich or poor, they were satisfied and well content.

Such was human nature, thought Charles wryly; and why should I wish to change it when it is so beneficial to myself?

He had made peace with the French, Danes, and Dutch at Breda in the summer, and soon he hoped to conclude the triple alliance by which England, Sweden, and Holland bound themselves to assist Spain against the French. The French had recently proved themselves no friends of his and although it had been deplorable that there should be open strife between them, Charles knew that the one man he must watch more carefully than any other was Louis XIV of France.

There were times when he was excited by the game of politics, but he tired quickly. Then he would want the witty gentlemen of his Court about him—and most of all the beautiful women—for during his years of exile he had grown so cynical that he found it difficult to have much faith in anything, or any man. Pleasure never failed him. It always gave what he asked and expected. So many times he had seen plans come to nothing through no fault of the planners; he had seen men work diligently towards an ideal, only to be cheated of it by a trick of fate. He could not forget the years of bitterness and exile, the heartbreak of Worcester. Then he had given all his youthful idealism to regaining his kingdom; the result—dismal failure and humiliation. He had changed after Worcester. He had gone back to his life of wandering exile, the excitement of his days being not the plans he made for the regaining of his kingdom but those for the conquest of a new woman; and then suddenly Fortune had smiled on him. Through little effort of his own, without conflict and bloodshed, he was called back to his kingdom. He was welcomed with flowers and music and shouts of joy. England welcomed the debauchee, the careless cynic; almost ten years before, after disastrous Worcester, they had hounded the idealist from their shores. Such experiences made a deep impression on a pleasure-loving nature.

So now, as he walked through his garden, his cynical smile expanded. He must keep disaster at bay and enjoy life.

But even in this matter of enjoyment life had changed. He was heartily tired of Barbara Castlemaine. In the first years of their relationship he had found her tantrums amusing; he no longer did so. Why did he not banish her from the kingdom? Her *amours* were notorious. He could not bring himself to do it. She would storm and rage; and he had formed a habit, long ago, of avoiding Barbara's storms and rages. It was simpler to let her alone, to avoid her, to let her continue with her love affairs. They said of him, in the language of the card tables: "His Majesty never discards; he adds to his hand." It was true. Discarding was such an unpleasant affair; you could keep the uninteresting cards in your hands even though you rarely used them. It was much the more peaceable method.

Frances Stuart had bitterly disappointed him. Silly little Frances, with her child's mind and her incomparably beautiful face and figure. In spite of her simplicity, he would have married Frances if he had been free to do so, for her beauty had been such that it haunted him day and night. But Frances had run away and married that sot Richmond. Much good had this done her. Now poor Frances was a victim of the smallpox, and had lost her beauty and with it her power to torment the King.

Then there was Catherine, his wife—poor Catherine, with her dusky looks and her rabbits' teeth and her overwhelming desire to please him. Why had his own wife to fall in love with him? It was a situation which the wits of his Court regarded as extremely piquant. Piquant it might have been, but he was a man of some sensibility and if there was one thing he hated more than having to refuse something that was asked, it was to see a woman distressed. He must live continually with Catherine's distress. She had been brought up in the strict Court of Portugal. He hated hurting her, yet he could no more help doing so than he could help being himself. He must saunter with his mistresses; his mistresses were more important to him than his crown. He was a deeply sensual man and his sexual appetite was voracious so that the desire to appease it surmounted all other desires.

Therefore with his countless mistresses he must displease his queen who had had the childish folly to fall in love with him.

He was beset by women. By far the more satisfactory mistresses were those who could be called upon when desired and made few demands. It was small wonder that the Dutch had made cartoons of him, clinging to his crown as he ran, pursued by women.

He it was who had brought change to England. Less than ten years ago there had been strict puritanism everywhere; he liked to think that he had brought back laughter to England; but it was often laughter of a satirical kind.

The conversation of the people had changed; they now openly discussed subjects which, ten years ago, they would have blushed to speak of and would have pretended did not even exist. Throughout the country the

King's example was followed, and men took mistresses as naturally as previously they had taken walks in the sunshine. The poets jeered at chastity. Maidens were warned of flying time, of the churlishness of holding out against their lovers; the plays were frankly bawdy and concerned mainly with one subject—sexual adventure.

The King had brought French manners to England, and in France a King's mistress—not the Queen whom he had married for expedience—ruled with him in his Court.

The men of letters who surrounded him—and his greatest friends, and those who received his favors, were the witty men of letters—were, almost every one of them, rakes and libertines. Buckingham had recently been involved in a brawl with Henry Killigrew in the Duke's Theater, where they had bounded from their boxes to fight in the pit while the play was in progress; and the cause of this was Lady Shrewsbury, that lady whose reputation for taking a string of lovers matched that of the King's own mistress, Castlemaine. Killigrew, himself a rake and a notorious liar, had fled to France.

Henry Bulkeley had fought a duel with Lord Ossory and had been involved in a tavern brawl with George Etherege. Lord Buckhurst had recently been making merry at Epsom in the company of Sedley and an actress from the King's own theater. Rochester, the best of the poets and the greatest wit and libertine, possessed of the most handsome face at Court, had abducted a young heiress, Elizabeth Malet. It had been deemed necessary to imprison him in the Tower for a spell—though not for long, as Charles liked to have the gay fellow at his side. There was not another who could write a lampoon to compare with his; and if they were most scurrilous and that scurrility was often directed against the King himself, they were the most pointed, the most witty to be found in the kingdom. Rochester, the most impudent and arrogant of men, had since married the very willing Elizabeth Malet, confounded her family, and taken charge of her great fortune.

All these happenings were characteristic of life at the Court.

As the King walked through his gardens he saw coming towards him a young man; and as he gazed at the tall and handsome figure, the cynicism dropped from his face. For this young man, who was by no means possessed of the wit the King loved, had the King's love as no other had at Court.

"Why, Jemmy!" he called. "You're early abroad."

"Following Your Majesty's customs," said the young man.

He came and stood before the King without ceremony, and Charles put his arm about the young man's shoulders.

"I had thought, after your revelry of last night, that you would have lain longer abed."

"I doubt my revelry equaled that of Your Majesty."

"I am accustomed to combining revelry and early rising—a habit few of my friends care to adopt."

"I would follow you in all things, Father."

"You would do better to follow a course of your own, my boy."

"Nay, the people love you. Thus would I be loved."

Charles was alert. James' words were more than flattery. James was looking ahead to a time when he might wear the crown; he was seeing himself riding through the Capital, smiling at the acclaim of the people, letting his eyes rest on the prettiest of the women in the balconies.

Charles drew his son towards him with an affectionate gesture.

He said: "Fortunate James, you will never be in the public eye as I am. You can enjoy the pleasures of the Court without suffering its more irksome responsibilities."

James did not answer; he was too young and not clever enough to hide the sullen pout of his lips.

"Come, Jemmy," said Charles, "be content with your lot. 'Tis a good one and might have been not good at all. You are more fortunate than you know. Do not seek what can never be yours, my son. That way can disaster lie—disaster and tragedy. Come, let us make our way back to the Palace. We'll go through my physic garden. I want to show you how my herbs are progressing."

They walked arm-in-arm. James was conscious of the King's display of affection. Charles knew he was glancing towards the Palace, hoping that many would see him walking thus with the King. Alas, thought Charles, his desire to have my arm through his is not for love of me; it is for love of my royalty. He is not thinking of my fatherly affection but implying: See, how the King loves me! Am I not his son? Does he not lack a legitimate heir? Will that rabbit-toothed woman ever give him one? He is rarely with her. With what passion could such a woman inspire a man like my father? See how he scatters his seed among the women around him. He has many children, but not one by Rabbit teeth to call his legitimate son and heir to the throne. I am his son. I am strong and healthy; and he loves me dearly. He has recognized me; he has made me Baron Tyndale, Earl of Doncaster, and Duke of Monmouth. I have precedence over all Dukes except those of the royal blood. I am empowered to assume the royal arms—with the bar sinister, alas—and all this shows how the King delights to honor me. Why should he not make me his legitimate heir, since it is clear that the Portuguese woman will never give him one?

Ah, Jemmy, thought Charles, I would it were possible.

But had he, in his affection, showered too much favor on this impetuous boy who was not twenty yet, and because of the love the King had for him was fawned upon and flattered by all?

How often did Charles see his mother in him! Lucy with the big brown eyes; Lucy who had seemed the perfect mistress to the young man Charles had been in those days of exile. Those were the days before he had suffered the defeat at Worcester. He had loved Lucy—for a little while, but she had deceived him. Poor Lucy! How could he blame her, when he understood so well how easy it was to deceive? Even in those days he had understood. And out of that relationship had come this handsome boy.

He was glad he had loved Lucy. He would long ago have forgotten her, for there had been so many mistresses, but how could he ever forget her when she lived in this handsome boy?

James had inherited his mother's beauty and, alas, her brains. Poor Jemmy! He could never pit his wits against such as Rochester, Mulgrave, Buckingham, and the rest. He excelled in vaulting, leaping, dancing; and had already given a good account of himself with the ladies.

Now Charles thought it necessary to remind James of his lowly mother, that his hopes might not soar too high.

"It was on such a day as this that Ann Hill brought you to me, Jemmy," he said. "That was long before I regained my kingdom, as you know. There was I, a poor exile confronted with a son only a few years old. A bold little fellow you were, and I was proud of you. I wished that your mother was a woman I could have married, and that you could have been my legitimate son. Alas, it was not so. Your mother died in poverty in Paris, Jemmy, and you were with her. What would have happened to you, had good Ann Hill not brought you and your sister Mary to me, I know not."

James tried not to scowl; he did not like to be reminded of his mother.

"It is so long ago," he said. "People never mention my mother, and Your Majesty has almost forgotten her."

"I was thinking then that I never shall forget her while I have you to remind me of her."

There was a brief silence and, suddenly lifting his eyes, the King saw his brother coming towards him. He smiled. He was fond of his brother, James, Duke of York, but he had never been able to rid himself of a faint contempt for him. James, it seemed to him, was clumsy in all he did—physically clumsy, mentally clumsy. He was no diplomatist, poor James, and was most shamefully under the thumb of his wife—that strongminded lady who had been Anne Hyde, the daughter of disgraced Clarendon.

"What!" cried Charles. "Another early riser?"

"Your Majesty sets such good examples," said the Duke, "that we must needs all follow them. I saw you from the Palace."

"Well, good morrow to you, James. We were just going to look at my herbs. Will you accompany us?"

"If it is your pleasure, Sir."

Charles grimaced slightly as he looked from one to the other of the two men who fell into step beside him: Young James, handsome, sullen, and aloof, unable to hide his irritation at the intrusion; older James, less handsome, but equally unable to hide his feelings, his face clearly showing his mistrust of young Monmouth, his speculation as to what the young man talked of with his father.

Poor James! Poor brother! mused Charles. Doomed to trouble, I fear.

James, Duke of York, was indeed a clumsy man. He had married Anne Hyde when she was to have his child, ignoring convention and the wishes of his family to do so—a noble gesture in which Charles had supported him. But then, being James, he had repudiated her just when he was winning the support of many by his strong action; and in repudiating her—after the marriage of course—he had deeply wounded Anne Hyde herself, and Charles had no doubt that Anne was a woman who would not easily forget. Anne was now in control of her husband.

Poor James indeed. Contemplating him, Charles was almost inclined to believe that it might have been a good idea to have legitimized young Monmouth.

Monmouth was at least a staunch Protestant while James was flirting—nay, more than flirting—with the Catholic Faith. James had a genius for drifting towards trouble. How did he think the people of England would behave towards a Catholic monarch? At the least sign of Catholic influence they were ready to cry "No Popery!" in the streets. And James—who, unless the King produced a legitimate heir, would one day wear the crown—must needs consider becoming a Catholic!

If he ever becomes King, thought Charles, God help him and God help England.

Charles was struck by the significance of the three of them walking thus in the early morning before the Palace was astir. Himself in the center—on one side of him James, Duke of York, heir presumptive to the crown of England; and on the other side, James, Duke of Monmouth, the young man who would have been King had his father married his mother, the young man who had received such affection and such honors that he had begun to hope that the greatest honor of all would not be denied to him.

Yes, thought Charles, here am I in the center, keeping the balance . . .

myself standing between them. Over my head flows mistrust and suspicion. This uncle and nephew are beginning to hate one another, and the reason is the crown, which is mine and for which they both long.

What an uneasy thing a crown can be!

How can I make these two good friends? There is only one way: produce a legitimate son. It is the only answer. I must strike the death knell of their hopes and so disperse that suspicion and mistrust they have for one another; remove that state of affairs and, in place of growing hate, why should there not be growing affection?

The King shrugged. There is no help for it. I must share the bed of my wife more frequently. Alas, alas! It must not be that for want of trying I fail to provide England with a son.

❁ ❁ ❁

Later that morning the Howards sought audience of the King.

Charles was not eager for their company; he found them dull compared with sharp-witted Rochester. It was typical of Charles that although he personally liked the Howards and disliked Rochester, he preferred the company of a man who could amuse him to that of those whom he admitted to be of better character.

Edward Howard had recently been subjected to the scorn of the wits who criticized his literary achievements unmercifully. Shadwell had pilloried him in the play, *The Sullen Lovers,* and all the wits had decided that Edward and Robert Howard should not be taken seriously as writers; only the mighty Buckingham who was, of all the wits, more interested in politics and diplomacy, remained their ally.

Now Robert said to Charles: "Your Majesty should go to the Duke's Theater this day. Pretty little Moll Davies never danced better than she has of late. I am sure that the sight of her dancing would be a tonic to Your Majesty."

"I have noted the lady," said Charles. "And mighty charming she is."

The brothers smiled happily. "And seeming to grow in beauty, Your Majesty, day by day. A good girl, too, and almost of the gentry."

Charles looked at the brother slyly. "I have heard that she has relations in high places. I am glad of this, for I feel sure they will do all in their power to elevate her, doubtless in compensation for her begetting on the wrong side of the blanket."

"It may be so," said Robert.

"And would it please Your Majesty to call at the Duke's this day to see the wench in her part?" asked Edward a little too eagerly.

Charles ruminated. 'Tis true, he thought; they are dunces indeed, these

Howards. Why do they not say to me: Moll Davies is of our family—a bastard sprig; but we would do something for her. She is an actress and high in her profession; we should like to see her elevated to the position of your mistress? Such plain speaking would have amused him more.

"Mayhap. Mayhap," he said.

Robert came nearer to the King. "The wench believes she saw Your Majesty look with approval upon her. The foolish girl, she was almost swooning with delight at the thought!"

"I was never over-fond of the swooning kind," mused Charles.

"I but spoke metaphorically, Your Majesty," said Robert quickly.

"I rejoice. I would prefer to keep my good opinion of little Moll Davies. A mighty pretty creature."

"And gentle in her ways," said Edward. "A grateful wench, and gratitude is rarely come by in these days."

"Rarely indeed! Now, my friends, I will bid you goodbye. Matters of state . . . matters of state . . ."

They bowed themselves from his presence, and he laughed inwardly. But he continued to think of Moll Davies. For, he said to himself, my indolent nature is such, I am amused that my friends should bring my pleasures to me rather than that I should go in search of them. There are so many beautiful women. I find it hard to choose, therefore deem it thoughtful of my courtiers to do the choosing for me. This avoids my turning with regret from a beautiful creature and having to murmur apologies: Not yet, sweet girl. I am mighty capable, but even I must take you all in turn.

❁ ❁ ❁

Buckingham presented himself.

"Your Majesty, have you seen Mrs. Nell Gwyn in the Beaumont and Fletcher revival of *Pilaster*?"

Charles' melancholy eyes were brooding. "Nay," he answered.

"Then, Sir, you have missed the best performance ever seen upon the stage. She plays Bellario. Your Majesty remembers Bellario is sick of love and follows her lover in the disguise of a page boy. This gives Nelly a chance to swagger about on the stage in her breeches. What legs, Sir! What a figure! And all so small that 'twould seem a child's form but for those delicious curves."

" 'Twould seem to me," said the King, "that you are enamored of this actress."

"All London is enamored of her, Sir. I wonder your fancy has not turned to her ere this. What spirit! What zest for living!"

"I am weary of spirit in ladies—for a while. I have had over-much of spirit."

"My fair cousin, eh? What a woman! Though she be my kinswoman and a Villiers, I pity Your Majesty. I pity you with all my heart."

"I conclude you and the lady have fallen out. How so? You were once good friends."

"Who would not fall out in due time with Barbara, Sir?" You know that better than any of us. Now Nelly is another matter. Lovely to look at, and a comedienne to bring the tears of laughter to the eyes. Nelly is incomparable, Sir. There is not another on the stage to compare with Nelly."

"What of that pretty creature at the Duke's—Moll Davies?"

"Bah! Forgive me, Sir, but Bah! and Bah I again. Moll Davies? A simpering wench compared with Nelly. No fire, Your Majesty; no fire at all."

"I am a little scorched, George. Mayhap I need the soothing balm that comes from simpering wenches."

"You'd tire of Moll in a night."

Charles laughed aloud. What game was this? he wondered. Buckingham is determined to put Barbara out of countenance; I know they have quarreled. But why should the Howards and my noble Duke have turned procurers at precisely the same time?

Moll Davies? Nell Gwyn? He would have one of them to entertain him that night.

He was a little put out with Buckingham, who had for most of last year been under a cloud, and, not so long before that, banished from Court for returning there without the King's permission. Buckingham was a brilliant man, but his brilliance was marred continually by his hare-brained schemes. Moreover the noble Duke gave himself airs and had an exaggerated opinion of his own importance and the King's regard for him.

Charles laid his hand on the Duke's shoulder. "My dear George," he said, "your solicitude for little Nelly touches me. It is clear to me that one who speaks so highly of a pretty actress desires her for himself. You go to my theater this day and court Nelly. I'll go to the Duke's and see if Moll Davies is the enchanting creature I have been led to believe."

❁ ❁ ❁

Nell heard the news; it sped throughout the theater.

The King had sent for Moll Davies. She had pleased him, and he had given her a ring estimated to be worth every bit of £700.

He was often at the Duke's Theater. He liked to see her dance. He led the applause, and everyone in London was talking about the King's latest mistress, Moll Davies.

Lady Castlemaine was sullen; she stayed away from the theaters. There were wild rumors about the number of lovers who visited her daily.

Then one afternoon, instead of going to the Duke's, the King came to his own theater.

In the green room there was a great deal of excitement.

"What means this?" cried Beck Marshall. "Can it be that His Majesty is tired of Moll Davies?"

"Would that surprise you?" asked her sister Ann.

"Indeed it would not surprise *me,*" put in Mary Knepp. "A more stupid simpering ninny I never set eyes on."

"How can the King . . . after my lady Castlemaine?" demanded Peg Hughes.

"Mayhap," said Nell, "because Moll Davies is unlike my lady Castlemaine. After the sun the rain is sweet."

"But he sends for her often, and he has given her a ring worth £700."

"And this night," said Beck, "he is here. Why so? Can it be that he has a taste for actresses? Has Moll given him this taste?"

"We waste time," said Nell. "If he has come here for a purpose other than watching the show, that is a matter which we soon shall know."

"Nell's turning to wisdom. Alas, Nell, this is a sign of old age. And, Nelly, you are growing old, you know. You're turned eighteen, I'll swear."

"Almost as old as you are, Beck," said Nell. "Of a certainty I must soon begin to consider myself decrepit."

"I'm a good year younger than you," cried Beck.

"You have a remarkable gift," retorted Nell. "You can make time turn back. This year you are a year younger than last. I have remarked it."

Ann interrupted: "Calm yourselves. You'll not be ready in time; and will you keep the King waiting?"

While Nell played her part she was conscious of him. All were conscious of him, of course, but Nell was playing her part for him alone.

What did she want? Another affair such as that in which she had indulged with my lord Buckhurst, only on a more exalted plane? No. She did not want that. But Charles Stuart was no Charles Sackville. She was sure of that. The King was libertine-in-chief in a town of libertines, yet he was apart from all others. She sensed it. He had a quality which was possessed by none other. Was it kingship? How could Nelly, bred in Cole-yard, know what it was? She was aware of one thing only; she wanted that night, above all things, to hear those words: The King sends for Nelly.

She was a sprite that night, richly comic, swaggering about the stage in her page's garb. The pit was wildly applauding; the whole theater was with her; but she was playing only for the dark-eyed man in the box, who leaned forward to watch her.

She made her bow at the end. There she stood, at the edge of the apron stage so close to the royal box. He was watching her—her only; she was aware of that. His dark eyes glistened; his full lips smiled.

She was in the green room when the message came.

Mohun brought it. "Nelly, you are to go to Whitehall at once. The King wishes you to entertain him in his palace."

So it was happening to her as it had happened to Elizabeth Weaver. She did not see the glances of the others; she was aware of a great exaltation.

Mohun put a rich cloak about her shoulders.

"May good fortune attend you, Nelly," he said.

❁ ❁ ❁

In the great apartment were assembled the ladies and gentlemen of the King's more intimate circle. Many of these were personally known to Nell. Rochester and his wife were there. She was glad, for, notwithstanding his often spiteful quips, she knew Rochester to be her friend. There was one thing he admired above all others—wit—and Nell, possessing this in full measure, had his regard. Buckingham and his Duchess were also present. The Duke's eyes were shining with approval. He had worked to bring this about, and he was enjoying the rivalry with the Howards who were putting forward Moll Davies. At last he had succeeded in getting Nell to the Palace, and he had no doubt that pretty, witty Nelly would soon triumph over pretty, rather spiritless Moll Davies.

Bulkeley, Etherege, Mulgrave, Savile and Scrope were also there. So were the Dukes of York and Monmouth, with several ladies.

Nell went to the King and knelt before him.

"Arise, sweet lady," said the King. "We wish for no ceremony."

She rose, lifting her eyes to his, and for once Nell felt her bravado desert her. It was not that he was the King. She had suspected it was something else, and now she knew it was.

More than anything she wanted to please him; and this desire was greater even than that which she had once felt when her ambition was to become an orange-girl, and later to act on the stage.

Nell, shorn of her high spirits, was like a stranger to herself.

But Buckingham was beside her.

"I trust Your Majesty will prevail on Mrs. Nelly to give us a song and dance."

"If it should be her wish to do so," said the King. "Mrs. Nelly, I would have you know that you come here as a guest, not as an entertainer."

"I am right grateful to Your Majesty," said Nell. "And if it be your wish, I will sing and dance."

So she sang and she danced; and her spirits returned. This was the Nell they had met so many times before—Nell of the quick wits; the Nell who could answer the remarks which were flung at her from my lords Rochester and Buckingham, neither of whom, she was sure, had any wish other than to make her shine in the eyes of the King.

There was supper at a small table during which the King kept her at his side. His glances showed his admiration, and he talked to her of the plays in which she had acted. She was astonished that he should know so much about them and be able to quote so much of their contents, and she noticed that it was the poetic parts which appealed to him.

"You are a poet yourself, Sire?" she asked.

He disclaimed it.

But Rochester insisted on quoting the King:

"I pass all my hours in a shady old grove,
But I live not the day when I see not my love;
I survey every walk now my Phyllis is gone,
And sigh when I think we were there all alone;
O then, 'tis O then that I think there's no hell
Like loving, like loving too well."

"Those are beautiful words," said Nell.

The King smiled wryly. "Flattery abounds at Court, Nelly," he said. "I had hoped you would bring a breath of change."

"But 'tis so, Your Majesty," said Nell.

Rochester had leaned towards her. "His Most Gracious Majesty wrote the words when he was deep in love."

"With Phyllis?" said Nell. "His Majesty most clearly says so."

"Some beautiful lady cowers behind the name of Phyllis," said Rochester. "I begin to tire of the custom. What say you, Sir? Why should we call our Besses, our Molls, and our little Nells by these fanciful names? Phyllis, Chloris, Daphne, Lucinda! As our friend Shakespeare says: 'That which we call a rose by any other name would smell as sweet.' "

"Some ladies wish to love in secret," said the King. "If you poets must write songs to your mistresses, then respect their desire for secrecy, I beg of you."

"His Royal Highness is the most discreet of men," said Rochester with a bow. "He's too good-natured. No matter whether it be politics, love, or religion."

Rochester began to quote:

"Never was such a Faith's Defender,
He like a politic prince and pious,
Gives liberty to conscience tender
And does to no religion tie us.
Jews, Turks, Christians, Papists, he'll please us
With Moses, Mahomet, or Jesus."

"You're an irreverent devil, Rochester," said Charles.

"I see the royal lip curve in a smile, which I trust was inspired by my irreverence."

"Nevertheless there are times when you try me sorely. I see, my lady Rochester, that you are a little tired. I think you are asking for leave to retire."

"If it should please Your Most Gracious Majesty . . ." began Lady Rochester.

"Anything that pleases you, my dear lady, pleases me. You are tired, you wish to retire. So I will command your husband to take you to your apartments."

This was the signal. They were all to go. The King wished to be alone with Nell.

Nell watched them all make their exit. This was performed with the utmost ceremony, and as she watched them she felt her heart beat fast.

When they had gone, the King turned to her, smiling.

He took her hands and kissed them.

"They amuse me . . . but such amusements are for those times when there are less exciting adventures afoot."

Nell said tremulously: "I trust I may please Your Majesty."

He replied: "My friends have put me in the mood to rhyme," and he began to quote Flecknoe's verse:

"But who have her in their arms,
Say she has a hundred charms,
And as many more attractions
In her words and in her actions."

He paused, smiling at her, before he went on: "It continues, I believe:

"But for that, suffice to tell ye,
'Tis the pretty little Nelly."

"And 'tis written of you, I'll swear, by one who knew you well."

"By one, Sire, who but saw me on the stage."

Charles drew her to him and kissed her lips. " 'Twas enough to see you, to know it were true. Why, Nell, you are afraid of me. You say, This is the King. But I would not be a King tonight."

Nell said softly: "I am but a girl from the Cole-yard, one of Your Majesty's most humble servants."

"A King should love all his subjects, Nell, however humble. I never thought to see you humble. I have noted your subduing of the pit."

"Sire, I do not now face the pit."

"Come with me and, for the sake of your beauty, this night let us forget that I am Charles Stuart, and you Nell of old Drury. Tonight I am a man; you a woman."

Then he put his arm about her and led her into a small adjoining chamber.

And here it was that Nell Gwyn became the mistress of the King.

❁ ❁ ❁

Nell left the Palace in the early hours of the morning. She was bemused. Never had her emotions been so roused; never had she known such a lover.

She was carried to her lodgings in a Sedan chair; it would not have been meet for her to have walked through the streets in the fine gown she had been wearing. She was no longer merely Mrs. Nelly, the play-actress. Her life had changed last night. People would look at her slyly; they would marvel at her; they would whisper about her; many would envy her; many would censure her.

And I care not! she thought.

When she reached her lodgings she kicked off her shoes and danced a jig. She was happier than she had ever been in her life. Not because the King had sent for her; not because she had joined the King's seraglio; but because she was in love.

There was never one like him. It was not that he was the King. Or was it? Nay! All kings were not kind, gentle, passionate, charming, all that one looked for in a lover. He was no longer Your Majesty to her; he was Charles. She had called him Charles last night.

"Charles!" She said it now aloud. And: "Charles, Charles, Charles. Charles is my lover," she sang. "The handsomest, kindest lover in the world. He happens to be the King of England, but what matters that? To me he is Charles . . . my Charles. He is the whole country's Charles . . . but mine also . . . especially mine."

Then she laughed and hugged herself and recalled every detail of the night. She wished passionately then that she had never known any other Charles, never known Charles Hart; never known Charles Sackville.

There have been too many Charleses in my life, she mused. I would there had been only one. Then she wept a little, because happy as she was there was so much to regret.

❁ ❁ ❁

The King forgot Nell for some time after that night. She was very pretty, but he had known many pretty women. Perhaps he had been disappointed; he had heard her wit commended by such as Buckingham; that did not count of course, as Buckingham had his own reasons for promoting Nell, which was the discomfiture of his cousin Barbara and doubtless the Howards. Yet Rochester seemed to have had some praise for her. Could it to be that Rochester had been or still was her lover?

The King shrugged his shoulders. Nell was just a pretty actress. She had been a very willing partner in an enjoyable interlude, as had so many. He fancied she was very experienced; he had heard of an escapade with Buckhurst. Doubtless the pretty creature was not averse to changing from Duke to King.

Moll Davies suited his present mood more frequently. Moll was so gentle; there had been no pretence of quick wits there; she was just a lovely young woman who could learn a part and speak it prettily; and she could dance as well as anyone on the stage.

He found he was sending more frequently for Moll than for any.

He had grown a little weary since the disasters. Was he ageing somewhat? Beneath the periwig he had plenty of silver showing among his dark hairs.

Now that Clarendon was gone he was missing him. He would have to form a new Council. Buckingham was pressing for a place and, of course, would have it.

State affairs claimed his attention; when he turned from them, little Moll Davies, who smiled so sweetly while speaking little, provided that which he needed. She was the completest contrast to Barbara. Then of course Will Chaffinch and his wife—who held the post of seamstress to the Queen—would often usher ladies up the back stairs to his apartments during the night, and lead them down to the river in the early hours of morning when their barges would be waiting for them. Chaffinch was a discreet and wily fellow, and his apartments were situated near those of the King. He had for long looked after his master's more intimate and personal business.

But now and then Charles remembered the sprightly little actress from his theater, and sent for her.

He enjoyed her company. She was mightily pretty; she was now becoming amusing, and often he would catch glimpses of that wit which had amused Buckingham.

Then he forgot her again; and it seemed that Moll Davies was going to replace Lady Castlemaine as the woman, among all his women, who could best please him.

❁ ❁ ❁

Nell was sad and her chief task during those days was to hide her sadness. She was nothing to him but just another harlot. She realized that now. She had been mistaken. The courtly manners, the charm, the grace—they were generously offered to any light-o'-love who could amuse him for a night.

She was nothing more than one of dozens. Tonight it might be her turn—perhaps not.

For her there was no £700 ring. Moll Davies had won. The Howards were triumphant.

As for Buckingham, he had forgotten his intention to promote Nell. His object had been achieved by the Howards and Moll Davies, for his cousin Barbara flew into a flaring rage every time the girl was mentioned. Barbara's pride had been lowered; Barbara knew that she must take care when she thought she might insult the great Duke of Buckingham—her cousin and one-time lover though he was. What part had Nell in Buckingham's schemes? None at all. He had forgotten he had ever exerted himself to bring her to the King's notice. Thus it was with all his schemes. He dallied with them for a while and then forgot. So Moll Davies was provided with beautiful clothes and jewels by the Howards, who brought her before the King whenever he seemed inclined to forget her, while Nell's benefactor ignored her.

So Nell was desolate.

In the green room the women laughed together, their eyes on Nell, Nell who had enjoyed the privilege of being sent for by the King.

"Cole-yard," whispered Beck Marshall, "could not go to Whitehall. 'Twas a mistake. His Majesty would be the first to realize it. Poor Nelly soon got her marching orders."

"She has been called back once or twice," said her sister Ann.

Peg Hughes, who was being courted by Prince Rupert, was inclined to be kind. "And doubtless will be called again. The King was never a man to fix his love on one. Nell will remain one of his merry band, I doubt not."

"She'll be in the twice-yearly class," said Beck.

"Well, 'tis better to play twice yearly than not at all," said Peg quietly.

When Nell came among them, Beck said: "Have you heard the latest news, Nell? Moll Davies is to have a fine house and, some say, leave the stage."

Nell for once was silent. She felt that she could not speak to them about the King and Moll Davies.

She had changed. She wondered: Shall I one day be like Elizabeth Weaver, waiting in vain for the King to send for me?

❁ ❁ ❁

Early that year the Earl of Shrewsbury had challenged Buckingham to a duel on account of the Duke's liaison with Lady Shrewsbury; the result of this was that Shrewsbury was killed. The King was furious. He had forbidden dueling, and Buckingham awaited the outcome in trepidation. He had now completely forgotten that he had decided to launch Nell at Whitehall.

In the summer she had the part of Jacintha in Dryden's *An Evening's Love; or the Mock Astrologer.* Charles Hart played opposite her.

Dryden, such an admirer of Nell's, invariably had her in his mind when he wrote his plays, and Jacintha *was* Nell, so said all, "Nelly to the last y."

The King was in his usual box and, as she played her part, Nell could not help gazing his way. Perhaps there was a mute appeal in her eyes, in her voice, in her very actions.

To love a King—that was indeed a tragedy, she had come to understand. She had no means of being with him unless sent for, no way of learning where she had failed to please.

Charles Hart as Wildblood wooed her on the stage before the King's eyes.

" 'What has a gentleman to hope from you?' " he asked.

And Nell, as Jacintha, must answer: " 'To be admitted to pass my time with while a better comes; to be the lowest step in my staircase, for a knight to mount upon him, and a lord upon him, and a marquis upon him, and a duke upon him, till I get as high as I can climb.' "

The audience laughed loud and long.

Many covert glances were thrown at the King in his royal box and pert Nell on the stage. She had had her lord; she had reached her King; but she had not kept her King.

There was no sign on the King's face to show how he received this piece of impudence. But Nell, intensely aware of him, believed he was displeased.

She went straight to her lodgings that night and wept a little, but not much. She had to show the world a bold front, and the next day she was a merry madcap once more.

"Nelly . . . the old Nelly . . . is back," it was said.

And after a while it was forgotten that she had ever changed. There she was, the maddest and most indiscreet creature who had ever played in the King's Theater, and the people crowded into the playhouse to see her.

Now and then the King came. Occasionally he sent for Nell. But Moll Davies had her fine house near Whitehall, and had left the stage.

All the actresses talked of Moll's good fortune, and many wondered why it was that pretty, witty Nell had pleased the King so mildly and Moll had pleased him so much.

❁ ❁ ❁

The company performed Ben Jonson's *Cataline.* Lady Castlemaine sent for Mrs. Corey who was playing Sempronia—a most unattractive character—and gave her a sum of money on condition that she would, when playing the part, mimic Lady Castlemaine's great enemy of the moment, Lady Elizabeth Harvey, whose husband had recently left London for Constantinople as the King's ambassador.

During the very first performance, when the question was asked, "But what will you do with Sempronia?" Lady Castlemaine leaped to her feet and shouted at the top of her voice, "Send her to Constantinople."

Lady Harvey was so incensed that she arranged that Mrs. Corey should be sent to prison for the insult. Lady Castlemaine then used all her influence, which was still great, to have her released. And when Mrs. Corey next played the part she was pelted with all manner of obnoxious objects, and men, hired by Lady Elizabeth, snatched oranges from the orange-girl's baskets to throw at the actors on the stage.

Each night the play was performed there was an uproar between men hired by Lady Elizabeth Harvey and those hired by Lady Castlemaine. It was bad for the play and the actors, but good for business; for the theater was filled each time that play was performed.

Later, Dryden's *Tyrannic Love; or the Royal Martyr* was produced; and in this Nell played Valeria, daughter of the Emperor Maximin who persecuted St. Catherine. It was a small part in which Nell stabbed herself at the end; then came the epilogue, which was to be her great triumph.

She felt exalted that day. She had escaped from the dismal creature she had become. She had been a fool to harbor such romantic thoughts about a King.

"Nelly, grow up," she said to herself. "Have done with dreaming. What are you to him—what could you ever be—but a passing fancy?"

She lay dead on the apron stage and when the stretcher-bearers approached with her bier, she leaped suddenly to her feet, crying:

"Hold! Are you mad? You damned confounded dog!
I am to rise and speak the epilogue."

Then she came to the very front of the apron stage—mad Nelly, the most indiscreet of all the actresses, pretty, witty Nell who had won their hearts.

The King, sitting in his box, leaned forward. She felt his approving eyes upon her. She knew that, try as he might, he could not withdraw them, and she believed then that neither Lady Castlemaine nor Moll Davies could have made him turn his eyes from her.

She cried in her high-pitched, mocking tones:

"I come, kind gentlemen, strange news to tell ye:
I am the ghost of poor departed Nelly.
Sweet ladies, be not frightened, I'll be civil;
I'm what I was, a little harmless devil . . ."

The audience was craning forward to listen as she went on with the lines which were setting some rocking with laughter, while others, fearful of missing Nelly's words, cried: "Hush!"

"O poet, damned dull poet, who could prove
So senseless to make Nelly die for love!
Nay, what's yet worse, to kill me in the prime
Of Easter term, in tart and cheesecake time!"

She had thrown back her head; her lovely face was animated. Many caught their breath at the exquisite beauty of the dainty little creature as she continued:

"As for my epitaph when I am gone,
I'll trust no poet, but will write my own:
'Here Nelly lies who, though she lived a slattern,
Yet died a princess, acting in Saint Cattern.' "

The pit roared its approval. Nell permitted herself one look at the royal box. The King was leaning forward; he was clapping heartily; and he was smiling so intimately that Nell knew he would send for her that night.

She felt light-headed with gaiety. She had tried to act a part because she had loved a King. In future she would be herself. Who knew, had he known the real Nelly, Charles might have loved her too.

❁ ❁ ❁

Charles did send for Nell that night, but secretly. Will Chaffinch came to her lodgings to tell her that His Majesty wished her to visit him by way of the back stairs.

In high good spirits Nell prepared herself for the journey and, very soon after Chaffinch had called at her lodgings, she was mounting the privy stairs to the King's chamber.

Charles was delighted to see her.

"It is long since we have met, Nell," said he, "in these intimate surroundings, but I have thought of you often—and with the utmost tenderness."

Nell's face softened at the words, even while she thought: Does he mean it? Is this another of those occasions when his desire to be kind triumphs over truth?

But perhaps his greatest charm was that he could make people believe, while they were in his presence, all the kind things he said to them. It was only after they had left him that the doubts crept in.

"Matters of state," he murmured lightly.

And indeed, he mused, that which had kept him from Nell was indeed a matter of greatest importance to the state. Of late he had been spending his nights with Catherine, his wife.

He had done his duty, he decided with a grimace. He fervently hoped that the exercise would bear fruit.

I must get a legitimate son, he told himself a hundred times a day. Every time he saw his brother James, every time he saw that handsome sprig, young Monmouth, swaggering about the Court eager that none should forget for a moment that he was the King's son, Charles said to himself: I must get me a son.

Here was a perverse state of affairs. He had many healthy children, sons among them, growing up in beauty to manhood, many of them bearing the stamp of his features—and all bastards. There was scarcely one of his mistresses who had not borne a child which she swore was his. Od's fish, I am a worthy stallion, he thought. Yet, in my legitimate bed I am sterile—or Catherine is. Poor Catherine! She yearns for a child equally with me. Why in the name of all that's holy should our efforts meet with no success?

And it was a great burden to follow the call of duty, to spend long hours of the night with Catherine—cloying, clinging Catherine—when superb creatures such as Barbara, charmingly pretty dolls such as Moll Davies, and exquisitely lovely sprites, such as this little Nelly, had but to be brought at his command.

When he had seen Nell on the stage this day, rising from her bier, looking the very embodiment of charm and wit and all that was fascinating and amusing, he had determined to evade his duty that night.

"My dear wife," he had said to Catherine, "I shall retire early this evening. I feel unwell."

She was startled, that good wife of his. He was never ill. There was not another at Court who enjoyed his rude health. In the game of tennis he excelled all others; and if he spent his afternoons in the theater and his evenings in amusing the ladies, his mornings were often devoted to swimming, fishing, or sailing. His laziness was of the mind—never of the body. He slept little, declaring that the hours a man spent in unconsciousness were lost hours; he had not yet had such a feast of the good things life had to offer that he could afford to waste long periods of his life in sleep. He merely disliked what he called "that foolish, idle, impertinent thing called business," and much preferred to take "his usual physic at tennis" or on horseback.

Mayhap he had been unwise to make the excuse of ill health. Catherine was all solicitude. She was a simple soul, who yet had much to learn of him; and he was his most foolish self in that he could not bring himself to say—as my lord Buckingham would have told his wife, or my lord Rochester his—that he needed an occasional escape from her company; he must tell his lies for, if he did not, he would hurt her, and to see her hurt would spoil his pleasure; and that was one thing he could not endure—the spoiling of his pleasure.

When they next met she would smother him with her concern and he would have to feign a headache or pain somewhere, and remember the exact position of the pain. He might even have to endure a posset of her making since the dear simple creature was ever eager to display her wifely devotion.

But enough of that—here was Nell, risen from her bier, prettier than ever, her eyes sparkling with wit and good humor.

This little Nelly grows on me, pondered the King; and lifting from the bed one of the many spaniels which were always in his bedchamber, he embraced her warmly; and Nell with delight gave herself up to that embrace.

They made love. They dozed, and they awakened to find Will Chaffinch's wife at their bedside.

"Your Majesty! Your Majesty! I pray you awake. The Queen comes this way. She brings a posset for you."

"Out of sight, Nelly!" said the King.

Nell whisked out of bed and, naked as she was, hid herself behind the hangings.

Catherine entered the room just as Nell was hidden; she approached the bed, her long and beautiful hair hanging about her shoulders, her plain face anxious.

"I could not sleep," she said. "I could do naught but think of you in pain."

The King took her hand as she sat on the bed and looked at him anxiously.

"Oh," he said, "the pain is to be deplored, only because it disturbed your slumbers. It has gone. In fact I have forgotten where it was."

"I very much rejoice. I have brought this dose. I am sure it will bring immediate relief should you need it."

Nell, listening, thought: here are the King and Queen of England, and he treats her in the same charmingly courteous way in which he treats his harlots.

"And you," he was saying, "should be resting in your bed at this hour. I shall be the one who has to bring you doses if you wander thus in your night attire."

"And you would," she said. "I know it. You have the kindest heart in the world."

"I pray you do not have such high opinions of me. I deserve them not."

"Charles . . . I will stay beside you this night . . ."

There was a sudden silence and, unable to stop herself, Nell moved the hangings and looked through the opening she had made.

She saw that one of the King's spaniels had leaped onto the bed and was bringing Nell's tiny slipper in his mouth and laying it there as though offering it to Queen Catherine.

Nell, in that quick glance, took in the scene—the King's discomfiture, the Queen's face scarlet with humiliation.

The Queen quickly recovered her dignity. She was no longer the same inexperienced woman who had swooned when she had come face-to-face with Barbara Castlemaine, and the odious woman had kissed her hand.

She said abruptly: "I will not stay. The pretty fool who owns that little slipper might take cold."

The King said nothing. Nell heard the door close.

Nell came slowly back to the bed. The King was gently stroking the ears of the little spaniel who had betrayed them. He stared moodily before him as Nell got in beside him.

He turned to her ruefully. "There are many strange things happening in the world," he said. "Many women are kind to me; but I am a King, and it pays to be kind to kings, so that presents little mystery. But there is one mystery I have been unable to solve: Why does that good and virtuous woman who is my Queen love me?"

Nell said: "I could tell you, Sire."

And she told him; her explanation was lucid and witty. She restored him to his good humor, and shortly after that occasion Nell discovered that she was to bear the King's child.

❀ ❀ ❀

Now that Nell was with child by the King, it was no longer possible for her to play all her old parts. She was helped by Will Chaffinch, who had charge of such items of the royal expenditure, and she moved into Newman's Row, which was next to Whetstone Park.

Nell was elated by the thought of bearing the King's child. Charles was only mildly interested. He had so many illegitimate children; it was a legitimate one which he so desperately needed. Even before he had been restored to his throne he had a large and growing family, of which the Duke of Monmouth was the eldest son. Some he kept about him; others passed out of his life. One of the latter was James de la Cloche who had been born to Margaret de Carteret while Charles was exiled in Jersey. He believed that James was now a Jesuit. Lady Shannon had given him a daughter; Catherine Pegge a son and a daughter. There were many others who claimed to be his. He accepted them all in his merry good humor. He was proud of his ability to create sons and daughters; and when some of his subjects called him "Old Rowley," after the stallion in the royal stables who had sired more fine and healthy colts than any other, he did not object. Barbara Castlemaine had already borne him five children. He loved them all tenderly. He adored his children; there was nothing he liked better than to talk with them, and listen to their amusing comments. He enjoyed his visits to Barbara's nursery more than to their mother's chamber. They were growing more amusing—young Anne, Charles, Henry, Charlotte, and George—than their virago of a mother.

He had an acknowledged family of nine or ten; he did what he could for them, raising them to the peerage, settling money on them, keeping his eyes open for profitable marriages. Oh, yes, he was indeed fond of his children.

And now little Nell was to provide him with another.

It was interesting; he would be eager to see the child when it put in an appearance; but meanwhile there was much elsewhere with which to occupy himself.

He was faintly worried once more by the shadows cast over his throne by his son Monmouth, and his own brother, the Duke of York.

Monmouth was turning out to be a rake. In the sexual field, it was said, he would one day rival his father. Charles could only shrug his shoulders tolerantly at this. He would not have had young Jemmy otherwise—nor could he have expected it with such a father and such a mother.

He wished though that his son did not indulge in so much street-fighting. Charles had given him a troop of horse, and when he had inspected fortifications at Harwich recently it was reported that he and his friends had had a right merry time debauching the women of the countryside.

It would be churlish of me to deny him the pleasure in which I myself have taken such delight, the King told himself. Yet he would have preferred young Jemmy to have had a more serious side to his character. It was true that the King's friends indulged in like pleasures; but these were men of wit; they were rogues and libertines, but they were interested in the things of the mind as well as those of the body—even as Charles was himself. So far it seemed to him that his son Jemmy had taken on himself all the vices of the Restoration and none of its virtues.

Jemmy was growing more arrogant, more speculative every day. He was providing the biggest shadow over the crown. Brother James also caused anxieties. He was very different from young Jemmy. James had his mistresses—many of them—and he visited them and got them with child whenever he could escape from Anne Hyde. James was not a bad sort; James was merely a fool. James had a perfect genius for doing that which would bring trouble—mainly on himself. "Ah," Charles would murmur often, "protect me from *la sottise de mon frère.* But most of all, protect my brother from it."

Now James was having trouble with Buckingham. There was another who was doomed to make trouble for others and chiefly for himself. Two troublemakers; if they could but put their heads together and make one brewing of trouble 'twould be easier, mused Charles. But they must busy themselves with their separate brews and give me double trouble.

Buckingham—by far the cleverer of the two—had decided that James should be his friend. He made advances to the Duke, suggesting that they sink their differences and work together. Buckingham wished to rid himself of his greatest rival in the Cabal, my lord Arlington, and had solicited James' help to this end.

James, with sturdy self-righteousness, had set himself apart from their schemes. He intimated that he considered it beneath him to enter into such Cabals; he was resolved to serve the King in his own way.

More tact should have been used when dealing with the wild and reckless Buckingham.

Buckingham now saw James as an enemy; and how could such an ambitious man tolerate an enemy who was also heir presumptive to the crown?

Buckingham raged, and mad schemes filled his imaginative brain. The

King must get legitimate children; the Duke of York must never be allowed to mount the throne.

So now it was that Buckingham brought out his wild plans for a divorce between the King—that mighty stallion, who had proved many times that he was capable of getting children with a variety of women—and sterile Catherine, whose inability to perform her duties as Queen could plunge the country into a desperate situation.

Charles had declined Buckingham's efforts on his behalf, which had ranged from the divorcing of Catherine to the kidnapping of her and carrying her off to some plantation where she would never be heard of again.

Moreover Charles had sought out James.

"My lord Buckingham's wild mind teems with wild plans," he said. "And the very essence of these plans is that you shall never follow me. Do not laugh at them, James. Buckingham is a dangerous fellow."

Buckingham was looking to Monmouth. What wild seeds could he sow in that wild mind?

So the shadows deepened about the throne, and the King had little time to think of the child which Nell would soon be bringing into the world.

❁ ❁ ❁

There was not a breath of air in the room. Hangings had been drawn across the windows to shut out the light; candles burned in the chamber. Nell lay on her bed and thought her last hour had come. So many women died in childbirth.

Rose was with her, and she was glad of Rose's company.

"Nelly," whispered Rose, "should you not be walking up and down the chamber? 'Twill make an easier birth, they say."

"No more, Rosy. No more," moaned Nell. "I have walked enough, and these pains seem fit to kill me."

Her mother sat by the bed; Nell saw through half-closed eyes that she had brought her gin bottle with her.

She was crying already. Nell heard her talking of her beautiful daughter who had captivated the King. Her mother's voice, high-pitched and shrill, seemed to fill the bedchamber.

"That little bastard my girl Nell is bearing the King's son. Who'd have thought it . . . of my little Nell!"

It is a long way, thought Nell, from a bawdy-house in Cole-yard to childbed of the King's bastard.

And where was the King this day? He was not in London. He was riding to Dover to greet visitors from overseas. "Matters of state," he would murmur. "Matters of state. That is why I cannot be at hand at the birth of our child, sweet Nell."

He would say such things to have her believe that the child she was bearing was as important to him as those borne by his lady mistresses. Actress or Duchess . . . it was the same to him. That's what he would imply. If he had been beside her and said it, she would have believed him.

"I always said," Mrs. Gwyn was croaking to Mary Knepp and Peg Hughes, who had come into the chamber to swell the crowds and see Mrs. Nelly brought to bed of the King's bastard, "I always said that my Nell was too little a one to bear children."

Then Nell suddenly sat up in bed and cried aloud: "Have done with your caterwauling, Ma. I'm not a corpse yet. Nor do I intend to be. I'll live, and so will the King's bastard."

That was so typical of Nell that everyone fell to laughing; and Nell herself kept them in fits of laughter until the pain grew worse and she called to Rose and the midwife.

Not long after that Nell lay back exhausted, with the King's son in her arms.

There was a fluffy dark down on his head.

The women bending over him cried: "He's a Stuart! Yes, you can see the royal stallion in Nelly's brat."

And Nell, holding him close, believed she was discovering a new adventure in happiness. She had never felt so tired nor so contented with her lot.

This tiny creature in her arms should never sprawl on the cobbles of Cole-yard; he should never hold horses for fine gentlemen; indeed he should be a fine gentleman himself—a duke no less!

And why not? Were not Barbara's brats dukes? Why should not Nell's most beautiful babe become one also?

"What'll you call him, Nelly?" asked Rose.

"I shall call him Charles," said Nell, and she spoke very firmly. "Charles, of course, after his father."

And as she lay there, for the first time in her life Nell knew the real meaning of ambition. It was born in her, strong and fierce; and all her hopes and desires for greatness were for this child who lay in her arms.

❁ ❁ ❁

Charles, travelling to Dover, did not give Nell and their child a thought. He knew that he was approaching one of the most important moments of his reign.

This meeting at Dover would not only bring him a sight of his beloved sister, but it would mean establishing that alliance which was to be forged between himself and France, himself and France rather than England and France, for the treaty which he would sign would be a secret treaty, the contents of which would be known only to himself and four of his most able statesmen—Arlington, Arundel, Clifford, and Bellings.

Secrecy was necessary. If his people knew what he planned to sign, they would rise against him. They hated the French; and how was it possible to explain to them that their country tottered on the edge of bankruptcy? How was it possible to explain that the effects of plague, fire, and a Dutch war lingered on? England needed France's money and, if France demanded concessions, these concessions must be made. Whether they would be kept or not was a matter with which Charles must concern himself when the time came for keeping them. Meantime it was a matter of signing the secret treaty or facing bankruptcy, poverty, famine, and that sorry state which invariably followed on the heels of these disasters and was the greatest of them all—revolution.

Charles had seen one revolution in England; he had no intention of seeing another. Ten years ago he had come home; and he was determined—if it were in his power to prevent it—never to go wandering again.

So he rode to Dover.

There were so many compensations in life. Here he was to meet his sweet Minette, that favorite of all his brothers and sisters, the youngest of them all, whom he had always loved so dearly and who, in the letters she wrote so frequently to him, seemed like a constant companion. She was married—poor sweet Minette—to the most loathsome Monsieur of France, who treated her shamefully; and she was in love—she betrayed this in her letters, and he had his spies in the French Court who had confirmed this—with Louis XIV, the brilliant and handsome monarch of France. It was Minette's tragedy that the restoration of her brother had come too late for her to marry the King of France, and that she had been forced to take Monsieur his brother.

But it would be wonderful to see his sister, to talk with her, to listen to her news and tell his, and to assure each other how much those frequent letters meant in their lives; to tell each other that brother and sister never loved as they did.

It was small wonder that Charles forgot that one of his minor mistresses was being delivered of a son. He fêted his sister and he signed the treaty which, if it had become universal knowledge, would have put his crown in as much danger as that which had surrounded his father more than twenty years before.

But he would not let the facts depress him. His dearest sister was his guest for two short weeks—that odious husband of hers would allow her to stay no longer—and Louis was to pay him two million livres within six months that he might, when the opportune moment arose, declare himself an adherent of the Catholic Faith. Charles shrugged his shoulders. There was no stipulation as to when Charles should make that declaration; had there been, he could never, however tempting the reward, have signed that treaty. He could declare himself a Catholic, at his own pleasure. That would be years ahead—mayhap never. And very badly England needed those French livres.

He was to declare war on Holland when Louis asked him to, and for his services in this respect he would receive three million livres a year as long as the war continued.

That gave him few qualms. The Dutch were England's enemies and, with the aid of pamphleteers, it was not difficult to rouse the country's hatred against an enemy who had recently sailed up one of England's rivers and burned the nation's ships under their very noses.

Nay, thought Charles, they'll go to war readily enough. 'Tis my turning papist they'd not stomach.

But he remembered the words of his maternal grandfather, the great Henri Quatre—when he had entered Paris and ended the wars of religion.

We are of a kind, thought Charles. A good bargain this. My country almost bankrupt, and myself to be paid two million livres to declare myself a Catholic at the right moment. Who knows, the right moment may never come, but my two million livres will, and prove most useful.

So he signed the treaty and delighted his dear sister, for Louis, whom she loved, would be pleased with her when she came back to France to make a present to him of her brother's signature on that treaty.

Sweet Minette. Back to France she must go. Back to her odious husband.

She held out her jewel case to him and said, "Choose what you will, dearest brother. Anything you may wish for I would have you take in memory of me."

Then he lifted his eyes and saw the charming girl who stood beside his sister, and who had brought the jewel case when Henriette had bidden her do so.

"There is only one jewel I covet," he said. "This fair one who outshines all in your box, sweet sister."

The girl dropped her eyes and blushed warmly.

Minette said to her: "Louise, my dear, I pray you leave me with my brother."

The child curtsied and was gone, but not before she had thrown a quick look over her shoulder at the King of England.

"Nay, Charles," scolded Minette, "she is too young."

"It is a fault easily remedied," said Charles. "Time passes, and those who are young are . . . not so young."

"I could not leave her behind."

Charles was somewhat regretful. He had rarely pursued women; it had never been necessary. Louise was a charming child, but he doubted not that here in Dover there were other charming children, his own subjects. The only time he had ever pursued a woman was during his infatuation for Frances Stuart.

"I shall regret her going," said Charles. "Had she stayed she could have provided some small consolation for your loss."

"Mayhap, dear brother, one day soon I shall come again to England, and I pray that next time I come it will not be necessary for me to depart so soon."

"My poor Minette, is life so difficult?"

She turned to him, smiling. "Life is full of happiness for me now," she said.

Then she embraced him and wept a little.

"When I return to France," she said, "write to me regularly, Charles."

"Indeed I will. It is the only solace that is left to us."

"Tell me all that happens at your Court, and I will tell you all that happens at Versailles. Louis is jealous of my love for you."

"And I of yours for him."

"It is different, Charles."

"I am but the brother and he . . ."

She smiled sadly. "Often there have been only your letters reminding me that I am entirely yours to make me feel my life is worthwhile."

He smiled at her tenderly; he understood so well. She loved him—but second to the King of France—and she had had to choose between them when she came on this mission as the agent of the King of France. Yet he loved her no less because of that.

❁ ❁ ❁

He saw his sister's young maid of honor before they left for France.

He came upon her suddenly in an antechamber as he was about to go to his sister's apartments. He wondered whether she had arranged that it should be so.

She curtsied prettily, and then as though wondering whether she complied with the English custom, fell on her knees.

"Nay," he said, "such obeisance is not necessary. Let not beauty kneel to any—not even royalty."

She rose and stood blushing before him.

"You are a charming child," he said. "I asked my sister to leave you behind that we might become good friends, but she will not do so."

"Sire," said the girl. "My English is not of the best, you see."

"You should be taught it, my child; and the best way to learn a country's language is to take up residence in that land. When I was your age and after, I spent many years in your country, and thus I spoke your country's language." He began to speak in French, and the young girl listened eagerly.

"Would you like to come and stay awhile in England?"

"But yes, Your Majesty."

"Stay at Court, shall we say, where I might show you how we live in England?"

She laughed childishly. "It would give me the greatest pleasure."

"Alas, my sister says she owes an obligation to your parents and must take you back with her." He placed his hands on her shoulders and drew her towards him. "And that," he said, "makes me desolate."

"I thank Your Majesty."

"Thank me not. Thank the Fates which gave you this beautiful curling hair." He fondled it tenderly. "This soft skin . . ." He touched her cheeks and throat.

She waited breathlessly. Then he bent gracefully and kissed her on the lips. There was a movement in the room beyond them.

He said: "Mayhap we shall meet again."

"I do not know, Your Majesty."

"Tell me your name before we part."

"It is Louise."

"Louise. It is a charming name. What other names have you?"

"I am Louise Renée de Penancoët de Kéroualle."

"Then adieu, sweet Mademoiselle de Kéroualle; I shall pray that ere long we meet again."

FOUR

When Louise de Kéroualle came to England with Charles' sister, Henriette, Duchess d'Orléans, she was already twenty years old. She looked much younger; this was due not only to her round babyish face but to her manners. These looks and manners were no indication of the real Louise, who was shrewd and practical in the extreme.

As the daughter of Guillaume de Penancoët, the Sieur de Kéroualle, a gentleman of noble lineage, she could not hope for a brilliant marriage, since her family had fallen into poverty and could not provide her with an adequate dowry. Louise, ever conscious of her lineage, was never tired of reminding those who seemed likely to forget it that, through her mother, she was connected with the family of de Rieux. Her position was an unfortunate one—so proud and yet so poor. Louise was older than her sister Henriette by some years, so her problem was the more immediate. She had one brother, Sebastian, who was serving abroad with the King's armies.

Men could distinguish themselves in the service of their Kings, mused Louise; there was only one way open to women: marriage. Or so she had thought.

She had remained at the convent, where she had received her education, so long that she had thought she would never leave it. She had had visions of herself growing old, past a marriageable age, perhaps taking the veil. For what was there left for noble women, who could not marry with their equals, but the veil?

And then, suddenly had come the summons to return to her parents' Breton home.

She would never forget the day she arrived at the great mansion, where all the family lived since none of them could afford to go to Court. She had wondered whether Sebastian had distinguished himself, whether the King had honored him, and their fortunes were changed, whether some miracle had happened and a man of wealth and family had asked for the elder daughter's hand in marriage.

It was none of these things, but it concerned herself.

Her parents received her ceremoniously. Never did her father forget that he was Sieur de Kéroualle, and ceremony in his house was as closely observed as it was at Versailles.

She curtsied before them both and received their embrace. Her father had waved his hand to dismiss the servants, and then he had turned his face to her and, smiling, said: "My daughter, a place has been found for you at Court."

"At Court!" she had cried, in her excitement forgetting that she should not show her surprise but accept all that was suggested, with the utmost decorum.

"My dear child," said her mother, "the Duchess d'Orléans is to take you into her suite."

"And . . ." Louise looked from one to the other, "this can be done?"

"Indeed it can be done," said her father. "Wherefore did you think we had sent for you if it could not be so?"

"I . . . I merely thought it might prove too costly."

"But it is a great opportunity, and one which we could not miss. I shall sell some land and make it possible for you to go to Court."

"And we hope that you will be worthy of the sacrifice," murmured her mother.

"I will," said Louise. "Indeed I will."

"In the service of Madame you will meet the very highest in the land. His Majesty himself is often in Madame's house. They are great friends. I hope you will find favor in the King's sight, daughter. Much good could come to our family if he found one of its members worthy of his regard."

"I see, Father."

They dismissed her then, for they said she was tired from her journey. She went to her room, and her mother followed her there. She made her lie down, and had food brought for her.

While she ate, her mother looked at her earnestly. She stroked the fine curling chestnut hair.

"Such pretty hair," she said. "And you are pretty, my dear Louise. Very pretty. Different from the Court ladies, I know; but sometimes it is a good thing to be different."

When her mother left her, Louise had lain staring at the canopy of her bed.

She was to go to Court; she was to do her utmost to please the King. There was something her parents were trying to tell her. What was it?

❁ ❁ ❁

She quickly discovered.

They talked constantly of the King. The most handsome man in all France, they said; and what a pleasure it was to have a young King on the throne, a King who looked as a King should look. They recalled his magnificence at his coronation; what a fine sight it had been to see him in the ceremonial cloak of purple velvet embroidered with the golden lilies of France, and the great crown of Charlemagne on his noble head. All who had watched in the great Cathedral of Notre-Dame de Rheims had said that this was more than a King; it was a god come among them. He was pink and white and gold, this King of theirs; and he had a nature to match his face—benign and beautiful. It was a pleasure for all to serve him—man and woman alike.

They recalled his love for Marie Mancini, how idealistically he had wanted to marry her; and he would have done so too, had not his mother and Cardinal Mazarin set themselves against the marriage. Of course it would have been quite impossible for the King of France to marry a woman who was not of royal birth, but did it not show what a kindly, what a charming nature he had, to think of the marriage?

What did the King look like? Anyone who wanted to know that only had to read the romances of the day. It was said that, when she described her heroes, Mademoiselle de Scudéry used Louis XIV as her model.

"He is married now, our King," said Louise regretfully; for she had begun to picture herself in the place of Marie Mancini, and she believed that had she been that young woman she would have married the King in spite of his mother, the unpopular Anne of Austria, and Cardinal Mazarin who was equally unpopular. She and Louis would have conspired together to bring about that marriage.

Marriage with a King! It was foolish to dream such dreams.

"He is married now, yes," said her mother. "He is married to the dumpy little Spanish Princess, Marie Thérèse. She looked well enough in her wedding garments. But divested of them! Oh, I shudder for our beloved King, he who is such a connoisseur of beauty. There will be others." Her mother lifted her shoulders and smiled tenderly. "How could it be otherwise? I have heard that, when he was very young, he loved Madame de Beauvais." She laughed aloud. "Madame de Beauvais! Years older than he was—a fat woman—and I have heard that she has but one eye. Yet . . . he has never forgotten her. He has shown her great favor. *There* is an indication of the kind of King we have. A King who never forgets to reward those who have pleased him . . . even if it was only for a short time and long ago."

Now Louise began to understand. She could not make a brilliant marriage because she had no suitable *dot*; but if she could become the good friend of the King, all sorts of honors might fall to her; and there were many men who then might wish to share her fortunes. How much more desirable was a royal mistress—even a discarded one—than a penniless virgin!

❁ ❁ ❁

So to Court came Louise. She was pretty enough, but this prettiness was due to her youthful appearance. Her hair was lovely, so was her complexion, unpitted by the pox and unmarked by any blemish. Her round plump face gave her an innocent expression rare at this time, and this was appealing. Her eyes were rather closely set, and there was a suggestion at times of a cast in one of them. However, she was accounted a pretty young girl; and, because her appearance was not one of conventional beauty, this brought her some attention.

She had been thoroughly schooled in social etiquette, both in her home and in the convent, and as a result of her training was possessed of a natural grace. Her education had not been neglected and she was considered to be a cultured young woman, though lacking in the imagination which would have made her an outstandingly clever one. Louise then, when she came to the Court, was a well-bred, well-educated girl with some pretensions to good looks, certain graceful charm, and shrewd ideas, beneath that calm and babyish brow, of making a comfortable existence for Mademoiselle de Kéroualle.

Louise was a born spy. Her poverty and pressing need had nourished this quality in her. She told herself that it was a matter of great urgency that she must understand all that was going on about her; she had no time to spare. She was already twenty, no longer very young; a place at Court might not remain open to her. Therefore she quickly grasped the state of affairs at St. Cloud.

Henriette d'Orléans, the wife of the King's brother, and sister to the King of England, was a charming woman—quick-witted, clever, and though no conventional beauty, one of the most attractive women in the Court of le Roi Soleil. Here, thought Louise, was a good model for herself. She studied Henriette and, watching her closely, being her intimate companion, she began to probe her secrets.

Not that Monsieur—Henriette's husband—made any secret of the life they led together. Monsieur had his *mignons,* his dear friends who meant more to him than any woman could. Monsieur was the most conceited man in France and Louise discovered that his wife pleased him very much in one respect. There were occasions when he felt proud of her.

Louise understood the meaning of this one day when Louis himself paid a visit to St. Cloud.

This was the first time Louise had seen him. She was prepared. She was looking younger than ever; she kept close to her mistress. Here was her first chance to shine before His Majesty. She wore the most youthful of her gowns and her magnificent hair was elaborately dressed but falling in curls over her shoulders, as a young girl would wear it. She was sure she did not look more than fifteen.

The King came into the apartment, tall and as handsome as he had been made out to be, dressed in cloth of gold trimmed with black lace, diamonds flashing in his hat; he strode to Henriette.

She would have knelt, but he would not allow her to do so. He was agitated, Louise guessed.

He said: "No ceremony, dear sister."

"Your Majesty has urgent business with me," said Henriette. "I had hoped to present my new maid of honor, Mademoiselle de Kéroualle."

Louis' eyes flickered lightly over Louise.

She came forward and fell to her knees.

He said: "Welcome to the Court, my dear. Welcome."

She lifted her eyes to his face; this was the moment for which she had longed and hoped. But he was looking at the Duchesse.

"You wish to speak to me alone?" asked Henriette.

"I do wish that," said the King.

It was the signal for attendants to retire.

One of her companions put her arms about Louise's shoulders. "Don't be hurt, my child," she said. "It is always thus. When he comes, he has no eyes for anyone but Madame. Moreover if you would have pleased him you should not have seemed such a very little girl. His Majesty once liked matrons—now he likes no one but Madame."

After that she began to understand a good deal.

Here was intrigue which interested Louise, not only because it was of vital importance to her, but because intrigue in any form fascinated her.

When her mistress danced in such a sprightly way, when she joked so readily, when she appeared to be gay, she was really full of sadness; and it was due to the fact that she had married the wrong man—Monsieur—when she loved the King himself.

Louise did not give up hope of attracting the King.

There was a great deal of gossip concerning Louis and his sister-in-law. Louise discovered that both the King's mother, Anne of Austria, and Henriette's mother, Queen Henrietta Maria, had pointed this out to the lovers.

It was at this time that the King began to show a little interest in that foolish and perfectly unworthy creature, Louise de la Vallière.

How could he look at the silly creature, Louise de Kéroualle wondered; then she began to understand. It was Madame who had decided that he should pay attention to La Vallière, Madame who had selected the girl. Louise de la Vallière was just the sort whom a woman who was in love would choose, if choose she must. Madame could feel confident that the King would never fall in love with the silly creature.

If only she had chosen me! thought Louise. How different it would have been then!

She thought of her family in their Breton home. They would hear the rumors from the Court. Such rumors always travelled fast. They would shake their heads and perhaps have to sell more of their possessions. Would they say: "Is it worth the expense of keeping Louise at Court?"

❁ ❁ ❁

One day Madame called Louise to her and said: "Louise, would you like to accompany me to England?"

"To England, Madame?" answered Louise. "Indeed I would!"

"It will be but a short visit." Henriette had turned away. There was, had she known it, no need for her to curb her tongue; she could have said all that was in her mind, because Louise knew it already.

Louise knew that she longed to get away from her husband, that she longed to see her brother who wrote to her so often and so lovingly. Louise was fully aware of the great affection between her mistress and the King of England. She had heard Monsieur, in one of his wild quarrels with Madame, declare that the love between his wife and her brother was more than that which it was meet and proper for two of such a relationship to share. She knew that, white-faced and horrified, Henriette had cried out to him that he was a liar, and that at that moment her self-control had broken.

Louise knew these things. She had a good pair of ears, and saw no reason why they should not be pressed into service. Those shrewd little eyes too were sharp. Louise trained them to miss nothing.

So if Henriette had decided to break free from that iron control which she kept on her feelings, and blurt out the truth to little Louise de Kéroualle, it would not have mattered. She would have told Louise very little that she did not already know.

"We shall stay no longer than two weeks," said Henriette. "My brothers will meet me at Dover. I doubt I shall have time to visit the Capital."

"Monsieur will not part with you for longer than that, Madame," said Louise.

Henriette looked at her quickly, but there was no trace of malice in the babyish face. She is a child, thought Henriette, who was unaware that she was twenty years old—not so very much younger than herself, Louise, looking so unconcernedly youthful, conveyed such an appearance of innocence. I must try to make a match for her before she loses that innocence which is so charming, thought the kindly Madame. May it be a happier one than my own, and may she preserve that faith in life for as long as it shall exist.

"My brother is most eager for the visit," said Henriette, and her face softened. "It is years since I have seen him."

"I have heard, Madame, that a great affection exists between you and the King of England."

" 'Tis true, Louise. My childhood was lived in such uncertain times. I saw so little of him. I was with my mother, a beggar almost at the Court of France, and my brother, the King of England, but a wandering exile. We saw little of each other, but how we treasured those meetings! And we have kept our love for one another alive in our letters. Hardly a week passes without our hearing one from the other. I think one of the most unhappy periods of my life was when France and England were not good friends."

"All France, and I doubt not all England, knows of your love for your brother, Madame. And all is well between England and France at this present time."

Henriette nodded. "And I hope to make that bond of friendship stronger, Louise."

Louise knew. She had been present on those occasions when King Louis had visited Henriette. Sometimes they forgot she was present. If they saw her they would think: Oh, it is but the little Louise de Kéroualle—a sweet child but a baby, a little simpleton. She will not understand what we talk of.

So it was that often they disclosed certain secret matters in her presence; often they betrayed themselves.

They loved, those two. Louis would have married Henriette had he not married dull Marie Thérèse before Charles Stuart regained his kingdom. Louise had heard it said that, before that time, Madame had been a shy girl who had not shown to advantage against the plump pink and white beauties so admired by the King of France. But when her brother regained his throne, Henriette's gaucheries had dropped from her and she emerged like a butterfly from a chrysalis, it was said—brilliant, exquisite, the most graceful, charming, amusing, and clever woman at the Court. Then Louis had realized too late what he had missed; now he contented himself with the shyness of La Vallière and the flamboyant beauty of Montespan, in an effort to make up for all he had lost in Madame.

This interested Louise and she rejoiced therefore when she was chosen to accompany her mistress into England.

❁ ❁ ❁

So she travelled with Madame to Dover, and all the pomp of a royal visit accompanied them.

She realized that Henriette was uneasy; and she guessed that it was due to the treaty which she was to induce her brother to sign.

Louis had prevailed upon Henriette to do this, and Louise surmised that the treaty, which would be signed at Dover, was one to which the King of France was very eager to have the King of England's signature. Henriette was uncertain. Louise knew by her abstracted air that she was torn between her love for her brother and the King of France; and Louise knew that the King of France had won. For all her professed love for Charles of England, Henriette was working for the King of France whom she regarded in the light of a lover.

There was one thing to learn from this: emotions should never become involved when it was a question of one's position in society. For all her cleverness, for all her wit, Henriette of Orléans was nothing but a weak woman, torn by her love for two men.

And so they came to Dover and were greeted, not only by the tall dark King of England, but by his brother, the Duke of York, and his natural son, the Duke of Monmouth.

There were banquets and dancing. The treaty was signed and dispatched to France. The days sped by. Henriette seemed to be indulging in frantic gaiety.

She loved her brother undoubtedly; yet, wondered Louise, how far had she sacrificed him to Louis?

She longed to know. The thought of such plots and counterplots was highly fascinating.

There came the time when they were due to leave the shores of England. Louise would never forget that occasion. It was a moment full of significance in her life, for it was then that new avenues of adventure were opened to her.

The King of England was looking at her with the approval which she had sought in vain to arouse in the King of France. He was referring to her as a brighter jewel than any in the casket which his sister was offering him. Those dark eyes, passionate and slumberous, were fixed upon her. Louise realized then that the King desired her.

This in itself was no unusual thing. The King of England desired many women, and it was rarely that his desires went unfulfilled. Yet Louise, the daughter of a poor Breton gentleman, had already deeply considered what the admiration of a King could mean.

She was blushing now, because the King was asking that she might stay behind in England, and her mistress was telling him that she had her duty to the child's parents.

Child! They seemed unaware that she was twenty years old.

Louise, considering her age, was filled with sudden panic. What if she failed to fulfill her parents' hopes? Would she have to return to the convent; perhaps make a marriage which would not lift her from the poverty from which she had determined to escape?

The admiration of kings could do a great deal for a woman. Her thoughts went to Louise de la Vallière—but all were aware that La Vallière was a simpleton who knew not how to exploit her lover. If ever the time came for Louise de Kéroualle to exploit such a lover, she would know full well how to do this to the best advantage to herself.

There was little time left, but she determined to do all in her power to see that the King of England did not forget her. She kept near her mistress because she knew that where Henriette was, there would Charles be.

And then there was that last encounter when she had stood before him.

Louis might like matrons, but Charles was clearly attracted by more youthful charms.

There was no doubt that he was attracted by her. He took her hands, and he spoke to her in her native French. He kissed her with a mingled passion and tenderness, and he told her he would not forget her and that he hoped one day she would come again to England, and that he would teach her the customs of the English.

She railed against the ill fortune which had brought her face-to-face with Charles such a short time before she was due to leave.

She longed to tell him that her parents would have no objection to her staying at the Court of England; that they had hoped she would become the mistress of the King of France, so they would not wish to refuse her to the King of England.

But how could she say these things? She could only stand on the ship, waving farewell and standing close to her mistress, so that the last Charles saw of the departing company was his dear sister and her maid of honor who had so charmed him.

❁ ❁ ❁

Louis welcomed them back with great rejoicing. He was delighted with his dear Duchesse. At all the balls and masques he was at her side.

On one of these occasions, Henriette turned to the girl beside her and said to Louis: "Louise greatly impressed my brother."

"Was that so?" said Louis.

"Indeed yes. He begged me to leave her with him in England."

Louis looked with amusement at Louise, who had cast down her eyes.

"And did you wish to stay, Mademoiselle de Kéroualle?" he asked.

"If Madame had stayed, I should have wished to, Sire," said Louise. "My wish is to serve Madame."

"That is as it should be," said Louis. "Serve her well. She deserves good service."

His gaze was kind and doting. His mother was dead now; so was Madame's mother, and he and Madame could not be reproved because they were so much together. None would dare reprove Louis now.

Louis laughed suddenly. "The King of England is governed by women, they say. I could tell you tales of the King of England, Mademoiselle de

Kéroualle, but I would not do so before Madame who loves him dearly, nor would I wish to bring the blushes to your cheeks."

"Your Majesty is gracious," murmured Louise.

❁ ❁ ❁

Louise was in her own apartments. She was stunned by the news. There had been a most unexpected turn of events, which she knew must affect the course of her life. Madame was dead.

It had happened so suddenly, though Madame had been frail for a long time. She had been dining with her women and, during the meal, they had thought how ill she looked; when it was over she had risen from the table and lain on some cushions; she felt exhausted, she had said. Then she had asked for a drink and, when Madame de Gourdon had brought her a glass of iced chicory water, she was in sudden and acute pain.

She had cried out that she was poisoned, and her eyes had turned accusingly to Monsieur who had come into the apartment. Everyone present had thought: Monsieur has poisoned Madame.

Louise, in extreme panic, had hurried out of the apartment to bring help. It was imperative that Madame be treated at once, for she looked close to death, and if she died what would become of Louise?

The doctors had come. The King had come. Louise witnessed the strange sight of the magnificent Louis kneeling by Madame, his handsome face distorted with grief; she had heard the sobs in his throat, and his muttered endearments.

But Louis could not save her; nor could the doctors. A few short weeks after her return from her brother's Court Henriette d'Orléans was dead.

And now, thought Louise, what will become of me?

She waited for the summons to return to her father's estate. She had failed. There was no place for her at Court; she realized that now.

Each day she expected the summons to come.

❁ ❁ ❁

There was a summons; but not from her home.

Madame de Gourdon came to her one day. Poor Madame de Gourdon! She was a most unhappy woman. She was not allowed to forget that it was she who had brought the glass of iced chicory water to Madame. Rumor ran wild throughout the Court. Madame was poisoned, it was whispered. Monsieur had done this; and his partner in crime was the Chevalier de Lorraine, his latest friend. But who had administered the draught? One of Madame's women. Why, it was Madame de Gourdon. In vain did Madame de Gourdon sob out her devotion to Madame. People looked at her with suspicion.

Now she spoke listlessly: "Mademoiselle de Kéroualle, the King wishes you to attend him immediately."

"His Majesty!" cried Louise, springing to her feet and smoothing down the folds of her dress.

"I will take you to him," said Madame de Gourdon. "He is ready to receive you now."

The King had come to St. Cloud to see her! It was incredible. She could think of only one thing it could mean. He *had* noticed her after all.

If he had come to see her all would soon know it. They would talk of her as they talked of La Vallière and Montespan. And why not? She was as good-looking as La Vallière surely. She touched her chestnut hair. The soft curls reassured her, gave her courage.

"I will go and prepare myself," she said.

"You cannot do that. His Majesty is waiting."

He was striding up and down the small apartment when Madame de Gourdon conducted her thither.

Madame de Gourdon curtsied and left Louise alone with the King.

Louise went hurriedly forward and knelt as though in confusion, but a confusion which was charming. She had practiced this often enough.

"Rise, Mademoiselle de Kéroualle," said the King. "I have something to say to you."

"Yes, Sire?" she said, and she could not keep the breathless note from her voice.

He did not look at her. He was staring at the tapestry which covered the walls of this small chamber, as though to find inspiration there. Louise took a quick glance at his face and saw that he was trying to compose it. What could this emotion of the King mean?

She was prepared to register the utmost surprise when he should tell her he had noticed her. She would be confused, overcome with astonishment and modesty. She would stammer out her gratitude and her fear. She believed that was what Louis would expect. She had the shining example of La Vallière to follow.

The King began to speak slowly: "Mademoiselle de Kéroualle, I have just suffered one of the greatest griefs of my life."

Louise did not speak; she merely bowed her head; the handsome eyes were turned upon her, and there were tears in them.

"And I know," went on Louis, "that you too have suffered. Any who had lived near her must feel her loss deeply."

"Sire . . ." murmured Louise.

The King raised his hand. "You have no need to tell me; I know. Madame's death is a great loss to our Court, and none in that Court suffers as I do. Madame was my own dear sister and my friend." He paused. "There is one other who suffers . . . almost as deeply as I. That is Madame's brother—the King of England."

"Indeed yes, Your Majesty."

"The King of England is prostrate with grief. I have heard from him. He writes harshly. He has heard evil rumors, and he is insisting that if it be true that Madame was hurried to her death those who are her murderers should be discovered and dealt with. But, as I am sure you will have heard, Mademoiselle de Kéroualle, at the autopsy which I insisted should be immediately performed, no poison was found in Madame's body. She had been in bad health for some time, and the very chicory water of which she drank was drunk by others, and these suffered not at all. We know that it was Madame's own ill health which resulted in her death, and no one here was in the least to blame. But the King of England bitterly mourns his sister whom he loved so well, and I fear we shall find it difficult to convince him. Now, Mademoiselle de Kéroualle, you are a very charming young lady."

Louise drew a deep breath. Her heart was beating so fast that she could scarcely follow what the King was saying.

"And," went on Louis, "I wish my brother of England to understand that my grief is as great as his own. I wish someone to convey my sympathy to him."

"Sire," said Louise, "you . . . you would entrust me with this mission?"

Louis' large eyes were benign. He laid a white, heavily ringed hand on her shoulder. "Even so, my dear," he said. "Madame herself has told me of a little incident which occurred while you were in England. King Charles was attracted by you; and, my dear Mademoiselle, it does not surprise me. It does not surprise me at all. You are most . . . most personable. I am going to send you to my brother in England to convey my sympathy and to assure him that Madame his sister has always been treated with the utmost tenderness in this land."

"Oh . . . Sire!" Louise's eyes were shining.

She fell to her knees.

"Rise, my dear Mademoiselle," said Louis. "I see you are sensible of the honor I would do you. I want you to prepare for your journey to England. I will acquaint King Charles of your coming. Mademoiselle de Kéroualle, you are the daughter of one of our noblest houses."

Louise drew herself up to her full height. There was pride in her eyes.

So the King himself recognized the standing of her family. It was only money that it lacked.

"And," continued the King, "it is from our noblest families that we expect and receive the utmost loyalty. I believe, Mademoiselle, that you loved your mistress dearly. But as in all good subjects of our beloved country there is one love which is above all others. That is love of France."

"Yes, Sire."

"I knew it. That is why I am going to entrust you with a great mission. To the King of England you will take comfort; but you will always serve France."

"Your Majesty means that during my stay in England I shall work for my country?"

"My ambassador across the water will be your very good friend. He will help you when you need help. Before you leave for England you will be further instructed. I have lost, in Madame, not only a very dear friend but one who, in view of her relationship to the King of England, was able to bring about great understanding between us two. Mademoiselle, I believe that such a charming and intelligent young lady as you so evidently are—and as one who has already attracted the attention of His Majesty of England—can, in some measure, give me . . . and your country . . . something of that which we have lost in Madame."

The King paused. Louise sought for words and could find none.

"I have taken you by surprise," said the King. "Go now and think about this."

Louise again fell to her knees and said in clear tones: "Your Majesty, I rejoice in this opportunity to serve my King and my country."

When she stood up, Louis placed his hands on her shoulders; then inclining his head with the utmost graciousness he kissed her lightly on both cheeks.

"I have the utmost confidence in you, my dear," he said. "France will be proud of you."

Louise left the apartment in a state of exaltation.

How often had she dreamed of being sent for by the King! At last it had happened.

The result was surprising, but no less promising for all that.

❁ ❁ ❁

George Villiers, Duke of Buckingham, presented himself at the French Court.

He had come to sponsor a treaty between his master and the King of France.

As several members of the Cabal were ignorant of the real Treaty of Dover, it had been necessary for Charles to devise another with which he might dupe them. This he had done, and Buckingham was selected to take it to St. Germain and at the same time to represent the King at the funeral of Madame. With Buckingham went Buckhurst and Sedley, and the Duke's chaplain, Thomas Sprat.

Buckingham had been chosen—as a prominent Protestant—because the King and those who were in the secret feared that the news of the King's promising to adopt the Catholic Faith might have leaked out. Since Buckingham was commissioned to sign the treaty in France, this would silence such rumors, as it would be generally believed that anything to which Buckingham would give his signature could not possibly concern the King's becoming a Catholic.

There was another matter with which he was entrusted. He was to escort to England the late Henriette's maid of honor who had attracted Charles when she had come to England in his sister's train.

This was a task after the Duke's own heart. It had been clear to him that his cousin Barbara was losing her hold over the King. Barbara's beauty, which had once been incomparable, was fading. None could live the life Barbara lived and keep fresh. Any but Charles would have turned her away long ago, tiresome virago that she was. It was true that in the heyday of her youth no one could compare with Barbara for beauty and for sensuality; the King had found her—tantrums and all—irresistible. But Barbara was ageing, and even with an easygoing man such as Charles she could not continue to hold the title of mistress-in-chief. Sooner or later Barbara must be replaced.

The King had his women—many of them. The chief mistress at the moment was Moll Davies, and Nell Gwyn was a close runner-up. But these were play-actresses, and Moll, aping the nobility, showed her origins as clearly as Nell who made no secret of her beginnings.

The mistress-in-chief should be a lady of high degree. She should feel at home at Court; and although Barbara's manners were atrocious, she was a noble Villiers and there could at times be no doubt of this.

But with Barbara fading from favor, someone else would soon be called upon to take her place. This Frenchwoman was surely the one to be selected for that task.

Louise de Kéroualle was a lady of noble birth. She had been educated and coached for a life at Court. She was not exactly beautiful. When Buckingham remembered what Barbara had been at her age he could call the new woman positively plain. But Louise had that which Barbara lacked—

poise, gracious manners, and a quiet charm. At this time he believed that Louise was destined to become the most important of the King's mistresses.

It was great good fortune that he had been sent to bring her to England, for it gave him a great advantage over all those who would later seek to reach the King's ear through his mistress. Buckingham would ingratiate himself with the woman and so establish himself as her friend.

The King of France was delighted to receive Buckingham. He had Madame's own apartments made ready for him at St. Germain. It seemed meet and fitting that Buckingham should be in France at that time for, ten years before when Henriette had visited her brother in England at the time of the Restoration, the Duke had professed to be deeply in love with her. He had, in fact, made something of an exhibition of these feelings which had been an embarrassment not only to Henriette herself but to others; Monsieur had declared himself jealous of the Duke, with the result that it had been necessary to recall Buckingham to London. Who, therefore, was better suited to attend the funeral of Madame as her brother's representative, than the Duke of Buckingham who had once loved her so madly?

Louis—anxious to show in what great esteem he had held Madame, and eager that the King of England should banish from his mind all thought that his sister had met her death by poison—greeted Buckingham warmly. He gave him one of the royal coaches and with it the service of eight royal footmen. All the expenses Buckingham incurred while in France were to be met from the King's exchequer.

Louis—being French—believed firmly in the power of a man's mistresses, and realizing Buckingham's infatuation for Anna, Lady Shrewsbury, offered to pay that lady a pension of four hundred pounds a year, because his ambassador in England had already warned him that the lady had said that she, for such recognition, would make sure that Buckingham complied with Louis' desires in all things. Louis also sent a bribe for Lady Castlemaine as, although the lady was no longer enjoying the favor she once had, it was clear that she would continue to wield certain influence as long as she lived.

Louis was fully aware of the power of these women. They were both deeply sensual; they had both enjoyed numerous lovers; therefore Louis believed that they were skilled in the arts of lovemaking. Each was a strong-minded woman. Barbara Castlemaine had proved this again and again. As for Anna Shrewsbury, she too had shown the world that she could be formidable—a good ally, a bad enemy.

Louis had heard of the duel which had been fought between Lord Shrewsbury and the Duke of Buckingham and which had resulted in Shrewsbury's death; he had heard rumors of how Anna Shrewsbury had been a witness of the duel; how, some said, she had acted as page to her lover so that she might be present; and how later, unable to forgo the immediate satisfaction of their lust, Buckingham and Anna had forthwith slept together, Buckingham still in the shirt spattered with her husband's blood.

There was another rumor concerning this woman. Harry Killigrew had been one of her numerous lovers, and there had been a notorious scene in the Duke of York's playhouse when Buckingham and Killigrew had fought together; as a result of that, Killigrew had been sent into exile, from which he had returned sullen and determined to be revenged on the Duke and his mistress. He had declared in many public places that Anna Shrewsbury would still be his mistress if he wished it, and that indeed she was any man's who cared to take her. She was like a bitch in season—only Anna Shrewsbury's season was every hour of the day or night.

Anna set out in her coach one dark night to see performed a certain deed which she had arranged. It happened near Turnham Green when Harry Killigrew was on his way to his house there. Harry Killigrew was set upon, his servant killed, and, only by a miracle it seemed, Killigrew escaped the same fate.

Yes, the King of France was certain that Anna Shrewsbury was worth a pension of four hundred pounds a year.

He was sure too that Buckingham was worth cultivating, even though the King had seen fit to keep him ignorant of the real Treaty of Dover.

So he arranged great treats for the Duke. Special banquets were prepared for him. He was presented not only with the coach, footmen, and living expenses, but with other costly gifts.

He was able to fit himself into the formal ceremony of Louis' magnificent Court. Handsome and witty, he was in his element. Mock sea fights on the Seine were arranged for his benefit and he was introduced to the splendors of Versailles.

The Comte de Lauzun—a man of diminutive stature and a great friend of the King of France—asked him to a supper party. A splendid banquet was prepared, and next to his host, in the place of honor, sat the Duke. Beside him was Louise de Kéroualle, formal and distant; but, the Duke assured himself, he would soon win her regard. She was a cold creature, he decided; not what he would have expected from the French, nor the sort he would have thought would find favor in his master's eyes. However, it was his task to ingratiate himself with her, and this he would do—all in good time. At the moment he was too busy being the guest of honor.

During that banquet three masked figures entered the banqueting hall. One was a man, tall and richly clad; the others were ladies. They came graciously to the table and bowed to Lauzun and Buckingham. The musicians, who had been playing in the gallery, changed their tune to a stately ballet, and the three began to dance with such grace and charm that all at the table held their breath—or pretended to—since all had guessed the identity of the masked cavalier.

There were murmurs of "Perfection!" "But who could dance with such exquisite grace?" "I know of only one I have seen to equal that dancer—His Majesty himself." "We must have the fellow perform before Louis. Nothing will content him but to see such perfection."

Now the ladies were miming charmingly. They had pointed to a sword which the masked man wore. All saw that its hilt was studded with brilliant diamonds. One of the masked ladies danced to Buckingham's side and implied, by her gestures, that the cavalier should bestow the sword upon their country's most honored guest. The cavalier retreated, clung to his sword, his gestures indicating that the sword was his dearest possession. The ladies continued to persuade; the cavalier continued to hold back.

The music stopped.

"Unmask! Unmask!" cried Lauzun.

With seeming reluctance the ladies did so first, and there was loud applause when one of these proved to be Madame de Montespan herself, the King's flamboyant and beautiful mistress.

Now Madame de Montespan turned to the cavalier. She removed his mask, and there were exposed the handsome features so well known throughout the country.

All rose; men bowed and women curtsied; and the handsome young Louis stood there smiling happily and benignly on them all.

"Our secret is out," said Louis. "We are unmasked."

"I could not believe that any but Your Majesty could dance with such grace," said Lauzun.

Now Madame de Montespan had taken the sword from the King and carried it to the guest of honor.

Buckingham stared down at the flashing diamonds, calculating its cost; then rising, fell on his knees before the King of France and thanked him, almost in tears, for his magnificent gift and all the honor which had been done to his master through him.

The King and his mistress took their places at the table; and the King talked to Buckingham of his love for the King of England, of his grief in Madame's death; nor did he forget to pay some attention to little Louise. Louise understood. He would have my lord Buckingham know that Mademoiselle de Kéroualle was to be treated with the same respect in England as in France.

How different had been her position when Madame was alive! Then she had been Madame's maid of honor—an insignificant post. Now she was the spy of the King of France, and that was indeed important.

"We have prepared many entertainments for you, my lord Duke," said the King. "There shall be masques and the ballet—we in France are devoted to the ballet."

"Your Majesty is the ballet's shining light," said Louise.

The King smiled, well pleased. "And we must show you our operas and comedies. They shall be acted in illuminated grottoes."

"I am overwhelmed by all the honor Your Majesty does unto me," said the Duke.

The King momentarily laid his hand over that of Louise. "And when you take this little subject of mine into England, you will give her the benefit of your care?"

"With all my heart," said Buckingham.

❁ ❁ ❁

Later he made plans with Louise.

"I would have you know, Mademoiselle de Kéroualle," he said, "that from henceforth I serve you with all my heart."

Louise accepted this outward profession of service with graceful thanks but she attached little importance to it. Since she was to act as French spy in England it had been necessary to acquaint her with certain political aspects of the state of affairs between the two countries. She knew that, although the Duke held a high position in his country's government and was a member of the famous Cabal, he was ignorant of his master's true plans.

He was quite unaware that the King of France was planning war with Holland in the spring of next year, and in this war the King of England would be his ally; and that as soon as it was satisfactorily concluded Charles was to declare his conversion to Catholicism.

Therefore she had little faith in Buckingham. Herself calm and rarely losing control of her emotions, she thought the Duke a tempestuous man who, clever though he might be, could be driven into great folly by his uncontrolled passions.

He was, he told her, although he had been so flatteringly received in France, looking forward to returning to his own country.

He talked of Anna Shrewsbury in glowing terms; he was indeed deeply infatuated with the woman. Louise listened and said little. He began to think her a little simpleton, one who would never hold his King's affection. He compared her with Anna, with Barbara, with Moll Davies and Nell Gwyn. Those four were possessed of beauty—outstanding beauty which would have marked them for notice anywhere. It seemed to Buckingham that Louise de Kéroualle lacked even that first essential. Why, there were indeed times when the woman positively squinted. And she was always so formal; he thought of Anna and Barbara in their rages, of Nell's wit and high spirits. It was true Moll Davies never raged, was never witty and rarely showed any spirits, but she was an extremely lovely woman. Nay, the more he pondered the matter, the more certain he became that Louise de Kéroualle would not hold the King's attention for long.

He was wondering whether he was not wasting his time in ingratiating himself with her. He was longing to be back with Anna.

He said to her: "There are certain matters to which I have to attend in Paris. My master, the King of England, is growing impatient to receive you. I think much time would be saved if you travelled to Dieppe in company which I will arrange for you and set out at once. I will conduct with all speed my business in Paris, arrange for a yacht to carry you to England, and I'll swear I'll be at Dieppe before you arrive there. Then I can have the great honor of conducting you to England."

"I consider that an excellent arrangement," said Louise, who was longing to set out on her journey and fearful, with every passing day, that the King of England might change his mind and, realizing that a young woman who came from Louis' Court might have been schooled in the arts of espionage, decide that he would be wise to content himself with the ladies of his own Court.

"Then let it be so," cried Buckingham. "I will inform His Majesty of my plans."

So it was arranged. Louise travelled to Dieppe; Buckingham lingered in Paris. He wanted to buy clothes, not only for himself, but for Anna.

Paris was always a step ahead of London with the fashions, and Anna would be delighted with what he would bring her.

❁ ❁ ❁

When Louise arrived in Dieppe—and the journey there from St. Germain had taken two whole weeks—it was to find that Buckingham had not yet arrived.

No one there had heard anything of the yacht which Buckingham had promised to have ready for her. Louise was weary after the journey from St. Germain and at first was not sorry to rest awhile—but not for long. She was fully aware of the importance of the task which lay before her. She had discovered all she could concerning the King of England, and she knew that, once she arrived in England, she would be well received. What terrified her was that, before she had an opportunity of being with the King, he might suggest that she did not cross the Channel.

She knew that Lady Castlemaine would do all in her power to prevent her arrival, and Lady Castlemaine still wielded some power.

So when the days began to pass she grew really alarmed.

Two days—three—a whole week, and there was still no sign of the Duke.

With the coming of the next week she grew frantic. She sent a messenger to Ralph Montague, the ambassador in Paris, and begged to know what she should do.

She waited most anxiously for news. Each time a messenger arrived at her lodgings she would start up in a sweat of trepidation. During those two anxious weeks in Dieppe the continual threat of failure was before her; she imagined herself being sent back to her parents' home in Finisterre, an ignoble failure, knowing that if she did not go to England there would now be no place for her at the French Court.

She watched the sea, which was rough and choppy, for a sight of the yacht which would come to take her away. Mayhap the weather was too rough for Buckingham to reach her. She clutched at any explanation.

And while she waited there, one of her maids came to tell her that a traveller had arrived from Calais and, hearing that she was awaiting the arrival of the Duke of Buckingham, had news for her if she would care to hear it.

The man was brought in.

"Mademoiselle de Kéroualle," he began, "I have heard that you are awaiting the arrival of the English Duke. He left Calais more than a week ago."

"Left Calais! For where?"

"For England."

"But that is impossible."

" 'Tis true, Mademoiselle."

"But did he say nothing of calling at Dieppe?"

"He said he was sailing for England. He filled the yacht with presents, which had been given him, and goods which he had bought. He said he hoped to arrive in England very soon as the tide was favorable."

Louise dismissed the man. She could bear no more. She shut herself into her room, lay on her bed, and pulled the curtains about it.

She knew that she had been deserted. She felt certain now that the King of England had changed his mind, that he had not been serious when he had asked for her to be sent to his Court, that he recognized her coming as the coming of a spy, and had commanded Buckingham to return to England without her.

It was all over—her wonderful dream which was to have saved her from an ignoble future. She should have known; it had been too wonderful, too easy. It was like something that happens only in a dream: To have gone to the Court in the hope that she would be chosen as the mistress of Louis Quatorze, and to have qualified for the same post at the Court of the King of England!

How long could she stay here in this desolate little seaport? Only until her parents sent for her or came to take her home.

❁ ❁ ❁

There was someone to see her.

She allowed her maid to comb back her hair from her hot face. She did not ask who the visitor was. She did not want to know. She guessed it was her father or someone from him, come to take her to her home, for they would know that the Duke of Buckingham had left without her.

Waiting for her was Ralph Montague, Charles' ambassador, whom she had often seen in Paris.

He came towards her, took her hand, and kissed it with great ceremony. "I came with all speed on receiving your message," he said.

"It was good of you, my lord."

"Nay," he said, " 'twas my duty. My master would never have forgiven me had I not come in person to offer my assistance."

"My lord Buckingham did not arrive," she said. "I have been waiting here for two weeks. I hear now that he left Calais some time ago."

"Buckingham!" Ralph Montague's lips curled with disgust. "I offer humble apologies for my countryman, Mademoiselle. I trust you will not judge us all by this one. The Duke is feckless and unreliable. My master will be incensed when he returns without you."

Louise did not say that his master would doubtless know of his return by now and had done nothing about arranging for her journey.

"I wondered whether he was acting on the King's instructions."

"The King is eagerly awaiting your arrival, Mademoiselle."

"I was led to believe that was so," said Louise. "But I doubt it now."

"And still is. Mademoiselle, I have already arranged for a yacht to call here in a few hours' time. It shall be my pleasure to make these arrangements. My friend, Henry Bennet, Earl of Arlington, will be waiting to receive you when you arrive in England. He and his family will look after you until you are presented to His Majesty. I trust you will give me this great pleasure in arranging your safe conduct."

The relief was so great that Louise, calm as she habitually was, was almost ready to break into hysterical tears.

She managed to say: "You are very good."

Montague said: "I will remain here in Dieppe and see you aboard if I have your permission to do so."

"I shall not forget this kindness," she replied. And she thought: Nor the churlish behavior of Buckingham. "My lord, have they offered you refreshment?"

"I came straight to you," said Montague. "I thought my first need was to impress upon you that all Englishmen are not so ungallant."

"Then will you take some refreshment with me, my lord?"

"It would give me the greatest pleasure," said Montague.

❁ ❁ ❁

Montague, as he took refreshment with Louise, was congratulating himself on the folly of Buckingham. What could have possessed the Duke to sail away from France, leaving the King's potential mistress in the lurch?

Surely Buckingham realized that, if ever Louise came to power, she would never forgive the insult.

He thought he understood, on consideration. His friend Arlington, with Clifford, was inclined towards Catholicism. Buckingham was staunchly Protestant. Buckingham would assess the influence the Catholic Frenchwoman would have on Charles, and mayhap had decided to do all in his power to prevent her arrival in England; so he had left her at Dieppe, hoping that careless Charles would forget her, as indeed it seemed he had. But Arlington, whose protégé Montague was, would hope to benefit from a Catholic mistress's influence over the King. Therefore it was Montague's duty to see that Charles had no chance to forget his interest in Catholic Louise.

He watched her as he took refreshment.

He admired her, this Frenchwoman, for her poise and calm. She looked almost a child with her plump, babyish face, and yet, in spite of the days of anxiety through which she had passed, she was completely controlled.

She was no beauty. At times it seemed as though she squinted slightly. Yet her figure was shapely, her hair and complexion lovely. Her charm was in her graceful manners; that complete air of the *grande dame* which the King would appreciate and would have missed in other mistresses.

Montague felt that if Louise de Kéroualle conducted herself with care she might find great favor with the King.

So while they waited for his yacht to arrive at Dieppe, he frequently talked to her. He told her of the King's character, that most easygoing nature, that love of peace.

"He has had little of that from those he loves," said Montague. "Even his Queen, a gentle, docile lady, was far from calm when His Majesty wished her to receive Lady Castlemaine into her bedchamber. It is my belief—and that of others—that, had the Queen been tolerant of the King's desire on this occasion, she would have won great love from him and kept it."

Louise nodded. This was friendly advice, and she took it to heart. It meant, Never be out of temper with the King. Give him peace, and he will be grateful.

"His Majesty greatly loved Mrs. Stuart before her marriage to the Duke of Richmond. He would have married her if he had been free to do so. But he was not free, and she held out until he was well-nigh maddened in his desire for her and would have offered anything, I verily believe, for her surrender."

"So many," said Louise, "must be ready to give the King all he asks, that it is small wonder that, when he finds one who holds back, he is astonished."

"And enamored . . . deeply enamored. If the Queen had died, many people believe, he would have married Mrs. Frances Stuart. And indeed that was the bait which was held out to him when . . ." He paused.

"When?" prompted Louise gently.

"It was my lord Buckingham with his wild schemes. He wished the King to divorce his wife and marry again."

"My lord Buckingham, it seems, would wish to run the affairs of his King's country," said Louise smoothly.

"A foolish man!" said Montague. "But he had his reasons. He did not like the Catholic marriage; he is a Protestant. Moreover, he was eager for the King to have an heir. One of his greatest enemies is the Duke of York."

Louise thought: From this moment he has a greater.

"And," went on Montague, "if the King does not get an heir, James, Duke of York, will one day be King of England. My lord Buckingham sought to replace the Queen with a fruitful woman who would provide the King with an heir and so ruin the Duke's chance of ascending the throne."

"It does not then seem that he is so foolish."

"He has moments of lucidity, superseded by moments of great folly. That is my lord Duke."

Louise was silent, looking into the future.

It was not long after that when the yacht which had been chartered by Ralph Montague arrived at Dieppe. As the tide was favorable, Louise left France for England, and when she arrived there, was greeted so warmly by Arlington and his friends that she no longer had need to complain of neglect.

Now she had two projects in view. The first and most important was to enslave the King; the second was revenge on the careless Duke who had given her so many hours of anxiety.

But, born spy that she was, cold by nature, calculating and in complete control, her eyes were now fixed on that distant goal which, she had suddenly made up her mind, should be marriage with the King of England. For if he had been prepared to marry Frances Stuart, why should he not marry Louise de Kéroualle?

❁ ❁ ❁

In the Palace of Whitehall Louise came face-to-face with the King.

When she would have knelt before him he raised her in his arms and there were tears in his eyes.

"Welcome," he said, "doubly welcome, my dear Mademoiselle de Kéroualle. It does my heart good to see you at Whitehall. But I cannot forget the last time we met, and I am deeply affected because I remember one who was with us then."

Louise turned away as though to hide her own tears. There was none; of course there was none; how could she regret the death of Henriette when it had given her a chance to reach such heights of glory as even her parents had not hoped for her?

The King was smiling at her now, his eyes alight with admiration. She was exquisitely gowned and wore fewer jewels than Castlemaine would have affected on such an occasion. Louise had the air of a queen, and Charles was reminded of Frances Stuart who had been brought up in France.

He was excited by the French girl, and he determined to make her his mistress with as little delay as possible.

He said: "The Queen will receive you into her bedchamber."

Louise murmured her thanks graciously; but she knew, of course, that Barbara Castlemaine had been a lady of his wife's bedchamber. Louise had no intention of going the way Barbara had gone.

She met the Queen; she met the courtiers; she met the Duke of Buckingham, and she betrayed not even by a gesture that she was in the least angered by his treatment of her; none watching her would believe that her anger rose so high that she feared that, if in that moment she attempted to speak, the effort might choke her.

She could content herself with waiting. The first task was the capture of the King; then she could proceed to annihilate the Duke.

The King had her sit beside him at the banquet which was held in her honor; he talked of his dear brother Louis and the French Court. All about them were saying, This will be the King's newest mistress.

The King himself believed it. But Louise, smiling so charmingly, looking so young and innocent, had other plans. Before her there was the shining example of Frances Stuart, the girl who had so plagued the King with refusals to surrender that, had he been able, he would have married her. She had seen the Queen—and it occurred to Louise that the Queen did not look over-healthy.

The King deceived himself if he thought he could make Louise de Kéroualle his mistress as easily as a play-actress from his theater.

He said to her: "So eagerly have I awaited your coming that I gave myself the pleasure of preparing your apartments for you."

She smiled into that charming face, knowing full well that his eagerness for her arrival was feigned. He had doubtless been so sportive with his play-actresses—and perhaps Madame Castlemaine too was by no means the discarded mistress she had been led to believe—that he had omitted to ask my lord Buckingham, when he arrived in England, what he had done with the lady whom he was supposed to be escorting.

"Your Majesty is good to me," she said with a smile.

He came closer; his eyes were on her plump bosom; his hands caressed her arm.

"I am prepared to be very kind," he murmured. "I have given you apartments near my own."

"That is indeed good of Your Majesty."

"They overlook the privy garden. I am proud of my privy garden. I trust you will like it. You can look down on the sixteen plots of grass and the statues. It is a mighty pretty view, I do believe. I long to show you these apartments. I have had them furnished with French tapestries, because I wished you to feel at home. No homesickness, you understand."

"I can see Your Majesty is determined to be kind to me."

"Would you wish me to dismiss these people, that you might be alone and . . . rest?"

"Your Majesty is so good to me that I crave a favor."

"My dear Mademoiselle de Kéroualle, you have given me the great gift of your presence here. Anything you might ask of me would be but small in comparison with what you have given me. And were it not, I have no doubt that I should grant it."

"I have had a long journey," said Louise.

"And you are weary. It was thoughtless of me to have given such a banquet so soon. But I wished to make you sure of your welcome."

"I am indeed grateful for the honor you have shown me, but my lord Arlington and Lady Arlington, who have been so good to me, have placed apartments in their house at my disposal."

"I am glad my lord Arlington and his lady have been so hospitable," said Charles a little wryly.

"I am very weary, and I fear that the etiquette of the Court, in my present state, would overtax my strength," said Louise.

Charles' glance was ironic. He understood. Louise was jealous of her dignity. She was not to be sent for like any play-actress. She had to be wooed.

Inwardly he grimaced. But he said with the utmost charm: "I understand full well. Go to the Arlingtons. His lady will make you very comfortable. And I trust that ere long you will be ready to exchange Lord Arlington's house for my palace of Whitehall."

Louise thanked him charmingly.

She believed she had won the first round. The King was eager for her; but he was realizing that a grand lady such as Louise de Kéroualle must be courted before she was won.

❁ ❁ ❁

Louise stayed with the Arlingtons. The King visited her frequently, but she did not become his mistress. Charles was often exasperated, but Louise attracted him with her perfect manners and babyish looks. There was in her attitude a certain promise which indicated that, once the formalities had been observed, he would find the waiting well worthwhile. Louise remembered other ladies from the past who, by careful tactics, had won high places for themselves. Elizabeth Woodville in her dealings with Edward IV. Anne Boleyn with Henry VIII. The latter was not a very happy example, but Louise would not be guilty of that Queen's follies; nor did Charles resemble in any way the Tudor King. The poverty of Louise's youth, the knowledge, which was always before her, that she must make her own way for herself had fired her with great ambition, so that no sooner did one goal appear in sight than she must immediately aim at another. King's mistress had been the first goal. She could achieve that at any moment. Now she was trying for another: King's wife. It might seem fantastic and wild. But there was the example of Frances Stuart. Moreover the Queen was ailing, and she could not produce an heir. These were the exact circumstances which had helped to put Anne Boleyn on the throne. Anne had had the good sense to withhold herself for a long time from an enamored monarch, but after marriage she had lost that good sense. Louise would never lose hers.

So she held back. She reminded the King by a hundred gestures that she was a great lady; she hinted that she found him very attractive but, because she was not only a great lady but a virtuous one, the *fact* that he was married prevented her from yielding to his desires.

Charles hid his growing exasperation under great charm of manner. He was ready to play her game, for he knew she would eventually surrender. Why else should she have come to England? And while he waited, he amused himself with others. Occasionally he visited Barbara, Moll, and

Nell; Chaffinch continued to bring certain ladies up to his apartments by way of the privy stairs. Thus he could enjoy the game of waiting which he must play with Louise.

Apartments were furnished for her at Whitehall; beautiful French tapestries adorned the walls; there was furniture decorated with the new marqueterie; there were exquisite carpets, cabinets from Japan, vases of china and silver, tables of marble, the newest kind of clocks with pendulums, silver candelabra and everything that was exquisite.

Louise moved into these apartments, but she made it clear to the King that such a great and virtuous lady as herself could only receive him at one time of the day. This was nine o'clock in the morning.

Colbert de Croissy, the French ambassador, watched uneasily. He even remonstrated with her. He greatly feared that she would try the King's patience too far.

Louise was determined.

She would serve, not only the cause of France, but her own ambition.

❁ ❁ ❁

Those three women who had been the King's leading mistresses watched the newcomer with apprehension. They knew that they owed the King's occasional company to the continued reserve of the Frenchwoman. They knew that, once she decided to surrender, the King's interest in them would wane. And what would be the effect of that waning? Barbara knew that she was fast losing her hold on the King. Her beauty was no longer fresh and appealing; her rages did not diminish with her beauty; she had taken so many lovers that she had become notorious on that account. Her adventures with Charles Hart and a rope-dancer named Jacob Hall had created the greatest scandal, because, it was said, she had chosen these men as lovers in retaliation for the King's preoccupation with Moll Davies and Nell Gwyn. Barbara still clung to her waning influence with the King, knowing that he would still be prepared to give way in some respect, if not for love of her, for love of peace.

Moll Davies was rarely visited now. She had her fine house and her pension, but the King was growing tired of her gentle qualities. It was due to his habit of "not discarding" that she remained his mistress.

As for Nell, her baby took up a great deal of her time, but her preoccupation with the little boy made her thoughts turn often to his father. The King must not tire of her; she must cease to be as frivolous-minded as she had previously been. There was the boy to think of.

"I'll get a fine title for you, my little man," she would whisper to the child. "You shall be a Duke, no less." She would laugh into the big wondering eyes which watched her so intently. "You . . . a Duke . . . that slut Nelly's brat—a royal Duke. Who would have believed it?"

But dukedoms were not easily come by.

The King was delighted with the child. Those were pleasant days when he came to visit Nell and took the boy in his arms.

"There is no doubt," cried Nell, leaning over him like any proud wife and mother, "that this boy is a Stuart. See that nose! Those eyes!"

"Then God have mercy on him!" said the King.

"Come, my little one," said Nell. "Smile for Papa."

The child surveyed the King with solemn eyes.

"Not yet, eh, Sir!" murmured Charles. "First wait and see what manner of man this is who has fathered you."

"The best in the world," said Nell lightly.

The King turned and looked at her.

"Od's Fish!" he cried. "I believe you mean that, Nelly."

"Nay!" cried Nell, ashamed of her own emotion. "I am sowing the first seeds which will flower into a dukedom for our boy."

"And strawberry leaves for yourself! Oh, Nell, you go the way of all the others."

Nell snatched the child from his father's arms and began dancing round the apartment with him.

"What do I want for you, my son? A coronet, a great title, all that belongs by right to a King's bastard. Already, my son, you have the King's nose, the King's eyes, and the King's name. Od's Fish! I trust His Majesty will not think you adequately endowed with these, for they will make little story in the world, I suspect."

Then she laid him in his cradle and bent and kissed him. The King came to her and put his arms about her shoulders.

He thought in that moment that, although Louise de Kéroualle was becoming an obsession with him, he would be loath to part with little Nell.

❁ ❁ ❁

Rose came to see Nell in her new house.

It was a small one at the east end of Pall Mall, not far from the grand mansion in Suffolk Street where another of the King's mistresses—Moll Davies—had her residence.

Nell's house was a poor place compared with that of Moll. Moll liked to ride past Nell's in her carriage and lean forward to look at it as she passed, smiling complacently, flashing her £700 ring on her finger.

"Keep your house, keep your ring, Moll!" called Nell from her house. "The King has given me something better still."

Then Nell would snatch up her child from one of the servants and hold him aloft.

"You've never got the King's bastard yet, Moll!" screeched Nell.

Moll bade her coachman drive on. She thought Nell a fool. She had had every chance to escape from her environment, and yet she seemed to cling to it as though she were reluctant to let it go.

"What a low wench!" murmured Moll in her newly acquired refined voice. "Why His Majesty should spend an hour in her company is past my comprehension."

Moll smiled complacently. Her house was so grand; Nell's was such a poor place. Did it not show that the King appreciated the difference between them? Nell went into the house where Rose was waiting for her.

Rose took the baby from Nell and crooned over him.

"To think that he is the King's son," said Rose. " 'Tis past understanding."

"Indeed it is not," cried Nell. "He made his appearance through all the usual channels."

"Oh, Nell, why did you move from your good apartments in Lincoln's Inn Fields to this little house? The other was far grander."

"It is nearer Whitehall, Rose. I have one good friend in the world, and I want to be as near him as possible."

"He acknowledges little Charlie as his own?"

"Indeed he does. And could you mistake it? Look! The way he sucks his finger is royal, bless him."

"It makes me wonder whether I ought to drop a curtsy to him when I pick him up."

"Mayhap you will have to one day," said Nell, dreaming.

Rose kissed the child.

"To think I've kissed where the King has kissed!" said Rose.

"If that delights you," Nell retorted, "you may kiss me any time—and anywhere—you wish."

That made them both laugh.

"You're just the same, Nell. You haven't changed one little bit. You have fine clothes, and a house of your own, and the King's bastard . . . and yet you're still the same Nell. That's why I've come to talk to you. It's about a man I met."

"Why, Rosy, you're in love!"

Rose admitted this was so. "It's a man named John Cassels. I met him in one of the taverns. I want to marry him and settle down."

"Then why not? Ma would like to have one respectable daughter in the family."

"Respectable! Ma cares not for that. She's prouder of you than she could ever have been of any respectably married daughter. She talks of you continually. 'My Nelly, the King's whore . . . and my grandson Charlie . . . the King's little bastard. . . .' She talks of nothing else. . . ."

Nell laughed. "Ma's one dream was to make good whores of us both, Rosy. I fulfilled her dreams, but you—you're a disgrace to the family. You're thinking about respectable marriage."

"The trouble with John is the way he gets his living."

"What is that?"

"He's a highwayman."

"A perilous way of making a living."

"So say I. He longs to be a soldier."

"Like Will. How is cousin Will?"

"Speaking of you often and with pride, Nelly."

"It seems that many are proud of the King's whore."

"We are all proud of you, Nell."

Nell laughed and threw her curls off her face. "Marry your John, if you wish it and he wishes it, Rose. Mayhap he will be caught. But if he should end his days by falling from a platform while in conversation with a clergyman . . . at least you will have had your life together, and a widow is a mighty respectable thing to be. And Rose . . . if it should be possible to drop a word in the right quarter . . . who knows, I may get my chance to do it. I do not forget poor Will and his talk of being a soldier. I often think of it. One day Will shall be a soldier, and I will do what I can for your John Cassels. That's if you love the man truly."

"Nell, Nell, my sweet sister."

"Nay," said Nell, "who would not do all possible for a sister?"

And when Rose had gone she thought that it would be a comparatively easy thing to find places in the army for Will and John Cassels.

"But, my little lord," she whispered, "it is going to be rather more difficult to fit a coronet onto that little head."

❁ ❁ ❁

Nell stayed on in her small house and the months passed. Louise had not surrendered to the King. Moll Davies still flaunted past Nell's house in her carriage.

My lord Rochester visited Nell in her new house, and shook his head over what he called "Nell's squalor."

He sprawled on a couch, inspecting his immaculate boots, and glancing up at Nell with affection.

He gave advice. "The King does not treat you with the decencies he owes to a royal mistress, Nell," he said. "That is clear."

"While Madam Davies rides by in her coach to her fine house, flashing her diamond ring!" cried Nell.

" 'Tis true. And poor Nelly is now a mother, and the infant's face would proclaim him as the King's son even if His Majesty had reason to suspect this might be otherwise."

"His Majesty has no reason to suspect that."

"Suspicion does not always need reason to support it, little Nell. But let us not discourse on such matters. Let us rather devote ourselves to this more urgent business: How to get Mrs. Nelly treated with the courtesy due to the King's mistress. Barbara got what she wanted by screams, threats and violence. Moll by sweet, coy smiles. What have you, sweet Nell, to put in place of these things—your Cole-yard wit? Alas, alas, Cole-yard is at the root of all your troubles. His Majesty is in a quandary. He is fond of his little Nell; he dotes on his latest son; but little Charles is half royal, half Cole-yard. Remember that, Nell. There have been other little Charleses, to say nothing of Jemmies and Annes and Charlottes. Now all these have had mothers of gentle birth. Even our noble Jemmy Monmouth had a gentlewoman for his mother. But you, dear Nell—let's face it—are from the gutter. His Majesty fears trouble if he bestows great titles on this Charles. The people accept the King's lack of morals. They like to see him merry. They care not where he takes his pleasure. What they do care about, Nell, is to see one of themselves rise to greatness through the King's bed. 'Why,' they say, 'that might have happened to me . . . or my little Nell. But it did not. It happened to *that* little Nell.' And they cannot forgive you that. Therefore, though you bear the King's bastard, they do not wish that titles should be bestowed on him. They wish it to be remembered that his mother is but a Cole-yard wench."

" 'Tis so, I fear, my lord," said Nell. "But it shall not stay so. This child is going to share in some of that which has been enjoyed by Barbara's brats."

"Noble Villiers on their mother's side—those little bastards of Barbara's, Nelly!"

"I care not. I care not. Who is to say they *are* the King's children? Only Barbara."

"Nay, not even Barbara. For how could even their mother be sure? Now listen to my advice, Nell. Be diplomatic in your attitude towards the King. When the Frenchwoman surrenders, as undoubtedly she will, there may be changes in His Majesty's seraglio. The lady may say, 'Remove that object. I ask it as the price of my surrender.' And believe me, little Nell, that object—be she noble Villiers or orange-girl—may well be removed. Unless, of course, the object makes herself so important to His Majesty that he cannot dispense with her."

"This Frenchwoman, it seems, would have great powers."

"She uses great diplomacy, my dear. She holds out hopes to our most gracious King, and then withdraws. It is a game such women play—a dangerous game unless the woman has the skill. She is skilled, this French Louise. It is her manners and this game she plays which make her so desirable. For the love of God I cannot see what else. The woman sometimes seems to squint."

"And so Squintabella will throw us all out of favor!" cried Nell wrathfully.

"Squintabella will, if she wishes to. Mayhap she will not consider a little onetime orange-girl from Cole-yard a worthy adversary. But listen to me, Nelly. For this time make no demands upon the King. Administer to his peace. Laugh for him. See that he laughs. He will come to you for refuge, as a ship comes into harbor. Squintabella will not rage and storm as Barbara raged and stormed, but yet I fancy he will have need of refuge."

Nell was silent for a while. Then she looked at the handsome dissolute face of my lord Rochester and said: "I cannot understand, my lord, why you should be so good to me."

Rochester yawned. He said: "Put it down, if you will, to my dislike of Squintabella, my desire for His Majesty's peace and enjoyment of the most charming lady in London, and my pleasure in helping a fellow wit."

"Whichever it should be," said Nell, "I'll follow your advice, my lord, as far as I'm able. But since the days when I sat on the cobbles in Cole-yard, I have never been in control of my tongue. And, as I know myself; I am certain I shall continue to ask favors for my young Charles until he is a noble duke."

"Aye!" cried Rochester. "Go your own way, Nelly. There is one thing that's certain. 'Twill be a way no other went before."

❁ ❁ ❁

So Nell continued at the eastern end of Pall Mall. The King came less frequently. Will Chaffinch regretted that his purse was not as deep as he would have liked, and Nell had developed extravagant tastes.

She would not dress young Charles in garments unsuited to his state. She had never been thrifty; debts began to mount.

One day she said to Rochester: "I cannot keep my little Charles, in the state to which I intend he shall become accustomed, on what I get from Chaffinch."

"You could remind the King of his responsibilities," suggested Rochester. "Remind him gently. Be not like Barbara with her demands."

"I'll not be like Barbara," said Nell. "And my son shall not be dressed in worsted. Nothing but silk shall touch his skin. It's going to be a duke's skin before he dies, and I want to make it duke's skin from the start. He was born high, and he'll stay high."

"Nell, I see plans in your eyes. What mad pranks do you plan?"

"Since what Chaffinch gives me is not enough, I must work for more."

"You would take a lover?"

"Take a lover! Nay, one man at a time was ever my way. I have my friend the King, and we have our child. We are too poor, it seems, to keep him in the state due to him. Therefore I must work."

"You . . . work!"

"Why not? I was once an actress, and it was said that many people crowded into the theater just to see me. Why should they not again?"

"But now you are known as the King's mistress and the mother of his son. King's mistresses do not work. They never have."

"This one will set a fashion," said Nell. "If his father is too poor to give young Charles his due, his mother shall not be."

"Nay, Nell. It is unheard of."

"From tomorrow it shall not be. For then I go back to the stage."

FIVE

James, Duke of Monmouth, was whipping himself to a rage. He strutted about his apartments before those young men whose pleasure it was to keep close to the King's son and applaud him in all that he did.

Monmouth was handsome in the extreme. He had inherited his father's physique and his mother's beauty; and there was just enough of the Stuart in his features to convince everyone that he was the King's son. All knew of the King's devotion to this young man, the liberties allowed him, the King's unending patience; for it had to be admitted that Monmouth was an arrogant fellow, proudly conscious of that stream of royal blood which flowed in his veins. At the same time he bore a great grudge against that fate which had made him an illegitimate son of such an indulgent father.

There was a hope, which never left him, that one day the King would legitimize him. There were many to surround him and tell him that this would be so, for the Queen's pregnancies continued to end in miscarriages, and the dislike of the country for the King's brother's religion was growing.

James, Duke of York, was suspect. He had not proclaimed himself a

Catholic, but it was clear by his absence from the church that he was uneasy in his mind concerning his religion, and rumor ran riot. It was for Monmouth and his friends to foster those rumors.

In the meantime Monmouth gave himself up to pleasure. He was a glutton for it. He had his father's interest in women, but he lacked his father's good-natured tolerance. Charles had the gift of seeing himself exactly as he was; Monmouth saw himself larger than life. Charles had had no need to bolster up the picture of himself, since his forbears were Kings of Scotland, England, and France. He was entirely royal. Monmouth had to link his royal ancestors with those of his mother; and, although he was the King's son, there were many who declared he would never wear the crown. There was a burning desire within him to override those who would stand in the way of his ambitions. This colored his life.

His education had not been of the best; he had left the environment of a simple country gentleman to become a petted member of his father's Court. His head was not strong enough for him to imbibe such a strong draught and remain sober.

So he strutted, raged, posed, and made many enemies; and those who were his friends were in truth either enemies of the Duke of York or those who thought to curry favor with the King because of the love he bore his son.

Monmouth's time was devoted to fortune-tellers, looking after his appearance, collecting recipes for the care of his skin, and keeping his teeth white and his hair that lustrous black which was such a contrast to his smooth fair skin; soldiering attracted him; he wished to be a famous soldier and to make great conquests; he pictured himself riding through the streets of London with his military glory like a halo about his handsome head; for thus, he believed, the people would realize his worth and, when they cried "Down with the Catholic Duke of York," they would add, "Up with the Protestant Duke of Monmouth!"

It was seven years since he had married the little Countess of Buccleuch, a very wealthy Scottish heiress whom his father had been pleased to bestow upon his beloved Jemmy. Monmouth had been fourteen then; Anne, his little bride, twelve. He remembered often how his loving father had merrily attended the ceremony of putting them to bed together, yet insisting on the ceremony's stopping there, since the pair were so young.

It had proved a far from happy marriage. But Anne Scott was proud. Monmouth thought her callous. She gave no sign of any distress, which her husband's wildness caused her, and some said she was as hard as the granite hills of her native land.

Monmouth was pursuing a lady of the Queen's bedchamber, Mary Kirke. It was not that Mary appealed to him more than any other; but he had heard that his uncle, the Duke of York, was enamored of the lady and, in his slow and ponderous way, was attempting to court her.

That was enough to inspire young Monmouth's passion, for it was necessary for him continually to flaunt what he felt to be his superiority over his uncle. He must do it in every possible way, so that all—including James, Duke of York—should realize that, should King Charles die without legitimate heirs, James II would not be James, Duke of York, but James, Duke of Monmouth.

Now, as he walked about his apartment, he was ranting to his companions on what he called an insult to royalty.

Sir Thomas Sandys was with him; also a Captain O'Brien. He had called these men in because he wished them to help in a wild plan which was forming in his mind. His great friends, the young Dukes of Albemarle and Somerset, sprawled on the window seat listening to Jemmy's ranting.

"My father is too easy-going by far!" cried Monmouth. "He allows low fellows to insult him—and what does he? He shrugs his shoulders and laughs. It is all very well to take that attitude, but insolence should be punished."

"His Majesty's easy temper is one of the reasons for the love his people bear him," suggested Albemarle.

"A King should be a King," said Monmouth boldly.

None spoke. Monmouth, as beloved son, had a right to criticize his father which was denied to them.

"Have you fellows heard what this insolent Coventry said in the Parliament?"

All were silent.

"And who is this John Coventry?" demanded the young Duke. "Member for Weymouth! And what is Weymouth, I pray you tell me? This obscure gentleman from the country would criticize my father and go free. And all because my father is too lazy to punish him. 'Tis an insult to royalty, I tell you; and if my father will not avenge it, then should his son do so."

The Duke of Albemarle said uneasily, "What was said was said in the Parliament. There, it is said, a man has a right to speak his mind."

Monmouth swung round, black eyes flashing, haughty lips curled. "A right . . . to speak against his King!"

"It has been done before, my lord," ventured Somerset. "What this man Coventry did was to ask that an entertainment tax should be levied on the theaters."

" 'Twas a suggestion worthy of a country bumpkin."

"He proposed it as a means of raising money, which all agree the country needs," said Somerset.

"My good fellow, the King must be amused. He loves his theaters. Why should he not have his pleasures? The theaters give much pleasure to His Majesty."

"That was said in Parliament," said Albemarle grimly.

"Aye," cried Monmouth. "And 'twas then that this John Coventry—*Sir* John Coventry—rose in his seat to ask whether the King's pleasure lay among the men or the women who acted therein."

" 'Twas an insult to His Majesty, 'tis true," admitted Albemarle.

"An insult! It was arrogance, *lèse majesté.* It shall not be permitted. All the country knows that the King finds pleasure in his actresses. There are Moll Davies from the Duke's and Nell Gwyn from the King's to prove it. Coventry meant to insult the King, and he did so."

"His Majesty has decided to allow the insult to pass," said Albemarle.

"But *I* shall not allow it to pass," cried Monmouth. "*I* shall make these country bumpkins realize that my father is their King, and any who dare insult him shall live to regret that day."

"What does Your Grace plan?" asked Sir Thomas Sandys. "That, my good friends, is what I have assembled you here to discuss," said the Duke.

❁ ❁ ❁

The King was very uneasy. He sought out his brother James in his private apartments.

James was sitting alone, a book before him.

James, thought Charles, so tall and handsome—far handsomer than I—and clever enough in his way; why is it that James is a fool?

"Reading, James?" said Charles lightly. "And the book?" He looked over his brother's shoulder. "Dr Heylin's *History of the Reformation.* Ah, my Protestant subjects would be pleased to see you reading such a book, James."

James' big dark eyes were puzzled.

He said: "I find much food for thought 'twixt these pages."

"Give over thinking so much, James," said Charles. "It is a task ill-suited to your nature."

"You mock me, Charles. You always did."

"I was born a mocker."

"Have you read this book?"

"I have skimmed its pages."

" 'Tis worth more than a skimming."

"I am glad to hear you say so. I trust this means your feet are set in what my Protestant subjects would call the path of the just."

"It fills me with doubts, Charles."

"Brother, when I die you will inherit a crown. The managing of a kingdom will take every bit of that skill with which nature has provided you. You will be at your wits' end to keep the crown upon your head, and your head upon your shoulders. Remember our father. Do you ever forget him? I never do. You are over-concerned with your soul, brother, when your head may be in danger."

"What matters a head where a soul is in the balance?"

"Your head is there for all to see—a handsome one, James, and that of a man who may well one day be King. Your soul—where is that? We cannot see it, so how can we be sure that it has any existence?"

"You blaspheme, Charles."

"I'm an irreligious fellow; I know it. 'Tis my nature. My mind is a perverse one, and to such as I am faith is hard to come by. But put away the book, brother. I would talk to you. 'Tis this affair of Coventry."

James nodded gloomily. "A bad affair."

"Young Jemmy grows too wild."

"The fellow will live?"

"I thank God that he will. But those wild young men have slit his nose and the Parliament is filled with anger."

" 'Tis to be understood," said James.

"I am in agreement with you and the Parliament, James. But my Parliament is displeased with me and it is a bad thing when parliaments and kings are not of one accord. We have a terrible example before us. When I came home I determined to live in peace with my subjects and my Parliament. And now young Jemmy has done this. He was defending my royalty, he proclaims."

"That boy has such a deep sense of Your Majesty's royalty, largely because he believes himself to have a share in it."

" 'Tis true, James. There are times when young Jemmy gives me great cause for anxiety. The Parliament has passed an act whereby any who shall put out an eye, cut a lip, nose, or tongue of His Majesty's liege people or in any other manner wound or maim any Parliament man, shall be sent to prison for a year, besides incurring other heavy penalties."

" 'Tis just," said James.

"Aye, 'tis just. Therefore I like not to see young Jemmy conduct himself thus."

"A little punishment, inflicted by Your Majesty, might be useful."

"Indeed it might. But I was never a punishing man, James, and I find it hard to punish those I care for as I do for that boy."

"Nevertheless he will bring trouble on himself, and on you one day."

"That is why I wish you to help me, James. Could not you two be friends? I like not to see this strife between you."

" 'Tis your natural son who causes the strife between us. He fears I shall wear the crown to which, in his heart, he believes himself to have prior claim."

"There is only one thing which can make you two become friends, I fear; and that is a family of healthy sons for me, so that there is no hope for either of you to wear the crown."

"Charles, there are some who say you love that boy so much that you would make him your heir in all things."

" 'Tis true I love the boy. He is my own flesh and blood. There are a thousand things to remind me of that each day. He is my son—my eldest son. He is handsome, he delights me. I'll deny it not. But you too, brother, are our father's son and you are my heir. Never would I make Jemmy legitimate, while there is one who, it is right and proper, should take my place. If I die childless, James, you are the heir to the throne. I never forget that. Light-minded though I may be, on this point I am firm and strong. But there is one other matter I must settle with you. It is this dabbling with the Catholic Faith."

"We cannot control our thoughts, brother."

"Nay, but we can keep them to ourselves."

"I could not be false to what I believed to be the true religion."

"But you could keep your thoughts to yourself, brother. Remember our grandfather, Henri Quatre. You're his grandson no less than I. Think of the control he kept on his religion, and because of this a country, which had known disastrous war, at last knew peace. England is a Protestant country—as firmly Protestant as France in the days of our grandfather was firmly Catholic. England will never again accept a Catholic King. If you would have peace in England when I am gone, you must come to the throne a Protestant."

"And if my heart and mind tell me the Catholic Faith is the true one?"

"Subdue the heart, dear brother. If you let the mind take control, it will say this: Worship in secret. Remain outwardly what the country wishes you to be. Remember our grandfather . . . the greatest King the French ever had. He put an end to civil war, because he, who had been Huguenot, professed to be a Catholic. Stop this flirting with the Catholic Faith, James. Show yourself with me in the church when the occasion demands it. Let the country see you as a good Protestant. Then, brother, we shall more quickly put an end to this unhealthy fostering of young Jemmy's ambitions. Do this—not for my sake—but for your own and that of an England you may one day rule."

James shook his head gravely. "You know not what you ask, brother. If a man follows the Catholic Faith, how can he go to a Protestant church and worship there?"

Charles sighed wearily.

Then he shrugged his shoulders. James was a fool . . . always had been a fool and, he feared, always would be. Charles could console himself with the thought that whatever trouble James brought on himself he, Charles, would be in his grave and not concerned with it.

He turned to a happier subject. "How fares your family?"

James' face lightened. "Mary is solemn as ever. Anne grows plump."

"Come, take me to them. I would have them know their uncle forgets them not."

In the Duke's apartment Charles met Anne Hyde. Anne's welcome was fond, and not entirely so because her brother-in-law was King. Anne was a clever woman, and she and Charles had ever been good friends. Anne did not forget that, when all had deserted her soon after her marriage and Henrietta Maria was demanding that she be ignored, it was Charles the King who had been her best friend.

"Your Majesty looks in good spirits," she said.

" 'Tis the prospect of talk with you," said Charles, ever gallant even to the over-fat and ageing. "Od's Fish! James is a gloomy fellow with his holy problems. Where are these children of yours?"

"I'll send for them," said Anne. "They'll be eager to come, now they know Your Majesty is here."

Charles, looking at Anne, thought she was more sallow than usual; her very fat seemed unhealthy.

He asked if she had news of her father, Edward Hyde, Earl of Clarendon, who was living in exile in France.

Anne had heard. He passed his days pleasantly enough, she told the King. He was finding compensation for his exile in writing his memoirs.

"They should make interesting reading," said the King.

Now the little girls were coming into the room: Mary and Anne, the only two who had survived, thought the King, among the seven—was it seven?—which Anne Hyde had borne the Duke of York.

Yet James, with his two girls, had been more fortunate than his brother. Why was it that royal folk, for whom it was so necessary to produce heirs, were usually so unfortunate? Lack of heirs was the curse of royalty.

Mary, the elder, took his hand and solemnly kissed it. Charles lifted her in his arms. He loved children and he was particularly fond of solemn little Mary.

He kissed her affectionately, and she put her arms about his neck and rubbed her cheek against his. Next to her father she loved her Uncle Charles.

Anne was tugging at his coat.

"Anne's turn," said Anne stolidly.

"Now, Mary, my dear," said the King, "you must give place to plump Anne."

He set Mary down and made as though to lift Anne from the ground. He wheezed and puffed, and both children shrieked with delight.

"Anne is too fat to be lifted," said Mary.

"I confess," said the King, "that this great bulk of my niece defeats me."

"Then give me sweetmeats instead," said Anne.

"It is because she eats that she is so fat, Uncle Charles," said Mary. "If she eats more she will become fatter and fatter, and *nobody* will be able to lift her."

Anne gave them a slow, friendly smile. "I'd rather have sweetmeats than be lifted," she said.

"Ah, my dear Anne, you present a weighty problem," said the King. "And knowing your fancies, and that I should be admitted to your ponderous presence, I came well armed."

Both little girls looked at his face; for he had knelt to put his on a level with theirs.

"Armed," said Mary. "That means carrying swords and such things, Anne."

"Swords made of sweetmeats?" said Anne, interested.

"Feel in my pocket, nieces, and you may find something of interest," said their uncle.

Anne was there first, squealing with delight, and cramming the contents of the King's pocket into her mouth.

Mary put her hand in that of the King. "I will show you Papa's greyhounds. I love them."

"I love them too," mumbled Anne as best she could; while the sweet juices ran down her plump chin.

"They are so thin," said the King, giving her his melancholy smile.

"I like others to be thin," said Anne. "It is only Anne who must be fat."

"You fear that if they grow as fat as you they will acquire similar tastes. If we all loved sweetmeats as does Mistress Anne, there would not be enough in the world to satisfy us all."

Anne was solemn for a while, then she smiled that affectionate and charming smile. "Nay, Uncle Charles," she said, "the confectioners will make more sweetmeats."

They went to look at the Duke's greyhounds. Their father forgot his preoccupation with religious problems and played games with his little girls. Charles showed them how to throw in *pelmel.*

And, as he guided Mary's hand when she would throw the ball and as little Anne toddled beside him, Charles thought: If these two were but mine I should end this dangerous rivalry between Jemmy and James; I should not need to feel concerned because I see my brother deep in doubt when he reads Dr. Heylin's *History of the Reformation.*

❁ ❁ ❁

Charles came to see Nell after she had been playing on the stage of the King's Theater for a few weeks.

He was amused by her return to the stage; but, as he pointed out, everyone knew that the child who was sleeping in the cradle was his son, and it was hardly fitting for that child's mother to remain an actress.

"It is necessary for that child's mother to provide food for the King's bastard," said Nell characteristically. "And if playacting is the only way she can do it, then playact she must. Should an innocent child starve because his mother is too lazy and his father too poor to feed him?"

"Have done," said the King. "Leave the stage and you shall not want—nor shall he."

"If I leave the stage I shall be obliged to see that this is a promise Your Majesty shall keep," said Nell. "For myself I ask no pension; but for my child—who is known by the name of Charles, and none other—I would ask a good deal."

"All that can be done for you and him shall be done," promised the King.

He was visiting her more frequently now. Louise de Kéroualle was still holding him at bay. He thought a great deal of Louise; she seemed to him infinitely desirable, indeed the most desirable woman in his kingdom, but he was too lighthearted to sigh on that account. Louise would succumb eventually, he felt sure; in the meantime there was Moll—still charming enough to be worth a visit now and then; Barbara on whom he still called occasionally, if only that he might congratulate himself on having almost broken with her; and Nell, who could always be relied upon to amuse and come up with the unexpected. The others—the ladies who provided amusement for a night or so—there would always be. He was well supplied with women.

Charles realized Nell's problems, and he had decided that it would be convenient if she lived even nearer to him at Whitehall.

He reminded her that he had given her the house in which she now lived.

"And that," retorted Nell, "I do not accept, since I discover it to be leasehold. My services have always been free under the Crown. For that reason, nothing but freehold will satisfy me."

"Nell," said the King with a laugh, "you grow acquisitive."

"I have a son to think for."

"It has changed you—becoming a mother."

"It changes all women."

The King was sober temporarily. "You do well," he said, "to consider the boy. You do well to remind me of your needs. Why, look you, Nell, it is a long step here from Whitehall."

"But Your Majesty's chief pleasure—save one—is sauntering, so I've heard."

"There are occasions when I would wish to have you near me. And now that you have left the stage, I am going to make you a present of a fine house—freehold. The only freehold in the district on which I can lay my hands."

"It is near Whitehall?"

"Nearer than this one, Nell. Indeed, it is nearer by a quarter of a mile. I do not think you will have reason to find this house unworthy of our son, Nell."

"And it is freehold?" insisted Nell.

"I swear it shall be."

❁ ❁ ❁

Nell was climbing in the world now.

She had her residence in the beautiful wide street at that end which was the home of many of the aristocrats of the Court. Nell's new house was three storys high, and its gardens extended to St. James' Park, from which it was separated by a stone wall. At the end of Nell's garden was a mound, and when she stood on this she could see over the wall and into the Park; she could call to the King as he sauntered there with his friends.

Now Nell was indeed treated with the "decencies of a royal mistress." Her near neighbors were Barbara Castlemaine, the Countess of Shrewsbury, and Mary Knight who had once been one of the King's favored mistresses. Lady Greene and Moll Davies were not far off.

There was a difference in the attitude of many people towards her now. She was Madam Gwyn more often than Mrs. Nelly; tradesmen were eager for her custom; she was treated with the utmost servility.

Nell of the old days would have ridiculed these sycophants; Nell the mother enjoyed their homage. She never forgot that the more honor paid to her the easier it would be for honors to find their way to that little boy, and she was determined to see him a Duke before she died.

There were some who often tried to remind her that she had been an orange-girl and an actress, bred in Cole-yard. Mary Villiers, the Duke of Buckingham's sister, had refused to receive her and this, Nell was delighted to learn, had aroused the King's deep displeasure. He had reminded the noble lady: "Those I lie with are fit company for the greatest ladies in the land." And Mary Villiers had had to change her attitude.

The Arlingtons were cool. They were all for the promotion of Mademoiselle de Kéroualle; but she, it seemed, was chained to celibacy by her virtue. Let her remain thus, thought Nell, while the rest of us enjoy life and grow rich.

There was some rivalry with Moll Davies.

Nell could not endure Moll's affected airs of refinement. She wondered that the King—a man of such wit—did not laugh them to scorn. He still visited Moll, and there were occasions when Nell, expecting him to call at the house or even vault the wall as he sometimes did, would see him passing on his way to visit Moll Davies.

Moll sometimes called on Nell after the King's visit. She would sit in Nell's apartment, displaying her £700 ring, and talking of the latest present the King had brought her.

"He even brings me sweetmeats such as I like. He says I am almost as great a glutton for them as the Princess Anne."

One day, early that spring, Moll called at Nell's house in a twitter of excitement expressly to tell her that the King had sent a message that he would be calling on her that night.

"It surprises me, Nelly," she said, "that he should come so far. *You* are nearer now, are you not, and yet he comes to me! Can you understand it?"

"All men, even Kings, at times act crazily," said Nell quickly.

She was anxious. Her son was without a name. She was not going to have him called Charlie Gwyn. He was growing. He needed a name. Many times she had suggested that some honor be given to the boy, but the King was always vague and evasive. He promised to do all that he could, but Charles' promises were more readily given than fulfilled. He was fond of the boy; yet to have ennobled him would have caused much comment. Rochester was right about that. The affair of Sir John Coventry was still remembered, and there were times when the King was eager not to arouse too much criticism in his subjects.

"Let be, Nell," he had said. "Let the matter rest awhile. I promise you the boy shall lack nothing."

And tonight he would go to that scheming Moll Davies. It was not to be borne.

"I am a good hand at making sweetmeats," Nell said to Moll.

"I was never taught to perform such menial tasks," said Moll.

"I used to make them to sell in the market," Nell told her. "Sweetmeats!" she cried in a raucous cockney voice. "Good ladies, buy my sweetmeats!"

Moll shuddered. She looked about her at the beautifully furnished apartment and wondered how such a creature as Nell had ever managed to obtain it.

Nell pretended not to see Moll's disgust. "I shall bring you some sweetmeats," said Nell. "My next batch shall be made especially for you."

Moll rose to go; she had preparations to make, she reiterated, for the reception of the King that night.

When she had gone, Nell picked up the baby.

A fine healthy boy; she kissed him fondly.

She was ready to fight all the duchesses in the land for his sake.

Now she went to her kitchen and, rolling up the fine sleeves of her gown, made sweetmeats; and as soon as they were ready she set out with them for Moll Davies' house.

Moll was surprised to see her so soon.

"I made these for you," said Nell; "and I thought I would bring them to you while they were fresh."

"They look good indeed," said Moll.

"Try one," suggested Nell.

Moll did so, flourishing her diamond under Nell's eye. Nell's gaze dwelt on it enviously, so it seemed to Moll.

"It's beautiful," said Nell simply.

"It is indeed! Every time it catches my eye it reminds me of His Majesty's devotion."

"You are indeed fortunate to have that outward symbol of the King's devotion. Do try another of these fondants."

Moll tried another.

"How clever to be able to make such delicious things! I was never brought up to be so useful."

"Nay," said Nell with a high laugh. "You were brought up to wear a diamond ring and play high-class whore to a merry King."

Nell went into peals of laughter which made Moll frown. Moll had never been sure of Nell since the impudent girl from Cole-yard had imitated her on the stage of the King's Theater.

"I laugh too readily," said Nell, subdued. "It was a habit I learned in the Cole-yard. I would I were a lady like yourself. Pray have another."

"You are not eating any."

"I ate my fill in my own house. These are a present for you. Ah, you are thinking, why should I bring you presents and what do I want in exchange? I see the thoughts in your eyes, Moll. 'Tis true. I do want something. I want to learn to be a lady such as you are." Nell held out the box in which she had put the sweets, and Moll took yet another.

"You know well what flavors appeal to my palate," said Moll.

"I'll confess it," said Nell. "I study you. I would ape you, you see. I would discover why it is His Majesty visits you when he might visit little Nell from the Cole-yard."

"Nell, you are too low in your tastes. You laugh too much. You speak with the tongue of the streets. You do not try to be a lady."

" 'Tis true," said Nell. "Pray have another."

"I declare I grow greedy."

" 'Tis a pleasure to please you with my sweetmeats."

Moll said: "You are good at heart, Nell. Listen to me. I will tell you how to speak more like a lady. I will show you how to walk as a lady walks, how to treat those who are your inferiors."

"I pray you do," said Nell.

And Moll showed her, eating the sweetmeats Nell had brought as she did so. When she had finished she had cleared the whole dish.

Nell rose to go. "You have preparations to make for His Majesty," she said. "I must detain you no longer. Pray keep the dish. When you look at it you will think of me."

Nell went out to her chair which was waiting for her.

"Hurry back," she said to her professional carriers whom she hired by the week. "I have certain preparations to make."

And when she reached her own house she went into the room where the baby was sleeping.

She picked him up and, kissing him fiercely, cried: "We must prepare for Papa. He will be coming here this night, I doubt not. And, who knows, when he is here I may be able to wheedle a nice little title from him for my Charley boy."

Then she laid him gently in his cradle.

There was no time to lose. She called her cook and bade him prepare pies of meat and fowl, to set beef and mutton roasting.

"I have a fancy," she said, "that His Majesty will be supping here this day."

Then she put on a gown of green and gold lace with slippers of cloth of silver.

She was ready; she knew that the King would come. Moll Davies would be unable to entertain him that night, for the sweets with which she had supplied her unsuspecting rival had been filled with jalap made from the root of a Mexican plant.

Moll had taken a good dose. Nell had little doubt that ere this day was out the King and she would be laughing heartily over Moll's predicament.

"It may be," said Nell aloud, "that Mrs. Moll will realize this night that there is something to be learned from my Cole-yard ways."

She was not disappointed. The King joined her for supper. He had discovered what had happened to Moll, and he had had a shrewd notion who had played the trick on her.

He could not contain his mirth as he and Nell sat over supper.

"You are the wildest creature I ever knew," he told her.

And she saw that he liked well that wildness, and was beginning to feel that, whoever came into his life, he must keep Nelly there to make him laugh and forget his troubles.

❁ ❁ ❁

It seemed to the King that, during that difficult year, Nell was his main refuge from his burdens. He was still pursuing Louise de Kéroualle who, although she was maid of honor to the Queen and had her apartments in Whitehall, still expressed her horror at the thought of becoming his mistress.

"How could that be?" she asked. "There is only one way in which Your Majesty could become my lover, and that way is closed. Your Majesty has a Queen."

In vain did Charles point out the irksomeness of royal lives. Queens were not to be envied. Look at his own Queen Catherine. Did she seem to be a happy woman? Yet look at merry little Nell. Was there a happier soul in London?

Louise appeared to be puzzled. It was a trick of hers when she wished to appear vague.

"I must work harder at learning to understand the English," she would say in her lisping voice which matched her baby face.

The King gave her more beautiful tapestries to hang in her apartments; he gave her jewels and some of his most treasured clocks. Still she could only shake her head, open her little eyes as wide as possible, and say: "If I were not the daughter of such a noble house, why then it would be easier for me to be as these others. Your Majesty, it would seem there is only one way open to me. I should go to a convent and there pass my days."

Charles was torn between exasperation and desire. He could not endure his lack of success. It was Frances Stuart's inaccessibility which had made her doubly attractive. Louise realized this, and played her waiting game.

It was many months since she had come to England. The King of France sent impatient messages. Daily the French ambassador warned her.

The Seigneur de Saint Evremond—who was a political exile from France and residing in England where, on account of his wit and literary qualities, Charles had granted him a pension—was eager to see his countrywoman an influence in the land of their adoption. He wrote to Louise—He had heard the rumor that she had declared her intention of entering a convent, so he wrote of the wretched life of nuns, shut off from the world's pleasures, with nothing to sustain them but their religious devotions.

"A melancholy life this, dear sister, to be obliged for custom's sake to mourn a sin one has not committed, at the very time one begins to have a desire to commit it.

"How happy is the woman who knows how to behave herself discreetly without checking her inclination! For, as 'tis scandalous to love beyond moderation, so 'tis a mortification for a woman to pass her life without one *amour.* Do not too severely reject temptations, which in this country offer themselves with more modesty than is required, even in a virgin, to hearken to them. Yield, therefore, to the sweets of temptation, instead of consulting your pride."

Louise read the advice with her childish smile, and her shrewd brain worked fast. She would surrender at the right moment, and that moment would be one which would bring great profit to herself and to France.

❁ ❁ ❁

The Duke of Monmouth, having been reprimanded by the King for the part he had played in the Coventry affair, was inclined to sulk.

"But, Father," he said, "I sought but to defend your honor. Should a subject stand aside and see slights thrown at his King's honor?"

"Mine has had so many aimed at it that it has developed an impenetrable shell, my son. In future, I pray you, leave its defense to me."

"I like not to see your royalty besmirched."

"Oh, Jemmy, 'tis so tarnished that a little more is scarce noticeable."

"But that these oafs should dare condemn you . . ."

"Coventry's no oaf. He's a country gentleman."

Monmouth laughed. "He'll carry a mark on his face all the days of his life to remind him to mend his manners."

"Nay, to remind us that we should mend ours," said the King seriously. "But have done with these wild adventures, Jemmy. I frown on them. Now let us talk of other matters. How would you like to come with me to Newmarket? You and I will race together and see who shall win."

Monmouth's sullen smile was replaced by one of pleasure. He was quite charming when he smiled. He brought such a vivid reminder of his mother's beauty that Charles could believe he was young again.

Jemmy was eager to go to Newmarket. Not that he cared so much for the racing, or for his father's company. What meant so much to Jemmy was that he should be seen at his father's side. He liked to observe the significant looks of courtiers, to hear the cries of the people. "See, there is the Duke of Monmouth, the King's natural son! They say His Majesty is so fond of the boy—and can you doubt it, seeing them thus together?—that he will make him his heir." Jemmy fancied that many people would be pleased to see this done. And why not? Did he not look every inch a prince? And was he not a Protestant, and were not the rumors growing daily concerning the King's brother's conversion to the Catholic Faith? Monmouth and his friends would see to it that there was no lack of such rumors.

Contemplating the trip to Newmarket, he was in high spirits. The King doted on him. There was nothing he could not do and still keep Charles' favor. And everyone would know it. More and more people would rally to his support. They would say he was the natural heir to the throne. All would know that, in spite of the affair of Sir John Coventry, he had lost none of his favor with the King.

He called to Albemarle and Somerset: "Come," he said, "let us go out into the town. I have a desire to make good sport."

Albemarle was eager to accompany his friend. He, with others, marveled at the King's softness towards Monmouth. The affair of Sir John Coventry was a serious one, yet the King had made as light of it as possible—because of who was involved. Albemarle was certain that his friendship with such an influential young man could bring him much good. Somerset shared Albemarle's ideas.

It was fun to roam through the city at dusk, to see what they could find and make good sport with. What excitement to come upon some pompous worthy being carried in his chair, turning it over, and rolling the occupant in the filth of the street! There might be a young girl out late at night, and if a young girl wandered late at night what more could she be expecting than the attentions of such as Monmouth and his friends?

They made their way to one of the taverns, where they dined. They sat about drinking, keeping their eyes open for any personable young woman who came their way. The innkeeper had taken the precaution of locking his wife and daughters away out of sight, and was hoping with all his heart that the dissolute Duke had not heard that these had a reputation for beauty.

Monmouth had not, so he contented himself with the innkeeper's wine and, when they staggered into the street, he and his friends were so befuddled that they lurched and leaned against the wall for support.

It was when they were in this condition that they saw an elderly man and a girl approaching them.

"Come," cried Monmouth drunkenly, "here's sport."

The girl was little more than a child and, as the three drunken men barred the way, she clutched at her grandfather in terror.

"Come along, my pretty," hiccupped Monmouth. "You are but a child, but 'tis time, I'll swear, you left your childhood behind you. Unless you already have . . ."

The old man, recognizing the men as courtiers by their fine clothes and manner of speaking, cried out in terror: "Kind sirs, let me and my granddaughter go our way. We are poor and humble folk . . . my granddaughter is but ten years old."

" 'Tis old enough!" cried Monmouth, and laid his hands on the child.

Her screams filled the street; and a voice called: "What goes on there? Who calls?"

"Help!" screamed the child. "Robbers! Murderers!"

"Hold there! Hold there, I say!" called the voice.

The three Dukes turned and looked; coming towards them was an old ward beadle, his lanthorn held high. He was so old that he could scarcely hobble.

"Here comes the gallant knight!" laughed Monmouth. "I declare, I tremble in my shoes."

The little girl had seized her grandfather's hand, and they hurried away.

The drunken Dukes did not notice they had gone, for their attention was now centered on the ward beadle.

"My lord," said the man, "I must prevail upon you to keep the peace."

"On what authority?" demanded Monmouth.

"In the name of the King."

That amused Monmouth. "Do you know, fellow, to whom you speak?"

"A noble lord. A gallant gentleman. I implore you, sir, to go quietly to your lodging and there rest until you have recovered from the effects of your liquor."

"Know you," said Monmouth, "that I am the King's son?"

"Nevertheless, sir, I must implore you . . ."

Monmouth was suddenly angry. He struck the man across the face.

"Down on your knees, sir, when you address the King's son."

"My lord," began the old man, "I am a watchman, whose duty it is to keep the peace . . ."

"Down on your knees when you speak to the King's son!" cried Albemarle.

"Kneel . . ." cried Somerset. "Kneel there on the cobbles, you dog, and ask pardon most humbly because you have dared insult the noble Duke."

The old man, remembering the recent outrage on Sir John Coventry, was seized with trembling. He held out a hand appealingly, and laid it on Monmouth's coat. The Duke struck it off, and Albemarle and Somerset forced the man down to his knees.

"Now," cried Monmouth, "what say you, old fellow?"

"I say, sir, that I but do my duty . . ."

Somerset kicked the old man, who let out a shriek of agony. Albemarle kicked him again.

"He is not contrite," said Monmouth. "He would treat us as dogs."

He administered a kick to the old man's face.

Monmouth's drunken rage was increasing; he had forgotten the girl and her grandfather, his first quarries. His one thought now was to teach the old man that he must pay proper respect to the King's son. Monmouth suspected all, who did not immediately pay him abject homage, to be sneering at him because of his illegitimacy. He needed twice as much homage as the King himself, because he needed to remind people of that in him which, in the King, they took for granted.

The watchman, sensing the murderous indifference to his plight in Monmouth's attitude, forced himself to get to his knees.

"My lord," he said, "I beseech you do nothing that would ill reflect upon your character and good nature . . ."

But Monmouth was very drunk; and he was obsessed with the idea that his royalty had been slighted.

He kicked the man with such ferocity that the poor watchman lay prone on the cobbles.

"Come!" screeched Monmouth. "Let us show this fellow what happens to those who would insult the King's son."

Albemarle and Somerset followed his lead. They fell upon the old man, kicking and beating him. The blood was now running from the watchman's mouth; he had put up his hands to protect his face. He cried piteously for mercy. But still they continued to inflict their murderous rage upon him.

Then suddenly the man lay still, and there was that in his attitude which somewhat sobered the three Dukes.

"Come," said Albemarle, "let us go from here."

"And be quick about it," added Somerset.

The three of them staggered away; but not before many, watching from behind shutters, had recognized them.

Before daybreak the news spread through the town.

Old watchman, Peter Virmill, had been murdered by the Dukes of Monmouth, Albemarle, and Somerset.

❁ ❁ ❁

Charles was worried indeed. People were saying that there was no safety in the streets. A poor old ward beadle murdered, and for keeping the peace!

All were watchful. What would happen now? My lord Albemarle who had recently inherited a great title, my lord Somerset who was a member of a noble house, and my lord Monmouth, son of the King himself, were all guilty of murder. For, said the citizens of London, the murder of a poor watchman was as much murder as that of the highest in the land.

The King sent for his son. He was cooler towards him than he had ever been before.

"Why do you do these things?" he asked.

"The man interfered with our pleasure."

"And your pleasure was . . . breaking the peace?"

" 'Twas a young slut and her grandfather. Had they come quietly all would have been well."

"You are a handsome young man, James," said the King. "Can you not find willing ladies?"

"She would have been willing enough once we had settled the old grandfather."

"So rape was your business?" said Charles.

" 'Twas but for the sport," growled Monmouth.

"I am not a man who is easily shocked," said the King, "but rape has always seemed to me a most disgusting crime. Moreover it exposes a man as a mightily unattractive person."

"How so?"

"Since it was necessary to make a victim of the girl instead of a partner."

"These people were insolent to me."

"James, you too readily see insult. Take care. Men will say, since he looks for insults, does he know that he deserves them?"

Monmouth was silent. His father had never been so cold to him.

"You know the penalty for murder," said Charles.

"I am your son."

"There are some who call me a fool for accepting you as that," said Charles brutally.

Monmouth winced. Charles knew where to touch him in his most vulnerable spot. "But . . . there is no doubt."

Charles laughed. "There is the greatest doubt. Knowing what I now know of your mother, I myself have doubts."

"But . . . Father, you have made me believe that you never had these doubts."

Charles stroked the lace on his cuff. "I had expected you to have your mistresses. That is how I would expect a son of mine to act. But to behave thus towards helpless people, to show such criminal arrogance to those who are not in a position to retaliate . . . these things I understand not at all. I am a man of much frailty, I know. But that which I see in you is so alien to my nature that I have come to believe that you cannot be my son after all."

The beautiful dark eyes were wide with horror.

"Father!" cried the Duke. "It is not true. I am your son. Look at me. Can you not see yourself in me?"

"You, such a handsome fellow—I, such an ugly one!" said the King lightly. "Yet never did I have to resort to rape. A little wooing was enough on my part. I think you cannot be a Stuart after all. I shall have you taken away now. I have no more to say to you."

"Father, you mean . . . You cannot mean . . ."

"You have committed a crime, James. A great crime."

"But . . . as your son . . ."

"You remember I have my doubts of that."

The Duke's face was twisted with his misery. Charles did not look. He was soft and foolish where this young man was concerned. He had made too much of him, spoiled him, petted him.

For Jemmy's own sake, he must try to instill some discipline into that turbulent proud nature which lacked the balanced good sense to understand the temper of the people he so fervently hoped to rule.

"Go to your apartments now," he said.

"Father, I will stay with you. I will make you say you know I am your son."

"It is an order, my lord Duke," said Charles sternly.

Monmouth stood uncertainly for a moment, a pretty petulant boy; then he strode towards Charles and took his hand. Charles' was limp, and the melancholy eyes were staring out of the window.

"Papa," said Monmouth, "Jemmy is here . . ."

It was the old cry of childhood which had amused Charles in the days long ago when he had come to see Lucy, this boy's mother, and the boy, fearing he was not receiving his due of the King's attention, had sought to draw it to himself.

Charles stood still as a statue.

"To your apartments," he said crisply. "There you will stay until you hear what is to be done."

Charles withdrew his hand and walked away.

Monmouth could do nothing but leave the apartment.

When he had gone, Charles continued to stare out of the window. He looked down at the river, beyond the low wall with its semicircular bastions. He did not see the shipping which sailed past. What to be done? How to extricate the foolish boy from the results of this mad prank? Did he not know that it was acts such as this which set thrones tottering?

There would be murmuring among the people. The Coventry scandal had not died down.

If he were strong, those three would suffer the just punishment of murderers. But how could he be strong where his warmest feelings were concerned?

He had to take a bold step. But he would do it to save that boy. There was very little he would not do for the boy. He must at all costs resist the temptation to give him what he so earnestly desired—the Crown. That he would not do—love him as he did, he would see him hanged first. Jemmy had to learn his lesson; he had to learn to be humble. Poor Jemmy, was it because he feared he was too humble that he strutted as he did? Had he been a legitimate son . . . then what a different boy he might have been. Had he been brought up with the express purpose of wearing the Crown, as he, Charles, had been, there would have been no need for him to make sure that everyone recognized him as the King's son.

I make excuses for him—not because he deserves them; but because I love him, thought Charles. A bad habit.

Then he did what he knew he must do. It was weakness, but how could he, a loving father, do aught else?

He issued a pardon "Unto our dear son James, Duke of Monmouth, of all murders, homicides, and felonies whatsoever at any time before the 28th day of February last past, committed either by himself alone or together with any other person or persons . . ."

There! It was done.

But in future Jemmy must mend his ways.

❁ ❁ ❁

While the King was brooding on the wildness of Monmouth, news came to him that his brother's wife, Anne Hyde, had been taken ill. She was so sick, came the message, and in such agony that none of the physicians could do aught for her.

Charles went with all haste to his brother's apartments. He found James distracted with grief; he was sitting, his face buried in his hands; Anne and Mary were standing bewildered on either side of him.

"James, what terrible news is this?" asked the King.

James dropped his hands, lifted his face to his brother's, and shook his head with the utmost sadness.

"I fear," he began, "I greatly fear . . ."

He choked on his sobs and, seeing their beloved father thus, the two little girls burst into loud wailing.

Charles went through to the bedchamber where Anne Hyde was lying, her face so distorted with pain that she was scarcely recognizable.

Charles knelt by her bed and took her hand.

Her lips twisted in a smile. "Your Majesty . . ." she began.

"Do not speak," said Charles tenderly. "I see that it is an effort."

She gripped his hand firmly. "My . . . my good friend," she muttered. "Good friend first . . . King second."

"Anne, my dear Anne," said Charles. "It grieves me to see you thus." He turned to the physicians who stood by the bed. "Has all been done?"

"All, Your Majesty. The pains came so suddenly that we fear it is an internal inflammation. We have tried all remedies. We have bled Her Grace . . . We have purged her. We have applied plasters to the afflicted part, and hot irons to her head. We have tried every drug. The pain persists."

James had come to stand by the bedside. The little girls were with him, Mary holding his hand, Anne clinging to his coat. Tears flowed from James' eyes, for Anne was half-fainting in her agony, and it was clear to all in that chamber that her life was ebbing away.

James was thinking of all his infidelities which had occurred during their married life. Anne herself had not always been a faithful wife. James thought bitterly of his repudiation of her in the early days of their marriage, and he wondered if his weakness at that time was responsible for the rift between them.

He could have wished theirs had been a more satisfactory marriage. Mayhap, he thought, had I been different, stronger when my mother was against us, if I had stood out, if I had been more courageous, Anne would not have lost her respect for me and mayhap we should have been happier together.

One could not go back. Anne was dying, and their married life was over. He wondered what he would do without her, for always during their life together he had respected her intelligence and relied on her advice.

There were his two little girls who needed a mother's care. If the King did not get a legitimate child, the elder of those little girls could inherit the throne.

"Anne . . ." he murmured brokenly.

But Anne was looking at Charles; it was from the King's presence that she seemed to gain comfort. She was remembering, of course, that he had always been her friend.

"Charles . . ." she murmured, "the children."

Then Charles bade the little girls come to him and, kneeling, he placed an arm about each of them.

"Have no fear, Anne," he said. "I shall care for these two as though they were my own."

That satisfied her. She nodded and closed her eyes.

James, weeping bitterly, flung himself on his knees. "Anne," he said. "Anne . . . I am praying for you. You must get well . . . you must . . ."

She did not seem to hear him.

Poor James! thought Charles. Now he loves his wife. She has but an hour to live and he finds he loves her, though for so long he has been indifferent towards her. Poor ineffectual James! It was ever thus.

Charles said: "Let her chaplain be brought to her bedside."

He could tell by her stertorous breathing that the end was near.

The chaplain came and knelt by the bed, but the Duchess looked at him and shook her head.

"My lady . . ." began the man.

James said: "The Duchess does not wish you to pray for her."

There were significant glances between all those who had come in to witness the death of the Duchess of York.

Anne half raised herself and said on a note of anxiety: "I want him not. I die . . . in the true religion . . ."

James hesitated. Charles met his eyes. The words which James was about to utter died on his lips. There was a warning in Charles' eyes. Not here . . . not before so many witnesses. He turned to the bed. Anne was lying back on her pillows, her eyes tightly shut.

"It is too late," said the King. "She will not regain consciousness."

He was right. Within a few minutes the Duchess was dead.

But there were many in that room of death to note her last words and to tell each other that when she died the Duchess was on the point of changing her religion. It seemed clear that, if the Duke was not openly a Catholic, he was secretly so.

Monmouth must lie low for a while. He must curb his wild roistering in the streets; but that did not prevent him from spreading the rumor that the Duke—heir presumptive to the throne—was indeed a Catholic. Had not the English, since the reign of Bloody Mary, sworn they would not have a Catholic monarch on the throne?

❁ ❁ ❁

Nell was now enjoying every minute of her existence. She had indeed become a fine lady.

She had eight servants in the house in Pall Mall, and from "maid's help," at one shilling a week, to her lordly steward, they all adored her. The relationship between them was not the usual one of mistress and servants. Nell showed them quite clearly that she was ever ready to crack a joke with them; never for one instant did she attempt to hide the fact that she had come from a lowlier station than most of them.

She liked to ride out in her Sedan chair, calling to her friends; and to courtiers and humble townsfolk alike her greeting was the same. She would call to the beggar on the corner of the street who could depend on generous alms from Mrs. Nelly, and chat as roguishly with the King from the wall of her garden. Nor would she care who his companions were. They might be members of his government or his church, and she would cry: "A merry good day to you, Charles. I trust I shall have the pleasure of your company this night!" If those who accompanied the King were shocked by her levity, he seemed all the more amused; and it was as though he and Nell had a secret joke against his pompous companions.

Nell entertained often. She kept a goodly table. And there was nothing she liked better than to see her long table loaded with good things to eat—mutton, beef, pies of all description, every fruit that was in season, cheesecakes and tarts, and plenty to drink. And about that table, she liked to see many faces; she liked every one of the chairs to be occupied.

Nell had only one worry during that year, and that was the King's failure to give her son the title she craved for him. But she did not despair. Charles was visiting her more frequently than ever. Moll Davies rarely saw him now, and it was not necessary to administer jalap in sweetmeats to turn the King from her company to that of Nell. He came willingly. Her house was the first he wished to visit.

Louise was still tormenting him and refusing to give way. Many shook their heads over Louise. She will hold out too long, it was whispered. Mayhap when she decides to bestow herself the King will be no longer eager.

Barbara Castlemaine, now Duchess of Cleveland, was growing of less and less importance to the King. Her *amours* were still the talk of the town, partly because they were conducted in Barbara's inimitable way. When Barbara had a new lover she made no attempt to hide the fact from the world.

That year her lustful eyes were turned on William Wycherley, whose first play, *Love in a Wood,* had just been produced.

Barbara had selected him for her lover in her usual way.

Encountering him when he was walking in the park and she was driving past in her coach, she had put her head out of the window and shouted: "You, William Wycherley, are the son of a whore."

Then she drove on.

Wycherley was immensely flattered because he knew, as did all who heard it, that she was reminding him of the song in his play which declared that all wits were the children of whores.

It was not long before all London knew that Wycherley had become her lover.

So with Barbara behaving so scandalously, and Louise behaving so primly, and Moll ceasing to attract, Nell for a few months reigned supreme.

Rose was a frequent visitor. She was now married to John Cassels, and when this man found himself in trouble Nell managed to extricate him, and not only do this but obtain for him a commission in the Duke of Monmouth's Guards, so that instead of having a highwayman for a husband Rose had a soldier of rank. Nell had also found *it* possible to bring her cousin, Will Cholmley, his heart's desire. Will Cholmley was now a soldier, and she hoped that ere long there would be a commission for him.

Rose came to her one day, and they talked of the old days.

Rose said: "We owe our good fortune to you, Nell. It is like you, Madam Gwyn of Pall Mall, the King's playmate and the friend of Dukes, not to forget those you loved in the old days. We have all done well through you. I'll warrant Ma wishes she had used the stick less on you, Nell. Little did she think to what you would come."

"How fares she?" asked Nell.

"She will not fare for long."

"The gin?"

"It is as bad as ever. She is more often drunk than sober. I found her lying in the cellar—that old cellar; how long ago it seems!—dead drunk. John says she'll not live long."

"Who cares for her?" asked Nell.

"There are plenty to care for her. She can pay them with the money you send her. But 'tis a foul place, that cellar in Cole-yard. The rats are tame down there. 'Tis not as it was when Ma used it as her bawdy-house."

"She will die there," said Nell. " 'Tis her home. I give her money. That is enough."

" 'Tis all you can do, Nell."

"She needs care," said Nell. "We needed it once. But we did not get it. We were neglected for the gin bottle."

" 'Tis true, Nell."

"Had she been different . . . had she loved the gin less and us more . . ."

Nell paused angrily. " 'Tis no concern of ours . . . if she be ill and dying of gin. What is that to us? What did she do to you, Rose? What would she have done for me? I'll never forget the day the flesh-merchant said you stole his purse. There she stood before you, and there was terror on your face . . . and she pushed you to him. Rose, she cared not for us. She cared for nothing but that you should sell yourself to pay for her gin. What do we owe to such a mother?"

"Nothing," said Rose.

"Then she will die in her cellar, her gin bottle beside her . . . die as she lived. 'Tis a fate worthy of her."

Nell was angry; her cheeks were flushed; she began to recount all the unhappiness and neglect she and Rose had suffered at their mother's hands.

Rose sat listening. She knew Nell.

And as soon as Rose had left, Nell called for her Sedan chair.

"Whither, Madam?" asked the carriers.

"To Cole-yard," said Nell.

That night Nell's mother slept in a handsome bed in her daughter's house in Pall Mall.

"Old bawd that she is," said Nell, "yet she is my mother."

Many were disgusted to discover the bawdy-house keeper installed in her daughter's house; many applauded the courageous action of the daughter, which had brought her there.

Nell snapped her fingers at them all. She cared not, and life was good. She was again pregnant with the King's child.

❁ ❁ ❁

That was a happy summer for Nell. She was with the King at Windsor, and it was a pleasure to see his affection for her little son.

Never, declared Nell, had she known such happiness as she had with her Charles the Third. Charles the First (Charles Hart) had been good to her and taught her to become an actress. Charles the Second (Charles Sackville, Lord Buckhurst) was a regrettable incident in her life, but with Charles the Third (the King) she found contentment. She did not ask for his fidelity. Nell was too much of a realist to ask for the impossible, but she had his affection as few people had; she knew that. She had discovered that she could keep that affection by means of her merry wit and her constant good humor. Charles had been accustomed to women who asked a great deal; Nell asked for little for herself, but the needs of her son were ever in her mind.

The little boy was now called Charles Beauclerk—a name given him by his father as a consolation while he waited for a title. He was called Beauclerk after Henry I, who had received it because he could write while his brothers were illiterate. This Henry I had been the father of a greater number of illegitimate children than any English King before Charles—Charles, of course, had beaten him. It was characteristic of the King to remind the world of this fact in naming Nell's son.

So temporarily Nell had to be content with the name Beauclerk which, while it brought no earldom nor dukedom for which she craved, at least was a royal name and a reminder to the world that Charles accepted Nell's son as his own.

Louise was growing a little anxious. Nell Gwyn was becoming too formidable a rival. It was rather disconcerting that, as in the case of his other mistresses, the King seemed to grow more rather than less affectionate towards Nell. It was incredible that the girl from Cole-yard should have such power to hold the elegant and witty King's attention where fine ladies failed.

Louise began to listen to the warnings of her friends.

Louis Quatorze had work for her to do. He was very impatient with her on account of her delay. Lord Arlington, who had Catholic inclinations and who had made himself her protector, was decidedly worried.

Louise had declared so frequently that she was too virtuous to become the King's mistress that, unless she made a complete *volte face,* she did not see how she could be. Yet she, too, had come to realize that to delay any longer would be dangerous.

"The King is an absolute monarch," she said to Arlington. "Why should he not, if he wishes, have two wives?"

Arlington saw the implication. He approached the King. Mademoiselle de Kéroualle loved His Majesty, said Arlington, and there was only one thing which kept her aloof—her virtue.

The King looked melancholy. "Virtue," he said, "is indeed a formidable barrier to pleasure."

"Mademoiselle de Kéroualle," mourned Arlington, "as a lady of breeding, finds it difficult to fill a part which has been filled by others who lack her social standing. If in her case an exception were made . . ."

"Exception? What means that?" asked the King, alert.

"If her conscience could be soothed . . ."

"I have been led to believe that only marriage could do that."

"A mock marriage, Your Majesty."

"But how is this possible?"

"With Kings all things are possible. What if Your Majesty went through a ceremony with the lady . . . ?"

"But how could such a ceremony be binding?"

"It would serve one useful purpose. It would show a certain respect to the lady. With none of those who pleased you has Your Majesty gone through such a ceremony. It would set Mademoiselle de Kéroualle apart from all others. And, although she cannot be Your Majesty's wife, if she were treated as such her pride would be soothed."

"Come, my lord, I see plans in your mind."

"What if, when Your Majesty is at Newmarket, you called at my place of Euston. What if we had a ceremony there . . . a ceremony which seemed in the outward sense a marriage . . . then, Your Majesty . . ."

The King laughed. "Let it be!" he cried. "Let it be! My dear Arlington, this is a capital idea of yours."

Arlington bowed. It was his greatest pleasure to serve his King, he murmured.

So, when the King set out for Newmarket, he did so with more than his usual pleasure. Racing delighted him. Monmouth, now fully restored to favor, was at his father's side most of the time. They went hawking together, and matched their greyhounds. They rode together against each other, and the King won the Plate although his young son was among the competitors. Charles, at forty-one, had lost little of the attractiveness of his youth. His gray hair was admirably concealed under the luxuriant curls of his periwig; there were more lines on his face, but that was all; he was as agile and graceful as he had ever been.

Every day he was at Euston; often he spent the night there; and all the time he was courting Louise who was growing more and more yielding.

And on one October day Arlington called in a priest who murmured some sort of marriage service over the pair, and after that Louise allowed herself to be put to bed with all the ribald ceremonies in which it was the custom to indulge.

Now Louise was the King's mistress and, in view of her rank and the high value she set upon herself, was being regarded as *maîtresse en titre*—that one, of all the King's ladies, to take first place.

Nell realized that her brief reign was over. There was another who now claimed the King's attention more frequently than she did; and because she was what Louise would call a vulgar play-actress, she knew that the Frenchwoman would do all in her power to turn the King's favor from her.

That December Nell's second son was born. She called him James, after the Duke of York.

As she lay recovering from the exhaustion of childbirth, which, because of her rude health, was slight, Nell determined to hold her place with the King and to fight this new favorite with all the wit, charm, and cockney shrewdness at her disposal.

She did not believe she would fail. Her own love for her Charles the Third strengthened her resolve; moreover she had the future of little Charles and James Beauclerk to think of.

SIX

Nell saw little of the King during the months which followed. He was completely obsessed by Louise, who gave herself the airs of a queen; she had only to imply that the apartments at Whitehall which had been hers before the mock ceremony were now no longer grand enough to house her, to have them remade and redecorated at great expense. With Louise it was possible not only to make love but to talk of literature, art, and science; and this the King found delightful. He realized that for the first time he had a mistress who appealed to him physically and intellectually. Barbara had been outrageously egoistical and her own greed and desires had shadowed her mind to such an extent that it had been impossible to discuss anything with her in an objective manner. Nell had sharp wits and a ready tongue, and there would always be a place for Nell in his life, but what did Nell know of the niceties of living? And Frances Stuart had been a foolish little creature for all her beauty. No! In Louise he had a cultured woman, moreover one who was well versed in the politics of her country, which happened to be at this time of the utmost importance to Charles.

It seemed that Louise had succumbed at exactly the right moment, for Louis Quatorze was about to undertake that war in which, under the terms of the Treaty of Dover, Charles had promised to help him.

Louise had received the French ambassador; she had been informed of the wishes of the King of France; it was for her to ensure that the King of England kept to his bargain. Louise was happy. She was pleased with her progress. She had held out against the King until it would have been dangerous to remain longer aloof. It had taken her some time to realize that her greatest rival could have been the common little play-actress, Nell Gwyn, simply because her aristocratic mind refused to accept the fact that one brought up in Cole-yard could possibly be a rival to herself. But at length she had realized that this play-actress—low as she was—had certain qualities which could be formidable. Her pretty, saucy face was not the most formidable of her weapons. Had Nell Gwyn received even the rudiments of education it might have been hopeless to do battle with her. As it was she must be treated with respect.

French soldiers were now crossing the Rhine and marching into Holland. The gallant Dutch, taken off their guard, were for a short time stunned—but only for a short time. They rose with great courage against the aggressors. In fury those men, the brothers De Witt who had advocated a policy of appeasement, were torn to pieces by the mob in the streets of The Hague. Dutchmen were calling on William of Orange to lead them against their enemies, declaring they would die in the last ditch. They were ready to open the dykes, an action which had the desired effect on the invaders by showing the French that no easy victory would be theirs when they came against Dutchmen.

Louise, in the King's confidence, assured him of the advisability of carrying out his obligations under the treaty. Charles had no intention of not carrying out this particular clause. He too badly needed the French gold which had been coming into his exchequer to offend Louis so flagrantly. Therefore Charles decided to send an expeditionary force of 6,000 men to aid the French.

Monmouth came to the King and asked if he might speak to him alone. Louise was with Charles, and Duke and King's mistress eyed each other with some suspicion. Each of them, favored by the King, was jealous of Charles' regard for the other. As yet they were unsure of the other's power. There was one great cause for dissension between them. Louise was Catholic, Monmouth Protestant. Monmouth knew—not that he had realized this himself, but those such as Buckingham whose interest it was to persuade the King to legitimize him had told him this—that Louise was an ambitious woman whose hopes went beyond becoming the King's mistress. Therefore she was dangerous. Monmouth did not believe for a moment that Charles would divorce Queen Catherine; but if the Queen died and Louise was able to fascinate the King enough, who knew what might happen? Louise was already pregnant, and she was delighted that this should be so. If she proved that she could give the King sons, as she was a lady of nobility there was a possibility that Charles might marry her. The thought that that child she now carried might one day take all that Monmouth so passionately longed for was unbearable to him.

Louise saw the King's natural son as an upstart. Monmouth's mother had been of little more consequence than the play-actress of whom the King was so fond. Little Charles Beauclerk had as much right to hope for the crown as this other bastard.

"You may speak as though to me alone," said the King.

Monmouth glared at Louise who, proud of her breeding, was clever enough to know that the King was so enchanted with her because he could be sure of decorous handling of any situation. Louise was determined to impress upon Charles that her manners were impeccable.

Now she inclined her head graciously and said with quiet dignity: "I see that my lord Duke would have speech with Your Majesty alone."

Charles gave her a grateful look and she was rewarded. She was smiling as she left father and son together. She would in any case very quickly discover what Monmouth had to say.

Monmouth scowled after her.

"Well," said Charles, "having succeeded in dismissing the lady, I pray you tell me what is this secret matter."

"I wish to go to Holland with the Army."

"My son, I doubt not it can be arranged."

"But as the King's son I wish to have a rank worthy of me."

"Oh, Jemmy, your dignity rides ahead of your achievements."

Monmouth's handsome face was flushed with anger. "I am treated as a boy," he protested.

Charles laid his hand on his son's shoulder. "Would you remedy it, Jemmy? Then grow up."

"There is only one post worthy of your son, Sir," he said. "Commander of the Army."

"You may command it, Jemmy. In time . . . in time . . ."

"Now is the time, Father. Wartime is the time to command an army."

" 'Tis true that at such times honors can be won. But disgrace can also be the lot of the commander who fails."

"I should not fail, Father. Always I have longed to lead an army. I beg of you, give me this chance."

He had thrown himself at Charles' feet, had taken his father's hand and was kissing it. The dark eyes with their curling black lashes were appealing. Lucy lived again in those eyes. Charles thought: Why is he not my legitimate son? What a happy state of affairs we should have if he were! Then he would have been trained with a difference; then he would not have been so eager always to maintain his dignity. We would have made a bonny King of Jemmy. Brother James could have continued to worship his graven images in peace, and none would have cared; there would not have been this enmity between them. What an unfortunate father I am! But how much more unfortunate is this pretty boy of mine!

"Get up, Jemmy," he said.

"Your Majesty will grant me this one small request?"

"You underestimate it, Jemmy. 'Tis no small one."

"Father, I swear you will be proud of me. I will lead your armies to victory."

"You know the temper of our enemies. You have seen what fighters these Dutchmen are."

"I know them, Father. They are an enemy worthy of the conquering."

"Jemmy, a commander of a great army must have more care for his men than for himself."

"I know it, and so would I have."

"He must be ready to face all that he asks his men to face."

"So would I face death to win my country's battles . . ."

"And glory for yourself."

Monmouth hesitated for a while and then said grudgingly: "Yes, Sir, and glory for myself."

Charles laughed. "I see new honesty in you, Jemmy, and it pleases me."

"And this I ask you . . . ?"

"I'll think of it, Jemmy. I'll think of it . . ."

"Father, do not put me off with promises such as those you give to others. I am your son."

"There are times when I think it had been better if you had been the son of another of your mother's lovers."

"Nay!" cried Monmouth. "I would rather be dead than own another father."

"You love my crown too much, Jemmy."

" 'Tis yourself, Sir."

"And I had just complimented you on your honesty! Nay, do not look hurt. 'Tis natural to be dazzled by a crown. Do I not know it? I was dazzled all through the years of exile."

"Father, you are turning me from my point. My uncle of York has the Navy. It is only right that I, your son, should have the Army."

"Your uncle is the legitimate son of a King, Jemmy. There is a difference. Moreover he is many years older than you; he is possessed of great experience. He has proved himself to be a great sailor."

"I will prove myself to be a great soldier."

Charles was silent for a while. He had never seen Jemmy so fervently eager. It was a good sign; he at least was asking for some means of proving himself to be worthy of a crown. Previously he had thought mainly of possessing it.

"There is nothing I would like better," said Charles, "than to see you at the head of the Army."

"Then you will . . . ?"

"I will do all that is possible."

Monmouth had to accept that but he was not satisfied. He was fully aware of his father's easy promises.

But Charles had decided that he would do something. He discussed the matter with Louise and she agreed with him that the young Duke should be given some duties. Moreover if he were sent with the Army there was the possibility of his disgracing himself or even being killed. It seemed to Louise an excellent way of getting the troublesome young man out of the kingdom for a while.

Charles sent for Arlington.

"Let the Duke of Monmouth have the *care* of the Army," he said, "though not the command of it. Make him a Commander—in name only. Then we shall see how he shapes as a soldier."

Arlington was very willing. He was eager not to be on bad terms with one so close to the King as the Duke was; he could see that Monmouth could save him a great deal of trouble without taking any of his power and profit from him.

So when the expeditionary force left England, Monmouth was with it.

And Charles, with fatherly devotion, waited to see how the young man would acquit himself.

❁ ❁ ❁

The war continued. It was popular in spite of the fact that press-gangs roamed the streets and, invading the taverns and any place where men might be gathered together, carried off protesting recruits. There came news of the successes achieved by Louis with the aid of Monmouth. Charles was proud to hear that Jemmy was proving himself to be both brave and daring in battle, harrying the enemy with the same abandon with which he had attacked innocent citizens of London.

Several of the Court gallants, considering the victories of Monmouth, planned to take a band of volunteers abroad to join the Duke. Buckingham, restless, always eager to be at that spot where he could enjoy most limelight, begged the King to be allowed to go as Commander-in-Chief.

Charles talked of this with Louise, as he talked of most things.

Louise smiled; she had visions of the Duke, returning to London a conqueror. It seemed as if that other Duke, Monmouth, might do this. Two Protestant Dukes to ride through the streets as conquering heroes! It would not do. Moreover she had a score of long standing to settle with Buckingham.

"Nay," she said. "Send not my lord Buckingham. He is as a weathervane. He turns this way and that, according to the winds that blow. Has it occurred to you, Charles, that the noble Duke is the most unreliable man in your kingdom?"

"Oh, George is a good fellow at heart. Wild he may be at times, and there has been trouble between us, but I have never doubted that George is my friend. We grew up together, shared the same nursery. I have a fondness for George, as I have for brother James."

"He has not Your Majesty's good heart. And forget not, he is a Protestant."

Charles laughed. "As are most of my subjects, and as I am . . . as yet."

"As yet," agreed Louise. "But you will not remain so."

The King was alert. He knew Louise spent occasional hours in the company of the French ambassador and he did not doubt that instructions for Louise would be continually arriving from Louis.

"I shall declare my conversion in my own time," said Charles. "That time is not yet."

"Nay, but mayhap after the war has been satisfactorily concluded. . . ."

"Who shall say when that will be! These Dutch are stubborn fellows. And we were talking of George's desires to lead the volunteers . . ."

"I long for Your Majesty to be a true Catholic in thought and deed."

"You share the desires of my dear brother Louis, which is mayhap not surprising since you are a subject of his."

Louise lowered her eyes and said quickly: "When one loves there is a wish for the loved one to share all things. This applies in particular to something so precious as Faith."

"Faith is one of the most difficult possessions for an honest man to acquire," said the King lightly. "Shall I give George his wish? Shall we turn him into a gallant soldier?"

This was characteristic. Stop this talk of my promise to declare myself a Catholic and you shall have your wish regarding Buckingham. Louise smiled gently.

"If my lord Buckingham left England, Lady Shrewsbury would miss him sorely," she said. "Is it kind to her ladyship to inflict such hardship upon her?"

The King laughed. She had given a witty turn to the discussion and that appealed to him.

He sent for Buckingham.

"You are not to lead the volunteers, George," said Charles, "for we could not bear to break Anna's heart. Therefore we will not deprive her of your company."

Buckingham's face was purple with suppressed anger. Louise was delighted to see him thwarted. It mattered not to her that he did not realize she was the one who had prevented his attaining his desires. Louise enjoyed working in the dark. Her aim was to destroy the man who had slighted her, not merely to enjoy the transient pleasure of snapping her fingers in his face.

❁ ❁ ❁

There came news of the battle of Southwold Bay which, while it proved indecisive, cost much in men's lives. Now the press-gangs were more rapacious, and mothers and wives were terrified when any able-bodied young man ventured into the streets. What was this war? it was asked. The English, sternly Protestant, were fighting Protestant Holland at the side of Catholic France. They were suffering great losses. For what reason? To spread the Catholic Faith across Europe. The King's brother, commanding the Navy, was almost certainly a Catholic. The King's favorite mistress was a Catholic. The King himself was so easygoing that he would adopt any faith if he were asked to do so prettily enough.

There were increasing scandals concerning the Court. That July, Barbara Castlemaine gave birth to a daughter whom she tried to foist on the King, but who everyone was sure was John Churchill's child. In spite of Barbara's importuning him, the King refused to acknowledge the girl.

Louise's son was born the same month. He was called Charles. Louise insisted on the name, although the King mildly protested that this would be his fourth son named Charles, and he feared he might at times be wondering which was which.

"My Charles," said Louise, "will be different from all the others."

She was certain of this, and she was furious when she saw the youngest of the King's Charleses—little Charles Beauclerk—amusing his father with his quaint manners which seemed to belong half to the Court and half to the slums of London.

Louise sighed over her Charles. He would be more handsome, more courtly than any. Only the greatest titles in the land would suit him.

"For I am different," she told Charles. "I am not your mistress. I am your wife, and Queen of England. That is how I see myself."

"As long as no others see it so, that is a happy enough state of affairs," said the King.

"I see no reason why you should not have two wives, Charles. Are you not Defender of the Faith?"

"Defender of the faithless sometimes," said Charles lightly. He was thinking of Barbara, who, since he had refused to acknowledge John Churchill's child, was making demands on behalf of those whom he had already accepted. She wanted her Henry, who was nine years old, raised to the peerage without delay. Earl of Euston, she thought, should be the title for him; then he would be fit to marry my lord Arlington's daughter, a charming little heiress. Charles had reminded her that her eldest was already Earl of Southampton, and young George was Lord George Fitzroy.

"I was never a woman to favor one child more than another," said Barbara virtuously. "And what of poor dear Anne and Charlotte? I must ask you to allow them to bear the royal arms."

Charles was beset on all sides.

Louise was less blatant in her demands than Barbara. But Charles knew that they would be no less insistent. Indeed, Louise's schemes went deeper than those of Barbara ever had. The Queen was ill, and Louise's small squinty eyes were alert.

It was not easy for her to hide her satisfaction as the Queen grew more languid. If the Queen died, Louise would get her little Charles legitimized at once through her marriage with the King. The little Breton girl, for whom it had been so difficult to find a place at the Court of France, would be the Queen of England.

Charles pointed out to Louise that he could not give her honors equal to those of Barbara's, for she was still a subject of the King of France, and therefore not in a position to accept English titles, so Louise lost no time in appealing to Louis. She must become a subject of the King of England, for England was now her home. Louis hesitated for a while. He wondered whether the granting of her request might mean the relinquishing of his spy. Louise assured him through the ambassador that, no matter what nationality she took, her allegiance would always be to her native land.

Louise's hopes were high. She believed she knew how to manage the King. She had shown him that she could bear his sons. She had all the graces which a queen should possess. And the Queen was sick. Once Louis had agreed to her naturalization she would be the possessor of noble titles, and with great titles went wealth. And she would never swerve from the main goal, which was to share the throne with Charles.

One of her minor irritations was the presence at Court of the orange-girl.

She suspected that the King often slipped away from her company to enjoy that of Nell Gwyn. He would declare he was tired, and retire to his apartments; but she knew that he slipped out of the Palace and climbed the garden wall to the house in Pall Mall.

Louise knew that she was often referred to as Squintabella because of the slight cast in her eye, and Weeping Willow because, when she wanted to make some request, she would do so sadly and with tears in her eyes. Both of these names had been given her by the saucy comedienne, who made no secret of the fact that she looked upon herself as Louise's rival. To Nell Squintabella was no different from Moll Davies or Moll Knight or any low wench to be outwitted for the attentions of the King.

She would call to Louise if their carriages passed: "His Majesty is well, I rejoice to say. I never knew him in better form than he was last night."

Louise would pretend not to hear.

All the same, Nell had her anxieties. Barbara's children flaunted their honors; it was said that the King was only waiting for Louise's naturalization to make her a Duchess; and meanwhile Nell remained plain Madam Gwyn with two little boys called Charles and James Beauclerk.

When the King called on her she indignantly asked him why others should find such favor in his sight while two of the most handsome boys in the kingdom were ignored.

Young Charles, now just about two years old, studied his father solemnly, and the older Charles felt uncomfortable under that steady stare.

He lifted the boy in his arms. Little Charles smiled cautiously. He was aware that his mother was angry, and he was not quite sure how he felt towards this man who was the cause of that anger. Little Charles looked forward to his father's visits, but his merry mother, who laughed and jigged and sang for him, was the most wonderful person in his world, and he was not going to love even his fascinating father if he made his mother unhappy.

"Are you not glad to see me, Charles Beauclerk?" asked Charles Stuart. "Have you not a kiss for me?"

Little Charles looked at his mother.

"Tell him," said Nell, "that you are as niggardly with your kisses for him as he is lavish with the honors he showers on others."

"Oh, Nelly, I have to be cautious, you know."

"Your Majesty was ever cautious with Madam Castlemaine, I understand. Those whom you fondly imagine to be your children—though none else does—are greatly honored. Yet for those who are undoubtedly your sons you have nothing but pleas of poverty."

"All in good time," said the harassed King. "I tell you this boy shall have as fine a title as any."

"Such a fine title that it is too fine for the human eye to perceive, I doubt not!"

"This is indeed Nelly in a rage. Fighting for her cub, eh?"

"Aye," said Nelly. "For yours too, my lord King."

"I would have you understand that this is something I cannot do as yet. If you had been of gentle birth . . ."

"Like Prince Perkin's mother?"

Charles could not help smiling at her nickname for Jemmy. He said: "Lucy died long ago, and Jemmy is a young man. There is plenty of time for this little Charles to grow up. Then I think he shall have as grand a title as any of his brothers."

"Should his mother be so obliging as to die then," cried Nell dramatically. "Shall I jump in the river? Shall I run a sword through my body?"

Young Charles, vaguely understanding, set up a wail of misery.

"Hush, hush," soothed the King. "Your mother will not die. She but acts, my son."

But young Charles would not be comforted. Nell snatched him from the King.

"Nay, nay, Charlie," she said, "'twas but a game. Papa was right. There's naught to fret us but this: You are a Prince by your father's elevation, but you have a whore to your mother for your humiliation."

Then she laughed and jigged about the room with him until he was laughing and the King was laughing too.

He was so delighted that he could not resist promising Nell that he would think what he could do for the boy. And he remembered too that her sister Rose suffered from her poverty, and he would grant her the pension of one hundred pounds a year for which Nell had asked him on her behalf.

As for Nell herself, she did him so much good even when she scolded for her son's sake that he would make her a countess, indeed he would.

"A countess," said Nell, her eyes shining. "That would please me mightily. Young Charlie and Jamie, having a King for a father, should indeed have no less than a countess for a mother."

The King wished he had been more discreet, but Nell went on: "I could be Countess of Plymouth. It is a title which someone will have ere long. Why should it not be Nelly? Barbara has done as well."

"All in good time," said the King uneasily.

But Nell was happy. Countess of Plymouth—and that meant honors for her boys. And why not? Indeed why not?

❁ ❁ ❁

Nell did not become Countess of Plymouth. Boldly she had applied for the documents which would have staked her claim to this title, only to be told that these could not be supplied. The King told her that he had but been jesting when he had made the suggestion; he asked her to understand the state of the country. They were engaged in a war which was proving to be more costly than they had expected; the Dutch were determined not to lose their country; not content with opening the dykes and causing the utmost confusion to the invaders, young William of Orange, Stadholder and Captain-General, was a determined young man who seemed to be possessed of military genius.

"Who would have guessed this of that gauche young nephew of mine!"

cried Charles. "Never will I forget his visit to my Court. A little fellow, pale of visage, afraid to dance lest it should make him breathless on account of his weak lungs. He was glum and I had to do something to rouse him, so I had Buckingham ply him with wine, and what do you think he did? Fall into a torpor? Not he! His true character came to the surface then. Before he could be prevented he had smashed the windows of those apartments which housed the maids of honor, so eager was he to get at them. 'Dear nephew,' I said, 'it is customary at my Court to *ask* the ladies' permission first. A dull English custom, you may doubtless think, but nevertheless one which I fear must be respected.' Ah! I might have looked for greater depth in a young man who appeared so prim and whom his cups betrayed as a lecher. Then he was drunk with wine. Now he is drunk with ambition and the desire to save his country. Again we see that this nephew of mine can be a formidable young fellow indeed."

"We talked of Plymouth, not of Orange," Nell reminded him.

"Ah, we talked of Plymouth," agreed the King. "Then let me explain that the war is costly. The people dislike the press-gang and the taxes; both of which are necessary to maintain our Navy. When the people are angry they look for someone on whom to vent their anger. They are asked for taxes, so they say, 'Let the King pay taxes, let him spend less money on his women, and mayhap that will serve to supply the Navy.' Nelly, I can do nothing yet. I swear to you that I shall not forget these sons of ours. I swear I shall not forget you."

"Swearing comes easy to a gentleman," said Nell, "and the King is the first gentleman in his country."

"Nevertheless here is one promise I shall keep. You know my feelings for the boys. 'Twould be impossible not to love them. Nay, Nell, have patience. Come, make me laugh. For with the Dutch on one side and the French on the other and the Parliament at my heels I have need of light relief."

Then Nell softened; for indeed she loved him, and she loved him for what he was, the kindest of men, though a maker of promises he could never keep; and she remembered too the words of my lord Rochester. She must soothe the King.

If she plagued him with her tongue, as Barbara had, she would drive him away. She, the little orange-girl and play-actress, had to be every bit as clever as the *grande dame* from France, who was her most formidable rival.

❁ ❁ ❁

Charles was now very anxious. He did not believe that his subjects would continue to support the war. He knew that he must act. Louis had taken possession of large tracts of Holland and had even set up a Court at Utrecht;

but Charles saw very clearly that, once he had beaten the Dutch, Louis would look for fresh conquests and that he would try to make his pensioner Charles, his slave.

He therefore planned to make a separate peace with Holland, doing all in his power to make them accept terms which would not displease Louis.

William of Orange was, after all, his nephew, and it was wrong, he declared, that there should be strife between them.

He decided to send two emissaries to Holland to sound young William; and he chose Arlington, one of the most able members of the Cabal, and the ebullient Buckingham of whom he still had great hopes. Moreover he wished to compensate poor George for his churlish refusal to allow him to take the troop abroad as its commander-in-chief.

He felt sure that twenty-year-old William would be ready enough to make peace on his terms. He did not ask a great deal; he wanted recognition of England's claim to be saluted by all ships of any other nation; he wanted a subsidy of £200,000 for the cost of the war, he would ask for the control of the ports Sluys, Flushing, and Brill; a subsidy for herring fishing; new arrangements regarding English and Dutch trade in the East Indies; time enough for the English planters in Surinam to sell their effects and retire; and as William was his nephew he would help him to enjoy favorable conditions in his own country.

Buckingham, ever ready to undertake some new venture, was delighted to convey these terms to Orange.

He landed in Holland, the benign peacemaker, and he and Arlington were greeted with expressions of joy by the people, for these two were the Protestant members of the Cabal, and the Dutch had hopes that they were in truth on their side. Monmouth joined them, and all knew that the King's natural son was a staunch Protestant even if only because his uncle, the heir presumptive to the throne, was suspected of Catholicism.

But the Princess-Dowager, Amalia, who was William's grandmother and had always been a power in the land, did not trust the English emissaries, and she made this clear.

Arlington's exuberance was quelled; Monmouth was silent; but Buckingham sought to assure her of their goodwill.

"We are good Hollanders, Your Highness," he told the Princess.

She answered: "We would not ask so much of you, my lord Duke. We would only expect you to be good Englishmen."

"Ah!" cried the irrepressible Buckingham. "We are not only good Englishmen but good Dutchmen. We do not use Holland like a mistress but like a wife."

"Truly," said the Princess, "I think you use Holland just as you do your wife."

Buckingham could say nothing to that; he knew that she had heard that when he brought his mistress, Anna Shrewsbury, to his wife, and that poor wronged lady had protested that there was not room for her and Anna under the same roof, he had replied: "*I* had thought that, Madam. Therefore I have ordered your carriage."

He felt therefore that he could not hope for a quick capitulation by the Princess, so he sought out young William over whom he imagined he would have an easy victory.

He remembered that it was in his apartments that William had become drunk during his stay in London. He remembered how difficult it had been to make the young man drink, for his opinions of wine seemed to be the same as those he had of gambling and the play; but he had managed it, and what fun it had been to see the solemn young Hollander smash the windows to get at the maids of honor! No! He did not foresee any great difficulty with young William.

"I rejoice to see Your Highness is in such good health," cried Buckingham, and went on to tell William that the King of France had seen the terms set out by the King of England and agreed that, as Holland was a conquered country, they were fair indeed. "It is because of your uncle's fondness for his sister who was your mother. His Majesty remembers that he promised his sister to keep an eye upon you. It is for this reason that, even though your country is a conquered one, His Majesty of England will insist that you shall be acclaimed King of Holland."

This young man was quite different from the youth who had tried to storm the dormitory of the maids of honor. His cold face was alight with determination to drive the conquerors from his ravaged country.

He said coolly: "I prefer to remain Stadtholder, a condition which the States have bestowed upon me; and I—and all Dutchmen—do not consider we are a conquered people."

"Your Highness would suffer not at all. You would be proclaimed King and accepted as such by France and England."

"I believe myself bound in conscience and honor not to prefer my interests to my obligations." The two Dutch statesmen who had accompanied him, Beverling and Van Beuning, nodded gravely, and William went on: "The English should be our allies against the French. Our countries are of one religion. What good would England reap were Holland to be made merely a province of France, myself a puppet—as I should certainly be—the French King's puppet? Picture it, my friends. Holland ruled by Louis through me. What is Louis looking for? Conquest. Why, having secured my country he might conceivably turn to yours."

"By God," murmured Buckingham, "there is truth in what His Highness says." The volatile Duke was immediately swayed to the side of the Dutchman. He saw a Catholic menace over England. He wanted to make new terms there and then which would make England and Holland allies against the French.

"But His Highness forgets," said Arlington, "that his country is already conquered."

"We in Holland do not accept that," said William hastily.

"You have called a halt to Louis," said Buckingham, "by flooding your land. But with the winter frosts it may well be laid open."

William said firmly: "You do not know us Dutchmen. We are in great danger, but there is one way never to see our country lost and that is to die in the last dyke."

There was no more to be said to such a fanatical idealist as this young Prince. It was vain to tell him that his ideals were part of his youth. William of Orange believed he had been selected to save his country.

Arlington, Buckingham, and Monmouth joined Louis' encampment at Heeswick. New terms were submitted to Dutch William; again they were rejected.

Then news came that the states of Brandenburg, Lüneburg, and Minster, determined to stem the conquests of Catholic Louis, were about to join William of Orange in his fight against the invaders. Louis, having found the war had brought him little gain at great expense, decided to withdraw, and marched his armies back to Paris, and there was nothing for the English diplomats to do but return to England.

Louise was contented.

Buckingham had failed miserably. He had wasted a great deal of money—the account he put in for his expenses amounted to four thousand seven hundred and fifty-four pounds and a penny—and he had brought nothing but ridicule to his country.

With Arlington he was accused by the people of England of making this disastrous war with the Dutch.

Louise was not the only one in England who had decided to bring about the downfall of the Duke.

❁ ❁ ❁

Charles could at last be proud of Monmouth. Whatever he had done at home, he had acquitted himself well abroad.

Charles liked to hear the account of how his son had fought at Brussels

Gate. Beside him had marched Captain John Churchill, and it had been hard to say which of the two young men—Churchill or Monmouth—had been the braver.

"Only one man could pass at a time," Charles was told by one who had witnessed the action. "We marched, swords in hand, to a barricade of the enemy's. There was Monsieur d'Artagnan with his musqueteers, and very bravely these men carried themselves. Monsieur d'Artagnan did his best to persuade the Duke not to risk his life by attempting to lead his men through that passage, but my lord Duke would have none of his advice. Monsieur d'Artagnan was killed, but the Duke led his men with such bravery and such contempt for death as had rarely been seen. Many will tell Your Majesty that they never saw a braver or more brisk action."

Jemmy came home, marching through the streets of London to Whitehall, and the people came out in their hundreds to see him pass.

He had grown older but no less handsome. There was a flush under his skin which made his eyes seem brighter and more lustrous. The women at the windows threw flowers to Monmouth, and the cry in the streets was: "Brave Jemmy's come marching home."

This was what he wanted. This acclaim. This glory.

And Charles saw with some anxiety that they were very ready to give it to this handsome boy—partly because he was handsome, partly because he was brave, but largely because the Duke of York was a Catholic and they had sworn that never again should a Catholic sit on the throne of England. Jemmy seemed more serious now, and Charles hoped his son might have realized it was better to jettison those dangerous ideas of his.

Jemmy had a new mistress—Eleanor Needham—who obsessed him. He was eager to found two packs of foxhounds at Charlton. His son—named Charles—was born, and the King himself with the Duke of York were godparents.

This was a happier way for a young man to conduct himself, thought the King. And the looks he bestowed on young Monmouth were very affectionate.

❁ ❁ ❁

There were rumors throughout England that the Duke of York was about to remarry, and that the Princess chosen for him was Mary Beatrice, sister of the reigning Duke of Modena. The girl was young—she was fourteen—beautiful, and seemed capable of bearing children. There was one thing against her: She was a Catholic.

This marriage had caused Louise a great deal of anxiety. Since she had left for England, Louis had given her three main tasks. She was to work for an alliance with France against Holland, make Charles give a public profession of the Catholic Faith, and bring about a match between the Duke of York and a Princess of Louis' choice.

Louis' choice was the widow of the Duc de Guise, who was worthy, being Elizabeth d'Orléans before her marriage, second daughter of Gaston, brother of Louis XIII. Louise had stressed to Charles and James the advantage of this match, but she was clever enough to know that she must not work too openly for France.

The Duke of York, in remorse on the death of his wife, had given up his mistress, Arabella Churchill, but he had almost immediately formed an attachment with Catharine Sedley, Sir Charles Sedley's daughter. Catharine was no beauty but, as his brother had said, it was as though James' mistresses were chosen for him by his priest as a penance. But James had perversely decided that although he would forgo beauty in a mistress, he would not in a wife, and that Madame de Guise, no longer young and beautiful, would not suit him. So failing a French wife, Louise was ready to support the choice of Mary Beatrice since she was a Catholic, and a Catholic Duchess of York would certainly be no hindrance to one of her main duties—the bringing about of that open profession of the King's acceptance of the Catholic Faith.

Louise felt therefore that, although she had failed to persuade the King and his brother to take Madame de Guise, she had not altogether displeased the King of France by throwing in her support for the marriage with Mary Beatrice, particularly as there was a great deal of opposition throughout the country to a Catholic alliance for the Duke.

A new wave of anti-Catholic feeling was spreading over England. It was long since fires had burned at Smithfield, but there were people still living who remembered echoes of those days.

"No popery!" shouted the people in the streets.

Louise had as yet failed to obtain any promise from Charles as to when he would declare himself a Catholic. He had, however, abolished certain laws against the Catholics. He wanted toleration in religious matters, he declared. But many of his subjects were demanding to know whether he had forgotten what happened to English sailors who fell into the hands of the Inquisition. Had he forgotten the diabolical plot to blow up the Houses of Parliament in his grandfather's reign? The King, it was said, was too easy-going; and that with his brother a Catholic, and the French mistress at his ear, he was ready to pay any price for peace.

"If the Pope gets his big toe into England," declared Sir John Knight to the Commons, "all his body will follow."

The House of Commons then asked Charles to revoke his Declaration of Indulgence. To this Charles replied that he did not pretend to suspend any laws wherein the properties, rights, or liberties of his subjects were involved, or to alter anything in the doctrine or discipline of the Church of England, but only to take off the penalties inflicted on dissenters.

The Commons' reply was to resolve not to pass the money bill until there was a revocation of the Liberty of Consciences Act.

Then Charles, finding both Houses against him, had no alternative but to give his assent to the Test Act, which required all officers, civil or military, to receive the sacrament according to the rites of the Church of England, and to make a declaration against transubstantiation.

Having done this, he immediately sought out James.

"James," he said, "I fear now you must make a decision. I trust it will be the right one."

" 'Tis this matter of the Test Act?" asked James. "Is that what puts the furrow in your brow, brother?"

"Aye; and if you were possessed of good sense it need be neither in mine nor yours. James, you must take the sacrament according to the rites of the Church of England. You must take the Oath of Supremacy and declare against transubstantiation."

"I could not do that," said James.

"You will have to change your views," said Charles grimly.

"A point of view is something we must have whether we want it or not."

"Wise men keep such matters to themselves."

"Men wise in spiritual matters would never enter a holy place and commit sacrilege."

"James, you take yourself too seriously in some ways—not seriously enough in others. Listen to me, brother. I am past forty. I have not one legitimate child. You are my brother. Your daughters are heiresses to the throne. You are to marry a young girl ere long, and I doubt not she will give you sons. If you want to run your own foolish head into danger, what of their future?"

"No good ever grew out of evil," said James firmly.

"James, have done with good and evil. Ponder on sound sense. You will come to Church with me tomorrow and by my side you will do all that is expected of you."

James shook his head.

"They'll not accept you, James," insisted Charles, "they'll not have a Catholic heir."

"If it is God's will that I lose the throne, then lose it I must. I choose between the approval of the people and that of God."

"The approval of the people is a good thing for a King to have—and even more important for one who hopes to be King. But that is for the future. You have forgotten, my lord High Admiral, that all officers, under the Test Act which I have been forced to bring back, must receive the sacrament according to Church of England rites, make a declaration against transubstantiation, and take the Oath of Supremacy. Come, brother, can you not take me as head of your Church? Or must it be the Pope?"

"I can only do what my conscience bids me."

"James, think of your future."

"I do . . . my future in the life to come."

"The life here on Earth could be a good one for you, James, were you to bring a little good sense to the living of it."

"I would not perjure my soul for a hundred kingdoms."

"And your soul is more important to you than your daughters' future, than the future of the sons you may have with this new wife?"

"Mary and Anne have been brought up as Protestants. You asked for that concession and I gave it."

"My solicitude was for your daughters, James. Has it ever occurred to you that if I die childless, and if you have no sons, one or both of those girls could be Queens of England?"

"It has, of course."

"And you jeopardize their future for a whim!"

"A whim! You call a man's religion a whim?"

Charles sighed wearily. "You could never give up your post as Commander of the Navy. You love the Navy. You have done much to make it what it is this day. You'd never give up that, James."

"So they are demanding that?" said James bitterly.

"It has not been mentioned, but it is implied. Indeed how could it be otherwise? Indeed, James, I fear your enemies are at the bottom of the desire to have this revocation of the Declaration for the Liberty of Consciences."

"Who would take my place?"

"Rupert."

"Rupert! He is no great sailor."

"The people would rather a Protestant leader who knew not how to lead their Navy, than a Catholic one who did. People are as fierce in their religion—one against the other—as they were in our grandfather's day."

"You constantly remind me of our grandfather."

"A great King, James. Remember his word, 'Paris is worth a Mass.' "

James opened his candid eyes very wide. "But that was different, brother. He . . . a Huguenot . . . became a Catholic. He came out of error into truth."

Charles gave his brother his melancholy smile. He knew that he had lost his Lord High Admiral.

❁ ❁ ❁

It was a misty November day when the royal barges sailed down the Thames to meet James and his new bride recently come from Dover. The people crowded the banks of the river to see the meeting between the royal barges and those which were bringing the bridal party to London. There was still a great deal of murmuring about this marriage. A strong body of opinion—set up by Anthony Ashley Cooper, Earl of Shaftesbury—had declared firmly against it. Charles had been petitioned by this party in the Commons to send to Paris at once and stop the Princess from coming to England to consummate her marriage.

"I could not in honor dissolve a marriage which has been solemnly executed," said Charles.

In a fury of indignation the Commons asked the King to appoint a day of fasting, that God might be asked to avert the dangers with which the nation was threatened.

"I could not withhold my permission for you gentlemen to fast as long as you wish," was the King's reply.

It was unfortunate that the anniversary of the Gunpowder Plot should have fallen at this time. When the feeling against Catholicism ran high, the ceremony of burning Guy Fawkes was carried out with greater zest than usual, and that year Guy Fawkes' Day was watched with great anxiety by the King and his brother. They feared that the burning of the effigies of Guy Fawkes, the Pope, and the devil would develop into rioting.

Arlington suggested then, since the King would not prevent the departure of the Princess of Modena from Paris, he might insist that, after his marriage, James and his new bride should retire from the Court and settle some distance from London, where he might enjoy the life of a country gentleman.

"Your suggestions interest me," said the King. "But the first is incompatible with my honor, and the second would be an indignity to my brother."

So Mary Beatrice of Modena had with regret left the shores of France where she had been treated with great kindness by many people in high places.

The young girl was terrified of her new husband. He was forty, and that seemed a great age. She had implored her aunt to marry the Duke of York, instead of her; she would be quite happy, she had declared, to go into a convent; any life would seem better to her than that which included marriage to a man, old enough to be her father, who had a reputation for keeping as many mistresses as his brother.

She was a lovely child; she resembled her mother who had been Laura Martinozzi, a niece of Cardinal Mazarin, and, like all the ladies of that family, noted for her beauty. But to be fourteen and torn from her home to start life in a new country with a man who seemed so old, was a terrifying experience, and she was too young not to show her repugnance.

James was fully aware of what his young bride's feelings might be and was determined to do all in his power to put her at ease.

He was on the shore at Dover to greet her in person, and he was touched when he saw her, for her youth reminded him of his own daughter Mary, who was not much younger than this child who had left her home and all she loved to come to a new country to be his wife. He took her into his arms and embraced her warmly. But Mary Beatrice had taken one horrified look at her husband and burst into tears.

James was not angry; he could only find it in his kindly nature to be sorry for her. He assured her that although he was old and feared he must seem mighty ugly to one so young and fresh and beautiful, she had nought to fear, as it would be his delight to love and honor her all the days of their lives.

He was fervently wishing that he had Charles' easy manner, which he was sure would quickly have put the child at ease.

But James' gaucheries were balanced by his gentle kindness, and he decided that until the child had grown accustomed to his company he would not force himself upon her.

"I would not add to your fears," he soothed her. "I think of my little Mary and Anne."

They set out from Dover, and the bride was glad that her mother and the Prince Rinaldo d'Esté travelled with them. They journeyed by slow stages to Canterbury, Rochester, and Gravesend, and the people came out of their houses to watch. The little girl charmed them so much that they were astonished to think that she might bring evil into their country.

At Gravesend they embarked and sailed to meet the royal barges. When they met these James took his bride to meet the King.

Charles was surrounded by the ladies and gentlemen of the Court. The Queen was there, ready to be tender and kind, remembering her own coming into this land to marry the most fascinating of kings only to discover that he was far from faultless, and to learn that it was impossible to fall out of love with him. Louise was beside the King, less flamboyantly dressed than most, yet seeming to be more richly clad; less heavily jeweled so that each jewel which adorned her person seemed to glow with a special luster. It was this lady whom Mary Beatrice took to be the Queen. Louise held herself like a queen, thought of herself as a queen. She had recently become naturalized and this meant that she had been able to accept the titles and estates with which the King had been pleased to endow her. She had now several resounding titles—Baroness Petersfield, Countess of Fareham and Duchess of Portsmouth. She was a lady of the Queen's bedchamber. She was, in all but name, the Queen of England. Nor did she despair of being entirely so. Her small eyes rested often on the pallid face of the Queen. She hoped the lady would not live long, for indeed what joy could there be in life for one such as Catherine of Braganza who could not adapt herself to her husband's Court? She could surely have no great wish to live. The Queen's death was what Louise ardently desired, for she knew the King would never divorce his wife. Louise had discovered something about Charles. Easygoing as he was, ready to make promises to all, once he made up his mind that he would take a firm stand on some point, he was the most obstinate man in the world. She must be continually grateful for his indulgence, but infatuated as she had managed to keep him, she did not forget that all others had a share in that indulgence—Catherine, the Queen, no less than any other. And if the King's desire was fixed on Louise, his pity went to Catherine his wife.

Mary Beatrice was aware of other ladies and gentlemen. She noticed beautiful Anna Shrewsbury with the Duke of Buckingham, and Lord Rochester, that handsomest of all courtiers, although debauchery was beginning to mar his good looks; and close to him a lively and pretty creature with chestnut curls and bright tawny, mischievous eyes, most flamboyantly dressed, and attracting the attention of everyone. Even the King's eyes strayed often towards her. Her name, it seemed, was Madam Gwyn. There were gentlemen whose names she had heard mentioned with that of the King: Earl of Carbery, Earl of Dorset, Sir George Etherege, Earl of Sheffield, Sir Charles Sedley, Sir Carr Scrope.

Then Mary Beatrice was aware of a pair of dark eyes watching her intently. She fell to her knees and she was raised by the King's elegant hands, and he, looking into her face, saw the too-brilliant eyes which suggested tears, noted the trembling lips.

"Why," he said in that gentlest and most musical of voices, "my little sister. I am mighty glad to see you here. You and I shall be friends."

Mary Beatrice put her hands in his. She did not care that he was the King; she only knew that his words, his smile, his infinite charm made her feel happy and no longer afraid.

The King kept a hold on her hand, and she felt that while he held it thus she could be almost pleased that she had come.

He kept her beside him during the festivities. He implied that he would be her special friend until she felt quite at home in her new country. He told her that she reminded him of her kinswoman, Hortense Mancini—one of the most beautiful women he had ever seen in the whole of his life. He had wanted to marry Hortense, but her uncle had put his foot down. "In those days I was a wandering exile. No good match at all. But I never forgot beautiful Hortense, and you remind me of her . . . with pleasure . . . with the utmost pleasure."

She was beside him as they sailed to Whitehall. She heard the people acclaim him from the banks, and she knew that they all loved him, that they felt that irresistible charm even as she did.

He pointed out his Palace of Whitehall whither they were bound.

She was relieved to stand beside him. Her mother was delighted to see the King's easy affability towards her daughter, delighted to see the lightening of her daughter's spirits.

The courtiers watched them.

"Am I mistaken?" drawled Rochester. "Is it Charles who is bridegroom or is it James?"

"His Majesty but puts the child at ease," said Nell.

"James has tried to do so," said Buckingham, "without success. Alas, poor James! It strikes me that in all things our gracious sovereign could, if he would; and his brother would, if he could."

Louise had strolled towards them. She glanced with some amusement at Nell's brilliantly colored gown.

Nell's eyes smoldered. It was galling to be reminded, every time she saw the woman, that she was now the Duchess of Portsmouth while her young Charles and James were merely surnamed Beauclerk and she was plain Madam Gwyn. The Duchess thought Nell scarcely worthy of notice. Yet she was kindly condescending.

"You are grown rich, it would seem by your dress," she said lightly. "You look fine enough to be a queen."

Nell cried: "You are entirely right, Madam. And I am whore enough to be a duchess."

The Duchess passed on; the laughter of Nell, Buckingham, and Rochester followed her.

Louise's face betrayed nothing. She was thinking that Rochester was a fool, continually banished from Court on account of his scurrilous attacks on all, including the King; his debauchery would soon carry him to the grave; there was no need to think of him. As for the orange-girl, let her remain—buffoon that she was. Moreover, the King delighted in her and would be stubborn if it were suggested she be removed; Nell Gwyn's attack was with words, an art in which Louise could not compete with her. Those quips never rose easily to Louise's lips even in her own language. But there was one who should soon feel the full weight of her displeasure. My lord Buckingham should not have long to flaunt his power if she could help it.

❁ ❁ ❁

The Duke of Monmouth was delighted with the marriage of the Duke of York.

"There is nothing he could have done," he told his cronies, "which could have pleased me more. The people are incensed. And do you blame them? My uncle is a fool if he thinks he can bring popery into England."

He was told that Ross, his old governor, wished to see him; and when Ross was admitted to him it was clear that the fellow had something to say which was for his ear alone.

Monmouth lost no time in taking the man to a place where they could speak privately. Ross was looking at him with that admiration which Monmouth was accustomed to see in many eyes.

"For this moment," said Ross, "I would but ask to look at Your Grace. I remember when you were a little fellow—the brightest, handsomest little fellow that ever came under my charge. It does me good to see Your Grace enjoying such fine health."

Monmouth was indulgent. He loved praise. "Pray continue," he said.

"There is but one thing which irks me concerning Your Grace."

"The bend sinister?" Monmouth prompted.

" 'Tis so. What a King you would make! How those people down there would line the streets and cheer, if only you were James, Prince of Wales, instead of James, Duke of Monmouth."

"Just a ceremony . . . just a signature on a document . . ." muttered Monmouth.

"And for that a country loses the best King it could ever have."

"You did not come merely to tell me this, Ross."

"Nay, my lord. When I watched you on your horse or learning how to use your sword, I used to let myself imagine that one day the King would acknowledge you as his legitimate son. I used to see it all so clearly . . . His Majesty sending for you when you were a year or so older . . . and that came true. His Majesty bearing great love for you . . . and that came true also. His Majesty declaring that in truth he had married your mother and that you would inherit the crown."

"And that did not come true," said Monmouth bitterly.

"It might yet . . . my lord."

"How so?"

"I feel in my heart that there *was* a ceremony between your father and Lucy Walter."

"My father says there was not, and I verily believe that since the Portuguese woman is barren he would most happily acknowledge me as his son if his conscience would let him."

"The consciences of kings often serve expediency . . . saving your royal presence."

"You mean my father would deny a marriage which had taken place. But why so?"

"Why so, my lord? Your mother was . . . again I crave pardon . . . a woman who took many lovers. She was not of state to marry with a king. Your father was young at the time—but eighteen—and young men of eighteen commit their indiscretions. She who was worthy to be a wife to an exiled prince, might not be owned by a reigning king."

"You know something, Ross. You are suggesting that my father was married to my mother."

"I asked Cosin, Bishop of Durham, to give me the marriage lines." Ross smiled slyly. "He could have had them. He was chaplain at the Louvre for those who belonged to the Church of England at the time of the association."

"Ross, you are a good fellow. What says he?"

"He insisted that there were no marriage lines. He asked me indignantly if I were suggesting that he should forge them."

"And . . . now he has promised to produce them?"

"He is dead."

"Then what good is he?"

Ross smiled slowly. "Friends of mine—and yours—are ready to swear that, as he died, he murmured of a black box which contained marriage lines proving that Lucy Walter was the wife of your father."

"Ross, you are the best friend a man ever had . . ."

"I looked on you as my son when I became your governor in the house of my lord Croft. There is nothing I would not do to give you your heart's desire."

"I thank you, Ross; I thank you. But my father lives . . . What will he say of this . . . black box?"

Ross was silent for a while; then he said: "The King, your father, loves you. The country does not want a Catholic King. The Duke of York, in giving up his post as Lord High Admiral, has exposed himself as a Papist. Now there is this marriage. The King loves peace . . . He loves peace more than truth. He loves you. He loves all his children, but everyone knows that his favorite is his eldest son. It may be that he—and I, feeling as a father towards you, understand his feelings—would accept this tale of the black box for love of you and for love of peace."

Monmouth embraced his old governor.

"Man," he said, "you are my good friend. Never shall I forget it."

Ross fell on his knees and kissed the Duke's hands.

"Long live the Prince of Wales!" he said.

Monmouth did not speak; his dark eyes glittered; he could hear the shouts of the people, feel the crown on his head.

❁ ❁ ❁

Rumor was raging through London as fiercely as, a few years before, the fire had raged—and, said some, as dangerously.

The King was married to Lucy Walter. The Bishop of Durham died speaking of a black box . . . a black box which contained the fateful papers, the papers which would one day place the crown on the head of the Protestant Duke of Monmouth.

"But where is the black box?" asked some. "Will it not be necessary to produce it?"

"It is in the interest of many to keep it hidden. The Duke of York's men will swear that it has no existence."

The country was Protestant and so hated the idea of a Catholic King. As for the wildness of young Monmouth, they would be ready to forget that. It was remembered only that he was young, handsome, and had acquitted himself with valor in the wars, that he was a Protestant and son of King Charles.

Monmouth awaited his father's reactions. He could not be sure what went on behind those brooding, cynical, and often melancholy eyes.

He had asked to be formally acknowledged as the head of the Army.

Meeting his uncle, he told him so. James, unable to hide his feelings concerning this nephew of his, knowing of the rumors which were abroad, gruffly told him that he thought he lacked the experience for the post.

"It could not go to you, my lord," said Monmouth with a smile. "You are disqualified under the Test Act. You know that all officers of the military services or civil ones must conform to the rites of the Church of England."

"I know this well," said James. "But your present position gives you as much power as you need."

"I am sorry I have not your friendship and support," Monmouth retorted sullenly.

James flushed hotly. "Indeed you are not sorry."

Then he left his nephew.

Monmouth sent for his servant, Vernon.

"Vernon," he said, "go to the clerks who are drawing up the documents which will proclaim me head of the Army. I have seen how these will be worded. The title of head of the armed forces is to go to The King's *natural son.* Vernon, I want you to tell the clerks that you have had orders to scratch out the word 'natural' if it has been already put in; and if the papers are not completed let it be that the phrase reads: 'The King's son, James, Duke of Monmouth.' "

Monmouth fancied that Vernon's bow was a little more respectful than usual. Vernon believed he was in the presence of the heir to the throne.

❁❁❁

James, Duke of York, was with his brother when the papers were put before the King. James took them from the messenger and looked sadly at them.

Charles was carelessly fond where his emotions were involved. Many believed, though, that Monmouth would do well in the Army. He had the presence, the confidence for it. Moreover his handsome looks and likeness to the King made people fond of him.

He spread the papers out on a table.

"Your signature is wanted here, Charles," he said.

Charles sat down and, as his eyes ran over the papers, the blood rushed into James' head.

He pointed to an erasure. The word "natural" had been removed.

"Brother!" said James, his face stricken. "What means this?"

Charles stared at the paper in astonishment.

"It is so then," said James. "This talk of the black box is no rumor. You admit that a marriage took place between you and Lucy Walter?"

"There is no truth in that rumor," said Charles. He called the man who had brought it to the chamber.

"Who commanded that that word should be erased?" he asked.

"It was Vernon, the Duke of Monmouth's man, Your Majesty."

"I pray you bring me a knife," said Charles, and when it was brought he cut the paper into several pieces.

"It will have to be rewritten," he said. "When that is done, I shall sign the paper giving my *natural* son the command of the Army."

Later that day, when he was surrounded by courtiers, ladies, and men from the Parliament, he said in a loud voice: "There have been rumors afoot of late which displease me. There are some who talk of a mysterious black box. I have never seen such a black box and I do not believe it exists' outside the imagination of some people. What is more important, I have never seen what that box is reputed to contain, and I know—who could know better?—

that these documents never were in existence. The Duke of Monmouth is my very dear son, but he is my natural son. I say here and now that I never married his mother. I would rather see my dear son—my bastard son, Monmouth—hanged at Tyburn than I would give support to the lie which says he is my legitimate son."

There was silence throughout the hall.

Monmouth's face was black with rage. But the King was smiling as he signed for the musicians to begin to play.

❁ ❁ ❁

Louise, walking in the gardens of Whitehall Palace, came upon the newly created Earl of Danby and graciously detained him. She had decided that the two men who could be of most use to her were Danby and Arlington. She had been eager to bring about the disgrace of Buckingham ever since he had humiliated her at Dieppe, but her nature was a cold one and she cared more for consolidating her position at Court and amassing wealth than for revenge.

Danby, it seemed to her, must be her ally if she were to enrich herself as she intended to, for Danby was a wizard with finance and it was into his hands that the King would place the exchequer.

Much as Louise delighted in her title of Duchess, there was one thing that was more important than any English title. It was at the French Court that she had suffered her deep humiliation, and one of her most cherished dreams was that one day she would return there to receive all that respect which had been denied her in the past. She would rather have a *tabouret* at the Court of Versailles, on which she would be permitted to sit in the presence of the Queen, than any English honors. The ducal fief of Aubigny had reverted to the crown on the death of the Duke of Richmond, on whose family it had been bestowed by a King of France as far back as the early part of the fifteenth century. Louise's acquisitive mind had already decided that she must be granted the title of Duchesse d'Aubigny—for with it went the *tabouret*—and she would need Charles' help to plead with Louis for the title; and if the pleas of a man who was rising, as Danby surely would, were added to that of the King, it would be helpful, for Louis would be pleased to grant favors to those who held influential positions at the English Court.

Arlington was ready to turn against Buckingham. Together they had supported the Dutch war, and together they had sought to make peace. The country was saying that both these activities had been conducted with incompetence and inefficiency. Therefore a man such as Arlington, to save himself, would be ready to throw the larger share of blame on his companion in misfortune. Buckingham had already done his best to weaken Arlington's position by trying to persuade the King not to proceed with the proposed marriage between Arlington's girl, Isabella, and Barbara's son, the Duke of Grafton. He had held out a better match as bait—the Percy heiress—and Arlington was furious at Buckingham's attempt to spoil the linking of his family with the royal one.

But Louise felt that Danby was the man who could help her most. He was quiet, a man who would be happy to work in secret, and he had come to his present place by quiet determination, working by devious ways towards his goal. If he lacked altogether the brilliance of Buckingham, he also lacked the Duke's folly which was ready to trip him at every step. As Sir Thomas Osborne, Danby had come to London when he was made member for York. He had first come to notice when he was appointed commissioner for examining public accounts some seven years before. Since then his rise had been rapid. He had been Treasurer of the Navy, Privy Councillor, and, with the reinstatement of the Test Act and the banishment of Clifford, he had become Lord High Treasurer.

Louise believed that he would rise to even greater power. She feared him. He founded his policy, she had heard, on the Protestant interest and thus he was opposed to the French. This meant that she and he must necessarily be in opposite camps. Yet at this point their interests were similar. Buckingham was to blame for the alliance with France and the Dutch war. Buckingham was even suspected of having Catholic interests, for he had received many costly presents from Louis Quatorze, and all knew that Louis did not give his presents for nothing.

Therefore she and Danby, who it would seem must follow diametrically different courses, could meet in one desire: to see the downfall of Buckingham. And Louise, ever fearful that she would fail to mold the King of England in the manner desired by the King of France, was ready to go to great lengths to secure the friendship of men whose animosity could ruin her. Her great dread was that she should be sent back to France without her *tabouret*—back to humiliation and obscurity.

"I trust I see you well, my lord Treasurer," said Louise.

"As I trust I see Your Grace."

Louise took a step nearer to him and lifted her eyes to his face. "You have heard the sad news of your predecessor?"

"My lord Clifford?"

Louise nodded. "He has grieved greatly since he resigned his post in accordance with the Test Act. He died—some say by his own hand."

Danby caught his breath. It was into Clifford's shoes that he had stepped. Was she warning him that a man held a high position one day and was brought low the next? He was bewildered. He could not believe that he could ally himself with the King's Catholic mistress. Was she suggesting this?

She smiled charmingly, and said in her quaint English: "There are disagreements between us, my lord Treasurer, but as we are both near the King, should we allow these to make us the enemies?"

"I should be sad if I thought I were Your Grace's enemy," said Danby.

Louise laid her hand very briefly on his sleeve. It was almost a coquettish gesture. "Then from now on I shall hope that we are friends? Please to call on me when you have the wish."

Danby bowed and Louise passed on.

❁ ❁ ❁

Shaftesbury had been dismissed. Clifford was dead. The Commons declared that the remaining members of the Cabal—Lauderdale, Arlington, and Buckingham—were a triumvirate of iniquity.

The result of the Cabal's administration was an unchristian war with Holland and an imprudent league with France. Protestant England had put herself on the side of Catholic France against a country which, entirely Protestant, should have been an ally. The King had been traitorously ensnared by pernicious practices.

Charles remained aloof. He could not disclose the clauses of the secret Treaty of Dover; he could not come to the rescue of his politicians by explaining that it had been necessary at one time to accept bribes from France in order to save England from bankruptcy. That clause in the treaty, referring to his conversion to Catholicism to be proclaimed at an appropriate moment, meant that it must never be disclosed while he lived.

If he attempted to defend his ministers, he could plunge his country into disaster.

He could only look on with the melancholy smile which came to his lips at times such as these, and await results. He could not regret the replacement of Clifford by Danby; Danby, juggling with figures, was beginning to balance accounts as they never had been balanced before.

So Lauderdale was indicted; Arlington followed; and Buckingham's turn came.

He was called to defend himself, which he did in person and, as ever being unable to control his tongue, answered questions put to him in his jaunty, witty, and fearless way. He spoke long of the misfortunes which had occurred during his administration of the Cabal, but declared that he felt it his duty to remind the assembly that this was not so much due to the administration as to those in authority over it.

He could not resist adding: "I can hunt the hare with a pack of hounds, gentlemen, but not with a brace of lobsters."

As this last epithet was flung at the King and the Duke of York, it was hardly likely that the reckless Buckingham would receive much sympathy in the only quarter from which at this time he could have hoped for it. Yet it was typical of the Duke that he would fling away years of ambition and all his bright hopes for the future for the sake of giving his tongue full play.

The result of this investigation was that Buckingham was dismissed, and the people clamored for peace with Holland. The clever young Prince of Holland asked for the hand of Mary, eldest daughter of the Duke of York, who, should the King and his brother fail to produce further offspring, would one day inherit the crown.

Louise was flung into a panic by this suggestion. She knew that she must exert all her influence with Charles to have it quashed. Louis would consider she had indeed failed in her duty if there was a marriage between Holland and England.

She talked to Charles. He was noncommittal. Easygoing as he always was, he was quick to sense the temper of the people. And the dissatisfaction with the Cabal had given rise to much murmuring among the people who knew that the King was involved, even as were his ministers. Charles wished to please those he favored, but not to the extent of angering his people against him.

Terrified that she would cease to find favor with Charles, picturing Louis' indifference if she returned humiliated to France, Louise turned in panic to Danby. She was ready to do anything—just anything—for a strong man who would help her hold her position at this difficult time.

❁ ❁ ❁

Buckingham's health collapsed rapidly. He suffered, said his doctors, more from fever of the mind than of the body.

Louise, watching, knew that the Duke had too many enemies for her to worry greatly about bringing about his downfall. Moreover she had more immediate troubles of her own.

A few days after he had suffered his ordeal and while he was a very sick man, the guardians of the fifteen-year-old son of Anna Shrewsbury arranged that the boy should bring a charge against Buckingham of the murder of his father and the public debauchery of his mother.

As the death of Shrewsbury had occurred six years before, and almost every man at Court was living in open adultery, this was dearly yet another of his enemies' moves to destroy the Duke.

He was aware that temporarily he was a defeated man, and he obtained absolution from the House of Lords only on paying a heavy fine, and promising never to cohabit with Lady Shrewsbury again.

The greatest of his troubles then was the knowledge that, now he was a defeated man, Anna Shrewsbury was finished with him. She had been faithful to him for many years, and had even been known as the Duchess of Buckingham, while Buckingham's wife had been called the Dowager-Duchess. Their relationship had seemed as though it would go on forever.

Now he knew that she too had deserted him—for had she not done so, nothing would have kept her away from him nor him from her—he was as low as he had ever been. Charles, no doubt finding it impossible to forgive the reckless Duke for referring to him and his brother publicly as lobsters, deprived him of the Mastership of the Horse. There was one waiting to receive it whose handsome looks would well become it: the Duke of Monmouth.

So Buckingham retired from Court. But his exuberant spirits would not let him stay long in exile. Little Lord Shaftesbury (who as Ashley had been a member of the Cabal and was now the leading light of the Opposition and secretly intriguing to legitimize Monmouth) made friendly advances; and Buckingham was already planning his return.

Louise had not betrayed by one glance how delighted she was in the Duke's misfortune.

But Nell knew it—although she knew nothing of politics—and decided that, since Louise was the enemy of the fallen Buckingham, she would be his friend.

SEVEN

Nell was a little sad at the beginning of that year. She had seen the disgrace of my lord Buckingham who had seemed such a brilliant ornament at the Court, and although she never really gave her mind to politics, she knew that even if Louise had not brought this about, she had had a hand in it. She was aware too of the growing friendship between the Lord Treasurer, the Earl of Danby, and Louise. Nell firmly believed that, while these two held their present positions, she would remain Madam Gwyn and never become a countess; and, what was more important, her two little boys would never be anything but Charles and James Beauclerk.

It was true that recently Charles had given her five hundred pounds for new hangings in her house, but even in this there was some cause for sadness. Charles was graciously apologizing for spending so little time with her.

She was not poor, but she realized that, compared with the establishments of Barbara in her heyday and Louise at present, her home was a comparatively humble one. Nell had never learned thrift, and money slipped through her hands. She was over-generous and never refused loans or alms. She had eight servants to feed, as well as her mother, herself, and her two sons. Rose's husband, Captain Cassels, had been killed while fighting with his regiment in Holland, and there was Rose to help along.

She had her own Sedan chair, and of course she must have her French coach; six horses were needed to draw it, and bills came in for oats and hay. She liked to have people around her and was a lavish hostess.

Nell's mother needed medicines from the apothecaries for her constant complaints, and Nell was continually paying for ointments and cordials, plague-water and clysters. The children were in need of sugar candy, pectoral syrup, and plasters. Charles was a healthy little boy; James was almost as healthy; but they suffered from the usual childish ailments and Nell was determined that they were both going to live to hold as great titles as any held by Louise's or Barbara's brats.

Nell had always loved the theater; she attended frequently, and the King's mistress must have one of the best seats. She was a gambler at heart and she enjoyed a flutter either on horses or gamecocks. Mr. Groundes, her steward, remonstrated with her but, as Nell said: "If I cannot pay for my fancies, then must the bills be passed on to Mr. Chaffinch."

She enjoyed riding forth in her coach, stopping at the Exchange to examine the goods for sale, her footman following her ready to carry her purchases. She would only buy the best for Charles and James. "Dukes' skins they were going to be from the start," she would declare.

But as she entertained her friends and was jolted forth in her coach, she was a little sad. It was a long time since the King had visited her, and although when they met he was friendly and always had a smile and joke for Nelly, his nights were spent with the Frenchwoman. It was almost as though he, like Louise, looked on that mock marriage as a true one and felt the need to treat it as such.

Lord Rochester, returned to Court after one of his many exiles from it, shook his head sadly.

" 'Tis a pity," he said, "that His Majesty is so enamored of the Frenchwoman."

"There are times when I think Charles bewitched," said Nell crossly. "When the woman isn't squinting she is weeping, and when she's doing both she's spying for France. What can he find so alluring in a weeping, squinting spy?"

"Novelty in the squint, mayhap, for though he has witnessed tears and spies in plenty, I have never before seen His Majesty enamored of a squint."

When he wandered through the Palace of Whitehall he thought of Nell who so sadly missed the King, and paused outside the door of that chamber occupied by Louise to stick on it one of those couplets for which he was renowned.

"Within this place a bed's appointed
For a French bitch and God's anointed."

Louise was furious, as she always was at any affront to her dignity, and as there was no doubt of the author of the couplet she demanded that Rochester be once more banished from Court.

The King agreed that the noble Lord took liberties, and that he should be dismissed. So Rochester's efforts to attack Nell's enemy gained her nothing and lost her the presence of one who—although in his scurrilous verses he did not spare her—she regarded as her friend.

Moll Davies now had a daughter, but the King's visits to her were rarer than those he paid Nell.

Louise continued to hold the King's attention. Louise was clever and she was cautious. She had made several attempts to turn the King from the suggested Dutch marriage, but she was quick to realize that it would have been unwise to be too insistent. Her strength lay in dignity; she must never rant as Barbara had; she must never be vulgar as Nell was. Moreover she had studied Queen Catherine, and from the appearance of the Queen she judged that she would not live long. If she could take the Queen's place Louise need never fear Louis again. The crown of England was preferable even to a *tabouret* at the Court of Versailles.

Nell Gwyn irritated her, but she would not lower her dignity by showing jealousy of a girl who had sold oranges at the King's Theater.

In spite of the shadow cast by the proposed Dutch marriage, Louise had never been feeling more sure of herself. Then, suddenly, a terrible misfortune befell her.

❁ ❁ ❁

Nell first heard of it through Rochester. Back from exile in the country, where the King never allowed him to stay for long, he called on Nell and, settling himself in one of the elaborate chairs, stretched his legs and smiling at his toes, said: "Nell, His Majesty is sick."

Nell stood up in alarm, but Rochester waved a white hand. "I pray you calm yourself. 'Tis naught but the pox. And he hath taken it lightly. 'Twas some slut brought to him by Chaffinch. The royal body will be submitted to the usual treatment. Rejoice in this, Nell. Out of evil cometh good. Charles has not visited you of late. Rejoice, I say. For although His Majesty hath taken the sickness but slightly, the French bitch hath it far worse. 'Twill be many months before she will share a bed with God's anointed."

Nell laughed aloud, suddenly remembering the jalap she had served to Moll Davies.

"You are sure of this?" she asked.

"I swear it. Our lady Duchess is in a fury. She strides up and down her apartment, wailing in her own language. Now is the time for the lucky Mrs. Nelly to leap into her shoes."

"And Charles?"

"A week or two, the usual course of pills, and all will be well. He was born healthy and, no matter to what he subjects the royal person, it remains healthy. Nelly, the enemy is *hors de combat.* Forget it not! Prepare to reign supreme. I hear that Louis Quatorze has sent her a diamond and pearl necklace—just to keep her spirits up. I heard too that she is to travel to Bath and Tunbridge Wells in the hope of a speedy return to health. Be ready to welcome His Majesty back to good health, sweet Nell. And remember what I tell you. Administer to His Majesty's comfort. Let him see that his merry Nell contributes more to his peace and enjoyment than Madame Squintabella. And then . . . only then . . . remind him of your brats."

"I will remember to remind him," said Nell grimly.

"Do not, dear Nelly, attempt to win the last battle first. 'Tis not the way to victory."

Then began a joyous spring and summer for Nell. She plunged right into the gaiety of the Court. The King was well again—not so Louise; and her frequent visits to Bath and Tunbridge Wells did little to relieve her. Her only consolation was to put on the magnificent necklace sent her by Louis—a reminder that she must get well quickly for there was work for her to do. But Louise knew that, if she failed to hold Charles, Louis would have little use for her. And there was nothing she could do but follow her doctor's advice and long to return to her place at Court.

The Court went to Windsor; and there was merry sport in the green fields. A mock battle was staged to represent the siege of Maestricht. Charles was particularly interested because that was the battle at which Monmouth had excelled.

He doted on that boy, thought Nell. 'Twas a pity he had not equal pleasure in little Charles and James Beauclerk. Not that he did not show the utmost affection towards them; not that it did not delight him to take the little fellows in his arms and lavish caresses on them.

Caresses! thought Nell bitterly. *They* won't make their fortunes.

Her anger against Charles' eldest son spurted out one day.

"Ha," she cried, "here comes Prince Perkin, to show us all how to win battles."

The color flamed in Monmouth's face. "Who are you to speak thus to me?" he asked. "You forget I am the King's son, whereas you . . . you belong to the gutter."

" 'Tis true," said Nell cheerfully. "I and your mother are much of a piece—both whores and both come up from the gutter."

Monmouth passed, cursing the low orange-girl whom his father was besotted enough to honor.

But Nell was not really angry with Monmouth. She found she could not be. She saw in him a resemblance to her own little Charles. They're half-brothers, she thought. She could understand Monmouth's ambitions. Had she not felt the same about her own boys?

Now she began to regard the handsome young man with a maternal eye. Strangely enough he found his arrogance quelled a little. Nell was low—none would deny that; but she was a born charmer; and to see those saucy eyes, momentarily sentimental and maternal as they rested upon him, could not but give the young Duke a feeling of pleasure.

He decided that, although she made the most outrageous comments and had no sense of the fitness of things, the little orange-girl was not without her attractions, and for the life of him he could not dislike her as he felt a young man in his position should.

Meanwhile Nell was back in high favor. Now Charles was wondering why he had neglected her so long. It was pleasant to escape from Louise's culture and enjoy a romp with Nell. Nell was so natural; moreover she learned quickly. She was already developing a taste for the kind of music which pleased the King.

It never failed to amuse him to see her in her apartments, the grand lady Madam Eleanor Gwyn. It grieved him that he could as yet do nothing for the boys, but he promised himself he would as soon as he felt it was safe to do so.

The King, recovered from his illness, was in good spirits. He recalled Rochester, for, although he could not entirely like the fellow, he knew of none who could write such witty verses and make him laugh so heartily—even though it was often at the King's expense.

The Court was merry. Charles refused to be worried by affairs of state. Louise was in retirement and, as there was no need to stand on dignity, there was much merrymaking during these months with Nell reigning supreme as the Queen of the Court, determined to enjoy every moment before that time when Louise must inevitably come forward and send her back a pace or two.

One day, when the King rose, it was to find one of Rochester's verses stuck on his door.

The courtiers gathered about him to read it.

Charles read aloud:

"Here lies our Sovereign Lord the King
Whose word no man relies on.
He never said a foolish thing
And never did a wise one."

There was an expectant hush when the King finished reading. A man must indeed have a lively sense of humor to be able to laugh at what he knew to be so true of himself.

There was Rochester in the background, debonair and reckless, not caring if the verses earned him another banishment from the Court he loved to grace. How could he, his expression demanded, refrain from writing such neat and witty verses when they occurred to him and happened to be so true?

The King laughed suddenly and loudly.

"Why, my friends," he said to the company, " 'tis true, what he says, but the matter is easily accounted for—my discourse is my own, my actions are my Ministry's."

Indeed it was a very merry Court during those months.

Nell gave a musical party in her finely furnished house; it was looking particularly grand, for if the King could not give her the titles she craved for her sons, he tried hard to make up for that with his gifts.

Nell, looking round the room, could hardly believe that this was now her home. It was not easy to conjure up the memory of that hovel in the Cole-yard now. Yet when she went up to that room where her mother would now be sleeping, the gin bottle not far out of reach, it was not so difficult.

But what a sight this was, with the candlelight gleaming on the rich dress of ladies and Court gallants! Nell glanced at her own skirts covered in silver and gold lace, at the jewels glittering on her fingers.

She, little Nell Gwyn of the Cole-yard, was giving a party at which the principal guests were the King and his brother, the Duke of York.

This was a particularly happy evening for Nell, because during it she would have a chance to do a good turn to a poor player from the theater. He had a beautiful voice, this young Bowman, and she wanted the King to hear it and compliment him, for the King's compliments would mean that London playgoers would crowd into the theater to hear the man; and it was a mighty pleasant thing, thought Nell, having had one's feet set on the road to good fortune to do all in one's power to lead others that way.

She watched the King's expression as he listened to the singing. She sidled up to him.

"A good performer, Nell," he said.

"I am delighted so to please Your Majesty," she told him. "I wish to bring the singer to you that you may thank him personally. It will mean much to the boy."

"Do so, Nell, if it be your wish," said Charles and, as he watched her small figure whisk away, he thought affectionately that it was like Nell, in the midst of her extravagant splendor, to think of those less fortunate. He was happy with Nell. If she did not continuously plague him about those boys of hers he would know complete peace with her. But she was right, of course, to do what she could for their sons. He would not have her neglectful of their welfare. And one day she should be rewarded. As soon as it was possible he would give young Charles all that he had given Barbara's and Louise's.

Nell was approaching with young Bowman, who nervously stood before the King.

"I thank you heartily for your music," said Charles warmly. He would not deny Nell the appreciation which she wanted. That cost nothing, and he wanted her to know that, were he in a position to do so, he would grant all her requests. "I thank you heartily again and again."

Nell was at his side. "Sir," she said, "to show you do not speak like a courtier, could you not make the performers a worthy present?"

"Assuredly yes," said the King, and felt in his pockets. He grimaced. He was without money. He called to his brother.

"James, I beg of you reward these good musicians in my name."

James discovered that he, too, had left his purse in his apartments.

"I have nothing here, Sir," he said, "naught but a guinea or two."

Nell stood, arms akimbo, looking from the King to the Duke.

"Od's Fish!" she cried. "What company have I got into?"

There was laughter all round; and none laughed more heartily than the King.

Nell was happy, delighting in her fine apartments, the favor she enjoyed with the King, and the love she bore him.

All the same she did not forget to make sure that the musicians were adequately rewarded.

It was a successful evening among many.

Thus it was while Louise nursed herself back to health.

❁ ❁ ❁

Louise was recovered, and now the King was dividing his time between her and Nell. Barbara, Duchess of Cleveland, although no longer in favor with the King, continued to fight for the rights of those children whom she declared were as much his as her own. Louise felt that by some divine right her own son should have the precedence over Barbara's. The King was pestered first by one, then by the other. Barbara's sons were to be the Dukes of Grafton and Southampton; Louise's was to have the title of Duke of Richmond, which was vacant on the death of Frances Stuart's husband. But Charles must arrange that the patents be passed all at the same time, to avoid jealousy.

Still there were no titles for Charles and James Beauclerk. Nell was unable to conceal her chagrin. She could not refrain from insulting Louise on every possible occasion. "If she is a person of such rank, related to all the nobility of France," she demanded, "why does she play the whore? I'm a doxy by profession, and I do not pretend to be anything else. I am constant to the King, and I know that he will not continue to pass over my boys."

But Louise had now managed to win Danby to her side, and Danby's position was high in the country. Charles could not ignore him because his wizardry in matters of finance had made such marked improvements in Charles' affairs. Nell knew that she owed her own and her sons' lack of honors to the Danby-Portsmouth league, and she was also wise enough to know that while Danby remained in power she would find it very difficult to get the recognition she so eagerly desired.

Danby was fast building up the Court party of which he was the head. He wanted to revive the Divine Right of Kings and the absolutism of the monarchy as in the days of Charles I. In opposition, the Country party, led by Shaftesbury with Buckingham as his lieutenant, aimed to support the Parliament. Danby's party called Shaftesbury's party Whigs, which was a term hitherto only applied to Scottish robbers who raided the border and stole their neighbors' goods under a cloak of hypocrisy. Shaftesbury retaliated by dubbing Danby's party Tories, a term used in Ireland for those who were superstitious, bloodthirsty, ignorant, and not to be trusted.

The King watched the rivalry with seeming indifference, but he was alert. He recognized the skill of Shaftesbury—the cleverest and most formidable member of the Opposition party. Charles and his brother James had nicknamed him "Little Sincerity." He was a small man who suffered much from ill health at this time; he had changed sides many times during the course of the last few years. When the civil war had started he had been cautious and retiring, waiting to see which side could serve him best. When it seemed the Royalists were winning he hastily joined them, and then was forced to desert to the other side with the greatest speed. He became a Field Marshal in Cromwell's armies; but while he kept close to Cromwell he took the precaution to marry a woman who was of a Royalist family. She died early, which was to the good, for Cromwell then became Lord Protector and the lady's background might have been an encumbrance to an ambitious man. Afterwards he married an heiress. He was clever enough to join none of the Royalist risings, but he was one of the first to present himself at Charles' exiled Court to welcome him back to England. He took a great part in the downfall of Clarendon, who held a post which he coveted. When the Great Seal was his, he was quick to see that the Opposition was likely to be very powerful; he had no wish to commit himself too hurriedly to support that which might prove to be a lost cause. But he was forced at this time to waver no longer. His way was clear. He must make Parliament supreme, for he clearly saw that his destiny lay therein. If Parliament were supreme, then Shaftesbury should be its head.

He did not underrate the King. Charles was lazy. As Buckingham had once said, "he could if he would," and never had Buckingham said a truer word. It was only poor James of York who "would if he could." Between lazy Charles and aspiring James, one must walk with caution.

Charles had once said to him: "I believe you are the wickedest dog in England."

Shaftesbury, whose tongue was as quick as his mind, retorted: "May it please Your Majesty, of a subject, I believe I am."

Charles could never resist a witty rejoinder; he knew "Little Sincerity" for a man without scruples, but he had to respect that quick and clever brain; in his continual tussles with his Parliament it was men such as Shaftesbury whom he must needs watch.

Nell, looking on, understanding little of politics, accepted Danby as her enemy because he and Louise were friends; Buckingham, friend of Shaftesbury, had been the means of bringing her to the attention of the King; so she looked upon Buckingham as her friend. The reckless Rochester was Buckingham's friend and therefore inclined to support the. Shaftesbury party. So to her house these men came, and it was at her table they sat and discussed their plans. One of these, which was formulating in the agile brain of Shaftesbury, was to have Monmouth proclaimed legitimate and, on the King's death, set upon the throne as a puppet who would do his bidding; Shaftesbury and Buckingham were formidable enemies of the Duke of York.

Monmouth, too, came to Nell's parties, and an affection sprang up between them. Nell continued to refer to the proud young man as Prince Perkin and the Pretender, but Monmouth had to accept such inroads on his dignity as "Nelly's talk."

Charles knew of Nell's Whig friends, but he knew Nell. She was completely loyal to him as a man. She saw him, not only as the King, but in that inimitable way of hers which made him feel half husband, half son. She was lustily ready for passion, but the maternal instinct was always there; and Charles knew that Nell was the one person in his kingdom who could be relied upon for disinterested love. It was true she pestered at times: titles for her sons, a grand title for herself. But he always remembered that she had not done this until her sons were born, and it was that maternal instinct which prompted her to do so now. Honors for her sons she must have. And she wanted the boys not to be ashamed of their mother.

He made no effort to stop those entertainments she gave to these men whom he knew were trying to shatter the doctrine of the Divine Right of Kings. Nell was careless; she did not realize that she was dabbling in high politics. Often unconsciously she gave away little bits of information which were useful. His affection for her, as hers for him, burned steadily, no matter what he felt now and then for others.

As for Louise, he had not felt the same for her since their enforced separation. She had forgotten her gentle manners when she realized that she had caught the sickness. She had railed against him in her fury; it had been necessary to give her a handsome present to pacify her. Not, she had declared, that anything could pacify her for the loss of her health, and for the terrible indignity of being forced to suffer from such a disease, and he believed that her manner of fretting, her anger and railings had impeded her recovery.

He would not have been altogether displeased if Louise had told him she intended to return to France. He could not, of course, suggest that she should go. That would offend Louis, and he dared not do that at this stage. Moreover it was well for Louis to believe he had a spy close to the King of England.

Charles would employ tactics not new to him in his relationship with Louise. He would placate and promise; but it did not mean that he would keep his promises.

He brooded on these matters as he attended race meetings at Newmarket or sat fishing at Windsor, or strolled in St. James' Park, feeding the ducks, his dogs at his heels, sauntering with the wits and ladies who delighted him.

He heard that Clarendon had died in Rouen, and that saddened him a little, for he had never forgotten the old man who had served him so well in the days of his exile. John Milton, who had written *Paradise Lost,* died also. No one greatly cared. The witty and scurrilous verses of Rochester were more widely read than Milton's epic poetry. These reminders of death turned the King's thoughts into melancholy channels. He recalled Jemmy's unhealthy thoughts. If it were true that Shaftesbury planned to make Monmouth heir, what of James, Duke of York? James was at heart a good man, but he was by no means a clever one. James would deem it his duty to fight for what he believed to be right, and he was a Stuart who believed that kings ruled by Divine Right and that they were God's anointed.

Trouble lies ahead, thought the King uneasily. Then characteristically: But it is my death that sets light to the train of powder. When I am dead what concern shall it be of mine?

So he fished and sauntered, divided his time between Louise and Nell, vaguely wished that Louise would go back to France, vaguely hoped that he could give Nell her heart's desire and make her sons the little lords she would have them be.

❁ ❁ ❁

With the coming of the new year there was a change at Court.

A small party on horseback came clattering through the streets. The leader of this party, wearing jacket, plumed hat, and a periwig, was Hortense Mancini, Duchess Mazarin. Her great eyes seemed black but on closer inspection were seen to be a shade of blue so dark as to resemble the color of violets; her hair was bluish-black, her features classic, her figure voluptuously beautiful. She was known throughout Europe as the most beautiful woman in the world, and all those who saw her believed that she was justly described.

She had brought with her a few of her personal servants—five men and two women—and at her side rode her little black page who prepared her coffee.

She drew up at the house of Lady Elizabeth Harvey, who came out to greet her and let her know that she was delighted to welcome her.

The citizens of London saw her no more that day. They stood about in the keen frosty air telling themselves that, the woman being so beautiful, and the King's reputation being what it was, she could have come to England for one purpose only.

They waited now to witness the discomfiture of Madam Carwell, as they had called Louise since her arrival in England. They refused to try to pronounce Kéroualle. Louise was Carwell to them, and no fine English title was going to alter that. It would please the Londoners to see her neglected whom they called The Catholic Whore.

Here was another foreigner, but this woman was at least a beauty, and they would be glad to see their King lured from the side of the squint-eyed French spy.

❁ ❁ ❁

Louise was worried. She believed that she had lost her hold on the King. She knew that that hold had largely been due to the fact that she had not been easy to seduce. She could not, of course, have held out any longer; to have done so might have made the King realize that he did not greatly desire her.

The sickness which she had contracted had not only taken its toll of her looks; it had left her nervous, and she wondered whether she could ever regain the health she had once enjoyed. She had grown fat and, although the King had nicknamed her Fubbs with the utmost affection, she felt the name carried with it a certain lack of dignity. She was beginning to fear that had Charles been less indulgent, less careless, she would have been passed over long ago.

She did not believe that he did half those things which he promised he would do and which she was commanded by the French King through Courtin, the French ambassador, to persuade him to.

He would look at her with that shrewd yet lazy smile and say: "So you would advise that, Fubbs? Ah, yes, of course, I understand."

She often heard him laugh uproariously at some of Nell Gwyn's comments and frequently these were uttered to discountenance herself. And now this most disturbing news had reached her. Hortense Mancini was in London.

There was no one in England whom she could really trust. Buckingham, her enemy, was in decline, but for how long would he remain so? Shaftesbury hated her and would want to destroy her influence with the King, since he was anti-Catholic and she had heard through Courtin that he was planning to expunge all popery from the country. It might have been that Shaftesbury knew of that secret clause in the Treaty of Dover concerning the King's religion; if so, he would know that she had her instructions from Louis to make the King's conversion complete and public as soon as she could.

She was trembling, for she had lost some of her calmness during her illness.

She decided that there was only one person in England who would help her now, and that the time had come for her to redeem those vague promises which she had held out to him. She dressed herself with care. In spite of her increased bulk she knew well how to dress to advantage and she had taste and poise which few ladies at Court possessed.

She sent one of her women to Lord Danby's apartments with a message which was to be discreetly delivered and which explained that she would shortly be coming to see him, and she hoped he would be able to give her a private interview.

The woman quickly returned with the news that Lord Danby eagerly awaited her coming.

He received her with a show of respect.

"I am honored to receive Your Grace."

"I trust that in coming thus for a friendly talk I do not encroach on your time."

"Time is well spent in your company," said Danby. He had guessed the cause of her alarm. "I hear that we have a foreign Duchess newly arrived among us."

"It is Madame Mazarin . . . notorious in all the Courts of Europe."

"And doubtless come to win notoriety in this one," said Danby slyly.

Louise flinched. "I doubt it not. If you know aught . . ." she began.

Danby looked at his fingernails. "I gather," he said, "that she does not wish to live in the Palace, as Your Grace does."

"She comes because she is poor," said Louise. "I have heard that that mad husband of hers quickly dissipated the fortune she inherited from her uncle."

" 'Tis true. She has let His Majesty know that she must have an adequate income before taking up her apartments in Whitehall."

Louise came closer to him. She said nothing, but her meaning was clear to him: You will advise the King against providing this income. You, whose financial genius enables you to enrich yourself while you suppress waste in others, you, under whom the King's budget has been balanced, will do all in your power to prevent his giving this woman what she asks. You will range yourself on the side of the Duchess of Portsmouth, which means that you will be the enemy of the Duchess Mazarin.

Why not? thought Danby excitedly. Intrigue was stimulating. Discovery? Charles never blamed others for falling into temptation which he himself made no attempt to resist.

He took her hand and kissed it. When she allowed it to remain in his, he was sure.

"Your Grace is more beautiful than before your illness," he said; and he laughed inwardly, realizing that she, the coldest woman at Court, was offering herself in exchange for his protection.

He kissed her without respect, without affection. He was accustomed to taking bribes.

❁ ❁ ❁

Hortense received the King at the house of Lady Elizabeth Harvey.

She had guessed that as soon as he heard of her arrival in his capital he would wish to visit her. It was exactly what Hortense wanted.

She lay back on a sofa awaiting him. She was voluptuously beautiful and, although she was thirty and had led a wild and adventurous life, her beauty was in no way impaired. Her perfect classical features would remain perfect and classical as long as she lived. Her abundant bluish-black hair fell curling about her bare shoulders; but her most beautiful assets were her wonderful violet eyes.

Hortense was imperturbably good-humored, lazy, of a temperament to match the King's; completely sensual, she was widely experienced in amatory adventures. She had often been advised that she would do well to visit England, and had again and again decided to renew her acquaintance with Charles; but each time something had happened to prevent her, some new lover had beguiled her and made her forget the man who had wished to be her lover in her youth. It was sheer poverty which had driven her to England now—sheer poverty and the fact that she had created such a scandal in Savoy that she had been asked to leave. The last three scandalous years had been spent in the company of César Vicard, a dashing, handsome young man who had posed as the Abbé of St Réal. When the letters which had passed between the Duchess and the *soi-disant* Abbé had been discovered, they, completely lacking in reticence, had so shocked those into whose hands they fell, that the Duchess had been asked to leave Savoy.

So, finding herself poor and in need of refuge, Hortense had come to England. She knew no fear. She had faced the perilous crossing in the depth of winter, and with a few servants had come to a completely strange country, never doubting that her spectacular beauty would ensure for her a position at Court.

Charles strode in, took her hand, and kissed it while his eyes did not leave her face.

"Hortense!" he cried. "But you are the same Hortense whom I loved all those years ago. No, not the same. Od's Fish, I should not have believed then that it was possible for any to be more beautiful than the youngest of les Mazarinettes. But I see that there is one more fair: the Duchess Mazarin—Hortense grown up."

She laughed at him and waved him to be seated with a fascinating easy gesture as though she were the Queen, he the subject. Charles did not mind. He felt that he should indeed forget his royalty in the presence of such beauty.

The long lashes lay against her olive skin. Charles stared at the beautiful blue-black hair lying so negligently on the bare shoulders. This languid beauty aroused in him such desire as he rarely felt nowadays. He knew that his bout of sickness had changed him; he was not the man he had been. But he was determined that Hortense should become his mistress.

"You should not be here," he said. "You should come to Whitehall at once."

"Nay," she said, smiling her indolent smile. "Mayhap later. If it could be arranged."

"But it shall be arranged."

She laughed. There was no pretence about her. She had been brought up at the French Court. She had all the graces of that Court and she had learned to be practical.

"I am very poor," she said.

"I heard that you had inherited the whole of your uncle's fortune."

" 'Twas so," said Hortense. "Armand, my husband, quickly took possession of it."

"What! All of it?"

"All of it. But what mattered that? I escaped."

"We have heard of your adventures, Hortense. I wonder you did not visit me before."

"Suffice it that I have come now."

Charles was thinking quickly. She would ask for a pension, and if it were large enough she would move into Whitehall. He must see Danby quickly and something must be arranged. But he would not discuss that with her now. She was Italian, brought up in France, and therefore, indolent as she seemed, she would know how to drive her bargain. It was not that he was averse to discussing money with a woman; but he feared she would ask too much and he be unable to refuse her.

He satisfied himself with contemplating that incomparable beauty and telling himself that she would be his mistress all in good time.

"We should have married," he said.

"Ah! How it reminds me. And what an enchanting husband you would have made! Far better than Armand who forced me to fly from him."

"Your uncle would have none of me. He did not wish to give his niece to a wandering prince without a kingdom."

" 'Twas a sad thing that you did not regain your kingdom earlier."

"I have often thought it . . . Now, having seen you, I regret it more than ever, since, had I been a King with a country when I asked for your hand, it would not have been refused me."

"Marie, too, might have been a Queen," said Hortense. "But our uncle would not let her be. Think of it! Marie might have been Queen of France and I Queen of England—but for Uncle Mazarin."

Charles looked into her face, marveling at its perfections, but Hortense's dreamy thoughts were far away. She was thinking of the French Court where she had been brought up with her four sisters, Laura, Olympia, Marie, Mariana. They had all joined in the ballets devised for the little King and his brother Philippe; and her uncle, Cardinal Mazarin, and Louis' mother, Anne of Austria, had ruled France between them. All the Cardinal's nieces had been noted for their beauty, but many said that little Hortense was the loveliest of them all. What graces they had learned in that most graceful Court!

She remembered that Louis—impressionable and idealistic—had fallen in love first with Olympia and then more passionately, more seriously with Marie. She remembered Marie's unhappiness, the tears, the heartbreak. She remembered Louis, so young, so determined to have his own way and marry Marie. Poor Louis! And poor Marie!

It was the Cardinal who had ruined their hopes. Some men would have rejoiced to see a niece the Queen of France. Not Mazarin. He feared the French. They hated him and blamed him for all their misfortunes; he believed that if he allowed their King to marry his niece they would have risen against him, and there would have been revolution in France. He remembered the civil war of the Fronde. Perhaps he had been wise. But what misery the young people had suffered. Louis had married the plain little Infanta of Spain, Marie Thérèse, whom he would never love, and now his love affairs were the talk of the world. And poor Marie! She had been hastily married to Lorenzo Colonna who was the Grand Constable of Naples; and he had succeeded in making her as unhappy as she had made him and as, doubtless, Marie Thérèse, the meek and prim little Spaniard, had made Louis.

And Charles, seeing the young Hortense, and connoisseur of beauty that he was even in those days, had declared that he would be happy to make her his wife. He had urgent need of the money which would have helped him to regain his throne, and it was known that the Cardinal's wealth would go to his nieces. To the penurious exile the exquisite and wealthy child had seemed an ideal match.

But the Cardinal had frowned on Charles' offer. He saw the young man as a reckless profligate who would never regain his throne, and he did not wish his niece to link her fortunes with such a man.

So the Cardinal had prevented his two nieces from becoming queens. He had torn them from two charming people that they might make marriages with unhappy results to all concerned.

"Those days are long ago," said Charles. " 'Tis a sad habit to brood on what might have been. 'Tis a happier one to let the present make up for the disappointments of the past."

"Which we should do?"

"Which we *shall* do," said Charles vehemently.

"It is good of you to offer me refuge here," said Hortense.

"Good! Nay, 'tis what all the world would expect of me."

Hortense laughed that low and musical laugh of hers. "And of me," she said.

"Od's Fish! I wonder you did not come before."

Hortense's dreamy eyes looked back once more into the past. César Vicard had been an exciting lover. It had not been her wish to leave him. There had been others equally exciting, equally enthralling, and she would have been too indolent to leave any of them had circumstances not made it necessary for her to do so.

Yet she had left her husband and four children. So in a dire emergency she could rouse herself.

"It is an adventure," she said, "to come to a new country."

"And to an old friend?" he asked passionately.

"It was so long ago. So much has happened. You may have heard of the life I led with Armand."

"Vague rumors reached me."

"You wonder why my uncle arranged that marriage," she said. "I might have had Charles Emmanuel, Duke of Savoy. He would have made a better husband. At least he was called Charles. Then there was Pedro of Portugal, and the Maréchal Turenne."

"The last would have been a little aged for you, I imagine."

"Thirty-five years older. But life with him could not have been worse than it was with Armand. Even the Prince de Cortenay who, I knew, concerned himself with my uncle's money rather than with myself . . ."

"The graceless fool!" said Charles softly.

"He could not have made my life more intolerable than did Armand."

"Your uncle delayed marrying you so often that when he was on his deathbed he acted without due thought in that important matter."

"To my cost."

"It was so unsatisfactory?"

"I was fifteen, he was thirty. Some I could have understood. Some I could have excused. A libertine . . . yes; I have never pretended to be a saint.

He had a fine title: Armand de la Porte Marquis de Meilleraye and Grand Master of the Artillery of France. Would you have expected such a one to be a bigot . . . a madman? But he was. We had not been married many months when he became obsessed with the idea that everyone about him was impure, and that it was his duty to purify them. He sought to purify statues, pictures . . ."

"Sacrilege!" said Charles.

"And myself."

"Greater sacrilege!" murmured Charles.

Hortense laughed lightly. "Do you blame me for leaving him? How could I stay? I endured that life for seven wretched years. I saw my fortune being dissipated—and not in the way one would expect a husband to dissipate his wife's fortune. He agreed to take my uncle's name. Uncle thought he would be amenable. We became the Duc and Duchesse Mazarin. Uncle would not allow him to use the 'de.' He said: 'Not Hortense, my fortune, and *de* Mazarin. That is too much. Hortense, yes. A fortune, yes. But you call yourself plain Duc Mazarin.' "

Charles laughed. "That is characteristic of the old man."

"And so to me came the Palais Mazarin. You remember it—in the Rue de Richelieu—and with it came the Hôtel Tuboeuf and the picture and sculpture galleries, those which had been built by Mazard, as well as the property in the Rue des Petits Champs."

"Such treasures! They must have been as good as anything Louis had in the Louvre."

"Indeed yes. Pictures by the greatest artists. Statues, priceless books, furniture . . . It all came to me."

"And he—your husband—sold it and so frittered away your inheritance?"

"He sold some. He thought it was wrong for a woman to adorn herself with jewels. He was verging on madness from the very beginning. I remember how I first came upon him before a great masterpiece, a brush in his hand. I said to him: 'Armand, what are you doing? Are you imagining that you are a great painter?' And he stood up, pointing the brush at the painting, his eyes blazing with what I can only believe was madness. He said: 'These pictures are indecent. No one should look on such nakedness. All the servants here will be corrupted.' And I looked closer and saw that he had been painting over the nudes. There were his crude additions, ruining masterpieces. That was not all. He took a hammer and smashed many of the statues. I dare not think how much he has wantonly destroyed."

"And you lived with that man for seven years!"

"Seven years! I thought it my duty to do so. Oh, he was a madman. He forbade the maidservants to milk the cows, for he said this might put indecent thoughts into their heads. He wanted to extract our daughter's front teeth because they were well-formed and he feared they might give rise to vanity. He wrote to Louis, telling him that he had had instructions from the Angel Gabriel to warn the King that disaster would overtake him if he did not immediately give up Louise de la Vallière. You see he was mad—quite mad. But I was glad later that he had written to Louis thus, for when I ran away from him he asked Louis to insist on my returning to him, and Louis' answer was that he was sure Armand's good friend the Angel Gabriel, with whom he seemed to be on such excellent terms, could help him more in this matter than could the King of France."

Charles laughed. "Ah, you did well to leave such a madman. The only complaint I would make is that you waited so long before coming to England."

"Oh, I was in and out of convents. And believe me, Charles, in some of these convents the life is rigorous indeed. I would as lief be a prisoner in the Bastille as in some of them. I was in the Convent of the Daughters of Mary, in Paris, and I was right glad to leave it."

"You were meant to grace a Court, never a convent," said Charles.

She sighed. "I feel as though I may have come home. This is a country strange to me, but I have good friends here. My little cousin, Mary Beatrice, the wife of your own brother, is here. How I long to see her! And there is you, my dear Charles, the friend of my childhood. How fares Mary Beatrice?"

"She grows reconciled to her aged husband. I have become her friend. That was inevitable because, from the first, she reminded me of you."

She smiled lazily. "Then of course there is my old friend, St. Evremond. He has long been urging me to come to England."

"Good St. Evremond! I always liked the fellow. He has settled happily here; I like his wit."

"So you have made him Master of your ducks, I hear."

"A task well suited to his talents," said Charles, "for there is nothing he need do but watch the creatures and now and then throw them something to eat; but to perform this task he must saunter in the Park and converse while he stands beside the lake. It is a pleasure to saunter and converse with him."

"I wonder does he grow homesick for France? Does he wish he had not been so indiscreet as to criticize my uncle at the time of the Treaty of the Pyrenees?"

"Does he tell you?"

"He tells me that he would never wish to leave England if I were there."

"So he has helped to bring you. I must reward my keeper of the ducks."

"He but spoke like a courtier, I doubt not."

"All men would speak like courtiers to you, Hortense."

"As they do to all women."

"With you they would mean the fulsome things they say."

She laughed. "I will call my blackamoor to make coffee for Your Majesty. You will never have tasted coffee such as he can brew."

"And while we talk, we will arrange for you to move to Whitehall."

"Nay, I would not do so. I would prefer a house . . . nearby. I do not think Her Grace of Portsmouth would wish me to have my quarters in Whitehall Palace."

"It is spacious. I have made improvements, and it is not the rambling mass of buildings it was when' I came back to England."

"Nevertheless, I would prefer to be nearby, you understand, but not too near."

Charles was thinking quickly. He was determined to lose no time in making this exciting addition to his seraglio.

With amusement he accepted coffee from Hortense's little slave, and as he sipped it he said: "Lord Windsor, who is Master of Horse to the Duchess of York, would most gladly vacate his house for you. It faces St. James' Park and would suit you very happily, I doubt not."

"It seems as though Your Majesty is ready to make me very happy in England."

"I shall set about that task with all my heart and soul," said Charles, taking her hand and kissing it.

❁ ❁ ❁

It was some months before Hortense moved to Whitehall. The question of money was a delicate one. Charles had placed himself in Danby's hands, for Danby had proved his worth in matters of finance.

Danby had summed up the character of the beautiful Hortense: Sensual, but by no means vicious; cultured, but by no means shrewd. She would let great opportunities elude her, not because she did not see them, but because she was too indolent to seize them.

He did not believe that she would long hold the King's undivided attention. She was more beautiful than any of the King's ladies, it was true, but Charles nowadays wanted more than beauty. Hortense desired a large pension because she needed it to live in the state to which she was accustomed. She had no wish to store up for herself great wealth as Louise did. She would not ask for honors, titles; she did not wish to reign as a queen in the Court. She wanted to be lazily content with good food, good wine, a lover capable of satisfying her. She would never intrigue.

Danby had decided that he would be well advised to support Louise. Therefore he held the King back from supplying the large income which Hortense demanded.

Hortense was, he knew, hoping that her husband would give her a bigger allowance than the four hundred pounds a year which was all he would allow her out of the vast fortune she had brought him. Danby believed that if Hortense received what she wanted she would accept Charles as a lover whether he supplied the income or not. That was Hortense's nature. She now asked £4,000 a year from Charles. But, as Danby pointed out, that would not be all she would ask.

Hortense was extravagant by nature. She had told Charles of how, one day shortly before her uncle's death, she had thrown three hundred pistoles out of the window of the Palais Mazarin because she liked to see the servants scramble for them and fight each other.

"Uncle was such a careful man," Hortense had said. "Some say my action shortened his life. But it did not prevent his leaving me his fortune."

Oh yes, Danby pointed out, if the King wished to keep his exchequer in order, they must be careful of such a woman.

But the whole country was talking of the King's latest mistress. Sir Carr Scrope wrote in the prologue to Etherege's *Man of Mode* which was produced in the King's Theater that year:

"Of foreign women why should we fetch the scum
When we can be so richly served at home?"

And the audience roared its approval of the lines, although most people declared that anything was worthwhile if it put Madam Carwell's nose out of joint.

But Charles was impatient. He insisted on the pension's being paid, and as there was no hope of Hortense's being able to persuade Louis to force her husband to increase her allowance, she accepted Charles' offer and became his mistress.

❁ ❁ ❁

Louise was distraught. Nell shrugged her shoulders. She was beginning to understand her position at Court. She was there when she was wanted, ready to make sport and be gay. She never reproached Charles for his infidelities. She knew she was safe and that no reigning beauty would be able to displace her. For one thing, Charles would never let her go. She was the buffoon, the female court jester, apart from all others. This was a battle between Louise and Hortense, and Hortense held all the cards which should bring victory. She was so beautiful that people waited in the streets to see her pass. She was deeply sensual. Louise was cold by nature, and had to pretend to share Charles' pleasure in their relations. Hortense had no need to pretend. Louise must constantly be considering instructions from France, and the King knew it. Hortense need consider nothing but her own immediate satisfaction. Hortense never showed jealousy of Louise; Louise continually showed jealousy of Hortense. Hortense offered not only sexual delight but peace. In this she was like Nell. But she lacked Nell's maternal devotion and she lacked Nell's constancy—although this was not apparent at this stage.

Edmund Waller wrote a set of verses called *The Triple Combat,* in which he portrayed the three chief mistresses struggling for supremacy. The country was amused; so was the Court. Charles acquired a new nickname—Chanticleer; and everyone was aware of how the affair progressed. Barbara had left for France, and Charles had at last made it clear that he wished to sever their relationship. "All that I ask of you," he had said, "is to make as little noise as you can and I care not whom you love."

Louise, who had been with child, suffered a miscarriage, and appeared at Court looking thin and ill. She had a slight affliction of one eye, and the skin round the affected eye became discolored.

"It would seem," said Rochester, "that Her Grace, aware of the superior attractions of Madame Mazarin's dark eyes, would seek to transform herself into a brunette."

The Court took up the story. Everyone was only too glad to jeer at Madam Carwell.

Louise was indeed melancholy. She feared that that nightmare, which had haunted her whenever she felt she was losing her hold on Charles, would become a reality. She was terrified that Hortense would persuade the King to send her, Louise, back to France and he, unable to deny his latest mistress what she asked, would agree. Louise need not have worried on that score, for Hortense would never bestir herself to make such demands.

Nell, as merry as ever, appeared at Court dressed in mourning.

"For whom do you mourn?" she was asked.

"For the discarded Duchess and her dead hopes," explained Nell maliciously.

The King heard of this and was amused. He wished now and then that Louise would go back to France, but he was determined that whatever happened he would keep Nell at hand. It was pleasant to remember that she was always there, ready, without recriminations, to make good sport.

❁ ❁ ❁

Louise lifted tearful eyes to the King. She had wept so much that those eyes, never big, seemed almost to have shrunk into her head. Her recent miscarriage and her illness of the previous year had undermined her health considerably. Charles would have been sorry for her had she been less sorry for herself. Although he was kind as always, Louise sensed that his thoughts were far away—she believed with Hortense—and she fancied she saw distaste in his eyes.

None of Charles' mistresses—not even Barbara—had been so acquisitive as Louise, and her great consolation now was that she and her sister Henriette, whom she had brought to England and married to the dissolute Earl of Pembroke, were very rich. But was that to be the only gratification of one who had sought to be a queen?

"I have served Your Majesty with all my heart," began Louise.

She did not understand him. Recriminations dulled his pity.

"You are the friend of Kings," he said.

She noticed that he used the plural, and her hopes sank.

A less kindly man would have called her Louis' spy.

She said: "I come to ask Your Majesty's leave to retire to Bath. There I think I might take the waters and regain my health."

Her eyes were pleading with him: Forbid me to go. Tell me that you wish to keep me beside you.

But Charles had brightened. "My dear Fubbs," he said, "by all means go to Bath. One of my favorite cities. There you will recover your health, I doubt not. Lose no time in going there."

It was a sorrowing Louise who made arrangements for the journey.

She did not know that the King was no longer as completely enamored of Hortense as he had been. She was beautiful—the most beautiful woman in his kingdom—he was ready to admit that. But beauty was not all. She had brought into her house a French croupier, Morin, and had introduced the game of basset to England. The King deplored gambling. He had always sought to lure his mistresses from the gaming table. It had always proved less costly in the long run to provide them with masques and banquets. He was therefore annoyed with Hortense for introducing a new form of gambling.

The little Countess of Sussex, Barbara's daughter, who was reputed to be Charles' also, was completely charmed by Hortense. She would not leave her side and Hortense, attracted by the little girl, gave herself up to playing games with her. This was very charming, but often when the King wished for Hortense's company Hortense could not tear herself away from his daughter.

There was another matter which was changing the King's attitude. She had a lover. This was the young and handsome Prince of Monaco who was visiting England. He had come, it was said, all the way from Monte Carlo with the express purpose of making Hortense his mistress.

Hortense was unable to resist his good looks and his youth. The young man became a constant visitor at her house, for Hortense was too reckless, too careless of the future, to hide her infatuation for him.

Barbara had taken lovers while she was the King's mistress, and he had gone back again and again to Barbara; but those were different days. He was almost forty-seven—no longer so young, and even his amazing virility was beginning to fade. Since he had recovered from his illness he appeared to be sterile, for he had fathered no child since the birth of Moll Davies' daughter.

He was growing old; therefore that immense infatuation he had felt for Hortense, and which had flared up so suddenly, as suddenly died down. He wanted to be amused. Louise was no good at amusing him. She would only weep and recount her ills. So he made his way to Nell's house in Pall Mall.

Nell was delighted to receive him. There she was, ready to act court jester, ready to laugh at him, the disconsolate lover who had been disappointed in his mistress, but ready to comfort, ready to show beneath all that banter and high spirits that she felt motherly towards him and was really very angry with the foolish Hortense for preferring the Prince of Monaco.

Buckingham was often at Nell's house. So was Monmouth. Shaftesbury was there. Nell was getting herself embroiled with the Whigs, thought Charles with amusement.

But it was pleasant to have Nell dance and sing for them and, when Charles saw her imitation of Lady Danby, and Buckingham's of Lady Danby's husband, the King found himself laughing as he had not laughed for some weeks. He realized that he had been foolish to neglect the tonic only Nell could give.

Then, with Louise recuperating at Bath, and Hortense relegated to being just one of Charles' more casual mistresses, Nell stepped into chief place once more.

Rochester warned her: " 'Twill only be for a while, Nell. Louise will be back to the fray—doubt it not. And she's a fine lady, while the dust of the Cole-yard still clings to little Nell. Not that I should try to wipe it off. That was where Moll failed. But do not be surprised if you are not number one all the time. Just fall back when required, but make hay, Nelly. Make hay while the sun shines."

So Nell made the King visit her not only for parties but during the day, that he might come to better acquaintance with his two sons.

One day she called little Charles to tell him that his father had come.

"Come hither, little bastard," she called.

"Nelly," protested the King, "do not say that."

"And why should I not?"

"It does not sound well."

"Sound well or not, 'tis truth. For what else should I call the boy since his father, by giving him no other title, proclaims him such to the world?"

The King was thoughtful, and very shortly after that one of Nell's dearest ambitions was realized.

Her son was no longer merely Charles Beauclerk; he was Baron Headington and Earl of Burford.

Nell danced through the house in Pall Mall, waving the patent which proclaimed little Charles' title.

"Come hither, my lord Burford," she shouted. "You have a seat in the House of Lords, my love. Think of that! You have a King for a father, and all the world knows it."

The new Earl laughed aloud to see his mother so gay, and little James—my lord Beauclerk—joined with him.

She seized them and hugged them. She called to the servants, that she might introduce them to my lord Burford and my lord Beauclerk.

She could be heard, shouting all day: "Bring my lord Burford's pectoral syrup. I swear he has a cough coming. And I doubt not that it would be good for my lord Beauclerk to take some too. Oh, my lord Burford needs a new scarf. I will go to the Exchange for white sarcenet this very day."

She fingered delicate fabrics in the shops. She bought shoes, laced with gold, for the children. "My lord Burford has such tender feet . . . and his brother, my lord Beauclerk, not less so."

The house echoed with Nell's laughter and delighted satisfaction.

The servants imitated their mistress, and it seemed that every sentence uttered to any in that house must contain a reference to my lord Earl or my lord Beauclerk.

EIGHT

Nell was busy during the months which followed. These were the happiest of her life, she believed. Charles was a frequent visitor; his delight in my lord Burford and my lord Beauclerk was unbounded; the little boys were well; and Nell's parties were gayer than ever.

It was true that there was no title for her, but Charles had promised her that as soon as he could arrange it, he would make her a Countess.

Nell allowed herself to shelve this ambition. Little Charles was an Earl, and nothing could alter that. She was ready to be contented.

Hortense was friendly and wrote to Nell, congratulating her on the elevation of her sons.

Nothing could have delighted Nell more.

"I have a letter here," she called to her steward, Mr. Groundes. "The Duchess Mazarin congratulates the Earl of Burford on his elevation."

"That is good of her, Madam."

"It is indeed good, and more than Madam Squintabella has had the good manners to do. Why, since the Duchess is so gracious concerning the Earl of Burford, I think I will call upon her and give her my thanks."

So Nell called for her Sedan and was carried to the apartments of the Duchess Mazarin, calling out, as she went through the streets, to her friends. "I trust I see you well?" "And you too," would come the answer. "And your family?" "Oh, my lord Burford is well indeed. My lord Beauclerk has a little cough." Then she would call at the apothecary's. "We are running short of pectoral syrup, and my lord Beauclerk's cough has not gone. I like to have it ready, for when my lord Beauclerk has a cough it very often happens that his brother, the Earl, catches it."

It was disconcerting, on arriving at the Duchess' apartments in St. James Palace, to find the Duchess of Portsmouth already there.

Louise, who was chatting with the French ambassador, Courtin, gave Nell a haughty look. Lady Harvey, who was also present, smiled uncertainly. Only Hortense was gracious. But Nell did not need anyone to help her out of an awkward situation. She went to Louise and slapped her on the back.

"I always have thought that those who ply the same trade should be good friends," she cried.

Louise was horrified; Nell was unperturbed. While Hortense smiled her sleepy friendly smile.

"It was kind of you to come," she said.

"Indeed I came!" declared Nell. "I was touched by your good wishes, Duchess. My lord Burford would have come to thank you in person, but he keeps my lord Beauclerk company."

"You must be very happy," said Hortense.

"And gratified," said Louise, "having worked so hard and so consistently to bring it about. Your son is fortunate indeed to have such a mother."

"And such a father," said Nell. "There has never been any doubt as to who my lord Burford's father is—although 'tis more than can be said for some."

Louise was taken aback although she could not believe the affront was meant for her. She had led an exemplary life—apart from that strange and somewhat tepid relationship she shared with Danby.

"And the same goes for my lord Beauclerk," said Nell.

Louise recovered her equanimity quickly. "I rejoice to say my own little Duke is well."

Nell at that moment was determined that before she died my lord Burford should be a Duke.

Hortense said to Nell quickly: "I have heard that you have petticoats which are the wonder of all that behold them."

"I have a good seamstress," said Nell. She stood up and, lifting her skirts, began to dance, twirling her lace petticoats as she did so.

Hortense laughed. "You twirl so we can scarcely see them. I pray you let us examine them more closely."

"You'll not find better work in London," said Nell. "And this woman will be making silk hoods with scarves to them for my lord Burford and my lord Beauclerk." She became alert; she could never resist the pleasure of doing a good turn. "Why, I doubt not this good woman would be ready to make for Your Graces if you should so wish it."

Hortense said that she did wish it; Louise said she feared she must go, and left while the rest of the company were examining Nell's petticoats.

Nell's eyes fell on the French ambassador. "Come, sir," she said, "like you not my petticoats? Portsmouth hath not finer, for all the presents that are sent to her by the King of France. Why, you should tell your King, sir, that he would do better to send presents to the mother of my lord Burford than to that weeping willow. I can tell you, sir, the King liketh me better than Fubbs. Why, almost every night he sleeps with me, you know."

Courtin hardly knew what to answer. He bowed awkwardly, fixing his eyes on the petticoats. Then he said: "Great matters need great consideration."

And after a while Nell took her leave and went back to her chair, stopping to buy shoestrings merely for the pleasure of telling the keeper of the shop in the New Exchange that they would grace the little shoes of my lord Burford.

❁ ❁ ❁

In Nell's house the Whigs gathered. Shaftesbury and Buckingham were excited. They believed that the country was behind them and that if they could bring about a general election they would have no difficulty in getting a majority.

Danby was nervous. He knew that, once Shaftesbury's party was in power, it would be the end of his career. He was determined to avoid the dissolution of the present parliament at all cost.

Shaftesbury and Buckingham planned to bring this about. And Nell, believing that Danby was the one who was preventing the King from giving her the patent which would make her a Countess, and knowing that he was the friend of Louise, assured them that she supported them wholeheartedly. Nell believed that once Shaftesbury was in power he would make her a Countess.

She did not realize that, in demanding a new election, Shaftesbury and Buckingham were going against the King's wishes, and that Charles' great desire was to rule without a Parliament, as he believed the Divine Right intended a King to rule. It was ever Charles' desire to put Parliament into recess, from which he only wished to call it when it was necessary for money to be voted into the exchequer.

Nell was awaiting the result of the meeting of Parliament and preparing for the banquet she would give that night. She believed that the diabolically clever Shaftesbury and the brilliant Buckingham would come back to her house to tell her how they had defeated Danby's administration, and how there was to be a new election which would certainly give them a majority over the Court Party in both Houses.

Then, she thought, I shall be made a Countess. Charles wishes to do it. It is only Danby who, to please Fubbs, prevents him.

While she waited a visitor called. This was Elizabeth Barry, a young actress in whom my lord Rochester was interested. He had found a place for her on the stage and was helping her to make a great career. He had begged Nell to do all she could for Elizabeth, and Nell, who would have been ready to give a helping hand to any struggling actress, even if she had not been a friend of Rochester's, had done so wholeheartedly.

Now Elizabeth was frightened.

"To tell the truth, Nell," she said, "I am with child, and I know not what my lord will say."

"Say! He will find great pleasure in the fact. All men think they are so fine that the hope of seeing a copy of themselves fills them with pleasure."

"My lord hates ties, as you know. He might look upon this child as such."

"Nay, acquaint him with the facts, Bess. They'll delight him."

"I understand him well," said Elizabeth uneasily. "He likes to laugh. He says that a weeping woman is like a wet day in the country. He hates the country as much as he hates responsibility. I once heard him say to a dog who bit him: 'I wish you were married and living in the country!' "

" 'Tis the way he has with words. He must ever say what he thinks to be clever, no matter whether he means it or not. Nay, Elizabeth, you should have no fear. He will love this child, and you the more for bearing it."

"I would I could believe it."

"I'll see that he does," said Nell fiercely. And Elizabeth believed she would, and was greatly comforted.

They talked of children then, and as Nell was discussing in detail her feelings and ailments while she was carrying my lord Burford and my lord Beauclerk, another visitor arrived. This was William Fanshawe, thin and poor, who held a small post at Court. He had married Lucy Water's daughter, Mary, over whom the King had exercised some care, although he had refused to acknowledge the child as his own, since everyone was fully aware that she could not be.

" 'Tis William Fanshawe," said Nell. "He is proud because his wife is with child. He will boast and try to convince you that Mary was in fact the King's daughter, I doubt not. It is the main subject of his discourse."

William Fanshawe was ushered in.

"Why, Will," cried Nell, "right glad I am to see you. And how fares your wife? Well, I trust, and happy with her belly."

Fanshawe said that his wife was hoping the child would bear a resemblance to her royal father.

" 'Tis to be hoped," said Nell, "that the baby will not take so long to get born as her mother did." This was a reference to the fact that Lucy Water's daughter was born far more than nine months after Charles had left her mother. But Nell softened at once and offered a piece of friendly advice. "And Will, spend not too much on the christening but reserve yourself a little to buy new shoes that will not dirty my rooms, and mayhap a new periwig that I may not smell your stink two storys high."

William took this in good part. He was delighted to be near one who was in such close touch with royalty.

But it was clear to Nell that he had not come merely to talk of his wife's pregnancy, and that he had something to say to her which was not for Elizabeth's ears.

So, finding some pretext for dismissing Elizabeth, she settled down to hear Fanshawe's news.

"Your friends are committed to the Tower," he said.

"What friends mean you?" asked Nell, aghast.

"Shaftesbury, Buckingham, Salisbury, and Wharton . . . the leaders of the Country Party."

"Why so?"

"By the King's orders."

"Then he has been forced to this by Danby!"

"They argued that a year's recess automatically dissolved a Parliament. They should have known that His Majesty would never agree that this was so, since it is His Majesty's great desire that Parliament be in perpetual recess. The King was angry with them all. He fears, it seems, that the fact that they make such a statement may put it into the members' heads to pass a law making a year's recess a lawful reason for dissolution."

"So . . . he has sent them to the Tower!"

"Nell, take care. You dabble in dangerous waters and you are being carried out of your depth."

Nell shook her head. "My lord Buckingham is my good friend," she said. "He was my good friend when I was an orange-girl. Should I fail to be his when he is a prisoner in the Tower?"

❁ ❁ ❁

The King took time off from his troubles to enjoy a little domesticity with Nell. These were happy times, for Nell's contentment was a pleasure to witness.

Charles took great delight in discussing their sons' future. Ironically he copied Nell's habit of referring to them by their full titles every time he addressed them or spoke of them to Nell.

"Nell, my lord Burford and my lord Beauclerk must receive an education due to their rank."

Nell's eyes sparkled with pleasure.

"Indeed yes. They must be educated. I would not like to see my lord Burford nor my lord Beauclerk suffer the tortures I do when called upon to handle a pen."

"I promise you they shall not. You know, there is one place where they could receive the best education in the world—the Court of France."

Nell's expression changed. "Take them away from me, you mean?"

"They would merely go to France for a year or so. Then they would come back to you. They would come back proficient in all the graces of the noblemen you wish them to be."

"But they wouldn't be my boys anymore."

"I thought you wished that they should be lords and dukes."

"I do indeed; and forget not that you have promised they shall be. But why should they not be with their mother?"

"Because it is the custom for children of high rank to be brought up in the households of noblemen, Nell. Had I left Jemmy with his mother, he would never have been the young nobleman he is today."

"Which might have been better for him and others. Mayhap then he would not have been strutting about as Prince Perkin."

"You speak truth. I would not press this. It is a decision you must come to for yourself. Keep them with you if you wish it. But if you would have them take their place in the world beside others of their rank, then must they follow a similar course of education."

"Why should I not have tutors for them?"

"It is for you to say."

When the King left Nell, she was disturbed.

She found the boys playing with Mrs. Turner, their governess, in charge of them. They ran to her as she entered.

"Mama," they cried. "Here is Mama, come to sing and dance for us."

Nell had rarely felt less like singing and dancing.

She dismissed Mrs. Turner and hugged the boys. They were so beautiful, she thought. They had an air of royalty which, no matter what education they received, must surely carry them to greatness. Charles was the image of his father. My darling, darling Earl of Burford, thought Nell; and little James? Nay, he had not the same air as his brother. There were times when Nell thought she saw her mother in him. This was not a new idea. She had settled her mother in a house in Pimlico, where she was very contented to be. Nell did not want her mother to influence those two precious lives.

"Mama," said Lord Burford, "are you sad?"

"Nay . . . nay, my little lord. I'm not sad. How could I be when I have two such precious lambs?" She kissed them tenderly. "Would you like to go to France?" she asked abruptly.

"Where's France?" asked Lord Beauclerk.

"Across the water," said his brother. " 'Tis a grand, beautiful place. Papa lived there a long time."

"I want to live there," said little James.

"Is Papa coming with us?" asked Charles.

"No," said Nell. "If you went, you'd have to go alone."

"Without you?" said Charles.

She nodded.

"Then I won't go," he answered haughtily—royally, thought Nell. The Divine Right of the adored child shining in his eyes.

She thought, Mr. Otway shall be his tutor. Poor Tom Otway, he'll be glad of a roof to his head and his food each day.

Little James had taken her hand and was staring into space. He was picturing himself in France.

Nell thought: Lord Beauclerk would not feel the break so much. Perhaps he should go to France. It is more important for a young son to have that air of nobility. Honors may not come so easily to him as to his brother. Nell snatched him up suddenly and held him tightly in her arms. I can't let him go, she told herself. He may be my lord Beauclerk, but he's my baby.

❁ ❁ ❁

Charles was relieved to have the troublemakers in the Tower. Their lodgings there were comfortable enough; they were allowed to have their own servants to wait upon them; they received visitors; in fact they lived like the noble lords they were; there was only one thing they lacked, and that was freedom.

Charles trusted none. To Danby, to Louise, he listened with sympathy; he visited Nell's house and talked with the utmost friendship to her Whig friends. But all the time he was playing the secret game. He had one great desire—to rule his country without the help of Parliament. Parliament, with its opposing parties, made continual trouble. The Whigs slandered the Tories and the Tories the Whigs. They were more concerned with their petty hatred for each other than their love of their country. Charles loved his country (as he would have been the first to admit, loving his country was tantamount to loving himself) and he was determined to use all his skill—which was considerable when he brought it into play—to prevent himself ever going on his wanderings again.

He supported Danby because Danby was a wizard who had managed his financial affairs as they had never been managed before. He did not believe he could afford to do without Danby. For the first time since he had come to England he felt his affairs to be in good order. He placated Louise because she was Louis' spy, and it was of the utmost importance that he should keep Louis' friendship. The bribes he was taking from France now, in exchange for which he kept aloof from the Continental war, were the very reason for his country's prosperity. Charles had always known that the country which stood aloof from war and concentrated on trade was the prosperous one. It was pleasant therefore to receive Louis' bribes for keeping a peace which in any case he had intended to keep. He pretended to take Louise's advice. Poor Louise! She must please Louis. He had to satisfy her in some way, and for the life of him he could not bring himself to visit her as often as he once had.

As for Nell, her dabbling in politics amused him so much that he could not keep away from her *salon.* She had as much understanding of politics as Old Rowley the stallion and Old Rowley the goat—who shared his nickname. Politics to Nell meant one thing: Who gives a dukedom to my lord Burford and makes the noble Earl's mother a Countess, shall have my support. Danby had been against elevating Nell—doubtless on account of Louise—therefore Nell was Danby's enemy.

So while Charles sympathized with Louise and Danby's Tories and turned a sympathetic ear to Nell's Whigs, he went his own way. And while he was accepting Louis' bribes he was trying to go ahead with the arrangements for the marriage between his niece, Mary, and William of Orange.

❁ ❁ ❁

James sought his brother. James' face was dark with passion.

"Charles, you cannot mean this. My daughter Mary to marry that man!"

"Forget that he is the Protestant leader of the Dutch, and you'll see what an excellent match he is."

"The man's a monster!" said James indignantly.

"The Prince is a brave soldier, Stadtholder of Holland, and our nephew."

"My little girl is too young."

"Your little girl is a Princess and therefore prepared for early marriage."

"Have you forgotten his conduct when he was here?"

"That is a long time ago, and we made him drink too much. When a man drinks too much he does wild things. That is why I like only to drink when I am thirsty."

"Brother, for the love of God do not give my little Mary to this man."

"But this marriage is a necessary part of the peace between our two countries."

"A man who smashed windows to get at the maids of honor. He is a lecher. He is debauched."

"Oh, come . . . no more than the rest of us."

James went away. He went to his little daughter and took her solemnly into his arms.

"Papa," said Mary, "what ails you?"

"My little one . . . my little one," sighed James.

Charles had followed him. He said: "Mary, a great future awaits you. You are to have a fine husband, and that is what every young lady—if she is wise—looks for."

But Mary's frightened gaze was fixed on her father's face. She stared at him and slowly the tears began to fall down her cheeks. She understood. She would marry, and when a Princess married she was forced to leave her home.

❁ ❁ ❁

The King liked to please Nell. Most of her requests—apart from the demand for that title which she felt should belong to the mother of her boys—were for others. She pleaded fiercely for Buckingham. His Majesty had so enjoyed the noble Duke's company. Could he ever be really angry with Lord Buckingham? Not for long, surely. They missed him at her parties; and had Charles forgotten how they had been friends together in their childhood?

Charles prevaricated. He was afraid of offending Louise and Danby, whom he wished to keep in the dark concerning the policy he was pursuing regarding the French. The fact that he wished to bring about the marriage of Mary and William of Orange would displease Louis and therefore Louise, though Louise, still unsure of her position, was giving little trouble concerning this marriage. He did not wish to sway too much to the side of the Whigs by releasing Buckingham.

But he hinted to Nell that if she visited Buckingham in his prison she might intimate that the King no longer wished his old friend and companion of his boyhood to remain in the Tower.

This Nell quickly did, with the result that Buckingham was granted leave for a month's freedom to help him throw off several indispositions which he had developed during his imprisonment. He did not return to prison, coolly taking up his quarters with his friend Rochester instead. They kept merry company with Nell Gwyn, and the King could not exclude himself from such entertainment as they gave.

Louise wept bitterly and told Charles that she feared he no longer had any regard for her. If he had, how could he show such friendship to those who sought to harm her?

The King softened towards Louise. He was more tender than he had ever been, because his love for her was gone. Poor Fubbs! She had never been the same since she had caught his sickness and she did not cease to remind him, with reproachful looks and hints, that she had suffered through him. He promised her that Buckingham should be dismissed from Whitehall; and he was as good as his word, knowing that Buckingham would not go far away. The Duke did indeed move to Nell's house in Pall Mall, and there the merry supper parties continued.

And the French ambassador was almost as concerned about the King's attendance at Nell's parties, those hotbeds of Whiggery, as he was about this proposed marriage between Mary and William of Orange.

❁ ❁ ❁

Meanwhile Charles was playing his lonely political game. The proposed marriage had thrown Louis into a fluster of anxiety. Louis, engaged in Flanders, was finding that the Dutch were a race of brave men, and stubborn fighters. William of Orange had proved himself to be a leader of genius, and Louis' hopes of quick victory were not fulfilled. There was one thing Louis dared not face—an alliance between England and Holland.

Charles went with apparent heedlessness to Newmarket. He went to Windsor to fish. He laughed and made merry at the parties his mistresses arranged for him. Danby reproved him for his friendship with the Opposition, but he merely laughed at Danby. "I declare," he cried, "I will not deny myself an hour's pleasure for the sake of any man."

Danby, bewildered and unable to understand on whose side the King was, wrote to Louis making fresh demands and promises. Charles read his Treasurer's letters. To all of these Charles gave his royal sanction. "This letter is writ by my order. C.R."

Louis continued to pay to keep England aloof to enjoy that peace which her King was determined to have. Louis was assured that the talk of a marriage between England and Holland was necessary to keep the people quiet and to prevent their demanding intervention in the war on the side of Holland.

But in October of that eventful year Charles announced the engagement of William and Mary. England and Scotland went wild with joy because they saw in this marriage an end to the menace of popery.

Not all rejoiced. In her bedchamber a fifteen-year-old girl sobbed bitterly while her father knelt by her bed and sought to comfort her.

❁ ❁ ❁

It was a misty November day, and in the Palace of St. James were assembled those who would attend the marriage ceremony of the little fifteen-year-old Princess Mary. In Mary's bedchamber an altar had been set up, for it was here in this room that the ceremony was to take place.

The bride's eyes were swollen; she had wept incessantly since her father had told her the news. She was terrified of the small pale young man with the grim face who seemed to her so cold and so different from her father and her Uncle Charles. They told her that she should be proud of her husband. He was a great soldier. He was called the "hero of Nassau." He had waged war on the invaders of his country; he had declared with such fervor his willingness to die rather than give in that his countrymen had rallied about him and followed his example. Nor had those been idle words. Mary was to marry a man whose name would be spoken of with awe every time military operations were mentioned. He was her cousin, her uncle had pointed out, his own sister's boy; and when that sister—Mary's own namesake—had died, Charles had promised his care of little Dutch William.

"And how could I relinquish that care to better hands than yours, my dearest niece?" asked Charles.

But Mary merely threw herself into the royal arms and sobbed bitterly. "Let me stay, Uncle. Please, please, dearest Uncle, Your Majesty, let me stay with you and Papa."

"Nay, nay, you'll be laughing at yourself in a short while, Mary. You are but a child, and we must all, alas, leave childhood behind us. You will rule Holland with your husband and, if this new child your new mother is to have should be a girl . . . well, then, one day you may rule England. If that became necessary, you'd have need of Dutch William."

But Mary could only sob and refuse to be comforted.

Now in her familiar room the King and the bridegroom were present, and the King was saying: "My little niece is the softest-hearted creature in the world. She and her sister Anne have been dear friends since their childhood. Poor Anne is suffering now from sickness, and her sister suffers with her. It is a pity that her dearest Anne cannot be present to witness the greatest moment her sister has yet experienced."

Mary wanted to cry out: "I do miss Anne. I would that she were here. But Anne will get well and, when she is well, I shall be far away. I shall lose all those I love, and in their place there will be this cold man who frightens me."

Her father had entered now. She suppressed the desire to run to him, to fling herself into his arms. There were tears in James' eyes. Dearest Papa, she thought, he suffers as I do. With James was Mary's stepmother, Mary Beatrice; she was large with child, and her beautiful dark eyes were fixed with compassion on her stepdaughter. Mary Beatrice had offered as great comfort as any could during the preceding days. She herself had not been long in England, and when she had first come she had been every bit as frightened as poor Mary was now. "That was different," said Mary. "You married Papa . . . my Papa . . . There is no one quite as kind as Papa." "I did not think so. I burst into tears when I first saw him. It is only now that I begin to know him that I realize there was no need for those tears. So you will find it with William."

Mary had allowed herself to be comforted, but now, in the presence of Dutch William, her courage was failing her again.

Charles, looking anxiously at his niece, was eager to have the ceremony done with. He called impatiently to Compton, the Bishop of London, who was to perform the ceremony.

"Come, Bishop," he cried. "Make all the haste you can, lest my sister here, the Duchess of York, should bring us a boy, and then the marriage will be disappointed."

William looked grim. His uncle's jovial cynicism astonished him. He was aware that Charles knew that, in marrying Mary, he was hoping that one day he would come to the throne of England, but he thought it astonishing that Charles should refer to it at the ceremony.

He looked with distaste at the poor blubbering child, in whom his hopes were centered. She did not attract him, but there would be others who did.

"Who gives this woman?" the Bishop was asking.

"I do," said Charles, firmly.

The Prince said the words required of him. He put a handful of gold coins on the book, as he endowed Mary with all his worldly goods.

"Put it in your pocket, Mary," said the King with a smile. "For that is all clear gain."

After that the ceremonies began. The bridegroom was aloof and indifferent to his bride, who continued to weep throughout the banquet in a quiet helpless way as though she had given up all hope of ever being happy again.

Charles was glad he had brought Rochester out of retirement. He found Dutch William and his friends a dull crowd, and was glad when the time came for him to officiate at the ceremony of putting the couple to bed.

Poor little Mary looked with dull eyes at those who crowded into the bedchamber to break bread and drink the posset, and cut her and her husband's garters.

At last Mary and William were in the great bed together, and the King himself drew the curtains.

He did not look at Mary. He could not trust himself to meet the appeal in the tear-drenched eyes of his little niece.

He glanced at grim William, who looked like a man at a funeral rather than at his own nuptials.

"Now, nephew, to your work!" cried Charles. "St. George for England!"

❁ ❁ ❁

Charles could no longer deceive Louis. The marriage with Holland was a fact, and the Parliament—Shaftesbury had now been released from the Tower and was back in the House—were demanding that an army be raised to assist Holland. Louis, through Danby and Louise, increased Charles' pension. Charles, in accepting this, continued to assure Louis that the raising of the army was being effected only to pacify his people and keep secret his friendship with France.

Louis was realizing that, in hoping to work through Charles, he had given himself a more difficult task than he might have had. There were others in England who could be of the utmost use to him. He considered the career of Shaftesbury, he whom Charles had named "Little Sincerity," and he felt that the leader of the Opposition might be as useful to him as the King. Louis was rich; he offered more bribes, and it was not long before the members of the Opposition—those stern Protestants—were on his pension list.

Thereupon Parliament refused to advance the money necessary for the troops, and there was nothing to be done but disband the army. Charles was forced to pay them out of his own pocket, which again put him in the power of the Parliament, for it was necessary to ask for a further grant of money.

The old struggle between King and Parliament was revived. The Commons made it clear that they wished to control the country's affairs. Shaftesbury demanded the expulsion of the Duke of York. And Louis, furious at the way in which Danby had made him his dupe, passed over to the Commons Danby's letters in which he had arranged for Louis' bribes to be paid to the King.

Now Danby's enemies were at his throat.

Charles assured the Parliament that all Danby had done had been at his command; and indeed at the bottom of each letter was written in Charles' hand, "This letter is writ by my order. C.R." The Commons decided to ignore the King's part in these communications with Louis. They were out for Danby's destruction; and his impeachment was imminent.

Nell tore herself from the domestic flurries concerning my lord Burford's shoelaces and my lord Beauclerk's cough, and gave way to rejoicing. Danby and Louise had worked together, and she was sure that but for them she would have been a Countess by now, and my lord Burford a Duke.

Louise was afraid for, as Danby and she had worked together, she knew that many of his enemies strove to strike at her through him.

Then throughout the city there were rumors. They penetrated Whitehall.

Plots were afoot to murder the King and set the Duke of York on the throne.

People began to talk of a man named Titus Oates.

NINE

Terror swept over England. No one was safe from the accusations of Titus Oates. The Queen herself was in danger. As for Louise, the lampoons which the Whigs had been accustomed to pass round the coffeehouses were replaced by demands that she be brought to trial or sent back to France.

The King, hating trouble and realizing as few others did that Titus Oates was a rogue and a liar, did all in his power to keep himself aloof from the troubles. He dared not expose Titus; he dared not attempt to prevent the cruel executions which were taking place, for he knew that revolution was in the air and that he was in as dangerous a position as his father had been before he had laid his head on the block.

Louise was now known as the "Catholic whore." No sin was too black to be imputed to her. She trembled in her apartments and played with the idea of abandoning all she had worked for and slipping back to France.

Nell, on the other hand, was unaware of danger. The King seemed fonder of her than ever before. She wept now and then because Lord Beauclerk was in France, and thus her happiness could not be complete. Since the birth of her children her thoughts had been occupied with them almost to the exclusion of all else. Nell wanted to have the King and her sons with her, like any cozy family; then she could be happy. Plots whirled about her, but she was scarcely aware of them. Her so-called friend, Lady Harvey, had recently tried to bring to the notice of the King a lovely girl named Jenny Middleton. Lady Harvey—urged by her brother Montague—had sought Nell's help in bringing this girl to the King's notice, and Nell, her mind being taken up with her grief in the absence of my lord Beauclerk and the promotion of my lord Burford to a dukedom, had been quite unaware of Lady Harvey's intention of bringing to the King's notice one who would turn him from Nell herself.

The Middleton affair had collapsed unexpectedly when Montague, its instigator, who was suspected of being Jenny Middleton's father, was recalled to England. He was in deep disgrace because he had seduced Anne, Countess of Sussex (the young daughter of the King and Barbara) while they were both in France. As Montague had previously been Barbara's lover, Barbara was furious with the pair and had lost no time in acquainting the King with Montague's defection. The resulting disgrace of Montague meant that all connected with him were out of favor; thus the Middletons found it necessary to leave Court in a hurry; and Nell was safe. Only she herself was sublimely ignorant of the danger through which she had passed.

She was a Whig because her friends were Whigs. Buckingham and Rochester had been good to her, and Nell was the sort never to forget a friend. She was fond of Monmouth because he reminded her of her own little Charles, and he was her children's half-brother. She always felt that she wanted to ruffle that black hair and tell Prince Perkin to enjoy himself and not worry so much about whether he would inherit a crown. He seemed to forget that, if he ever received it, it could only be at the death of that one who, Nell believed, must be as beloved by his son as he was by her—King Charles, the fount of all their bounties.

She enjoyed life as best she could taking into account the absence of little James. She had a bonfire on November 5th, just outside her door in Pall Mall, and there she had a Pope to burn with the longest red nose that had ever been seen. The people rejoiced, calling her the "Protestant whore." And she was one of the few people at Court who was not in danger from Titus Oates.

Little Charles ran excitedly from the bonfire to his mother. He was throwing fireworks of such beauty that few had seen before.

"Now watch, good people," cried Nell. "My lord Burford will throw a few crackers."

So Lord Burford let off his fireworks and threw squibs at the long red nose of the burning Pope, and all the people about Nell's door that night rejoiced in her position at Court. They remembered that those who were poor had no need to ask help twice from Nell Gwyn. "Long life to Nelly!" they cried.

Nell went into her house that night when the celebrations were over, and as she herself washed the grime from the little Earl's face, he noticed that she was crying; and to see Nell cry was a rare thing.

He put his arms about her and said: "Mama, why do you cry?"

Then she hugged him. She said: "It has been a good day, has it not, my lord Earl? I was wondering what my lord Beauclerk was doing in the great French capital. And I was crying because he was not here with us."

Little Lord Burford wiped away his mother's tears. "I'll never go," he said. "Never . . . never. I'll never go to France."

❁ ❁ ❁

The fury continued, and Charles temporized. He gave way to demands. He did all he could to save Danby, but was forced to submit to his imprisonment in the Tower. He found it necessary to dismiss the Duke of York and send him into temporary exile in Brussels. Louise, sick both mentally and physically, could not make up her mind whether or not to leave for France. Hortense continued to play basset and amuse herself with a lover. The people realized that Hortense should not give them cause for concern. It was Louise, the spy of Catholic France, who was the real enemy of the country.

There was talk of the Queen's attempt to poison the King. Charles characteristically intervened and, although he would have welcomed a new wife and a chance to get a son which he felt would have solved most of his immediate troubles, gallantly stood by the Queen and saved her life.

Nell continued to receive the Whigs at her house. She was cheered wherever she went. People crowded into a goldsmith's shop, where the goldsmith was making a very rich service of plate, admired this greatly and were pleased because they believed it was to be presented to Nell. When they discovered it was for Portsmouth, they cursed the Duchess and spat on the plate.

Nell was immersed in family affairs. Rose had married again on the death of John Cassels. This time her husband was Guy Forster, and Nell was working hard to get a bigger pension for Rose and her husband.

While Nell was at Windsor news came to her of her mother's accident.

Madam Gwyn had moved to Sandford Manor where, at the bottom of her garden, was a stream which divided Fulham from Chelsea. One day she had wandered out to her garden and, well fortified with her favorite beverage, had slipped and fallen into the stream. It was a shallow brook but, being too drunk to lift herself out of it, she had lain facedown and drowned.

Nell hurried to London where Rose was waiting for her. They embraced and wept a little.

" 'Tis not," said Nell, "that she was a good mother to us, but she was the only mother we had."

So Nell gave the old lady a fine funeral and many gathered in the streets to see it pass. Madam Gwyn was buried in St. Martin's Church, and Nell ordered a monument to be erected over her grave.

Whigs and Tories gathered in the streets. The Whigs called attention to the virtues of Nell; the Tories jeered. There was a new spate of Tory lampoons on Nell's upbringing in her mother's bawdy-house.

Nell snapped her fingers and went back to Windsor to join the King.

❁ ❁ ❁

Charles knew that he was passing through the most dangerous time of his life. As an exile he had longed to regain his kingdom, but then he had been young. Now he was aging; he had enjoyed almost twenty years of that kingdom, but he knew that if he did not walk with the utmost care he would lose it again; and he wondered whether, if he lost it, he would ever have the strength to recover it.

He tried to lead the life he loved—sauntering in his parks, his dogs at his heels, feeding his ducks, exchanging witty comments as he went. He sat for long hours fishing on the banks of the river at Windsor. He wished that he could prorogue Parliament and prevent its ever sitting again. If he had enough money with which to manage the affairs of the country, he believed he could rule in peace; he could put an end to this terror which hung over his country. He would demand freedom of thought in religious matters for all men. He saw no peace for any country when there was religious conflict. He wished to say: Think as you wish on these things, and let others go their way. He himself would never feel bound to any religion; he merely wished for freedom for all his subjects.

He wanted peace, and while Whig was at Tory's throat, and vice versa, there would never be peace. Let a pleasure-loving man such as himself rule; let the people take their pleasures as he did; give him enough money to fit out a navy which would hold all enemies from his shores, and there would be peace and plenty throughout the land.

But this terror had come upon the country, and there was nothing he could do to prevent it. He was powerless in the hands of his Parliament; he was caught between the Whigs and Tories, the Protestants and the Catholics.

James had reproved him for wandering too freely in his parks alone. "Would his little spaniels protect him from an assassin's bullet?" James demanded. "Do not worry on that score," Charles had said. "They will never kill me to make you King."

He had said it with a laugh, but there was a great sadness in his heart. He feared for James; he greatly feared for James.

Oh, James, he mused again and again, if you would but turn from your holy saints, if you would but declare yourself a Protestant, England would accept you as my successor, and young Jemmy's nose would be out of joint. All this unrest would die down, for it flows out of the curse of this age—religious conflicts, and the curse of Kings: the inability to get sons.

He went to Nell for comfort.

Young Charles—my lord Burford, thought the King with a chuckle—came running to greet him.

"It is long since you have been to see me, Papa," said Charles.

" 'Tis but a few days."

"It seems longer," said the boy.

Charles ruffled the hair so like his own had been when he was a small boy roaming in the grounds of Hampton Court or lying on the banks at Greenwich watching the ships sail by.

"It was wrong of me."

"You should pay a penalty for your sins, Father."

"What would you suggest for me?"

"Stay all the time."

"Ah, my son, that would be my pleasure, and penances are not for the pleasure of the sinner, you know. You and I will go to Portsmouth to watch the launching of one of my ships, shall we?"

Charles leaped into the air. "Yes, Papa. When? . . . When? . . ."

"Very soon . . . very soon . . . I'll tell you something else. Ships have names, you know, just as boys have. What shall we call this one?"

Little Charles looked shyly at his father, waiting. "Charles?" he suggested.

"There are so many Charleses. Who shall say which is which? Nay, we'll call her Burford."

"Then she will be my ship?"

"Oh, no, my son. All those which bear our names do not necessarily belong to us. But the honor is yours. It will show the world how much I honor my son Burford. 'Twill make your mother dance a merry jig, I doubt not."

"Shall we tell her?" asked small Charles with a laugh.

"Come! We'll do so now."

And hand in hand they went to find Nell.

❁ ❁ ❁

Charles, determined to follow the old life as far as possible, gave up few of his pleasures. He could not stop the execution of the accused, though he had managed to save the Queen. The mob had allowed him that, for such was his charm that he had only to appear before them to subdue their anger, and he had gone in person to Somerset House to bring Catherine to Whitehall at the very time when the mob was howling for her blood. But he could not save others, for Titus Oates, it seemed, was King of London during those days of terror.

So he sauntered and fished and played games, as he had always done. He had forgotten that he was fifty, he had enjoyed such robust health that he seemed to have a notion that he always would.

He had played a hard game of tennis and, walking along by the river, he had taken off his wig and jacket to cool down.

This he had done effectively enough at the time, but when he went to bed that night he became delirious and his attendants hurried to his bedside, to find him in a high fever.

Shaftesbury, Buckingham, and the whole of the Parliament were filled with consternation. If Charles should die now, there could be no averting civil war. James would never stand aside, and, although Monmouth had his supporters, there were many who would die rather than see a bastard on the throne.

James' friends sent word to Brussels, telling him that the King was on the point of death and that he should return immediately. James left Brussels at once, leaving Mary Beatrice there and taking with him only a few of his most trusted friends—Lord Peterborough, John Churchill, Colonel Legge, and his barber.

He dressed himself in simple dark clothes and wore a black periwig, so that on his arrival in England none would recognize him. This was very necessary, for with his brother, as he believed, dying, his life would be worth very little if he fell into the hands of his enemies.

James believed that a great ordeal lay before him and, as John Churchill advised him, it was imperative that he should be at hand when his brother died, that he might be proclaimed King before Monmouth could be helped to the throne. James was very sad. He was a sentimental man and very fond of every member of his family. It seemed a terrible thing that a Stuart should be forced to fly the country while his brother was reigning King. Time and time again Charles had said to him: "Give up your popery, James, and all will be well." But, thought James, my spiritual well-being is of greater importance than what happens to me here on Earth.

He prayed and meditated on the future as he made the crossing in a French shallop, and when he arrived at Dover none knew that the Duke of York had come home.

Reaching London, he spent a night in the house of Sir Allen Apsley in St. James' Square, and Sir Allen immediately brought his brother-in-law, Hyde, to him with Sidney Godolphin.

"It is necessary, Your Grace," they told him, "to make all haste to Windsor where the King lies. He is a little better, we hear. But for the love of God ride there, and ride fast. As yet Monmouth and his followers know nothing of His Majesty's indisposition."

James set out for Windsor.

❁ ❁ ❁

Charles' barber was shaving him when James burst in.

He rushed to his brother and knelt at his feet.

"James!" cried Charles. "What do you here?"

"But you are yourself, brother. I had heard you were dying."

"Nay, 'twas but a chill and touch of fever. The river breezes cooled me too quickly after tennis. And kneel not thus. Let me look at you. Why, James, did you think to find me a corpse and yourself a King?"

"Brother, I rejoice that it is not so."

"I believe you, James. You have not the art of lying. And indeed you are wise to wish it at this time. I dare not think what would happen if I were so inconsiderate as to die now. I should leave the affairs of this country in a sorry state. Think of it, brother: The English persecute the Jesuits and they owe my life, and what is more their concern the peace of their country—if this present rule of Titus can be called peace—to the Jesuits' powder, quinine. I swear this drug has cured me."

He asked after Mary Beatrice and life in Brussels.

" 'Tis a sorry thing that you must be an exile, James," he said. "It would seem our family is cursed to be exiles. But, James, if you persist in acting as you have, and you should come to the throne, I'd not give you four years to hold it."

"I would hold it," said James, "were it mine."

"You must leave the country ere it is discovered that you returned."

"Brother, is it justice, I ask you, that I should be exiled? Monmouth remains here. You know that were it not for Monmouth there would not be this trouble. This illness of yours has brought home to me how dangerous it is for me to be so far away when Monmouth is so near."

Charles smiled wryly. James was right. It was unhealthy to have Monmouth in England during the Popish terror. Monmouth should go to Holland where he had so distinguished himself against the Dutch; and Catholic James should go to Protestant Scotland. It might be that both these men—both dearly beloved, but both recognized as sadly foolish—should learn something they both needed to learn, against a background which should be alien to them.

❁ ❁ ❁

Shaftesbury and his Whigs were determined on the downfall of the Duke of York. They did not wish Monmouth to remain abroad and, believing that the King's love for his eldest son was as strong as ever, they brought him secretly back from Holland.

Monmouth was nothing loath. He was now certain that he was to wear the crown. It was true he had been sent to Holland, but that was only that the King might have an excuse to be rid of the Duke of York. The foolish and criminal exploits of his youth had been forgiven him. He knew how to placate the King, and Charles was never annoyed with him for long at a time.

It was the anniversary of Queen Elizabeth's coronation, and the Whigs had chosen this occasion as an opportunity for staging a demonstration which they believed would induce the King to legitimize Monmouth and make him his heir. It was easy to whip up the people of London to a state of excitement. They had already been shown the villainy of the papists by Titus Oates, according to whom new plots were continually springing up. It was therefore not difficult to rouse them to fury, and they were soon parading the streets holding aloft effigies of the Pope and the Devil which it was their intention to burn.

For several days these scenes took place; then they gave way to rejoicing. Charles, watching from a window of Whitehall, having heard the bells ring out, saw his son riding triumphantly at the head of a procession, holding himself as though he already wore the crown.

He stopped at Whitehall, and a message came to Charles that his dearly beloved son craved audience.

Charles sent back a message.

"Bid him go back whence he came. I have no wish to see him. I will deprive him of all his offices since he has disobeyed my wishes in returning to England when I commanded him to stay abroad. Tell him, for his own safety, to leave the country at once."

Monmouth went disconsolately away.

Charles heard the crowds cheering him as he went. He shook his head sadly. "Jemmy, Jemmy," he murmured, "whither are you going? The path you are taking leads to the scaffold."

Then he recalled long-ago days in The Hague, when he had lightly taken Lucy Water as his mistress. From that association had sprung this young man, and in him had been born such ambition as could set a bloody trail across this fair land and plunge it into civil war as hideous and cruel as that which had cost Charles' father his head. And all for the sake of a brief passion with a light-o'-love.

I must save Jemmy at all costs, Charles decided.

✿ ✿ ✿

Nell was giving my lord Burford his goodnight kiss when she was told a visitor wished to see her.

She hoped it was my lord Rochester. She had need of his cheering company. Charles was melancholy. It was due to all these riots in the streets, all this burning of the Pope and the Devil. Poor Charles! She wished everyone would go about his business and let the King enjoy himself.

The visitor was shown in. He was wearing a long cloak which he threw off when they were alone.

"It's Perkin," cried Nell. "Prince Perkin."

He did not frown as he usually did when she used that name. Instead he took her hand and kissed it. "Nell, for the love of God, help me. The King has refused to see me."

"Oh, Perkin, it was wrong of you to come. You know His Majesty forbids it."

"I had to come, Nell. How can I stay away? This is my home. This is where I belong."

"But if you are sent abroad on a mission . . ."

"Abroad on a mission! I am sent abroad because my uncle must go."

"Well, 'tis only fair that if one goes so should the other."

"My uncle goes because the people force him to. You have seen they want me here. Did you not hear them shouting for me in the street?"

Nell shook her head. "All these troubles! Why cannot you all be good friends? Why are you always seeking the crown, when you know your mother was no better than I am. I might as well make a Perkin of little Burford."

"Nell, my mother was married to the King."

"The black box!" said Nell scornfully.

"Well, why should there not have been a black box?"

"Because the King says there's not."

"What if the King tells not the truth?"

"He says it all the same, and if he says 'no black box,' then there should be none."

"Nelly, you're a strange woman."

"Strange because I don't bring my little Earl up to prate about a black box which carries my marriage lines?"

"Don't joke, Nell. Will you keep me here? Will you let me stay? 'Twill only be for a short while, and mayhap you can persuade the King to see me. I've nowhere to go, Nell. There's no one I can trust."

Nell looked at him. Dark hair, so like my lord Burford's. Dark eyes . . . big lustrous Stuart eyes. Well, after all, they were half-brothers.

"You must be well-nigh starving," said Nell. "And there'll be a bed for you here as long as you want it."

❀❀❀

Monmouth stayed in her house, and the whole of London knew. It was typical that the King, knowing, should have said nothing. He was glad Nell was looking after the boy. He needed a mother; he needed Nell's sharp common sense.

Nell pleaded with Charles to see his son.

"He grows pale and long-visaged, fearing Your Majesty no longer loves him."

"It is well that he should have such fears," said Charles. "I will not see him. Bid him be gone, Nelly, for his own sake."

Nell was universally known now as the "Protestant whore." In the turmoil that existed it was necessary to take sides. She was cheered in the streets; for the London mob, fed on stories of Popish plots, looked upon her as their champion.

They loved the King, for his easy affability was remembered by all, and in this time of stress they sought to lay blame for everything that happened in his name on the people who surrounded him. The Duchess of Portsmouth was the enemy; Nell was the friend of the people.

One day, as she was riding home in her carriage, the mob surrounded it, and, believing that it was Louise inside, they threw mud, cursed the passenger, and would have wrecked the vehicle.

Nell put her head out of the window and begged them to stop. "Pray, good people, be civil," she cried. "I am the Protestant whore."

" 'Tis Nelly, not Carwell," shouted one and they all took up the cry: "God bless Nelly! Long life to little Nell."

They surrounded the coach, and they walked with her as she was carried on her way.

She was stimulated. It was pleasant to know that Squintabella, from whom it had been impossible to turn the King's favor, was so disliked and herself so popular. Nell enjoyed dabbling in their politics, even though she understood so little. Still she had understood enough to keep her place; she knew that she was no politician; she knew that the King could not discuss politics with her as he could with Louise. As she had said on one occasion: "I do not seek to lead the King in politics. I am just his sleeping partner."

So she was carried home.

❁ ❁ ❁

The troublous winter had passed into spring and now it was June. Nell never forgot that June day, because some joy went out of her life then, and she knew that no matter what happened to her she would never be completely happy again.

A messenger arrived at her house. Her servants looked subdued and she knew at once that something had gone wrong and that they were afraid to tell her.

"What is this?" she asked.

"A messenger," said her steward, Groundes. "He comes from France."

"From France. Jamie!"

"My lord Beauclerk was suffering from a sore leg."

"A sore leg! Why was I not told?"

"Madam, it happened so quickly. The little boy was running about happily one day, and the next . . ."

"Dead," said Nell blankly.

"Madam, all was done that could be done."

Nell threw herself onto a couch and covered her face with her hands. "It is not true," she sobbed. "There was nothing wrong with Jamie. He had a cough at times, that was all. Why was I not told? . . . My little boy, to die of a sore leg!"

"Madam, he did not suffer long. He died peacefully in his sleep."

"I should not have let him go," said Nell. "I should have kept him with me. He was only a baby. My little boy . . ."

They tried to comfort her, but she would not be comforted. She drove them all away. For once Nell wanted to be alone.

Her little James, Lord Beauclerk, for whom she had planned such a glorious future, was now dead and she would never see those wondering dark eyes looking at her again, never hear the baby lips begging her to dance a jig.

"I let him go," she said. "I should never have let him go. He was only a baby. But I wanted to make him a Duke, so I let him go, and now I have lost him. I'll never see my little lord again."

They sent Lord Burford in to comfort her. He wiped her eyes and put his arms about her.

"I'm here, Mama," he said. "I'm still here."

Then she held him fiercely in her arms. She did not care if he was never a Duke. The only important thing was that she held him in her arms.

She would keep him with her forever.

❁ ❁ ❁

Nell shut herself in with her grief. Life seemed to have little meaning for her. She blamed herself. She had so wanted the child to be educated like a lord. How thankful she was that she had kept one of her sons at home.

She was still mourning the death of James when the news of another death was brought to her. It was that of the Earl of Rochester. Rochester had been a good friend to her; his advice had always been sound; and because he was merry and wicked and, although three years older than she was, had seemed but a boy to her, she grieved for him. It seemed a sad thing that he, after only thirty-three years of life, should have died, worn out by his excesses. Poor Rochester, so witty, so brilliant—and now there was nothing of him but the few verses he had left behind.

Death was horrible. Her mother was gone, but she was old and Nell had never loved her. It was a marvel that the gin had not carried her off long before. But these deaths of such as Rochester and little Jamie moved her deeply. She might laugh; she might dance and sing; but she was aware of change.

She was glad she had known nothing of that fever which had attacked Charles so recently. There had been no need to feel anxiety then, because he was well again before she heard of it. But it could happen suddenly and mayhap next time it would not end so happily.

Rochester . . . Jamie . . . She could not forget.

Charles, sharing her grief in the loss of their son though not by any means feeling it as deeply as she did, was sad to see the change in her.

He wanted his merry Nell back again.

He took her to Windsor and showed her a beautiful house not far from the Castle.

This was to be Burford House, and it was the King's gift to Nell. It was a delightful place. "And so convenient to the Castle," said the King with a smile.

It was impossible not be charmed with the house. It seemed a fitting residence for my lord Burford. And Nell showed her gratitude by trying to dismiss all thoughts of her lost child from her mind. She had the interior of Burford House decorated by Verrio, the Court painter, who was also working on the Castle at this time. And Potevine, her upholsterer in Pall Mall, furnished the place to her satisfaction. The gardens, facing south, were a delight, and she and the King planned them together, with my lord Burford running from one to the other, happy to see his mother more like herself, and his father with her in the new home.

❁ ❁ ❁

With the terror at its height, the Whigs made an effort to force Charles to legitimize Monmouth. Thus only, they argued, could the King protect his own life and save his people from the Catholic plotters.

Charles, in the House of Lords, patiently pointed out that what they asked of him was illegal. He assured them that he intended to take great care of himself and his people.

It was pointed out to him that laws could always be changed in emergency.

"If that is your conscience," said Charles, "it is far from mine. I assure you that I love my life so well that I will take all the care in the world to keep it with honor. But I do not think it is of such great value after fifty to be preserved with the forfeiture of my honor, my conscience, and the law of the land."

Monmouth was present and Charles watched the young man as he spoke. He saw the bitter look in Monmouth's face; and he thought: I was a fool to think he loved me. What did he ever love but my crown?

The King won the day. But Shaftesbury would not give in. He had gone so far he could not draw back and he knew he had proved himself to be such an enemy to the Duke of York that he must at all cost prevent his coming to the throne. He now tried to bring a new bill to force Charles to divorce the Queen. Charles retaliated with his old gambit: the dissolution of Parliament.

Louise meanwhile had been in constant touch with the new French ambassador, Barrillon, who had replaced Courtin. She believed she saw a chance to reinstate herself with Charles.

She had made herself aware, during the recent years of terror, of every twist and turn in the complicated policy of the King and Parliament. Now that Danby was a prisoner in the Tower she had turned her attention to Lord Sunderland, one of the most important men in the country. She had used all her wits to save herself and had found it convenient to turn to anyone who she thought could be of the slightest use to her. She even helped Shaftesbury to reinstate himself; she made friendly overtures to Monmouth, though she secretly hoped that her son, the Duke of Richmond, might be legitimized and named heir to the throne; but she said nothing of this to Monmouth.

Louise was desperate and, being full of crawling as well, she began to sidle back to the King, and her ability to discuss with intelligence any new political move made him seek her company. He was visiting her every day, although he was spending his nights with Nell. Louise did not greatly care that this should be so, because she was beginning to realize that if she were clever enough both Louis and Charles could come to look upon her as a person important to the policies they wished to pursue. For Charles she was that one to whom he could confide what he wished for from the King of France; to Louis she was the person who wielded an influence over the King of England which she could use as he bade her.

She sought out the King very soon after the dissolution of Parliament and, seeing that she wished to speak with him alone, he allowed her to dismiss all those about them.

One of his little dogs leaped into his lap, and he fondled its ears as they talked.

"What great good fortune," said Louise, "if it were never necessary to reassemble Parliament!"

"I agree with all my heart," said Charles. "But alas, it will be necessary ere long to do so."

She had moved nearer to him. "For what reason, Charles?"

"Money," he said. "I must have money. The country needs it. I need it. The Parliament must assemble and grant it to me."

"Charles, what if there were other means of filling your exchequer . . . would you then think it necessary to call the Parliament?"

He raised his eyebrows and smiled at her, but he was alert.

"If I could make certain promises to Louis . . ." she began.

"There have been promises."

"Yes, and the Dutch marriage and your failure to confess yourself a Catholic angered Louis."

Charles shrugged lightly. "I was forced into the first," he said. "The people wished it. As for the second—that is something my people would not tolerate."

"And you yourself, Charles?"

"I am an irreligious fellow. I cannot conform, you know. I think that the Catholic Faith is more befitting to a gentleman than gloomy Presbyterianism certainly. But I am my grandfather again. England is worth a principle, as Paris was with him."

"In the Treaty of Dover you promised to proclaim yourself a Catholic."

"At the appropriate time," said Charles quickly.

"And that will be . . . ?"

"When my people will accept a Catholic King."

"You mean . . . never as long as you live."

"Who can say? Who can say?"

Louise was silent for a while. Religion, as with his grandfather who had saved France from the disaster into which religious conflict was plunging the nation, would always be for Charles a matter of expediency. She must shelve the great desire to fulfill that part of her duty to France. But she must seek to bind Charles closer to the country of her birth, not only to please the French King, but to make her own position secure.

"If you had money," she said, "if you had, say, four million livres over three years you would be able to manage your affairs without calling Parliament."

"You think Louis would pay . . ."

"On conditions which me might arrange . . ."

Charles put down the lapdog and held out his hand. "Louise, my ministering angel," he said, "let us talk of those conditions."

❁ ❁ ❁

Before the next Parliament was called Charles was to receive £200,000 a year for a promise of neutrality towards Louis' Continental adventures. Charles saw his chance to rule without a Parliament, which in the past he had needed merely to vote him the money he required for governing the country.

When the new Parliament met, the King's expression was inscrutable.

He called to the Lord Chancellor to do his bidding, and the Lord Chancellor declared that the Parliament was dissolved.

Charles left the chamber, where everyone was too astonished to protest. When he called to his valet to help him change, Charles was laughing. "You are a better man than you were a quarter of an hour since," he said. "It is better to have one King than five hundred."

He continued in high good humor. "For," he said, "I will have no more Parliaments, unless it be for some necessary acts that are temporary only, or to make new ones for the general good of the nation; for, God be praised, my affairs are now in so good a position that I have no occasion to ask my Parliament to vote me supplies."

Thus Charles, true ruler of his country through the French King's bribes, determined not to call a Parliament for as long as he lived. Nor did he.

Now he began to deal with the terror. Shaftesbury was sent to the Tower. Oates was arrested for slander. Monmouth was arrested and, although he was soon released, and Shaftesbury escaped to Holland, gradually there was a return to peaceful living.

TEN

In a house not far from Whitehall a little group of men sat I huddled about a table. They spoke in whispers and every now and then one of their number would creep to the door and open it silently and sharply, to make sure there was no one listening outside. At the head of the table sat a tall handsome young man whose brilliant eyes were now alight with ambition. Monmouth believed that before the year was out he would be King of England.

He listened to the talk of "Slavery" and "Popery," from which these men were swearing England should be freed forever. Popery and Slavery had special meanings; one referred to the Duke of York, the other to the King.

Monmouth was uneasy. He hated Popery. But Slavery? He could not stop thinking of eyes which shone with a special affection for him, and he pretended to misunderstand when they talked about the annihilation of Slavery.

Rumbold, one of the chief conspirators, was saying: "There could not be a spot more suited to our purpose. My farm—the Rye House—is as strong as a castle. It is close to the road where it narrows so that only one carriage can pass at a time. When Slavery and Popery ride past on their way to London from the Newmarket races we will block the way."

Colonel John Rumsey said: "We might overturn a cart. Would that suffice?"

"Amply." Rumbold looked round the table at the men gathered there: Richard Nelthorpe, Richard Goodenough, James Burton, Edward Wade, and many more—all good countrymen; and the nobility was represented by the Earl of Essex, Lord William Russell, and Algernon Sydney.

Essex said: "We would have in readiness forty armed men. They will quickly do their work."

"And should there be trouble?" asked Captain Walcot, another of the conspirators. "What if the guards come to the aid of Popery and Slavery?"

"Then," said Rumbold, "we can retire to the Rye House. As I said, it is as strong as a castle and can withstand a siege until the new Government is set up. My lord Monmouth will be in London."

"And," said Sydney, "he will but have to go into the streets and proclaim himself King."

They were all looking at the young Duke, but Monmouth did not see them. He was remembering a room in a foreign house, a blowsy and beautiful woman upon whose bed he had climbed. He remembered playing soldiers with her sweetmeats; he remembered the arrival of a tall man who had tossed him to the ceiling and caught him as he fell. He remembered his own choking laughter of excitement; he remembered that wonderful feeling—the thrill of being thrown, and the certain knowledge that those hands which caught him would never fail.

Now they were asking him to aid in the murder of that kind father.

"You cannot," said a voice within him.

But he could not shut out the thought of the glittering crown and the power that went with it.

❁ ❁ ❁

Charles had settled into a life of ease.

Less vigorous than he had been, he had three favorites, and they were adequate. There was Louise—and he never forgot that it was Louise's advice and her negotiations with the French which had brought him the pension enabling him to rule without a Parliament—and he looked upon Louise as his wife. It was Louise who received foreign visitors, for she understood politics as poor Catherine never could. Louise looked upon herself as Queen of England, and acted the part with such poise and confidence that many had come to consider her as such. She felt herself to be so secure that she did not hesitate to leave England and take a trip to her own country. There she had been received as a Queen, for the French King, even more so than the King of England, was sensible of her services. She had demanded the right to sit on a *tabouret* in the presence of the Queen of France, and this had been granted her. Louis had done great honor to her and everywhere she had been received with the utmost respect. Louise, practical as ever, had set about wisely investing the great fortune she had amassed while in England. This was her real reason for coming to France. And, strangely enough, on her return to England she had been received with more honor than ever before. The people of England, hearing of the homage paid to her by the King of France for acting so ably as his spy, were ready to accord her that respect which hitherto they had always denied her.

Then there was Hortense—serenely beautiful, cultured, easygoing, very like the King in character—who was still the most beautiful woman in the kingdom, for her beauty was such that nothing seemed to mar it; and, although she took lovers and sat late at the basset table, she did all these things with such serenity, never departing from a mood of contentment, that there were no lines of dissipation to mark the beautiful contours of her perfect face. So lovely she was that men of all ages fell in love with her. Even her own nephew, Prince Eugéne de Savoy-Carignan, when he visited London, did so, and had fought a duel for her sake with Baron de Bainer who was the son of one of the generals of Gustavus Adolphus; in this duel Bainer was killed, and at the Court of Versailles there was amazement that a woman who was a grandmother could arouse such passion in the heart of a young man who was moreover her nephew. But Hortense went on calmly playing basset, taking lovers, receiving the King now and then; not seeking power as Louise did; content with her position as casual mistress, that she might not be denied the right to take another lover if so she wished.

Then there was Nell. Nell's role, Charles came to realize, was the more maternal one. It was to Nell he went for amusement and for comfort. Nell's love was more disinterested than the others'. Nell loved him, not always as a lover, not as a King; but understanding that in him which—cynic though he was—had never quite grown up, she was his playmate; she was his mistress when he desired her to be; she was his solace and his comfort.

Recently he had laid the foundation stone of Chelsea Hospital, which was to be a refuge for disabled old soldiers, and it was Nell who, with Sir Stephen Fox—for so many years Paymaster to the Forces—had urged him to this benevolent act. He smiled often remembering her enthusiasm and how, when she had seen Wren's plans of the hospital, she had protested angrily that it was too small. Then with a roguish laugh she had turned to the King. "I beg Your Majesty to make it at least as big as my pocket handkerchief," she had pleaded. He had answered: "Such a modest request could not be denied you." Whereupon she confounded him—and Wren—by tearing her handkerchief into strips and making a hollow square into which she fitted the plans. Charles was so amused that he agreed to increase the size of the proposed hospital.

He had come to know, in these years when he was aware of the slight ailments which must attack a man even as healthy as himself; that Nell was more important to him than any of his mistresses. Louise he admired as a clever woman who had risen from obscurity to be the power behind the throne; Hortense must be admired for her beauty; but it was Nell whom he could least bear to lose.

But he was a fortunate man. There was no need to lose any one of them. His pension from Louis enabled him to meet his and his country's commitments. He could dabble in scientific experiments in his laboratory; he could sit by the river and fish; he could go to the play with Louise on one arm and Nell on the other. He could spend his time between Whitehall and Windsor, Winchester and Newmarket.

Many of his friends were no longer with him. Buckingham, after the defeat of the Country Party; had left public life and retired to Helmsly in Yorkshire. He regretted George's gay company, but wherever George had been there also had been trouble. Rochester was dead. There would be no more witty verses stuck on bedroom doors; but those verses of his had been scurrilous indeed and had doubtless done much to dissatisfy the people. James, his brother, was back in England and, though he prophesied trouble for James when he came to the throne, and feared that James would not last long as King, he advised him now and then on ruling as he was ruling, keeping Parliament in recess and thus preventing that deadly rivalry between Whig and Tory which had almost brought the country to revolution. In any case he could tell himself that the ruling of the country would be James' affair, and any trouble that ensued could not reach him in the grave. His dear son, Monmouth, realized now that he had been foolish. He knew that he could never have the crown. "Why you, Jemmy?" Charles had said.

"Think of all the sons I have who might as easily lay claim to the throne." And Jemmy had looked sheepish, while Charles put his arm about his shoulders. " 'Tis my wish," he had said, "that you thrust such thoughts from your mind since they can bring nought but suffering to you and to me."

Then Jemmy had looked at him as the young Jemmy had when he had plunged his little hands into his father's pockets for sweetmeats. Charles remembered saying then: "Why, Jemmy, is it the sweetmeats you are glad to find, or your father?" And the young Jemmy had considered this and suddenly thrown his arms about his father's neck. Jemmy, the young man, had not altered, thought Charles. He longs for a crown. But he knows it is dangerous longing.

Thus was his state when he travelled down to Newmarket for the season's races. The Duke of York was with him and they were seen together, the best of friends, the most loving of brothers. Charles wanted the whole country to know that, now that he had given up all hope of getting a son, his brother James was the only man who could follow him to the throne.

They planned to leave Newmarket on a certain day, and the journey home would be, as usual, through Hoddesdon in Hertfordshire and past the Rye House.

At the Rye House a group of men eagerly awaited the coming of the coach in which the royal brothers would be riding. All plans were completed. There was the cart which would be set across the road. There were the conspirators waiting in the Rye House. In London the Duke of Monmouth waited. He could scarcely contain his impatience.

But the conspirators waited in vain for the coach to ride into the trap, for the day before Charles was to leave Newmarket there was a great fire in that town and many houses were burned down. That in which Charles and James were staying did not escape, and the King decided that they might as well set out for London a day before they had intended to.

Thus, when they came to that narrow stretch of road through which it was only possible for one coach to pass at a time, they went straight through, having no idea that, in the house close by, their enemies were preparing to murder them on the following day.

❁ ❁ ❁

It was some weeks later when important documents were brought to Charles. It appeared that a letter from a certain Joseph Keeling to Lord Dartmouth had been discovered, and in this letter was set out an account of the conspiracy which had been planned to bear fruit near the Rye House. Some of the minor conspirators, then feeling that it might be gainful to expose the plotters now that the plot had failed, were ready to come forward, explain all that had been planned, and incriminate those who has taken part in the plot.

There had been much talk of such plots. Only a short while ago the country had been roused to fury by the Meal-Tub plot, which had been concocted by the Papists as a retaliation for all the Popish plots which had grown out of the fevered imagination of Titus Oates. In that case papers relating to the plot, which was to raise an army and set up a Presbyterian republic, were supposed to have been discovered in a meal-tub. Therefore it was felt that the King would laugh to scorn this discovery of a new plot unless there was really tangible evidence to support it. Fortunately some letters of Algernon Sydney, as well as that of Keeling, were discovered, and when these were brought to Charles he could not doubt the existence of the Rye House plot.

Essex, Russell, and Sydney, with others, were arrested. But there was one name concerned in this which filled Charles with horror. There was no doubt that murder had been intended, and Jemmy was involved; Jemmy was one of the conspirators who had plotted the murder of his father.

The country was roused to fury. The death of all the traitors was demanded. The King was as popular now as he had been on the day of his restoration. Easygoing and affable, his people delighted in him, for he was never too proud to speak to the humblest of them, man to man; that was what they loved best in him. They laughed at the gay life he led. Why should he not? they demanded. Who would not support a seraglio if it were possible? All feared his death, for it was realized that he had but driven the threat of civil war underground. It was Charles with his disregard of Parliaments, his determination to keep England at peace, and living on the bribes of Louis, who was responsible for the peaceful state now enjoyed.

Russell and Sydney were executed. Essex took his own life in prison, and a new Lord Chief Justice was appointed to mete out justice to these men. His name was George Jeffreys and he had a reputation for severity.

The Rye House plot sealed Charles' triumph, for the Whig party was now completely out of favor. Nothing could have been more opportune than the discovery and frustration of such a plot.

Charles was safer than he had been since the early days of his Restoration; but his triumph was a bitter one.

He could not keep his eyes from that name which occurred again and again in the documents: James, Duke of Monmouth. James . . . Little Jemmy . . . who had plotted to murder his own father.

On the failure of the Rye House plot, Jemmy had hastily gone into hiding, but he was writing appealing letters to his father. "I was in this plot, Father," he wrote, "but I did not understand they meant to kill you."

Then how else, my son, said Charles to himself, could they have put you on the throne?

He knew that, had he cared, he could have drawn Jemmy out of his hiding place. He could have put Jemmy in the Tower with those other would-be murderers. But he could not bring himself to do it. He could not shut out of his mind the memory of little Jemmy, bouncing on his mother's bed, holding up imperious arms to his father.

He did not want to know where Jemmy was. If he did he must take him from his hiding place and put him in the Tower.

It was to Nell he turned for comfort. Nell was ashamed and angry because at one time she had helped "Prince Perkin;" she had kept him in her house and asked the King to see him. Now she realized she had preserved him that he might live to attempt to take his father's life.

"I want no more of him," said Nell; yet she could understand the King's grief. He loved the boy. He was his son. He was as dear to him as little Lord Burford.

Louise expressed anger against Monmouth, but the King sensed her pleasure. There were secrets in Louise's eyes, and Charles knew that at one time she had entertained hopes that her son, the Duke of Richmond, might be a possible heir to the throne. Louise was afraid because he had come near death, but that fear was really for the security of her own position.

Hortense expressed horror in her serene way. But Hortense was too careless of the future even to ponder what would become of her should her benefactor die.

And there in Charles' hands was the letter from Jemmy.

"What good can it do you, Sir, to take away your own child's life that only erred and ventured his life to save yours?"

That made the King smile. It was Jemmy's assurance that he had entered into the plot only to save the conspirators from violence. He would never have agreed to murder the father who had done everything for him.

"And now I do swear to you that as from this time I will never displease you in anything, but the whole study of my life shall be to show you how truly penitent I am for having done it. I suffer torments greater now than your forgiving nature would know how to inflict."

The Duke of York came to him as he sat with the letter in his hand.

"James," said Charles, "I have here a letter from Jemmy."

James' face hardened.

"Oh, I know you find it hard to forgive him," said Charles. "He is but a boy. He was carried away by evil companions."

"Evil, indeed, since 'twas murder they plotted."

"He had no intention to murder. He was there to restrain the others from violence."

"Then," said James grimly, "he knew not the nature of the plot."

"I like not to see this enmity between you two, James. I think of when I am gone. Why, brother, if you persist in your religion, I give you but four years as King—and mayhap then I am being over-generous. Peace between you and Jemmy would be a beginning of better things."

"You would call him back?" said James incredulously. "You could find it in your heart to forgive him when he has stood beside those who plotted to take your life!"

"He is my son," said Charles. "I cannot believe he is all bad. He was led away. And I do not think he intended to murder his father."

"I think he intended to murder his uncle!"

"Nay, James. Let us have peace . . . peace . . . peace. Meet the boy half-way. If he begs humbly for your pardon, if he can assure us that he had no intent to murder . . ."

James smiled wanly. Charles would have his way. And James understood. He was a father himself.

❁ ❁ ❁

Charles embraced his son. The young Duke had been brought secretly into the Palace, and Charles had prepared a letter which he would require Monmouth to sign.

"Father," said the young man with tears in his eyes.

"Come, Jemmy," said Charles. "Let bygones be bygones."

"I would never have let them kill you," sobbed Jemmy.

"I know it. I believe it. There! Sign this, and I will see that a pardon is issued to you."

Monmouth fell to his knees and kissed his father's hand.

"Jemmy," said Charles, "you do not remember, but when you were a small boy you tried to catch hold of a burning log. I stopped you in time and I did my best to make you understand that if you attempted to touch the fire you would be badly hurt. You did understand. I am telling you just that now."

"Yes, Father, and I thank you from the bottom of my heart."

"Now you must leave me," said Charles. "It would not be well for you to be discovered here now. The people do not forgive you as readily as your father does."

So Monmouth left his father, but, even as he moved quickly away from the Palace, he was met by some of his old friends. They knew where he had been and what he had done, and they pointed out to him that he had deserted those who had supported him and sought to put him on the throne, and once the confession he had signed was made public none of his supporters would ever plan for him again. He would be deemed but a fair-weather friend. Indeed, by signing the letter his father had prepared for him he had gone over to the enemy.

Monmouth, hot-blooded and impetuous, went back to Whitehall.

He faced his father. "I must have that confession," he said.

"Why so?" asked Charles coldly.

"Because it would do me great harm if it is known I signed it."

"Harm you to have it known that you did not plot against your father's life?"

"I must have it," persisted Monmouth.

Charles handed him the paper. Monmouth grasped it, but as he lifted his eyes to his father's face he was looking at a new man. He knew that Charles had thrown aside his illusions, had forced himself to accept his Jemmy for what he was—the son who would have murdered the father who had raised him up to where he was, and had done nought but what was for his own good; and this son would have murdered that father for his crown.

"Get out of here," said Charles.

"Father . . ." stammered Monmouth. "Where should I go?"

"From here to hell," said Charles.

He turned away, and the Duke crept out into the streets. He was holding the confession in his hand.

There were crowds in the streets. They were talking of Rye House. He listened to them. He took a look at his father's Palace, and he knew that at this time there was no place for him in England.

That night he took ship for Holland.

❁ ❁ ❁

Charles no longer thought of Monmouth. The Rye House plot had lost him his son, but it had brought an even greater power to him and with that power was peace. He was ruling as he believed a King, endowed with the Divine Right, should rule. His brother, the Duke of York, was reinstated as Lord High Admiral and, as James would not take the Test, Charles merely signed an order that, as brother to the King, he should be exempted from this.

Then began the happy months. His private life was as peaceful as his public life. All his children—with the exception of the one whom he had loved best—brought great pleasure to him.

He looked after their welfare, delighted in their triumphs, advised them in their troubles. He took charge of his brother's children's future, and married Anne to the Protestant George of Denmark—a not very attractive young man, no gallant, no wit, no scholar; but as his chief interest in life seemed to be food, Charles doubted not that Anne would be satisfied with him. He was over-fat, but Charles merrily advised him, "If you walk with me, hunt with me, and do justice to my niece, you will not long be distressed by fat."

It was Louise, strangely enough, who gave him cause for a slight attack of jealousy—but this was assumed more than deeply felt. A grandson of Henri Quatre and la Belle Gabrielle, one of the most notorious of his mistresses, came to England. This was Philippe de Vendôme, the Grand Prior of France. Louise appeared to be experiencing real passion for the first time in her life, for she seemed blind to the danger in which she was placing herself. Charles, indifferent, happy with Hortense and Nell, had really no objection to Louise's amusing herself elsewhere; he who had given his affection to Louise more for her political significance than for her physical attractions, would have stood aside. But Louise's enemies, who had gone under cover, now came forward to do all they could to make trouble between her and the King. In the end Charles arranged that the Grand Prior should be expelled from England.

It was Louise who suffered most from the affair. She was terrified that the Grand Prior, on returning to France, would make her letters public and expose her, if not to Charles' displeasure, to the ridicule of her fellow countrymen. Louis, however, realizing the importance of Louise to his schemes and not ungrateful for what he considered the good work she had done for France, forbade the Grand Prior to speak of his English love affair, and eventually the matter was forgotten.

That winter was the coldest for years. The Thames was so thick with ice that coaches were driven across it. A fair was set up on the ice which was firm enough to bear both booths and the weight of merrymakers. There was skating, sledging, and dancing on the frozen river.

London was now springing up, a gracious city, from the ruins of the great fire. The King's architect, Christopher Wren, had long consultations with His Majesty, who took a personal interest in most of the building.

On the Continent there were continual wars. Charles, absolute monarch, kept his country aloof. He had introduced, as far as he could, freedom of religion.

"I want everyone to live under his own vine and fig tree," he said. "Give me my just prerogative and for subsidies I will never ask more unless I and the nation should be so unhappy as to have a war on our hands and that at most may be one summer's business at sea."

And so his subjects, dancing on the ice at the blanket fair, blessed Good King Charles; and the King in his Palace, with his three chief mistresses beside him, was contented, for indeed, now that he was approaching fifty-five and suffered an odd twinge of the gout, he found these three enough. His Queen Catherine was a good woman; she was docile and gentle and never gave way to those fits of jealousy which had made such strife between them in the beginning. She was as much in love with him as she ever was. Poor Catherine! He feared her life had not been as happy as it might have been.

Nell was happy now, for Charles had given Lord Burford his dukedom and the boy was the Duke of St. Albans, so that Nell could strut about the Court and city, talking constantly about my lord Duke.

Dear Nelly! She deserved her dukedom. He would have liked to have given her honors for herself. And why should he not? It was others who had withheld them. Why should not Nelly be a Countess? She was his good friend—perhaps the best he ever had.

Yes, Nelly should be a Countess; and there was only one thing he needed to make him feel perfectly content. He thought often of Jemmy in Holland. It was such a pity that he could not have every member of his handsome family about him. He was so proud of them all. He was even honoring Moll Davies' girl—the last of his children, for there had been none after that bout of the disease which had robbed him of his fertility.

Ah, it was indeed a great pity that Jemmy was not there in this happy circle.

Poor Jemmy! Mayhap he had been led astray. Mayhap by now he had learned his lesson.

❁ ❁ ❁

Charles was in his Palace of Whitehall. It was a Sunday and he felt completely at peace.

In the gallery a young boy was singing French love songs. At a table, not far from where the King and his mistresses were sitting, some of the courtiers were playing basset.

On one side of the King sat Louise, on the other, Nell; and not far away was the lovely Hortense. And as Charles watched them all with the utmost affection, he was thinking that soon Jemmy would be home. It would be good to see the boy again. He could not let his resentment burn against him forever.

He bent towards Nell and said: "And how is His Grace the Duke of St. Albans?"

Nell's face was animated as she talked of her son's latest words and actions. "His Grace hopes Your Majesty will grant him a little time tomorrow. He says it is long since he saw his father."

"Tell His Grace that we are at his disposal," said Charles.

"The Duke will present himself at Whitehall tomorrow."

"Nell," said the King, "methinks His Grace deserves a Countess for a mother."

Nell opened her eyes very wide; then her face was screwed up with laughter. It was the laughter she had enjoyed when she sat on the cobbles of the Cole-yard with Rose, the laughter of happiness rather than amusement.

"Countess of Greenwich, I think," said the King.

"You are good to me, Charles," she said.

"Nay," he answered. "I would have the world know that I have both love and value for you."

❁ ❁ ❁

It was late that night. The King's page, Bruce—the son of Lord Bruce, whom Charles had taken into service, having a fondness for the boy, and had declared he would have him close to his person—helped him to undress and went before him with the candle to light him to his bed-chamber.

There was no wind in the long dark gallery, yet the flame was suddenly extinguished.

" 'Tis well we know our way in the dark, Bruce," said Charles, laying his hand on the young boy's shoulder.

He chatted awhile with those few whose duty it was to assist at his retirement for the night. Bruce and Harry Killigrew, who shared the bedchamber, said afterwards that they slept little. A fire burned through the night, but the King's many dogs, which occupied his sleeping apartment, were restless; and the clocks, which struck every quarter, made continual clangour. Both Bruce and Killigrew noticed that, although the King slept, he turned repeatedly from side to side and murmured in his sleep.

In the morning it was seen that Charles was very pale. He had had a sore heel for some days, which had curtailed his usual walks in the park, and when the surgeon came to dress the sore place he did not speak to him in his usual jovial manner. He said something which no one heard, and it was as though he were addressing someone whom they could not see. One of the gentlemen bent to buckle his garter and said: "Sir, are you unwell?"

The King did not answer him; he got up suddenly and went to his closet.

Bruce, terrified, asked Chaffinch to go to the closet and see what ailed the King, for he was sure that his behavior was very strange and it was unlike him not to answer when spoken to.

Chaffinch went into the closet and found the King trying to find the drops which he himself had made and which he believed to be efficacious for many ailments.

Chaffinch found the drops and gave them to Charles, who took them and said he felt better. He came out of the closet and, seeing that his barber had arrived and that the chair by the window was ready for him, he made his way to it.

As the barber began to shave him, Charles slipped to one side and Bruce hurried forward to catch him. The King's face was distorted and there was foam on his lips as he slipped into unconsciousness.

Those present managed to get Charles to his bed, and one of the physicians hastily drew sixteen ounces of blood. Charles had begun to writhe and twitch, and it was necessary to pry open his jaws lest he should bite his tongue.

James, Duke of York, wearing one shoe and one slipper, hurried into the apartment. He was followed by gentlemen of the Court.

"What is happening?" demanded James.

"His Majesty is very ill, mayhap dying."

"Let this news not go beyond the Palace," said James.

He looked at his brother and tears filled his eyes. "Oh, God," he cried. "Charles . . . Charles . . . what is happening, my dear brother?" He turned to the surgeons. "Do something, I implore you. Use all your skill. The King's life must be saved."

Those about the King now began to minister to him. Pans of hot coal and blisters were applied to every part of his body. Cupping glasses were brought and more blood was withdrawn. They were determined to try all cures in order to find the right one. Clysters were administered, emetics, purgatives, a hot cautery, and blistering agents were applied to the head, one after another.

In spite of these attentions Charles regained consciousness.

It was impossible to keep the news from leaking from the Palace. In the streets the people heard it in shocked silence. It could not be true. Such a little while ago they had seen him sauntering in the park with a mistress on either arm, his dogs at his heels. It could not have been more than a week ago. There had been no indication that he was near his end.

The Duke of York took charge and ordered that the news must be stopped at all ports. Monmouth must not hear what was happening at home.

The King smiled wanly at all those about his bed; he tried to speak to them, but could not.

The doctors would give him no rest. They began forcing more drugs down his throat; they gave him quinine which had served him well before; they set more hot irons on his head; they put spirit of sal ammoniac under his nose that he might sneeze violently. They proceeded with their cupping and blistering all through the day.

By nightfall he had lapsed into sleep and, mercifully, while he slept, those about him ceased their ministrations.

The next day he was weak but a little better. Still his physicians continued to plague him. He must drink broth containing cream of tartar; he must take a little light ale. He must submit to more clysters, more purging, more bloodletting, more blisters. He gave himself into the hands of his torturers with that sweetness of temper and patience which he had shown throughout his life.

To add to his discomfort, all through the day crowds entered his bedchamber to look on his suffering. He lay very still, in great pain, trying to smile at them.

In the streets the citizens wept and asked what would become of them when he was no longer there. They remembered the Popish terror; they remembered that the heir presumptive was a Catholic and that across the water the Duke of Monmouth was waiting perhaps to claim the throne.

This King of theirs, this kind-hearted cynic, this tolerant libertine, had stood between them and revolution, they believed. Therefore they must wait in fear for what would happen were he taken from them.

In the churches special services were held. Prayers were delivered that this sickness might pass and that they might see their King sauntering in his park once more.

By Wednesday he seemed better, and the Privy Council issued a bulletin to this effect. In the streets the people cheered wildly; they embraced each other; they told each other that he was a man with the strength of two; he would recover to continue to reign over them.

Although he was in great pain and was allowed no rest from his physicians, Charles managed to appear cheerful. But soon after midday on Thursday it became clear that he could not recover.

He joked in his characteristic way. "I am sorry, gentlemen," he said, "to be such an unconscionable time a-dying."

They sought new remedies, and it was hard to find one which they had not tried upon him. They gave him black cherry water, flowers of lime and lilies of the valley, and white sugar candy. They administered a spirit distilled from human skulls.

He asked for his wife. She had come earlier, they said, and now so prostrate with grief was she that she was fainting on her bed.

She had sent a message to him, begging his forgiveness for any faults she may have committed.

And when they told him this, they saw the tears in his eyes. "Alas, poor woman," he said. "She begs my pardon? I beg hers with all my heart. Go tell her that."

❁ ❁ ❁

Louise was waiting outside his apartments. The attitude towards her had changed subtly, and there were many to remind her that, since she was not the King's wife, she had no place in that chamber of death. She had hung over him when he was unconscious, but he had been unable to recognize her, and a great terror possessed Louise.

What will become of me now? she asked herself.

She was rich; she would return to France, to her duchy of Aubigny. But the King of France would no longer honor her, having no need of her services. He would remind her that she had failed in the one great task for which she had been sent to England. Charles had been paid vast sums of money to declare himself a Catholic at the appropriate time. Now he was dying and he had not done this. But he must do it. Louise must return to France victorious. She must say to Louis: "I came to do this and, although it was delayed to that time when he was on his deathbed, still I did what I set out to do."

She thought of Charles, only half conscious in his agony, made more acute by the attention of his doctors. It might well be that now was the time, when he could not be fully aware of what he did.

It must be done. Only thus could Louise serve the King to whose country she must soon return.

She sent for Barrillon.

"Monsieur L'Ambassadeur," she said, "I am now going to reveal a secret which could cost me my head. The King is at the bottom of his heart a Catholic. There is no one to administer to his need. I cannot in decency enter his room, for the Queen is there constantly. Go to the Duke of York and tell him of this. There is little time in which to save his brother's soul."

Barrillon understood. He nodded admiringly. It was in the interests of France that the King should die a Catholic.

By great good fortune, when Bishop Ken had come to the King's bedside to administer the last rites of the Church of England, Charles had turned wearily away. He had submitted to too much. He had never been a good churchman and he was not the man to change on his deathbed. He had lived his life as he had meant to live it; he had declared that the true sins were malice and unkindness and, within his limits, he had done his best to avoid these sins. He had said that the God he visualized would not wish a gentleman to forgo his pleasures. He had meant that; and he was no coward to scuttle for safety at the last moment.

The Duke of York came into his bedroom. He knelt by the bed and whispered in his ear. "For your soul's sake, Charles, you must die in the Catholic Faith. The Duchess of Portsmouth has told me of your secret belief. She will never forgive herself if it is denied to you."

At the mention of Louise's name Charles tried to turn his glazed eyes to his brother, and a smile touched his lips. Then he said, half comprehending: "James . . . do nothing that will bring harm to you."

"I will do this," said James, "though it cost me my life. I will bring a priest to you."

Into the chamber of death an altar was smuggled, and with it came a priest, Father Huddleston, a man who had helped to save Charles after Worcester and whom Charles had saved from death during the Popish troubles. In spite of his drugged and dazed state, Charles recognized him.

"Sir," said James, "here is a man whose life you saved and who is now come to save your soul."

"He is welcome," said Charles.

Huddleston knelt by the bed.

"Is it Your Majesty's wish to receive the final rites of the Catholic Church?"

The glazed eyes stared ahead. Charles was conscious of little but his pain-racked body. He thought it was Louise who was beside him. Louise making her demands on behalf of the King she was really serving.

"With all my heart," he said wearily.

"Do you desire to die in that communion?"

Charles nodded.

He repeated all that Huddleston wished him to.

His lips moved. "Mercy, sweet Jesu, mercy."

Extreme unction was administered. Charles could scarcely see the cross which Huddleston held before his eyes. He was conscious for brief intervals before he swooned with the pain and the exhaustion which was in part due to the terrible ordeal through which his physicians had caused him to pass.

When the priest left, those who had been waiting outside burst into the room.

❁ ❁ ❁

From her house in Pall Mall Nell looked out on the street. She saw the people silently standing about. London had changed. It was somber out there in the streets.

She could not believe that she would never see him again. She thought of the first occasion she had seen him at the time of his Restoration, tall, lean and smiling, the most charming man in the world. She thought of the last time she had seen him when he had taken her hand and promised to make her a Countess that all might know what love and value he had for her.

And now . . . never to see him again! How could she picture her life without him?

She sat still while the tears slowly ran down her cheeks.

She thought, I shall never be happy again.

Her son came and threw himself into her arms. He was sobbing wildly.

He knew, for how could such things be kept from children?

She held him fast against her, for in those moments of desolate grief she could not bear to look into that face which was so like his father's.

She did not think of the future. What did the future matter? Life for her was blank since her King and her love would no longer be there.

❁ ❁ ❁

Charles lay still, uncomplaining. He was aware that he was dying and that those who crowded into his apartment had come to take their last farewell.

They knelt about his bed, his beloved children, and he blessed them in turn. He looked in vain for one, for he had forgotten that his eldest son was still in exile.

He called his brother to him.

"James," he said. "James . . . I am going. . . . It will not be long now. Forgive me if I have been unkind. I was forced to it. James . . . may good luck attend you. Look to Louise. Look to my poor children. And, James, let not poor Nelly starve."

He sank back then; he was conscious of those weeping about his bed. Scenes from his past life flitted before his eyes. He thought he was sore from riding so far to Boscobel and Whiteladies. He thought he was cramped because he was hiding in an oak while the Roundheads searched for him below.

But then he knew that he was in his bed and that soon this familiar room would be his no more.

"Open the curtains," he said, "that I may once more see the day."

So they drew them back, and he stared at the window. He listened to the sounds of his city's waking to life, and he slipped into unconsciousness again.

He was breathing so painfully that his gasps mingled oddly with the ticking of the clocks. His dogs began to whimper. Then, just before noon, he fell back on his pillows and ceased to live.

Bruce, who had loved him dearly, said as the tears rolled down his cheeks: "He is gone . . . my good and gracious master, the best that ever reigned over us. He has died in peace and glory, and may the Lord God have mercy on his soul."

Author's Notes

The Wandering Prince

My plan is to write the story of Charles II, and as he was a King to whom women were of great importance, I propose to do so through the lives of those few women—among so many—who played the most significant parts, not only in his life, but in history.

It is in his dealings with women that Charles is usually seen at his best, for, rake though he was, he was invariably courteous and kind. He loved women, so naturally women loved him—a universal corollary, since the misogynist is always unpopular with women, while their constant admirer, even if he be as profligate as Charles himself, is treated with indulgence. People—men or women—are generally predisposed to love those who love them. That is why—certainly among women—England's Merry Monarch is England's most popular King.

The Wandering Prince, complete in itself, deals with the early life of Charles II as it is reflected in the lives of two women who were to have a far-reaching effect not only on Charles' life but on the history of these islands—his sister, "Minette" (Duchesse d'Orléans), and his mistress, Lucy Water.

Among the many books I have read in the course of my research I should like to acknowledge my debt to the following:

History of France. M. Guizot. Translated by Robert Black, M.A.

Madame. Memoirs of Henrietta, daughter of Charles I, and Duchess of Orléans. Julia Cartwright (Mrs. Henry Ady).

Diary of John Evelyn. Edited by William Bray, Prefatory Notes by George W. E. Russell.

Diary and Correspondence of Samuel Pepys.

Early Life of Louis XIV. Henri Carré. Translated by Dorothy Bolton.

Political History of England, 1603–1660. F. C. Montague, M.A.

History of England. William Hickman Smith Aubrey.

King Charles II. Arthur Bryant.

The Gay King. Dorothy Senior.

Old Paris. Its Courts and Literary Salons. Catherine Charlotte Lady Jackson.

Lives of the Queens of England. Agnes Strickland.

British History. John Wade.

A Health Unto His Majesty

Any novel dealing with the days of the Restoration must inevitably be impregnated with one characteristic which was a feature of the times: licentiousness. Therefore I feel that, when presenting this middle period of Charles' life beginning with the Restoration, I must remind my readers that England had suddenly emerged from several years of drab Puritan rule. Bull-baiting and such sports had been suppressed, not from any consideration for the animals concerned, but solely because the people were known to enjoy those sports, and, in the opinion of their rulers, enjoyment and sin were synonymous; the taverns had been abolished; the great May Day festival was no more; Christmas festivities—even the Christmas services in the churches—were forbidden; the theaters were closed and their interiors broken up, and anyone caught playacting was tied to a cart and whipped through the streets. It was therefore natural that, when the King returned, there should follow a turnabout, and it was only to be expected that the repressed population should swing violently in the opposite direction. Accordingly, no picture of Restoration days which ignores the fact would be a true one.

There may be some who will feel that my portrait of Charles is too flattering. I would say that excuses must be made for Charles' weaknesses as for those of his people. His fortunes had been subjected to a similar abrupt change; he had grown cynical during his exile and was determined never to "go a-travelling again." He was the grandson of Henri Quatre, the greatest King the French had ever known, the man who had united France and put an end to the civil wars of religion when he had declared that "Paris was worth a mass." It was understandable that Charles should regard his grandfather as an example to be followed. Henri Quatre had the same good nature, the same indifference to religion; he was known to have declared that conquest in love pleased him more than conquest in war, and he had more mistresses than any King of France had ever had—or ever has had—including the notorious François Premier. I would say that Charles was unlucky in living when he did. The great plague and the great fire ruined the commerce of the country while it was engaged on a major war. If he appeared flippant and preoccupied with his mistresses, while his country was in danger, he was not really so. His demeanor of indifference had been acquired during the hardening years of exile when disappointments had quickly followed one another; he did not show his feelings, but the real man is to be seen when, during the fire, he worked as hard as any, standing with water up to his ankles, passing buckets, shouting orders and witty encouragement, so that it was said that what was left of the City owed its survival to Charles and his brother. Charles wins my sympathy as the man whose kindness makes him unique in his times, the man who declared he was weary of the hangings of those men who had killed his father and been responsible for his own exile, as the man who visited Frances Stuart to comfort her when he no longer desired her and her friends had deserted her, and again as the husband who held the basin when his wife was sick—the kind and tolerant King. For this King, careless and easygoing as he might be, and licentious as he certainly was, remains unique in his age on account of his kindness and tolerance.

In the research I have undertaken to write the book I have read a great number of works. I list below those which have been most helpful:

The National and Domestic History of England. William Hickman Smith Aubrey.
Bishop Burnet's History of his Own Time.
King Charles II. Arthur Bryant.
Diary of John Evelyn. Edited by William Bray.
Diary and Correspondence of Samuel Pepys. Edited by Henry B. Wheatley.
The Diaries of Pepys, Evelyn, Clarendon and other Contemporary Writers.
Personal History of Charles II. Rev. C. J. Lyon.
Beauties of the Court of Charles II. Mrs. Jameson.
Lives of the Queens of England. Agnes Strickland.
Great Villiers. Hester W. Chapman.
Titus Oates. Jane Lane.
Political History of England. F. C. Montague, M.A.
British History. John Wade.
The Gay King. Dorothy Senior.

Here Lies Our Sovereign Lord

It is so generally believed that Charles died a Catholic that I feel I must explain why I do not hold that belief. The deathbed scene has always worried me a great deal because I have felt it to be out of line with Charles' character. Therefore I was anxious to find a convincing explanation.

It is true that Father Huddleston came to him on the night before he died, and that Charles made no protest when it was suggested that he be received into the Catholic Church; but when all the facts are considered I think there is a viewpoint, other than the accepted one, which serves to explain his acquiescence.

On that Sunday, February 1, 1685, he ate little all day; he passed a restless night and next morning, while he was being shaved, fell down "all of a sudden in a fit like apoplexy." He never fully recovered, although he had periods of consciousness during the next five days, which were spent in great pain aggravated by the attention of his physicians who, not knowing what remedies to use, applied most of those of which they had ever heard. During those five days, hot irons were applied to the King's head, pans of hot coals to all parts of his body, and warm cupping glasses to his shoulders while he was bled. Emetics, clysters, purgatives, blistering agents, foul-tasting drugs, and even distillations from human skulls were given to him—not once but continually. Spirit of sal ammoniac was put under his nose that he might have vigorous sneezing fits, and when he slipped into unconsciousness cauteries were applied to revive him. So that in addition to the pain of his illness he had these tortures to endure.

He knew that he was dying on the Monday, yet he made no effort to see a priest. When Bishop Ken begged him to receive the rites of the Church of England he turned away; but this was a natural gesture, for he was suffering great pain and discomfort, and he had never been a religious man. All through Monday, Tuesday, Wednesday, and Thursday he had been, as he said, "an unconscionable time a-dying," and on Thursday night the Duke of York and the Duchess of Portsmouth (who both had their reasons) brought Huddleston to his bedside; and at this late hour, according to those few people who were present, Charles joyfully received Huddleston's ministrations.

I believe that Charles was too ill to resist the importunings of his brother and his mistress. I believe that in that easygoing manner which had characterized his entire life he gave way as he had so often before. That is if, after four days of acute agony, discomfort, and intermittent unconsciousness, he was even aware of what he was doing.

According to Burnet, Ken pronounced the absolution of his sins over the King's bed, and in his last hours Charles said that he hoped he should climb to Heaven's gate; "which," goes on Burnet, "is the only word savoring of religion that he was heard to speak."

Charles' attitude to religion had always been constant. He had modeled himself on his maternal grandfather, Henri Quatre, who had ended religious strife in France when he changed from Huguenot to Catholic, declaring that Paris was worth a Mass. Charles believed that religious toleration was the way to peace. He was tolerant to Catholics, not because he was a Catholic, but because they were being persecuted. He had said of Presbyterianism: " 'Tis no religion for gentlemen." This was during his stay in Scotland when he had been forced to hear long prayers and sermons every day, and repent of so many sins that he said: "I think I must repent that I was ever born." He had declared: "I want every man to live under his own vine and fig tree." But this did not mean he was a Catholic.

His attitude to the Church was often frivolous. He had in his youth been hit on the head by his father for smiling at the ladies in church; and as Cunningham says, "he had learned to look upon the clergy as a body of men who had compounded a religion for their own advantage."

To his sister Henriette he wrote: "We have the same disease of sermons that you complain of. But I hope you have the same convenience that the rest of the family has, of sleeping most of the time, which is a great ease to those who are bound to hear them." He greatly regretted that he had not been awake to hear delivered to Lauderdale a reproof from the pulpit: "My lord, my lord, you snore so loud you will wake the King." Burnet, who was a large and vehement man, had once when preaching thumped his pulpit cushion crying: "Who dares deny it?" to which Charles answered audibly: "Nobody within reach of that devilish great fist."

It was Charles' belief that God would never damn a man for a little irregular pleasure; and he had declared his conviction that the greatest sins were malice and unkindness. Such a man would, in my opinion, never "play safe" at the eleventh hour. He had borne great pain with immense courage and patience which astonished all who beheld it. He was not afraid of death. If he believed that malice and unkindness were the greatest sins he must also have believed that he had sinned less than most men of his age.

I list below some of the books which have been of great help to me:

Bishop Burnet's History of his Own Times, with notes by the Earls of Dartmouth and Hardwicke and Speaker Onslow, to which are added The Cursory Remarks of Swift.

Diary of John Evelyn. Edited by William Bray.

Diary and Correspondence of Samuel Pepys.

A History of English Drama. (Restoration Drama 1660–1700.) Allardyce Nicoll.

The Private Life of Charles II. Arthur Irwin Dasent.

Royal Charles—Ruler and Rake. David Loth.

King Charles II. Arthur Bryant.

The Court Wits of the Restoration. John Harold Wilson.

The Story of Nell Gwyn. Peter Cunningham.

Nell Gwynne, 1650–1687. Her Life Story from St. Giles's to St. James' with some account of Whitehall and Windsor in the Reign of Charles II. Arthur Irwin Dasent.

Nell Gwyn. Royal Mistress. John Harold Wilson.

Great Villiers. Hester W. Chapman.

Louise de Kéroualle. H. Forneron.

Rival Sultanas: Nell Gwyn, Louise de Kéroualle and Hortense Mancini. H. Noel Williams.
Lives of the Queens of England. Agnes Strickland.
British History. John Wade.
History of England. William Hickman Smith Aubrey.

About the Author

JEAN PLAIDY is the pen name of the late English author E. A. Hibbert, who also wrote under the names Philippa Carr and Victoria Holt. Born in London in 1906, Hibbert began writing in 1947 and eventually published more than two hundred novels under her three pseudonyms. The Jean Plaidy books—ninety in all—are works of historical fiction about the famous and infamous women of English and European history, from medieval times to the Victorian era. At the time of Hibbert's death in 1993, the Jean Plaidy novels had sold more than fourteen million copies worldwide.

A Reader's Guide

THE LOVES OF CHARLES II

Jean Plaidy

About the Book

Charles II reigned during one of the most turbulent eras in England's history. Returning from exile after Cromwell's death-grip on the British Parliament, Charles was faced with the task of rebuilding the monarchy's respectability and restoring morale to the populace against a backdrop of Bubonic plague, antipapist hysteria, humiliating wartime defeat, and the tragic Pudding Lane fire that decimated two-thirds of London. Miraculously, however, Charles is remembered less for manning the helm during a succession of national disasters than he is for unleashing the joie de vivre of a people exhausted from the rigors of Puritanism. Perhaps the original "good-time Charlie," Charles gained the adoration of his subjects through his relaxed, convivial style and his unapologetic appetite for the many pleasures in life. Charles' reputation as a gifted lover threw dozens, if not hundreds, of women into paroxysms of lust, and, wittingly or not, he led by example a large-scale revolt against the sanctity of marriage, ushering in a culture of licentious freedom previously considered "French" and scandalous.

This extraordinary trilogy of short novels celebrates six of Charles' most beloved and influential partners, women with diverse backgrounds and agendas, each of whose tumultuous relationship with the king offers a singular glimpse into the psyche of England's "Merry Monarch." *The Wandering Prince* introduces Henriette d'Orléans, Charles' adoring younger sister and Lucy Water, his wanton mistress. Caught between her passionate devotion to Louis XIV of France and her misery-drenched marriage to his sadistic, homosexual brother, Philippe, Henriette turns to Charles for succor and sanity—when she is not busy spying on him for Louis. Lucy, meanwhile, spirals slowly from pampered courtesan to ruinous degenerate, thanks to her unchecked libido. *A Health Unto His Majesty* pits Charles' wife, Catherine of Braganza, a timid, barren Portuguese princess, against his lover, Barbara of Castlemaine—"an Amazon of incomparable beauty . . . of a deep sensual kind." As Catherine navigates the uncertain terrain of her husband's loyalty and grapples with her inability to provide him an heir, Barbara enjoys unprecedented power over the king through the sheer force and stamina of her temper tantrums. *Here Lies Our Sovereign Lord* presents the infectious and delightful Nell Gwyn, thespian and hoofer, whose charms on the royal stage buoy Charles' lascivious spirit to new heights. Nell resentfully shares Charles with the alluring Louise de Kéroualle, a visitor from France, whose hard-to-get ploy drives Charles to obsession. With Nell as a bawdy playmate, and

Louise as a pleasant tactical challenge, Charles survives the treason and assassination attempts that would derail a lesser king.

Jean Plaidy interlaces watertight historical research, elegant prose, and a lively sense of character in each of these mesmerizing stories. With her vivid handle on the pageantry, hypocrisy, and heartache inherent in courtly living, she creates an indelible portrait of Charles II and his fiery cadre of women. Entertaining and uniquely insightful, this trilogy of novels reveals why Charles inspired his closest advisors to conclude, "Oddly enough . . . though one believes him to be in the wrong, one desires above all things to serve him."

Questions for Discussion

I. *The Wandering Prince:* Henriette d'Orléans and Lucy Water

1. Henriette is introduced as a garrulous, opinionated, two-year-old political refugee masquerading as the son of a peasant. That feisty personality does not reemerge until page 216, when Henriette exiles La Vallière in a vociferous fit of rage over the girl's dalliance with Louis. In between these episodes, Henriette cuts a meek and tolerant figure, mild and forgiving even in the face of her husband's flagrant indiscretions, her mother's ruthless political ploys, and her lover's repeated infidelities. Is Henriette a wimp, or does she display exquisite control over her emotions? Either way, is she likeable?

2. What classical figures does Plaidy draw on for her characterization of Louis's and Henriette's affair: "In those weeks it was enough for Louis—as it was for Henriette—to know themselves loved by the loved one. Their relationship seemed to them the more perfect because, as they saw it at this time, it could never reach its natural climax. It was romantic love which seemed to gain beauty from the fact that it could not reach that climax and therefore would go on forever at the same high level"?

3. The long-suffering Henrietta Maria plays both the tragic figure and the villain throughout this novel. Do her constant harangues intensify—or offer comic relief from—the relentless tension of the story? Do any of her wishes for her children come about?

4. Louis's love for Henriette is increasingly tainted by his jealousy over her relationship with her brother. At what point does his obsession turn omi-

nous? Does Henriette recognize the shift? How does Anne of Austria's death affect Louis's attitude toward leadership and love?

5. Why does Henriette acquiesce to a rigorous Catholic education, when she knows it is against the express wishes of her late father and most of her siblings?

II. *A Health Unto His Majesty:*
Catherine of Braganza and Barbara, Countess of Castlemaine

1. This story is largely that of the timid, miserable, and misunderstood Catherine. However, Plaidy makes it abundantly clear that her sympathy lies with the bumbling, jovial Charles who continuously breaks Catherine's heart. Does Catherine read as an innocent victim or a masochist? In modern parlance, does her behavior "enable" Charles? Does Charles' insensitivity occlude his likeability as a character?

2. Charles embraces a social tolerance that is out of step with the politics of his time. While his ministers call for the blood of his father's enemies, Charles "was the one who alone . . . desired that these men should remain unpunished . . . Revenge . . . was enjoyed by the failures of this world." While Presbyterians and Anglicans wrangle loudly over who should enjoy the king's favor, Charles wonders "Why could they not . . . be easy in their minds? Why should not men who wished to worship in a certain way worship that way? What should another man's opinions matter to the next man . . . ?" When and how does this enlightened but unpopular attitude get Charles into trouble? Do his laissez-faire ideals ever catch on among his subjects?

3. Lord Chesterfield provides a great deal of mirth to his peers by his thwarted attempts to court his own embittered wife. What does Chesterfield's saga reveal about the sexual politics of Restoration England?

4. Catherine spends the entire novel ruing—and paying for—her initial inflexibility on the issue of Charles' infidelity. She is deemed "willful," "stubborn," "obstinate," "narrow-minded," full of "vanity and self-love," "foolish," "rigid," "simple and ignorant," and "jealous," not only by Charles, but by nearly everyone, when she refuses to gracefully and publicly allow him his mistress. Even when Catherine later tries to reverse her position, the damage is done, and no one takes her seriously. Does the author insert a bias on this topic into the text? The novel was written in

1956; do you think this issue would be handled any differently if the novel had been written thirty or forty years later?

III. *Here Lies Our Sovereign Lord:* Nell Gwyn and Louise de Kérouałle

1. Plaidy paints Nell as an especially appealing character through her sense of humor. Nell christens Louise "Squintabella," for example, and delights in crowing publicly to her rival: "His Majesty is well, I rejoice to say, I never knew him in better form than he was last night." Where do we see a similar gift for comedy in the king? Does it come as a surprise in this novel, or is the king's levity apparent in the first two books of the trilogy?

2. Chief among Nell's vibrant qualities is her fresh, of-the-moment attitude. Plaidy writes, "Nell knew how to live gloriously in the joyous moment, and to remember from the past only that which made pleasant remembering." Why, then, does Nell pass such harsh judgment on herself after her six "mad, feckless weeks" spent with Charles Sackville at Epsom, "which Nell was often to remember with shame"? How does she regain her self-respect after this rare bout of regret?

3. As "libertine-in-chief in a town of libertines," Charles revolutionizes not only sexual politics in London but unleashes a new, sexualized jargon as well. Ordinary citizens "now openly discussed subjects which, ten years ago, they would have blushed to speak of and would have pretended did not even exist." Much is made of Charles' male imitators: "Throughout the country the King's example was followed, and men took mistresses as naturally as previously they had taken walks in the sunshine." Does Plaidy suggest that this new era of liberation was beneficial to women as well? If not, how does she show otherwise?

4. Nell's reaction to motherhood is euphoric: holding her new infant, she "believed she was discovering a new adventure in the game of happiness. She had never felt so tired nor so contented with her lot." Motherhood looms large throughout the trilogy, whether Plaidy focuses on the agony of Catherine's childlessness, or the emotional tyranny Henrietta Maria wields over her children. What aspects of motherhood does Plaidy explore through Anne of Austria, Barbara of Castlemaine, Lucy Water, and Eleanor Gwyn, as well as the many young women separated from their mothers in the stories?

5. Upon reaching the English court from Paris, Louise immediately plots the downfall of the Duke of Buckingham: "The first task was the capture of the King; then she could proceed to annihilate the Duke." What grudge does she hold against Buckingham? Is he aware of her hatred? Does she achieve her two goals?

MURDER MOST ROYAL

Jean Plaidy

The tragic, entwined stories of Anne Boleyn
and Catherine Howard come to life
in Jean Plaidy's masterpiece,
MURDER MOST ROYAL,
in bookstores January 2006.

The King's Pleasure

In the sewing-room at Hever, Simonette bent over her work and, as she sat there, her back to the mullioned window through which streamed the hot afternoon sunshine—for it was the month of August and the sewing-room was in the front of the castle, overlooking the moat—a little girl of some seven years peeped round the door, smiled and advanced towards her. This was a very lovely little girl, tall for her age, beautifully proportioned and slender; her hair was dark, long and silky smooth, her skin warm and olive, her most arresting feature her large, long-lashed eyes. She was a precocious little girl, the most brilliant little girl it had ever been Simonette's good fortune to teach; she spoke Simonette's language almost as well as Simonette herself; she sang prettily and played most excellently those magical instruments which her father would have her taught.

Perhaps, Simonette had often thought, on first consideration it might appear that there was something altogether too perfect about this child. But no, no! There was never one less perfect than little Anne. See her stamp her foot when she wanted something really badly and was determined at all costs to get it; see her playing shuttlecock with the little Wyatt girl! She would play to win; she would have her will. Quick to anger, she was ever ready to speak her mind, reckless of punishment; she was strong-willed as a boy, adventurous as a boy, as ready to explore those dark dungeons that lay below the castle as her brother George or young Tom Wyatt. No, no one could say she was perfect; she was just herself, and of all the Boleyn children Simonette loved her best.

From whom, Simonette wondered, do these little Boleyns acquire their charm? From Sir Thomas, their father, who with the inheritance from his merchant ancestors had bought Blickling in Norfolk and Hever in Kent, as well as an aristocratic wife to go with them? But no! One could not say it came from Sir Thomas; for he was a mean man, a grasping man, a man who was determined to make a place for himself no matter at what cost to others. There was no warmth in his heart, and these young Boleyns were what Simonette would call warm little people. Reckless they might be; ambitious one could well believe they would be; but every one of them—Mary, George and Anne—were loving people; one could touch their hearts easily; they gave love, and so received it. And that, thought Simonette, is perhaps the secret of charm. Perhaps then from their lady mother? Well . . . perhaps a little. Though her ladyship had been a very pretty woman, her charm was a fragile thing compared with that of her three children. Mary, the eldest, was very pretty, but one as French as Simonette must tremble more for Mary than for George and Anne. Mary at eleven was a woman already; vivacious and shallow as a pleasant little brook that babbled incessantly because it liked people to pause and say: "How pretty!" Unwise and lightsome, that was Mary. One trembled to think of the little baggage already installed in a foreign court where the morals—if one could believe all one heard—left much to be desired by a prim French governess. And handsome George, who had always a clever retort on his lips, and wrote amusing poetry about himself and his sisters—and doubtless rude poetry about Simonette—he had his share of the Boleyn charm. Brilliant were the two youngest; they recognized each other's brilliance and loved each other well. How often had Simonette seen them, both here at Hever and at Blickling, heads close together, whispering, sharing a secret! And their cousins, the Wyatt children, were often with them, for the Wyatts were neighbors here in Kent as they were in Norfolk. Thomas, George, and Anne; they were the three friends. Margaret and Mary Wyatt with Mary Boleyn were outside that friendship; not that they cared greatly, Mary Boleyn at any rate, for she could always amuse herself planning what she would do when she was old enough to go to court.

Anne came forward now and stood before her governess, her demure pose—hands behind her back—belying the sparkle in her lovely eyes. The pose was graceful as well as demure, for grace was as natural to Anne as breathing. She was unconsciously graceful, and this habit of standing thus had grown out of a desire to hide her hands, for on the little finger of her left one there grew the beginning of a sixth nail. It was not unsightly; it would scarcely be noticed if the glance were cursory; but she was a dainty child, and this difference in her—it could hardly be called a deformity—was most distasteful to her. Being herself, she had infused into this habit a charm which was apparent when she stood with others of her age; one thought then how awkwardly they stood, their hands hanging at their sides.

"Simonette," she said in Simonette's native French, "I have wonderful news! It is a letter from my father. I am to go to France."

The sewing-room seemed suddenly unbearably quiet to Simonette; outside she heard the breeze stir the willows that dripped into the moat; the tapestry slipped from her fingers. Anne picked it up and put it on the governess's lap. Sensitive and imaginative, she knew that she had broken the news too rashly; she was at once contrite, and flung her arms round Simonette's brown neck.

"Simonette! Simonette! To leave you will be the one thing to spoil this news for me."

There were real tears in her eyes, but they were for the hurt she had given Simonette, not for the inevitable parting; for she could not hide the excitement shining through her tears. Hever was dull without George and Thomas who were both away continuing their education. Simonette was a darling; Mother was a darling; but it is possible for people to be darlings and at the same time be very, very dull; and Anne could not endure dullness.

"Simonette!" she said. "Perhaps it will be for a very short time." She added, as though this should prove some consolation to the stricken Simonette; "I am to go with the King's sister!"

Seven is so young! Even a precocious seven. This little one at the court of France! Sir Thomas was indeed an ambitious man. What did he care for these tender young things who, because they were of an unusual brilliance, needed special care! This is the end, thought Simonette. Ah, well! And who am I to undertake the education of Sir Thomas Boleyn's daughter for more than the very early years of her life!

"My father has written, Simonette. . . . He said I must prepare at once . . ."

How her eyes sparkled! She who had always loved the stories of kings and queens was now to take part in one herself; a very small part, it was true, for surely the youngest attendant of the princess *must* be a very small part; Simonette did not doubt that she would play it with zest. No longer would she come to Simonette with her eager questions, no longer listen to the story of the King's romance with the Spanish princess. Simonette had told that story often enough. "She came over to England, the poor little princess, and she married Prince Arthur and he died, and she married his brother, Prince Henry . . . King Henry." "Simonette, have you ever seen the King?" "I saw him at the time of his marriage. Ah, there was a time! Big and handsome, and fair of skin, rosy like a girl, red of hair and red of beard; the handsomest prince you could find if you searched the whole world." "And the Spanish princess, Simonette?" Simonette would wrinkle her brows; as a good Frenchwoman she did not love the Spaniards. "She was well enough. She sat in a litter of cloth of gold, borne by two white horses. Her hair fell almost to her feet." Simonette added grudgingly: "It was beautiful hair. But he was a boy prince; she was six years older." Simonette's mouth would come close to Anne's ear: "There are those who say it is not well that a man should marry the wife of his brother." "But this is not a man, Simonette. This is a king!"

Two years ago George and Thomas would sit in the window seats and talk like men about the war with France. Simonette did not speak of it; greatly she had feared that she, for the sins of her country, might be turned from the castle. And the following year there had been more war, this time with the treacherous Scots; of this Anne loved to talk, for at the battle of

Flodden Field it was her grandfather the Duke of Norfolk and her two uncles, Thomas and Edmund, who had saved England for the King. The two wars were not satisfactorily concluded, but wars have reverberating consequences; they shake even the lives of those who believe themselves remote. The echoes extended from Paris and Greenwich to the quiet of a Kentish castle.

"I am to go in the train of the King's sister who is to marry the King of France, Simonette. They say he is very, very old and . . ." Anne shivered. "I should not care to marry a very old man."

"Nonsense!" said Simonette, rising and throwing aside her tapestry. "If he is an old man, he is also a king. Think of that!"

Anne thought of it, her eyes glistening, her hands clasped behind her back. What a mistake it is, thought Simonette, if one is a governess, to love too well those who come within one's care.

"Come now," she said. "We must write a letter to your father. We must express our pleasure in this great honor."

Anne was running towards the door in her eagerness to speed up events, to bring about more quickly the exciting journey. Then she thought sadly once more of Simonette . . . dear, good, kind, but so dull Simonette. So she halted and went back and slipped one hand into that of her governess.

❁ ❁ ❁

In their apartments at Dover Castle the maids of honor giggled and whispered together. The youngest of them, whom they patronized shamefully—more because of her youth than because she lacked their noble lineage—listened eagerly to everything that was said.

How gorgeous they were, these young ladies, and how different in their own apartments from the sedate creatures they became when they attended state functions! Anne had thought them too lovely to be real, when she had stood with them at the formal solemnization of the royal marriage at Greenwich, where the Duke of Longueville had acted as proxy for the King of France. Then her feet had grown weary with so much standing, and her eyes had ached with the dazzle, and in spite of all the excitement she had thought longingly of Simonette's strong arms picking her up and carrying her to bed. Here in the apartment the ladies threw aside their brilliant clothes and walked about without any, discussing each other and the lords and esquires with a frankness astonishing—but at the same time very interesting—to a little girl of seven.

Also by Jean Plaidy

The Sixth Wife
0-609-81026-X
$13.95 paperback

Dangerous court intrigue and affairs of the heart collide as renowned novelist Jean Plaidy tells the story of Katherine Parr, the last of Henry VIII's six queens.

Katharine of Aragon
0-609-81025-1
$14.95 paperback

The story of Henry VIII and the House of Tudor begins with the story of his first wife, Katharine of Aragon. This book combines Jean Plaidy's three short novels about Katharine's life into one volume for the first time in paperback.

Royal Road to Fotheringhay
0-609-81023-5
$12.95 paperback

The haunting story of the beautiful—and tragic—Mary, Queen of Scots, as only legendary novelist Jean Plaidy could write it.

In the Shadow of thc Crown
0-609-81019-7
$13.95 paperback

In this dark and fascinating tale, Jean Plaidy brings to life the story of Mary Tudor, daughter of Henry VIII, whose long road to the throne was paved only with sorrow. Written as a memoir, in Mary's own voice, it is a gripping account of a tragic life.

Queen of This Realm
0-609-81020-0
$14.95 paperback

Jean Plaidy presents Elizabeth I in all the many stages of her dramatic life, from bewildered, motherless child of an all-powerful father to monarch who launched England into the time of its greatest glory.

The Thistle and the Rose
0-609-81022-7
$12.95 paperback

Margaret—Princess of England, but Queen of Scotland—finds herself torn between loyalty to the land of her birth and to that of her baby son, now king of the Scots.

Mary, Queen of France
0-609-81021-9
$12.95 paperback

The story of Princess Mary Tudor, a celebrated beauty and born rebel who would defy the most powerful king in Europe—her older brother, Henry VIII.

The Lady in the Tower
1-4000-4785-4
$12.95 paperback

Anne Boleyn, second wife of Henry VIII and mother of Elizabeth I, was one of history's most complex and alluring women. Her fascinating, tragic story comes to vivid life in Jean Plaidy's classic novel.

The Rose Without a Thorn
0-609-81017-0
$12.95 paperback

Born into an impoverished branch of the noble Howard family, young Katherine is brought by fate into the court of Henry VIII, where she soon catches the eye of the unhappily married king. But her bliss is short-lived as rumors of her wayward past force her destiny to take another turn.

THREE RIVERS PRESS • NEW YORK

Wherever books are sold
For reader's group guides, author interviews, and free excerpts, go to:
www.maidenscrown.com
Historical fiction from the Crown Publishing Group